Praise for Hannah Fielding's first novel, *Burning Embers*:

'An epic romance like Hollywood used to make ...'
Peterborough Evening Telegraph

'*Burning Embers* is a romantic delight and an absolute must-read for anyone looking to escape to a world of colour, beauty, passion and love ... For those who can't go to Kenya in reality, this has got to be the next best thing.'
Amazon.co.uk review

'A good-old fashioned love story ... A heroine who's young, naive and has a lot to learn. A hero who's alpha and hot, has a past and a string of women. A different time, world, and class. The kind of romance that involves picnics in abandoned valleys and hot-air balloon rides and swimming in isolated lakes. Heavenly.'
Amazon.co.uk review

'The story hooked me from the start. I want to be Coral, living in a more innocent time in a beautiful, hot location, falling for a rich, attractive, broody man. Can't wait for Hannah Fielding's next book.'
Amazon.co.uk review

APHRODITE'S TEARS

HANNAH FIELDING

LONDON
WALL
PUBLISHING

COPYRIGHT

First published in hardback and paperback in the UK in 2018
by London Wall Publishing Ltd (LWP)
24 Chiswell Street, London EC1Y 4YX

Digital edition converted and distributed in 2018 by FaberFactory

EB ISBN 978–0–9955667–8–1

To my loving son, Christian, whose knowledge of ancient Greek and love of mythology was the wind beneath my wings in the writing of this book, such was his support and encouragement.

…There is the heat of Love, the pulsing rush of Longing, the lover's whisper, irresistible — magic to make the sanest man go mad.

Homer, *The Iliad*

CONTENTS

PROLOGUE

Kent, England, April 1977

'*U*rgently wanted: experienced archaeologist to supervise licenced subsea exploration around a small, private Ionian island. Candidates to show impeccable academic credentials and experience of underwater archaeology. Apply to: The Administration, PO Box 7520, Athens, Greece,*' read the newspaper advertisement. Strangely, it carried no more details than that, although there was a phrase in bold letters at the end: **'Do not waste your time or ours if you are not qualified for this job.'** It had certainly caught Oriel's eye, not only because it mentioned Greece but also because of the arrogant turn of phrase. She could almost hear the autocratic voice that had dictated those words.

Still, it was an intriguing idea, working on a private island, Oriel thought as she let her gaze wander over the dreary Kentish view that extended beyond her window. It was the middle of spring, yet the weather behaved as if the countryside was still steeped in midwinter. She had come down from the house she shared in London with some of her old university friends for a few days' holiday at her family home in Cranbrook, hoping for some sunshine so she could relax beside the pool. As she was an only child, her parents were always delighted to see and spoil her, particularly given that for most of the year Oriel worked abroad, travelling to archaeological sites that took her all over the world.

She sipped her steaming coffee, sitting at the desk in her old bedroom, which hadn't changed since she was a teenager, and smoothed the page of the folded newspaper thoughtfully. Nostalgic memories haunted the edges of her mind.

Greece. It was a long time ago since she'd been back to that part of the world.

She sighed wistfully, remembering her faraway moonlight experience that night six years ago on the small Greek island of Aegina. The sky had been a velvet-dark tapestry, illuminated by a full moon that cast a breathtaking staircase of light on a midnightblue sea; a night for lovers' meetings, not for goodbyes. She had been conscious of the pervasive silence, broken only by the whispering, rhythmic lapping of the Mediterranean on the sable shore – a soothing sound. *How strange it is, the way our memories are selective,* she thought, as that episode of her life came back to her in every pulsing detail.

At the age of twenty-two, Oriel had been on Aegina as part of her year's placement, studying the Saronic islands for her MA in archaeology and anthropology. It had been a long day on the dig, made even longer by the anticipation of her fiancé Rob arriving that evening. Oriel had been excited about their week's holiday, during which they were to make plans for their wedding. Kind, dependable Rob, who treated her like an equal and totally understood her drive to succeed in a man's world. At Cambridge, she had fended off the attentions of many young men who underestimated her, but then Rob had come along. It hadn't been just his good looks, intelligence and charming manner she had fallen for, they had been firm friends since their first meeting on campus.

When Oriel had returned to her hotel late that afternoon and saw the envelope addressed to her in Rob's familiar scrawl, her reaction had been one of surprise and delight. An incurable romantic, she had resisted the urge to rip it open there and then, and instead had strolled down to the beach as the sun was setting to read his letter during that magic hour.

Maybe that was why the impact of its contents had been so devastating.

She had stood a long time with the letter in her hand, shocked and feeling sick. Scanning past the preamble of excuses and explanations, she'd gone over his final lines again and again, hardly believing what the words were spelling out: *'I don't know how to write what I have to tell you, but I have no choice. I know you will understand and forgive us, sweet Oriel. Please believe me that Alicia and I fought our attraction for months, but eventually it became something neither of us could deny. We couldn't help it, we just fell in love. Alicia is carrying my child and we will be married next month.'*

Rob and Alicia. Her fiancé and her best friend – how very unimaginative! She had trusted them both so implicitly. Staring at the innocent piece of paper that held such a cruel and bitter shock, a nauseous wave of disbelief had engulfed her. Later on, she acknowledged that she had been partly to blame, but it hadn't made the sense of betrayal any better at the time. She had no doubt that her idealistic and rather old-fashioned attitudes to love and sex had been, to a great extent, the cause for Rob's succumbing to Alicia's alluring charms. Oriel had wanted the white dress and veil that she would be wearing on her wedding day to carry the authentic symbol of sexual purity, in the same way it had in her mother's day. Rob had seemed patient and decent – but in the end had gone looking for greener pastures. Now, with the benefit of hindsight, she acknowledged that there had always been something missing: his kisses had not stirred her in the way she'd imagined they would, his touch didn't move her to lose control as she thought it should. There was a passionate streak in her that was left untapped and unreleased. Perhaps that's why she had found it easy to wait to surrender her virginity …

Now her eyes returned to the bold advertisement. To be in Greece again was an enticing thought. *Subsea exploration.* Her pencil circled the words aimlessly over and over again. A job tailor-made for her! She had just finished an excavation assignment in the medieval city of Trondheim in Norway and was shortlisted for another position in the North Sea, off the Shetland Islands. *Another dark and dreary place,* she thought, without enthusiasm. Still, the imperious words of the advert, the sun and the beautiful, ever-changing colours of the Mediterranean beckoned. Besides, this wasn't Aegina, and she was twenty-eight now: older and wiser than the young woman who had been hurt all those years ago.

After all, it wasn't just Rob who had caused her pain …

Her mind slipped back into those distant memories. In one night she'd been forced to grow up, her whole philosophy in life coloured by a determination never to be hurt again. She could still remember it all so clearly: sitting on a boulder with Rob's letter in one hand and the photograph from her wallet of the two of them in the other, trying to control the shaking that possessed her as the numb sickness had given way to anger. While looking blankly towards the horizon, where the lanterns of fishing boats danced on the dark waters like fireflies, Oriel had been blinded with sudden self-knowledge and the most terrible scorn: scorn for herself. What a colossal, naïve fool she'd been with her hopes and her dreams and her unrealistic idealism. '*I know you will understand and forgive us,*' he had said presumptuously. So they were an 'us'. A double betrayal. How they must be laughing at her. The humiliation of it all was too deep for tears. Oriel found herself shaking with a terrible anger – and not all of it directed at them, she realized. She was furious at herself too, with a rage that screamed for an outlet.

Oriel had been sitting on the boulder for a long time, gazing distractedly towards the water, when she became vaguely aware of something moving in the shallows. The moon had by now disappeared behind a bank of cloud, extinguishing the glitter of the waves and the silvery patina on the rocks. The shift in darkness of the night sky made it difficult to see what had rippled the surface of the water. Frogmen night diving, she thought, or the slight undulation of the sea in the warm, salty breeze. She didn't give it another thought, returning her attention to the winking lights of fishing boats on the horizon – and then, abruptly, he emerged …

It was a man, but not one wearing a wetsuit, fins or diving mask; this one was almost naked, his modesty barely protected by what could only be defined as an apology for a low-rise brief. He was no mere trick of the light. Sleek and glorious, he was suddenly hurtling out of the water, throwing spray off his body like Poseidon rising from the waves.

Oriel's breath caught in her throat as she watched him, a small frown crinkling her brow. A curious sense of apprehension seeped into her veins. In the near-darkness he looked large, somewhat menacing and disturbingly masculine as he strode through the shallows. There was an air of unquestioned dominance about this man, an arrogant power that expressed itself in the controlled motion of his body as he sauntered on to the beach.

For that fateful minute, she was totally helpless, in the grip of emotions too basic to be controlled by rational thought. Instead of turning to leave quickly, she continued to stare at the stranger who had materialized like a Greek god wading from the depths of the sea. The moon slid into view again, throwing a wash of silver over long muscular legs and narrow hips, wide shoulders and a sculpted torso, all combined in a vibrantly athletic stance. As his approaching form became more discernible, each smooth, fluid curve of muscle, each long line of sinew and bone, and each angular feature glistened with a radiance that stabbed Oriel straight to the heart. Hair as dark as the devil's soul was dripping wet across his forehead and he lifted his hand to slick it away from his face, the moonlight catching every droplet that glittered like tiny diamonds across his skin.

All at once, Oriel gathered her wits, conscious that she too was only lightly clad, just a muslin sarong covering her bikini. She remembered her mother's warning that it wasn't wise for a woman to venture out alone on a deserted beach, and she stood up to hurry back to her hotel, quickly tucking the letter and photograph into her sarong.

Too late! She had barely taken a step before she found herself confronted by the tall, dark figure. Well above the average height of other Greek men, he towered over her, a dark silhouette against the moonlit sky. His eyes gleamed like steel against his deeply tanned skin as his gaze wandered over her and then rested upon her hair, which cascaded heavily down her back, pale and shining as the moon on the water. He had a strong masculine face, rather insolent and somewhat primitive – so much so that despite the tinge of fear fluttering through her, Oriel couldn't help but feel mesmerized by this Adonis.

'What brings a beautiful girl to such a deserted place on this enchanting night?' he asked in English. His obvious Greek accent gave a delightful, smoky edge to his deep voice and sent an involuntary warmth up her spine. Slicking back his wet dark hair once more, he studied her openly. 'You look like the ocean nymph, Calypso, waiting for Odysseus on your island, ready to bewitch him with your mesmerizing voice.'

Oriel had been too startled, too alarmed, to reply at first. His comment was unexpected, and those glittering grey eyes seemed to hold her prisoner, flickering with amusement and something more intense. It was she who was bewitched.

'I thought I was alone,' she murmured, finally finding her voice.

His mouth quirked. 'So did I.' He nodded behind him. 'I

dropped anchor back there to come in for an evening swim. It's been a hot day.' His eyes returned to her, intent and appraising.

Oriel's gaze flitted away and caught sight of a small boat, moored next to the rocks to her left. Partially obscured by the craggy ridge that shaped the deserted cove, only the top of the sail was visible, billowing gently in the balmy breeze. She'd been too preoccupied by her brooding thoughts to notice its arrival.

She felt an urge to push past this handsome stranger and run away to the safety of her hotel bedroom, but something about this man had held her there, transfixed. The intriguing power of his personality gripped her imagination. This stranger could have stepped straight out of Homer's *Odyssey*.

A silky platinum lock slipped from the scarf Oriel had tied around her head in a band to keep her heavy, tumbling mane in place, and the breeze blew it across her face. He reached out a bronzed hand with tapering long fingers and lightly pushed the strand away, before caressing the length of her hair almost reverently. There was a sultry burn now in the gaze that wandered from her hair to her mouth and then settled on Oriel's wild doe eyes, which stared back at him. Her stomach curled with instinctive heat.

She felt the impulse to escape, like a fawn fleeing into the brush. Instead, she stood there, pulse racing, her legs trembling as an unfamiliar and exquisite sensation flooded the lower part of her body. It was madness! Never before had this sense of danger – of seduction – hit her with such potency. Surely it was the island air that had gone to her head like an enchanted potion.

The dark waves murmured on the sand, their gently rolling edges lit a luminous blue under the moonlight. Everything was cloaked in unreality and it was as if the two of them were caught in a dream. Oriel sensed that the mysterious stranger before her was also aware of the extraordinary atmosphere that engulfed them.

His fingers were still touching her hair and she backed away. This man was so overwhelming, and she was disorientated. In a sudden, desperate panic, Oriel turned to run, hardly looking where she was going, her bare feet stumbling through the wet sand in the silver-washed half light. Before she had time to register it, her foot came into contact with something hard and she tripped and went sprawling forwards. In the same split second she was jerked sideways by a pair of muscular arms as the Greek god sprang forward and caught hold of her, their bodies colliding in mid-air.

Oriel gave a choked cry. The stranger fell with her, holding her, his body going into a complicated twist just before they hit the sand so that she landed on top of him, the fall softened for her by his body. She lay winded for an instant; then, before she was over the shock, he took her by the shoulders and gently slid her from him sideways. She found herself on her back, staring up at the milky moonlit sky. His bulk arched over her, blotting out the moon with the dark circle of his head, and she looked wildly up at him as the weight of his muscled body pressed down, splaying her against the sand.

'Don't!' she cried out, struggling in his arms. His skin was hot and smooth, and she fought the impulse to relax and let herself melt into him.

The stranger's eyes glittered and held hers beneath the perfect arc of black eyebrows. 'You were headed for a nasty fall on that rock, you should look where you're going.' His was a face out of Greek tragedy itself. It was so close to hers that Oriel felt his warm breath on her cheek and her pulse quickened; with it came an acute awareness: the needs she had suppressed for years were suddenly rushing to the surface. An aching feeling was invading her lower limbs, a strange weakness. It was magnified a hundredfold when he leapt to his feet and a strong brown hand helped her up, his powerful frame looming over her. His silver eyes skimmed the taut curve of her breasts and she prayed her flimsy bikini top was displaying no signs of her arousal.

He didn't let go of her hand as his eyes bored into hers. 'You're trembling, beautiful Calypso.'

Oriel blinked. He was terrifyingly attractive. She pulled her hand from his, now embarrassed at her clumsy attempt to flee. 'It's nothing. Thank you.'

His sensuous lips stretched into a slow smile, uncovering a row of pure white teeth. 'You must have been here centuries ago, waiting for me on your island.' Even his speech was theatrical. She found herself returning his smile and entered into the spirit.

'And who were you?' she breathed, the question almost catching in her throat; she already knew the answer.

'Odysseus, of course. Remember? I was shipwrecked and washed up on the shore of this island. You fell in love with me and held me prisoner, but you weaved your magic spell over me with your beautiful long hair, spun from moonbeams, your mesmerizing voice and enticing body, and your manipulative ways.'

Oh, he was daring and arrogant – and irresistible, too. Despite herself, Oriel took up his allusion of the ancient Greek myth and ventured boldly down the same path, perilous though it was. 'And even though I promised to make you immortal, you refused and wanted to return to Ithaca and your wife.'

Now it was the stranger's turn to look surprised. He regarded her with amusement. 'We made love and I was lost for seven years.'

'But it was me who saved you and built the boat that eventually took you home.'

Finally he laughed, transforming the hardness of his features into an expression that was devastating, making Oriel's heart leap. Even the sound of his laughter was huskily exotic. 'Maybe you do not believe in the reincarnation of souls,' he said.

'I've never really thought about it.'

The images he evoked made Oriel long for him to take her in his arms, to be clasped by those strong hands that had stroked her hair with such gentleness … To lose herself beneath that powerful body again.

Surrounded by such beauty and serenaded by the sea, it was as though they were trapped in time. Maybe it was the lingering adrenaline of her anger at the contents of the letter and her heightened nervous system. Perhaps it was the nature of this deserted place that made everything seem like an alluring fantasy. Or maybe it was simply that this man was unlike any other Oriel had ever met. He was no Odysseus, she decided: that Greek hero had been a mere mortal. Indeed this man seemed the personification of Poseidon himself.

His eyes glinted darkly and pinned her with their glimmering steel, setting her nerves tingling. Had he read her thoughts? Was he aware of the emotions he had stirred up as he plucked at needs deep within her that no one had yet aroused? Oriel's throat was dry, her lips parched, and she passed the tip of her tongue over them.

Oh Lord, there was no sense to this!

Shocked at her disturbing reaction, she stepped forward to move past him. 'I'm sorry … I need to go,' she murmured, but his fingers caught hold of her wrist. She felt the strength of them, before his thumb brushed sensually against her skin, caressing it, melting her very insides.

'Don't break the spell,' he said faintly, his voice low and hoarse. Close to this man, every sensible instinct told Oriel that she had been right to make a run for it, but as the shifting moonlight caught and held in his irises, she stared into them, profoundly aware of his dark masculine beauty and power. Sometimes it took only a single glance to say everything and, in that moment, she felt her old beliefs crumble inexorably around her. She lowered her eyes and a frisson of emotion ran through her body.

'You feel the magic as I do, yes? Anything might be possible on a night such as this.' His voice was slow and heavy, tinged with the unmistakable edge of male desire.

A pulse beat fast in Oriel's throat. She lifted her face and her huge green eyes gazed up at him, a delicious thrill coursing through her veins like brandy. She swayed slightly, her legs threatening to give way, and he pulled her against the hard wall of his chest. The bare heat of him seared her again. She could feel his heart beating and, as he tightened his embrace, the hardness of his need against her made her gasp imperceptibly. She could smell a mixture of soap and dried salt water on his skin, mingling with the manly scent of his body.

A sweet insanity was stealing over her. Shocked, Oriel felt her whole being jerk abruptly in physical response to him, as though he had already touched her in the most intimate way. The desire she felt for this unknown man brought in by the sea, the delight of his warm contact against her trembling flesh as his hands moved over her bare arms, was intoxicating. The unfamiliar sensations that were taking over every nerve in her body were so intense that she could think of nothing else but him and, in that moment, she wanted more than anything to give her virginity to the dark Greek god with silver eyes.

Oriel shuddered wildly. She felt the fear of something primitive and unpredictable racing through her and yet, obeying that sixth sense without question, she thrust herself even closer to this divine figure, hungry and demanding.

As if reading her mind, the Greek god's steel-grey eyes darkened to almost charcoal, scanning her face until they settled on the sensitive curves of her lips. Without a word, he lowered his head a fraction but did not kiss her. Oriel's breath caught sharply in her throat as she read the look in his piercing gaze that glittered with deep, adult fires.

Stars burned in the dark sky, a great silvery drift of them that seemed to hold the pair in stunned wonderment while they stared at each other as though bemused by an enchanted spell. Oriel had lost all sense of what had gone before or what might happen in the future. She simply thought to herself: *Damn the consequences!*

So that night, Poseidon, god of the sea, took his beautiful young virgin to that overwhelming, dazzling place where the world and everybody else in it ceased to exist. There were only the two of them and the blazing combustion they created between each other. When the heat built to that point of no return, she knew he felt her innocence. For a moment he paused over her, his diamond eyes now black with passion, questioning, waiting. In answer, Oriel drove her hands into his hair and pulled him towards her, urging him on. 'Regret nothing,' he'd whispered just before taking full possession of her with exquisite gentleness … then with a fire that consumed her, mind, body and soul.

She would never regret it, Oriel knew, even though what happened had violated all the principles she had so far held dear.

It had been a moonlit night of hedonism and passion. Spent and satiated, they slept in a small cave off the beach. When Oriel forced her heavy lids open the next morning, her Greek god had gone and she almost wondered whether the ecstasy she remembered just a few hours before had been real. As a new kind of desolation filled her, she fought back tears of bitter disappointment.

He had left her just as Rob had done – by stealth.

After that night, Oriel knew two things for certain: it was the last she would ever see of the stranger, and she would never let any other man abandon her again.

CHAPTER 1

Athens, May 1977

Clad in a cool coral shirtwaist dress that showed off her exquisitely proportioned hourglass figure and long shapely legs, Oriel stood on a scorched sweep of airfield above the glittering Mediterranean. Colourful sailboats made bright etchings against the far-off horizon. The Greek sun beat down upon her platinum-blonde head and her fingers tightly gripped the handles of her overnight bag as her dark-fringed green eyes, hidden behind large sunglasses, looked around her.

It had been less than a month since she had seen the advertisement in the newspaper and she had wasted no time in sending out her résumé to Stavros Petrakis, works manager of the subsea excavation project. She'd had no difficulty securing the role: a few exchanged faxes, including her references, and within a week an engagement letter and contract had arrived and all arrangements had been made. Clearly these people were organized and efficient, she had thought, which perhaps wasn't surprising, given the imperious tone of the original advert. Yet Petrakis had sounded very pleasant in his correspondence, making Oriel suspect that the person responsible for outlining the job specification had been the name signed at the bottom of her contract, 'D. Lekkas' himself. Anyhow, boss or not, already she didn't like the sound of him. Hopefully he would keep out of the way and let her get on with her job.

The project was certainly exciting: an ancient wreck, possibly dating from Roman times, calcified and half buried in the sand, awaited a proper salvage operation. She had never worked on an argosy of such antiquity and was itching to find out more. Stavros Petrakis had sent her the basic works specification but assured her that once she was on site, she would be briefed further. He had given her all the particulars: Oriel would be met in Athens and taken on

1

her employer's private plane to Helios, a small island in the Ionian Sea, privately owned by the Lekkas family.

Oriel scanned her surroundings. Light aircraft of various sizes stood in orderly rows on the tarmac, their iron carcasses glistening in the afternoon haze. It all felt so familiar: the way the air smelled of pine trees, brine and sienna-coloured earth, the shimmering blue of the sky. Even the sunlight seemed to have a particular quality of its own.

I'm in Greece again, she thought. *I'm really here at last.*

She was about to approach a man who was busy painting a logo on to one of the jet planes when she heard someone behind her call out her name.

'*Despinis* Anderson?'

Oriel turned abruptly. 'Yes, that's me.'

A polite smile greeted her from the wiry-framed Greek man with slicked-back hair and sideburns who was now extending a brown hand towards her. He was older than Oriel, with slightly pockmarked skin; his dark eyebrows slanted sharply away from a wide nose like two circumflex accents, giving his face a fox-like appearance. Neatly dressed in a short-sleeved white safari shirt and dark trousers, he would have seemed rather nondescript were it not for the large, expensive gold watch that glinted on his wrist. '*Kalós ílthate stin Elláda,* welcome to Greece. I am Yorgos Christodoulou, estate manager for *Kyrios* Lekkas.'

Oriel's face broke into a smile as she held out her hand. '*Chairō,* pleased to meet you.'

Jet-black eyes that were small and beady skimmed an appreciative look over the young woman's slim figure and her delicate Englishrose complexion.

'Did you have a pleasant journey?'

'Yes, thank you. I must say, arriving in sunny Athens after the dreary weather in England is truly uplifting.'

'Your luggage has already been picked up by our courier and will probably arrive at Helios tonight.' As he said this, Yorgos Christodoulou took Oriel's overnight bag from her.

'*Efharisto.*'

'*Parakaló,* my pleasure.' He took up a brisk pace, leading Oriel along the airfield towards a cluster of small aircraft. 'You have learnt a few words of Greek, I see. It is always wise when going to a foreign country to have some knowledge of the language.'

'I'm fluent in Greek,' Oriel told him, switching to his own language. Something in the way he spoke made her suddenly feel the need to justify herself. 'I read Classics at university before my Masters in archaeology, so I'm familiar with both ancient and modern Greek.'

He raised an eyebrow, answering her in Greek. 'A clever young lady, I see. Very impressive. You speak our language well, *Despinis* Anderson, for a foreigner.' He nodded ahead of them. '*Kyrios* Lekkas's private plane is waiting to fly us to the island. It's just a short walk from here. I imagine this isn't your first visit to our country?'

'No, I've visited various parts of Greece throughout my academic courses, including a few of the islands.'

'You look very young for such extensive studies.'

She smiled brightly, trying to ignore his condescension. 'Appearances are often misleading.'

He shot her a sideways glance. 'I have nothing to do with the archaeological side of the island, that is Stavros Petrakis's field, but if you don't mind my saying so, as you are young and attractive, I think the *Kyrios* will find you unsuitable for the job so be prepared.'

Oriel was used to this – the perception, in a largely patriarchal society, that she had a man's job. There was nothing new in the estate manager's attitude. Still, this didn't prevent her being irritated by his comments. 'I stated my age on my résumé, I gave *Kyrios* Petrakis all the information he needed, and I have excellent credentials and references,' she retorted. 'My age and appearance are surely immaterial.'

Yorgos raised his eyebrows. 'You certainly sound very confident, *Despinis* Anderson, and I wish you the best of luck.'

She nodded but felt an amused sort of mockery in his words. It was evident that the male population of this part of the world was still untouched by the sexual revolution. To most Greek men, a woman's place was in the kitchen, and to be outdone by a female threatened their egos. Undoubtedly, Yorgos Christodoulou's condescending attitude might well be typical on this job, Oriel mused. But what if he was right and the island's owner took one look at her and sent her packing? Anything was possible if Stavros Petrakis had hired her without the sanction of his boss. She sighed inwardly. Was this to be a complete waste of her time?

The Lekkas Piper Saratoga prop plane was one of the smaller craft on the asphalt, yet its elegant steel frame stood out among all the other, more imposing planes. The tail and the top of its wings were adorned with a modern image of the sun, painted in glistening warm shades of orange, red and yellow, clearly designed to represent Helios, the sun god of Greek mythology, after which the island was named.

Yorgos signalled to the pilot, who waved back from the cockpit, before clasping Oriel's elbow firmly and helping her up the steps and into the cabin. The twin-engine piston aircraft seated four passengers in a cosy but sleek cabin. The decor was elegant, pure and understated in its luxury, with an ivory-coloured interior that contrasted beautifully with the lacquered walnut of the pull-down tables and window frames. Oriel sat down in one of the leather seats.

'Are you comfortable?' the estate manager asked once she had fastened her seatbelt. 'Can I get you something to drink? A glass of ouzo, maybe?'

'No, thank you.'

'Perhaps a little wine?'

Oriel shook her head. After the brazen heat of the airfield, the cool cabin was welcome but her throat felt dry and her lips were parched. 'Just a glass of water, please.'

He reached into a large coolbox tucked behind the seats at the back of the plane and poured some water, placing the chilled glass in front of her on the table. 'Better to have your wits about you when you meet the *Kyrios*. I warn you, he takes no prisoners. Never has a man's name been more appropriate.' He poured himself a glass of ouzo and sat down opposite her, fastening his own seatbelt.

She frowned. 'I don't understand.'

Yorgos gave a short laugh, seeming to relish her confusion, and his teeth gleamed against the dark olive of his skin. '*Kyrios* Damianos Lekkas.' He regarded her with an assessing stare that she sensed was meant to intimidate her. 'In ancient Greek, Damianos means master, tamer and conqueror. The name suits him well, you'll find.'

4

Oriel was well aware of the meaning of the word but she also knew it would be a waste of time pointing that out to him. Instead, unflinching, she said: 'I didn't realize *Kyrios* Lekkas's name was Damianos. On the contract I signed, his forename was only an initial. So, you say his name suits him well?' She hardly wanted to ask but curiosity got the better of her: forewarned was forearmed.

'Put it this way, the islanders call him *Drákon* Damian, Dragon Damian. Feared by everyone, he is himself fearless. He seems to have six heads, each with a pair of eyes. Nothing on the island escapes him.' Yorgos appeared to look straight through her for a moment in reflection before his gaze fixed on her again. 'It would be a brave and clever man who outwitted the *Kyrios*.'

Drákon Damian. The rather gothic epithet didn't bode well, Oriel thought wryly. 'You make him sound quite formidable.'

'Of course the *Kyrios* is formidable. He is the island's leader, a tough one, who demands respect.' Yorgos's obsidian eyes regarded her closely, making Oriel feel as if she were being pinned under a microscope and put in her place. There was something self-important about the estate manager; she had the sense that a weak and dull personality was being animated by guile and the affectation of substance.

Oriel schooled her features into an inscrutable mask, one that she was used to adopting when asserting herself at work. 'I see how Damian Lekkas is the master of the island but "tamer" and "conqueror" are surely not adjectives he warrants,' she said mildly.

Yorgos took a large gulp of ouzo and cleared his throat. 'You think I exaggerate? He is both of those things. He hunts in the moonlight with the wolves and swims with the sea monsters in the deep and dark waters surrounding the island. The waters around Helios are known to be particularly dangerous.' He leaned forward slightly. 'Do you know that he once fought a shark and actually killed it?'

Oriel raised an eyebrow. No deep-sea diving excavation project was without its dangers and the way Yorgos Christodoulou was speaking was overblown; still, it made her feel uneasy. As for Lekkas himself, she was becoming increasingly intrigued by the enigmatic figurehead of Helios, despite her growing sense of foreboding. 'A courageous man,' she said in a neutral tone.

Yorgos regarded her suspiciously, clearly wondering if he were being mocked. 'Yes, *Despinis* Anderson, a courageous man and a powerful one, too. He can be totally merciless with his enemies and when it comes to defending his property.'

'Owning an island must bring a great deal of responsibility,' she conceded. 'Security being paramount, naturally. I suppose for that one needs to be hard.'

Yorgos sat back in his deep leather chair. 'Hard, yes. Some people would say there is also a coldness about him. Even so, that doesn't stop him exerting a strange power over women.' He gave Oriel another calculating look. 'In that way, he's the conqueror, *Despinis* Anderson, since you ask. He just has to set his cap at a woman for her to kneel at his feet in submission.' He shrugged, looking down into his glass. 'I've seen it many times. Each year it's the same. Another girl here, another girl there, all of them drawn to him like a magnet. And the *Kyrios* responds as any man would.' Yorgos's glittering eyes snapped back to Oriel's face. 'Oh, he will bed them, but he doesn't care one iota for them. There's only ever been one woman for him.' At this, he gave a half smile and shrugged. 'But the *Kyrios* is easily bored. As soon as a girl starts demanding things of him, he casts her out. He's a man of stone, with a dead heart.'

Oriel tried to hide her distaste for the estate manager's vulgarity, not to mention his disloyalty. Even if *Kyrios* Lekkas was all the things Yorgos Christodoulou was describing – although she put much of it down to Greek melodrama – she disapproved of the way he was criticizing the person on whom she depended for his livelihood.

'That's a harsh thing to say. Why do you work for him if you dislike him so much?'

Yorgos gave a forced smile and held his hands up as if to correct her misapprehension. 'You misunderstand, *Despinis* Anderson. I don't dislike him, I grew up with the man and understand his ways better than any other. We Greeks have a saying: if you do not praise your own home, it will fall on you and squash you. We do not speak badly about our own kind. But it is the Greek way to talk plainly, you'll find out soon enough. There's a difference.'

Is there? Oriel wondered. It sounded to her as if there were skant difference at all where Yorgos Christodoulou was concerned, but she bit her tongue.

'I admire the *Kyrios*, of course,' he continued, 'but he's a man to be feared. Everyone is wary of the *Drákon*. The locals all bow and raise their hats but behind their smiles, people whisper when he passes. Some say that, if crossed, he would be capable of anything. Even murder.' A shiver rippled down Oriel's back. She didn't answer, glad that the plane's engines were now rumbling to life, providing a distraction.

'Ah, we're about to take off.' Yorgos finished off his ouzo and set his glass down. 'The flight isn't long.'

Oriel turned and looked out of the window as the aircraft began to taxi down the runway, avoiding further eye contact with the estate manager and concentrating instead on the golden landscape beginning to move faster outside. Then suddenly they were in the air. She gazed down on the shining surface of the emerald and cobalt waters of the sea with its rippling surf, drowsy lagoons and islands, so brilliantly green, floating in the vast ocean under the Mediterranean sun. The people became midgets; the palms looked like aspidistras; everything on earth a child's toy set in the endless blue lake of the sea.

They had been flying for forty minutes in silence – Oriel having made it clear that she was disinclined to continue a conversation that she considered in poor taste – when Yorgos got up and leaned over her to the window. He pointed to an island that had suddenly come into view.

'Helios,' he announced.

Standing out with breathtaking detail in the dazzling afternoon sunlight, like a primitive red-and-green sculpture arising from the depths of a peacock-blue sea, the island of Helios seemed like an inhospitable rock, a place out of time. And as the small prop plane began its descent, a sense of apprehension tightened its grip on Oriel. Damian Lekkas – a man with a dead heart, who fought sharks, played with wolves and whose brutal magnetism made women fall at his feet! The leader of Helios was beginning to sound more like a medieval overlord by the minute. Did she really want to work for someone who was feared, almost as a god, by his people?

Lower and lower, the plane moved down towards the stretch of glistening sand that curved alongside the ocean like the undulating tail of a snake. The remains of a round tower, which in centuries past must have protected the harbour, sat jagged at the edge of a grey stone quay, whose crumbling walls extended to an old lighthouse, a grim sentinel guarding the toilers of the sea. Behind were mountains, topped by a huge cratered peak, shadowed with deep ridges as if the rock had been pulled and stretched towards the sky by a huge hand.

They flew over a group of low trees edging the quayside before heading for a clearing, where a wide strip of asphalt had been laid as a runway. Oriel's heartbeat quickened as the small craft touched down smoothly.

'We're here,' announced Yorgos.

Oriel unfastened her seatbelt, looking forward to seeing this astonishing island close-up. 'Helios is volcanic. I hadn't realized,' she said.

'Yes. We're not far from the island of Kythira, almost opposite the south-eastern tip of the Peloponnese peninsula. Like Kythira, Helios has a history of earthquakes, but we've been lucky so far. Apart from a few tremors from time to time, we haven't had any major quakes for two hundred years.' Yorgos stood up and swung open the door to the plane, letting in a blast of hot air, the heat rising in waves from the baked runway outside. He was about to pick up Oriel's overnight case but, before he could come to assist her, she slid from her seat and grabbed the bag, alighting swiftly on her own. He frowned as he followed her out.

'The Lekkas residence is about ten kilometres away as the crow flies, almost on the opposite side of the island. I'm going to drop you there,' he told her, leading her towards a Jeep parked under a stretch of gnarled olive trees.

It was cooler here than in Athens, with the breeze coming off the sea, but still sweltering enough to feel uncomfortable. Oriel's first impression of Helios was one of blazing light, naked rock, cacti and thorns. Apart from the sparse olive trees, it was virtually without shade, unprotected from either sun or wind, and although the light was almost white in its brightness, this part of the island looked as desolate as any place she had ever seen.

Oriel experienced an unfamiliar sense of nervousness as she followed the estate manager, who, she had to concede, had disarmed her with his remarks. Hundreds of questions raced through her mind. What if she didn't hit it off with her new employer? He sounded like a dreadful womanizer and a complete despot to boot. Even if he didn't hold any reservations about her having the job, what if she wasn't up to it? She'd handled difficult and complicated assignments before, and had plenty of diving experience, but maybe this time she wouldn't be so lucky. Then she quickly berated herself: it was not like her to be so self-doubting.

When they reached the open-sided Jeep, Oriel let Yorgos take her case, which he stashed in the back of the vehicle. She looked around her at the remoteness of the landscape. This island was so very different to the others she'd seen, with its dry, red soil and scattered, shrivelled-up trees. To her, its almost derelict lighthouse and ruined round tower somehow seemed aggressive, guarded by flocks of screaming gulls that hovered menacingly overhead. It felt like an archaic place, desolate – cut off from the rest of the world.

'This area of the island hasn't yet been developed,' Yorgos told her, as if uncannily reading Oriel's mind. 'It used to be part of a harbour, but approaching Helios by sea from this side is dangerous as there are fifteen miles of shifting sands. It's been the graveyard of many a ship bound for the island.'

'How eerie,' she murmured, looking out to sea. Yet the archaeologist in her was fascinated by the imprints of the past that must lie undiscovered in such treacherous waters.

Yorgos gestured for Oriel to get in before climbing into the driver's seat of the vehicle. 'A few years ago, the *Kyrios* decided to develop a new harbour on the eastern side. It was just a tiny fishing village but now it's a small port with a marina and much safer since it lies in a sheltered bay.'

She stared out at the bleak and timeless vista. 'The island is certainly very wild.'

'It's not like this everywhere. Helios was divided between the two Lekkas brothers, Damian, the eldest, and Pericles, after the death of their parents and their uncle Cyrus not long after. *Kyrios* Damian's part was planted with olive trees, and the plan had been to introduce blackcurrants to make something of Pericles's portion.' He paused, before adding: 'If you ask me, Pericles was given the worst end of the bargain. It's no surprise he didn't make anything much of his part of the island.'

Yorgos pulled a packet of cigarettes out of the top pocket of his shirt and lit one, squinting through the strong plume of smoke as he exhaled. 'He was a fun guy to hang around with … very misunderstood. Anyhow, that's another story.'

'And the brother, Damian, what did he achieve with his part of Helios?' asked Oriel, fascinated as this almost feudal story unfurled.

'He actually took over the running of the whole of Helios and ended up paying an annual income to Pericles, as he also did for their cousin, *Kyria* Helena.'

'Why didn't she have a share of the land?' Oriel wanted to know.

'That's how it's done here, the rules of the island.'

'The rules of the island?'

'On Helios, a girl does not inherit land, she receives an annuity. That's how families keep their land intact. Now, since the murder two years ago, it all belongs to the *Kyrios*.'

Oriel's head turned sharply. '*Murder*? You mean the brother, Pericles?'

Yorgos put the key in the ignition and paused. 'Not only Pericles, God rest his soul.' He took a quick drag on his cigarette and crossed himself with the same hand.

Oriel's eyes widened. 'What are you saying?'

'What I'm saying is that the Lekkas family has been touched by tragedy more than once,' he replied solemnly, watching her intently.

It was on the tip of Oriel's tongue to ask more questions, but prying felt wrong. Clearly the estate manager revelled in being the keeper of knowledge about the Lekkas family and she didn't want to give him the satisfaction of providing a too-willing audience. Yet, inevitably, her curiosity was piqued. If there were a grisly story involving the Lekkas family, no doubt she would find out soon enough.

Yorgos stared into Oriel's eyes with a curious little smile. 'You are beginning to think that it wasn't such a good idea to come to this island after all, eh?'

Though her apprehension was increasing steadily, Oriel lifted a defiant chin. 'Not at all, I have come here to do a job. What happens on this island, the gossip, the rumours, is not my concern.'

'Well, let me know if you want to return to the mainland,' he persisted. 'I've seen others turn tail once they find out what living on Helios, with its accursed ruling family, is like.'

He added slowly: 'The island has a history, *Despinis* Anderson. A dark, passionate history, just like the tragedies of our ancient mythology, which cannot be ignored. Whoever lives here cannot help but get caught up in the dramas of Helios. They are part of everyday life.'

Yorgos studied her, one hand on the steering wheel where his cigarette smouldered between his thick fingers, the other still on the ignition, waiting to turn on the engine.

Oriel felt her heart thud quickly with a combination of excitement, indignation and fear. Was this some kind of warning? It seemed bizarre and melodramatic. She made her voice sound cool enough not to divulge her inner turmoil: 'I have signed a contract, *Kyrios* Yorgos, and I'm not in the habit of reneging on my word.'

Her reply seemed to annoy him, and he threw away his cigarette half smoked. 'What can I say? A very commendable trait in normal circumstances, I admit, but I wouldn't speak too soon.' Then the Jeep's engine came to life and they were off.

The road towards the other end of the island took them over harsh terrain, Oriel's hair streaming behind her as the Jeep bucked its way over the bumps and stones. She almost forgave the arrogant presumption of Yorgos Christodoulou – although she hoped she would have little to do with him in the weeks to come – as he turned out to be a remarkably knowledgeable guide. Above the grinding noise of the Jeep's engine, he pointed out the cliffs rearing up with ravaged-looking remains of buildings on their crest. Somewhere inside these great rocks there were grottos, he said, where the islanders had on occasion taken refuge from pirates in times gone by. Towering precipices rose sheer from the sea, and the slashes in the rock, he told her, were believed to have been cut by St George's sword.

Before them, the hills rolled like waves of an angry ocean and to the side of them lay rocky escarpments and steep gorges. It was just the sort of place where, in the language of Dodwell and other early nineteenth-century travellers through Greece, 'a false step would mean death,' Oriel thought, as they bumped along the road at an almost vertiginous speed.

It was like a dark fantasy world from an adventure book, and Oriel was all for adventure! She was the only child of ageing parents, who had tried to cosset and protect her for most of her life. This had, no doubt, bred in her a desire for escape and excitement. She had simply rebelled against her mother's and father's good intentions, finding every opportunity to assert her independence from them.

It was partly why she had been drawn to archaeology in the first place. As a young girl, she had spent many nights under her bedcovers with a torch, reading about the lost civilizations of the past, intrepid explorers and their tales of derring-do, imagining what it might be like to be a heroic adventurer who could travel back in time and experience those worlds for herself. Her mother was conventional down to her bones and although she had been proud that Oriel had secured a place at Cambridge, she was nevertheless alarmed at her choice of profession. Muriel Anderson had looked at her daughter with a slightly dismayed expression. 'Are there any lady archaeologists, darling? Isn't that what men usually do?' From that day onwards, Oriel had been even more determined to follow her own star.

Oriel lifted her eyes towards the mountain she'd noticed from the air, which had been looming over their ride up the cliffside; it was huge and dominated the scenery, almost bewitching in its monstrosity. Yorgos followed her gaze.

'You are looking at Typhoeus, our volcano. The great dragon!' he said dramatically.

Now that he had mentioned the volcano, Oriel realized there was a pervading smell of sulphur that hung in the air, giving a diabolical flavour to the scenery. Yes, she could see its resemblance to a hideous behemoth. Or rather, a vast mouth with a good many teeth missing, like the model of a monster's jaw made by an infernal dentist. White wisps rose from the top like the fumes that give away a secret smoker hiding behind a wall. Grim and forbidding, it frowned over the island.

'The volcano has been dormant all my life, but the history of the island tells of angry gods turning our beautiful blue sky charcoalgrey for months,' Yorgos told Oriel, who stared back at it, transfixed.

'People have always created myths to explain acts of nature,' she answered.

'Myths are the food and drink of Helios.' He pulled the steering wheel left and right as the Jeep lurched over uneven ridges in the road. 'The people of our island have lived in near seclusion for many years. Few outsiders visit.'

Soon the aspect of the island began to change. The road had meandered towards a tiny natural port where the light was indescribably keen, yet soft. Here, Oriel could see that the volcanic soil of the island was highly pigmented: the rich brown earth was streaked with the emerald and jade of olivine, the dark pink of quartz, the silver-grey of chrome and the warm yellow of gold. On the right, the Ionian Sea sparkled invitingly, gentle waves ruffling its surface. Another road led down to a small marina, where a handful of brightly coloured boats bobbed imperceptibly, as if quite content to remain at their moorings instead of braving the open sea. Houses were set among tumbling cascades of jasmine that scented the air, their gardens leading down to the beach where the iridescent waters lapped softly against the sand. In the distance Oriel could distinguish gently rolling hills and dizzying mountain ranges: sheer needles of rock shot with veins of mineral pigmentation, shimmering in a halo of late afternoon haze. They passed a small chapel that lay dozing in the still heat. There was no movement anywhere, of man or beast, except for a few butterflies fluttering lazily among the cypress trees.

Everywhere Oriel looked conjured sharp pangs of memory, taking her back to her last visit to a Greek island. Not for the first time since that far-off night in Aegina, she wondered what had happened to the Greek god who had ravished her in the moonlight and then vanished like a dream. Who was he and where had he come from?

Her thoughts were interrupted by the estate manager's voice. 'Though the *Kyrios* won't have returned yet, I've been told to take you straight to Heliades, the Lekkas residence, so you can wait for him there,' he said.

'I would prefer to use the time to book into a hotel for a couple of days while I look for an apartment to rent,' she replied.

'You won't find any on the island, I'm afraid. And the only hotel is a two-star hovel,' he said, casting her a sideways look, 'which a sophisticated lady like yourself would not appreciate. This is a private island and the *Kyrios* doesn't encourage tourists.'

'Where do the other members of the team live, then?'

'At the staff house.'

'Then that's where I would like you to take me, so I can tidy myself up before meeting *Kyrios* Lekkas.'

A mocking twist appeared on Yorgos's mouth as his dark, unsettling eyes flicked over her. '*Kyrios* Damian wouldn't allow that. The staff house is too primitive for a young lady like yourself.'

Oriel was becoming increasingly annoyed. It felt like the estate manager was dreaming up obstacles at every turn. Perhaps he simply didn't like women. Or, at least, not when they were taking on a 'man's' job. 'For heaven's sake,' she said, exasperated. 'I've lived under canvas before now, on a job! I know how to rough it, if that's what you're worried about.'

He smiled unpleasantly. 'I still need to take you to Heliades. What you do after that is none of my business.'

Oriel set her chin defiantly. The sooner she had her meeting with Damian Lekkas the better; then, at least, she would know where she stood. After all, he was her employer and she suspected that the insecurity of her position was merely a fabrication on the part of Yorgos Christodoulou to put her off the job for some reason of his own. Still, if anyone reneged on the contract, it wouldn't be her …

'Very well then, I'll wait for him and take it from there.'

Again, he looked amused. 'Persistence overcomes resistance, we say in Greece. You think that you will convince the *Kyrios*, eh?'

'Isn't he the one in authority here?'

At this the manager looked pensive. 'Indeed he is,' he said in a low voice and Oriel felt that she had at least won the first round.

Within another twenty minutes the Jeep was heading north along the eastern coastline, which offered magnificent views of the sea below and terraces of silver-green olive groves that led like a giant staircase down to the water's edge. Oriel's impression was of a fabled land. Yorgos slowed to point out Heliades – the name meant 'children of the sun' – and the Lekkas *kahstro*.

The mansion looked like a shimmering white temple in the crystallized light, standing proudly on the crest of the rocky cliffs that towered above the island, surrounded by clusters of cypresses, Judas trees, twisted olives and wild lemon. Oriel drew a sharp breath. *A pagan prayer to Zeus.* One would have to be a painter to capture the primitive appeal of everything she saw. Appearing to have been built in ancient times, it was a striking edifice; a sort of dazzling, arrogant challenge to all the untamed beauty of the island, she thought.

She turned to Yorgos. 'How far back does it date?'

'It was built in the nineteenth century, but over the years parts have been added to the original house.'

Oriel could hardly contain her excitement – how could she resist the chance of working in such fabulously archaic surroundings? The building was a perfect study in neo-classicism and the whole island breathed mystery and historical secrets. She could just imagine the archaeological wonders she would be discovering here. Yet there was a warning voice at the back of her mind that counselled her to think carefully before she made an irrevocable decision. *First impressions are often the truest, as we often find to our cost,* went the saying, and on arrival here, her initial reaction had hardly been favourable, she reminded herself.

The Jeep picked up speed again as they drove past fields of vines and barley. Some women were reaping barley with sickles, while others with baskets on their hips were bent over picking *hortas*, leafy greens, or plucking tomatoes from vines. Oriel stared, fascinated, at this rural scene which looked as though it could have existed over a hundred years ago. The women wore white Turkish breeches tucked into long boots, their skirts looped up while they toiled, and each worker covered her head with a black handkerchief decorated with coloured flowers. One woman had a baby slung in a bundle on her back, where it was gently rocked by the movement of her body.

A different world. Oriel's eyes lingered on the infant as the Jeep sped on and she wondered what it must be like to have been born in such a remote place. Perhaps that child would spend his or her entire life on Helios and never see what lay beyond its shores.

Soon the road followed a high brick wall that enclosed the lemon orchards and olive groves leading up to the great house.

Oriel's thoughts moved to the lord and master of this intriguing place.

'Does the *Kyrios* live on his own?' she asked.

'No, his cousin Helena lives there, too. She has a whole section of the house to herself,' said Yorgos. 'Pericles's wing was closed for a long time after the murder, but the *Kyrios* has had it totally refurbished. It has a fabulous view over the sea and the island and has its own private beach.'

Oriel looked round sharply at this mention of the tragedy again. Curiosity and unease plucked at her in equal measure. She was on the verge of asking the estate manager more when they came upon a pair of tall bronze gates that interrupted the line of the boundary wall. They were of the imposing, curved kind with wonderful spiral and leaf detailing, topped by an arch with scrolled corners. Yorgos got out and pushed them open, pulling them shut again once the Jeep was inside the grounds, and the vehicle began its ascent up the long driveway to the house, which was still hiding behind a curtain of tamarisks and eucalyptus trees.

As the residence came into view closer up, Oriel nearly gasped. It was a house befitting a great dynasty; no one setting eyes on Heliades would deny that. It appeared to have been built originally in honey-coloured stone, which over the years the sun had mellowed to a soft yellow. A mantle of climbing plants reached up the walls to the roof. Across the façade a pink-stemmed spreading pellitory with bright green leaves unfurled its delicate flowers, the petals of which had the rosy tint and fineness of a baby's skin, and these entwined with the more vivid fuchsia of bougainvillea. The grand edifice had two rows of tall windows with beautifully carved shutters and wrought-iron balconies gracing the top floor. Its front was pillared in a neo-classical style, topped with a pediment decorated with a sculpture of Helios, the glowing sun god, represented here in its Greek interpretation by a gigantic eye surrounded by a halo, observing everything his light could touch. The magnificent home of the Lekkas family was a spectacular monument that looked as if it had been there from the beginning of time and would survive as long again.

The Jeep passed through the gates into an inner paved area that ran the whole width of the building, with a fountain warbling at its centre, while lines of tall cypress trees stood like willowy sentries on the outer edges. The marble steps and balustrades that led to the front door were massive but well kept, gleaming white in the brilliant sunshine. Oriel's wide-eyed gaze swept up to the top of the steps, where a broad paved terrace stretched with carved statuary standing in niches, dividing rooms at the front of the house, and huge urns spilled over with fuchsias and geraniums. Towards the rear of the main property huge wings had been added, each of them big enough in themselves to accommodate a man of substantial means.

As Yorgos brought the Jeep to a stop, the arched front door to the house opened and a servant came out to meet them. Short and dark, with a clipped beard following the line of his jaw, he was dressed in green and gold with a golden sun embroidered on the front of his coat. At a nod from Yorgos, he took Oriel's hand luggage from the back seat. 'Show the lady into the *salóni* and serve her some refreshments,' the estate manager commanded brusquely. Then, turning to Oriel, he said more gently: 'Would you prefer tea or coffee? Have you had any lunch?'

'Thank you, but I'm not hungry. A cold glass of water would be greatly appreciated though.'

'Are you sure? You might be in for a long wait.'

'Thank you, but water will do.' Oriel stood at the foot of the marble steps and looked up at the outside of the vast mansion. It felt as if she'd stepped back in time, and the awed child in her that had dreamed of visiting worlds gone by felt a thrill of excitement as well as trepidation.

At that moment, she caught sight of a shadow at one of the tall windows on the ground floor. Was it a person moving or a trick of the light? Then it was gone. She was conscious again of that uneasy prickling down her spine. 'Is there anywhere I can wash my hands and tidy myself up a little?' she asked quickly.

'Yes, of course. Kyrillos here will show you to the downstairs guest room. It has a bathroom and everything you'll need. Irini will bring some towels.'

Oriel thanked him and made to follow the wordless servant. Yorgos excused himself then with the same unctuousness he'd shown throughout, but it seemed he couldn't resist a small gibe before he went: 'I'm afraid I must leave you now, I have some work to attend to. No doubt the *Kyrios* will call me when he has decided whether or not to give you the job.'

Oriel answered him tightly, prickling with irritation. 'He has already agreed to give me the job. We have signed the contract. I thought I made that clear.'

'Maybe,' Yorgos said with an unpleasant fox-like grin, 'but that was before yesterday's incident. Didn't I tell you? It seems another one left us last night. The *Kyrios* has had enough of unreliable females. They unsettle the men and then run off, leaving the team short.'

Oriel bristled. 'Who has left the team? Which women are you referring to?' Was there yet more gossip that he was delighting in dangling before her?

He seemed about to answer her question but then paused, his eyes narrowing. 'I'm sure you'll find out all you need to know from the *Kyrios*,' he said with a brisk arm gesture of farewell, his back to her now as he climbed into the Jeep.

With a frustrated exclamation under her breath, Oriel turned on her heel and followed Kyrillos into the great tiled entrance hall. As she went in, her attention was immediately diverted. The sheer size of the room with its high, ornate domed ceiling, supported by delicately veined marble pillars, gave the impression she was entering a cathedral. Her eyes then took in the floor, which was paved with fabulous marble tiles arranged in a huge mythological picture: Pegasus the winged white horse surrounded by the Muses – the nine daughters of Mnemosyne and Zeus, each depicted in a dress of a different hue and presiding over an art or science.

The imposing grandfather clock that stood at the far end of the hall struck five o'clock, making Oriel jump. Kyrillos glanced at her covertly as he showed her into the guest dressing room and gave her the bag.

'Irini will bring the towels. When you have finished, ring the bell. I'll take you to the *salóni*.'

Entirely wordless in his dealings with Yorgos, the manservant now revealed a rich, well enunciated voice. His eyes, however, remained guarded. Oriel thanked him and Kyrillos closed the door gently behind her.

The circular room was luxurious to say the least, painted blue with tiled panels of fantastic murals all over the walls, interspersed with floor-to-ceiling mirrors and tall windows. In the middle of the room stood an elaborately carved wooden dressing table, painted in antique gold, with a matching stool. There was also an original *klinai*, a couch used by dinner guests in ancient Greece to recline upon during a symposium or a meal, with two matching bijou armchairs and a sofa, covered in a royal blue and gold silk brocade. The place was strongly redolent of expensive scents and body lotions, presumably used by other guests of Heliades. If the guest dressing room was this sumptuous, and decorated with such antiquated elegance, Oriel could only wonder what the rest of the house looked like.

There was a jug of water on a marble washstand, next to the basins, and Oriel poured herself a glass. It felt cool on her parched lips and she downed it in one go. Opening her bag, she was just rummaging around for her hairbrush when she heard murmurings in the hall outside the door.

'It's happening all over again, I tell you, Kyrillos,' whispered a woman's voice. 'One minute she was there, the next she was gone. Without a goodbye or anything. Just like that Dutch girl last year. The *Kyrios* was so angry. But she looked more afraid than anything, when I saw her outside his study.'

Oriel stilled, in reluctant fascination. Much as she didn't like eavesdropping, she could not help herself. Then she heard Kyrillos's voice. 'What do you expect, with these loose foreign women carrying on the way they do? It's not good that they stay here.'

'Yes, they must have excited the anger of Hades, *To Aórato*, the Unseen One.'

Kyrillos grunted. 'More like the anger of the *Kyrios*. I'd rather face Hades any day.'

'Even the *Kyrios* is under the power of the lord of torment. After all, look at the *Kyrios*'s wife and how she carried on ... And then the poor *Kyrios*, having to deal with that terrible business.'

'Hush, Irini, it's not good to speak of the dead that way.'

Oriel put her hairbrush down carefully on the dressing table, listening intently. Since all of Yorgos's cryptic remarks, her curiosity had been aroused and now what she was hearing seemed to be another tiny piece of the puzzle.

So Lekkas had a wife. Where was she now? Yorgos hadn't mentioned her at all. How did she fit in to the accursed ruling family that the estate manager had described so melodramatically?

'It's all the doing of *To Aórato*,' the woman went on. 'He is displeased, you mark my words. And today, this new lady is here and …'

'Enough, Irini,' Kyrillos hissed. 'That tongue of yours is so loose, one day it'll fall out of your head. Go, go! She's waiting.'

There was the sound of the manservant's hastily departing footsteps and then a pause. Knuckles rapped at the door.

Oriel composed herself. *'Erchontai se*, come in.'

Irini came in with a set of blue towels, which she put down on a small table. She was young, probably in her late twenties, brown-skinned with great jet-black eyes that blinked cautiously at Oriel but were warm and kindly. Her hair was also black, rich and shiny, cut in a short bob with a fringe. She wore an attractive navy uniform with a frilled and embroidered collar, an apron and a small cap.

'Kalispera, Despinis, I am Irini, the *kamariera*, the maid. I have brought you clean towels.'

'Kalispera, Irini. *Efharisto*, thank you.'

The Greek woman went to one of the stone cabinets recessed into the wall. 'Here you will find shampoo and all sorts of creams and perfumes for your use.' She moved to another cabinet, 'Here there is a hairdryer.'

Despite her earlier unease, Oriel couldn't help but smile at the *kamariera*'s fastidious and caring manner. 'Thank you very much, Irini, but I only need a quick shower to refresh myself. It's much hotter in Greece than in England.'

'Yes, today has been particularly hot. We've never had a May like it. Maybe there will be a storm. Do you need me to press anything for you?'

'No thanks. I have a change of clothes in my overnight bag which won't need ironing.'

'As you wish, *Despinis*. I will leave you now. When you have finished, ring the bell and Kyrillos will take you to the *salóni*. You will need something to eat.'

'I'm really not hungry at all, but thank you.'

Irini went to the door and then hesitated before turning round.

'The *Kyrios* might be very late. He had to go to Athens urgently.' She glanced at Oriel nervously. 'Did *Kyrios* Christodoulou mention it?'

Oriel guessed that Irini probably knew a great deal about what went on in this house and, if the maid were as indiscreet as Kyrillos had intimated, perhaps she might find some more answers by speaking to her.

Oriel nodded. 'He told me I would need to wait here for *Kyrios* Lekkas, yes.' Then she added casually: 'He also mentioned that there was a woman who left last night. Who was she?'

Irini shifted uneasily, her hand on the door handle. 'It was a French lady, Chantal.'

'Did she work for *Kyrios* Lekkas?'

Irini nodded. '*Né.* She was a student helper, part of that group who are digging up the old temple. Sometimes she helped at the olive press, too, in the office.'

Oriel remembered Stavros Petrakis explaining in his letter that there was another site being excavated inland. Some members of her dive team would be helping out there when the weather was too rough to be down on the wreck.

'Why did the woman leave? Did she receive bad news from France?'

Irini shrugged. 'I don't know, but it was very sudden.' She stared at Oriel with large, dark eyes. 'It is a sign of *kaki tichy*, bad luck.'

Oriel bit her lip, as superstitious beliefs were not part of her own thinking, but she wondered how far the maid would go in elaborating on what she had been saying to Kyrillos. 'What do you mean?' she asked.

'The old gods are still powerful on Helios. They control people's fate here. It is so, *Kyria*, trust me.' Seeing Oriel's barely concealed sceptical expression, Irini lowered her voice. 'I know that it is better to lose an eye than to get a bad name, and I don't wish to speak out of turn, but you seem like a nice young lady and—'

Irini broke off mid-speech as they heard Kyrillos calling her, and she scurried out of the dressing room with a sheepish expression on her face. The door closed behind her and Oriel pressed a hand to her throat, feeling the quickening of her pulse. What had

21

Irini been about to say? Then her mind drifted back to what she had overheard earlier: the maid's whispered mutterings about Hades. Surely Irini didn't believe that the ancient mythological god of the underworld had been responsible for scaring people off the island? Ignorance and superstition. Was it possible that in this day and age people were still ruled by the gods of myth and legend?

Oriel felt in a curiously divided mood. This place was riddled with dark secrets. Phrases had a dramatic quality – omens seemed to be hidden in every word; a sense of Greek tragedy fluttered in the air. She was glad to be here, on this savagely beautiful island that beckoned with its sense of mystery and antiquity, yet a strange feeling clutched at her heart, a sort of enchantment that made her feel uncomfortable.

Shrugging off her gloomy thoughts, Oriel took out a jade-coloured sleeveless dress from her overnight case and shook it loose. It was understated and well cut but feminine, and just right for a meeting. The steam of the bath would help the few creases drop out. It was an old trick her mother had taught her and it had never let her down. Oriel then proceeded to take out miniature samples of shampoo, conditioner, soap and body cream from a make-up bag. Her hand luggage always contained everything she would need if she were stranded somewhere for forty-eight hours. With her job, Oriel was often sent to places off the beaten track and so had learnt to be prepared. There were certain creature comforts she found it hard to be without.

Oriel went into the adjoining bathroom. It was smaller but just as luxurious as the main dressing room, with similar tilework on the floor and walls. It had a sunken bathtub in the middle, with a sink in blue stone. Her limbs ached. She had been travelling since the early hours of the morning and felt hot and sticky. The bath looked like heaven. Oriel had always preferred baths to showers, even in the heat – there was something so much more relaxing about having a long soak.

She hung up her dress and let the hot water run, filling the small room with steam for a few minutes, and then added the cold with the bubblebath she'd found on the side. Then she lay in the blue tub in a deliciously scented warm veil of bubbles, soaking away the fatigue of the day, lulled by the soft, persistent chorus of the cicadas outside the window as evening began to fall, singing their farewell to the setting sun. She'd better get dressed – it would be mortifying if Damian Lekkas came back and she was not ready for their meeting. According to Yorgos Christodoulou, she was already on shaky ground and, having learnt that one woman had just fled the island in unceremonious haste, Oriel did not want to give her prospective employer any reason to annul her contract. True, the *kamariera*, Irini, seemed even more dramatic in her pronouncements than Yorgos with his dark insinuations. Still, why had this woman, Chantal, left the island so hastily?

Oriel stepped out of the tub and wrapped herself in one of the huge towels. All the dust and grime of the journey was gone, and her skin felt smooth and silky as she stepped into white lace lingerie. After sitting down at the dressing table in the main room, she dried her long, pale-blonde hair with the dryer, then brushed it until it was shining, weaving it into a plait that she twisted and pinned at the nape of her neck, all the while pondering on the gossip she had heard since her arrival only a few hours ago.

Oriel looked at herself critically in the mirror, wondering whether or not to put on make-up. Having good skin, she often didn't bother with it, particularly as it was not practical for work. Perhaps because of that, she delighted in having the opportunity to indulge her feminine side and having lovely clothes was her specific weakness. If she were to spend her days knee-deep in dirt and covered in dust, Oriel reasoned, she could at least take pleasure in dressing nicely in her time off.

Large green eyes with glittering brown flecks stared back at her from the glass, their long dark lashes in arresting contrast to her hair. Deciding less was more, she touched some pink gloss to her soft full lips and some highlighter to her high cheekbones, emphasizing the good bone structure of her heart-shaped face. Finally, she slipped on her dress. As expected, the steam had relaxed the few wrinkles and the rich material moulded her slim figure to perfection, hugging her slight curves in all the right places. The warm jade of the silk jersey was well suited to her colouring, reflecting her eyes and giving them a mysterious quality. Yes, she thought, she looked older than her age and subtly sophisticated enough to meet the island's dragon. Confidence was what she needed; now she looked the part.

Oriel walked out of the bathroom and back into the domed hall. The whole place looked deserted, unwelcoming and somewhat sinister. *You're being ridiculous*, she told herself. *It's just a house.* She was about to retreat to the guest room, remembering she'd been told to ring the bell, when a voice stopped her.

'Ah, *Despinis* Anderson. I see that Kyrillos and Irini have looked after you well. I hope you found everything you needed.'

Oriel looked up abruptly to find Yorgos coming down the stairs, back from whatever business he had left to attend to. His hands were in his pockets, his black eyes crinkled in a cordial smile.

'Yes, thank you.'

'The *Kyrios* is on his way. He went to Athens by boat and is already back at the island. There's a mooring at the foot of the cliff, behind the house, so he won't be long now. I'll take you to the *salóni*, where you will be comfortable waiting for him. Were you given a glass of water?'

'Yes, thanks, I'm fine.'

'Irini makes delicious lemonade, and what about some of our special *melomakarona*? They're our traditional walnut biscuits made with currants grown on the island.'

'I will gladly try Irini's lemonade, thank you, but no biscuits. Perhaps later.'

A rush of footsteps sounded on the flagstones and, as if by magic, Irini appeared. Yorgos gave her his orders, then, turning to Oriel, he smiled again. 'I hope your meeting with the *Kyrios* goes as well as you hope. Remember, he can be difficult and moody so if you're successful today, be assured you can always come to me directly with any problems as he is not always so approachable. I'm sure I'll be able to sort things out for you.'

Oriel almost winced at his quietly patronizing speech. Oh, how self-satisfied the man was! 'How very magnanimous of you,' she said softly.

Yorgos either missed the edge of sarcasm in her voice or chose to ignore it. 'We have a saying in Greece: help me, so that I can help you, so that we can climb the mountain. Cooperation is everything, *Despinis* Anderson.'

Seeing as he was so eager to be helpful, Oriel decided to put it to the test. There was another thing she'd been wondering about. 'I've not seen *Kyria* Lekkas as yet. Am I to meet her as well?'

He gave a vacant smile and shook his head. 'The *Kyrios*'s cousin usually rests at this time of the day.'

'No, his wife, I mean.'

The estate manager raised an eyebrow, his jet-black eyes reflecting a curious hint of mockery. 'The *Kyrios* is a widower, *Despinis* Anderson. Has been for the past two years. Come, I'll take you to the *salóni* now.' With that, he set off across the hallway, leaving Oriel following in his wake, thoughtfully digesting this new piece of information. Damian Lekkas was becoming an increasingly complicated figure by the minute.

Oriel followed Yorgos down a spectacular passage paved in beige-coloured marble, past white statues and busts standing on plinths, the figures seeming to watch their progress like mute sentinels. Paintings of mythological characters hung on the walls, and Oriel's eyes drank in the exquisite neoclassical renderings as they moved past each one. At one point they turned a corner and she concluded she must be in another wing of the imposing residence, somewhere at the back of the house. Eventually Yorgos stopped at a pair of tall walnut doors and opened them with a flourish. Oriel understood the ceremoniousness of this gesture once she was in the room, and she gave a small gasp.

The drawing room was long and high and very large, its many windows facing the sea. It opened on to an enormous terrace with steps to the sprawling garden beyond. Like the hall, the ceiling was reminiscent of the vaulted roof of a church, and striking paintings, rare banners and fabrics covered the white walls. At the far right was a niche crowded with ancient Greek vases and terracotta urns. Priceless-looking antique jugs and figurines had place of honour on the white marble mantelpiece of an enormous fireplace. Sofas, cushions and chairs, upholstered in blue floral fabrics that reflected the ocean and the vivid azure sky, gave the room a serene elegance that to some might have appeared austere. In a corner by one of the tall windows stood a very large bronze telescope, presiding over a magnificent view of the island and sea. Not for the first time Oriel tried to imagine what the master of this vast domain must be like, owning everything he surveyed. One of the feudal *agrótes*, no doubt: landowners who ruled in these remote parts of the Ionian

Sea. Yes, she was sure that Damian Lekkas was very much lord and master of this land – a daunting thought in the twentieth century.

Yorgos had been standing silently beside her while she surveyed the room. 'I see that you are impressed,' he said finally.

Oriel nodded slowly. 'Yes, it is very grand. So many treasures …' she said, almost pensively. What had she signed up for? Surrounded by such awesome antiquities, her previous hesitancy returned as she wondered if she would be up to the job.

'I'd better leave you now,' announced Yorgos. 'By all means have a look at the garden. It is full of exotic trees and plants that the *Kyrios*, and his ancestors before him, imported from far-off lands. It's a great source of pride to him and he often tends to the plants himself. At this time when the sun is setting it is even more impressive.' With that, he retreated to the double doors and closed them behind him, leaving her alone.

Oriel moved on to the terrace with its imposing columns and wrought-iron lanterns and stood by the stone balustrade. The sun had sunk below the horizon and given place to a rosy twilight. An iridescence glowed across the whole sky. Drenched in golden light, the view was stunning: beyond the garden and the sea, the outline of green hills and crags fell away to the dark blue waters, while in the distance the island's houses seemed to rise straight from the living rock; the picture was so surreal that she wondered if she was dreaming. Dominating the view, the mountain Typhoeus seemed closer from here, shrouded in a cloud of haze, like a blot on the horizon. *The Secret Mountain,* she thought, remembering the Enid Blyton adventure book she had read again and again as a child, where for years a secret and strange tribe of people had made their home in the centre of a mountain.

She descended the polished white marble steps and wandered into the shadowy garden, weaving her way between the dark green foliage of the lemon trees and bushy mastics. In the tangled undergrowth the birds were sleepily gossiping while the short dusk lasted. Oriel passed a small pond with the statue of a beautiful nymph standing among the water lilies and an old weeping willow spilling into the shiny water. A breeze brought in gusts of scent: of blue sage and thyme, wild jasmine, frangipani and magnolia, which lingered in the air, teasing her senses. It was a wild heart of a garden, the kind you would find in ancient Greek legends, where fauns and satyrs fluted to each other in the dusk. Oriel took a deep breath and the atmosphere of Helios seemed to flow into her veins like a heady wine. The almost deafening sound of the cicadas matched the excited beat of her heart, held by the magic of the island.

It was getting dark. The last green tint of evening had disappeared, but Oriel still moved further into the garden among the dense green masses of exotic foreign trees and giant-fronded ferns. From the terrace she had noticed that there were steps beyond the lush grounds she was walking through, which she presumed led to the sea. She moved onwards as if seduced and unable to help herself. The whispering waves called to her and she could feel the salt on her lips.

She had almost emerged from the dense part of the garden into a moonlit clearing when suddenly her heart was in her throat …

CHAPTER 2

A shadow moved among the green leaves. A rush of heat prickled all over Oriel as, in that moment, she recalled the dark rumours she had heard about this place: the women who had decided suddenly to leave the island, superstitious fears … murders. The shadow moved again and she stared up at the tall, dark figure that stood a few feet away from her, framed by the splayed branches of two lemon trees. Though his features were shrouded in darkness, she could just make out his square broad shoulders. He took a step forward and, as he did so, moonlight fell on one half of his face.

Oriel felt as if she had been struck by invisible lightning, the blood draining from her body, and her legs seemed made from cotton wool. It couldn't be! Those bright and glowing slate-grey eyes were quite unmistakable … *once seen, never forgotten*, she told herself with stunned bewilderment, at least not by her.

'It *is* you,' he murmured, his eyes glinting with something unfathomable. He spoke impeccable English in that deep foreign voice imprinted on her memory. 'But then how could it be any other, with that flaxen hair that looks as if it's been woven with the silver rays of the moon?' He smiled languidly. 'It's good to see you again, Calypso. Or should I say *Despinis* Anderson? We never were properly introduced, were we?' He didn't bother to come forward but remained where he was, his shoulder propped against one of the trees, arms folded across his chest.

His eyes narrowed like those of a jungle animal as he watched Oriel standing there, holding her breath as if suspended in time. He spoke again quietly, coolly now, a sardonic veil covering whatever expression had kindled at the first stunned impact of their meeting. 'Remember me?' Struck dumb, Oriel's eyes were wide with disbelief. Surely *this* wasn't the man she'd agreed to work with for the next few months? It couldn't be! Her mind had to be playing tricks on her.

'Let me refresh your memory, dear Calypso.' He spoke again, this time in an even tone, and there was a touch of flint in his gaze that belied his smile. 'A brief, but hopefully pleasant, interlude in your carefree student days. We hardly spoke, of course, on that enjoyable night in question but, if I remember correctly, you were on a dig.'

Oriel fumbled for something to say. Of course she remembered. The way her heart raced just from his proximity was testament to that. The sheer size of him, with those broad shoulders and massive chest … his mere silhouette had a thrilling familiarity.

How many times in the past had she wished that he would walk into her life again? How many nights had he haunted her dreams as she searched hungrily in the dark for his lips, his arms, craving his touch? And now he was here, standing in front of her after all these years, opening the floodgates to all those memories and dreams, and she felt nothing but cold shock and panic. She stepped away instinctively, her heart thudding beneath the silk of her dress.

'Why are you hiding from me, Calypso? Haven't you missed me?' There was a glint of mockery in his smile.

At this, Oriel found her voice. 'Of course I remember you,' she answered, ignoring his second question. She made a valiant attempt to pull herself together, stepping forward and trying her best to give a professional smile of greeting. 'Although it would be easier, in the circumstances, if we could start off on a new footing, don't you think?'

He paused, his gaze assessing. 'New beginnings, mmm? In that case, welcome to my island, *Despinis* Anderson,' he said in his rich, whisky voice, suddenly pushing away from the tree.

Oriel caught her breath. Her attempt at a calm professionalism was cut straight through, and the smile was torn from her face. The dark stranger had moved sideways out of the shadows and, almost as though he'd planned it, in that second the moonbeams shone upon him, revealing a long, thin, jagged scar that stretched across the left side of his face, from the base of his temple down to his jawbone and the side of his neck, giving him an almost sinister look. He was watching her closely, she knew, to see if the sight of the disfigurement repelled her. She realized with some surprise that it didn't at all; it merely accentuated the strength and arrogance of his features.

What had happened to him?

Oriel didn't give his face more than the briefest glance, not trusting herself to surrender to the sudden longing to do so but, in that second, she took in the high-planed contours of it, the well defined lips – now set in a sardonic twist as he watched for her reaction – and the head of thick, raven-black hair. He was dressed in a close-fitting, crisp white shirt, which was expensive-looking but rolled up casually at the sleeves, revealing those strong muscular forearms that had once held her all night. The line of his lean torso tapered to long legs clad in tan trousers. She swallowed, her mouth suddenly dry, remembering how much she had known of the powerful frame beneath those clothes. He was as magnificent as ever. Even fully clothed, he still looked as if he had walked out of a pagan legend.

Yet as she looked at him, Oriel saw he was different in one respect. It wasn't just the scar that had changed him. There was a ruthless set to his jaw that had not been there before, a maturity in his bearing, a bitter cast to those unusual silver eyes.

'Not as you remember me, eh? Afraid of me, Calypso?' Damian Lekkas raised a hand to his temple and drew the length of his scar with his forefinger and a brief smile twisted his lips. 'Perhaps you find me repulsive now.'

Oriel couldn't help her gaze dropping to his granite-like thighs. 'Not at all,' she found the courage to murmur. 'You're just a little different, that's all.'

The moonlight shone down, so terribly clear it almost turned night into day. Damian's eyes flashed and, moving towards her, he caught her wrist in his iron grip, standing above her like doom itself. He lowered his voice. 'Want to bet?'

Oriel gasped and jerked her hand away, not because she was repelled by him but she could feel the old spell working its charm and she knew that this man was as compelling as ever, if not more so. She stepped back against the gnarled trunk of a nearby mastic tree, her mind reeling at how unbelievable all of this was.

Oh, God, what have I got myself into?

Looking down at her, he smiled sardonically. 'At night all cats are grey, goes the old proverb. Everything is equal in the dark.'

Oriel felt his words like a cold, hard blade, crude in their implication. As if she could so easily be seduced under the cover of darkness, like an alley cat yowling for a mate – any mate. Did he think he had a right to her all over again? She recoiled, bristling and, not for the first time, tried to control the trembling in both her body and voice.

'I wouldn't know, but what I do know is that I never mix work with pleasure. Ever.' Her tone was quietly emphatic, and she was relieved that her voice didn't betray her this time.

He gave a short, mirthless laugh. 'An excellent principle, but tonight you will dine with me, Calypso. We need to discuss work, there's much to talk about.' It was almost an order, coming from someone who wasn't used to having his demands turned down.

Oriel met his arresting gaze, those silver irises so pale in a face so tanned, and darkened further by moonshadow. They watched her, an arrogant glint shining in their depths. With his autocratic chin tilted slightly up, Damian's resemblance to a mythological Greek god had never been so marked. Now, though, he had a more forbidding presence, and she wondered how this aloof and intimidating figure had ever been the same man she'd met on another moonlit night like this in Aegina.

'No, I don't think I'll impose on your hospitality. It would be better to discuss the job tomorrow. Perhaps you can fill me in on everything in the morning and we can go over the plans then?'

Oriel was pleased with herself for drawing a line in the sand. She knew that it wouldn't take much – especially with wine and moonlight – to step over into the abyss. She would only succeed in embarrassing herself and, in the process, end up without a job as well. By tomorrow, she would have had more time to gather her wits and, in the sobering light of day, more fortitude, she hoped.

Damian looked taken aback and frowned. This was a man not used to people refusing him anything, least of all a woman, Oriel guessed. 'Come, I'm sure a proper meal and a glass of our excellent island wine will do you the world of good.' He spoke briskly.

'Actually, I would prefer you to drive me to the staff house, *Kyrios* Lekkas, if you please. I've been travelling all day and I would like to have an early night,' she retorted, pride strengthening her voice. 'Has the rest of my luggage arrived?'

Abrupt silence followed and, for the first time, Oriel saw a flash of the devil in Damian's eyes and a muscle tense in his jaw. She was sure she had angered him. Then the most surprising thing happened: he burst out laughing, a low husky sound that brushed her with heat from head to toe. *This man,* she thought, *is as fierce and unpredictable as the island itself.*

'The staff house, eh? Do you have any idea what it's like? Definitely unsuitable for a woman.'

'In what way?'

'In many ways, *Despinis* Anderson.' The night shadows played across his face as he moved closer to Oriel and stood in front of her, his arms folded across his broad chest once more, exuding brute strength. 'It's a primitive house, roughly built, and only meant to last for the duration of the dig. Nothing more.'

'I really don't see what all the fuss is about,' she went on stubbornly, trying to ignore how close he was.

His eyes gleamed. 'I will spell it out for you then, in one word. Sex. My team is now solely made up of men. Men with healthy libidos who will make mincemeat out of a woman like you. We've tried it once before and it seemed impossible to keep appetites in check, if you understand my meaning.'

Was he insinuating that she couldn't keep her own appetite in check? That *she* was insatiable?

Her eyes sparked and her response was clipped. 'I wouldn't worry about that, *Kyrios* Lekkas, I'm used to roughing it, and I'm perfectly capable of living and working with men. I know how to look after myself, I assure you.'

'Oh, I'm not worried about you,' he returned, with a cool smile. 'I'm sure *you* are quite capable of looking after number one. It's my men that I'm thinking of.' An edge of dry amusement entered his voice as he boldly looked her up and down. 'Remember, I've known the softness of that fine porcelain skin of yours. I wouldn't want anything to upset the balance of the team.'

Despite the undercurrent of sensuality in his words Oriel felt their sting, and even the hint of contempt behind them. Why had this man hired her if this was his attitude? She sensed his strange ambivalence towards her and his determination to remain distant and unfeeling. Did he simply want to see her discomfited for some reason? Perhaps he was looking to find a kind of twisted enjoyment in playing a sadistic little game of lord and master over one of his previous conquests, she thought. None of it made sense. Whatever the reason, her hopes for the job of her dreams were disintegrating with every minute in her new employer's presence. Her shoulders dropped slightly; suddenly she felt weary and filled with self-doubt.

The air had cooled and the cicadas chirped their evening song. Against the inky vault of night, the stars and the moon shone with lustrous brilliance, as if to remind her that even in the darkness there is light.

Damian's formidable masculine face softened in the moonlight, as though he realized he'd been too harsh on her and was getting less pleasure from his sport than he had expected. Like a weather-vane turning in the opposite direction, his eyes lost their flintiness and his voice became kinder.

'Look, I want to know you're safe,' he murmured with a small smile. 'We'll discuss where you'll stay tomorrow but allow me to be the host tonight. Have dinner and sleep in comfort here at the house.'

Now all Oriel knew was that with so much travelling, and the excitement of the past twelve hours, she felt exhausted. For tonight, there was no fight left in her. Besides, she hadn't eaten since the morning, she loved Greek food, and no doubt Damian's kitchen was as impressive as the rest of Heliades.

'Do me that honour,' he continued, 'and I assure you, I'll be nothing but the gentleman.' He raised an amused eyebrow and held out his forearm, like the upright hero of a Victorian novel. Oriel relaxed and couldn't help but laugh at this unexpected change of de-meanour, placing a mock-formal hand on his arm in acquiescence.

As she did so, his eyes flew to hers and Oriel felt the hard mus-cles stiffen involuntarily under her fingers. He stared at her while the silence of night deepened in the penumbra, lit only by the pure silver beams of the moon. A sudden weakness spread all over her body and echoes of old sensations, buried deep inside her, instantly resurfaced. She watched his silvery eyes blaze with the hidden fire of diamonds. His breathing was heavy, matching the rapid rise and fall of her breasts as he turned towards her, and his gaze locked on hers in the silence that followed.

'Calypso …' he murmured, so softly she almost wondered if she'd heard it. His eyes were searching her face. Gone was the grey stone in his expression. For one brief moment, a flicker of something else was there, a glimpse of smouldering turmoil. Then it was gone. Damian turned back to face the house, his hand grasping her elbow to guide her. He took a breath that was almost a shudder. 'Come, we need to eat. It's been a long day.'

As they approached the veranda, Kyrillos emerged from a side door, a pair of large hounds at his heels, one grey, the other brindle. Both animals clearly knew who was their master. They bounded over to Damian, leaping around him, until he controlled them with a word. '*Kátw!* Down!' They sat, heads erect, ears pricked, waiting on his next word or move. He bent down to scratch behind their ears. 'Oriel, meet Heracles and Peleus.'

She realized with a jolt that it was the first time he'd called her by her real name and she felt a rush of responding warmth, as well as relief, intuiting that it indicated a truce had been offered. 'They're Cretan hounds, *Kritikos Lagonikos*. One of the oldest hunting breeds in Europe. Two of the most faithful companions a man could ever wish for,' he said proudly.

Oriel eyed the great beasts apprehensively. *He runs with the wolves*. Wasn't that what Yorgos Christodoulou had said?

As he cast a paternal eye over the two dogs, Damian paused, a frown furrowing his brow. A dark look came over him. 'Kyrillos, why is Heracles still limping?' he asked sharply. 'Have you kept him in as I instructed? I ordered you to be sure not to let him exercise.'

Oriel was startled at the lightning change of tone and expression in Damian. Although the words had not been directed at her, she felt a sudden frisson of something close to fear. Damian stood, flanked by the great beasts, looking fierce and imperious. He was impressive to behold and she could see how commanding a leader of the island he must be.

At the same time, other words from Yorgos drifted into her mind: *Some say that if crossed, he would be capable of anything … even murder*. Her gaze travelled over Damian's towering form and she shuddered imperceptibly.

Oriel watched as Kyrillos snapped to attention, almost as if he were facing the wrath of a general about to issue a court martial.

'Yes … I mean no, *Kyrios*.' Kyrillos's words tumbled over themselves in a stammer. 'The dog was kept in, as you instructed.' And then venturing a little further in the naked hope of placating his master: 'The foot, I am certain it is getting better. I was only saying so this afternoon.'

'And you've been applying the antibiotic cream as ordered?' Damian's tone was still autocratic but his manner had relaxed just a little.

'Yes, *Kyrios*. Twice a day, as instructed.' Kyrillos's head was nodding vigorously as he spoke.

'Good, keep it up. If anything happens to the dog, it will be on your head.'

'Yes, *Kyrios*. Of course, *Kyrios*.'

Damian's face became impassive. 'And now, take *Despinis* Anderson inside and check if her luggage has arrived. We'll be having dinner in twenty minutes. Make sure she gets to the dining room on time.'

Saying nothing, still aghast at this feudal lord-and-master tirade, Oriel allowed herself to be led away, following in the footsteps of the manservant. Behind her, she could hear Damian whistling for his dogs. Damian Lekkas was definitely someone who expected to be obeyed, and who was used to having his way in everything. Not for the first time since setting foot on the island, a shiver ran down her spine at the thought of him but whether it was one of apprehension or – somewhat to her shame – something closer to arousal, she wasn't entirely sure.

* * *

'Happy is he who like Ulysses travels far' was the first thing that came to Oriel's mind as she stepped into the dining room. Kyrillos had fixed her a drink of iced lemon and, with a solicitous look, had left her to await the *Kyrios*. Now she stood gazing around her.

This room was in keeping with the other parts of the house that she had seen so far, crammed with objets d'art from all over the world. Damian Lekkas may be many of the things Yorgos Christodoulou had described, but the estate manager had not done justice to his master's love of antiquity or his refined eye for beauty. The wide room, with its white walls and marble floor, was bathed in candlelight. The circular nineteenth-century dining table, with a hundred years of polishing, reflected the candle-glow like still water. Its leaves were down, so it was smaller and more intimate, and set for two, with glittering crested silver and the finest crystal and bone china Oriel had ever seen. An ancient Corinthian bowl, with black geometric designs painted in a wide band around it, stood in the centre, filled with red roses, eloquent with romance. Arched French doors were wide open to the garden, letting in the sweet fragrances of the island and the noises of the night.

'You must be hungry.'

Oriel spun round and he was there. Standing in the doorway, Damian had now donned a black fitted waistcoat that hugged his muscular torso, accentuating the broadness of his chest and slim hips. He smiled politely and, despite the dramatic appearance of his scarred profile, he looked every bit the courteous host.

Oriel's heart gave a jolt as she stared back at him. He had lost that ferocious edge she'd witnessed back in the garden, but his eyes were piercing in their silent scrutiny of her and the force of his masculine presence was still intimidating. 'Yes, I'm famished now, actually,' she conceded with a self-conscious smile.

He crossed the room and pulled out a chair for Oriel, then sat down next to her, proffering the unmarked side of his face.

'I love the classical proportions of these rooms,' Oriel said, switching to Greek. After all, if they were to end up working together, it would be more professional to use Damian's own language, she thought.

He gave a surprised smile and nodded, obviously pleased. 'That's the first time I've heard you speak Greek. I'm impressed.'

She arched an eyebrow. 'Although you didn't stipulate it in the advertisement, I assume you need someone with fluent Greek. Isn't that the case?'

'Of course,' he answered, his mouth twitching a fraction.

Oriel looked up at the ceiling of the elegant room, which was decorated with a mixture of hunting and landscape scenes, then her gaze travelled to the large mosaic on one of the walls, representing fishing and seascapes.

'I was brought into the *salóni* earlier this evening and saw some of your beautiful artefacts and paintings,' she continued. 'It's like a sanctuary for valuable relics of antiquity here. Even from the outside, your house looks like a temple.'

'It was modelled on an old Byzantine villa,' he said, reaching for a chilled carafe of water and pouring them both a glass. 'It is very large, as you will have probably gathered from the exterior. My ancestor, Gjergj Lekkas, built it in the nineteenth century, when he seized this isle. At the time it was just a load of hills and scrub. He turned it into a prosperous island. This room, like the *salóni*, is part of my wing.'

'From what I've seen of your house, I gather that you're a great collector.'

'These are all pieces bought on my travels and from auctions around the world, where I try to buy up the treasures of my country. They're part of our history, of our identity, and shouldn't be scattered to the four winds.'

Oriel gestured to one of the two marquetry cabinets that stood against the wall at each end of the room. They held clay pots, vases, pitchers, fruit stands and what she identified as baby feeding bottles, some of them resembling contemporary sculptures. 'Those are antique cooking utensils, aren't they?'

'Yes, for the most part. Some are just items that were used around the house in ancient Greece.'

'Fascinating! I did extensive studies on domestic objects during my MA.' Her green eyes became animated. 'The amount of artefacts we unearthed on Aegina was staggering. So many glazed and fired cooking pots from an ancient Greek kitchen are just like the ones used today. It really was an amazing opportunity being there.'

Damian gazed at her intently, the corner of his mouth curving in a wry smile. 'Yes, being in Aegina must have given you many memorable experiences.'

'Yes, in fact …' Oriel stopped abruptly, realizing too late that in her gushing enthusiasm for her subject, she had inadvertently mentioned her time in Aegina and Damian had wilfully misinterpreted her meaning. She took a sip of water, suddenly tongue-tied. However, any prolonging of her embarrassment was mercifully interrupted as the door opened at that moment. A servant with a green cap and full green trousers came in, bearing a tray with a dozen small dishes and a large plate of flatbread, which he placed on the table with a wide smile. He was dark-skinned, with gentle black eyes and very white teeth. Oriel could see that he wasn't Greek. Probably Egyptian or North African, she thought, and smiled back at him, grateful for the distraction. 'Thank you.'

The man bowed his head twice but did not speak.

'This is Hassan,' Damian told her. 'He comes from Aswan in Upper Egypt. Because he is mute, he was being ill-treated in his village so I brought him over here to work for me.'

For some reason, the information surprised her. Hardly the gesture of the man they called *Drákon* Damian. Her eyes slid back to him with renewed curiosity. 'That's very kind,' she said.

Damian ignored the compliment. 'These are *mezedes*. You have probably been served them in one of the restaurants in Athens or on the touristic islands. Maybe even Aegina.' His mouth quirked as he registered Oriel's blush. 'The *krasomezédhes*, I hope, will be a totally different experience. They are homemade, each using a different vegetable cooked in olive oil and the herbs of our island. They go particularly well with wine.' He turned to Hassan to thank him and, as the servant left the room, Damian picked up a crystal decanter and began pouring some red wine into two fine-stemmed glasses.

'Are you familiar with traditional Greek cuisine?'

'I'm afraid my only experience comes from *tsipourádika* or tavernas.'

'The food served in those places is designed to please the ignorant masses,' he said with a dismissive gesture. He spooned small mounds of the appetizers on to Oriel's plate and passed her the bread before helping himself.

Oriel found herself watching him as he started to eat. Damian's mouth was so sensuously sculpted that it gave her a jittery feeling deep inside.

He looked up and flinty sparks of amusement lit his eyes. He waved a hand. 'Come, eat! I thought you were famished? We can't have you wasting away now, can we?'

Mortified he'd caught her staring, to cover her awkwardness Oriel picked up a piece of bread and dipped it in some hummus.

'I'd like to talk about the job, if you don't mind,' she said, almost abruptly.

'Yes, of course.' Damian's face instantly assumed a blank professionalism. 'There's plenty to brief you on. It's an exciting wreck. We've had full cooperation from the Minister of Culture in Athens. In fact, I may have to travel a bit to the mainland while you're here. There's another site on land that my colleague, Vassilis, is in charge of. A joint project with the Ministry to uncover a Minoan temple.' He took another forkful of food. 'As for the underwater excavation, I'd like to take you down to the wreck in the next day or two. So far, progress has been slower than I'd have liked. As soon as there's a storm out at sea, it can throw the whole project for a few days. With all the debris and silt, you can't see a thing. The currents can be treacherous too.'

'How did you find it?' asked Oriel, relieved to be once more on safe ground.

'The usual story,' said Damian. 'It's almost always fishermen who tip off divers about wreck sites.'

'Yes, of course. Wrecks make rich feeding grounds for fish.' Oriel skewered a morsel of the *krasomezédhes* with her fork, appreciating the delicious food that was far superior to anything she'd tasted elsewhere in Greece.

'Exactly. For that reason, a fisherman will often keep the information close to his chest. After all, knowing the best places to fish makes the difference between having a family fed and clothed or not.' Damian gestured at the food in front of them. 'We're a self-sustaining community on Helios and we all work together. Still, life can sometimes be tough on the island, especially in winter. You can't afford to have a rival vessel encroaching on your patch.'

'So how did you discover this wreck in the end?' Oriel asked.

'A tongue loosened by too much ouzo in the bar one night,' Damian smiled. 'Although I've known the fisherman in question since I was a boy and I think he felt honour-bound to reveal what he'd seen. He'd been bringing up pieces of amphorae in his nets for quite a while, you see. Those earthenware pots were clearly ancient and the islanders are well aware how passionate I am about preserving our heritage.' He jutted his chin, the hard and autocratic look returning to his face. 'They certainly don't want to cross me.'

Oriel shifted her gaze uneasily from Damian, aware once again just how powerful a force this man wielded. Perhaps if she didn't look at him, she could behave normally.

'That was what attracted me to this job,' she explained, determinedly fixing on the bowl filled with red roses in the centre of the table. 'So many dive teams behave like pirates, smashing and grabbing the moment they find a wreck. Most of them have such callous disregard for history and heritage.' Her voice became heated. 'They couldn't care less about preserving a site, so long as they can get their hands on the spoils.' She took a gulp of water, as if to douse the fire in her cheeks – whether caused by Damian's proximity or her own righteous outrage, she wasn't quite sure.

Her next words were still impassioned, but there was a wistful quality to them. 'Just think what we've lost, the provenance of these ancient relics. All those clues as to how people lived and worked thousands of years ago.'

She placed her glass down and moved it distractedly in a slow circle in a bid to settle back to the calm professional once more, failing as she did so to notice how Damian's expression had softened during her tirade.

'Do you know how old it is?' Oriel raised her eyes to his again.

'I think it's Roman, but we haven't brought anything to the surface yet so I can't give you a precise age. It must have been a big argosy, though. There are numerous amphorae littered about the area.'

'Thank goodness for that.' Oriel shoulders relaxed a little. 'I was terrified that you'd already been cutting into the wreck and sucking everything up with an air-lift. I don't suppose a cartographer has made a map of the site?'

'Oh, doubting Calypso!' Damian grinned. 'Don't worry, it's all been done. There's a floating grid secured over the whole area and the map has been drawn. You'll be able to plot your finds accurately, never fear.'

He paused, contemplating Oriel for a moment, his eyes roving over her lazily. She felt an answering warmth suffuse her, infuriated at the way her body stirred whenever he turned that penetrating gaze in her direction.

'… Although I'm half wishing I *had* done something to annoy you,' he continued sardonically, then lowered his voice as his gaze held hers. 'The way those emerald eyes of yours flash like sharp jewels when your blood's up … your chest heaving in righteous indignation …' Oriel's heart jumped into her throat as he looked her up and down almost insolently. 'Have you any idea, Calypso, just how alluring that whole schoolmistress act is?' He gave a smoky laugh and her heart almost stopped. 'In fact, I almost wish I'd used some explosives on the wreck. That way you might have told me to stay behind after class.'

His eyes were hooded, with an almost sleepy leonine quality, but Oriel wasn't fooled for one moment. This man was alert to every move she made, every word she said. Her new employer was determined to have the upper hand. If before, just for a moment, Damian had forgotten himself – lost in his passion for Helios and its history – he was back again now. A cat with a mouse.

She sensed – with a ripple of excitement mixed with dread – that he was intent on subduing her; but before he did, he wanted the pleasure of toying with her. Well, she refused to be intimidated by him. Oriel's pulse skittered but she willed it to calm. 'If I were to reprimand you, something tells me that you're hardly the kind of man who accepts being told he's made a mistake. Not by a woman, anyway.'

'That depends on the woman … and the reprimand.' His mouth gave that little twist of a smile as he faced her. He had deliberately misinterpreted her words.

Oriel's eyes met the slits of glittering steel watching her between dark lashes, reminding her of what had passed between them on Aegina. She felt the hot colour rise in her cheeks.

Could she really do this job? She wanted it so badly. Her own Roman wreck, what archaeologist wouldn't welcome this opportunity? But she was fearful too. She intuited the iron control, the strange pleasure he took in her discomfiture, and she quailed at the thought of what her total subjugation might bring. If she were to let her guard down, what then? Damian was different in so many ways to the man she had met all those years ago and there was indeed a cruel edge to him now. Yet he was drawn to her, that she could tell. He had hired her, after all. But she sensed in every bone of her body that his fascination was something to be afraid of, to avoid if she valued her peace of mind, her career … her own self.

Knowing that the conversation needed deflecting as soon as possible, Oriel grasped wildly at the first thing she could think of. 'Is that taramasalata?' she asked, pointing to a dish in front of Damian.

'Here, taste it,' he said, tearing a piece from the large oval of flatbread and spreading it with a dollop of the dark pink paste. 'It is carp roe, but what you're likely to have tasted is a poor substitute. This dip is the real thing, the way Greek families eat it in their home. It's made with roe, potato, olive oil and lemon.'

'Thanks.' Oriel took the canapé from him and popped it in her mouth. 'Delicious! You're right, quite different from what I've had before. This seems to have bits in it,' she said after a pause.

'Yes, it is our family's own method of preparing it, borrowed from the Turkish recipe where the roe must remain substantially intact.'

'I've just noticed, the other *mezedes* we're eating are mostly vegetable or cheese based. The ones served up in restaurants are often primarily meat.'

He nodded. 'We don't eat much meat on Helios. The land is hard here. Men live close to the earth, and even today they exist very much as they did in ancient times. Our milk, cheese and meat come from our black goats. Our fishermen provide the fish, and the land gives us plenty of olives, figs and grapes. The islanders trap birds in nets and still look for wild honey but they are mostly vegetarians, like our ancestors who only ate meat when a sacrifice of an animal was made to the gods. Some would say that Helios is a very primitive island.'

Oriel remembered Irini's bizarre superstitions that still clung to a belief in the ancient gods. 'I hope that doesn't mean the primitive custom of sacrifice is still practised on the island?' she asked wryly, lifting her wine glass and putting her lips to the rim.

Damian watched her, a mischievous smile tugging at his lips. 'Only occasionally, I assure you, though we do call this wine you're drinking the Rapture of the Virgins.' His gaze sparked with amusement and intensity. It held her as if it were meant to magnetize her. 'The sacrifice, in those cases, is the most primitive of all.'

Oriel's eyes shot to his face, hot awareness flaring in her at this deliberately provocative remark, then suddenly the door opened and Hassan came in with the main course and started clearing away the appetizers.

In the shadows of the candlelit room, Damian's and Oriel's eyes locked over the blood red of the wine in the glass she was holding.

Don't look at me like that, she thought. *Dear God, I must forget that night if this is going to work.*

Yet forgetting him hadn't worked in all those years. However hard she tried, Oriel had never been able to surrender herself to another man. Whether it was the cruel desertion by two men in such quick succession that had shocked her into celibacy, or no man had thrilled her sufficiently to succumb since Damian, she wasn't entirely sure. Meanwhile, she travelled the world, seeking one exciting assignment after another, partly because it was in her nature but also because she needed to channel her restless energy. That night, she had to acknowledge, had released something in her and she had been running from it ever since.

Perhaps now it had found her.

Had this dinner been set up before her arrival, before Damian even realized that she was the one – his one-night stand of six years ago – whom he had employed? Or had he recognized the photograph she had attached to her résumé? Yes, that was it: he had known all along who she was. Perhaps Yorgos Christodoulou had some inkling about this and had tried to protect her, in his own way, by putting her off the job. But what was Damian's game?

'Are your thoughts private or can anyone join in?' Damian's lightly bantering voice broke the silence.

'Sometimes I find it best to keep my thoughts to myself, don't you?' she countered.

'Usually, yes,' he shrugged. 'But you look as though you have something on your mind.' Then, uncovering the earthenware pot Hassan had placed on the table, he continued without waiting for her answer. '*Katsíka youvetsi* is a real Greek speciality, usually made with beef, though sometimes with *arni*, lamb, but on Helios we make it with *katsíka*, goat, which gives it a much stronger flavour. Here, give me your plate.'

Damian stood up and served her a spoonful of the aromatic dish. The wick of the candle flared and threw his imposing shadow on to the dining-room wall. She tensed as if this Greek god towering over her as he piled food on to her plate might suddenly bend his head and brush her skin with his lips. Or was that merely wishful thinking? She shook off the thought, struggling for equanimity.

Damian helped himself and sat down. A benign smile quirked at the edges of his mouth but his eyes were darkly intent behind the half-lowered lashes. 'Relax,' he said in a deep voice that sent an involuntary wave of heat rushing through Oriel, and she found with dismay that she couldn't prevent the sudden languorous melting between her thighs at its caress and the innuendo it conjured up.

'We have good food and wine, and this is a perfect Helios night. What else is important, *agápi mou*?' He filled her empty glass with more of the Rapture of the Virgins elixir and topped up his own. Oriel noted once again the strong grace of his well kempt hands, the subdued ripple of muscle as he poured the vermilion liquid.

'You like to shock, don't you?' she murmured. The question came out of the blue, surprising even her. The wine must have made her bold, or foolish – she wasn't sure which it was.

He didn't miss a beat. 'In my experience, people like to be shocked. Besides, one is usually shocked by the truth, eh?'

Damian was suddenly turning on the charm and she was finding it hard to keep up with his lightning changes in mood. The surroundings were beautiful, the food was delicious and the wine had a velvet, moreish quality. He was right: nothing else was important. Her gloomy thoughts were being gradually dispelled and replaced by a wonderful languor that was taking over her senses.

She could hear the distant whisper of the waves and the subtle rustle of the leaves in the breeze that had just come up. They were both silent for a while. Outside, all sounds were similarly muted and there was hardly a breath of wind coming through the wide-open windows. Oriel could see the mass of starlight shining in the distance. How far away England seemed to her tonight, even though she had only left it that morning.

The candlelight flickered on Damian's face and Oriel's eyes skimmed the fearful scar which, in the shadows of the room, appeared then disappeared as he moved his head, one minute giving him the semblance of a god and the next of a devil. She wondered how he had come by it. Perhaps the shark attack that Yorgos

Christodoulou had told her about?

Now as she studied him she saw other alterations. There was a fine network of crow's feet around his eyes. Deeper creases were etched between his nose and the corners of his mouth, making him seem older than he was. Every feature of his face suggested pride and dominance and a hard, unyielding will, she thought; everything but his mouth, which was oddly gentle, with its full lower lip. His jaw was more set than she recalled, and only his eyes remained as brilliant and arresting as she remembered them.

She was looking at the scar when Damian turned and caught her eye. His brows arched derisively, his teeth flashing white against the dark bronze of his skin.

'Why not ask if you're curious?' he said softly.

Oriel flushed. 'I'm sorry, I didn't mean to stare.'

'I don't mind … Do disfigurements have a fascination for you?'

'No, of course not,' she said quickly. 'Anyway, yours isn't a disfigurement. It gives you a rather … piratical look.'

Damian chuckled. 'Pirate indeed!' He tilted his head back a little and looked at her directly. 'And you like pirates?'

Her eyes dwelt on the dark head and the broad shoulders of the man sitting beside her. The deep gash on the side of Damian's face didn't bother her in the least – she barely noticed it now. She was only aware of his fiercely masculine appeal – it made her tingle from neck to toe as if she had been numb for a long time and every limb, every nerve in her body, was just beginning to come alive.

She smiled enigmatically, taking another sip of wine and feeling the beneficial warmth of the liquid trickle through her veins, then gave her undivided attention to the goat stew.

'This is delicious,' she said, deliberately ignoring his question. Her gaze meandered around the elegant room. 'Tell me about this house. It seems enormous, a real labyrinth.'

Damian took a swig of wine. 'Gjergj Lekkas, my ancestor, built this mansion in the first quarter of the nineteenth century over the imprint of a Roman palace, which had been almost burnt to the ground. The site was enormous. He was able to save parts of the central area. Some of the frescoes and all the statues that decorate the front of the house are nearly as vivid as the day they were created.'

'Who inhabited the island before your ancestor took possession of it?'

'It was abandoned. There were rumours about it that frightened the people away.'

'Rumours?'

'Stories about people disappearing on the island, never to be found again.'

Oriel's eyes widened slightly. *Disappearing*? Shadowy thoughts of the murders crept into her mind again.

Damian shrugged. 'But there's a very logical answer to that. The terrain on this island is mostly clay, and some sandy parts, like many of our beaches, are treacherous. Boards have been placed over areas where quicksand might be a hazard,' he shook his head and spread his hands, palm upwards, in a gesture entirely Greek, 'but unfortunately there are still accidents. Especially when twigs and leaves gather on the surface.'

Oriel looked apprehensive. 'Helios *is* a dangerous place, then.'

'Of course, but doesn't danger have its fascination?' he said, giving her a long, hard look.

Her brows drew together in an irritated frown. 'Can you ever say anything without it having a double meaning?'

Damian looked at her over the rim of his glass. 'And can you never take my words at face value?' he countered, apparently unruffled.

The tension between them seemed to turn her bones into fluid. Every inch of Oriel was aware of him, of his powerful frame and those long, elegant brown hands that were now idly playing with the stem of his glass.

Hassan came in again, this time bearing a beautiful golden cake. He took away the earthenware crock of goat stew, changed the plates, and placed the cake in the middle of the table.

'*Karydopita*, our national walnut cake,' Damian told her. 'Quite delicious. It is made with breadcrumbs, crusted walnuts, cinnamon and cloves, and then drenched in syrup. We have our own recipe, of course,' he smiled. He placed a slice of the gooey cake on a plate and passed it to Oriel, then proceeded to open another bottle of wine.

'Not for me, thank you,' she said, raising a hand. 'I've already had too much to drink.'

'What are you afraid of now?' he queried, his expression faintly amused but almost detached as he assessed the graveness of her face.

Oriel met his eyes determinedly. 'I'm not afraid, but I think that I've already indulged myself too much tonight.'

'Do you not like our wine, or is it your English restraint that holds you back?'

'No, it's my common sense,' she answered quietly, attempting cool civility. Of course she had lied when she said she was not afraid of him. He did frighten her a little, not because of his scars, or even his overbearing manner – but because she was tempted by him, just as much as before. Perhaps even more so.

He filled his glass and took a sip of wine. 'There's no harm in indulging oneself from time to time,' he said, his voice tinged with a slight drawl of amusement. His deep gaze embarrassed her suddenly and she picked up the small silver fork to start on her cake.

From somewhere far away in the night came the faint echoes of a flute, floating like a breath over the hills. The low woody sound was almost as spellbinding as Damian's voice, Oriel thought. 'I like that sound … a flute. Who would be playing at this time of night?'

'Oh, a shepherd sitting on the hill outside his shed.' He was silent for a moment. 'I see no wedding ring on your finger, are you not married?'

'No, I'm not.'

'Engaged?'

She glanced at him. 'Nope.'

'I would have thought with your beauty, and the impressive credentials I read on your résumé, you would have been snapped up by now. In Greece, a girl of your age would already be a wife and mother,' he said in his usual forthright manner.

It was on the tip of Oriel's tongue to retort that it was none of his business what she did with her life, but she bit it back. 'I've not found the right partner, that's all.'

'On Helios, it is for the parents to find the right person to take care of their daughter. They are the best judge of what is best for her. That way, it's very rare for a woman to stay unmarried.'

Oriel shot him an ironic look. 'Really? How very convenient for everybody except for the lady concerned. What about love?'

Only then did she remember something else. *He's been married. His wife had died.* Was theirs an arranged match? Had he loved her? Yorgos had mentioned that Damian only ever had feelings for one woman. Was it his wife?

Damian continued, seemingly ignorant of her unease. 'You see, love is a sweet and savage combat, more so in a land like mine. Women need protection against the softness of their heart and that is why, here, a woman always belongs to a man. He is her shield, her protector. Her father first, then her husband.'

'The sexual revolution has clearly passed Helios by,' Oriel noted drily.

'Modern women are losing their femininity. By doing away with those womanly characteristics with which God has endowed them, they have thrown to the wind everything that makes them different, secret, mysterious,' he pinned her with an unwavering look, 'and therefore desirable to a real man.'

She stared at him. Such words were demeaning to any woman, yet she couldn't deny a tremor of arousal that made her curse herself. She lifted her chin. 'I really don't much care for those sorts of ideas, they belong in the dark ages. The world has moved on, in case you hadn't noticed. As owner of this island you should be trying to enlighten your people instead of holding them back.'

'Tell me, Calypso, have you ever let a man have the last word?'

'Rarely, if I could help it,' she replied, with a raised eyebrow.

At this he laughed out loud, and Oriel was caught off guard once more, as earlier in the garden. This was different, however. She remembered this husky, exotic sound and now she saw a flash of the old Damian, the warmth of the man she'd known so briefly before.

'Anyhow, to return to what we were saying,' she said, endeavouring to focus her mind again, 'I don't see what all this has to do with my being married or not.'

He smiled. 'It definitely has to do with whether you have any attachments. This could turn into a long assignment. Is there someone in England waiting for you?'

'I didn't say that I would take the job.'

Damian seemed to be idly watching the wine in his glass, its changing colour as he moved it gently in the candlelight. 'Really?

You've signed a contract. Breaking it would cost me a lot of money and heartache. Without wishing to flatter you, archaeologists of your calibre, especially those trained to work underwater, aren't easy to come by.'

She enjoyed the triumph of hearing him acknowledge her worth. Still, that didn't solve all her problems. 'I admit that I find the job description very interesting and the experience it'd give me would help further my career beyond anything I've done before.'

'But?'

Oriel finished her cake and, putting down her fork, looked him straight in the eye. 'I would like to be treated like the rest of your employees. The fact that we knew each other almost a decade ago is irrelevant.'

'I don't think so. *Moira*, fate, *le destin, destino, maktoub* … the word exists in every language. The hidden forces that are at work behind the scenes, arranging our lives ahead of our own decisions.'

'That notion exists only in Greek tragedies.'

'I disagree, I believe things happen for a purpose. Sometimes they are there to test us, other times to give us a second chance. Fate has thrown us together in a particular way. Who are we to say there isn't some purpose behind it?'

She glanced at him dubiously. 'The only coincidence here is that I read your advert. As you said yourself, archaeologists with my sort of background are not common, and this promises to be the job of a lifetime, so obviously I would have applied for it.'

'Actually, we received a very good response.' He gave her a rakish smile. 'But I recognized you from your photograph. You haven't changed that much … though now I detect a touch of pain in those emerald eyes of yours, and a bitter edge to your voice.'

Did he not see the irony of his own words?

'No one can assume life to be all smiles and no scratches, don't you think?'

Oriel was a little shocked at her own bluntness but Damian had ruffled her feathers with his patronizing assessment of the woman she had become.

He ran his hand over his scar pensively. '*Touché,*' he murmured. 'I expect so.' He then pushed his wine glass to one side. '*Katanoitó,* now then, I have told you about the job, and you have admitted that this would be an opportunity not to be missed. What is your answer? Do we have an agreement that you will stay?'

Oriel looked at him squarely. She would give him his answer, but on her own terms. 'I'd be grateful if we could discuss it in the morning. I'll sleep on it.'

Hassan came into the room to clear the table, interrupting what was turning into an awkward conversation.

'Ah, coffee,' said Damian, rising from the table. 'Shall we have it outside? The night is balmy and now there's a light breeze from the sea.'

Oriel acquiesced and they went out on to the vast terrace, lit by wrought-iron lanterns, with its comfortable Lloyd Loom armchairs. Huge terracotta pots, set at different levels, overflowed with brilliant blooms of honeysuckle and roses that lent a sweet fragrance to the air.

She moved to the wide balustrade and stared down at the spectacular landscape spread out below. The moonlight shone clearly, illuminating the terrace and falling brilliantly on the garden, etching the trees in a graceful silhouette; it was a world of peace and beauty, so still that in the distance beyond them she could hear the song of the sea on the outer reef, breaking with a soft rhythm. The scents of the night-bound island hung in the atmosphere, and the croaking of bullfrogs from the pond could be heard plainly. Oriel found it intoxicating. The enchantment of Helios was upon her, that spell by which this ancient place made her own those whom she elected; the kind of sorcery from which there is no escape, which lifts men and women to heaven or drags them down to hell.

'This place is quite unique,' she murmured, almost imperceptibly.

'You like it?'

'How can one not?' she whispered, hugging her arms around herself and inhaling deeply.

He came to stand beside her. 'I'm happy that at least one aspect of this assignment has met with your approval. I hope, by morning, others will seem equally favourable and you will cease your ...' Damian hesitated and his lips gave that little twist of a smile, '... prevarication.'

'If I'm prevaricating, it's with good reason. I need to think about it.'

'What is there to think about?'

She eyed him sideways with a wry smile. 'Oh, I can think of a few things.'

'Is all this about your pride, because I recognized your photograph? I can assure you that your résumé was the most impressive among the twenty applicants who applied for the job.' Damian waved a hand as if to dismiss her objections. 'Besides, Stavros Petrakis, my head of works, was the one to shortlist you. Your credentials made quite an impression on him. When your résumé was brought to me, there was only one other candidate who seemed suitable and he couldn't start until next month. It was a no-brainer.'

Oriel said nothing but just stared out into the starlit sky. He seemed to have an answer for everything and she no longer knew what to think. The air vibrated with tension. Damian took a packet of cigarettes out of his pocket and offered her one.

'Do you smoke?'

'No, not any more. I used to. Bad habit.'

'Do you mind if I do?'

She glanced at him briefly. 'No, go ahead, please …'

Damian lit his cigarette and the flame from the lighter illuminated his face, accentuating the deep indentation marring its once beautiful symmetry. He looked at Oriel for several long, lingering moments. 'You really don't trust me, do you?' he said softly, his eyes narrowing on her tense expression behind the spiral of smoke.

She picked her words carefully. 'Your estate manager thought you'd find me unsuitable and would send me back immediately. In fact, he almost tried to dissuade me from staying. He told me strange things have happened on the island. That a young woman who'd been working on the site had decided to leave very suddenly last night.'

Damian's face darkened. 'Yorgos has his own agenda. He is very efficient at his job and I've known him all my life, which is why I allow him more latitude than I do most, but he's somewhat unpredictable.' He drew on his cigarette and switched his gaze to the shadowy outlines of the garden. 'I admit that a young lady, who had been contracted to help on the dig and in the estate office, decided to leave. That was her decision and I couldn't stop her.'

Now that she had him on the defensive, Oriel decided to press him further. 'Apparently, a similar incident occurred last year, when another student also left in a hurry.'

Damian muttered something under his breath. 'I'm impressed! You haven't been here twenty-four hours and you're already well informed about the trivia that occupies the wagging tongues and idlers of this island.'

'But a similar incident did occur, didn't it?'

He paused and put one hand in his pocket as he smoked, as if deliberating whether or not to answer her question. 'You seem very interested in the local gossip. What does it matter why these women left?'

'It matters if I'm to be working in the same conditions. They were both part of your team.' Perhaps it was inappropriate for her to pursue this line of questioning but he hadn't given her a direct answer. Nothing he'd said had contradicted her fear that these women had been used by him and then cast aside when he'd become bored.

'Yes, they were, but they were unpredictable enough to leave without working their notice ... so perhaps it's for the best that they're gone.' He glanced at her, the moonlight making his eyes glow even more brightly. 'You're different.'

'Am I?' Something in the way he spoke made Oriel search his face. She wanted so badly to believe that was true; that she wasn't just another employee that Damian intended to use as his plaything.

Hassan appeared on the terrace with a tray of coffee and a plate of sweetmeats, which he placed on the table. Neither Damian nor Oriel said a word as he moved about soundlessly before leaving them alone once more.

'How do you take your coffee?'

'Black. No sugar, please.'

Damian went over to the table, lifted what Oriel recognized as an antique Persian Qajar silver pot and poured the coffee from the long curved spout. There arose a delectable aroma as the fresh coffee whirled ink-black into the cups. 'It's strong and bitter,' he said, 'not like the brown-coloured water you get served in some restaurants abroad. Are you sure you won't have sugar or milk?'

'Quite sure, thank you.' Oriel smiled. She herself wasn't fond of the weak brew they called coffee in England either. 'I've travelled in Greece, as well as Turkey and Egypt, where the coffee is much stronger and thicker than this. In fact, in Greece I've always been served Turkish coffee, especially in shops. Shopkeepers are always keen to offer you a cup of coffee. Everyone is so very hospitable here.'

'It's what we call *philoxenia*, an awareness of the needs of strangers. "If it were not for guests, all houses would be graves," that's what Khalil Gibran says. A truth which the Greeks firmly believe.' He motioned to the chairs. 'Would you like to sit?'

'Actually, I'm happy here with this wonderful view,' she answered, turning to look at the garden.

The breeze blew warm, carrying upon it the intoxicating fragrance of flowers and shrubs. From her vantage point, Oriel could see a pergola in the form of a small temple, its shallow steps descending between high hedges of Surinam cherry and oleander like an overgrown classical ruin in an eighteenth-century folly garden. A tangle of plants flowed over its stone terrace and the surrounding trees wrapped in passion-flower vines created a breathtaking view. The night was hushed save for the trickle of water in the nearby pond, filled with arum lilies and water lettuce.

Damian moved back to the balcony, handing Oriel the cup and studying her with open intent for a few moments. 'In the moon your hair shines like silver.' His eyes remained fixed on her while he drank his coffee, and once again she felt that she was being magnetized by his silvery gaze, so vitally piercing it was almost surreal.

She knew that look – oh yes, she knew it too well. It had hypnotized her years ago, and now its captivating power was washing ripples of weakness along her spine, arousing a clamouring desire deep inside her that threatened to force her to her knees and, along with it, an emotion she dared not indulge.

Oriel blinked. She didn't know how she felt any more. She was wound up, jumbled inside like a disordered jigsaw puzzle. Her mind told her to run from this Greek god as soon as she had the opportunity; her body was longing to surrender to him. If only she could think clearly. If only she could convince herself that her body, as well as her mind, was equally able to resist Damian's devastating sensuality.

'It has been a long day, eh?'

Oriel drained her cup. 'It's been an interesting day, certainly. Thank you for your hospitality, it was a delicious dinner.'

'The first of many, I hope.'

'Perhaps. Though if I take the job, I'm sure I'll be happy eating at the local taverna with the rest of the team,' she said mildly.

His brow furrowed. 'If you take the job, we'll be discussing this stubborn idea of yours about staying at the staff house.' He took the empty cup from her and placed it with his on the broad surface of the balustrade.

Oriel wasn't in the mood to enter into another argument about it now. 'Really, there's no need for your concern,' she said. 'I've already told you, I've worked on many excavations around the world. There were only ever a handful of women on the digs. Most of the teams I've worked with were male-dominated.'

'It's true, this is a man's world.'

The moonlight and the night shadows played over his face and revealed the hint of wickedness in his smile. He moved towards her and braced his arm against the balustrade, caging her between the stone balcony and his body.

'I'm used to it.' She held his gaze defiantly. 'But times are changing, didn't you know?'

'Ah yes, women's lib, isn't that what you call it in England? I'm guessing you subscribe to their point of view, that you want to be … liberated.'

She swallowed, painfully aware of his proximity. 'If you mean that I want equality at work, the same rights and freedoms as a man, and to be treated with respect, then, yes, I'd call myself a feminist. I take it you don't believe in those things? Judging by your earlier remarks, you see a woman as merely a wife and mother.'

'On the contrary, if that were the case, I wouldn't have hired you for this job. You were the best around.'

'I'm glad you think so.'

His mouth curled at the edges in a lazy, sensual manner. 'Still, that doesn't mean I think a woman should lose her softness and femininity. If you were to go to the staff house, I can't vouch for how the men would react. You would be too much of a temptation for them, I think.'

She felt his glance almost like a physical caress as it passed over her platinum-blonde hair. She instinctively knew how fascinated he was by her fairness, just as she was by the glittering silver blades of his eyes, which now flicked back to hers. Although the neckline of her dress was not low-cut, she felt bare and vulnerable.

Oriel was no shrinking violet; she was tall and slim but strong with it – she had to be in her line of work – but he made her feel delicate, fragile. What's more, deep down, that's how she really was, despite her outward appearance of fierce independence and self-sufficiency.

'I would indeed live up to my nickname, *Drákon*, if I let you spend a single night in that place.' His voice became husky and intimate. 'A woman like you, with flaxen hair, pearly skin and a curvaceous body … Yes, that would be too much of a temptation.' Damian's taunting eyes scanned Oriel's face until they settled on the sensitive contours of her mouth, and she felt the shock of his sensual words all through her body.

As she gazed back at him, Oriel felt his power, his confidence and his danger. Still, the spring-like tension that she sensed in Damian was in her too – an explosive force that would blow to atoms every barrier she had erected. Where had her cool persona disappeared to? Were a few provocative words by her Greek god – who had ravished her so unforgettably during one night of madness – sufficient to melt her iron resolve and turn her into putty in his hands?

No! She would not give in to him and let herself down.

'I can handle myself,' she said with a confidence that was nevertheless starting to wane.

Damian leaned in a fraction. 'Shall we put it to the test, *agápi mou*?'

Oriel's head snapped up and she met his glittering gaze directly. '*Kyrios* Lekkas, may I remind you that I am here as your employee, nothing else. Ever heard of the phrase "sexual harassment"? Your cheap allusions could be construed as exactly that in a court of law.'

They were brave words, yet she didn't move back. In fact, every time he made a provocative suggestion, it merely caused her pulse to dance in a most troublesome fashion.

Damian's smile was subtle. 'I don't think so, my dear Calypso. There would have to be witnesses and, to my knowledge, the only attesters to our friendly conversation here are the moon and the sea, much like the night of our other little encounter.'

'You're wicked,' she murmured, still unable to look away.

'The wicked are often truthful, eh?'

'You're also presumptuous, arrogant …'

'You can save your charitable descriptions, Calypso. I've heard them all before. They're true, of course.'

Despite herself, amusement curved her lips at his roguish conceit. 'So there's no point in telling you how to behave like a gentleman when clearly you don't wish to do so?'

'Clearly.'

Her smile faded as his eyes, dark as volcanic glass, locked with her own. Oriel's cheeks flamed and she tried to stand tall, deeply aware of him only inches away from her, tensed and unpredictable; but his hypnotic stare was mesmerizing. Dominance and defiance clashed like silent blades.

An owl hooted, startling her for a moment, and she glanced up. The stars, so alive and numerous, burned above the treetops and the white moon lit to silver the tender blue curtain of darkness that brooded over them. Then, in the distant depths of the night, the sound of the shepherd's flute took up again, and to Oriel it seemed as if she were truly in the ancient garden of the wanton god Pan, who was hiding among the tangled groves with his entourage of nymphs and fellow satyrs, and had chosen that moment to manifest his seductive powers.

'Your shepherd is back,' Oriel said breathily, still looking up at the night sky.

'He will be serenading us a while yet.'

Oriel willed herself to withstand the sheer force of Damian's magnetism. He was standing so close that she could feel the heat of his body.

The lissom, mellow notes of the flute drifted through the air, treacherously beguiling.

'You love the wildness and the mystery of Greek islands, don't you?' he added, his voice low and gentle.

Her gaze fell back on his face. 'The nights, especially, are very beautiful.'

Damian's smile was wry, and it twisted the scarred side of his face, nevertheless lending it an unexpected, compelling charm as his eyes gleamed down at her. 'It is a magical sort of night. I feel almost a different person. It must be you, beautiful Calypso,' he told her with an almost sorrowful laugh. The pitch of his voice had matured; it was even deeper, richer than it had been all those years back. The sound of it still had the power to send a shiver down her spine, though now it was a shiver slightly different to that of six years ago.

He turned his disfigured cheek away from her, a fleeting and unreadable look shadowing his expression. Suddenly she felt a deep ache at the core of her heart for her Grecian god, who looked as though he had been struck by lightning. A curious weakness assailed her. Then he looked back, and she was paralyzed by yearning and by fear.

Before she could protest, Damian had drawn her to him; his warm palm had run the length of her spine and was pressing into its base where her body curved. He gripped her so fiercely that the skirt of her dress was pulled up, his tight, strong body leaning into hers.

Every nerve ending in Oriel was ablaze. She was enthralled by his smouldering silver gaze as his mouth inched towards hers. His breathing came in rasps as her breasts crushed against him. His need for her was obvious and she was aroused beyond her control, revelling in the sensation of his hands holding her against his rigid groin. She placed her hand flat against his broad chest, knowing she should push him away, and felt the frantic pounding beneath her touch.

That was her undoing.

It was madness to allow these feelings swamping her to drift up to her brain, dulling the nagging voice that warned her not to get herself involved with a man like Damian Lekkas. But there was the ethereal glow of the stars and the moon above them, and the breeze of the night carried an aroma of fruit trees that was dizzying in its sweetness, mingling with Damian's warm male scent enveloping her – all of it an overwhelming enchantment. In that moment, Oriel's lips parted softly, knowing this was inevitable.

Damian's damaged face came down and his hungry mouth sought out hers, pushing her against the balustrade until she felt the cool stone at her back. One of his hands moved up and tangled it-self in her hair, pulling her head back, and she arched towards him, exposing her smooth neck. Oriel heard his sharp intake of breath and felt him tense, every part of him telling her of his wild desire to possess her. His kiss was ocean deep, a torrent of fire that plunged through her senses, and even though it was the worst thing to do, she let him explore her mouth, tasting and filling her until her mind and body were a riot of sensations. He was like a fever in her blood. His hot mouth trailed down to the pulsing vein at the hollow centre of her throat, palpitating like a minute blue flower on a bed of snow. She trembled uncontrollably, acutely aware of the hard male body pressing so tightly against her soft curves as he licked and kissed and bit, finding nerve centres she had never even dreamed existed.

'You've missed me, I can feel it,' Damian whispered hoarsely, his breath like scorching flames against Oriel's sensitized skin. 'I want to rip off this dress and love you, right here,' he murmured against her neck as his other hand slid upwards to her breast and cupped its soft fullness, moving his thumb across the taut, aching nipple.

At that moment, a dog barked somewhere in the distance, star-tling a bird that flew out of the undergrowth with a scream that tore through the night. The spell was broken.

Oriel gasped, jerking away from him.

'It's only a bird, *zoi mou*,' Damian said, his voice thick, drawing her back towards him, his breathing still laboured.

'No, no, Damian, this is wrong … this is madness,' she mur-mured, her heart still beating fiercely against her breast. Among the seething tangle of emotions she was feeling, the reality of her situa-tion came flooding back. This man was a virtual stranger to her. He had a scarred face, a dead wife, a murdered brother … What else had happened to him since that night they had met on Aegina? Who was he really?

'Madness …' she repeated to herself.

Damian's hand tightened on her waist. 'How can you say that, eh? Every inch of your body is on fire, like mine. You're still trem-bling.'

'No,' Oriel repeated, trying to sound firm. She pulled back and separated herself from him, knowing that he was right and hating herself for not holding out against the arousal of her own body. She was still tingling all over with the exquisite feel of his touch.

For a moment they stared at each other, both stunned by the instinctive, carnal haze of lust that had overcome them. Then Damian swore under his breath. He ran a hand through his hair, as though trying to gather his wits.

He let out a frustrated breath. 'You kissed me as though you had been waiting for someone to kiss you properly all these years. Waiting for *me*.'

Oriel almost winced at the truth of it, but her chin went up. 'I didn't kiss you, *you* kissed *me*.'

'You let me.'

'You're an egotist.'

'Perhaps, but there are signs that don't lie. I can still read you like a book, Calypso.'

'You think so? Oh yes, you're such an expert on women,' she threw at him resentfully.

A tiny muscle jerked at the side of Damian's jaw. 'You enjoyed every minute, *matia mou*, don't deny it ...' She could tell that he had jolted back to his previous cynical self, as if he had realized that he had lost control and was now re-establishing it.

His eyes glowed like molten silver coals as he stood haughtily in front of her and Oriel took in his strong, dark, mutilated face with its ridges of pale scars that gave him an almost devilish quality in the moonlight – *Mephistopheles*, she thought. He was right. Every sinew in her body yearned for him to take her with the same wild passion he had shown in Aegina, but he was the last person in the world to whom she would reveal that information.

This man would never love her.

'I think it's best I go now,' she said.

Mockery slid into his voice. '*Go*? Because you're afraid of being alone with me ...? But maybe you're right to be wary.' His glance held an unexpected touch of humour. 'I am, as you might say, in the driving seat.'

But Oriel found nothing amusing in the situation. 'Not for long, *Kyrios*,' she retorted impulsively. 'Tomorrow I'll be leaving your island.'

His expression didn't change. 'We'll talk about that in the morning.'

'Will you have someone drive me to the staff house now, please? I'm tired and I want to go to bed.'

'Where you will sleep all alone … such a waste.'

'Do you never stop?'

'When the world says, "Give up," hope whispers, "Try it one more time."'

'Not all women are the same.'

'Are you inviting me to find out if you are different?'

'The reason I came here was to do a professional job. I have no interest in other distractions.' She stopped abruptly, realizing she was starting to sound very pompous indeed.

He stared at her, amusement lurking in the corners of his mouth. 'Then take the job. And if you decide otherwise tomorrow, then so be it.'

Oriel took a deep breath. Damian couldn't stop her from leaving the island the next day, if that was what she really wanted. The fuss she was making was almost ridiculous. True, he was dangerous, but only because of the physical chemistry that still flared between them. Furthermore, if she did decide to stay, Oriel had no doubt he was too proud a man to force himself on any woman that rejected him. On the contrary, she suspected it would be almost a challenge to his manhood to make a woman really want him, now that a terrible scar distorted what had once been an almost flawless face. Damian was right, she wanted him – more than that, she craved him just as strongly as ever, his kisses and his caresses. The memory of that night of love in Aegina had always haunted her. She couldn't deny, even to herself, that since then she had sought in every man she met the Greek god who had made love to her with such passion.

All she knew now was that, with all the travelling and the excitement of the past twelve hours, she felt exhausted. For tonight, there was no fight left in her.

'Fine, we'll discuss everything tomorrow.'

'And you stay here for tonight,' he said emphatically. 'You're not leaving now, it's too late.'

She sighed, shaking her head and looking up at him. A weary smile played uncertainly on her lips. 'You are one hell of a persistent man, and tonight I am too tired to argue.'

The steel in Damian's irises held wicked glints of triumph and awareness. 'Ah! That's better, *koukla*,' he said. 'Come, I will show you your apartment. Your baggage has arrived and is waiting for you there,' he told her as they left the terrace and made their way through the labyrinth of the house.

Finally they arrived at a pair of huge double doors. 'We're here,' Damian said as he turned the key in the lock. Oriel found herself in a magnificent room with a high painted ceiling representing heroes of antiquity, and tall arched windows that opened on to a magnificent terrace. She let out a little gasp of appreciation. Everything was grand, from the age-polished, carved-wood furniture and the shining marble floor to the pretty voile curtains fluttering in the windows. A touch of the sensuous intermingled with the austere. 'It's lovely!' she exclaimed, going further into the room.

Some hint of emotion crossed his face before he spoke. 'I had it refurbished not that long ago,' was all he said.

The middle window was wider than the four others, with spiral stone columns reaching from floor to ceiling on either side, creating a focal point. The three walls were covered with large murals, each depicting one of the Fates.

'The Moirae,' Damian told Oriel, leaning towards her, eyes glowing. 'Clotho, Lachesis and Atropos. The sisters who determine when life begins, when it ends and what happens in between. Undoubtedly, they were there on the island of Aegina that night we met …'

The way he looked at her made Oriel drop her gaze quickly. In a crystal-clear flash of memory she recalled the frenzied night they had spent together. 'That's a little far-fetched perhaps,' she murmured, hoping he hadn't noticed the way her cheeks had coloured.

Ignoring her comment he crossed over to the central window. 'There's a wonderful view from here,' he said, standing aside to let her past and, as Oriel stepped on to the terrace, the breath caught in her throat and she blinked in disbelief. It was as if she were standing on the deck of a boat with the sea stretching into infinity. She looked up at the sky. These were the same stars that greeted the ancients, the same that would be here in millions of years' time. It must have been a night just like this that inspired Van Gogh, she thought.

'Incredible,' she murmured. 'An absolutely beautiful sight.'

Damian appeared beside her. 'The stars of Helios are unusual, so close they look like they can be plucked from the night sky.' He leaned on the balcony, staring into the night. 'The saying goes that each star is a lover's dream, and when a star falls out of the heavens …'

A voice came from behind them. 'Ah, there you are, my dear cousin! Still not averse to spinning fairy tales to wide-eyed young women, I see … I would have thought you'd have learnt your lesson by now.'

The pair turned abruptly. A young woman in a wheelchair was framed in the doorway, staring fixedly at them. Then she rolled a little further on to the terrace and gazed straight at Oriel, a certain curiosity dwelling in her large pale-grey eyes that made the golden colour of her skin seem all the more dark and her features strong and defined – a beautiful raven-haired goddess, the female counter-part of Damian.

CHAPTER 3

'I am Helena,' the dark goddess said in a carefully cultivated husky voice, 'and you, I presume, are the new *archaiolgos*.' She spoke English with a pronounced Greek accent.

In a moment's confusion, Oriel looked from Damian to this striking woman who was glaring up at her haughtily. Yorgos Christodoulou had never mentioned that Helena was confined to a wheelchair and, come to think of it, Damian had never even mentioned his cousin all through dinner.

She was dazzling. Dressed in a long, royal blue evening dress of chiffon, she looked positively regal. Gold bangles on her arms glowed in the shaded light, jewels scintillated on her lobes, and upon her neck and fingers. Although it all seemed a little overdone, Oriel had to admit that the bright gold jewellery suited her dark beauty. Her eyes, however, were shinier than Damian's, with an odd brightness that was disconcerting.

Oriel swiftly recovered her composure. 'How do you do, yes, I'm …'

'Helena, I thought you would have been resting,' Damian cut in. Oriel would have been irritated by this interruption but then caught sight of his guarded expression as he eyed his cousin; there was a hint of uncertainty in the furrow of his brow. '*Despinis* Anderson is going to be a great help with the underwater excavations south of the marina,' he added.

Helena regarded Oriel somewhat scornfully. 'She looks sort of ethereal. I don't say it isn't becoming, but are you quite sure she's cut out for this job, especially now you've lost yet another member of your team?'

'Ethereal!' Oriel laughed, determined not to take offence. She held up one finely rounded arm, where the sleek outline of muscle could be discerned under the flawless white skin, and tapped it. 'Hardly. I've worked on some pretty tough sites in my time.'

Damian gave his cousin a pointed look. '*Despinis* Anderson's credentials are quite impressive. Stavros would not have chosen her if that hadn't been the case.'

Helena looked at Damian almost resentfully. 'The wilds of Helios are quite unlike the suburbs of England. Besides, Stavros's decisions, as yours, are made by his hormones, not by his brain.'

Oriel could feel undercurrents of tension vibrating in the air. Damian had the look of a nervous racehorse as his cousin's bright and suspicious gaze fastened upon him.

'Helena,' he warned, his tone charged with irritation. 'It's getting late, we can discuss this in the morning.'

It was Oriel's turn to interrupt. Cousin or not, this woman was taking liberties. 'I can assure you, *Kyria*, that I am perfectly capable of holding down this job. I have worked on considerably more taxing sites in Norway and Ireland. While fascinating, this project doesn't seem too difficult.'

Helena's large grey eyes flickered from Oriel to Damian and flashed like diamonds – it was clear that she was furious. Though there was an arrogant disdain in her whole poise, her voice was cool as she stated: 'I don't suppose that *Despinis* Anderson knows that the site is near a wall of reef that is known to be frequented by sharks.'

'Oh, come on, Helena! Sharks are very rare in the Mediterranean, as you well know,' Damian answered, clenching his jaw.

A sneer crossed Helena's beautiful face, distorting her features into an almost ugly mask as she glared back at him. 'Danger is everywhere, haven't you learnt that by now?'

'Really, Helena,' Damian muttered, 'let's not have a scene, shall we?' Something in his tone had changed, stiffened even – or so it sounded to Oriel – although there was a fleeting shade of sad resignation at his cousin's seemingly nonsensical remark. Then, having delivered her parting shot, the beautiful Greek goddess turned her wheelchair round, leaving Oriel staring after her in bewilderment as Helena swept back through the terrace doors, the creaking murmur of the wheelchair fading as she disappeared. Was every inhabitant of Helios so keen to encourage Oriel to leave?

The ocean whispered and a night bird called from the cliffs. Damian shook his head and sighed. 'I must apologize for my cousin's behaviour, she likes to shock.'

'I think it might be a trait that runs in your family.'

He quirked a jagged, distorted eyebrow, a touch of humour returning to his expression. 'Ah yes, I forgot that you think so highly of me.' His teeth glinted in a smile. 'Come, I think you've had enough excitement for one night, eh?'

They went back inside and walked through the *salóni* to the bedroom next door. Like all the other rooms in the house, this one was huge – a study in beauty and luxury. An iridescent eight-light opaline chandelier hung delicately from a lofty ceiling, on which a mural showed sketches of birds flying in a pale-blue sky. The walls were panel paintings with vignettes of seashells against a backdrop of sugared whiteness to represent a sandy beach, or fish swimming in a turquoise sea. As in the *salóni*, the curtains were of pale, airy voile, softening the vastness of the space.

The room was furnished with turn-of-the century furniture: a pedestal table and a couple of curvy Thonet chairs, plus a rocking chair. Oriel was pleased to see that there was a small escritoire where she could write her letters or read her notes. Facing the tall windows, a high-beamed recess with a stone platform had been created to accommodate an old brass four-poster bed, from where you could gaze out at the Ionian Sea and the surrounding landscape. Instinctively, Oriel moved further into the room towards the window, and only then did she notice the golden cage hanging from a beam in the far corner. Inside, a canary suddenly chirped and fluttered nervously as she approached.

Oriel gasped and froze for a second. Ever since childhood, when she had seen a bald eagle snatch a goat, its talons ripping into the kid's back while it bleated a desperate call, she had been wary of birds of any kind. It hadn't helped that her nanny used the event as a warped cautionary tale: 'The eagle will snatch you up if you don't do it now …'. And now, anything about birds – their fluttering wings, gleaming eyes, hard beaks and ugly, curved claws – filled her with dread.

'Is something the matter?' Damian asked.

'Everything is so beautiful, it takes my breath away!' An innocent white lie, she thought, to save her pride. She wasn't going to admit her fears to him. It was just a canary, she'd get a grip on herself and live with this little creature if she had to.

To distract herself, Oriel crossed quickly to the adjoining dressing room. It had a huge walk-in cupboard with mirrored doors which, when opened, revealed all her clothes neatly put away and her cases stored overhead. Behind her, in a corner alcove, she spied a bentwood vanity table with a small matching chair, positioned to benefit from the sunlight.

Next door, the bathroom was beautiful in its minimalistic simplicity: just pink iridescent marble with mosaics adorning the floor and walls. A sunken bathtub set in the middle took up most of the area, leaving enough space for a separate shower. The only adornment was a plaster cast of a goddess's head, hidden in a shallow niche.

Damian was leaning against the doorframe with folded arms, awaiting her verdict. His slate eyes danced under dark brows. 'You like the apartment?'

'Like' was hardly the word, Oriel thought: awe-inspiring was a more appropriate description of its effect on her at this moment. 'It's magnificent, like the rest of your house.'

Damian moved closer and placed his wide hand on her shoulder. 'So you'll stay?' His eyes were bright with expectation and there was a subtle quirk to his lips. 'After all, from your comments to my cousin, you seem to have made up your mind. Am I right?'

Oriel knew it was useless to deny: she didn't want to leave. True, this job was too good an opportunity to pass up and she was competitive enough to want to prove her worth; also, there was Damian himself. The effect he had on her was intoxicating.

She nodded. 'If it's not working after two weeks, though, I reserve the right to hand in my notice.'

'Excellent.' Damian's mouth widened into a heart-stopping smile that made Oriel give in to a quiver of excitement in the pit of her stomach. His eyes then glinted wickedly. 'Two weeks … A lot can happen in that time. You said it yourself, tomorrow will be a new beginning, eh?'

Oriel could read his intention in those eyes. He wanted to prove how weak she was, how firmly caught by his masculine power over her. And he was right: if he touched her, she would be lost. She was overwhelmed by his aura of sensual virility. God! If he could see inside her right now, he'd realize that her heart was hammering like a pounding machine, her blood near to vaporizing with the heat of her desire.

She moved past him quickly and went back into the *salóni*.

'Oh good, my diving gear has arrived too.' Oriel went over to a round table under which sat a large canvas holdall. She crouched down to unzip it quickly, satisfying herself that everything was there, and rose to find Damian standing next to her.

'And here, Hassan has left you something in case you get hungry. You should try one of these,' he told her as he took a sweetmeat from the plate on the table. He unwrapped the paper foil around it and held out his hand. '*Medjool dáctulos*, what some on the island call *mikrés fantasióseis*, small fantasies. Have you ever had one?'

Now why did she feel this was a loaded question? She shook her head.

'Dates dipped in rich milk chocolate are a powerful aphrodisiac, given to young brides on their wedding night to arouse and intensify their sexual desire.' Damian moved nearer to her, almost closing the gap between them. 'Here, take a bite,' he said, his voice suddenly low, his eyes turning into piercing beams of intensity.

Oriel's pulse was racing at an extraordinary pace, and she was dimly conscious of an overpowering contrast: her female vulnerability against iron-hard male muscle. She knew this was foolhardy; still, staring into his cruelly scarred face and feeling the warmth that emanated from him, her resistance weakened. As she opened her mouth, he placed the cylindrical fruit between her parted lips, grazing them with his fingertips. She bit off a piece and he put the remainder in his own mouth, savouring it slowly, his gaze never faltering, caressing each one of her features.

Kiss me, Damian, she willed him silently, although another voice, the voice of reason, told her she might regret it. An electric current shivered through her. She could feel his inner tension. He was a coiled spring: motionless but ready to quiver into life at the faintest touch. She sensed the power of those eyes, boring into her, flooding her veins with tingling heat. Her skin burned where his fingers had touched her mouth.

Oriel breathed an unsteady sigh, aware of that familiar dampness between her thighs. The peaks of her breasts were so taut she could feel them pushing against the fine material of her dress. Her heart was beating quickly, half with the fear of where this moment was leading, and half with panic that he would sense her acute reaction to his physical closeness.

Damian gave her a dazzling white smile. 'Good, eh?'

'Yes, it's good.' Her voice was inadvertently husky. She had to fight the urge to fling her arms around his neck once again, to give herself up to that delicious, treacherous sweetness and let tomorrow take care of itself.

Damian lifted his hand and smoothed a wisp of hair away from Oriel's cheek then took a deep breath, seeming to gather himself in some way. He stepped away from her and helped himself to another date, which he placed in his pocket. Oriel stared at him nonplussed as she felt a stabbing thrust in her breast. Having toyed with her emotions and her senses, he was now letting her go. The warm quivering in the pit of her stomach had spread over her body and she tightened all her muscles in an effort to deny it, to stop herself from betraying her disappointment.

'It's late, I should be going. You need your sleep.' His voice was neutral now and that wide, sensual mouth seemed to firm in resolution. 'Goodnight, *Despinis* Anderson. We shall speak at nine-thirty tomorrow morning.'

Oriel watched Damian's tall lithe frame move towards the door, while curiosity and desire still skittered through her blood. There was a rigid finality in the stiffness of his back. Perhaps he regretted his impulsive action of kissing her earlier on the terrace, after promising to be a gentleman, and now thought she would leave if he tried it again? Yet she felt weak at the thought of how much she wanted him.

As he was closing the door, Oriel was almost tempted to call him back. *But to what end?* she thought. This wasn't a man you could tangle with and come away unscathed – he had made love to her once, six years ago, and had taught her more about pleasure in a few hours than most women experience in a lifetime; and she had realized tonight that she had never recovered from that one night in paradise.

This man had the power to hurt her. Oriel knew she should feel relieved that he had left her alone just now. Remaining on the island was one thing, but entering into an affair with Damian Lekkas was out of the question. The job she'd been offered was a dream come true, the reason why she'd gone through so many years of studying – an opportunity of a lifetime. She would not throw it away just because she couldn't keep a grip on her hormones.

Oriel's eyes scanned the room. There was nothing but comfort, spaciousness and beauty around her, yet beneath it all there remained that sinister, intangible atmosphere: the same feeling that had hit her as soon as she had arrived on the island, and to which she could give no name. Maybe it was the quietness after the bustle of London, or perhaps merely the odds-and-ends of words, sentences and hints dropped by Yorgos Christodoulou and Irini, the maid, and of course there was the obvious animosity of Damian's cousin … but probably, she decided, all these misgivings were just a reaction to tiredness.

Still, as Oriel moved to one of the windows, a shiver ran through her from head to toe, partly fearful but shot with excited anticipation. She gazed out into the night, made luminous by the moon. The velvet warmth, the exotic scents, the shape of the far-off mountain, a shadow just discernible against the sky. Despite herself, she was gripped again by the enchantment of Helios: this alien, mysterious island to where she had been spirited by fate, like a figure on a chessboard. Was it really destiny? Damian seemed to think so. Perhaps he was right. The compelling feeling she had was that, in a certain sense, this was a journey she had to make. Even if this job hadn't been there, she would have had to come here … which was absurd, of course.

Moira, Damian had said, *the hidden forces that are at work behind the scenes, arranging our lives ahead of our own decisions.* Could it be that her fate, whatever it might prove, lay here on Helios?

Am I going to love it or hate it? Oriel didn't know. She only knew that she stood ready and waiting for what lay in store.

Before preparing for bed, she thoroughly checked each item of her diving gear. It was unlikely that they would be diving immediately the next day but she wanted to be prepared for anything.

* * *

On the half-lit terrace, the dogs paced and sniffed around Damian's heels as he tried to examine Heracles' paw one last time. He patted their sides and straightened up. The hounds were restless, as was he. They must have picked up on his mood tonight, he thought.

He left them lying in their usual spot at the side of the house and strode back along the terrace to his apartment, slamming the door behind him. His head was full of Oriel and his body was frustrated beyond belief.

As Damian had walked across Oriel's room to leave, he'd felt her fiery green eyes dwell on him and he had been tempted to look back. But that would have been fatal. He wouldn't have been able to control his libido and he knew that if he set his mind to it, he would be able to destroy all the misgivings that kept her from him. He could have walked back into the room and told her there and then why he had disappeared that night, tasted those soft rosy lips, and she would surely have given in to the desire that he'd seen glowing in her eyes. But when Oriel came to him – *if* she came to him – it must be of her own free will, not because he had seduced her.

He pulled off his clothes and walked into the bathroom. As he went in, the tall mirror showed a reflection that, since his accident, never ceased to shock him. Still, he refused to turn away from the unsightly image that stared back at him; it was part of him now and somehow he was proud of it, proud of how he had acquired it. Tonight was different: he was viewing it through Oriel's candid gaze. He shuddered as he took in the damage the shark had done and swore quietly.

The incident was still live in his mind and he often relived the nightmare, as he did now. The piercing pain as the cruel jaws sunk into the flesh of his chest, almost tearing a chunk out of it; the sickening lurch in his stomach when he'd become aware that the water around him was stained with ugly rust-like streaks of blood. At first, his panic had surpassed the pain of his lacerated body. His lungs were tight and dry and hot, and he could only hear the splash of the water as he churned it, the clamour of his heart and the thudding beat of blood in his head. The water had become a live thing, the sea and the shark one great amalgamated beast holding him back, and when finally he'd killed it, his body had jerked but the impulsive instinct for survival had carried him on towards the coral reef and his cheek ripped against its razor-sharp edge as he slumped, exhausted, hearing shouts from the boat and feeling arms coming up around him as he lost consciousness.

It had taken three operations to perform the small miracle of repairing his savaged torso; the shark's vicious teeth had ripped the skin off Damian's chest, including a nipple and a part of his stomach. The gory wound had run deep, very close to the heart, and despite the ability to minimize the mutilation, the surgeons had not been able to reconstruct the nipple. Damian was left with a scar in the form of a cross that went down from the middle of his abdomen to his groin.

How had Oriel felt when she'd seen his face? Surely any woman would be repelled by his disfigurement, even if they didn't show it. There had been a flash of something in her eyes when he'd stepped out of the moonlight and had appeared to her with his scarred face, but she hadn't shrunk from him in distaste as Cassandra had, and he'd read no pity in her eyes – he was an expert at detecting that sort of compassionate response. It made him flinch inwardly even more than he did when he sensed repulsion. But how might she feel if she saw the rest of him?

Damian showered but, before turning out the light, he went to his cupboard and took out a yellow-and-orange silk scarf he had jealously stowed away. The fragrance Oriel wore, mixed with the scent of her own skin, made him dizzy; it always had and he had never forgotten it. She still smelled the same, and it made his senses run wild. After that night in Aegina, when he left her sleeping at dawn, he'd taken her scarf – a token of the woman who had shown him a paradise he'd never dreamt existed. Since then, he had searched for Oriel in every woman he had met, and in each woman he'd bedded, but he had never found in them the blend of innocence and carnal instinct that she embodied in her lovemaking: a mesmerizing quality that had excited and confounded him in equal measure.

He pressed the cherished scarf to his lips and breathed in its scent, faint but still detectable. The sexual response in his body was instant. He shouldn't be doing this, he knew, it would only lead to fresh tortured urges. He knew he would dream of her tonight and would find release in her arms as he had so many times before.

Damian turned off the light and threw himself on the bed, physically and mentally exhausted. Through the huge window that ran from wall to wall, the night sky showed stars but mostly the moon – a moon as bright as it had been on Aegina.

Memories flooded back of that night of madness, as he knew they would: those shadows that walked beside him, mocking shadows of the past. He had been travelling for so many months on his own, before returning home to Helios and to a life of responsibility. The island of Aegina was where he had sailed to spend a few hours before moving on the next morning to Athens; and there she was, looking like the water nymph, Undine, sitting on a rock with the sea at her feet, her ashen silk hair shining under the silver light like spun moonbeams. Her smile had revealed a deep dent at the left side of her soft, pink mouth that made him lose his senses. She was lovely and desirable, a warm-blooded, intoxicating woman, full of fire and passion. Almost like wine she had gone to his head at first glance and, like wine, he had become drunk on her.

When his mouth had touched those fresh soft lips, their kiss had blotted out everything that had gone before, everything that could happen in the future; there had been no time or place or boundary to the fullness of the moment. Damian had felt Oriel trembling in his arms like a frightened fawn, afraid of some unknown power, and he had sensed her inexperience. Yet, by looking into those enormous green eyes that reflected the depths of the sea, he had also known that she was as enthralled by the chemistry between them as he was.

He would have prolonged his stay to get to know her better, not to mention try to satiate his body's endless hunger for this exquisite, sensual woman, had it not been for the photograph he had found lying on the beach. She was smiling into the eyes of a young man with fair hair and a goatee, who had his arm around her. Damian had turned the snapshot over and had read: *Night of Rob's proposal in Venice.* His opinion of the female gender had already taken a knocking – this had added the decisive blow. So she was one of the hordes of Northern European women who flocked every year to Greek beaches looking for a holiday adventure. He knew the type; he had bedded many since the age of sixteen. Still, that hadn't stopped him thinking about her over the years that followed and wondering if he might have been too hasty in his judgement of her, too quick in his decision to leave her that night.

And then Stavros had brought him Oriel's résumé, with her photograph attached, and his whole body had frozen. Surprise and incredulity had then morphed into something else: hope had flared in his heart. The status on her details showed she was single. Had she never married this 'Rob'? Had she married anybody else? And if not, why not? Was fate giving him another chance? Of course he was not the man he had been when they first met, but somehow he had felt in his heart that it wouldn't matter: their bodies spoke the same language. It had been true then – why not now?

Tonight he had been proved right. The chemistry between them was as potent as ever. On the terrace, despite her protests during the few moments he had held her, Oriel had shuddered with the same abandoned passion she had demonstrated on that one night in Aegina. The moans and delicate sighs were the same sounds she had made in his arms all those years ago; and yet alongside the intensity of her responses, he had detected an almost shy, restrained element that was at odds with her instinctive sensuality. He remembered thinking at the time that maybe she always limited the expressions of her pleasure that way.

Damian was sure that Oriel's rebuff had been half hearted; he had felt her need blossoming under his touch. She still wanted him but she wasn't going to give in to him without making him work for it. Of course not. Did he expect she'd just fall into his arms? After all, he had left like a thief in the night, without a word, and how was she to know that his pride had been too wounded to stay when he'd discovered she was attached? Still, why had he lost control of himself in the first place? He cursed inwardly, his hands scrubbing over his face as he lay on the bed. Oriel had only just got here and already he was acting like a weak schoolboy. No woman had ever got under his skin like this, he needed to pull himself together before he became too distracted.

He would let her be for now. Besides, they had work to do; although, he admitted, the fact that Oriel stimulated him intellectually as well as physically merely stoked his desire. Working side by side with her would be hard, and he would have to fight the urge to drag her into his arms every time she came within an inch of him. Still, he knew enough about her that to try his luck again might end in disappointment.

His thoughts turned to Helena … jealous, possessive, uncompromising Helena; the cousin he had vowed always to look after despite her deeply troubled nature. She would not make this easy.

Damian sighed. Why was it that at every turn in his life the gods seemed to be set against him?

* * *

Oriel wasn't sure what time of night it was when something woke her. The silver-white moon spilled its beams through the window opposite her bed. Half-caught in slumber, she opened her eyes. Someone was there, she was sure of it. The pattern of light and shadow had changed disturbingly in the room.

Focusing her sleepy gaze, she peered at the French doors that led on to the terrace. She thought she had shut them, but they were wide open and the flimsy curtains were gently lifting in the breeze.

It was then that she looked down and saw a shadow stretched across the floor – the figure of a man or a woman, she couldn't tell. She tried to smother a soft cry of terror but it slipped through her lips and the dark shape moved at once. There was a faint sound, no more than a shuffle, yet it had a frightening reality, and then the shadow vanished and the band of moonlight lay unmarred upon the floor. Horror washed through her body and for a moment she was paralyzed, her heart thudding with sickening speed. Then, with a sudden jarring movement, Oriel reached for the light and switched it on, which made the canary suddenly fly up in its cage with a loud chirrup. She instinctively flinched at the noise and then stared wildly around, but there was nothing there.

The canary settled on its perch and the room seemed quiet and peaceful again; the only sounds were the low nocturnal clicking of cicadas and the distant gentle murmur of the sea. Oriel breathed deeply, then she got up and closed the windows and went to the bathroom to wash her face and drink a glass of water. Perhaps she had been dreaming. The unsettling atmosphere of Helios – beautiful though it might be – was clearly getting to her more than she expected.

Oriel slipped back in bed and sighed: she was becoming too jumpy, she told herself, it was not like her. She settled down, pulling a pillow up under her cheek. Before she knew it, she had fallen back into a deep and exhausted sleep.

* * *

To her surprise, Oriel slept extraordinary well for the rest of the night. The bed was comfortable and the silk sheets were a pleasurable new experience – a nice change from the continental quilt she had just bought at home, whose practicality appealed to her busy lifestyle and lack of time for making beds. She awoke to the song of the canary, hopping and chirping away happily in its gilded cage. Oriel found that it didn't overly bother her now morning had come; perhaps it was that the little creature seemed to fit in well with the extraordinary exotic surroundings, or that she was simply getting used to its presence. Either way, her attention was now drawn to the sight of the distant horizon through her window, where the pale blueness of the sky met the intense azure of the Ionian Sea. She had forgotten to close the shutters last night and was now glad of it: this was a view to which she could grow accustomed.

She lay for a while listening to the sound of distant waves whispering outside her window, just savouring the sense of wellbeing the sound produced, so different from the familiar London noises. Oriel glanced at her watch; it wasn't yet eight o'clock. Damian had set their meeting for nine-thirty; she had time to relax a little longer.

The night before, tiredness and the shock of seeing Damian again had overwhelmed her. The strain on her nerves had caused a kind of mental and physical exhaustion that no doubt explained why she'd been seeing things in the middle of the night, but this morning her mind was rested and she had a more rational view of her situation and was now, in fact, relishing the task ahead.

A knock at the door jolted her out of her reverie and she sat upright, instinctively pulling the sheet up to her chest to cover the curve of her breasts that the deep V in her nightdress revealed. '*Ella mesa*, come in,' she called out.

To Oriel's relief, it was Irini with her breakfast.

The maid smiled cheerfully. '*Kaliméra, Kyria,*' she said, proceeding to set out an extensive set of dishes on the round table.

'*Kaliméra*, Irini.' Oriel pushed back the covers, slipped out of bed and grabbed her dressing gown.

'I hope the *Kyria* slept well. It is always difficult to sleep in a new place.'

Oriel laughed. 'I've never slept in a place like this before, I must admit. I have no complaints.' Her mind fleetingly conjured up an image of the shadow in her room but she decided to make nothing of it. After all, she'd probably been dreaming. She smiled at the *kamariera*. 'I was very comfortable and I slept like a baby till the morning. It must be the sea air.' Her eyes then took in the mountain of food that Irini had placed before her.

'This is not a Greek breakfast,' the maid explained, seeing Oriel's surprised look at the bacon, sausage and egg. 'The *Kyrios* thought that you would feel less homesick if you were greeted this morning with an English breakfast.'

'It smells delicious and I'm ravenous. That is very thoughtful of *Kyrios* Lekkas. I will thank him when I see him this morning.'

Irini looked at her apologetically. 'The *Kyrios* has left this morning for the mainland. Some business in Athens. He will be back tomorrow, but he has set up a meeting for you with *Kyrios* Stavros. Stavros Petrakis, the *Kyrios*'s right-hand man.' Irini tapped the folded sheet that was lying on the tray. 'It is all outlined on this piece of paper, which *Kyrios* Yorgos asked me to give you.'

Oriel nodded at the maid's words, although was it a tinge of disappointment she felt pinching her heart? Had she secretly been looking forward to seeing Damian this morning and starting over on a friendlier footing? 'Thanks, Irini,' she replied, forcing a bright smile.

'*Kyrios* Stavros will be over from the staff house at nine-thirty. He said not to bring any diving gear today, as you will not need it. I'll come and get you five minutes before, otherwise you might get lost. This house is big and you are not used to it yet.'

'*Efharisto*. I'll be ready.'

'*Parakaló*. Enjoy your breakfast.' Irini left the room, closing the door behind her.

Oriel looked down at the copious breakfast set in front of her. Orange juice, cereal, egg, bacon, sausage, grilled mushroom and tomato, steaming coffee, toast and marmalade – it had all been prepared as though by an English chef. What luxury! She had been ravenous when Irini brought it in, so why was she suddenly not at all hungry? She poured herself a cup of coffee and went to the window. The night before she hadn't noticed the small terrace adjoining her bedroom, which had steps leading down to an area of flat rocks. It was a blue morning and the air was still fresh.

Leaning over the parapet, Oriel glanced down at the narrow sandy beach that seemed to border the edge of the property uninterruptedly; from here she could see the crystalline water and the uneven seabed visible beneath it, diapered with long weedy patches, fragments of fallen rock and brighter patches of sand. She inhaled the pungent odour of sea wrack on the sand and listened to the breathing of the waves, which lapped softly against the shore like a herd of nodding mythological beasts emerging from the deep.

To her right, Oriel could see the garden in which she had walked last night. In daytime, the clumps of tall trees with their glossy green foliage and colourful flowers stood motionless in the warm air, with that peculiar entranced appearance leaves and blossoms take on under the sunshine. Beyond the garden was the terrace with its steps that led to a stone wharf, where a long quay jutted out into the sea. The view in front of her held a vision of mythological splendour; here was a landscape where one could imagine the omniscient acts of divine beings, the spilling of golden plenty and the thunderbolt of punishment. This was a legendary sea, steeped in age and tales of heroic voyages. It was difficult not to look around and think: *anything can happen here …*

Oriel showered and dressed casually for a working day in a pair of dark-blue jeans and a plain navy cotton shirt that unconsciously drew attention to her extreme fairness. Picking up the paper that Irini had left behind, she glanced at the schedule, which confirmed they would not be diving today. She put away her diving gear in the walk-in cupboard, chiding herself for being upset at the idea of not seeing Damian that morning. She was an employee and she had demanded – yes, demanded – to be treated as such, and his whereabouts were really none of her business. She would just do as she was told; follow the schedule.

Oriel was ready to go when Irini knocked on her door just before nine-thirty, and together they walked through the cool house with its closed shutters to the hall. A tall man in jeans and a white T-shirt was waiting at the bottom of the marble stairs, a welcoming smile lighting his weathered face.

'Welcome to the island of Helios, *Despinis* Anderson,' he said, shaking Oriel's hand. 'I am Stavros Petrakis, *Kyrios* Lekkas's head of works. He sends his apologies for not being here himself but he is seeing the Minister for Culture in Athens, who could only meet with him today.'

Oriel gave an imperceptible start as she met the steel-grey gaze of the man that had just covered her hand with his two large palms and was regarding her with evident pleasure. Greek eyes were usually jet black, like those of Yorgos Christodoulou and most Mediterranean people, or sometimes blue – but rarely grey. In other countries, she had often encountered grey eyes, but they were almost always rather dull and had left her cold. Before coming to Helios, only once had she come across steel irises with such cutting brilliance that they had taken her breath away, and that was six years back on Aegina. *Was Stavros Petrakis related to the Lekkas family somehow?* Although now she looked more closely, *Kyrios* Stavros's eyes were less vibrant than those of either Damian or Helena, and not as large, but they still had that strange luminous glitter.

Oriel smiled. '*Kaliméra.*'

'We'll drive down to the temple site where we are still finishing the digging and reconstruction. It will be a good opportunity to introduce you to some of the crew,' Petrakis told her as they walked down the steps together.

Her face lit up with interest. 'Ah yes, the Minoan temple excavation. *Kyrios* Lekkas mentioned the other dig. Is it far?'

'No, only a few kilometres north. One of the team left yesterday, but we don't need so many for the underwater job that you've joined us for. We're very lucky to have found someone with your credentials, I was very impressed.'

'*Efharisto.*'

They climbed into the waiting Lekkas Jeep and the inner gates of Heliades closed behind them as they made their way down the long drive. 'We'll visit the underwater excavation site tomorrow. It's further down the island, not far from the marina.'

'Not close to the shark-infested reef then?' Oriel innocently put in, remembering Helena's parting bombshell of the night before.

Stavros pulled a face. 'Sharks? No sharks, *Despinis* Anderson. I see that you are familiar with the geography of Helios.'

'It's the only privately owned island in the Ionian Sea, isn't it? How come the Lekkas family manage to own it?'

'Ah, through hard work and determination,' said Stavros. 'Gjergj Lekkas was originally an Albanian who lived in Greece. He was a shipbuilder by trade and a soldier who fought many wars under the Ottoman Empire. Badly injured at the beginning of the nineteenth century, he couldn't fight any more and so he roamed the seas on a boat he built, selling goods from island to island.'

Oriel remembered something Damian had said about Helios being abandoned, stories of people vanishing that gave the place an eerie reputation. 'Was the island completely uninhabited?' she asked.

'Almost. Originally monks lived here, although their numbers were dwindling by the time Gjergj happened upon Helios. Funnily enough, the walls of the old monastery are still standing and the *Kyrios*'s grandfather turned part of it into an olive press, and the other into offices. Damian now runs the olive oil business as well as his archaeology projects.'

'So how was the island populated?'

'Gjergj appropriated Helios gradually, first becoming a successful shipping owner and then rebuilding the island. The Ionian Islands at that time were more or less independent, which made them popular with Greek intellectual exiles, freedom fighter politicians fleeing the country, and foreigners.'

'And Helios became one of the places the settlers chose?' Oriel thought about those agricultural workers she had seen on the way to Heliades the day before and wondered what the rest of the islanders were like and where they had hailed from originally.

Stavros nodded. 'This place flourished under the Lekkas dynasty. Gjergj was a great visionary and, with the aid of these men and women, he made something of the island. You could say with his ideas and their labour Helios really began to develop. Because Gjergj was a mariner, he shipped the produce of his island to markets more distant than Athens: ports in Egypt and especially Albania, from where his ancestors came.'

Oriel's mind conjured an image of Damian's face, with its mixture of strength and arrogance; one could see the unending line of his forebears and imagine a similar man in Gjergj Lekkas, a bold and reckless soldier, sailing his ship through perilous waters to build the glory of his island. Oriel smiled to herself. A fanciful view, she realized, but it was so easy here to get caught up in the romance and storybook feel of Helios.

Unaware of Oriel's meandering thoughts, Stavros continued: 'Under British rule, your country used part of the island as a naval base. Then, when Britain decided to transfer the islands to Greece, sometime in the 1860s, I think, Gjergj bought Helios from the British government and officially registered the rights to the island, changing his original Albanian surname, Leka, to the Greek Lekkas. Just before he passed away in 1870, he bought his Greek nationality. The family have been here for almost two centuries and they continued to prosper up until the death of Damian's grandfather. When *he* passed away, the island's fortunes deteriorated somewhat under Damian's father, Konstantin, until Damian himself took over and built them up again.' Stavros glanced at her as he drove. 'I tell you, Damian Lekkas is the best thing that could have happened to this island. You'll find him a dedicated and brilliant man to work with.'

Oriel's gaze flickered to him before her eyes returned to the view. 'He's certainly an impressive figure,' she said, choosing her words carefully.

Stavros laughed. 'Yes, he is that. He's a good friend. I've known him all my life. Damian knows what he thinks and he doesn't suffer fools gladly. He wants what's best for the island. It's beautiful and unspoilt, but it's not easy living here sometimes. Sitting on the edge of *ena ifaísteio*, Helios is not regarded as a safe place. That's what made it so easy for Damian's ancestor to buy it from the British all those years ago.'

As if on cue, the volcano loomed into view. With the morning light on it, the form and texture of Typhoeus appeared much paler than the almost sinister dark shape of the night before. Mottled here and there with a hint of pink, it stood out in the clarity of the intense Greek light, against the two blues of sky and sea.

'But apparently the volcano isn't still active, isn't that right?'

'True, it hasn't erupted since the end of the eighteenth century, but it takes up a significant part of Helios. Some believe that it rose from the sea, deposited its lava on one of the mountain flanks and that was how Helios was born. The islanders named the volcano Typhoeus after the fire-breathing dragon with a hundred heads that never rests. It's part of our mythology and there's a shrine on the way up to the smoking mountain where some of our people still deposit gifts in the hope of circumventing its fury. But even so, from time to time it grumbles.'

He caught the look in Oriel's eye and gave a half smile. 'I know, superstitious foolishness, that's what you're thinking, eh? But trust me, *Despinis* Anderson, when I tell you that it is not a pretty sound … *freektoh*, horrible … the sleeping fire.' Stavros made a negative gesture with his hand and shook his head.

It was a different route to the one she had taken with Yorgos the afternoon before. The orange trees were in bloom and the air was drenched with the sweet and piercing scent of the blossom. Peasants in the fields, whose skins had turned to leather through long hours spent in the scorching sun, stopped working and stared with shrewd, doubting eyes as the Lekkas Jeep carrying the new foreign *despinis* hurtled by. Many were saddling up donkeys and leaving their baskets as a church bell sounded nearby.

'The scene is almost biblical.'

'This is a primitive island, riddled with myths and superstitions. Forgive me if I'm being too personal, but it is your blonde hair that makes them stare. It's so seldom seen on the island and it points out your foreignness, which fascinates people. In Greek mythology only the nymphs, the mermaids and the gods had hair as fair as yours.'

'Are they anti foreigners?'

'*Oyhee,* no, they are only a little wary of what they don't know. They are simple but kind people.'

They were passing through a small village and had now come up to a chapel. A bell was ringing wildly in the breeze. The pavement, the chapel and its surrounding wall were crammed full of people, while others were still arriving, and about a score of mules and donkeys that had brought workers from the fields at the top of the cliffs stood very reverently on the cliffside, their heads bowed. Beasts waited in the shade under a tree, men under another.

As the Jeep travelled through the streets, a ring of staring faces greeted them when they passed a café, shaded by plane trees, where fishermen at one table were playing cards. At another, musicians with a violin, a zither, lyres and a lute were singing *mandinádhes,* improvised rhymes of bittersweet love and tricks of fate. The swaying rhythms and throaty warbling of the singers had a mournful, eastern exoticism to them. Oriel would have liked to stop and listen some more to this timeless sound but they needed to get to the temple site and so the Jeep sped on.

Soon they turned off and went up a steep, dusty road, immediately after which Oriel's eyes took in fallen pillars scattered like confetti on the flanks of a towering slab of grey rock. She raised her eyes and saw that it was crowned by a small acropolis in a semi-ruined condition.

Stavros explained that, for months, the senior archaeologist and his team had made their way to the site each morning and worked there until late afternoon. Initially, they had taken measurements and made careful drawings of every part of the acropolis, at the centre of which stood part of small Minoan temple. Then, once every detail of the construction of the buildings and the art they contained had been clearly understood and logged, the work of reconstruction had begun.

'We're here,' Stavros announced as he pulled the Jeep off the road in front of the site and stopped. The landscape seemed wilder here, with the sea-bathed shores in the distance and pungent herbs scenting the air. Oriel stepped out of the car and surveyed the scene appreciatively. Everything on the site looked orderly and well run. Brightly coloured pin flags tidily marked out a couple of rectangular areas under excavation. At one of these, three men were absorbed in their tasks and she could see from the way they were working together that whoever was overseeing them must be an accomplished leader. One man with a bushy beard, his muscled arms covered in tattoos of mermaids and other mythological creatures, was on his knees in the earth, shaking dirt through a mesh screen, while a second was bagging and labelling artefacts taken from it. The third, a wiry, animated young man, was documenting the finds in an oilskin-covered field notebook, occasionally making comments and gesticulations that made the other men laugh.

Stavros explained that it was a settlement site of about 500 BC.

It covered a wider area than Oriel expected. The remains of a temple and two palaces with other small residences had been uncovered but some were still in very poor condition.

'We've only completed about half of it,' he told her. 'As you can see, the stone is so worn in places that even re-erecting the temple hasn't been easy.'

'It all looks very organized,' said Oriel, turning to Stavros. 'The archaeologist leading the team must be good.'

'Vassilis,' said Stavros, nodding his agreement. 'Damian is lucky to have him. They knew each other in America. Friends from college days, I think.'

Just then, a man in his early thirties, in a blue shirt and jeans, sleeves rolled up to reveal lean forearms and an unshowy but expensive-looking watch, strode towards them. With his long legs, he covered the ground swiftly like one of the panthers Oriel had seen in Africa. He held out his hand and shook hers warmly. His black hair retreated from his forehead in a series of seductive waves, although the front flopped a little over his forehead and he pushed it away with the back of his wrist so he could survey her properly.

'This is *Despinis* Anderson,' said Stavros. 'She's helping with the undersea excavation of the amphora wreck. I've brought her to look at your site today though, if you don't mind. We should have been out on the boat, as you know.'

'Of course,' said the man warmly, his dark eyes having never left Oriel's face. 'Vassilis Markopoulos, at your service. It will be a pleasure to show you around.' His voice had a pleasant ring with subtle shadings in it, made even more appealing by his pronounced accent. *What was it with Greek men?* They exerted such sex appeal and were so devastatingly handsome, Oriel thought.

'I've heard that you're quite an accomplished young lady,' Vassilis continued. 'Rare in our field, if you don't mind my saying so.'

Oriel flushed with pleasure at the tactful compliment. 'You have a good-looking site here,' she said as she moved to stand beside him.

'Wait until you see some of the things we've found,' he said with an engaging smile, showing a row of white teeth, bright against his tan. There was definitely something flirtatious in his manner, she noticed, but this was offset by a boyish enthusiasm that put Oriel at her ease.

She fell in step as Vassilis headed towards the remains of the small Minoan temple, Stavros following in their wake.

'We're reconstructing it piece by piece,' explained Vassilis. 'There's a fresco that's in surprisingly excellent condition, quite as good as the ones on Crete.'

Inside the temple they moved along a corridor that extended the width of the building but was, as yet, only walled on one side. Three rooms opened off the walled part, each one lined with large earthenware oil jars; then, just as they must have reached the heart of the building, Oriel's eyes widened. At the end of the corridor was the mural. She almost gasped at the sheer power of the hunting scene laid out before her. At the centre stood a bull in its death throes, a spear and a ribbon of bright blood emanating from its flank. The reddish hue of the hunters' muscled torsos stood out boldly against a vivid cerulean sky.

'It's almost as if it had been painted yesterday,' she murmured.

'You can see why Damian's so excited by the site, eh?' said Vassilis. 'He's poured a lot of time and money into the project.'

'And with impressive results,' said Oriel admiringly.

'Ah, that's not all, by any means. Wait till I show you something else we found.' He led Oriel and Stavros further down the corridor to an inside portico, half of it resurrected in all its elegant glory with a row of graceful arches and stone pillars, the other half still under reconstruction, including the fallen portions of a beautiful triangular tympanum with carvings of rearing horses. Two men were bent over a large marble head and torso on the ground, working carefully with a brush and small chisel. Next to them, on a trestle table, various fragments were laid out, each one numbered and catalogued neatly. A bare-chested brawny local was in the act of loading rubble into a wheelbarrow when he saw Oriel, instantly dropping the handles and staring at her, his mouth gaping in an involuntary leer.

Oriel didn't think to speculate on whether Damian had been right about the somewhat uncouth behaviour of his team or whether it was altogether sensible to insist on staying in the staff house. Instead, she was transfixed by the gigantic torso on the ground.

'The Prince of Lilies!' she gasped, kneeling to look at it more closely, her hand reverently and gently outlining the necklace of carved flowers and the curling peacock feather of his headdress.

'This is the only marble one,' explained Vassilis. 'But we've found twelve pottery versions, too. Buried when the pediment came down. Typhoeus did a great deal of damage when it erupted, but it preserved some things that would only have been looted in time.'

'Where are the others?'

'They're at the lab in Athens. This is the last, Damian wants to keep it here at the temple.'

Oriel's mind was spinning. 'You know, I've seen an ancient record of a shipment of pottery Lily Prince statues but I never thought I'd see the real thing. It must have been a veritable factory here.'

'Exactly,' said Vassilis. 'Damian reckons they were probably part of a consignment bound for a festival in Crete. Then disaster struck.'

Oriel stood up, straightening her back, and looked around. The late afternoon light glowed on the walls and pillars, bathing them in gold. 'Nothing much can have changed in the past three and a half thousand years,' she thought wonderingly.

One of the young men who had been crouched down by the statue – a student, Oriel guessed, as he didn't share the same weathered, rough look of his workmates – now got up and walked over to the trestle. He came back bearing something in his hand, which he held out to her shyly. It was a bronze knife, about fourteen inches long. Each side of the handle was carved in the shape of an animal head, a surreal-looking thing with the snout and tusks of a boar, ears shaped like butterfly wings and the slanted eyes of a fox. Oriel drew her thumb along the blade: it was still sharp.

'I've handled one of these in a museum but this is a much finer specimen,' she told the shy student. 'We think they were used to kill bulls in the Minoan blood rituals but no one really knows.'

'Probably used by a jealous husband on his wife,' laughed Vassilis. 'Some rather lurid family blood feuds have gone on in these parts.' Then he caught Stavros's eye and the laughter died on his lips. 'You're right, of course, *Despinis* Anderson. No one knows, but it's likely to be a blood sacrifice tool. It's good to have someone with your knowledge on board.' At that moment, another young man appeared and asked Vassilis for help with a cataloguing problem, glancing at Oriel curiously as he did so. With that, Vassilis excused himself. 'I hope to see you later, *Despinis* Anderson,' he said, his eyes twinkling, and strode off with his colleague.

'Come,' said Stavros. 'I'll show you round and you can meet some of the team. If you'd like to join us for the day, we'd be very happy to have your help.'

'Yes, of course, I'd be fascinated to see more of what you've found,' replied Oriel.

There was an air of informality as Stavros made the introductions and, although the men couldn't help their eyes lingering on Oriel, they were all respectful, particularly with Stavros looking sternly at them as he presented her to each one with the utmost care.

After he had shown her around, Stavros took Oriel to a long table under a shelter of woven palms, where maps and sketches were laid out. There was also a large notebook in which the team members documented any finds before marking them on the map of the site.

'You said that one of the team left yesterday,' Oriel said suddenly, wondering how another female archaeologist would have felt among these men. 'Was that the Frenchwoman?'

Stavros nodded. 'Yes, Chantal Hervé. An archaeology student.'

'*Kyrios* Yorgos said it was all very sudden. Something to do with *Kyrios* Lekkas,' she ventured carefully, trying to sound casual. 'Was there a problem?'

'That's what Yorgos said, was it?' Stavros lit a cigarette and snapped shut one of the notebooks with what seemed to Oriel an air of irritation. 'I've no idea why she decided to go so quickly. To be honest, she was one of the best helpers we've had, sharp as anything.' He dragged on the cigarette and gestured around them.

'Some students think this is a glamorous job to enhance their CV, believing they can just turn up and coast, not do too much. Damian is an exacting boss and has no time for that. We can't afford to carry anyone here. Chantal wasn't like that at all, and Damian rated her highly. I don't know why she decided to leave, it may have been that she did something to annoy him.' Stavros gave a lopsided smile. 'As you say, *Despinis* Anderson, Damian can be rather "impressive", particularly when angered.'

She smiled at him. 'Yes, I can see that.'

Still, Yorgos's opaque remarks rang in Oriel's head: *Each year it's the same ... and the Kyrios responds like any man would ... he's had enough of unreliable females ... they unsettle the men and then run off.* Somehow, she had the impression that there was something more salacious going on than a work dispute. Of course, she was more inclined to believe the easy-going openness of Stavros than the Machiavellian air of the estate manager. Then again, was Stavros used to turning a blind eye to his old friend's womanizing practices? They were both Greek men after all.

Stavros was looking at her as if reading her mind. 'What else did Yorgos say about Damian, might I ask?'

'That the islanders are afraid of him,' she blurted out without thinking.

'Heh,' Stavros shrugged. 'We have a saying here: *Ópios yínetai próvato ton tróei o líkos*, he who becomes a sheep is eaten by the wolf. Damian is the leader of Helios, so he does what he needs to do. I would say that the islanders respect him, rather than fear him. They know he has their best interests at heart.'

'Yorgos seems to think he has no heart,' Oriel murmured, turning to stare at the team of people moving back and forth across the site.

'And do you believe that, *Despinis* Anderson?'

Oriel glanced back and caught him watching her thoughtfully. 'Yorgos never told me that Damian was a widower,' she said, not replying to his question. 'And please, call me Oriel.'

'Very well, and likewise you must call me Stavros.' He wiped his forehead with the back of his hand before answering slowly. 'Yes, Damian's wife, Cassandra, died just a few years ago. His brother, Pericles, too. It was a dark time in his life, he's been through a lot.'

Without elaborating further, he suddenly threw his cigarette to the ground, crushing it under his heel, and gave her a guarded but friendly smile. 'So, Oriel, there's much you can help us with today. Where would you like to start?'

* * *

Oriel was glad when they finally broke up for the day. She was terribly hot, her skin felt clammy and her hair seemed full of sand. Although she'd applied suncream earlier, she had forgotten to bring her hat and so, after lunch, Kostas, one of the Greek archaeologists, had given her his baseball cap. 'With that fine white skin, you'll burn under our sun,' he had told her, dark eyes riveted on her face.

Oriel had thanked him without taking it, and now she was regretting her stubbornness as she wiped her face with a handkerchief dipped in water. Stavros needed to stay behind to check over some plans with Vassilis, so she decided to stretch her legs by walking down the arid hill to the shade of a small copse. Beside it, a few wild fig trees and moth-eaten cypresses stood beside a couple of white-washed stone dwellings with lines of washing outside.

As she neared the cluster of trees, she came upon four little boys playing football with a ball made out of rolled rags and wool. An old woman was sitting under one of the cypresses, a large basket at her side. She lifted a withered hand and signalled to Oriel to approach. One of the boys, taller than the others, with an olive complexion and extraordinary, deep brown eyes, came up to her and, gently taking her hand, pulled her across to the old woman resting under the tree. Curious, Oriel followed him. The basket was covered with large, dark green leaves. The old woman's lips stretched over toothless gums into a smile as she uncovered the basket full of large, freshly picked ripe figs. She motioned to the boy, pulling out a wide square scarf from under the basket and nodding encouragingly towards Oriel. Silently, the boy filled the scarf, as full as it could hold, with the luscious ripe fruit and bound it up, tying it with a knot.

'*Efharisto polý*, thank you very much.' Oriel smiled at the old woman, who nodded back.

'*Parakaló.*'

Oriel took out a handful of coins and offered them to the woman, who only chose a couple. In England, she reflected, that amount of figs would have cost a great deal more. The woman waved away Oriel's protest and put the coins in the front pocket of her apron.

'American?'

'No, English.'

The old woman gestured towards the acropolis. 'You are with

the men digging up the old temple?'

'Yes, that's right,' said Oriel.

Her wrinkled face looked concerned. 'The gods will be angry, mark my words.'

Oriel smiled politely, familiar with the tendency of locals to be suspicious, as well as superstitious. She'd encountered it before on other Greek islands. 'They are being very respectful, I assure you. Everything is being restored carefully to the way it was before it was destroyed.'

The old woman swatted a fly away with a red handkerchief that had been lying in her lap. 'You're not an islander, you don't know what Helios has suffered. It was the same when Poseidon's anger swallowed them up, took everything beneath the sea.'

Oriel frowned. 'What do you mean?'

'*Oi aiónes antigráfoun allílous,* the centuries copy each other.' The old woman peered up at Oriel, not unkindly. 'It is the same, you see, eh?' she repeated. She lifted a crooked hand and gestured from side to side. 'Poseidon here, the *Drákon* there. No good will come of it. The *Drákon* already knows about the vengeance of the gods.'

Shaking her head, she sighed, raising herself creakily from her chair. She called to the boys that it was time to go in for their supper then turned back to Oriel, eyeing her almost sadly. 'May you have good luck. A dove has no place among the crows.' With that, she hobbled off towards one of the cottages, lurching from side to side and shooing the boys along in front of her.

It left Oriel pensive. The old woman was clearly speaking about Damian. It seemed that the islanders' leader was almost as caught up in the legends of Helios as the old gods themselves. This place was extraordinary. There was so much she still had to piece together about the Lekkas story, she mused. She split open one of the figs and took a bite from its lusciously sweet interior as she started to walk back.

Oriel waved to Stavros as she reached the top of the hill and they both climbed into the Jeep, leaving the site as daylight was softening. She was tired and could feel a headache starting up across her eyes. Mild sunstroke, she thought, but that didn't worry her. Her grandmother had a trick against it; all she needed was some salt and water. Some people drank it but, when she was a child, Granny

Heather used to pop some in each of Oriel's ears for half a minute and it always worked. Nevertheless, she was looking forward to a cool bath, a real soak in the sunken tub of her luxurious marble bathroom. Again, she was grateful to Damian for his thoughtfulness. He had been on her mind on and off all day and she wondered if he would be at the dive the next morning.

'We often start work before dawn,' Stavros told her as they finally turned into the driveway leading up to the great house, 'but tomorrow, being your first day on the job, we'll be leaving later, at nine-thirty. We can provide you with diving gear but I'm guessing you'll want to use equipment that's familiar to you. You do have your own?'

'Yes, of course. I always use my own apparatus.' Oriel smiled. 'We are inseparable. When I'm on a job it goes where I go.'

'Good. Have you checked that it is all in good order, especially your regulator and your buoyancy compensator?' He hesitated, checking himself. 'My apologies, Oriel, I forget, you've dived many times before, it's just that …'

'You've never had a woman on the dive team before?' she said, raising her eyebrows.

He smiled apologetically and nodded. 'Né, that's right. We'll be diving quite deep and your safety is of the utmost importance.'

'Yes, yes, of course, I understand. Don't worry, Stavros, I'm used to it,' she told him. 'Rest assured, it's all checked and ready to go.'

'*Exairetiki*, excellent!'

A little later, at the door to her apartment, Oriel asked Irini, who was hovering in the corridor, for some salt. In no time, Granny Heather's remedy had worked miracles – as usual – and Oriel's headache had almost vanished. She then soaked for twenty minutes in her bath, wondering what to do with her evening. On her return to Heliades, Stavros had given her the keys to a Volkswagen Beetle cabriolet, which he said had been appointed for her use. Should she drive down to the port or perhaps walk there? Oriel would see much more of the island if she walked but it was already starting to get dark and, from what she had gathered, the walk would take twenty-five minutes. On an unlit road it might not be the wisest thing to do.

Once out of the bath and wrapped in a dressing gown she felt better and began drying her hair, seated at the vanity table. Her gaze settled on a stack of magazines, presumably left out by Irini. Selecting the one on top of the pile, she began flicking through the pages with one hand. A moment later, her fingers stilled; there was a picture of a well dressed woman with dark glasses, hair pinned up stylishly, getting out of a limousine. Yet it wasn't this image that made Oriel pause, it was the name 'Damian Lekkas' that caught her eye in the column beneath.

GREECE'S SWEETHEART YOLANDA HEADS BACK HOME
Singer Yolanda is heading back to her childhood home of Helios after sell-out tours all over Greece and Italy. The stunning singer claimed exhaustion after her gruelling tour, but many are speculating about the real reason for Yolanda's return to Helios, the island run by elusive tycoon, Damian Lekkas, her childhood sweetheart. Her long-time association with Lekkas has kept the gossip columns guessing for years. Perhaps one day she'll be queen of Helios, as her fans on the island have always wanted. Will wedding bells finally ring for Yolanda?

Oriel turned off the hairdryer, her face flaming. Hot jealousy spiked through her, unfamiliar and unwelcome. Of course, it was foolish of her not to expect that Damian would have a woman hovering in the background. He probably had many. After all, he was ferociously handsome, the wealthy owner of an island and apparently had women queuing up to be 'conquered' by him, as Yorgos had put it. That was not difficult to believe, she thought, brushing her hair with irritated, vigorous strokes.

Before she could settle her thoughts, there was a brisk knock at the bedroom door.

'*Ella mesa.*'

The door opened and there, framed in the doorway, sat Helena Lekkas in her wheelchair.

'*Kalispera, Despinis* Anderson. I have come to ask if you would have dinner with me tonight.' Helena's smooth poker face was enigmatic, her pale, glassy eyes fixed on Oriel, but there was a caressing softness in her voice quite different to the sarcastic tone she had adopted the night before.

Oriel hesitated then nodded. In the face of Helena's apparently genuine friendliness, words were not coming easily to her. The last thing she wanted was to spend the evening with Damian's cousin. Desperately, she sought a tactful way to refuse without giving offence.

The Greek woman's perfectly drawn eyebrows went up in puzzled interrogation. '*Well*? Do you have anything better to do?'

'No … Yes … I mean yes, of course, thank you very much,' Oriel replied quickly.

'*Poli kaló*, very good. Irini will come and fetch you, say … in one hour?'

'*Né, efharisto*, thank you. That'll be fine.'

Helena backed out of the doorway and disappeared. Oriel went to the door and closed it behind her. How had Damian's cousin entered her flat? Irini obviously had keys. Did that mean anyone could have access to the apartment, and at any time? She felt uneasy and promised to investigate the matter.

Despite the seeming affability Helena Lekkas had shown, Oriel sensed a menacing hint in the woman's mien: the way she sat stiffly in her chair, her long fingers holding on to its arms in an unnecessary death grip, as if Helena was trying to control some inner tension. Oriel wished suddenly that Damian was there to parry any unpleasantness that might occur. She thought of what Stavros had said about Helios's dormant volcano, and she had a hunch that under the smooth, impassive mask of Helena's beautiful face lurked a temper that, like Typhoeus, could cause horrendous damage if unleashed.

Oriel went to her wardrobe. She wasn't sure what the dress code was here but, if she had to go by the way Helena had decked herself out the night before, she figured that the etiquette was to dress up for dinner. She concluded that a conservative approach would be wise and chose a long turquoise chiffon dress, which she had worn many times in London, with a wide antique Chinese spinach jade bangle and a pair of matching hoop earrings bought in a small shop in Hong Kong on one of her Asian holidays. She slipped on a pair of stiletto-heeled sandals and surveyed her reflection in the mirror, satisfying herself that she looked elegantly respectable.

An hour later, accompanied by Irini, she made her way to Helena's apartment. She was surprised to find it was next door to hers: she had presumed that it would be in a different wing entirely. Irini explained why, before she could ask.

'*Kyria* Helena's quarters are being redecorated so, for the time being, she has borrowed part of the apartment you are living in. That is why yours is so small.'

'Small?' Oriel smiled. 'It seems perfectly spacious to me.' Yet, now she thought about it, her own quarters did look as if they could have been part of a larger apartment. There was no kitchen or dining room and the *salóni*, while large enough, had a certain imbalance to it for such a vast mansion.

Irini glanced at her and said in hushed tones: 'The *Kyrios* decided to do up this wing, which had been closed since the death of *Kyrios* Pericles. The *Kyria* was very upset, you see, and insisted she had her wing totally refurbished too.' The maid seemed unable to stop herself from elaborating further. 'The *Kyrios* was not happy about this situation, I think, but when his cousin asks for anything, *Kyrios* Damian always bows to her wishes. There's no one else he would do that for,' she added, as they halted outside a doorway and the maid quietly pushed open the door.

The room Irini took Oriel through had tall narrow windows that mirrored the ones in Oriel's own sitting room and bedroom, and a vaulted, frescoed ceiling. She gave a little start when she realized that the frescoes were, every one of them, representations of the perverse and violent decadence of mythological gods. One part showed an image of Zeus, in the guise of a swan, violating Leda, and Oriel almost gave a shudder at the swan's thick neck and great beating wings, depicted in vivid detail, while Leda swooned in terror. Elsewhere, the king of the gods appeared as a muscular black bull, carrying away a naked Europa to ravish her. Every portrayal on the ceiling had a lurid fascination with sexual conquest and, unbidden, Damian's scarred face appeared in Oriel's mind's eye, his forbidding gaze heavy with desire, making her stomach tighten in reflex.

As for the walls, Cerberus, the dog with three heads, Centaur, the half man, half horse, Chimera, the amalgamation of goat, lion and snake, Medusa the Gorgon and many of the darker creatures of Greek folklore were pictured in the brown wood panelling or on the furniture, carved in thick relief. It was a celebration of the hideous over the beautiful, the grotesque over the normal, and Oriel was suddenly filled with a sense of foreboding.

As she walked through the drawing room, Oriel noticed almost all the shelves and tables bore black-and-white photos in gilded frames of a beautiful young man in various close-ups, smiling or pensive. A few of the images, displayed in prime position, showed him crouching beside Helena in her wheelchair. His face had such a familiar look – the bright, piercing eyes and shape of the jaw – that Oriel realized instantly that this must be Damian's brother, Pericles. The frames were interspersed with flowers and on top of one cabinet she spied what looked like a shaving brush in a glass jar and, next to it, what appeared to be a rolled-up silk tie in a jewel-encrusted box surrounded by lit candles, as though part of some odd shrine.

Dressed in a scarlet evening gown, Oriel's hostess was waiting for her on an enclosed terrace, sitting in a damask-silk-covered chair at the dining table. The place was shady, the branches of lemon trees extending high over one side of the terrace. Oriel hardly took in her surroundings, though, and instead smothered a gasp. Everywhere … everywhere … there were cages of birds: they rested on tables, on pedestals and stands. Even the yellow fruit that hung like little lanterns from the branches of the trees had to make space for ornamental cages full of twittering coloured birds, which every now and again flew at the curving bars of their prisons, beating their delicate wings against them. A shiver ran down Oriel's spine at this eerie spectacle and, despite her near-revulsion, she felt pity for the small captive creatures that longed, she was sure, to be free.

'Good evening, *Despinis* Anderson. Do you like birds? You seem fascinated.'

Damian's cousin smiled. Oriel saw the hard stare of the Greek woman's eyes and the curious expression beneath the smile, as Helena's gaze took in the platinum-blonde hair that fell loose about her shoulders. For a split second she could feel a tension in the atmosphere so acute that she was convinced this glamorous woman, for some unknown reason, disliked her.

'They're striking, I must admit,' said Oriel evasively, hoping her face didn't betray her discomfort.

Helena Lekkas's gaze roamed distractedly over the cages then flicked back to Oriel, watching her intently. 'I love them. They keep me company. In a way they remind me of myself, captive in their golden cages. You see, even though I am taken out in my wheelchair twice a day, I feel as though I am a prisoner of this magnificent temple, my home.' She gestured to a chair. 'Please, have a seat.'

At a loss for words, and feeling more than a little awkward, Oriel murmured her thanks as she sat down.

Helena's incredible hair was gathered into a forties' vintage snood hairnet that matched her dress. Her neck, earlobes and her silken tanned arms were adorned with expensive jewellery that, Oriel suspected, was likely the work of well known Greek goldsmiths – Lalaounis or Zolotas perhaps. She too loved gold and had bought some of these Greek creations at auction over the years. Helena was stunning – like one of the mythological daughters of the night – and suddenly Oriel pitied this beautiful crippled woman. Her moment's misgiving she decided to put down to unreasonable fears and a fertile imagination. Anyway, she would try to have a pleasant evening and even found herself wondering if, perhaps, she and Damian's cousin might actually become friends.

'I thought it would be more enjoyable to dine in the fresh air,' explained Helena. 'The weather is pleasant at this time of the evening. It's not so hot and there is an agreeable breeze blowing from the sea.'

'Yes, I think so too. It's a great treat for me, especially as we don't often have the opportunity to sit outside in England, even during the summer.'

'Will you join me in a glass of ouzo?' Helena asked, pointing to a bottle in an ice bucket that stood on a tray beside her with two glasses. 'It's a stronger version of the French Pernod, distilled from the residue of the grapes left after the wine is made.'

'Oh yes, I've had ouzo before, the last time I was in Greece.'

'So this is not your first visit to our country?' Helena murmured as she poured a little of the clear liquid into the glasses.

'No, I've studied and worked in Greece before.'

'Ice?'

'Yes, please.'

'You speak Greek with almost no accent. Foreigners usually

have great difficulty pronouncing some of our words.' She added a couple of cubes of ice and some water to the drinks, which immediately turned milky white.

'I read ancient Greek at university before extending my studies to archaeology. I've always been fascinated by the Greek civilization.'

A waiter, an ageless-looking black man of colossal frame and stature, bald and with African features, appeared with small plates of *mezedes*, which he placed in front of them with some bread before withdrawing as silently as if shod in velvet. Oriel thought he looked rather like one of the eunuchs who guarded the harems in *A Thousand and One Nights*, a fairy-tale figure lost in time, just as this house seemed to be.

Had Helena read the curiosity in Oriel's face as she had stared at the servant? Anyway, she smiled at the young woman, seemingly amused, and said: 'Beshir has been with us since the age of twelve. My father brought him back from Turkey, where he was being mistreated. He is a eunuch, an extinct treasure from a different era. Even the Turks and Persians wouldn't have them in their households today.'

Although Helena's clarification had proved her analogy right, Oriel was shocked all the same. But was she so surprised? These people seemed to be living in an age almost as old as the antiquities they were excavating.

Helena clinked her glass against Oriel's. '*Yassas!*' she said, with that enthusiasm so typical of Greeks. 'Your health! Did you know that this clinking of glasses originates from an ancient Greek belief that wine should be savoured with all the senses? Its bouquet pleases the nose, its colour the eyes. It delights both touch and taste with its body and flavour, and when we clink our glasses the crystal sound charms our ears.'

Oriel smiled. 'I must say, I do like the idea that the habit propagated from Greece to the rest of the world. So much more appealing than the other, more grim, medieval theory.'

'And what is that?'

'That the sloshing of the wine into each other's cups was a symbolic gesture of trust between enemies, that one man trusted the other not to poison him.'

Helena tilted her head to one side, regarding Oriel as though she was a curious exhibit behind glass. 'How enlightening! I never knew that.' She took a sip of ouzo and smiled sweetly. 'You see, you're quite safe with me, *Despinis* Anderson.'

Oriel laughed, though to her own ears it sounded a little uneasy. There was something about Helena Lekkas that seemed wholly unpredictable. 'Have you travelled much outside Helios?' she asked, then wondered if she had been tactless, glancing at Helena's slender brown wrist on the armrest of her wheelchair.

Again, her hostess seemed to read her thoughts. 'Being in a wheelchair does not stop me from seeing the world, I can assure you. My cousin and I go away for two months every year, July and August, when the weather becomes too hot here. Damian does the rounds of auction houses and antique shops looking for our Greek heritage, while I go shopping for clothes and jewellery.' A cloud swept over Helena's beautiful features. 'Though this year it's different – Damian's busy with the new excavations,' she sighed sadly, but the dangerous glitter in her grey eyes, belying an outward calm, didn't escape Oriel.

'I think travel is one of the most liberating pastimes of all,' Oriel said brightly, trying to keep the conversation light. 'That's one of the attractions of my job, I suppose. I love seeing different cultures.'

'I envy you your freedom. I have always wondered what it must be like to go wherever one pleases, whenever the mood takes you. If not for this,' Helena gestured to her wheelchair, 'I might have had a different life, away from Helios.' She looked at Oriel with interest. 'It is impressive that you have achieved so much as a woman when we live in a man's world.'

Oriel smiled. 'It hasn't been easy but I've always been addicted to challenges.' She began to relax a little. The antagonism Damian's cousin had shown her on their first meeting now seemed to be replaced by an unexpected cordiality. 'If women don't push themselves in a man's profession, how will progress ever be made?'

'Yes, but it's different here,' Helena said thoughtfully. 'Still, let us drink to progress. As Heraclitus said: "There is nothing permanent except change."' Yet it seemed to Oriel there was a melancholy tinge to her expression as she said it.

Both women raised their glasses once more and clinked them

together.

With the onset of evening, a glory of colour came out in the light of the setting sun. The earth and sky were suffused with a delicate pink tinge – the closer to the earth, the deeper the pink. And then the boundless cloth of gold was tarnished suddenly with darkness. The night was soft and cool. The moon came up and from where Oriel sat she could see that it had carved a brilliant pathway of light across the sea to the edge of the world.

The waiter, Beshir, a silent shadow despite his great stature, came over and lit the candles, which stood on the dining table in their pink-coloured glass globes, thinly etched with gold. Genuine treasures from the Ottoman Empire days, no doubt, Oriel thought.

Dinner was delicious with *avgolemono* soup, a concoction of egg and lemon mixed into a chicken broth, which Oriel had never tasted before, and *stifado*, a stew of wild rabbit and bay leaves that was richly flavoured. It was a much less elaborate menu than the one Damian had given her the night before but just as enjoyable – if not more so – because its simplicity put her at ease.

They talked about Greece and their travels, and Oriel had the distinct impression that her hostess lived for those times when she could escape the confines of this 'beautiful prison', as she called Heliades. By the time Beshir brought in a plate of baklava and the coffee, Oriel was beginning to take a genuine pleasure in the evening.

'Will you have some Turkish coffee or would you prefer instant?'

'I would love Turkish coffee, please.'

'How do you take it?'

'*Métrios*, medium, thank you.'

There was a lull in the conversation while they ate the sweet pastries with their coffee, enjoying the peaceful night as the moon hung high above them.

Then Helena put down her coffee cup. 'So, how do you find my cousin, *Despinis* Anderson?'

Oriel glanced at her in mild surprise, not expecting the question. 'What do you mean?'

'Damian usually has an effect on people, whether it's good or ill.' Helena stared at her expectantly.

Oriel turned her attention to her coffee, her finger tracing the ornate silver handle of the cup. What could she say? There was no way to describe her feelings about Damian. She could hardly voice the thought of how his broad shoulders, tanned muscular chest, long, firm thighs and arms with their strength of steel made her lose control of her own body. Or that his eyes had a way of glittering enigmatically when he looked at her. Yet none of that explained the power he had over her; the sense that only he could unlock a part of her she had never known existed, if only she could trust him. Her mind went back to the picture of the singer she'd seen in the magazine in her room. The thought of him with another woman made her stomach twist painfully again.

'He's a very charismatic man, that's true.' She glanced at Helena, hesitating. 'I didn't realize that he may soon be engaged to Helios's most famous inhabitant,' she added, deftly redirecting the conversation.

But Oriel's tactic to deflect worked too well. Helena's eyes became flints of steel. 'Yolanda is a nobody! In spite of her vulgar fame, she has not been distinguished by noble birth. Damian cannot marry such a woman.' Her response was coldly dismissive, but a spark of something volatile lurked in her expression.

'I suppose arranged marriages have been the tradition with your ancestors,' Oriel replied carefully.

'Exactly, my dear.' Despite the cool breeze, which made the leaves on the lemon trees waft gently behind them, Helena dabbed at her upper lip with a napkin as if she were feeling hot. She clearly viewed marriage as a union of rank and breeding as far as her family's dynasty was concerned. If Damian was expected to marry into a high-class Greek family, Oriel thought ruefully, that was yet another reason why the two of them could never be together.

Helena breathed deeply and placed her napkin down. 'Damian may be the head of this island, but the poor man doesn't see what's good for him half the time. That's why he needs me to protect him from his own mistakes. No one understands what it is to be a Lekkas. Damian must keep his focus.' She had been speaking almost as though to herself but when she looked at Oriel her gaze suddenly became penetrating. 'When he's not distracted by his own weakness, he does great things for Helios.'

Oriel blinked. Was this a veiled threat aimed at her?

Her hostess smiled pleasantly once more. 'So you are starting the important excavations tomorrow?'

Oriel's feeling of wariness had begun to creep back. 'Yes, I'm really looking forward to it.'

'My cousin is obsessed with these antiquities. He studied archaeology at the University of Athens, and then worked for the same institution for three years. It took him five years to get an excavating permit from the Ministry of Culture and Tourism. There are very strict laws that control the sea around these islands and inspectors come to Helios every now and then to make sure that we are observing them.'

'I didn't realize until I came here that *Kyrios* Lekkas was himself an archaeologist.'

'A passionate one. He dives almost every day during the hot months, and once or twice a week in winter. He's never so happy than when he is grubbing around in the mud, looking for broken jugs.' Helena's proud demeanour instantly gave way to an oddly theatrical look of distain. 'But I don't understand all this interest in the dead. I find it much more exciting to concentrate on the living.'

Oriel looked down at her coffee. She couldn't have disagreed more. 'I can understand him. I find it thrilling to walk where ancient feet have trod.'

'This time it's that shipwreck Damian discovered a few months ago,' Helena went on, not listening to Oriel. 'It's Roman, apparently. He brought up a beautiful bowl the last time he was down there, quite intact. Of course, he had to hand it in to the museum. What a waste! He doesn't seem to mind the risk of being eaten alive in those deep waters when there are such treasures for the taking.'

Oriel decided it might be best to humour her. 'Do you really think there are sharks around here? Have there been any incidents?'

Helena burst out laughing, an hysterical sort of laugh. 'I see you took on board my unfortunate remark yesterday evening. Oh, you mustn't worry too much about that.' She shrugged. 'I only said it to wind up my cousin. Damian has a thing about sharks.' She laughed again and the high-pitched sound of it rippled through the silent night, causing a shiver to run up Oriel's spine. For a brief, shocking moment, as if glancing into a private room, she glimpsed a raw blaze of cruelty in those magnificent grey eyes and in the twist of those sculpted red lips.

The Greek woman's gaze glittered as it searched Oriel's face speculatively. 'This is a harsh island, *Despinis* Anderson, and if you are going to live among its people you must be prepared to face the primitive occurrences that knock us down from time to time.'

Shallow hollows lay about Helena's cheekbones. Her features now held a strangely placid expression so that, in the moonlight, her face became like a mask of blackened and tarnished copper. Something had shifted in her expression as she stared vacantly ahead. It was as if her poise was beginning to slip, like wax melting from a candle.

'Helios makes everyone suffer its primitive urges,' she went on, 'generation after generation. The island rules us all. But it is home … *my* home. Pericles has always understood that. He would never let me live anywhere else but here. Not any more, not now he is the ruler of Helios. He brought me home again, where I belong.'

'Pericles?' Oriel looked confused at these ramblings. She was talking as though Pericles were still alive. 'You mean Damian?'

Helena turned to Oriel. 'Mmm? Pericles, yes. He was such a beautiful man, so strong. He could have been an athlete, you know.' Her eyes sparkled almost girlishly and her voice became lighter, like a teenager struck by her first crush. 'He used to visit me and take me out. He was so kind to me. And no one understood him the way I did. All the things they said he did … not true, not true. Pericles was a slave to his passions, that is all.' She turned away, her eyes gazing at nothing as she muttered: 'It was the women … they threw themselves at him in a disgusting way. He was a pure spirit, too good for this world.'

Oriel was intrigued. Helena seemed lost in her own world, and it was clear her capricious moods were completely unpredictable. Still, not once had Damian talked to her about his brother, so perhaps this was her chance to piece together more of the mystery of this claustrophobic family, she thought. She knew she had to tread carefully with Helena Lekkas but her curiosity was now aroused.

'Were you close to him?' she asked softly.

'Close?' Helena looked dreamily at Oriel. 'Oh yes. We were in love … We were always meant to be together, even as children.

Bound by the tragedy that struck us all.' Her face fell. 'The curse of our family took my father, then my dear Pericles.'

Oriel reached for her coffee cup slowly, watching her hostess. 'Curse?'

Helena looked surprised and leaned forward, her expression becoming almost comically earnest. 'The curse, my dear, yes. Can you not see it? It's there in my cousin's scarred face. The Lekkas family is doomed to a life of tragedy. Every one of us. Ah, Beshir, my saviour,' she said, smiling beatifically once more.

The manservant had come back to clear the table and on a silver tray was bearing a bowl of the fat chocolate-covered dates that Damian had offered Oriel the night before. Beshir glanced at Helena. Scanning her expression with his midnight eyes, he frowned. Had he picked up on her change of mood from that single look? Oriel found her eyes meeting those of the waiter and she sensed that behind his impassive features lay the brain of a powerful and intelligent man. She couldn't help thinking of Ajax, from Homer's *Iliad*, who, loyal to a fault, would lay down his life for his mistress. Beshir held the tray to his chest and bowed, melting back into the shadows.

She wanted to know more about this so-called curse though dared not ask Helena how Pericles had been murdered. Had it happened before Damian's wife, Cassandra, had died? Had she also fallen prey to this 'curse' too? But she was distracted just then by Helena's voice. 'You'll have a chocolate date,' her hostess pressed as Oriel set down her cup. 'Pericles used to love these. Have you tried one? With your fine frame you don't need to avoid sweet things, or do highly strung nerves keep you slim?'

Oriel was a little taken aback by what seemed a double-edged compliment. 'I'd love one, but it was a delicious dinner and I'm afraid I over-indulged myself. In England, I'm not used to eating a meal at night. I usually have just a slice of fruit or some yoghurt.'

Helena smiled condescendingly. 'You need all your strength to face up to the challenges that will come at you on Helios. A few kilos more will do you no harm at all ...' She tipped her head to one side again in that strange way, and regarded Oriel with a pout of exaggerated concern. 'You have a worrying fragility that I don't think will withstand the taxing work that awaits you.'

Oriel glanced at Helena but decided to ignore the gibe. 'I'm sure I'll manage somehow,' she answered, her tone as friendly as she could muster. She didn't feel like lingering any longer around Damian's cousin, but she was itching to probe a little further about the dead wife and there was no easy way to introduce the subject. She hesitated, then said: 'Damian – *Kyrios* Lekkas, I mean – he seems to enjoy challenging work. There's a great deal for him to supervise, the family business as well as the excavations. Your family seems to have suffered a great deal. I expect he finds solace in keeping busy, particularly since he lost his wife. Cassandra, wasn't it?'

Helena flinched as if she'd been struck. 'Agamemnon's concubine!' she hissed and something feverish shifted in her gaze. 'The Lekkas dynasty is the lifeblood of Helios. That blood cannot be tainted by the offspring of whores and harlots!' Helena's knuckles were white as they gripped the handles of her wheelchair; her breathing picked up, a red flush staining her cheeks. 'She tried to take him away from me!' Helena became more and more agitated, her chest heaving as she gulped for air. Fumbling at the top of the wheels of her chair, she pushed herself away from the table.

'I'm so sorry, I didn't mean to upset you, *Kyria*. It's getting late and I should go,' said Oriel, horrified at this excessive reaction.

'Oh yes, I agree.' Helena's pale eyes bored into her. 'You should indeed go. A woman needs her beauty sleep, especially when surrounded by so many healthy and virile-looking men, but I don't need to tell you that. You know it already, don't you?' She sneered vituperatively, her words tumbling out in a gravelly wheeze.

Oriel's instinctive, angry reaction gave way almost immediately to pity – pity and fear. The beautiful Greek goddess might have been the perfect hostess earlier that night, but it was plain to see that Damian's cousin was a troubled soul, endowed with unstable passions.

As she stood up hastily from the table, Beshir appeared as if from nowhere, gliding on to the terrace like a towering, dark apparition.

'Beshir, my medication. Take me inside!' Helena hand was clenched against her chest, her eyes still narrowed on Oriel.

Taking her leave with an awkward smile and eager to return to her room, Oriel hurried away from the terrace as if the devil himself were at her heels.

'Goodnight, *Despinis* Anderson. Sweet dreams,' Oriel heard her hostess rasp behind her, followed by an unsettling, high-pitched laugh.

With a little shiver, Oriel crossed the narrow corridor that separated Helena's apartment from hers, the heels of her shoes tapping intrusively on the black-and-white Greek tiling. Shadows gathered beneath the high stone arches leading to the moonlit garden; the lacy foliage of the flame tree, trembling in the soft breeze, seemed to be whispering to her to run from the island.

Once in her bedroom, she flooded it with light and stood a moment against the closed door, her heart in turmoil. She glanced at the canary, twittering briefly at her arrival before settling quietly on its perch, and took a deep breath. Not for the first time since her arrival it seemed that she'd been on the island for ages – England seemed so far away.

She undressed and prepared for bed, but found she was still wide awake. Her thoughts drifted to the Frenchwoman who had left the team so suddenly. There were two women, weren't there? Hadn't there been a Dutch girl in a previous year, as well as Chantal Hervé? She should have pressed Stavros about the other student, too. Oriel couldn't help but wonder what was behind their hasty departures. Maybe they had left for family reasons, something as simple as that, but wasn't it a strange coincidence that only women had left the team? Was it anything to do with Damian? He was still extremely handsome, despite his scarred face. His rough sort of arrogance and his flirtatious manner were just the sort of traits that a woman could fall for, if she wasn't careful – Oriel knew that only too well. Had he made a pass at them? Maybe they had fallen for him, or for one of the crew, or another islander, and had been hurt? Perhaps … although two women on the team succumbing to unbearable heartache in a relatively short space of time seemed unlikely.

Oriel sighed. She knew she wouldn't sleep if she went to bed now. She shouldn't have had that Turkish coffee, she thought – caffeine didn't suit her, she was so jumpy. Yes, it must be the caffeine; normally it took quite a lot to unnerve her. Anyhow, better to unwind and relax before trying, and failing, to get to sleep – otherwise she would be tired for her dive the next day.

She went out on to the terrace and paused at the balustrade, looking up at Typhoeus. The vast, conical peak of the volcano stood darkly against the firmament, the myriad points of the distant stars like a vast infinite curtain, pulling Oriel's own small world close on this perfect night. Her wrestling emotions, almost too much to contain, were caught and held by this vivid theatre of nature; the grandiose, spectacular sight seemed to reflect back to Oriel her own limited experience of love and romance. The air was heavy with the scent of iodine, algae and stone pines. The wildness of Helios – in the cliffs, the sea, the threatening slumber of the island's volcano – was at odds with the sophisticated, modern comforts of Heliades, she thought: a volatile contrast that reflected the character of the people who lived in this house.

Suddenly she heard a noise – the humming drone of a motor as the darkness was speared by a distant splash of light, growing nearer and larger, and which now seemed like a giant firefly skimming slowly over the waveless sea. Rounding the bay, the form of a boat appeared, its white mainsail furled around the mast, motoring towards the quay of the Lekkas domain.

Oriel's heart leapt in her breast and she gave a sigh of relief, knowing that Damian was back and that she would see him tomorrow. Keeping her eyes peeled in the darkness, she observed him getting off the boat and mounting the stairs to the terrace, noting the details of his movements, the proud lift of his head, the energetic step, the sway of his broad shoulders and the way he swung his arms when he walked; and then he disappeared into the garden and was gone. Even from a distance and in dim light she would always know that silhouette. She stayed a little longer out on the terrace and then went in, pulling the shutters to before climbing into bed and slipping into a deep sleep as soon as her head hit the pillow.

It felt like only minutes later that Oriel suddenly woke up panting. She was almost certain she had heard the rhythmic sound of Helena's wheelchair as it moved around the room. Was it an actual noise that had disturbed her sleep or had she had a nightmare? She listened, without turning on the light; the house was silent. She glanced at the shining dial of her travel alarm clock on the bedside table: three o'clock. The little canary was also awake, fluttering nervously in his cage. Without turning on the light, she went to the door and listened but there was no one there. *It must be my imagination,* she concluded, but that made it no less disturbing.

Back in her bed, Oriel tossed and turned restlessly, hovering between sleep and wakefulness as glimpses of Damian's and Helena's faces, alternating with volcanoes and sharks, kept flickering before her closed eyes. Conversations she'd had since her arrival whirled round and round in her tired brain and she found herself sitting up several times in a cold sweat. It wasn't until nearly dawn that those voices ceased, the disturbing images melted away and she fell into a sound slumber.

CHAPTER 4

Stavros and Oriel arrived at the marina just as the sun was rising. Helios had the subdued quiet of dawn and the sea was a metallic grey, glistening as the occasional spear of light pierced through the clouds and danced over the surface. The air felt fresh and new; a gentle breeze caressed Oriel's skin, soothing her. The marina was set in a small bay pinched into the coast between high pine-clad shores. There was a tiny taverna with a loggia surrounded by a trellis of vines, and a rickety wooden jetty at which Damian's boat was moored with a scattering of other colourful craft, all almost motionless on the bluest of blue water. A slipway was littered with lobster pots and gnarled rope while, further along, brown nets stood drying on the white sandy beach, one of the many that scalloped the ultramarine sea and were generally empty. All was quiet, save for the noise of the hulls gently knocking against the jetty and the men's voices discussing the day's agenda.

Damian and the rest of the crew were already onboard the dive boat *Ariadne*, a twenty-five-metre blue-and-white wooden *caique*-style vessel, moored stern-on. Oriel stepped aboard and made her way to the wheelhouse, where she could see Damian standing with a couple of the dive team. He was half turned away, head down, scrutinizing some plans laid out on a small table in front of him, looking so handsome and virile that she caught her breath. His body was superb in his clinging wetsuit, giving the impression of indomitable strength. His dark curling hair, usually brushed back, fell across his forehead softly as if he hadn't combed it since he woke.

As she walked across the wide deck that was comfortably equipped with wooden benches, Damian turned and their gaze met for a single searing moment before he turned once more to his plans.

The two men beside him weren't so absorbed in the task not to stare at Oriel, who, despite her height, looked almost fragile in her wetsuit, which was moulded to her like a second skin, emphasizing her slim waist and the curve of her hips. She recognized the pair from the temple site the previous day. One was the tattooed bearded giant with the wheelbarrow who had leered at her; the other the wiry young man who had been laughing while writing in his field notebook. He was now nudging the gawping giant, who remembered his manners enough to stammer '*Kaliméra*' in greeting.

Oriel smiled in what she hoped was a business-like fashion. '*Kaliméra.*'

Damian, still not looking her way, folded the map carefully. Finally, he turned to Oriel and Stavros. 'I think you've all met. Yanni and Spyros,' he said briskly, motioning to the giant and the impish-looking young man in turn. 'Spyros is from Kalymnos and this is his first dive with us. Normally he's with Vassilis's team but he's pestered me so often about getting involved with this excavation, he's worn me down.' The gruffness of his tone didn't quite match the amused glint in his eye as he glanced at the young man, who grinned sheepishly back.

They all followed Damian out of the wheelhouse on to the deck. Two more men were seated on one of the benches, crouched over their kit bags. 'Alexis, Mohammed, this is *Despinis* Anderson, who is joining us on the dive today.' His hard gaze swept over the men before he glanced at Oriel, seeming almost aloof. 'We're a diverse team. Alexis here is from Crete, Mohammed from Algeria.' The Cretan looked up and gave a wide snag-toothed smile, while the young Algerian, who already looked eager to start the dive and was pulling out his gear, nodded in Oriel's direction.

'Now,' Damian continued, 'before we set sail, I would like everyone to check their gear. We will be diving to a depth of thirty metres, half a mile offshore. The currents can be a little wayward and it's just deep enough that observing the correct decompression stages will be vital. We don't want anyone getting the bends.'

The wiry young man shrugged, and Damian fixed him with a gimlet eye. 'And that means you too, Spyros,' he barked with authority. 'I know your sponge-diving ways are time-honoured in Kalymnos but this is my boat and my crew, and what I say goes.'

'With all due respect, sir, people got along perfectly well before all these fussy scientific safety rules,' Spyros argued, seemingly immune to the thunderclouds in Damian's eyes and the dig in his ribs from the towering Yanni. 'All you do if you get the bends is get your partner to take you back to the same depth. Then back to the surface slowly, five feet every five minutes. Then *presto*, you're cured.'

'If you want nitrogen bubbles in your bloodstream and a life of paralysis, that's your issue, Spyros. But remember one thing, I am your captain and your employer, and you will do me the courtesy of obeying my orders. Or you can leave now,' Damian instructed him firmly.

Spyros shrugged self-consciously. 'Yes, sir.'

'You can still back out.'

The young man smiled. 'No, sir, I wouldn't miss this expedition for anything.'

Damian's expression changed and he gave the youth a hearty slap on the back. 'Well, in that case, Spyros, welcome aboard the *Ariadne*. But, as I said, no improvising and no bright ideas.'

'Understood.'

Satisfied, Damian asked Stavros to pull up the anchor, and the *caique* slid smoothly away from the jetty. Oriel watched Damian's tall, lean figure move from one group to another, exchanging a few words with each man on his crew. She noted the friendliness with which they all responded, even Spyros, the young man from Kalymnos whose manner, though naturally playful and rebellious, was still tempered with respect. She went to sit on one of the wooden benches with her dive bag, where Damian soon joined her. For a long moment she sat silent, electrified by his closeness and unable to check through her kit, knowing she'd be fumbling around with trembling fingers. Finally she took a deep breath and spoke, saying the first thing that came into her head.

'You've got a fine dive boat here.' She looked around as she said the words, taking in for the first time the sheer scale of the vessel, with its two decks and state-of-the-art hoists and suction equipment. 'I've rarely seen one as modern and well equipped.'

It must have cost a small fortune, she added silently to herself.

Damian nodded, looking less aloof now, obviously pleased by her comments. 'Cousteau helped me fit it out,' he said. 'We met at a dive conference and he showed me around his boat. His is a converted American Second World War minesweeper but I wanted mine to be more Greek in style. Below deck, the cabins have every convenience. I like things to be comfortable as well as functional.'

Oriel's eyes sparkled, her awkwardness forgotten. 'I would love to meet Jacques Cousteau,' she exclaimed. 'He was one of my childhood heroes. I once heard him interviewed and he said he'd almost killed himself as a child, weighing himself down with bricks in his family's swimming pool, staying underwater until he lost consciousness.'

'I think that kind of obsession in a man can accomplish great things,' said Damian, smiling slightly. 'And now, if you'll excuse me, I'd better go and check the course has been correctly set.'

Oriel held on to the wooden rail behind her while the *Ariadne* made for the open sea. Despite the brilliant blue sky, the *meltémi* wind roared as the boat heavily beat and bashed its way against the rolling waves, the bow spray billowing up at each impact. This was normal May weather, though hot, and most of the divers were used to it, but as Oriel glanced across at the assembled men on the opposite bench she saw that the two younger divers were clearly feeling the harshness of the voyage.

They had been motoring for about twenty minutes when Alexis came to stand next to Oriel with a set of plans. 'These are the plans of the wreck site that the *Kyrios* went through with us. I thought you might want to look at them,' he said. He leaned in close to point out various features, devouring her with his eyes.

'Thank you, Alexis,' she answered politely. He was so closely invading her space that she could feel his warm breath on her cheek. On purpose, Oriel turned away as she assessed the map carefully. 'I'm glad Damian thought to get a good underwater cartographer, it makes life a lot easier.'

'Any problem, Alexis?' Damian cut in before his crew member could answer. Oriel hadn't heard him approach, and obviously neither had Alexis, who flinched a fraction at his employer's tone. She turned her head and stared at Damian. There was a sardonic lift to his eyebrows and an arrogant tilt to his head as her gaze met the chips of ice that were watching her, as if to say, *You see why I didn't want you staying at the staff house?* 'No, no problem, Kyrios,' Alexis answered hastily. 'I was just making sure *Despinis* Anderson was familiar with the layout of the site.'

Oriel felt her cheeks grow hot. How on earth was she expected to work in a team if this was going to be how they behaved? She followed the two men to join the others, who were assembled for the captain's briefing. They would go down in pairs, Damian explained. Each would have forty-five minutes underwater, and no more than two dives that day.

'You must stick close to your dive partner,' he instructed. 'It's very easy to get so absorbed in what you're doing that you forget the time.'

Oriel thought of the other danger inherent in diving at thirty metres or more. All it takes is one ambitious or greedy moment – the desire to search further or finish digging out some artefact winking beguilingly – and before you know it, you are lost to narcosis. Yet a diver wouldn't feel his senses growing confused: the hazy feeling comes upon you stealthily like a drug. Oriel had felt it herself before – the slower reactions, the impossibility of logical or rational thought – but she'd been lucky enough to have an experienced dive partner who had read the signs and helped her to the surface. The 'Martini effect', as nitrogen narcosis was often termed, had been fatal to plenty of others. Before too long, you might be moving senselessly in the wrong direction, away from the dive rope that guides you safely to the surface, or lashing out at your partner, even if they are in the very process of trying to save your life. Oriel gave an involuntary shiver. As she did so she met Damian's intent gaze. Had he read her mind?

Damian now detailed who would partner whom. He assigned Oriel to himself, which made her think for a moment that perhaps all hope of them becoming friends again was not lost. As she took a seat a little away from the rest of the crew, it occurred to her that this was the first time she had found herself working in an all-male group. Although she hated to admit it, she increasingly understood Damian's reluctance for her to live at the staff house. The men around her were coarse, relaxed and at ease. There was no compulsion to be on guard with their language or their jokes, which Oriel didn't mind. However, sometimes she noticed one or other ogling her without shame and, although the men seemed respectful enough under Damian's watchful eye, she was happy that she didn't need to spend her evenings at the staff house, sharing the sitting room and the kitchen, or choosing to be either cooped up in her room or to go out to escape the men.

By now the boat had skirted a headland and had moved closer again to the shore, following it in parallel. Gentle gusts of wind were filled with a briny tang as they made Oriel's hair flutter across her face. The sea was translucent and she gazed through the blue water at the little silver fish that darted in shoals, first one way, then the other. Looking up, she caught the glare of brilliant whiteness between the two bands of blue. There was the deeper one of the water, moving in a dance of lights and shadows, and the great upper band of the burning blue sky above the hilled islands they were passing by. It made the white structure of the little cliff-side villages, with their white walls and roofs of reddish tiles, their ridged slopes rich with pines, olives and pointed cypresses, stand out in such a picturesque way.

From time to time, Oriel slanted a glance at Damian but he ignored her, never speaking to her directly. His eyes, she couldn't help noticing, were empty of expression whenever they met hers. It was as if he had retreated once again into himself and away from her.

Now the high-up villages thinned, becoming few and rare, and then petered out altogether into empty mountains and wild shores. Soon they came to a fringe of reef that ran parallel to the coast in a long line, about half a mile from the shore. As could be seen by the noticeable difference in the colour of the water, the reef fell perpendicularly into the depths of the sea and it was here, where the much deeper water suddenly turned into an intense blue, that Damian gave the signal to weigh anchor.

Glancing across at his hard profile, Oriel saw that in daylight the scar appeared rather more defined, but Damian himself projected such charisma that one could almost forget about it. He was gazing out to sea, smoking. As she studied him through half-closed lashes, she could see that he was determined and ambitious, someone used to taking command – a leader of men who, if angered, would make a fierce enemy. Still, he seemed stressed, she decided, as she eyed his taut, muscular frame in his wetsuit, sitting there on the edge of the boat, curiously lonely-looking as he drew on his cigarette: a man apparently without the need of human warmth, a man fighting secret demons …

'*Despinis* Anderson and I will be going down first,' he announced to the crew. He strode towards Oriel, who was tightening the straps of her weight belt. Her heart gave an uncontrollable lurch. She was about to protest when he bent over her and took the straps from her hands to examine the quick-release fastening, but then she saw that the other divers were all engaged in checking out each other's gear. 'We want you to be able to float easily to the surface if you get into trouble,' he murmured as he tinkered with the mechanism, locking and releasing it until he was satisfied it was in good working order. The potent maleness of him so close made flames dance inside her.

'Thank you,' she said, 'but I'm perfectly familiar with my gear.'

But Damian ignored her and examined her compressed-air cylinder. 'The stopper isn't tight enough,' he told her. 'The loss of gas is very slight, but we can't risk it.' He unstrapped the cylinder, made the necessary adjustment, and helped her buckle the straps tightly once more. Oriel's heart was thudding uncontrollably as he stared down into her face, his expression granite, his mouth grim.

'Spit into your mask,' he ordered.

She hesitated for a second, annoyed at being dictated to, but most of all unsettled by the effect Damian's closeness was having on her as an intense unrequited longing fought for supremacy in a raging storm inside her. This was crazy: he was a stranger. How was it possible to be sucked so deeply into another's powerful personality?

'It'll keep your mask from fogging up.'

She silently obeyed, meeting his lidded gaze with a surge of resentment, the green in her eyes flaring. No one had any right to upset her equilibrium quite so thoroughly.

Damian took the mask from her and rinsed it out again. 'Spit keeps the air on the inside of the mask from condensing on the glass,' he explained.

'I'm well aware of that. I've dived before,' she shot back.

'Yes, but I wasn't sure if your delicate sense of fastidiousness would preclude your doing such a vulgar thing, eh?' His face suddenly broke into a grin that was crooked and shatteringly attractive; still, she glared at him.

'Come on, *Despinis* Anderson, let's go. We have work to do,' he announced gruffly but, as he looked at her, his dark, rugged features held an enigmatic quality, half mocking, half intense. There was a glitter of some emotion in the steady steely eyes, but Oriel was either too confused or too defensive to decipher it.

Turning to his crew, Damian gave them his final orders. 'We have enough air to stay under the water for two hours, although I'm giving each of the four teams a strict forty-five-minute limit. If we need any help, I will send *Despinis* Anderson up and two of you will come down. I would prefer it if Stavros stayed up here today to man the boat and deal with any inspectors from the Ministry of Culture, should they visit. They have been told that we're excavating, and they usually come across on the first day.'

Damian went first in order to secure the line to the seabed, which was marked at carefully calculated intervals to help them decompress in the correct stages on their ascent. A few minutes later he was up again and he waved to Oriel, who obediently dropped backwards into the sea.

She swam alongside Damian as, fathom by fathom, she let herself sink deeper into the sparkling blue water beneath her. It was uncommonly clear, so much so that it was impossible to gauge the depth. The sea dust that she stirred on her descent slowly drifted away, leaving her suspended free in space. For several seconds that seemed an eternity, she felt herself hurtling downward, conscious only of the upward rush of bubbles around her. She loved this three-dimensional world and felt as free as a bird in the sky.

The pounding of the surf grew softer and softer. The brilliant colours of the algae, sea anemones and sponges on the cliff-like formation that composed the edge of the reef were followed by bizarre bushes of gorgon coral. A startled scorpion fish withdrew its red head into a grotto, spines extended. Oriel passed through a school of blue-black sea swallows … and then suddenly she saw it.

The huge wreck loomed beneath her. She had excellent visibility; still a few metres above it, Oriel could see the entire length of the cargo vessel, which lay on its side. As she approached it was like a vast rock, not ten feet from her, covered in calcite and barnacles. Here and there its body was creviced by fissures. Everywhere it was festooned with sea vegetation – seaweed, kelp, anemones – and, together with the coral and calcite fingers, the great wreck rose up like some surreal piece of Gothic architecture. Oriel floated motionless a moment, entranced. She turned to look at Damian, who shone his torch on the coral, alive with seahorses. Their angled heads and tubular mouths bobbed and swayed in the current, transparent fins fluttering in waving motions. Each of them was clasped to the branches by a fragile tail, hardly looking more robust than a child's finger. Magic!

The sand was loose as Oriel's feet touched the bottom and, although she was careful not to disturb it, the particles were so fine that the silt rose up anyhow in pale grey clouds around her legs. Unknowingly, she stepped on a stingray that was the same grey colour as the sand. As her foot touched it, it lifted its long, rat-like tail, ending with a dark venomous spike, and whipped her violently. Fortunately, her soft-sole high boots were of an excellent heavy quality so the spike did not pierce them.

As she and Damian made their way to the stern of the half-buried argosy, her heart beat a little faster and her fins beat the water more urgently. She could see the pottery littering the area around the mound: amphorae – masses of them, by the looks of it. She spotted the necks of the large earthenware pots poking out from the silt, encrusted with barnacles and calcite. Definitely a large trading vessel – Roman, as Damian had surmised. He gave her the okay sign, and she returned the gesture.

Oriel felt pumped, more alive than she had ever thought possible. Every fibre of her being was vibrating with anticipation. Adrenaline was coursing through her veins. All the mundane worries of her life had been muted and all there was to know about was this moment: no worrying about Damian and the past, no anxiety about the future.

They set to work methodically, working at one end so as not to disturb the rest of the site unnecessarily. Damian was taking photographs with his Nikon, the very latest underwater model, Oriel noticed. He had stopped now and was clearing mud and sand carefully from some small artefact he had spotted. Oriel left him to it – intent on finding a good amphora specimen she could send to the surface for closer inspection. She knew well enough that the seal could provide the clue they needed to date the vessel … or vessels. As she poked among the fragments, she began to see a far more various cargo than she would have expected. Campanian dishes, bowls, oil lamps, statue fragments and differing styles of amphorae littered a fairly wide area. *This could be more than one ship,* she thought to herself wonderingly. It wouldn't be too unusual if a wreck site was near dangerous rocks amid a busy trading route – plenty of ships could have sunk to their doom in storms over the centuries. *But is this the case here?* she pondered.

A few minutes later she had found the perfect specimen. The amphora was whole, its seal intact. She pulled a large dive balloon from the bag on her back and attached it to the pot before filling the balloon with compressed air from her tank. Minutes later the balloon, with its cargo, was floating towards the surface.

She glanced over at Damian, busy attaching his own finds to a balloon. As she waited for him to join her, she looked around wonderingly. Nearby, in among the rocks, damselfish and clownfish were playing about, swimming in and out of anemones' tentacles as if they felt totally at home there. Just then, a shoal of silver fish obscured Oriel's vision and for a moment she lost sight of the dive line, the wreck, and Damian too. All of a sudden she felt alone and vulnerable, before the muscular wet-suited figure was visible once more. Again he gave her the okay sign and made his way over to her, kicking long, muscular legs. *Why do I feel so reassured?* Oriel wondered. This strange, brooding, unpredictable Greek man was so disturbing, and yet she felt safe just knowing he was near.

She and Damian ascended slowly, holding the dive rope and stopping at regular intervals along the way, a barrage of bubbles breaking the surface as they finally rose to the top. They were helped into the boat and immediately surrounded by the other divers, who were all talking at once, everyone wanting to have a look at the antique finds. '*Thavmahsios, thavmahsios*, wonderful, wonderful!' they cried out excitedly as they examined Damian's Roman seaman's knife and a perfectly intact drinking cup with a rudely fashioned face leering from its side. When Stavros saw that Oriel's amphora had an unbroken seal, he laughed, eyes twinkling. 'We need to celebrate, and we've got the wine right here!'

'Not sure what it'll be like after two thousand years,' Damian observed wryly, putting down his mask. 'I've heard Cousteau talk about trying some from an amphora he'd raised from a wreck near Cap Ferrat. It tasted worse than vinegar and there was no alcohol left at all. But this one might be worth a toast, I suppose,' he added with a lopsided grin.

'Wait a minute, everyone,' laughed Oriel, 'not until it's been properly cleaned and documented. I don't want anyone touching that seal!'

'How's the wreck looking?' asked Mohammed, the keen young Algerian who was due to go down next.

'Most of the artefacts are embedded in the calcite that's formed around the wreck,' answered Damian. 'It's going to be impossible, working underwater, to extract them without breaking them. I suggest you only pick up the smaller, accessible items for now.' He turned to Oriel. 'I propose we cut the wreck into blocks of about two hundred pounds apiece, which is the maximum our winches can raise.'

'I think that's the only course open to you,' she agreed, 'so long as all the necessary drawings, maps and photographs have been made first. There's a lot to do before we can even think of carving up the argosy.'

Damian nodded and turned to Stavros, 'This is such a big job, I think we might have to ask Vassilis and his crew to help us bring the big pieces up.'

'Yes, he's just bought some sophisticated equipment from America. He was boasting about it at Manoli's last night,' Stavros told him.

As the next pair of divers was seen off, Damian turned to Oriel. 'I take it that Vassilis looked after you well at the temple site yesterday?'

'Yes, he's very thorough. I was impressed.'

Damian glanced at her. 'Not too impressed, I hope,' he said, devilment in his eyes. He paused, then added: 'You did well down there. There's something methodical in how you work. Good under pressure too, I'd guess. Not a *thermokéfalos* hothead like Spyros over there. He'll need to be watched.'

Oriel glanced over at the wiry young Greek who was showing off, arms gesticulating wildly, his excitable voice rising above the laughter of his companions. She was glad to have an opportunity to turn her face away so that Damian couldn't see the pink hue rise in her cheeks. There was something very intoxicating about approval, and she felt a heady warmth at the remarks he'd made about her.

'I think we're in need of a drink,' Damian added, glancing at his watch. 'Plenty of time before the next divers come up.'

Oriel pulled a T-shirt out of her kit bag and followed him below deck.

The sitting area in the cabin was very wide; there were no hard edges, no corners, everything was rounded. There was an overall effect of dark mahogany and bright brass with inviting sun-yellow curtains and cushions and sea-blue fabrics covering the built-in so-fas. The polished wooden shelves and cupboards were all inbuilt. It seemed fully equipped with refrigerator and ice-maker, and electric cooker. The general feel was warm, modern and luxurious without being ostentatious.

'What would you like to drink?' he asked, crossing over to the fridge.

'Just a glass of water, please.'

Oriel self-consciously turned her back to him and quickly un-zipped her wetsuit, pulling it down to her hips. She slipped the T-shirt over her bikini top. When she turned back, Damian's eyes were watching her intently as she laid a dry towel on the sofa before taking a seat.

'Ah yes, the glass of *nehro* of Henry Miller fame, eh?' At Oriel's puzzled look, Damian laughed as he opened the fridge and took out a bottle of Greek still mineral water. He poured a long glass of it, handing it to her while he drank straight from the bottle. 'Henry Miller, the American writer, became obsessed with our wa-ter when he came to Greece. It's true that if you knock on any door in Greece, whether it belongs to a rich or poor house, you will al-ways be offered a glass of water accompanied by a spoonful of sweet preserve. It's a gesture of hospitality, a Greek way of welcom-ing the guest.'

'Yes, I've always found that a wonderful tradition. I love the water in Greece, it tastes unlike water anywhere else.'

'It tastes of our air, and our light.'

That made her smile. 'I love that comparison,' Oriel told him as she sipped the icy liquid. Yes, it did have a sort of ethereal flavour, now that she came to think of it.

Damian fixed her with a look touched with amusement. 'And

most of the time, especially on the islands and in villages, the water comes from our natural springs. Mount Hymettus, just outside Athens, has a spring that is legendary because it was known to increase fertility.' He took another swig of water, and her eyes were drawn to the masculine set of his jaw and neck as he swallowed.

'Yes, I've been there.'

He gave her a calm, appraising glance. Oriel shifted awkwardly and tried to dismiss all the erotic associations of his words and the chaos of her thoughts in that direction.

Damian unzipped his own wetsuit, peeling it down to his waist, revealing his muscled torso and arms. Oriel suppressed a gasp and had to will herself not to stare. Running up the front of his abdomen was a livid scar that reached his chest, and extended across what would have been one of his nipples. Her shocked gaze moved up to his face questioningly, wondering what on earth could have inflicted such terrible damage.

He took in her obvious unease, and his level stare seemed to challenge her to look away. Then, sinking down into the chair opposite, devilment flashed in his eyes. 'You should see the other guy.'

She ignored this flippancy and held his gaze. 'What happened, Damian?' she asked softly.

'It's a long story. Maybe one for another time.'

Oriel paused, and something told her not to push him further for now although she couldn't help but steal one last glance. She remembered how her hands had explored that rock-hard body one night long ago when it was smooth and perfect and hadn't been ravaged by goodness knows what; and yet she found nothing ugly in his disfigurement – it merely added to his aura of primitive masculinity.

There was a moment's silence. 'So,' said Damian, clearing his throat roughly before changing the subject, 'now you've had a chance to inspect your find, what does it tell you about the wreck?' He leaned back in his seat and crossed his legs at the ankles. The stressed look of earlier had vanished, although his dark eyes were engaged, alert to her every word.

Oriel kept her eyes resolutely on his face. 'Once I've managed to scrape away some of that encrustation I'll be able to get a better look at it. I can just make out something on the seal. There is definitely a trader's mark there, which is good. Roman, as you thought.' Then, as an afterthought, she turned her clear green eyes to him questioningly. 'I was interested in why you chose the pieces you did, humble everyday artefacts.'

'I like the ordinary domestic items. Sometimes they fire my imagination the most. I suppose I must be an anthropologist at heart, not a treasure hunter after all.' He gave a crooked smile. 'Just think, over two thousand years ago a Roman sailor was using that knife to shuck an oyster or clean his nails. Doesn't that thought excite you?'

'Definitely.' Oriel gave a warm smile, a light bringing fire to her emerald eyes. Damian's gaze lit instantly with answering flames. They stared at each other for only a second and yet there was time-lessness in it. It was as if the two of them were the only people on the boat. Oriel's muscles tightened and she felt her body grow rigid. For an instant she thought he might make a move towards her, and her heart beat a little faster, but then he seemed to think better of it and, with some reluctance, pulled himself up out of his chair. In a moment he was the cool, efficient captain again.

'We'd best go up and join the others.'

Mohammed and Yanni had returned to the boat when they emerged on deck; both men glanced at them fleetingly and Oriel felt distinctly self-conscious about disappearing below deck with Damian, although he himself looked as self-possessed as ever. Alexis and Spyros were up next, almost tumbling over each other in their haste to get to the water first.

'After those two hotheads come back, we'll break for lunch,' announced Damian, who was eyeing the wire-mesh basket which Mohammed and Yanni had elected to take down with them, and which Stavros had hauled up to the boat with the winch. The pannier was full of large earthenware fragments covered in sea violets. Oriel had never seen these blackish creatures, which were a special-ity of Mediterranean waters. They had the shape of a smallish potato with a dark and leathery exterior. The divers had also brought up a whole load of sea urchins.

Damian gave both men a slap on the back to mark his appre-ciation. 'Ah! *Fouska! Poli calo*. We'll have them raw as *mezedes* for lunch with a twist of lemon.' He was standing next to Oriel and immediately shot her an enquiring look, a smile tugging at the corners of his mouth as he stared at the generous curve of her pink lips. 'Have you tasted these delicious creatures? They're a powerful aphrodisiac.' He had lowered his voice when he'd thrown out the flirtatious remark, but clearly not enough.

Yanni, the large tattooed giant, nudged Alexis with a snort of laughter. 'Is someone getting the bridal chamber ready, eh? On Helios, we never fail to put a bowl of them in the bedroom to …' here, he winked at Oriel '… get the bride's juices flowing.'

The men burst out laughing but Oriel didn't join in; instead she calmly lifted her chin, furious with Damian for starting this. She seared him with a blaze of her huge green eyes. 'No, I've never tasted them before,' she said evenly, knowing by instinct as she met the intense silver glint of Damian's irises that he too had been rocked by Yanni's words and regretted his insensitive quip; it seemed he had been caught at his own game.

Oriel moved away, crossing the deck to study the items Mohammed and Yanni had collected: a large clay bowl in good condition and fragments of marble statuary, as well as another oil lamp. She turned the pieces slowly in her hand. Some of the other artefacts were eroded by the water, encrusted with salt and mussels, but given careful restoration they would provide small but vital clues to the wreck's provenance. She picked up her notebook and began to log and sketch each piece.

A while later, she was roused from her task by a shout from the water. It was Alexis, holding aloft a large light-grey object, which Stavros almost tore from his hands. Hastily he wiped off the mud. It was a small bronze statue of a figure holding a lance. Oriel drew closer. Damian was beside her and the smile that cracked his face was like the expression of a small child with an especially large Christmas present. Stavros handed it to him and his eyes sparkled with excitement as he smeared more mud from the dull metal. 'Do you see what it is?'

'It's Alexander the Great, isn't it? Thousands of these statues were made. He was a very popular subject for many artists. This is a lovely find.'

'Yes, but look at the detail. Surely only one man was capable of such exquisite perfection?' There was a tremor in Damian's voice as he spoke.

Oriel looked up at him with doubtful eyes. 'You honestly think Lysippos, the court sculptor of Alexander, made this one?'

'Exactly.'

'Except for the one found near Anticythera, not one of his works has been preserved. To my knowledge, not even Roman copies survived.'

'Well, I think this one escaped being melted down and recast into church bells or whatever other crimes they committed in the Middle Ages.' He grinned. 'I need to get it to Athens. You know we're going to create quite a stir with such a find, don't you, if I'm right?'

Although Oriel had no desire to take the wind out of his sails, she didn't think it would be right to play along with him. The piece was definitely of a superior quality but to leap to the conclusion it was a work of Lysippos? 'You might be right but remember, his work was much copied and there were other sculptors around, like Scopas and Praxiteles, any one of whom might have made this.'

Damian had a stubborn tilt to his chin and was about to respond when Stavros tapped his shoulder. The man's face was creased with worry. 'Damian, Spyros hasn't surfaced. Alexis just told me he thought he was following behind. Spyros had stayed down to dig out another piece and apparently the lad gestured he was coming up.'

Oriel guessed that in Alexis's excitement, having found the statue, he'd forgotten to double-check his partner was indeed bringing up the rear.

Damian swore violently and shoved his arms into his wetsuit. 'I knew Spyros needed a close watch. Alexis, statue or not, what the hell did you think you were doing not waiting for him?' he barked at the other diver, who stammered an apology. Damian grabbed his kit and scrambled to put it on. 'Damned fool, he'll have the narcs by now and be all over the place. Help me with this. I'd better get down there at once!'

'I'll come with you.' Oriel had already flung down her T-shirt and was zipping up her wetsuit.

'No, you stay here. It's dangerous enough already.'

'I've experienced narcosis, I know what to look out for.'

Damian threw her a speculative glance and then scowled. 'All right, let's go.' He turned to Stavros, gesturing in the direction of Oriel. 'I'll take *Despinis* Anderson with me. Fit her with a fresh tank, will you?'

Moments later, the pair were dropping quickly to the seabed. As they swam, powerfully beating their fins, bubbles and sediment swirled around them in the murky grey-blue depths. At first they could see no sign of Spyros, and Oriel had to quell a sense of panic. What if he had swum in the wrong direction, left the security of the wreck and the line, which was their guide to the boat above? He could have swum out of sight by now, disorientated, moving further and further, carried on the currents or a rip tide right out to sea. She took a breath and steadied her nerves. Damian gestured that she should look on the other side of the wreck. She swam a little further, reluctant to lose sight of her dive partner even for a moment; she had come to trust him in the deep water like a beacon in a storm.

As Oriel swam round to the far side of the sunken wreck, her eyes pierced the glinting water, head moving from left to right, scanning every inch of the ground within sight. The mound of the argosy loomed to the right of her, every crevice and cave in the great fossilized hulk of the wreck a dark and threatening maw, which she felt might swallow her whole given the chance.

Her head spun sideways as she detected a movement in the shadows. A fat grouper with mouth agape emerged from one of the caves in what was left of the ship's hull. Oriel's heart was beating violently and she willed herself to breathe steadily, not to let panic take hold.

By now she had traversed the side of the boat and was coming round the bow. Still no sign of either Damian or Spyros. She knew better than to leave the security of the wreck, from where at least she knew she would be able to find the line to the dive boat above. She hoped that Damian hadn't swum too far from the argosy. On the other hand, they had to find Spyros. The headstrong young diver must be out of air by now, surely?

Then her eyes caught a beam of light, irradiating the small pieces of coral and shards of pottery on the seabed a few feet away. She swam over: it was Damian's torch, lying in the sand. *Oh, where is he?* Oriel cried silently. Her mind flicked wildly over the possibilities: he might have been in a fight with a giant eel, a tiger shark, something with tentacles … or perhaps, more likely, he had needed both hands to wrestle a violently out-of-control Spyros, the young diver's brain made paranoid by the effects of narcosis so that he couldn't recognize help when it was at hand.

She picked up the torch and continued to swim down Damian's side of the wreck, methodically looking right and left and refusing to let panic take hold. *Damian put his trust in me as his dive partner*, she told herself. *I will not let him down. I can't behave like a frightened schoolgirl.*

She'd done all the courses, every bit of first aid training – she'd been here before. *Get a grip!* she remonstrated with herself.

Then she saw them.

Damian was half carrying the young diver, who was flailing in his arms like a drunk. He was behind Spyros, holding him with both arms in a chest grip, and he was struggling in the direction of the line. Oriel swam hard to catch up, fins kicking the water desperately. Her mind was already calculating: Spyros must be almost out of air; he wasn't convulsing yet, thank goodness, so they would still be able to do the required decompression stops.

She caught up with Damian at the line. He had wrapped his legs around Spyros's torso, leaving his hands free to hold the rope and control buoyancy at the same time. He motioned in sign language for Oriel to bring up the rear, tapping his watch to indicate that she would need to monitor their decompression stops. It felt like an age before they reached the surface. Oriel could only wonder at the sheer power of Damian's thighs, locked around the prone body of Spyros. She marvelled at his adept control of their buoyancy, maintaining a steady ascent without his arms having to take any strain. Initially, Spyros was still moving sluggishly but, halfway to the surface, he must have lost consciousness and then he became a dead weight, hard to manoeuvre, like a floppy rag doll. Between watching the clock and timing their ascent, Oriel had little time to panic or pray, but relief surged through her when the three of them broke the surface and she saw Stavros and Yanni bent over the deck rail, in the process of lowering a stretcher into the water.

From then on everything became a whirl. The crew helped to haul Damian and Oriel up on to the deck. Once on the boat, Damian ripped off his mask, chest heaving from his exertions, and shouted for extra oxygen for the boy, before directing Oriel to administer first aid. The rest seemed to happen as if she were on autopilot. She was on her knees beside the young diver in a moment, checking for breathing before engaging in resuscitation and chest decompressions. Above them, the sky was still a clear blue, the gulls wheeling in slow circles, but here on deck the pressure was intense, the air almost vibrating with it.

Later, Oriel could only wonder at the strange way the mood changed seamlessly, almost in a heartbeat, as Spyros groggily came to. Suddenly the crew was laughing, slapping him on the back and joking that he must have done a deal with the devil; either that or he had gills and his mother was a mermaid. Spyros himself even managed to muster some of his cocksure spark, boasting that his sponge-diving credentials really had made all the difference in the end, 'I'm from Kalymnos, after all!'

Damian cast a glance at Oriel as the extrovert diver continued to laugh down the Grim Reaper. He rolled his eyes and an exhausted smile appeared on his face as he dropped down on to a bench, raking a hand through his dripping hair. Oriel grinned back, half elated now that the ordeal was over. This had been a close one, and neither of them ever wanted to experience an event like that again.

Damian cast a black look at Alexis and Spyros. 'If you two ever do that again, I'll drown you myself, got it?' The two men nodded furiously. 'Right, young man,' he said to Spyros. Relief dispelled any trace of sternness he might otherwise have aimed at the rebellious youth. 'Stavros has us on course for the port and we'll get you to the clinic for a thorough check-up, although you have to thank *Despinis* Anderson here for her admirable skills in first aid, as well as helping me get your remarkably cumbersome body to the surface.'

At this, the whole team raised a cheer and Oriel blushed to the roots of her hair. *Well,* she thought to herself, *if nothing else, this sorry escapade has brought me closer to the men I'm going to be working with, and that has to be a good thing.* But what she barely allowed herself to acknowledge was the closeness she now felt to Damian. Yet it was so much more than that. Warmth flooded her with longing: she yearned to feel his arms around her, his burning mouth on hers. Maybe the almost primal urge she was feeling was simply a reaction to the intense moments of strain they had jointly experienced in the rescue but, whatever was the cause, her legs almost felt like giving way.

Damian was smiling at her and she blushed again. His eyes crinkled at the edges and the brightness of them intensified in the glare of the overhead sun. Then he broke the tension quite suddenly and turned to the crew.

'What do you all say to a bit of lunch?' he asked them with a grin. 'I think we've deserved it, don't you?'

There was a loud noise of agreement from the men and Damian moved over to Oriel. Despite the hubbub of voices behind him, he lowered his own as he said: 'You did well out there, Calypso. Thank you.'

'So did you.' Oriel's clear green eyes gazed up at him, and she was lost for more words.

'Maybe you would like to change before lunch. We'll not be going down again this afternoon and we can head back early afterwards. We'll take the artefacts to the warehouse to be catalogued.' He searched her face as if wanting to say more but refrained, knowing they were not alone. 'Come, there's a place with more privacy below.' His voice was even and Oriel felt that he was making a supreme effort to keep his distance, despite what they had just been through.

He showed her into a spacious cabin with en suite facilities. Again he had treated her with privilege and she was grateful to him. The crew's quarters were completely separated from this part of the *caique*.

Once he had disappeared, Oriel stripped and stepped gratefully under the shower. Temporarily freed from the turmoil Damian stirred, she enjoyed the coldish water trickling down her burning skin: it was revitalizing and she felt good as she mulled over the events of the morning. Throughout, Damian couldn't have been more gentlemanly and considerate towards her. There had been no physical touching she could object to, no phrases in bad taste. Still, the looks that they had exchanged and the remark about the violets proved to Oriel that, like her, he was struggling to keep his desire under control. Now the shared experience of intensity in rescuing Spyros only added to the crackle of electricity between them.

She could hear Damian whistling as he moved around in the bathroom next door and she wondered whether he would bring down his barriers again once they were alone. What did she really want? She had never been stirred by a man in this way – not before Aegina, and certainly not since.

Oriel had often wondered at her motives that night. It was so unlike her to do something so promiscuous, and she always came up with the same answer. She had not given herself to Damian simply because she had just been let down by Rob, and not even in rebellion against her own conservative principles, but because she had felt a compulsive desire to be possessed by Damian himself. This mythological god had suddenly come to her out of the darkness as a gift from the sea, and it seemed to her now that he had appeared in her life for a reason: to teach her about herself. There had been something downright fateful about the whole thing, and now she wasn't afraid to admit such a foolish thought. She had never forgotten the magic of that night and – although Oriel had felt devastated at his desertion – had never regretted it.

The magic was still there, the desire to be possessed by Damian just as overwhelming, if not more so – every nerve ending remembered his passionate onslaught on her aching body. But then he had disappeared without a word, without a backward glance. It had hurt her, but she had come to terms with it: what else could she have expected on a moonlit night from a stranger on a deserted beach? She had engaged in what was known as 'casual sex' and she had got what she deserved.

If Oriel was tempted by Damian's body just as much as before, now her heart was dangerously beguiled, too. This could be a different situation altogether: love could be knocking at her door, couldn't it? Still, she didn't think that Damian would ever love her. Desire her, yes. She had no doubt that the fire that had consumed her all those years ago had been mutual. Men, unlike women, couldn't feign passion.

How easy it would be to throw caution to the wind again and simply let herself be carried away, to stop thinking about tomorrow, live for the moment; to have a hot, no-strings-attached affair with Damian and damn the consequences. Wasn't that what he was proposing when he had taken her in his arms the other night?

But for Oriel, the repercussions of such foolish behaviour would indeed be damning – devastating! Another night like the one they'd spent together on Aegina and she wouldn't only be engaging her body, she would be giving him her whole being. Damian would have his fun and then, after the job had ended, she'd go back to England with a broken heart and he would continue his life on Helios, awaiting a new student conquest, no doubt. It was obvious: Damian's presence in her life was only temporary, a fact to keep in mind. Always.

Oriel changed into a pair of white shorts and an orange halterneck top. She tied her hair into a French braid and looked in the mirror. Still wet, it seemed darker, almost golden, and her eyes had a jade tinge in them that made them look almost turquoise. Without make-up and with this sort of hairstyle, Oriel looked about sixteen but then, with an all-male crew on board, she hardly wanted to emphasize her womanliness, even if a secret part of her wanted Damian himself to find her attractive. She put on a pair of flat white sandals and, after a last glance at herself, slipped out of the bathroom … and started violently as she bumped into Damian. He had shaved and his dark hair was wet from his shower. He wore a white T-shirt and a towel was hitched nonchalantly around the lower part of his body.

Oriel stood completely tongue-tied as his eyes slipped to her mouth, to her throat and slender bare shoulders with a sensual reminiscence that turned her limbs to water. They were standing only inches apart and Damian's heated gaze was riveted on her. He smiled wryly. 'The sun is in your hair, the sea is in your eyes and the roses are on your lips, mesmerizing Calypso.' He lifted a hand as though to touch her cheek and then let it fall again. 'How do you expect a man not to lose his head, eh?' His voice sounded ragged, and he shook his head, adding almost gruffly: 'We'll be having lunch on deck. You go up, I'll join you in five minutes.' He moved past her through a door to the crew quarters, leaving Oriel standing there, her chest rising and falling rapidly as she fought to catch her breath.

Oriel went on deck to join the men, all of whom looked as if they had scrubbed up, their dark curly hair still wet. Even the giant Yanni's bushy beard had a clean look about it. An appetizing spread had been set out on the table under an awning. They were already drinking either ouzo or retsina.

'Would you like a drink?' Stavros asked as she appeared on deck.

'Yes, please. I'll have a small glass of ouzo.'

'Ah, you know our national drink then?' Yanni noted, looking pleased as he tossed back a glass of the clear liquid.

Oriel didn't hear Damian approaching from behind and she almost gasped when his hand lay suddenly and heavily on her shoulder.

'*Despinis* Anderson knows our country well,' he told them. 'Is that not so?'

Oriel half turned to look up at him and met the glimmer of enigmatic amusement that had leapt into his eyes.

'And such a fascinating country it is,' she said with a smile, trying to sound natural.

'To *Despinis* Anderson, then,' said Yanni, filling the glasses of the crew who seemed to have a new-found respect in their gazes as they smiled at Oriel.

'She can rescue me again any time,' grinned Spyros, causing a raucous cheer from the rest of the men.

The crew all called out, '*Yassas!*', clinking glasses exuberantly before they began a barrage of jokes at Spyros's expense once more.

Damian dropped his hand from Oriel's shoulder, but not before sliding it the length of her back, then he thrust both hands deep into the pockets of his denim shorts and moved away from her. 'Let's sit down and have lunch, I'm starving.' Again, Oriel felt his eyes come to rest on her as they all found a place along the benches on deck.

The air was sweet with a long stretch of empty, melting blue sea and sky, looking as if both were merged together in one sapphire expanse. Shimmering with a white-gold haze, the not-too-distant landscape of Helios looked mysterious and otherworldly, almost like a mirage. Oriel was jerked back to earth by Damian presenting her with a violet that was split in half along the length.

'The poor man's oyster,' he told her as he squeezed a twist of lemon juice over the gelatinous, purple-veined pulp. 'Here, try one. I can assure you it tastes like heaven.' Oriel caught the devilish glint in his eye, his gaze dipping for a second to her mouth as he handed it to her. She almost blushed again at the awareness between them, but held his gaze steadily. She had always had a predilection for shellfish – oysters, mussels, sea urchins – and if one of them was on the menu, she was sure to order it. Now would be no different, she determined.

'Thanks, I'll have a go,' she murmured, smiling and taking the small crustacean from him. She scooped out the shiny orange flesh with the special spoon that was next to her plate and popped it in her mouth. The men all clapped and hailed her, admiring her lack of squeamishness, obviously not realizing that she was well travelled and an old hand at sampling all sorts of different food. Then there was total silence for a moment; Oriel felt like an exhibit at the zoo as all their stares focused on her while they awaited her verdict.

The texture was luscious, the flavour strong and briny: heavenly, just as Damian had described it. Oriel smiled. '*Nóstimo*, delicious, really delicious.'

There was a very Greek exclamation of '*Ópa!*' and another round of clapping and appreciative sounds, then they were all passing around the small dishes of *mezedes*, the bread and the lemon. This little interlude seemed to have broken the ice and soon there was a hum of voices around her, a composite sound, deep and masculine, which she was welcome to join in and she did. Everybody was relaxed and at ease.

Still, Oriel couldn't help but be most conscious of Damian. From time to time she felt the power of his gaze upon her, setting her pulse beating uncomfortably faster. Through her lashes she watched him talking to his men and saw the friendliness with which they all responded and the admiration in their eyes whenever he voiced an opinion. When Damian spoke, the others listened.

After lunch, the *Ariadne* headed back and soon the marina with its little jetty was in sight. The scene looked sleepy, no one about except for a couple of fishermen sitting outside the taverna enjoying a late lunch and a skinny cat chewing on a fish head on the slipway. They slid on to their mooring almost noiselessly, barely disturbing the gull roosting on the canvas of a neighbouring yacht, its beady eyes keeping a sharp watch on the water. While Damian went ashore to call Yorgos from the telephone in the taverna, ordering him to fly Spyros to the mainland for a health check, Stavros monitored the other divers, who were engaged in logging and packing away all the items retrieved from the wreck that morning. The boxes were then unloaded on to the quay and carried to a windowless wooden building not far from the taverna.

Damian caught up with Oriel as she followed the others, holding one of the containers of amphorae. 'You haven't seen our lab yet, have you?' he said. 'We call it the lab, but it's not much more than a warehouse. From the outside it looks like a humble fishing shed, but it has surprisingly modern security systems in place. Everything we find from the various archaeology sites on Helios is brought here.'

Oriel stepped inside, on to the concrete floor of a large room, illuminated by strip lighting. To her left, a wall was lined with several tall lockers, each one numbered and padlocked. To her right stood a stainless steel lab bench and stools. Glass-fronted cupboards extended along the right-hand wall, holding chemicals, measuring equipment, scraping tools and a pair of microscopes. It was here that the men were now depositing their boxes.

Oriel went over to where the intact amphora she had recovered from the argosy had been lifted on to the steel bench. She peered at it thoughtfully, then retrieved tools and a chemical solution from the cupboard behind her and set to work, carefully scraping encrustation from the seal. Damian was equally absorbed, laying out the contents of one of the boxes opposite with Alexis.

Finally, Oriel straightened up and Damian, sensing her movement, raised his eyes enquiringly. She beckoned him over and he came to stand beside her. She was acutely aware of his closeness as he bent over to look at the seal. 'Look, here,' she said, just managing to keep her voice even. 'This is the trader's mark. I think it's a trident …'

'You're right. Wait, it looks as if something's wound around the shaft. Could be a sea serpent. Do you see?'

Oriel had to lean in close, so that their heads were only inches away from each other. She forced herself to quieten her beating heart and her breathing. 'Oh, yes, so there is. Look, here at the base. SES … see there?'

Damian nodded pensively. 'You should research the insignia.'

'Yes, each Roman shipping magnate had their own individual two- or three-letter name abbreviation. We'll know a great deal more about the wreck if I can discover who SES was.'

Oriel and Damian spent the rest of the afternoon working alongside the other men, sorting, photographing and cataloguing the treasures. No words were exchanged between them that did not concern work and, when he looked at her, it seemed as if he was no longer reacting to her as a woman. She was one of the men now.

'Go home and rest,' Damian told the crew at five o'clock. 'I'll choose a night during the week to celebrate at Manoli's.' His suggestion was met with roars of hurrahs.

As Oriel was heading towards one of the Jeeps with Stavros, Damian called out: '*Despinis* Anderson, you're coming with me, or have you forgotten that you live at Heliades?' She followed Damian to his Jeep, where he held open the door for her. 'I hope you're not too tired after all the excitements of today?'

'I think I'll survive. If you're a diver, it rather goes with the territory,' she observed as he took his place beside her. 'It was a little scary, yes, but I enjoyed every minute of it. Very different from the last job I had in Norway. Much more exciting!' She grinned at him as he put the key into the ignition.

Damian put the car into gear and accelerated out of the warehouse's small parking area. As the Jeep made its way back to Heliades, they were absorbed in talk of the finds of that day, and the wreck itself, until they fell into companionable silence. Soon they had the cliff in sight, bathed in a most translucent naked light that flashed off the sea.

Damian finally spoke. 'I hope that the incident with Spyros didn't put you off diving with the team,' he said. 'You're just what this project needs.' Oriel shook her head, smiling. For a moment, she thought of Yorgos's doomladen predictions regarding Damian as a boss; in many ways his words were unfounded and certainly disloyal. Damian seemed perfectly prepared to give praise where it was due, whether he was dealing with a man or a woman. True, he could be hard on his employees but only – she suspected – when faced with incompetence. As Stavros had so rightly said, his boss was not a man who suffered fools gladly.

As if he could read her mind, Damian arched a brow enquiringly and Oriel resumed the conversation quickly. 'The wreck is the most exciting project I've ever handled,' she acknowledged. 'I can't wait to dive it again. After Alexis brought up the Alexander bronze I knew we were dealing with a very special site indeed. A once-in-a-lifetime chance for any archaeologist.'

Damian glanced at her with a half smile as he steered the Jeep, and she couldn't help reflecting that he looked like a basking lion – luckily for her, at this moment, uninterested in bringing down a prey animal, even one who'd strayed so close. 'Tell me, Calypso,' he asked, 'how did you become so keen on archaeology?'

'My father used to tell me tales of Atlantis as a child,' she said. 'After that, I read anything I could lay my hands on, especially stories about lost cities … Bells tolling mysteriously under the water, that sort of thing.'

'We have more in common than you might think,' said Damian, his voice a caress, 'although my lost cities were always Greek. Have you heard of Helice?'

'The seaport mentioned by Homer, the one no one has ever found?'

'Yes. It's supposedly somewhere on the Gulf of Corinth. We know it was engulfed by a giant tidal wave and that the Ionians had built a temple there, dedicated to Poseidon, but little else.' Damian's eyes had a look of boyish excitement as he recollected his childhood passion. 'Although there was a ferryman who was quoted a century after the disaster saying that he could remember seeing a massive bronze statue of Poseidon lying there, like a hazy mirage under his boat, in the midst of the drowned ruins.'

'Under many feet of mud now, I imagine,' noted Oriel wryly. 'Mind you, it's the dream of such finds that keeps us archaeologists going.' She paused, his mention of Poseidon setting off a recollection in her mind. 'Near the Minoan Temple site there was an old woman who gave me some figs from her garden. She said something obscure about Poseidon submerging everything under the sea.'

Damian nodded. 'We have a strong oral tradition here on Helios. People are always telling stories about the gods. Given the seismic activity of the place over the past decades it's not surprising that so many of our local stories contain fire and brimstone, people being swallowed up by the angry gods and suchlike. It could have been any one of our legends.'

Oriel wrinkled her brow, trying to remember the old woman's words. It was more than that, she was sure … something specifically about Damian and the vengeance of the gods. She glanced at him, wondering what could have caused the woman to look so troubled. Pure superstition perhaps? 'She seemed very wary of us digging around and disturbing the dead.'

'But that's our job, isn't it?' he said, flashing her a broad smile.

Oriel's gaze drifted back to the passing landscape. 'Yes, of course. We're a strange mix of boring scientist, sifting and recording, and romantic adventurer, I always think.'

'I imagine the romantic adventurer in you was uppermost, Calypso, the night we first met,' he said silkily, taking his eyes off the road for a second and, not for the first time that day, a faint pink hue rose in her cheeks.

Luckily she was able to refrain from replying as suddenly Damian swerved the Jeep to avoid a goat that had stumbled across the road. He swore robustly, making Oriel give a breathless laugh despite herself. Raking a hand through his hair, he glanced at her sheepishly, then grinned, looking straight ahead.

Oriel looked silently at the disfigured profile of the man sitting beside her. She could see it clearly now, the badly maimed skin that had turned the once-beautiful classical Greek face into something that some women might find repellent. Still, Damian appeared neither self-conscious nor embarrassed by it, and that was maybe why she, like others, seemed able to forget the shock of it. She turned away, hoping he wasn't aware of her scrutiny.

'Like my face?' he asked after a few minutes, as the car climbed up the cliff road. His tone of voice was ultra-mocking, yet Oriel caught the flare of fiery arrogance in his eyes as he turned to look at her.

She shrugged. 'I've told you before, it's neither here nor there. When you don't draw attention to it, you have enough charisma to make your scars almost unnoticeable,' she told him quietly.

'So kind … so kind and patronizing, dear Calypso. Or should I stick to calling you *Despinis* Anderson?'

'I'm telling you the truth.'

Damian fell silent for a moment.

'Charisma or not, I'm no longer the man you knew in Aegina,

am I, eh? You were adventurous enough for a one-night stand with a stranger back then, but now … now you cannot bear to let me make love to you, isn't that so?'

Oriel felt the heat rise in her cheeks and had to steady her voice before she answered. 'I am an employee, and you can just imagine the gossip any intimacy between us would raise, especially on a pagan sort of island like Helios.'

He cocked an eyebrow. 'Pagan?'

Oriel winced slightly at her own choice of words but it was too late to take them back. 'You have to admit, there's a touch of primitive superstition embedded in the islanders' view of their world …' She began stumbling over her words. 'I mean, the people here seem primitive, as if they belong to a different era.'

'And you're unnerved by pagans, eh?' he asked softly. 'You have changed then, dear Calypso. I seem to remember a young woman who made love with a certain uninhibited primitive instinct that some might describe as almost pagan.' He laughed, the sound low and sensual, and infinitely disturbing.

A quiver ran through Oriel at his outrageous remark. Damn the man! He knew exactly what those words, those evocative memories, were doing to her. Later, when it was too late, the appropriate stinging retort to his insolence would undoubtedly come to her; at the moment, however, even if she had had the presence of mind to know what to say, Oriel could not trust her voice to remain steady.

Damian's gaze dwelt on her face with its shocked look. His silver-grey eyes were brilliant with cynical mockery. 'Don't worry, beautiful, irresistible Calypso, I will stick to our bargain and not lay a finger on your delectable silk-like skin,' he said with a sardonic smile.

They had arrived at Heliades, and Oriel leapt out of the car, not waiting for Damian to come round and open the door for her.

'I'll meet you here in an hour. We're going to Santorini for dinner,' she heard him say to her back.

Oriel turned and paused on the terrace steps. 'What? No, I don't think—'

'That's right, Calypso, don't think, just come with me. It's been an exciting day. We both need to unwind and celebrate our finds.'

She hesitated. If she refused then it would seem as though he

135

had got under her skin. At least that's what she told herself. 'Santorini? That's quite far from here.'

Damian grinned. 'Not by plane it isn't.'

'Plane?'

'Yes, I'll fly us there in the Saratoga. I just feel like getting out of Helios tonight and the island of Santorini seems a good idea. Just wait until you see the magnificent views of the caldera, Santorini's active volcano crater, and the surrounding islands of the Aegean.'

'It's another of those places linked to Atlantis because of its massive volcanic eruption,' Oriel murmured almost to herself, her interest genuinely piqued.

'Indeed. More to the point, I know of a charming place in Oia, where they serve excellent crustaceans. The sunsets there are spectacular. Every evening in Oia, it's a special event to watch the sun go down from the Sunset Serenade point, high up in the village. I've seen it myself. For a few moments, the view of the white houses and the caldera capturing the colours of the setting sun is breathtaking … something not to be missed.'

'I've never been to Santorini. I must admit I've always wanted to go.'

Damian ambled up the front steps until his gaze was level with hers. 'Well then, you've just given me another excellent reason for us to go there tonight.'

Oriel was falling into that silvery gaze that pinned her to the spot, the way it always did. Her mind stumbled backwards. 'Did you say you personally were going to fly us there?'

'Yes, that's right. I'm a fully qualified pilot.'

She laughed and shook her head. 'Why does that not surprise me?'

He gave a wolfish grin. 'Because I'm hugely talented, and with me you've learnt to expect the unexpected?'

Secretly she *was* thinking something similar but had no intention of adding to his arrogance by admitting to it. Instead she rolled her eyes, but couldn't help smiling. 'How long does it take to get there?'

'Only an hour. If we want to catch the sunset, we can just make it if we leave within the hour. It's usually crowded with couples at this time of year, especially at sundown, but I'll ring my friend

Demetris, whose nightclub overlooks the caldera and the sea. His restaurant has already acquired two Michelin stars and I think he's hoping to receive another one this year. VIPs from all over the world come by yacht or fly down for the evening to dine there. He has a landing strip for small aircraft where I'll be able to put down.'

After only a moment's hesitation Oriel nodded, suppressing a smile as she tried to hide the excitement bubbling up in her chest. 'It sounds great, I'll be ready.'

She hurried into the house and went straight up to her apartment. Her body was on fire, her mind in turmoil as fears and hopes chased inexorably around it. More than ever, it was clear that Damian wanted her with the same passion that was driving her crazy, too. His eyes, his voice, his evocative words had been as powerful in arousing her as if he had trailed his scorching mouth all over her flesh. And now he was whisking her away to Santorini for dinner in time to watch the spectacular Oia sunset. Oh, this could be so dangerous!

Would it be wrong to give in to this overwhelming desire, just for one night? Who was she fooling? Things were never that simple. There would be another night, and then another; the nights of passion would turn into a fully fledged affair and, before she could blink, this assignment would be over in a flash and she would find herself going back to the drawing board, her dreams in pieces. Damian would have no interest in her after the job was finished. It was a litany that Oriel had repeated to herself umpteen times since her arrival on Helios, but sensible words did not relieve her fever–this obsession had become a sickness.

She rushed into the bathroom, tore off her clothes and stepped into the shower, turning on the cold water. As it trickled over her she trembled and shuddered. It felt refreshingly icy against her burning skin and she stood there for a long while, savouring the calming sensation as the tension gradually seeped out of her. Next, she dried her hair and gave it the one-hundred-strokes treatment, which she did from time to time when she was giving particular care to her appearance, but tonight her brushstrokes were much more vigorous, as though she was trying to brush her feelings for Damian out of her system. At the end of it her heavy platinum mane looked even shinier and silkier than usual, hanging loose over her shoulders. She glanced at herself in the mirror and gave a little shiver of anticipation. Yes, this could be a dangerous evening indeed.

* * *

Oriel was deliciously aware of her own feminine power as they sat on the wide terrace of the nightclub, Kallísti, in Oia, waiting for the day to die, while drinking a fresh lime *pressé* and eating oversized olives that came from the trees in Demetris's garden. An array of appetizers was laid out before them, with delicious pita bread that must have been baked that evening. Kallísti was a whitewashed building, like most on Santorini, with a domed glass ceiling designed to capture the view of the starlit night; inside, everything was black-and-white minimalist chic, with huge photographic prints adorning one wall of the club and a large semicircular window opposite, framing the vista of sea and horizon beyond. Another entire side of the club opened on to the terrace, and here a raised platform formed a dancefloor, stretching from the interior out into the open air.

The setting was perfect: the sky was flushing from blue to lavender as the time of sunset drew near. Here, at the top of the cliffs, the heat was fading to an agreeable coolness as the day began to decline. A smouldering warmth lay upon the sea, which looked like beaten gold in the light of the dying sun.

Damian's compelling silver eyes glittered with fires that Oriel recognized only too well as they gazed insistently on her lips and dipped to the rounded fullness of her chest. His mouth quirked. 'For an archaeologist, you have a very enticing evening wardrobe, may I say, *Despinis* Anderson?'

Oriel smiled shyly, her cheeks dimpling. 'I like to have a few emergency nice outfits in my travel case. It's a weakness of mine.'

His gaze intensified. 'And is this an emergency?'

She laughed. 'I'm not sure yet.' She took a sip of the lime to cool her throat.

Oriel knew that she looked good, and it gave her a thrill to see such undisguised masculine appreciation in Damian's gaze. The form-fitting black jersey maxi dress she had chosen had a deep V halter neckline at the front, hinting at the curve of her breasts, and an open back. It was held up by straps in a diagonal cross design and with cut-out detailing. The day spent on the boat had given Oriel a healthy, golden tan which made her wide eyes appear even greener than usual.

She had hesitated before trying on a chunky Zolotas necklace, sculpted as a twenty-two carat gold undulating collar of stylized horns. Oriel had bought it three years ago for a bargain price at an auction in New York with the bonus she had received for a difficult job well done on a Spanish wreck in Florida. It was part of a set, comprising a necklace, a bangle and a pair of earrings and, though she hadn't had the chance to wear it often, she really loved it. The necklace fitted perfectly over her slender décolletage and the warm colour of the gold reflected in her eyes, giving their greenness an almost amber sparkle. The horns on the earrings were designed as wings, covering a great part of her earlobes. The bangle was equally heavy, its simple classic lines tasteful and chic. Oriel had wondered if she might be overdressed, yet no one could be called overdressed in Greece.

She placed down her glass. 'Once I was invited spontaneously to an embassy dinner in Italy while I was on a job with a colleague and, luckily, my self-indulgent packing served me well as I had this very dress rolled up in my case at the time. Since then, I've never regretted being prepared. Besides, you said this nightclub was frequented by VIPs from all over the world.'

'Indeed it is, Calypso, and you outshine all of them in both sophistication and glamour,' Damian said, his voice almost a purr.

In a silver flurry, a star fell out of the sky, breaking his gaze. 'Look, a shooting star. They're rare around here, it's a good omen.' He tried to take her hand, but Oriel moved it away before he had a chance to touch her.

'In that dress, *omorfiá mou*, you look like those stars, so striking and mysterious,' he murmured. 'Unreachable, untouchable.' His eyes returned to her face, scrutinizing it intensely. 'Is that what you really want?'

His predatory gaze made Oriel's pulse skitter but she tilted her chin slightly. 'You know the score. I agreed to stay on the job on certain conditions and I was happy to come here with you tonight, knowing we had laid down a set of rules that I hoped you would respect,' she said in a calm, even voice that belied the heartbeats she could feel in her chest like warning drums as she looked at him.

He was so handsome in his dark suit, white silk shirt and burgundy tie. It was the first time Oriel had seen Damian formally dressed and the animal grace that made him stand out among all other men was never so potent. He was beautiful. Somehow the scar on his face, instead of diminishing his appeal, enhanced that masculine beauty by disturbing the symmetry of his features and giving them a stronger, primitive sexiness. Just as the scars on his body made him seem like some warrior from the ancient past, she thought, and then berated herself inwardly for such wistful romanticism.

'Rules were made to be broken.' Damian smiled with his lips but his eyes, so astoundingly silver, had an inscrutable look behind soot-thick lashes.

Oriel went utterly still. It was as if every nerve in her pulsating body had gone into emergency red alert. The reality of her situation confronted her with painful force. Suddenly she was afraid that if he did step over the line, she wouldn't be able to resist. She was flying too close to his heat like some foolish Icarus with wings of wax and feathers. There would only be herself to blame if she plummeted into the sea.

Was he determined to have his way with her before the end of the project? Would she have the strength to reject him? Her eyes held a silent plea for him to understand as she said softly: 'Please don't make me regret that I trusted you.'

The gasp of awe that rose from the crowd, which had gathered outside the nightclub a few metres down the cliff to watch the sunset, kept Damian from answering her, and Oriel turned her attention to the incredible view that stretched endlessly as far as the eye could see.

Long tongues of fire spread from the sun's dazzling rays over the twisted rocks, the houses of the beautiful white town ablaze with a transparent copper glow that reminded her of barley sugar. Smouldering, the molten flames in the sky moved further, changing its smooth azure to violet streaked with apricot, to apple green blending into scarlet, bright yellow and cobalt blue. Within this veil of complex, glorious colour, the golden globe seemed alive with a magnificent sort of agony. Suddenly it faltered, tumbling down behind the horizon – a burning death. The drama and the splendour of it all filled Oriel with a wistful emotion and she sighed.

'It takes your breath away … really,' she murmured. 'Even the Caribbean, which is famed for its sunsets, can't compare to this.' She knew now why Kallísti was decorated in such a starkly minimalistic fashion; even the large prints adorning the wall inside were imbued with the same subdued monochromatic character. The star here was the sunset.

'Our island sunsets are legendary and Santorini's are particularly spectacular. There's hardly anything to rival their beauty.' Damian's voice dropped lower, a brush of rich velvet against her ear. 'Fire and beauty, they often go hand in hand. I know that you don't want to hear it, *agápi mou*, but I learnt that in Aegina. I've searched for what we had together ever since.'

Oriel turned to face him again. His irises were like smoke: grey and full of heat as they slid over her features. Their eyes locked and it seemed to her that a strange hypnotic spell had been cast over the two of them, as if memories of yesteryear suddenly filled their universe. Without thinking, she put a hand to her cheek and felt its warmth. Damian's stare held a silent, intense communication: yes, she had no doubt now – that night in Aegina haunted them both. Everything about Damian – his provocative words, his masculine presence – was reawakening her to a wild, strange ecstasy that could not be called love but was certainly hunger: a driving need that annihilated any coherent thought.

She was grateful for Demetris's interruption, which put an end to this dangerous conversation.

'*Yassou*, Damian, *ti kánete?* How are you? *Keró éhume na ta púme!* Long time, no see.'

'I know, but I've been very busy. Not enough hours in the day.'

Demetris was a short, rotund man with a thick moustache and balding head, whose face seemed relentlessly jovial. 'So who is your beautiful companion? Scandinavian this time, eh?' The restaurateur winked at Damian, obviously not realizing that Oriel spoke Greek.

She flashed Damian a pointed look and smiled thinly at Demetris. 'I'm English, actually.'

'*Despinis* Anderson is an English archaeologist well versed in Greek language and literature.'

Undaunted, Demetris beamed at her. 'So you are acquainted with our language. You've lived in Greece a long time, eh?'

'No, I studied Greek at university.'

'*Polý entyposiakó!* Very impressive!' the man exclaimed, while ogling Oriel's décolletage quite unashamedly.

'So, now that we've made the introductions, let's move on,' said Damian curtly. 'What are you recommending tonight?'

Oriel observed the note of irritation in Damian's voice and, looking at him, she could see that his colour had risen under the copper tan.

Demetris seemed oblivious. 'Our *soupia me melani,* squid in ink, tonight is especially good as our chef has tried a new recipe and the *soupia* is really fresh … brought in by the fishing *caiques* this evening. We serve it with bread as a starter and with pasta as a main dish. The sauce is *nóstima,* delicious.' Demetris bunched his fingers together and brought them to his mouth, smacking his lips.

'The *mydia,* mussels, have just arrived this evening, too. Then, of course, the house speciality this week is our *ortikia se klimatofila,* quail in vine leaves. The quail is Hydra wild quail, the best, of course. I am sure the beautiful *Despinis* here would enjoy this delicate dish served with our pilaf rice and pomegranate sauce.'

'And fish?'

'*Psari plaki.* Our snapper is exceptionally large tonight. Depending on your appetite it can serve one or two people, and we cook it with a tomato and herb crust and serve it with rice cooked in aromatic herbs.'

'And meat-wise?'

'Our usual *vithelo me melitzana ke elies,* veal with eggplant and olives, and *kleftiko,* which is always a favourite with foreigners.'

'It all sounds delicious. Calypso?'

'I think I'll have the squid in ink and the Hydra wild quail with rice.'

Demetris grinned. 'I must congratulate you on your choice, *Despinis.* That is what I would have recommended.'

'I'll also have the squid to start, and then *psari plaki* to follow.'

'Ah yes, good choice, large portion.' Demetris winked at

Damian again and gave him a meaningful look. 'A man needs his strength, eh?'

No one could have missed the vulgar innuendo and a forbidding look passed over Damian's face. 'We'll have the wine list now, please.'

His expression was enough to make the restaurateur's smile drop. Demetris clearly realized that he'd overstepped the mark on this occasion and he cleared his throat. 'I will recommend Sigalas Barrel Santorini, which has had a particularly good year.'

'Calypso? White or red?'

'White please, but what about you?'

'I'm piloting, remember? I'll have just half a glass, to taste it.'

The restaurateur hastily moved away and Damian shook his head. 'I apologize for Demetris's manners. He is a vulgar man, always has been.'

'Human nature … I wouldn't worry about it.'

Damian almost growled his annoyance. 'I can't bear it when men look at you like that.'

'Trust me, I don't like it either. But men will be men, driven by their baser instincts.' She glanced at him meaningfully.

'Not *all* men, *agápi mou.*'

His expression turned to seriousness and she knew he was trying to hold himself in check now, to prove to her that she could trust him.

A question that still needled Oriel swam into her head. Her gaze sharpened. 'You never did tell me why the Frenchwoman left the team so suddenly. And the Dutch student the previous year.' Stavros had said Damian was not to blame, but he had avoided her question before. Now she wanted to hear the truth.

He gave her an arrested glance. 'No, I didn't. What of it?'

'Did you have problems with them?'

'You think *my* baser instincts were the issue, is that it, eh?'

She looked uncertain. 'Well, I …'

He crossed his arms over his chest. 'Ah, Calypso, I see you have been listening to island gossip too much. You really want to know what happened?'

Oriel held his gaze. 'I've said so before, yes. We are working together after all.'

Damian made a gruff noise in his throat and sat back in his chair. 'All right. The woman, Chantal Hervé, who left just before you joined, was perfectly competent and I had no problem with her at all. I was perplexed and a little annoyed when she suddenly handed in her notice. Things were really busy at the olive press, you see, and she'd been a great help in the office. A natural with numbers, and kept the accounts up to scratch. She seemed upset about something but she didn't want to talk about it, so I took her to Athens myself.' His dark lashes looked down as he searched in his pocket for his cigarettes. 'Whatever her reason for leaving, I assumed it was probably the same as the Dutch student's.'

Oriel listened attentively, relief and curiosity mingling. 'And what reason was that?'

He fixed her with a look. 'Like I've said before … men.'

'You think she got mixed up with one of the team?'

Damian lit a cigarette, the flame illuminating his scarred cheek as he regarded her evenly. 'I can't be sure, unpleasant things can occur anywhere. It's unfortunate that this time it might have involved one of our employees. I wouldn't be surprised if one of the men had gone after her in a heavy-handed way.'

'And you think the same thing happened to the Dutch student,' Oriel summarized.

'They wouldn't be the only foreign students who didn't have a clue how to conduct themselves on the more conservative of the Greek islands.' His mouth curved sardonically. 'Your women's lib doesn't work here.'

Her brow creased into a frown. 'By that, I suppose you mean they deserved whatever unpleasant experience they got, is that it?'

'That's not what I said, no. Look, some of them get drunk in our tavernas, they flirt quite openly with the married men of the island, who are dazzled by their forward ways. You can't behave on Helios as you would in your own country.' Damian gestured with outstretched hands.

'The community on Helios is conservative … most of the islanders have never left its sanctuary. The people here are simple folk who lead uncomplicated lives, and for the most part are happy. This is the main reason why Helios has never welcomed tourism. Like my ancestors, I don't want to corrupt the island.'

'Corrupt?' Oriel's brows lifted.

'Let's just say it's a conservation island, an island of notable environmental and historical importance that I'm protecting against undesirable change, like any other conservation area in the world.'

She nodded, considering. 'Somehow, I can understand that. The island feels so remote, it's like living in another world. But my concern is that you're not giving your people a choice. Your attitude is almost feudal.'

'Feudalism is a negative label. Paternalism would be a better word to describe what we have on Helios. Stay a while, and you will understand. But you're right, it is another world, in so many ways.'

Something in the way he spoke made Oriel search his face. There was no change in his expression and she didn't feel like questioning him further. It was enough to know that Yorgos's insinuations had been misplaced. She could see it in Damian's eyes, which now watched her intently; there was honesty there, even though part of him was still guarded.

The questions perched on the tip of her tongue: *How and why was your poor brother, Pericles, murdered? How did your wife die?* It was so tempting to ask him but she sensed tonight was not the time. The way he was looking at her was making her whole body languid and the night was too beautiful for talk of such dark and tragic matters. The waiter came over and lit the candle that stood in a globe on the table. He poured half a glass of wine for Damian, and filled Oriel's glass. Damian met her gaze '*Yassas!*'

They clinked glasses and Oriel smiled shyly as she sipped the crisp aromatic white wine. She looked around her at the dimly lit room with its atmospheric white spotlights in each discreet, curved alcove holding tables of diners. 'This place is very stylish.'

'Demetris, for all his faults, has a nose for business. He used to be a merchant seaman but came into an inheritance ten years ago and opened a small taverna down on the beach, here at Santorini. His wife is a good cook and his restaurant gradually became well known. Five years ago he capitalized on the taverna by selling it in an auction at a considerable price, and he opened this place.'

'It's stunning.' She gazed at the groups of chattering people who were a mix of young couples, glamorous partygoers and older, wealthy-looking Greeks out for dinner. All, she noticed, had one thing in common: they were expensively dressed in eveningwear, and gold and diamonds didn't seem an issue. This was a place frequented by the rich and famous, and everything about it – the silverware, the eggshell chinaware and the Baccarat glasses – bore witness to this. She hadn't been given a menu so she could only imagine the price of the food here. 'It's clearly the place to be seen.'

Damian nodded. 'The name of the restaurant, Kallísti, the beautiful one, had originally been that of Santorini itself. It's a name that's easy to remember,' he said, with a suggestive smile that Oriel didn't miss. 'Demetris had already gained a substantial clientele from his taverna and decided this nightclub would have a limited number of members, which immediately put it on the map. There is a two-year waiting list to join, and now anyone who is anybody in Greece wants to become a member.'

The moon shone clear, almost white in colour, a full round orb of splendour. The sea was light green, the stars above glistening as if they had been specially polished, Oriel thought fancifully. Their table overlooked the cliffs with a view right down to the beach, where the sea lay darkly gleaming, whispering like silk, and though the very air breathed romance, there was now a distance and restraint about the night that seemed to touch them both, making them subdued.

Oriel studied Damian in the candlelight. In his classic dinner jacket, tailored to fit him to perfection, and with his strong, unique face, marred down the right side of his profile, he seemed to her suddenly unapproachable. His eyes appeared dark in the shadow of his brow, just as the sea darkened when night fell.

Apollo carved in teak, she thought.

What was this man about? What did she know about him? So much was rumour and hearsay, or shreds of information, hinted at and unsubstantiated. What was that secret magnetism about him she seemed unable to escape? She had slept with him once, a long time ago, but the close acquaintance with his body hadn't given her access to his mind; he was a stranger from a foreign land who was taking control of her emotions and thoughts. Many women she knew had one-night stands and managed to walk away unscathed. Yet she didn't seem able to do that …

As if reading the questions in her mind in his usual uncanny way, Damian answered, his voice soft and caressing: 'You and I have never needed words to communicate, *agápi mou*. Our eyes speak to each other before our lips have had time to utter a sound.'

At once, Oriel felt the pink rise to her cheeks and she could not control it. She saw a glint beneath his lashes, like flickers of fire seen way back in a forest clearing. Something had re-emerged in his gaze, as though he could no longer keep his distance.

Her finger traced the rim of her glass. 'We're almost strangers and, even if we hadn't been, I guess you're far too shrewd to disclose yourself to anyone.'

'To you, if you wanted, I would bare my soul.' Their gazes locked. 'As I have my body.'

His provocative words were intoxicating, bringing a wave of heat to her body. 'Stop it,' she murmured, lifting her glass and swallowing her wine deeply. 'You're deliberately ...'

'Inflaming you? Exciting you? Making you realize what you desire more than anything, but stubbornly persist in denying?' He leaned forward a little in his chair. 'Why are you wary of me, Calypso *mou*? Do you wonder why some islanders call me *Drákon* Damian behind my back? Or are you unable to look me in the face without wondering how I came to get slashed into the semblance of a devil?'

'No, no!' Oriel protested immediately. 'I hardly notice that about you.'

'Then what?'

'If you must know, yes, you are like some kind of demon ... always tempting!' She could not control the words: they leapt from her mouth and hung in the silence that followed them.

Damian leaned back into his chair again, his eyes slumberous, almost closed. With deliberation, he sipped his wine in silence for a brief moment. 'And you? Are you such an angel?'

'No, I'm just an ordinary human being.'

He arched one eyebrow in lazy sarcasm. 'Do you really believe that, or is it me you are trying to convince, eh? Who is tempting whom?' His eyes flickered over her sophisticated silhouette. 'In that black dress of yours, with your beautiful silvery hair and your fine porcelain skin, and those pools of green emerald that look at me with such yearning,' his gaze dropped to her mouth, his voice condensing to a rough whisper, 'and those soft pink lips, that seem to be begging for my kisses, you are a temptress, Calypso. Like the sirens of our mythology, desirable, with a fatal beauty.'

'Why are you saying this to me?' Oriel breathed. Her heart was thudding and a hot blush had spread from her chest to her throat.

'You are my passion, *agápi mou*. And each time you reject me, dousing my fire, my desire, like the phoenix, rises from the ashes, stronger and more determined.'

Oriel willed the surging heat in her body not to continue its downward course. She needed to gather her wits. It was as though they were both playing a game of hide-and-seek, and she was beginning to yearn to give up and be found. Thankfully, she was saved from finding a response to Damian's unnerving words. Their conversation was interrupted by the waiter bringing them the first course and Demetris, following in his wake, bearing a bottle of pale pink wine and two glasses.

The restaurateur smiled flamboyantly as if trying to make amends for his previous faux pas. 'You must taste this new rosé. My guests can't get enough of it and this is my last bottle. Ovilos Rosé from the Biblia Chora Estate. It has all the freshness of the sea breeze of the Aegean and the sparkle of our dry summers and our cool nights. Enjoy, with the compliments of the house!'

Damian smiled graciously at the nightclub owner. '*Efharisto*, Demetris, but not tonight. I'll take it back to Helios, where I'll be able to enjoy it without feeling guilty.'

'Sure, sure, my friend! But let me know what you think and, if you need to order a crate or two, no problem. I will be receiving a new delivery at the end of the week.' With that the host gave a small bow and hurried off.

The squid was delicious and they ate for a while in silence. Oriel took a slice of pita bread, fresh and fragrant from the oven, and broke it in half. Damian handed her a small bowl of olive oil and she noticed how brown his hand was in contrast to the creamy colour of hers.

She glanced at him to see his lips curve into a brief smile. 'Opposites attract each other … complete each other, *agápi mou*. That's why we are so good together. You see? I read you like a book and you always know what I'm thinking, isn't that so?'

'That's because you're one-track minded.'

Damian's laugh was rich and deep and the sound of it made Oriel's eyes dance. 'And you are too, *matia mou*, if you would only admit to it.'

Oriel tried to suppress a smile. 'You think you're so sure you can see into my mind as if it were a crystal ball.'

He leaned forward and grinned. 'It is true … I have the Greek oracles' power of eating the thoughts of those who are important to me, didn't you know?' He tapped the side of his nose conspiratorially. 'It's all part of the *Drákon* Damian myth.'

She didn't answer – Damian's banter only served to confuse her. The waiter came by again to take away the empty plates and placed the main dish in front of them.

While Damian tucked with gusto into the impressive portion of fish he'd been served, Oriel looked down at her plate with the little fowl wrapped in vine leaves. 'I do enjoy game but I never eat quail in England, somehow it doesn't seem right there.'

Damian looked up from his food. 'Why not?'

Oriel cut into the dish, releasing a fragrant wisp of steam. 'My parents hold a shoot every year, pheasants and partridge. I used to beat when I was younger. We'd have house parties every weekend, and friends of my parents and their children would attend. The young ones would beat while the grown ups did the shooting.'

He grinned. 'Pheasant shooting, very English. Did you enjoy that?'

'No, not really. But I'm an only child, you see, so it was quite fun having friends of my own age to stay.'

'Your parents didn't want more children?'

'They had tried for so long before they had me, and were quite old by then, so it was too late. I think that's why they dote on me rather too much.' She smiled. 'It's a little suffocating at times, but they mean well.'

He studied her. 'I'm sorry you grew up on your own, that must have been lonely. In Greece, we are always surrounded by family.'

She shrugged. 'Oh, I didn't mind really. It forced me to be adventurous, just to get away from home.'

'So that's another reason why you became an archaeologist.'

'Yes, I suppose so.' She watched him look back at his food as he ate, as though reluctant to travel further down this path of conversation. 'But what about you? Why did you become an archaeologist?'

He looked up at her, his gaze holding a trace of something guarded. 'For similar reasons. I wanted to see the world, get away from Helios.' He gestured towards her plate. 'Try the sauce, it's good with the quail.'

Oriel could see he was deftly steering the talk away from himself and, although it gave her a twinge of disappointment, she decided to let him have his way. She took a sip of wine and tasted some of the rice with the pomegranate sauce. 'Mmm, yes! I love the fruit tang it adds to the food.'

'Pomegranate is used a lot in Greek and Turkish cuisine. Traditionally, we adorn our tables with the fruit, setting it out in honour of the fertile land and its bounty. We use it as decoration in all our celebrations. Our legends are filled with the image of the pomegranate.'

Oriel glanced at him, a momentary glint of humour sparkling in her eyes. 'Yes, indeed they are. They're a symbol of fertility in many cultures. Which particular drama surrounding the pomegranate tree do you find the most appealing?'

His mouth quirked in a lazy smile. 'Are you really interested? I wouldn't want to bore you.'

'Stories never bore me. It's only when you try to make them personal that I object.'

'But these myths are about human nature and the passions of us mortals. How can anyone deny seeing in them the reflection of their own shortcomings, eh? But I grant you, these are not happy tales.'

'Are any of your legends happy? Your gods were a vengeful and cruel lot.'

They both laughed heartily.

'Of course, the best myth associated with the pomegranate is the most famous one.'

'The story of Persephone?'

'Yes. Do you know it?'

'I should do, I read it as part of my degree course. But there were so many of those tales and so many gods that my recollection of all the details is a little hazy.'

'Then I will refresh your memory. Persephone was a beautiful maiden desired by Hades, god of the underworld. When she refused to be his wife he kidnapped her to live with him in his dark world of the dead. Demeter, Persephone's mother and the goddess of harvest, was so distressed, she killed every plant on earth. To avoid the devastation of the world, Zeus commanded Hades to allow Persephone to return home. However, before letting her go, Hades tricked her into eating four pomegranate seeds, which ensured she had to live in the underworld for four months every year.'

'Yes, that's it, and it was how the ancient Greeks explained the change of the seasons, the eternal cycle of death and rebirth in nature.'

'Indeed. While Demeter was mourning her daughter's absence, she let the earth die, and that is why we have our winters.'

'As I said, an unforgiving bunch, your gods and goddesses. I'd hate to have been on the wrong side of their wrath.'

Damian chuckled and reclined in his chair. 'The gods shared the same weaknesses and violent passions as mankind. Anger, jealousy … desire. We are made in their image.' His gaze, palpable as heat from the sun, held hers and refused to let go. 'Hades was consumed by his hunger for the beautiful Persephone and wanted to live with her forever. It's no surprise that he would do anything to keep her, even kidnapping.'

He was doing it again: trying to fluster her. Well, he wouldn't succeed. Oriel took a sip of wine, enjoying the relaxing tingle of it seeping gently through her. She smiled playfully. 'That's what power can do to men, whether gods or mortals. It turns them into barbarians.'

'And you disapprove of barbarians?'

'Wholeheartedly.'

His expression glinted with amusement. 'Are you sure, Calypso?'

They had finished their main course and people had started moving to the dancefloor. Music drifted across the club – a popular, moody love song that started with a trembling *bouzoúki* mandolin and fell into sultry drums and soaring violins as a man's sonorous voice began to sing imploringly of his lost love.

Damian leaned forward. 'This is one of my favourites. Shall we dance?'

Before Oriel had time to respond, he had risen, laughing at her shocked expression as he pulled her to her feet, his eyes like flaming steel in his tanned face. She shivered with pleasure when he brushed his fingertips against her naked shoulder as he led her to the dancefloor outside on the terrace, lit only by the stars and the moon. The feel of his palms was slightly rough, belonging to working, not idle hands, so that when something smoother touched her shoulder again, she knew it to be his lips. The kiss was a brief flame that came and went and her excitement made her hold her breath until Damian took her in his arms.

Then the rhythm and the sweet throbbing insistence of the music caught at Oriel, calling to an answering chord within her that she was unable to resist. She was a born dancer and her light, supple body melted into Damian's hands as she moved against him. Now and again, her breasts pressed lightly against his chest and his eyes flashed with fire, riveted to her face. He pulled her tighter. His hand moved over her naked back and she gasped, quivering at his touch.

Damian moved differently to any other man Oriel had danced with before; his natural rhythm and grace were compelling her body to join the sensual tempo of his own, so that she knew with every cell of her being the things he wanted to tell her, the things her usual common sense refused even to consider. Dancing with Damian was infinitely disturbing, maddening and sweet. She didn't know herself any longer … this new Oriel, who was growing more reckless by the minute, who hadn't the strength to refuse the delicious physical contact of his body even though something whispered that it was more dangerous than anything she had ever faced before.

She sighed, leaning into him, and half closed her eyes, revelling in the guiding pressure of Damian's hand at the small of her back as they danced without words. There was a roaring in her brain and ears; her heart was beating so that she could feel it everywhere, and the physical delight was overwhelming. Their bodies spoke to each other as the music went on; the disturbing emotions raging through her were shared by him, she could feel it.

They moved among the shadows that were the other dancers, gliding in their own world, dancing high above a sea that was lit by the moon like an ocean of molten silver. The languorous voice of the singer and the gently pulsing music swept over them, lulling them into their own private paradise, oblivious to everyone around them. Oriel heard the sea, distant, yet at the same time close, as it came and went between the rocks down below.

They moved together for song after song, like an intimate, silent conversation where their bodies were getting to know one another in a different way, asking, exploring, feeling for the other's responses. The edge of the terrace was darker where giant potted palms marked the balustrade and they found themselves secluded in a corner of it.

Damian was so close that his mouth brushed against her hair. 'Ah, *agápi mou*, you smell of flowers, you feel like satin. What are you doing to me? I want you so much it's driving me insane.' He was now whispering beautiful, sensual words into her hair almost incoherently, one hand moving up and down her back; shock waves of desire ran over her skin as his fingers played, ripples of acute sensitivity that made her want more – much more.

Oriel succumbed, savouring his body against hers, loving his breath in her ear. She was desperate for him to kiss her. His gaze caught hers in the moonlight and her eyes widened. Their lips were mere inches apart. She watched those silver irises darken almost to glistening black under his ebony lashes. Her breath quickened in anticipation, her nipples brushing against Damian's strong torso, making them harden to tight peaks. She wanted him to plunder her, to feel no responsibilities or cares about tomorrow.

They both caught their breath before his mouth crushed down on hers and though she gasped against him, she parted her lips readily, allowing his tongue to chase hers with hungry abandon. His kiss explored every sweet, secret corner of her mouth. His hot lips began to trace a path over her fluttering eyelids, finding the racing pulse beneath her temple, and swirling into the delicate shell of her ear, his every touch fiery and demanding, challenging her to match his heat. Oriel did so, her body melting into his arms, a deep, honeyed warmth flowing through her veins, reducing her to a state of mindless bliss.

His mouth returned to hers and she coaxed him eagerly, wanting more and more of this hot, wet taste of him. They kissed as though telling each other what had not yet been expressed in words. Her hands tangled in his hair while his gripped her back and pulled her tightly against his swelling groin.

They kissed until they realized that they were the only ones left on the dancefloor and the music had died down. Silently they gathered their belongings and left. They flew back to Helios, their hearts beating wildly, bodies on fire, hardly speaking.

Time seemed almost unreal, so caught up in each other were they, anticipation hanging silently between them. They went up to Oriel's apartment and she put the key in the lock of the door with a trembling hand. She looked up at him, not knowing the right thing to say. 'Thank you for an unforgettable evening, Damian,' she murmured, her voice thick with an overwhelming need for him.

The glitter of his eyes told her what he'd been fighting all evening, and what had come out in that kiss – a kiss that had rocked her world. She stared at him knowing what her senses wanted but that she still tried to deny herself.

'Surely this isn't goodnight?' he murmured in a trembling voice, searching her face. Damian's hands played with the frail straps on her shoulders as if he wanted to pull them off. Then he bent his head and took her lips with his own, crushing them with a bruising passion that seemed to have been pent-up forever. His strong arms lifted her from the floor so she was held completely to him, her feet off the ground.

'Do you like to torment me, Calypso?' he asked, his eyes heavy-lidded with desire. Was it her tormenting him? Oriel couldn't deny her need, or his, any more. The time for pretending was over. She heard herself moaning his name as she yielded to her body's demands, hugging him to her aching breasts. 'Please, Damian,' she whispered urgently as his mouth moved over her neck. 'Make me yours again tonight.'

'*Agápi mou* … no other man can make you feel as I can do. Let me show you.'

'Yes,' she panted for breath. 'Show me.'

CHAPTER 5

Damian lowered Oriel down but kept his arm tightly round her waist. His hand reached for the key, ready to turn it in the lock of her apartment, when he froze as someone behind them laughed – the sort of cackle that later reminded Oriel of Carabosse, the wicked fairy godmother in a pantomime version of *Sleeping Beauty* that she had seen as a child.

The deep, mocking laughter echoed like a broken note that died away in the great hall, shattering their sweet wild harmony. 'Well, well, what have we here?'

Shocked out of their daze, Damian and Oriel broke apart and turned to find Helena in her wheelchair, her face a mask in which the eyes alone were alive and seething with livid flames. Oriel recoiled from the antagonistic look fixed upon her.

'Helena, what are you doing up at this hour?' Damian's voice was low and calm, although he was clearly fighting to regain his composure.

'And it's a good thing too that someone is awake to stop our home becoming a whorehouse. First your brother, and now you! Has neither of you any shame?' his cousin cried in anger.

'Please, Helena, control yourself.'

'What about you, eh? Have you thought of controlling your disgusting, lustful desires?' Her expression shifted, becoming almost imploring. 'Can't you see, no good will come of it? Pericles was the same. They all tricked him with their manipulative ways. You and I understand each other, don't we, cousin? No one has seen what we've seen.'

He fixed his eyes on her as though trying to calm a frightened horse. 'That's all in the past, Helena. You're tired. I'll get Beshir ...'

But Helena wasn't listening to him. Like quicksilver she turned her bitter gaze on Oriel. 'And you, little English upstart, with your innocent wide eyes, does it excite you to lie with Frankenstein? You haven't been in this house two days and already you're trying to worm yourself into his bed,' she sneered.

'Don't think that I can't see what you're up to. Like all these women he carries on with, you want to marry him so you can have the run of this island.'

'That's enough, Helena,' Damian said quietly, going to his cousin and laying a hand on her shoulder, which she sent flying off with a knock of her clenched fist.

'Get off me!' Her eyes flashed furiously. 'You're just a pawn that these women use to reach their goal.' The words seemed to choke in her throat. 'They know your weakness, they know you can't keep your trousers on.'

As he stood before her, Damian's intense gaze burned brightly, caught between disgust and pity. Oriel could see that he was appalled by the naked anger in Helena's eyes and the venomous words that had just rolled out like an irrepressible torrent, but his bearing had changed and he became taller, more distant and imposing. The shadow of *Drákon* Damian had returned.

Helena looked up at him now with a submissive kind of fear. 'Just like *him*. Lust, always lust. What is it with this family?' Suddenly she threw her hands over her eyes and a cry of pain broke from her. 'I can't stand it, I can't stand it!' Then, pushing her head back, her features racked with some sort of anguish that tortured her, she turned her wheelchair and rolled out of the room.

Although he didn't go after her, Damian's gaze was fixed upon Helena until she had disappeared into her apartment. The unmarked side of his face was turned to Oriel, tired lines etched deeply in his brown skin. He seemed to have aged ten years in a few seconds, and she could see behind his rigid expression that his heart was bleeding. Oriel wasn't so much surprised by his concern for Helena, what startled her was the discovery that the exterior look of hardness he showed wasn't necessarily proof that he was a hardened man. It was an armour, making him aloof, unapproachable. This realization made a nerve leap against her fingertips as she touched them to the skin of her throat. She inhaled sharply and he stole a quick glance at her, his gaze going down inside her, holding her as if on a steel hook.

'You must forgive my cousin,' he said, his voice low and even.

'Being confined to a wheelchair, day in, day out, makes her mind wander sometimes. She has these turns, brought on by tension and nerves. It makes her behaviour … unpredictable at times.' His intense gaze softened, and he sighed and shook his head.

'This is my fault. I didn't drop in and see her before we went out tonight, as I usually do. She had probably been waiting for me, hoping that I would have dinner with her. I didn't even warn her that I was going out, my mind was on other things.' His eyes bore into Oriel's. 'It's totally my fault, and I hope you can forget her unfortunate outburst.'

Oriel smiled reassuringly and stared up at him, standing there so dark and powerful, and evoking in her the wild despair of a creature that finds itself in a trap. She laid a hand on his arm, trying to push away her own feelings of shock and disturbance at what had just occurred. 'It is already forgotten. Don't give it another thought.'

The glitter of steel showing through Damian's lashes was soft but his gaze upon Oriel was still penetrating. 'Thank you, *agápi mou*. I'll make sure this doesn't happen again.' Intense emotions hung in the air between them and the look they exchanged was one of silent understanding: their moment of passion had been brutally crushed, and whatever individual demons they were both harbouring had reared up to prevent them from being together that night.

As she went to turn the key to her apartment, Damian added with a tired smile: 'It's already the early hours. You'd better get some sleep. I think we'll be too tired to dive tomorrow, I'll tell Irini not to wake you. Perhaps I could show you around the island. Maybe take you to visit the Lekkas Press, we make the best olive oil around here.'

She nodded quickly. 'That sounds like a good plan. I'll see you later then. Goodnight.'

'Yes, I'll send Hassan or Irini to fetch you at two o'clock, after lunch. *Kalinýchta*.'

Oriel went into her room and, after watching his dark figure disappear down the corridor, closed the door behind her, leaning against it. From the outside no one could have guessed how upset she was, though inside she was still trembling. Thwarted desire, frustration, anger and a strange kind of relief all vied for prominence within her. This whole evening had been a roller-coaster ride, and now she felt as though she had been sent hurtling through the air only to come crashing to the ground in a bruised heap.

Oriel had lied, of course, when she had said that the incident with Damian's cousin was forgotten. She was dismayed and outraged by Helena's accusations. This woman was clearly unbalanced, and she knew in that moment that getting involved with Damian Lekkas, tempting as it might seem, would be pure madness. Even if she could be sure of his feelings for her, she couldn't shake off the uneasy feeling she had around this household, blighted by tragedy and scandal. Did she really want to get pulled into its shadowy grasp?

She glanced over at the darkened windows. Beyond them it was still night but dawn would be breaking soon … Yet there would no dawn for the feelings that she could feel budding in the innermost recesses of her heart. If she were to protect it, Damian must remain forbidden to her.

* * *

Oriel didn't wake up until she heard a light knock on the door. It was Irini bringing in a tray of food.

'*Kaliméra, Despinis.*' The maid smiled. 'The *Kyrios* gave instructions not to wake you until lunchtime. Did you sleep well?'

Oriel raised herself up on one elbow, rubbing her eyes. 'Yes, thank you, Irini. I can't believe I slept for so long.'

'The *Kyrios* said to tell you he will come by to collect you at three o'clock, not at two. He said to give you this.' Irini put down the tray on the little writing table under the window and removed a cream envelope from it, handing it to Oriel, who had propped herself up against her pillows. The maid lowered her voice confidentially. 'That will give him time to have lunch with the *Kyria*, his cousin. She has had one of her bad turns and was awake most of the night. She's been crying all morning and didn't want to see anybody … not even Beshir.'

Oriel didn't respond, as her mind flashed back to the previous night and Helena's vituperative comments. It was clear that Damian's cousin, if it pleased her to do so, could wind herself up into such a state that the entire household was thrown into disarray.

Evidently, the woman wasn't quite right in the head but, even so, it was also plain that she could still muster the power to manipulate.

Oriel sighed inwardly. Whatever Helena's intention, her arrival last night, hysterical and unpleasant though it was, had in fact been timely, saving her from making a terrible mistake: she had come perilously close to giving in to the passion that Damian ignited in her. However, now it seemed he would have to spend his lunchtime dancing to Helena's tune, calming her down, making things manageable again.

'Has the *Kyria* always had these bad turns?' asked Oriel, as she opened the envelope from Damian.

Irini shook her head. '*Den xéro*, I don't know. I have only been working here a few years but, from what I hear, she has always had these sudden changes of mood.' The young woman shrugged her shoulders. 'I have to go now, they'll be wondering where I am in the kitchen. Eat your lunch, or it will get cold.'

Irini went out of the room, leaving Oriel to read Damian's note. It was a brisk missive, informing her that he had woken early and had flown straight to Corfu. He had decided to show the Alexander bronze to an archaeologist he knew who had retired on the island, a former professor at the Aristotle University of Thessaloniki. If anyone could say with confidence who had sculpted the bronze, it was he. Damian added that he would see Oriel in the afternoon for a trip to the olive press.

Oriel put down the note and brought her lunch tray back to bed, settling herself once more against the pillows. She was too preoccupied to touch the food, her mind pensive and distracted. So, Damian had gone to Corfu this morning … he can't have had much sleep. Her thoughts turned wistfully to the night before. They had breathed and moved on that dancefloor as though meant for each other. Still, Helena had made every effort to let Oriel know she was merely one in a line of many, raising the spectre of other women Damian had presumably brought to the house, other women he'd no doubt carried on with in the same seductive way he had with her – and it wasn't just Helena who cast him as a philanderer: Yorgos had called him a conqueror of women … Was Damian Lekkas really the man who had seemed so honest with her last night? Something twisted inside Oriel. Was he a womanizer, just a practised seducer who was toying with her?

She looked down at the tray of food; she wasn't really hungry. It was too hot to eat anyway; even the salad of baby artichokes and zucchini didn't tempt her. Maybe some fruit? Oriel helped herself to a bunch of grapes and a slice of melon – sweet and refreshing. How sensitive her lips were, still a little bruised from the feel of his. She must get a grip now, before seeing him again.

Oriel treated herself to a scented bath. The steam crept all over her – it was a delicious, soothing feeling and she soaked among the bubbles for ten minutes, her eyes closed, trying to make a void in her mind, allowing herself to do nothing more than appreciate the sheer physical comfort of the hot water as the bubbles broke around her, their sweet scent filling her senses.

Afterwards she dressed quickly, revived by the relaxing heat of the bath. She chose a simple navy cotton mini dress, then swept her hair up into a high ponytail, slipped on a pair of flat golden sandals and studied herself in the mirror. She seemed a little pale, and her eyes were overly bright as though she were running a fever, so she added some blusher to her cheeks and gloss to her lips. There was still plenty of time before three o'clock.

Oriel had already decided to do a little research of her own before Damian came to take her to see the olive press. There was a friend from her college days she planned to call, Cynthia Albright, who now worked at the Bodleian Library in Oxford. Her friend would be the ideal person to help her research the trader's brand on the seal of the amphora she had brought up from the wreck. Walking downstairs with Cynthia's phone number on a scrap of paper, she caught sight of Irini arranging a vase of flowers in the hall, and asked if it was possible to make a call.

'I'll take you to the *Kyrios*'s study. You can use the one in there. That way, you won't be disturbed,' the maid told her. Oriel was led down corridors to Damian's wing and a set of tall doors. Inside, she found herself in a cool room, shaded by Venetian blinds, which smelled of wax polish and a hint of mustiness emanating from the shelves of leatherbound books that lined the walls.

She settled herself at Damian's large oak desk, feeling a little awkward inhabiting his space in that way. Stacks of papers were piled up neatly to one side and, opposite, was a single photo in a silver frame. Oriel peered closely at it and saw two grinning teenage boys with fishing rods squatting down, knee-to-knee, over a giant fish. Their faces were so similar – tanned and arrogantly youthful – there was no mistaking that they were brothers, Damian and Pericles. She gazed, fascinated, at this snapshot of Damian's past self, looking so boyish and yet, even then, as she looked more closely, there appeared something more sombre in his smile than the wilder expression of his younger brother.

Finally, she snapped her attention away from the photo and lifted the receiver, waiting patiently while she was connected to her friend.

'Cynthia! Yes, it's me, Oriel. I wonder if you can help me …'

A few minutes later she put down the receiver with a feeling of satisfaction. Cynthia had said she would be on the case that very afternoon to unearth the information needed. Oriel had described the trident motif, with what looked like a snake curled round the shaft at its base, and the three letters – SES – inscribed beneath. Having told her friend that she would be out that afternoon, Oriel agreed that they should speak again at the weekend, probably Sunday morning when they were both most likely to be around.

In the meantime, Oriel decided to make the most of the bookshelves in Damian's study. Soon she was curled up on a red leather Chesterfield with a large book of photographs that charted the decades of dedicated work that archaeologist Arthur Evans put in to unearth the mysteries of the ancient city of Knossos in Crete. So engrossed was she that she was a little startled when there was a knock on the study door and Hassan appeared. She glanced at her watch, realizing it was already three o'clock. The servant gazed at her benignly and smiled, holding the door open in an unspoken message that she was expected elsewhere. She quickly replaced the book on the shelf and followed him.

Damian was waiting for her in front of the Jeep, looking his usual handsome self in a pair of tight-fitting white jeans and a crisp white shirt. He must have just showered, because his raven-black hair was sleekly swept back, with only a single unruly lock caressing his wide forehead, giving him a roguish air. As he saw her, his gaze skimmed appreciatively down her figure, taking in her long shapely legs in the cotton mini dress.

'*Kaliméra, matia mou*, did you sleep well?'

Oriel smiled. 'Yes, very well, thank you.'

As Damian came to kiss her, she drew away from him. 'No,' she whispered.

His brow knitted together. 'What's wrong?' he murmured.

'What almost happened yesterday would have been a grave mistake,' she told him, glancing up at his enquiring frown. 'We were under the influence of the romantic atmosphere of Santorini.' She waved a hand self-consciously. 'The wine, the music, the beautiful moonlit night.' She hesitated, and added in a faltering voice: 'Maybe it was the fate you always talk about … I mean, that Helena appeared to wake us up before we did something we would both regret.'

He stared down into her eyes with a questioning look, his darkness filling her vision until everything else was blotted out and, for a moment, it was as if the sun had gone in. An invisible fist reached inside her, seizing her heart, for never before in her life had she been cruel to anyone. She hated cruelty, but she had to defend herself from the onslaught of feelings this man evoked. The seeds of something treacherously tender had already been germinating slowly inside her for six years, but she must not allow them to flourish.

'*Katalavaíno*, I understand,' Damian said, without emotion, and then, helping her into the Jeep, he climbed into the driver's seat.

They drove in silence for a while. Although the sun was smiling on this balmy day, Oriel's heart felt cold, the flames that had warmed it the night before quashed by inhibitions and fear. She considered asking after Helena, but decided against it in case Damian thought she was prying.

They progressed up the hillside through a series of hairpin bends, at times skimming the very edge of the steep drop down to the treetops and the sea. Then the road dipped down again, passing a double row of white cottages that clung precariously to the cliffside, bright with geraniums and vividly painted shutters. A group of men in rough working clothes sat together outside one building and followed the progression of the Jeep with lethargic interest, hands clasped about glasses of ouzo or retsina. There wasn't a woman or child in sight, only a mangy ginger cat, licking itself lazily in the sun.

'I went to Corfu early this morning to see a colleague of mine,' Damian announced nonchalantly. 'I took the bronze with me. I'm taking the whole team to Manoli's tonight to celebrate what I think will be a significant find.'

Oriel glanced at him with instant eagerness. 'Of course, sorry, I almost forgot to ask. What did he say?'

'Oh, once we've identified who owned the argosy the job of finding the provenance will be much easier. But he'll need time to delve into the historical writings and shipment records of that era.'

She nodded. 'I've already got my friend, who works at the Bodleian, on the case. I rang her earlier.' His eyes met hers as she spoke and she noticed the shadows under them. 'You must have had virtually no sleep.'

He smiled at her. 'It wouldn't do if I shirked my responsibilities just because of one late night.'

'You don't spare yourself, do you?'

'I enjoy what I do. I'm lucky, so many people in this world hate their jobs.'

'True.' She gave him a speculative glance. 'Though I always think that we make our own luck.'

'To a certain extent I agree. Anyway, it's good that you've got your friend involved with the research.' The side of Damian's mouth curved upwards in amused approval. 'I knew I wouldn't regret bringing you in on this job.'

Oriel bit back a pleased grin as her gaze followed the undulating landscape. 'So, tell me, I've never known anyone who owned an olive press – certainly not another archaeologist. You seem to have many strings to your bow.'

He shrugged. 'It's part of my family's history. When my ancestor bought this island, there were already many olive trees growing on it, despite the devastation the volcano eruption had created. In those days, there was only a handful of monks living in the monastery and the surrounding olive trees were largely neglected. Gjergj decided to develop the existing groves into a commercial plantation, the produce of which he sold to the neighbouring islands.

'By the time my grandfather took over the island, the last of the elderly monks had passed away, leaving the monastery empty, so he began work on the restoration. It seemed the perfect place to house the press and our estate offices. In those days, they worked with the same kind of olive presses the Greeks were using more than five thousand years ago. My father continued using this same process and started to market our olive oil further afield, to the Greek mainland and Italy. When I took over the island, the business passed to me.'

He slowed the Jeep as they turned down a long dusty track with cypress trees on either side. 'Archaeology is my passion but I need to make money for Helios to prosper. Plus, I enjoy the challenge. I've just found a very modern way to produce good oil. Cheaper to make, so it's at a competitive price for the mass market, but still gives an excellent quality. We can maintain an expensive high-end artisanal product, still using the traditional methods, while distributing a mass-produced version to other global markets. The new machines will be delivered next month.'

'You're quite entrepreneurial, aren't you?'

He threw her a sideways glance. 'I have only my work in this life to light my fires and keep them burning,' he told her as they entered a gated domain.

Was this the key to what drove him? Like so many times before, Oriel's eyes fell on the hard, scarred profile of the man next to her and recognized in him such strength and lonely determination that it made her heart swell with emotion.

Damian stopped the car. 'We're here.'

Oriel gazed up at him. For a brief moment the atmosphere between them was alive with vibrations, swift arrows of thought and feeling that darted from his eyes into hers, delivering little shafts of awareness throughout her body. And then Damian smiled.

'*Éla*, let me show you around.'

Oriel slid out of the Jeep and looked around her. They had driven up to a building that looked like an old Roman monastery, its domed tower presiding over thick stone walls of pale pinkish ochre, different sections covered with tiled, pitched roofs. It was a strange and beautiful place. Surrounding the building, row after row of noble olive trees surged up from a parched, rocky, calcareous soil, gnarled in the calm stillness, their silvery-green leaves shimmering against the bright Greek sky in the sun-drenched afternoon.

'My olive heaven,' he murmured.

'It's so quiet here, so peaceful, as though we're in another world,' Oriel remarked.

'It's a couple of miles out of town. Maybe that's why the monks chose to build their monastery here.'

Orderly lines of trees marched up and down the great expanse as far as the eye could see. Damian and Oriel walked in venerable silence under the cover of their branches, basking in the serenity of the place. The light flashed silver in some spots; in others it tinted the grove in shades of pink, peach and cobalt blue.

'There are sixty-four varieties of olive. Some are as big as walnuts, others as small as berries, and believe it or not the small ones yield proportionately more oil. We only grow twelve varieties on Helios,' Damian explained

'The bees must be happy when the trees are in flower.'

'The bees don't pollinate them, the wind does: the *ponenta*, west wind. I love the olive. I love trees in general, but I think this is my favourite.'

'It's not exactly beautiful though, is it?' She brushed a hand over a gnarled trunk. 'With this bark it could appear rather sinister, don't you think?'

'On the contrary, it's their tortured body I find most beautiful, as though they have grown in pain, like human souls looking for delivery.'

Oriel laughed. 'That's a rather grim image.'

Damian shrugged and twisted his lips wryly, 'I don't think so. It's rather poignant …'

She nodded. 'Grim …' and they both laughed. They had left the olive grove and were now in a clearing next to the cloisters of the old monastery, which seemed to be a larger replica of Damian's garden, where Oriel had walked on the night of her arrival. There were birds flitting among the trees and sunshine caressed the sweet, fragranced petals of honeysuckle and climbing roses. Marble statues gleamed white in the golden rays and fountains made a rainbow of colour before cascading down into their different-shaped bowls.

'How do you keep all your gardens so green?'

'It rains in winter over the Ionian, it even snows on the mountains of Kefalonia. I'm thinking of adding units of desalination for some parts of the island, where it's still quite barren. The water would come straight from the sea, or we'd dig wells. It's an expensive procedure, but we would be able to plant more, vines especially. It would almost double the produce of Helios, affording a better life for the islanders.'

Oriel nodded, impressed. 'A wonderful project that would be.'

Among other statues, she spotted a striking one of Apollo in all his naked beauty.

Damian followed her eyes. 'A reproduction, of course. If it hadn't been, I wouldn't have been allowed to keep it.'

'It's still a work of art.'

'It was actually sculpted by a blind man. Kostis lost his sight when a jealous woman threw sulphuric acid in his face.'

Oriel shivered. 'How dreadful!'

'Jealousy, *agápi mou* … Passions can make the human heart monstrous.' Damian had spoken in a low, cavernous voice without looking at her, but she could see his eyes had a harrowed and faraway expression.

What was he thinking? Her gaze wandered over the scarring of his beautiful face. There was so much about him that she didn't know.

Close by, Oriel noticed the tallest bay tree she had ever seen. 'Oh, what a magnificent bay,' she said, trying to bring back Damian's former cheerful mood.

It worked, and his expression brightened. 'We call it a laurel in Greece. It's been here ever since I can remember, I think it was my grandfather who planted it. We revere the laurel because it's associated with Daphne and Apollo, and Daphne taking its form to avoid her own human feminine one being so attractive to the male sex.' He smiled mischievously. 'You might say we Greeks are unhealthily obsessed by stories of gods chasing virgins.'

He was being provocative again, Oriel knew, and she turned away and walked around the tree to the fountain. 'Yes, I know the myth.'

'Daphne didn't escape Apollo, you know, even as a laurel tree. She stabbed him with her leaves when he tried to embrace her.' Damian sauntered over to the laurel and reached up to rub a leaf between his fingertips. 'But he didn't give up, you see. He tended her as his own tree and made her evergreen.' He came to stand next to her. 'Don't run from me, *agápi mou.*'

'Then stop messing with me, Damian.'

His silver gaze clashed with hers. 'Would you stab me with your leaves?'

How could she, when every cell in her body cried out for him – every sigh, every breath secretly exhaled his name? Her senses were tingling with the scent of him so close, a heady fusion of soap, clean skin and pure masculinity. Oriel attempted to scowl at him.

'Yes, I probably would, if you don't leave me alone.' The lie almost stuck in her throat.

'And so both our souls would be damned forever. What a waste.'

Oriel stepped away from him again. The wide oval archways of the cloisters were each punctuated by other trees that stood against the stone pillars, their thick, twisted branches laden with spiky violet flowers. She was now closer to them and, in sharp contrast to the alluring scent of Damian, they gave off a pungent fragrance that tickled Oriel's nose, making her almost sneeze.

'What's that?' she asked, moving back quickly. 'The smell is really strong.'

Damian gave a brief laugh, deep in his throat, almost a chuckle. 'What is it with you and trees today? It's called Monk's Pepper, also known as the Chastity Tree. In ancient times it was believed to be an anti-aphrodisiac.' He folded his arms and leaned back against stone edge of the fountain, regarding Oriel in a way that unsteadied her. 'Women used part of the plant on their bedding, in Pliny's words "to cool the heat of lust" during the religious festival of the *Thesmophoria*, when Athenian women left their husbands' beds to remain ritually chaste. Monks also sat under it to quieten their libidos.'

'Then maybe you should sit beneath it yourself.' The words had flown out of Oriel's mouth impulsively and she blushed, not quite sure how Damian would take her snappy retort.

'No amount of Monk's Pepper would succeed in calming the turmoil I feel whenever you're near me. I just have to look at you, *agápi mou*, for my senses to riot out of control. I know that it's the same for you, even if you keep denying it.'

Oriel swallowed. He was right, she couldn't deny it. The intensity of his gaze told her that he might move closer to her again, and she didn't know if she would be able to stop herself from letting him press that powerful, hard body against her. *Please don't come any closer*, she silently willed him. Damian gazed at her with eyes that seemed veiled in a hundred secret thoughts. He pushed a hand through his hair.

'Come, let's walk on before I break my promise and lose control of myself.'

Oriel let out a quiet breath and followed him as he strode off, her eyes on his broad back. Now that he had moved away she was relieved, although part of her was disappointed that he hadn't simply pulled her into his arms and made them *both* lose control.

They crossed the front gardens of the enclosed courtyard, heading towards a large wooden door at the far end. The stone walls of the monastery rose high above them and Oriel could see where the centuries had rounded every edge of the crenulations and the belfry. The roofs were dark ochre, as were the turrets and chimneys. A long, arched gallery extended around the upper floor, above the arched cloisters that surrounded the building. Pines and beech trees had been planted around the building, separating it from the rest of the grounds, so that it appeared almost secluded.

'How old is the monastery?' she asked, happy to talk about anything other than this unbearable tension between them.

Damian barely turned his head as they walked together. 'It dates from the sixteenth century. It survived the earthquake and volcanic eruption that destroyed most of the island. Ever since the press was set up, I've had a bishop come up from Athens twice a year to hold a service in our family chapel, and he blesses our olive press. In return, he receives twelve gallons of olive oil. A great tradition, don't you think?'

'Yes, that makes sense given the press is housed in an old monastery. It is a most beautiful building. The lines are rather austere, but that lends a certain grandeur.'

As they approached the front door, Yorgos Christodoulou appeared on the threshold.

'Ah, Yorgos, *kalispera*. I didn't know that you'd be here today.'

The estate manager fiddled with the heavy watch on his wrist, regarding them both with his impenetrable black eyes. 'I was told you were coming to visit so I decided to stay in case you needed me for anything. Some of the men are working overtime today because we had a large harvest of olives last week and, if we don't turn them into oil quickly, they'll rot.'

Damian nodded. 'Good, well done. You've obviously met *Despinis* Anderson.'

Yorgos flashed Oriel a smile. '*Né*, yes, of course. *Kalispera, Despinis.*'

Oriel nodded politely, but there was still something about this man she didn't like.

'Perhaps you'd like me to give *Despinis* Anderson a tour of the press?'

'Thank you, Yorgos, but I'm happy to show her around.'

'As you like, *Kyrios*, but I'll be in my office if you change your mind.' He nodded lightly and was just about to disappear into one of the dark corridors of the building when Damian called him back.

'Actually, there is one thing you can do for me. Bring the Jeep round and park it outside the monastery. I left it at the entrance. It'll save us walking back. Here …' He threw him the keys.

'Of course, I'll do that immediately.'

Oriel looked after the estate manager as he left the courtyard. She didn't like his subservient manner towards Damian, which, she felt, jarred with the rather underhanded way he had described his boss on the day she had arrived. Plus, she hadn't forgotten how he had tried to put her off the excavation job in the first place.

Damian turned to Oriel. 'From the look on your face, I can see that you don't care much for Yorgos,' he remarked.

'I find him rather creepy, to be honest.'

'He's an odd character, I must admit. He was the best friend of my younger brother. They'd always hung around together, since childhood.' Damian's face went blank. 'Pericles died a few years ago, as you probably know, and although Yorgos wasn't someone I even liked much as a boy, I wanted to honour the connection my brother had with him.'

Oriel looked up at Damian, trying to read his expression, but it was closed. 'I'm sorry about your brother,' she said softly. 'Yorgos

169

did tell me that he'd died.'

Damian nodded brusquely, obviously unwilling to be drawn further into conversation about Pericles, the only hint of emotion a slight furrow in his brow. 'I do sometimes wonder about Yorgos. He's certainly not an open book, it's hard to tell what his honest opinion is sometimes.'

'If you're not sure about him, why do you entrust him with your estate?'

'It's not that I distrust him, as such. Besides, he runs a tight ship and is very efficient so I've no real reason to get rid of him. I just don't have the easy, open relationship with him as I do with, say, Stavros. But you can't have it all, I suppose.'

He smiled at Oriel and took her arm. 'Come, let's forget about him. First, I'll show you the traditional stone mill that my grandfather used. It requires real craftsmanship and expertise to run it properly.'

They entered a big room where machines were thundering away noisily. At the entrance there was a queue of men carrying baskets loaded to the brim with green olives. Each placed the fruits of his harvest on a conveyor belt, which took the olives through a stream of running water before tipping them into the grinding mill. They greeted Damian with obvious respect; he, in turn, thanked them for working overtime to safeguard the crop, slapping them on the shoulder with encouraging approval.

Oriel moved over to a large trough, where three pairs of great revolving millstones were rotating laboriously, grinding whole olives into a brown, gluey pulp.

'This traditional way of producing olive oil has many advantages over the modern mill. The good thing about this open vat is that the paste is visible. That way, the miller can watch what's going on and assess the pulp.'

Oriel watched, fascinated, as bright beads of extra virgin oil began to appear along the edges of the palm-fibre bags of pulp, now in the presses. As the pressure increased, it became a rich, bright golden stream. 'It glitters like liquid gold.'

'It *is* the gold of this island. Presses like these may not have changed for millennia but they're still perfectly efficient. Nothing is wasted,' he told her as they left the room. 'The final dregs of liquid, after several pressings, are stored in large cans and we sell that lower-grade oil cheaply on the island. As for the desiccated brown pulp, it's used to make soap.'

They moved to the next room, where stood a modern version of the stone mill and six huge containers. 'This is the second process we use. Much slower, as we simply let the oil, mixed with water, drip down from the crushed paste. Then the liquid remains in those containers, where they're left to separate naturally.'

'The oil is lighter than water, so floats to the top.'

'Exactly. When I first travelled around the world to learn how other olive oil producers worked, I came upon this process in Italy. The Italians call it *affioramento*, afloat. They refer to it as *olio fiore*, the flower of oil. It yields a much more delicate oil but takes almost twice the time and needs a lot of patience and supervision. It's sold at a premium, of course.'

'So why do you use two methods?'

Damian smiled broadly. 'Both require a great amount of labour, and that suits me because it provides jobs for the islanders. Some of these artisans have had their craft handed down from their fathers and grandfathers.' He put his hands in his pockets and surveyed the room with satisfaction.

Oriel looked up at him, her eyes smiling. 'You have a beautiful island, and you're clearly the king of it, Damian.'

He gave a small, self-derisive laugh before adding: 'With no queen to share it.' The gently mocking note in his voice held an edge of something else; it sounded almost like pain. When he turned to look at her, his eyes stabbed hers with such scorching intensity it seared through Oriel, making her wince.

They went upstairs and walked through the office area, a light and airy space with white painted walls and arched windows, where an accountant and various administrators worked. Oriel was ushered into Damian's private office, where he spent most of his time when he was not working on the archaeological sites, he told her. It was a simple but very large, rectangular room with six narrow windows and had a classically elegant feel to it, the colour scheme all honey brown and cream. It was totally devoid of decoration or clutter. A large oak desk and captain's chair covered in tan leather had pride of place in the centre of the stone floor, an island of industry in this sober room. The view from the narrow windows was spectacular, too, on one side stretching over the garden to the olive grove and, on the opposite, framing the intense blue of the bay.

In front of one of the windows stood a beautiful walnut lacquered ball-and-claw chess table with dovetailed solid hardwood drawers, flanked by a couple of upright chairs. It was an imposing piece of furniture that had already lasted for centuries and would see out many more generations, Oriel supposed.

'Do you play?' Damian asked, coming to stand beside her as she leaned forward to look at the ivory and ebony chessmen.

'Unfortunately not.' She shot him a smile. 'I've never really been interested in board games.'

'I would have thought you'd like chess. A game in which knights storm castles and challenge queens ought to have natural appeal for someone like you.' He picked up a piece, turning it idly in his hand.

'You make me sound rather foolish,' Oriel protested, 'as though I still believed in fairy tales and flying carpets.'

'Don't you?' His keen silver gaze was on her, intent but pensive, quizzing her face.

'If what you mean is that I have unrealistic principles, then you're wrong, it's just that life hasn't jaded me yet.'

'Yes, indeed, I think deep down, you're a romantic, Calypso, through and through.'

'Why would you say that? Because I believe in love?' The words tumbled almost furiously from her lips and she glared at him, appalled at the depth of her yearning.

He put the chess piece down, his eyes darkening. 'Love?'

'Yes,' she said unsteadily, cursing herself for having started down this path, but feeling she had no choice but to soldier on. 'I still believe in love, in its strength and purity.'

Damian studied her with a kind of ruthless deliberation, and she was caught in his gaze like a pin drawn to a magnet 'How can a man and a woman explore all the mysteries of love if they don't give free rein to their emotions?' he said thickly. 'This pure, strong love you talk about, which is smothered in your rules of restraint, is a barren and cold thing, denuded of all passion.'

Oriel was mesmerized by his vital, masculine presence. She

could feel the heat radiating from his body as he stood close to her, and made the mistake of glancing up at his sensual mouth. He caught her look, a gleam deepening in his eyes. Her mind cast around desperately for a defence against this invasion of her senses. 'The mythology of your country is teeming with tales of unleashed passions, drawing in their wake the most horrific tragedies.'

He moved closer still, his face now only inches away. 'The passion we feel for each other, *agápi mou*, can only lead to fulfilment, never tragedy.'

'Fulfilment of the body, never of the soul.'

'We are the victims of our own biology, aren't we? A nun or a monk can ignore the temptations of desire, but only provided there is a stone wall protecting them from being physically touched. You are not one of those, *matia mou*. You are aware of your body and its merciless demands. More than once you have given into it with me … and if I want, I can prove it to you again and again.'

'Oh yes, you're so sure of yourself. I suppose you think—'

In the next instant Damian silenced her words by jerking her into his arms as his lips came down hard on hers, crushing her to him in the most thrilling way. His electrifying response almost winded her. Her hammering heart gave in to it as her arms went around his neck, better to feel him and enjoy the violent onslaught of his mouth. Oh, the bliss of this man's possessive kisses! It was like a hurricane sweeping her away to a land of rapturous delirium. Oriel had heard it said that some men could ravish with a kiss but at that moment, kissing was not enough.

What happened next was as natural as day following night. His skilled, hot mouth moved down and brushed the pulse that throbbed in her throat, sliding gently across to the fragile slope of her shoulder. To Oriel's untutored body, Damian's touch was dark magic and smooth, sweet fire. She had no thought of saying no, no desire to rein back the fierce excitement that ran like forked lightning through her veins.

His hungry exploration went further, became bolder, his warm palms skimming over her shoulders, sure, gentle, yet unrelenting as they moved over the silky skin of her arms till, at last, they reached the curves and the points of her breasts, barely touching them, but oh, so much more tantalizing!

Oriel looked up into eyes that blazed into hers, burning away inhibitions until she was left at the mercy of her long-repressed hunger. She trembled, every part of her pulsating and alive to his burning gaze. Her thighs quivered, her stomach tingled and her breasts became heavy, the nipples upstanding. As the heat of desire burned between her legs, she was aware of her vulnerability to this man, now every part of her craving his possession of her; and so, instinctively, she half lifted herself towards him, arching her back as she did so, wanting to feel the muscled, potent hardness of him.

It was a provocative gesture like a red rag to a bull. Damian's hands grasped the cheeks of her bottom through the thin material of her dress. Pulling Oriel even closer to him, he leaned into her, the swell of his arousal rising hard against her thigh and she smothered a small cry of need when he gently rubbed himself against her in silent imploration. She could sense his impatience; she could feel the intolerable desire tightening his body and the knowledge excited her. She clung to him, wanting, revelling in the strength that held her imprisoned.

Once more, Damian's head came down, the heat of his mouth scorching her lips as he began to kiss her. Deep, hungry kisses of consuming intensity; kisses of exploration and discovery, seeking and exulting in every tingling nuance of sensuality.

Such a warm lovely mouth, she thought as her own opened to it in instinctive response, welcoming, savouring, pleading to be loved. His marauding tongue was fierce and urgent, but his searching hands were gentle and caressing as they shaped the back of her head, her neck, then sliding down, sensuously fondling her breasts through the thin cotton fabric, with more urgency this time. Then, lifting the short skirt of her dress to gain access to the more intimate part of her, his fingers made their way slowly up her thighs, stroking her skin.

Moisture flooded Oriel's loins, the swollen bud throbbing as she craved release. Fighting her growing need to give him access to that place, she felt she would explode in fireworks if he so much as touched it. Her body stiffened and she brushed his hand away silently but forcefully, without breaking their kiss.

Damian didn't insist. When his lips finally pulled free of hers and he looked down into her eyes; they were both breathing hard.

She felt as she always did when he touched her: so confused, her mind and body fighting a storm that was getting out of control. How much longer could she ignore her passion for him?

Oriel stared at Damian, her every nerve ablaze, quivering with yearning, and the desire to be possessed by him was stronger than ever. 'I've told you before, you're the devil,' she choked.

His hand stroked her cheek as he held her tight. 'Maybe, *agápi mou*, but then a woman's face is the devil's mirror when she has eyes green and deep as the darkest jungle, where they say a man should never get lost,' he said hoarsely, his thumb tracing over the bottom edge of her mouth. '… And lips, *Theé!* Smooth and soft as the sweetest roses.'

Damian's arousing words left her helpless beneath the torrent of feeling that flooded her as she met the smouldering gaze beneath his dark brow. Whether she liked it or not, heart, mind, body and soul she belonged to this Greek god who, one night years ago, had swept her away to his heaven, while today she was burning in the hellish flames of her self-imposed abstinence. 'I will never force myself on you, *agápi mou*,' he murmured, his mouth still so near to hers. 'But you must know that our bodies are made for each other. You are fighting a losing battle, Calypso, and I will prove that to you.'

He was still holding her against his powerful, hard frame when there was the sound of knocking at the door. Quickly loosening her arms from around his neck, Damian moved away from her. With equal haste, Oriel stepped around the table and smoothed down her dress, flushed with frustrated desire, her mind in disarray.

'Yes, what is it?' Damian barked. He was already at his desk and, even while Oriel was trying to unravel her tangled thoughts at the same time as straightening her rumpled dress, she could see that he was equally disconcerted. The door opened and the wiry figure of Yorgos appeared.

'Sorry to disturb you, *Kyrios*. I'm sure you're already aware, but Yolanda is back on Helios. She wanted me to tell you that she's singing tonight at Manoli's. Her tour has been a sell-out so the place will be packed.'

Oriel turned to see a slight smile on the estate manager's face as he spoke, one she found deeply irritating. Suddenly her mind registered the name: *Yolanda*. It was her, the childhood sweetheart. Her scalp prickled with apprehension as she stared at Damian, whose face had paled.

'Perhaps you'd like me to get you and Yolanda a table after her act tonight?' Yorgos continued smoothly. 'You must have lots to catch up on.'

Damian ran a hand through his hair. 'I'm taking the team out tonight,' he said brusquely. 'We'll talk about this later, Yorgos.'

'Of course, as you like. If you want some privacy, just let me know.'

Damian looked at Yorgos, stony-faced. 'I said we'll talk later.'

Yorgos's obsidian eyes narrowed to two slits in a way that put Oriel in mind of a cornered fox. Then he nodded and retreated, closing the door behind him.

Oriel stood there, frozen to the spot, still feeling as if Damian's kiss was burning into her lips. She only managed a few words to break the oppressive silence between them. 'I'd like to go now.'

Then she turned her face from him and silently headed for the door as quickly as she could.

* * *

As she showered, Oriel couldn't seem to shake the combination of fear and excitement that stirred within her. There were no words to describe the soul-wrenching intimacy she felt with Damian and the debilitating confusion he created in her. Her skin, her limbs, her entire femininity had wanted to be crushed to every male inch of him. She had responded to this carnality with a savage abandon that, in retrospect, made her blush in shame.

Then, once again, her bubble of self-delusion had been burst. This time by the news that Damian's old flame, Yolanda, would apparently be performing to her adoring fans at Manoli's tonight. Was Damian still carrying a torch for her? She had seen how his face had paled at the mention of the singer's name.

Jealousy lanced through Oriel painfully. She winced under the stream of water as it cascaded down her face, willing it to wash her mind clean of all those tormenting thoughts. Why did she lack the self-discipline to stay away from Damian Lekkas? Why on earth could she not control this masochistic impulse to let him back into her life? Today was another reminder that she could never be with this man who was a 'conqueror of women', who had a childhood sweetheart waiting in the wings … a man who would one day fulfil his duty and choose a suitable Greek wife to carry on the family dynasty. No doubt he would keep this Yolanda woman as his mistress.

Still, despite all her misgivings, Oriel couldn't help but think about the alarming depths of passion between them. Her mind skittered back to that moment in his office, and the overwhelming sensual upheaval she felt in his arms; the way he looked at her, kissed her and touched her, as though he couldn't stop himself. It had left her shaken and speechless. Now, the sense of anticipation she felt at seeing Damian again tonight stalked her like a guilty secret, and her heart hammered with a thrilling ferocity that made her whole body tingle.

Oriel spent a long while showering, drying and brushing her hair, creaming her body and polishing her nails, all the while deep in thought. The sun was setting when finally, wrapped in her bath towel, she moved to her walk-in cupboard to select something to wear. She chose a sun-soaked yellow dress made of delicate chiffon with a strapless sweetheart line: almost a beach dress but with a sophisticated, classic cut. The ruched styling of the low bustier enhanced the curve of her breasts, and the softly pleated skirt that skimmed the tops of her knees swung as she walked, showing off her long legs. Her only adornment was a bold hammered-bronze handmade cuff that she had bought at a second-hand shop while on holiday in Turkey. She wore no make-up, apart from a touch of gloss on her lips and a hint of dark-brown mascara on her lashes.

Slipping into dainty gold stiletto sandals, she stroked some of her favourite fragrance behind her ears, at the centre of her throat and on her wrists, and then went to survey herself in the full-length mirror of her walk-in cupboard. It was casually elegant, she decided, even if it did expose quite a bit of skin.

A slight frown wrinkled her brow. A little voice in the recesses of her mind chided: *Why are you trying to keep Damian's fire burning when you've already rejected what he's offering?* Even so, she pushed the thought away determinedly. Another more impulsive part of her wanted Damian to find her attractive, particularly if his old girlfriend, Yolanda, was singing at the bar that night.

She glanced at her watch: it was almost eight o'clock. She grabbed her thin copper-coloured wrap and a small clutch bag then stepped out of her apartment, nearly colliding with Helena's wheel-chair.

'Out on the town, *Despinis* Anderson?'

She met the appraising steel-grey eyes that fixed on her face. Helena's cold gaze was unnerving. 'Yes, yes,' Oriel answered quickly, trying to sound natural.

'And who will you be trying to seduce tonight with that reveal-ing dress, eh?' the other woman jeered, her voice becoming ugly as she stared up at Oriel's suddenly pale features.

'Sorry?'

Helena's eyes narrowed. 'That harlot, his wife, was the same, walking around half naked, bringing shame on our family. While you're a guest in this house, you will cover yourself up, do you hear me? We have standing on this island, and we can't have any women of loose morals besmirching our good name.' She looked Oriel up and down, her expression sneering. 'You Englishwomen have no shame, you flaunt your flesh for all to see and then you cry rape if a man shows any interest.'

Oriel's chin snapped up and she glared frostily into the other woman's eyes. 'I'm sorry you feel that way, *Kyria*, but if you'll ex-cuse me, I must go now or I'll be late.' And without waiting for an answer she hurried past Helena and down the corridor, not looking back as she descended the stairs into the hallway. She stood a mo-ment at the bottom of the steps to regain her composure; she was trembling. Then, taking a deep breath, she walked out of the house and with a brisk step went to join her date.

Damian was waiting for her, leaning against his Jeep, smoking. He had swapped his casual outfit of earlier for a pair of black trousers – a cross between jeans and chinos – which caressed every line of his body, from his belted slim waist and narrow hips to his lithe, springy legs. The small gold medal on a necklace he wore drew attention to the dark down on his chest, which flirted with the edges of his thin, black, open-necked shirt. Tall, lean and tanned, his appearance was a veritable assailment of masculinity and it was all Oriel could do not to stare.

'Sorry if I'm late, Damian,' she said awkwardly as she came

up to him, 'but I was ambushed by your cousin on my way out.' Suddenly, she felt irritated; she was already trying to tamp down feelings of vulnerability about this evening, and Helena's appearance hadn't helped.

He eyed her cautiously. 'Everything all right?'

Oriel paused. Should she tell Damian about his cousin's vitriolic outburst? No, Helena's comments were just the embittered words of a jealous and deranged woman. Besides, talking of it to Damian now would just make her feel worse, she decided, and she needed to pull herself together. 'It's fine,' she answered blithely. 'I'm here now.'

His glance swept her figure as she stood in front of him in her golden dress. 'Yes, you are, beautiful Calypso, and looking so glamorous,' Damian said, still leaning against the car, his speech – like his gaze – slow, lazy and sensual as it moved over her body.

Undercurrents shimmered between them, almost visible in the silence of the night. For a moment Oriel found herself trapped in the quicksilver of Damian's steady regard, so that she pulled her wrap instinctively around her shoulders, feeling as if the embarrassed heat of her body would come right through the material.

'No need to do that, *agápi mou*, and deprive me of the pleasure of looking at so much of your beautiful velvet skin, even if you have forbidden me to touch it.'

Oriel would have loved to come up with some clever snippet of repartee, but Damian's disturbing allusions almost always left her speechless. A pink hue stole into her cheeks. He was only trying to bait her because she wouldn't let him take her to bed. Still, as always, he had taken her composure and snuffed it out, as he might a candle flame, between his strong fingers. He was no doubt adept at using his sensual way with words on women through plenty of practice, Oriel thought, as a swirl of emotion shot up inside her to a sharp and almost painful degree.

Straightening up, Damian regarded her now with an unreadable expression. He raked a lazy hand through his raven-black hair and then opened the door to the Jeep to let her in. Oriel watched him stroll round to the other side to take his seat next to her, all the while making a huge effort to drag her distracted senses back into line.

The door slammed and they shot away into the night. Oriel

looked out into the semi-darkness, trying to concentrate on the view as they took the coastal road. The shore was broad, and beneath the moonlight it appeared as white as snow, spread in tones of marble and velvet shadows, while on the hills above there was a grove of black trees.

Damian glanced at her. 'Manoli's is built on the site of an ancient Greek temple that overlooks the sea. I think you'll find it a magical scene.'

Oriel kept her head turned away as she stared into the night. 'That's what I love about these islands, the past is still so evident … though the modern world is impinging day by day and more buildings are appearing. Not here though.'

'How so?'

'From the minute I set foot on Helios, it struck me as different. Here, time seems to have stopped. Everything is as it would have been thousands of years ago. I love it.'

He shot her a wry look. 'You love the land but you despise its people.'

Her gaze snapped back to him. 'That's outrageous! Don't put words into my mouth, I never said that,' she exclaimed. Her eyes flashed olive-green, glittering as the baleful glare of a cougar. 'Just because I disapprove of arranged marriages, where a woman is merged into the possessions of a man, doesn't mean that I despise the people here. I only resent the rules that govern them, rules you talked about on the night of my arrival. *Your* rules!'

'They are not *my* rules, but customs and traditions that have held hard and proved effective over thousands of years. Who am I to dispute them, eh?'

Damian's passive attitude made Oriel bristle again. 'You should try at least to reform them. You're the educated one.'

'A wise man does not interfere with nature. Have you read *To Kill a Mockingbird?*'

'Yes, of course.'

'Atticus Finch says about nature: "Love her, but keep her wild." I've tried to apply that as much as I can in my life. I would no more try to change these people than I would attempt to tame a wild cat or force a woman into bed.' Damian gave her a knowing glance before he turned the car off the road. 'But we've arrived, *méli mou,* and so we'll have to postpone this interesting conversation to a later date,' he told Oriel as he brought the Jeep to a halt.

She let herself out of the car and immediately caught her breath. They were at the top of a cliff with their backs to the sea. Massive patches of black shadow scarred a broad expanse of earth and, here and there, she could make out where lines of rock and tumbled columns lay. All was still. The view was naturally limited by the light, and she found it difficult to assess space and the distance in the semi-darkness, but it seemed to her as if a miniature city, sliced off by time, was sprawled before her, reposing in a breathless trance. The moonlight lay like a dream of beauty on the ruins.

'What have we here?' she whispered, her eyes taking in the soulful mystery of the place.

Damian came to stand beside her. 'It's the site of an old acropolis. Legend has it that the city and its temple were built as a hideaway for Aphrodite and Ares, the illicit lovers.' A thread of amusement ran through his voice. 'Unfortunately, there's not much left of it, and Manoli has built his taverna inside what's left of the old palace. He's managed to make a feature of the temple, even though the columns are in bad condition and its roof has long gone. Even though I've been here many times, I've never had time to do a proper study of the site. Perhaps one day you could take a look at it. I'd value your opinion.'

He took a step forward and looked down at her with his intense, argent stare. Some distracted part of her mind registered that, in the evening light, his eyes shone like those of a hungry wolf.

'I'll make sure I make time for it,' she answered, tearing her gaze from his. They began walking side by side. As far as Oriel could make out, the ground was strewn with stone, brick and bits of wall. On her high heels she was struggling not to fall.

'Here, let me help you. I wouldn't like you to twist your ankle.'

Oriel felt the touch of his hand on hers and this time she didn't jerk away. They mounted a small slope, crushing wild herbs under their feet, filling the air with a tangy fragrance. Silence dragged between them, but Oriel knew that they were both aware of the current of physical attraction running directly from their fingers straight into one another's veins.

The cool breath of night blew Oriel's hair from her brow and played caressingly around her neck and across her face. She withdrew her hand from Damian's to push the strands away and, in so doing, lost her balance, and would have fallen if he hadn't moved instantly to catch her arm.

'You see what happens when you let go of me?' he admonished softly.

Oriel looked up at him and met the glinting slits of granite and saw the tension in his face as he slowly dropped his hands to his sides. She could tell that he was fighting with his senses, trying to control his need for her and, in response, it was as if a slim flame burned within her body. The moonlight played over the width of his shoulders and gleamed in the medal half buried in the dark hairs of his chest.

More than ever Damian reminded her of a pagan god and she felt the yearning deep in her belly, even as she hated him for making her feel so insecure around him. Oriel's hunger for Damian consumed her, just like the mouth of a great sea anemone devouring its prey of little fish. She pulled away, forcing herself to avert her gaze in case what she felt for him was showing nakedly in her eyes.

Already the loud music of the taverna could be heard from afar, floating on the air. They entered through an arch in the ancient wall and walked along a vast corridor, down which spilled a broad pathway of golden light from the taverna. From a distance, its glowing lights beneath the moon's soft splendour gave Manoli's the outward appearance of a serene bethel at heaven's door. Inside, though, it was almost a shock to find whitewashed walls decorated with crude drawings of fish, crayfish and a giant mermaid. There were shelves of hollow gourds and empty wine bottles filled with dried herbs. Copper pots and pans hung from the ceiling, interspersed with strings of garlic and large bunches of red onions. Brightly coloured chequered cloths covered the tables and in the far corner stood a gleaming copper brazier. There were a surprising number of people inside, seated at the tables, enjoying good food and wine or at the bar that took up a whole wall at the end of the room.

Some of the men, Oriel noticed, were wearing the Greek traditional costume, which consisted of a shirt with very wide sleeves, knee-length baggy trousers supported by a cummerbund, and leather sandals worn over short black stockings. Men and women alike seemed all to be in high spirits, talking at once, arguing and roaring with laughter, their voices competing with the blasts of Greek pop music coming from a 1950s jukebox. Beside her, Damian gestured to it and leaned in, speaking into her ear in a raised voice. 'Manoli's new acquisition,' he explained. 'He's very proud of it.'

The noise was horrendous; the whole place looked as if it had been overcome in a delirium of wine and song, and Oriel was relieved when, taking her arm, Damian guided her to the open courtyard.

'Our table is outside,' he told her as they walked towards a tall arched doorway and stepped out again into the fresh air.

The first thing Oriel saw as they left the crowded room were the remains of a temple set on a promontory, jutting out to sea. Although roofless and almost in ruins, its twenty-four Ionic columns of incomparable grace and beauty still stood, braving the harshness of time and weathered by the winds of more than two thousand years. They seemed to possess a life of their own as they caught the silver beams of the moon. The phosphorescent light, the glory of night, poured down on to the whitened stone of the monument where once stood the foundations of an ancient civilization, chipped out of the earth's rock.

'This site is enormous, and those columns … twenty-four of them, so white, so pure, so intimidating. Awesome!' Oriel gasped.

Damian gazed out at the distant ruin. 'The temple is usually lit up at night, except when the moonlight is as bright as it is tonight. But this isn't the best time to see it. Its true beauty appears at dusk and at sunrise when colour floods over the columns. I've seen them pearly pink at dawn and golden at sunset, when bathed in the ver-milion shades of twilight. They're like actors taking on the character and personality of their surroundings.'

A long table was set further down, next to the parapet that looked over the cliffs to the sea. It stood on a wide paved terrace, surrounded by tall cedar pines and old gnarled olive trees, dimly lit by lamps hanging from low branches. A large group of about twenty or so islanders was already seated, including Stavros and the rest of the crew, who raised their glasses as Damian and Oriel appeared, and the whole table began clamouring.

Someone she didn't recognize called out above the noise of greetings: 'Hey, Damian, we've been waiting for you!' Then another voice: 'You haven't shown up here for months, where have you been? These evenings aren't the same when you're not around!' And at that, all the others started to stamp their feet and bang the table, shouting out his name.

Oriel glanced at him. This was a man who was clearly loved, giving her, once again, a totally different picture from the one Yorgos had painted of him on the first day, and much more akin to the person she had discovered in the past two.

Damian laughed at the affectionate reception of his friends. Suddenly he looked happy, relaxed and so much younger, Oriel thought. 'Absence makes the heart grow fonder, isn't that the way the saying goes?' he called out, his deep, strong voice rising above the noise.

'Not always,' came the booming shout from the giant Yanni, winking at Spyros and giving him a playful slap on the back, making the young man nearly choke on his drink. 'This sprat's just got back from the mainland, and I'm wishing he'd stayed there.'

'Clean bill of health!' Spyros coughed and lifted his glass to Damian and Oriel, grinning.

Some of the group left their places and came to greet Damian, pulling him away towards the table and, for a few minutes, there was a lot of hugging and kissing amid the outburst of chatter, while Oriel stood, a little awkwardly, where he'd left her. Though she had witnessed this custom of tactile greeting many times in Mediterranean countries, as well as in the Middle East and Latin America, the fact never ceased to surprise her; it was so alien to England, where some fathers still never kissed or even hugged their sons. She loved the warmth of these people of the sun, as she called them; she'd always believed that the weather had a lot to do with their behaviour.

As she waited for the euphoria to calm down, a man wearing chinos and a black T-shirt detached himself from the group and came towards her. The slight tension she felt at standing alone, mostly among strangers, waiting for Damian to return, melted away as she realized that the man was Vassilis Markopoulos, the archaeologist friend of Damian's she'd met at the temple site, and a smile of recognition lit up her face. He strode up to her, grabbing both of her hands in his, an answering grin showing even white teeth against his tanned skin.

'*Despinis* Anderson!' he said, kissing her on both cheeks. He stood back to admire her outfit. 'You look fabulous.' His eyebrow quirked. 'That's not to say you don't look ravishing in your work clothes, but this takes a man's breath away.'

Oriel couldn't help but laugh. She had been warned so vociferously about the men in Damian's crew and their vulgar ways, not least of all the unwanted attention she was bound to receive from them, yet there was something honest and straightforward about Vassilis. She found his boyish charm appealing – the black curls that flopped over his forehead, the cleft chin and the college-boy mannerisms that he must have picked up in the States when he was studying there. It helped too that, having spent an afternoon working with him at the Minoan excavation site, Oriel was certain he respected her. She did not doubt for an instant that he thought of her as anything but an equal, so she entered into the relaxed flirtation willingly.

'You don't look so bad yourself. Amazing, isn't it, how different we look once the dust has been brushed off?' She beamed at him. 'Actually, I'm very happy you're here. It was a little intimidating standing here among all these strangers.'

'Well, if Damian's foolish enough to leave you untended for a moment, then he has only himself to blame if I spirit you away.' He winked and gave her another engaging smile. 'Here, let me get you a drink and we can sit down. What will you have, ouzo, retsina, or would you prefer a gin and tonic, or perhaps a Martini?'

'Ouzo will be perfect, thank you.'

Vassilis snapped his fingers at a waiter who was hovering, ready to take orders. '*Ena ouzo, parakaló,* for the young lady here,' he said, before guiding her to the table where he had been seated. Oriel was just about to take her place next to him when a large hand gripped her arm in a vice.

'Ah, Vassilis, you moved fast, my friend. I leave *Despinis* Anderson for one moment and she's already been appropriated by you, I see. Always on the lookout for a pretty woman, eh?' The deep voice that had spoken sounded friendly enough, but as Oriel turned her head to look at Damian's fingers curled around the bare skin just above her elbow, she felt something hard as flint beneath his words. She lifted her eyes with express slowness to meet his, colliding with the laser-sharp irises. The look she gave him was almost as cutting as his, and he let go of her arm.

'Where would men be without women, eh? You tell me, my friend,' Vassilis joked, still relaxed on the surface, but Oriel was sure the undercurrents hadn't escaped him either.

'Oh, I'm sure we'd manage,' came the laconic answer.

'Then you'll not object if I monopolize *Despinis* Anderson tonight.'

'It depends if *Despinis* Anderson wants to be monopolized, eh?' He was studying Oriel, his grey eyes sweeping her with the slow deliberation that never failed to send colour flooding her cheeks.

An involuntary sound of protest escaped her lips and she smiled at Vassilis. 'I'm perfectly happy here with *Kyrios* Markopoulos, thank you.'

Damian bowed mockingly. 'Your wishes are my command, *Kyria*,' he laughed, the sound low and sensual, and infinitely disturbing. 'I'll leave you then. Have a pleasant evening.' Then, turning on his heel, he went to join the group sitting at the other end of the table, leaving Oriel with a hollow feeling in her stomach.

Vassilis grinned and pulled a chair out for her. 'Now that's settled, let's enjoy the evening. By the way, do call me Vassilis. And I will, if I may, call you Oriel?'

'Of course. I've been carefully trying to follow the Greek code of politeness, but it'll be a relief not to have to be so formal.'

The long table was soon covered in small plates of *mezedes*, displayed like works of art on the red chequered tablecloth. There were little pies of spinach, cheese and seafood wrapped in filo pastry, chunks of *saganaki*, a fried yellow cheese, black Kalamata olives, cod's roe, *tzatziki* and *kolokythoanthoi*, zucchini flowers stuffed with rice and herbs.

Once they had both helped themselves from the plates of food, Vassilis continued their conversation. 'This can't be your first visit to Greece as you speak the language so fluently.'

'*Oyhee*, no, six years ago I spent months travelling all over Greece, although my main base was Aegina.'

'Well, you must have had a good teacher. You've hardly any accent at all.' His eyes sparkled mischievously. 'A Greek boyfriend too, eh?'

She almost rolled her eyes at the comment, refusing to take the bait. 'No, I'm afraid it wasn't a Greek boyfriend who taught me how to speak your language. I read classical and modern Greek at university because I wanted to become an archaeologist, and I was fascinated by Greek history in particular.'

'Of course,' Vassilis had the good grace to look sheepish at her slightly pointed tone. 'That makes sense. By the way, congratulations on bringing up the Alexander bronze. What a find!'

'Yes, it was very exciting.' She lowered her voice. 'We'll have to keep it under our hats, though. We don't want treasure hunters appearing from all directions.'

'Absolutely. Just the close team,' nodded Vassilis.

After the *mezedes* they ordered *briàm*, an oven-baked Greek version of ratatouille and *kleftiko*, which Vassilis explained was cooked 'bandit-style'. 'The lamb is first marinated in lemon juice and garlic, and then slow-baked on the bone in a pit oven. The story goes that the Klephts, who were bandits in the hills and didn't have flocks of their own, used to steal the lambs in the valley and cook the meat in a sealed pit to avoid the smoke being noticed.'

The night air was fresh and cool on Oriel's face. The atmosphere was relaxed and carefree. Some of the crew came over to speak to her and Vassilis from time to time, and clinked glasses with them before staggering off to find more ouzo or brandy. It felt good having people talk to her warmly and without restraint – she was made to feel part of the group, not a mere stranger.

Vassilis was entertaining and witty. He told her about his years spent in the United States after studying archaeology there, and how he'd set up his own company, getting commissions on sites all over the world. His flirting was subtle and he made Oriel laugh. He wasn't the first sophisticated man she'd spent an evening with. Over the years she had been wined and dined, and had received her fair share of compliments. She'd been flattered by some and left cold by others, but none had touched a special chord in her soul as Damian had.

Oriel was enjoying her evening, and yet she found that her thoughts turned often to the man who was sitting at the head of the table, and to whom her eyes were drawn from time to time, despite herself. But he seemed oblivious to her and appeared to be half listening to two young women clearly competing for his attention.

As he threw back small glasses of ouzo, she noticed he smoked one cigarette after another, the famous Gitanes. The brand suited him well, she thought; the sensual blue graphic of a gypsy dancing archly against a cloud of smoke, her wispy undulations in space casting imaginative and passionate reveries before the smoker's vacant gaze. Oriel's eyes travelled to Damian's face. What was he thinking? What was he dreaming of? The shadows hid his expression but somehow she felt his loneliness. Angry with herself now for thinking about him again, she made a concerted effort to push him from her mind, but to no avail.

Midnight was on the threshold. Inside, the taverna had become noisier as people were dancing the *sirtaki*, a dance that had become popular after the film *Zorba the Greek*, for which it had been invented. Oriel had tried it once, a long time ago, when she was still engaged to Rob, and had found it fun. Even in an isolated place like Helios, it seemed some influences from the outside world had penetrated, she thought to herself. Perhaps the island wasn't so trapped in its own time bubble after all.

Once the dancing had finished inside, more people spilled out on to the terrace. In the corner, a couple of musicians, one on the *bouzoúki*, the long-necked Greek mandolin, and another on the clarinet, now struck up a song. Oriel watched as men and women gathered to dance in a ring, holding their hands high in the air, feet crossing nimbly as they stepped from side to side with the swinging rhythm of the music. Another group of women joined in, singing along in unison with a meandering melody. She suddenly saw that Damian had moved from his seat and was now taking his place on the right end of the curved line of dancers to whistles from the crowd.

He led the circle of dancers, pulling a twisted handkerchief from the back pocket of his jeans that were slung above his hips with a belt, and Oriel couldn't help but notice how they showed the tapered outline of his torso. The appearance of the handkerchief was a signal that the men were dancing alone, and the women fell back into the throng of onlookers who clapped in time to the lilting music.

Damian's body was gracefully masculine, his hips swivelling with each bouncing step as he waved the handkerchief, swaying along with the other men. He kicked up his foot in front then behind the other leg, as the others followed suit. Oriel's eyes were fastened on Damian's back, the muscles rippling visibly under his shirt as he lifted his hands to place them on the shoulders of his fellow dancers while they all did likewise. Every now and then, a man would detach himself from the circle and leap up, slapping his heel to the approving cries of '*Ópa!*' from the ring of dancers, who dragged their feet smoothly with a skip and a hop along to the beat. The music began speeding up and the men began shouting '*Ópa! Ópa!*' with glee as they got caught up in the relentless pull of the dance.

As she watched, a group of people moved to obscure Oriel's view and she shook herself, sighing. Her gaze wandered upwards. The moon was low; it looked so close, touching the landscape with silver, accentuating the mystery around them. As the breeze swept through the trees and echoed against the stone of the nearby temple, a hint of nostalgic sadness hung in the velvety night sky, where alien stars blazed in place of the more familiar Southern Cross that spread its kite-like shape over the Thames. Oriel wondered, was she homesick? No, she was heartsick from hankering after a man to whom she was fatally attracted but who would never love her, even though he lusted after her, and who would eventually break her heart if she ever gave in to the enchantment of their chemistry.

It was getting late. Wine, retsina and ouzo were still flowing freely. The meal went on endlessly as more and more appetizers were brought to the table. Some of the locals, who had been sitting in the taverna, were beginning to spill out on to the courtyard and, not for the first time tonight, Oriel noted that the Greeks were a happy lot, liking to be surrounded by their friends, laughter and music.

Vassilis glanced at his watch. 'Ah, it is almost time for Yolanda to sing.'

Oriel tensed. In the noisy atmosphere of the taverna and her conversation with Vassilis, she'd almost forgotten about the nightclub singer, but not quite. 'I hear she's quite something,' she murmured. Her gaze caught Damian, who had returned to the table and had lit up another Gitane. After the boisterous dancing, he was now oddly distracted once more.

Vassilis refilled his glass. 'She's certainly got an incredible voice. Very Greek,' he answered. 'You just wait until you hear her. She's sung all over the world, you know. She has a recording deal, too, but she still likes to return home in the summer months. She is the *aidóni*, the nightingale of the island, well known for her improvised *rebetiko* songs, a sort of urban blues.' He took a gulp of retsina. 'She's been courted by millionaires, film stars, even royalty. But Yolanda Christodoulou has only ever had eyes for one man ... Damian Lekkas.'

Even though this wasn't news to her, the name brought a swift, sharp pang to Oriel's stomach; still, she managed to laugh. 'Yes, he seems to be quite the ladies' man.' A thought then struck her. 'Christodoulou ... the same surname as *Kyrios* Lekkas's estate manager.'

'Yes, Yorgos is Yolanda's brother. Some people say he's there to keep an eye on Damian, who's always had women vying for his attention. He's a very good catch, even more so since he became not only a widower but the sole heir to a great fortune. Trust me, more women than I care to count fight like cats over him, and Yorgos is hoping that Damian will eventually marry Yolanda.'

'How awkward for him.' No wonder the estate manager took such evident glee in pointing out that the singer would be here at Manoli's tonight.

'Oh, I wouldn't worry about Damian. So far he's managed to elude them all and, apart from Yolanda, no one has had a hold on him ... yet.'

'I think I heard somewhere that they were childhood sweethearts.'

Vassilis nodded, sipping his retsina. 'But they were forbidden to marry because Yolanda comes from a totally different background. There were rumours at the time that she had no intention of marrying because her career was just taking off and she didn't want any ties. Who can say? Anyhow, he ended up marrying the rich heiress, Cassandra. And we know how that ended.'

Oriel forbore from quizzing him on the subject of Cassandra. Besides, she was too busy processing the information about Yolanda. Instead, she couldn't help herself asking: 'He's a widower now, so what stops him from marrying Yolanda?'

'I don't think Damian will ever marry again. This is a small island and there's always gossip floating around. Some say Yolanda is his mistress, and always was, even when he was married.'

Before Oriel could utter a rejoinder, Vassilis nudged her. 'Speak of the devil,' he said in a low voice. 'Here she comes. Ravishing, isn't she?'

At first, all that Oriel could wonder was how a woman so petite could emit such a strong charisma. There was subtlety there too, as if the singer knew that her striking looks needed nothing more than a simple black dress, with no other embellishment, to set off her beauty. Everything about the young woman was feminine and she had an aura of dark sensuality that Oriel realized, with a uneasy twinge, reminded her of Damian's.

Oriel and Vassilis continued to watch Yolanda as she made her way sinuously through the groups of standing drinkers, some of whom broke off from their conversation and laughter to stare, while others were bold enough to engage her in a word. A moment later, the dark beauty was standing beside Vassilis, who had enough presence of mind not to look flustered by her attentions.

Oriel couldn't help staring at Yolanda's face as she spoke to Vassilis. The elegant outline of the woman she'd seen in the paparazzo photo only hinted at her full impact. There was something imperious about the singer's perfect Greek profile – almost austere – and, together with the mass of shining hair, dark as a raven's wing, that tumbled down her back in luxuriant waves, she looked almost as if sculpted by some ancient master.

That illusion of coolness was banished, however, by her striking, velvet-black eyes, fringed with thick dark lashes and flashing a blaze in their depths that countered that first impression. Flawless copper skin added extra warmth to the singer's beauty, and Oriel's eyes moved instinctively to Yolanda's vermilion mouth as she spoke to Vassilis, taking in the perfect white teeth. She reflected for a moment that the canines had a sharpness to them that gave the singer an almost mustelid quality; indeed there was something mink-like in the quick, neat gestures Yolanda made as she spoke, and a rapaciousness in the way her pointed little tongue darted over her teeth when she laughed.

'So, Vassilis, it's good to see you here,' Yolanda was saying. 'I miss all the fun we used to have with Damian. Wasn't it wild? He's more intense these days, don't you think? Though I can't say that doesn't have its attractions.' She gave a dimpled, wicked little smile, and Vassilis laughed. She had that way, Oriel realized, of making the person she was addressing feel like they were the centre of her world. It seemed that Vassilis wasn't immune to such flattery, but he didn't forget himself so far that he failed to remember his manners.

'Yolanda, I don't think you've met Oriel Anderson,' he said, breaking the intimacy of the *tête à tête* the singer had orchestrated. 'She's joined the dive team as archaeologist.'

Yolanda held out a perfectly manicured hand with crimson nails, offering it almost regally. Oriel found herself holding it for a split-second before it was sharply withdrawn, and the singer's eyes were once more fixed on those of Vassilis. 'Another of Damian's lovely interns.' She dimpled again as she spoke, and Oriel couldn't be certain if Vassilis was aware of the rudeness of Yolanda's appraisal, or the fact that the singer couldn't be bothered to look at her when she spoke.

Vassilis gave Oriel a reassuring wink. 'Goodness, no. Oriel outdoes any of us when it comes to her knowledge of archaeology. The team is more than a little impressed. We're finding it hard to keep up with her, isn't that right, Oriel?'

Oriel laughed, a little embarrassed, but glad to see that Vassilis's comments had been met with a swiftly veiled look of annoyance in Yolanda's eyes. It was then that she realized that he had the exact measure of Yolanda and was perfectly happy to thwart her.

Yolanda gave a tight smile. 'I hope you are being looked after. Vassilis has always had perfect manners, and would never let a wallflower stand around on her own.' Oriel and Vassilis's eyes met for a brief second, both acknowledging the rudeness implicit in Yolanda's words.

'I'm certainly not doing my gentlemanly duty tonight,' said Vassilis smoothly. 'I couldn't see another person in the room whom I would rather be with, so I got in quickly and monopolized Oriel,' he said, smiling deep into her eyes.

He turned back to Yolanda, with a little grin of devilment.

'Damian is making sure to look after her, too. Oriel's lucky enough to be staying at Heliades,' he said.

For the slightest moment Oriel thought she could detect a narrowing of Yolanda's eyes, as if the diva were sizing her up. Then, once again, the singer showed her dazzling row of perfect pointy teeth in a bright smile, although now her eyes held ice rather than fire. 'Well, I'll leave you both to it then,' she said shortly, before walking away towards the stage, her hips moving fluidly as she went.

Vassilis laughed, his eyes gleaming with amusement. 'Well, that showed her. I couldn't resist winding up the little vixen. To be honest, I don't know what Damian sees in her.' He paused before qualifying his statement. 'Of course, I do see she has some rather obvious attractions, but he should know better by now. She's had him dancing to her tune for far too long.'

Oriel, her spirits dampened, suddenly imagined Yolanda's perfect caramel-coloured body entwined with Damian's and the muscles in her stomach contracted painfully again. Luckily she was saved from responding. A hush had fallen over the courtyard. Waiters were setting chairs in a semicircle and a man with an aquiline face and black moustache appeared, wearing a black-beaded kerchief on his forehead and jackboots on his feet. With almost reverential respect, he announced: 'The great Yolanda Christodoulou will sing to you *Agapi Pou Gines Dilopo Maxairi*, which Oriel mentally translated as: My Love You Turned into a Double-Edged Knife, a well known song that Melina Mercouri had made famous twenty years before in the film *Stella*.

A more extensive band now appeared and took up their places around an imaginary stage. The ensemble was a traditional lineup of two *bouzoúkia*, a *baglamadaki*, the long-necked bowl-lute, a guitar, an accordion, a set of *cochilias* seashells that the Greeks use as percussion instruments, and a portable piano. The silence was so profound you could have heard a pin fall. And then the diva appeared to a shower of applause.

The song was full of passion and melancholy, a plaintive melody with an exotic, flagrant Mediterranean feel to it. Without shame, Yolanda sung of her yearning and her nostalgia for the man who filled her soul with fire. Her dark eyes fixed on Damian, glittering almost with tears, and it seemed as though her heart spilled out her desire and pain.

> *Once upon a time you gave me nothing but joy,*
> *But now you drown the joy in tears.*
> *I can't find a way out of this, I can't find a cure.*
> *I can see fire burning in his eyes,*
> *The stars disappear when he looks at me.*
> *Turn off the lights, turn off the moonlight,*
> *Don't let him see my pain when he takes me …*

Damian had turned his chair, his back to Oriel. He was still smoking but the expression on his face and his eyes were hidden from her. What was he feeling? Was he moved, like Yolanda's audience, who watched spellbound by her half-vampish, half-waiflike image and that languid look that transferred itself to her voice? Was he mesmerized, electrified under the magic she seemed to weave around her, like every man in the taverna who stared at her, goggle-eyed, with undisguised longing, tugging at their moustaches and sucking on their cigarettes? Or, unlike them, was he unaffected by that sexual frenzy she was stirring in her male admirers? Oriel hoped fiercely it was the latter.

An involuntary shiver ran down her spine as, nevertheless, for one horrifying moment, she held a clear vision of their bodies interlocked in lovemaking. Images of Damian lying with this diva flashed before her: his strong, beautiful, masculine body stretched against hers, his muscled arms holding her, clasping her, moulding her to his hardness. Oriel was not a jealous person by nature. Never before had she experienced the piercing pain that was twisting in her heart now and the need for this man whom she hardly knew.

Her eyes were stinging; involuntary tears poured down her cheeks. Vassilis's hand covered hers. She glanced at it but couldn't move. How ironic. He probably thought that she had been moved by Yolanda's song, like other members of the audience who had taken out their handkerchiefs. It brought her abruptly back to reality and she told herself staunchly not to think about Damian's love life; he could sleep with whomever he pleased and it was absolutely nothing to do with her. Still, who was she fooling? Deep down, Oriel knew those were empty words and she hated herself for being so weak.

The night was wearing on. The song had ended now to a shower of applause and flowers. Yolanda bowed and blew kisses to her fans, who were shouting and asking for more. And then, suddenly, Damian stood up and approached the band. As he slipped a banknote to the bandleader, he whispered something to him. The musician nodded and he stepped away.

Almost immediately there was a noticeable quieting of the crowd as the familiar notes of the *rebetiko* song demanded everyone's attention. Oriel recognized it immediately. She had heard it many times in the tavernas around Greece. *Sa Maghemeno To Myalo Mou* – As if Enchanted, my Mind – it told the story of a man who loves a woman who shuns him, and he languishes over his ill-fated love.

What Oriel had not expected was that Damian was going to dance the *zeibekiko*, a highly expressive, freeform dance performed by a solo male dancer for himself, which she had read about but had never seen.

Damian stretched out his arms as though they were the wings of a bird, and started his slow-moving circular dance, his manner introspective, eyes downcast as though in a trance, while a group of men and women knelt around him, clapping their hands to the rhythm, symbolizing the friends that would not leave a man alone with his pain.

Yolanda sang the emotional words: 'As if enchanted my mind hovers, and my every thought dangles around you,' and Damian, his eyes still fixed on the floor, danced around an imaginary antagonist, bending to touch the ground and hissing from time to time like a hawk on attack. His motion kept within limited movements to start off with, then evolved into more elaborate ones as the song became more poignant. It was a dance of passion and sorrow, full of sighs and heartbreak, of fears and pain, full of despair and unfulfilled love; the grief of a tortured soul in a dreamlike, slow-motion rhythm. The mixture of deep introspection and flamboyant display was as enticing as a peacock's tail.

Looking at them from a distance, Oriel sensed a strange current at war between Damian and Yolanda. Proud-boned, their silent dialogue seemed cruel at times. They were two of a kind, meant by all the laws of Greek blood to be together instead of held apart by conventional traditions, she thought. The passion in Damian's dance told of homage to the thwarted love he felt for his old flame, who stood before him, serenading his pain.

There was no applause at the end; it didn't seem to be expected. Some of Damian's friends came up and hugged him, and kissed Yolanda.

'Did you enjoy it?' Vassilis asked, turning to Oriel.

'Yes, immensely,' she said, distrait, and forcing a smile to her lips.

'Have you seen the *zeibekiko* performed before?'

'Yes, no … but I've read about it.'

Vassilis was talking to her, but Oriel was not really listening any more, answering him in monosyllables. She longed to run away and find some dark corner so she could gather her thoughts privately but, instead, the dictates of convention, not to mention her own pride, demanded that she should stay in this crowded, noisy place, sipping wine and talking to Vassilis as if her heart weren't being sliced into pieces. She could not possibly have said what subjects they talked about; it was enough that she *did* talk, that she was giving the impression that she was thoroughly enjoying herself with no hint at all of the turmoil inside.

Oriel never knew that she had it in her to be such an accomplished actress. Damian and Yolanda were two charismatic people, childhood lovers whose passion had defeated the passage of time and she had seen it for herself – her Greek god's heart was already given to a glamorous Greek goddess. The force of this reality suddenly hit home with a hard, cruel blow.

How very naïve of her, she thought. Common sense dictated that Damian must inevitably have someone in his life to whirl to the very heights of heaven with one of his special kisses, to bewitch utterly with his sensual words, to capture body, soul and spirit by the sheer magic of his personality. And still, she'd been sure that his desire for her was equal to her own. The moments when he had held her in his arms, Oriel had felt his tall, lean body tremble with emotion like an aspen quivering in the breeze, and had been aware of the tumultuous pounding of his heart. How could he at the same time justify these feelings for Yolanda, his all-time love? Was he so fickle that he could court one woman while swearing undivided love to another?

Now groups of people were dispersing, and Oriel looked at her watch: it was past two in the morning. The air was warm, and the stars burned hazily overhead. Moonlight lay on the temple, and the smooth black waters of the Ionian were broken only by the long bands of phosphorescence lighting their lapping darkness.

'Can I give you a lift back to Heliades?' Vassilis asked as he saw Oriel gathering her shawl and bag.

'Thanks, but since I came with *Kyrios* Lekkas, I think it's only polite to leave with him.'

Vassilis raised an eyebrow. 'I understand. But consider too that maybe it would be a relief for Damian if he didn't have to drive you. Yolanda's villa is in the opposite direction to Heliades …'

Vassilis had a point: the last thing she wanted was to be a burden. She glanced over at Damian, and saw him bidding farewell to his friends. Oriel watched him toss back a last glass of wine abruptly, and then he was coming towards her. He resembled a dark, brooding force – lethal, she acknowledged, noting the long strides he took and the glitter in his gaze, which was riveted on her for the first time since she had sat at the table with Vassilis.

'That was a moving performance you and Yolanda gave us tonight,' Vassilis told him.

Damian's nod was almost indifferent. 'Thanks. I'm afraid we haven't had time to discuss the wreck tonight, too many people and too many distractions.'

Vassilis folded his arms. 'Stavros started to put me in the picture earlier today. Sounds exciting.'

Damian shifted his gaze away from Oriel to his friend, his expression impassive. 'We need to have a serious talk to decide how we're going to go about it. Some of the items will be difficult to extricate, and I don't want to damage the wreck.'

'I spoke to Stavros about it. We think, with your approval, we should buy a new pump. If we go about it carefully we shouldn't disturb the site too much. I can get the latest model from the US.'

'Great. Go ahead with that. We'll talk again after the weekend.'

Vassilis agreed then turned to Oriel. 'Are you sure you don't want a lift back, Oriel?'

She saw Damian wince at his friend's deliberate familiarity, and before she could answer he cut in: '*Despinis* Anderson came with me and I will take her back.' There was a leashed quality in his stance that boded ill should she dare consider rebellion.

'I thought you might have had other interests to pursue tonight,' Vassilis said, with eyes that twinkled with innuendo.

Damian chose to ignore his friend's remark. 'Goodnight, Vassilis. See you next week.' Then he linked his arm firmly through Oriel's. 'Shall we go?' His touch was impersonal yet flames burned within her, with every separate nerve-end quivering into vibrant life, each individual skin cell craving his contact.

'Goodnight, Vassilis, and thank you for making me feel so welcome this evening,' she said over her shoulder. Damian's grip tightened on her skin, letting her feel the pressure of his strong fingers as he began manoeuvring her firmly through the crowd.

They went back to the car in silence, Oriel having difficulty keeping up with Damian's long stride – he was almost dragging her along. They sped back to Heliades, racing unsteadily round hairpin bends, each wrapped in thought, the island stretching away in deep mystery on either side of them as the stars winked above.

Oriel's eyes glanced at the dark, proud outline of the man seated next to her. The easy feeling that had existed between them the day of the dive, as they worked side by side, had evaporated, replaced by a familiar tension. The tanned, capable hands that held the wheel were tight-knuckled; the rugged profile of the driver was taut. She wondered what was he thinking at this precise moment. Why was he so angry? Had he really been offended that she had chosen to sit with Vassilis instead of with him? What did he care? After all, he had other fish to fry, as she had discovered this evening. Or was it just his macho Greek pride niggling at him?

They arrived at the house much quicker than it had taken them to get to Manoli's earlier that evening. Oriel's bag had slipped to the ground and, by the time she had bent over to pick it up, Damian was already opening the door of the Jeep to let her out. Ice crossed with flame as she stepped out and faced him. The cutting, diamond edge of his gaze was drawing her into its unfathomable depths and, despite herself, she stood mesmerized for a few seconds like a small animal caught in the powerful glare of headlights. Her eyes dropped down to the open neckline of his shirt that revealed the curling black hairs on his chest. It evoked an overwhelming desire in Oriel to slip her hands under the thin material and feel the warmth of his skin and the hardness of his muscles. It was a heady thought, one that sent her reeling backwards, away from him.

'Thank you, Damian. Goodnight.' Turning abruptly, she ran up the steps to the front door. Hassan, who had stayed up for his master, stood there waiting like a statue in the shadows, and Oriel detected something like a protective, vigilant glance in her direction too as she approached. She slowed down as she entered the house, expecting Damian to follow her inside but, seconds later, she heard the engine start up and the sound of the Jeep drawing away, dwindling into the nothingness of the night.

* * *

Damian drove off in a savage mood. He couldn't remember the last time he'd felt this angry. He was furious at Oriel and Vassilis – and at the world in general – but most of all, his anger was directed towards himself. Oriel had looked stunning in that yellow dress but he had felt the blood boil in his veins as he thought of all the men at Manoli's who must have ogled her and fantasized about her incredible body. When he'd seen her with Vassilis he couldn't have stopped the words that had tumbled out of his mouth if he'd tried. Vassilis was his friend but, *me to Theó,* by God, Damian had wanted to punch him tonight. It was all he could do to feign an air of indifference when hot jealousy was burning his insides like lava.

They'd had two such wonderful days, he and Oriel, working side by side the day of the dive and walking through the grounds of his olive press this afternoon; and now he had gone and spoilt it all with his snide comments. All day he had been looking forward to the time when, after dinner at the taverna, he would take her on to the beach and kiss her senseless, telling her how she made him feel. Oh, at first, of course, she would push him away as usual but then she would submit and her body would yield to its needs – a fire that only he could assuage. But he had blown it and, consequently, had

199

spent the evening in a foul temper.

As usual, he had been a target for unattached females, and there had been plenty of them, all beautiful and ready for a little fun. Even Yolanda, who had looked particularly enticing tonight, had left him cold. Yolanda … now there was a thorny issue. Why hadn't she told him she was returning tonight? Her song had made no secret of the way she felt about him, but that was another story.

The headlights slashed across the quiet countryside, which had long gone to sleep as the Jeep roared through the night. The air was hot with a heaviness that sat oppressively upon Damian. He stared at his fingers, clenched hard on the steering wheel. Where was he going? Anywhere, nowhere, what did it matter? He would just drive until he'd calmed down.

He drove for hours around the island, with fantasies of Oriel naked and needing him flashing through his mind like an erotic film. Oriel in his arms, her body moulded against his, her head thrown back exposing her throat, eager for his caresses. Oriel moaning against his mouth as he tasted her lips and drunk thirstily; Oriel's breasts in his hands, the lush curves and the hard peaks igniting his need; Oriel whispering to him of the places she wanted him to stroke and then parting her legs so he could better explore the mystery of her delicate, warm flesh. His loins throbbed as he imagined her crying out his name, words of passion and love on her lips when he filled her, opening up to him as he moved deeper and deeper into the heat of her damp softness – she, desperate and wild, shuddering underneath him, begging for more.

Damn it! He wasn't angry any more but totally aroused.

Her words came back to him.

I've told you before, you're the devil.

Well, the devil had taken hold of him tonight. Lust pounded in his veins and Damian glared at the road, feeling the straining arousal in his trousers. A muscle in his jaw jerked. If he went to bed now, even after a cold shower, it would be hours before he found sleep … that was *if* he found sleep. He dragged one hand down his face. He must stop this. No more memories, no more fantasies; he had to either convince Oriel that they were made for each other or erase her totally from his mind, otherwise he would go mad.

He finally found himself at the port. Damian swung out of

the car. Nothing but peace lay around him and above his head. The beach was deserted and the sea monotonously calm, its little wavelets the only whisper in the overall hush. The night sky was paling to blue, the moon fading away, and the stars that had burned all night were beginning to extinguish their winking light; it was almost dawn, and land and sea were covered in a thin transparent mist that gave the scene an almost ghostly, unreal impression.

Damian paused for a moment, taking in the heady sense of isolation. He inhaled huge gasps of the salted air, pure and crisp at this hour; then, tearing off his clothes, he ran into the sea. He gave a powerful shudder as the cold water came into contact with his burning skin then plunged into the clear bosom of his friend. He swam vigorously, using every muscle of his hard body, forcing the tension to seep out of his aching limbs and raging senses.

When he came out of the water, his frustration had exhausted itself and the night had gone – gone like a passing shadow and with it his anxieties, misgivings and the torturing edge of his desire. The sun had sprung suddenly into the throne of purple and rose-coloured clouds that the mist had left for him. Damian walked back to the car, pulled out a towel from the back and dried himself. Then, taking his pack of Gitanes, he walked back to the beach and propped himself up against a rock. Sitting naked on his towel, he lit a cigarette and quietly watched nature rise. This was the time he liked most, when everything quivered with freshness and hope – the virgin page of a brand-new dawn.

As Damian smoked, his gaze settling in front of him, his mind emptied. The rising sun grabbed the scenery and at once turned it to woven gold. All of nature seemed to have woken up now; flights of doves and seagulls were whizzing round in the sky; dogs were calling the flocks of sheep and goats to pasture, distant cockerels were crowing, donkeys braying. A big sailing boat, her torn sails wrinkled like ancient skin, came in with barely perceptible movement as the current brought her towards the island.

A smaller boat, further south, did little more than stem the current. She was loaded deep with raw, red brick and seemed to have no more than six inches of freeboard. It was one of his, he noted absent-mindedly. Odd that it didn't have its red and green lights on or even a foglight. He made a mental note to tell the harbour master and check with Yorgos later.

He stood up and threw away his cigarette. The harbour waters were getting busier by the minute, with fishing *caiques* gently trawling out into the open sea to tempt their luck as they had every day for more than a hundred years. Figures were beginning to move on the shore. It was time to go back.

* * *

Oriel lay awake, staring up at the ceiling. She was shocked at her reaction on hearing about Damian and Yolanda. It wasn't a surprise to her, and yet it still twisted her heart when Vassilis had talked about them. She didn't like feeling that way. It was out of character and she found it demeaning. Damian didn't care for her really. Oh, he definitely desired her, she had no doubt about that, but there was nothing else, no warmth, no tenderness; she was just another seductive piece of flesh to him and that thought was even more degrading. He wasn't the first man to hurt her, but he would be the last.

Forget him, she told herself angrily. *He's gone off now to slake his passions, no doubt, with Yolanda. Driving Oriel back to Heliades had been an inconvenience. No wonder he'd driven so fast – he couldn't wait to get back to the siren, who had drawn him back to her with impassioned song.*

A brief fury flared in her, but then was snuffed out and replaced by a mix of pain and frustration. The reason Damian could still hurt her was because she had never let go of him, never let him fade into her past ... and the past could only hurt her if she let it stay in the present. Sleep evaded Oriel. Twisting and turning, she found her search for its temporary oblivion disrupted by tormenting thoughts and images, which even chased her into her dreams. A tall man, with skin like copper and eyes like flint, moved through those dreams, lay beside her, touched her with fire ... made her shudder. She could feel the warmth of his body moulding her to him, the fever of his lips brushing her skin, the shameless coaxing of his hands as they explored her. She found herself reaching out in turn for him, murmuring his name; seeking him in vain in the still heat of the night.

CHAPTER 6

It was mid-afternoon by the time Oriel left Heliades. As it was Saturday, she had the day to herself to do with as she pleased and, after a night spent tossing and turning, a quiet morning writing letters in her sitting room had been restorative. Her spirits now revived, she set out on foot, heading for the marina.

It was good to stretch her legs and to feel the sun on them as she walked. She was wearing a pair of denim shorts with a sleeveless blouse and flat, golden sandals. Over her shoulder she carried a canvas beach bag, into which she had hastily shoved a long-sleeve shirt, some sun cream and a bottle of water.

The landscape became starker the further from Heliades she went: the great sandy expanses were peppered with wild carob, fig and olive trees that seemed to grow out of the rocks. Here, the barbaric sun had drained the countryside of colour and etched shadows, sharp and black, on the place. Goats were champing the sparse vegetation; one doe hadn't long dropped a kid and it lay soft-eared, nuzzled by its mother.

Elsewhere a lithe country girl in her ankle-length skirt, thick raven-black plaits falling down her back and a voluminous black handkerchief swathing her head, carried a dark-eyed baby on her back while picking some figs. At one point a team of ox carts and mules went by with jangling bells. Oriel noticed that the peasant men in their black-and-white costumes, walking at the head of their beasts, kept their eyes to the ground as they passed her. It was a silent procession that carried her right out of the twentieth century into a remote, undated past.

Even the clusters of cottages here were timeless-looking, whitewashed under sun-dried bricks of brown clay. Most of the doors were open to the sunshine and outside a few of them were women dressed in black, with scarves over their heads, seated on rickety chairs gossiping and knitting, while others swept their front steps, the harshness of their arid land etched in their features. Their dark, watchful eyes looked up at the pale foreign lady passing by with a mixture of curiosity and suspicion. Some would smile and politely murmur '*Kalispera*' as she strolled past.

As she neared the outskirts of the little port, the road dropped downhill and she delighted in unexpected glimpses of the sea through sun-drenched olive groves. She was on the outskirts now, the wide road narrowing and becoming steeper. Oriel's footsteps rang on the cobbles of crooked streets, some only wide enough for a donkey. Gone was the bare, dry terrain of before: this part of the island was decorative and almost poetic in its quaintness. The walls of some of the houses were whitewashed; others were the red of the bare volcanic limestone tufa. Their windows were aflame with cacti, carnations and begonias, and the high walls of the gardens were draped in bougainvillea and jasmine. The doorways, with their cheerful, coloured porches, were festooned with green vines and everywhere she looked, it seemed, bright flowers and foliage climbed and tumbled in a wild and heady tangle.

Oriel then caught her first sight of the bay, which seemed almost scooped out of the pine-forested cliffs, with a swathe of ivory-coloured beach fronting it. The slopes of green hills behind were rich with tall cypresses and tortured olive trees, their distant ridges gleaming with the dazzling white of a few scattered cottages. As she came down to the front, she passed a boatyard, which she hadn't noticed previously, cluttered with half-finished *caiques* and all kinds of gear. Its small pontoon was at the outside edge of the harbour, so that craft could be launched straight into deep water. She inhaled that indescribable smell of freshly sawn timber, paint and varnish, so typical of a place that has its feet in water.

A little further away stood a row of fishing smacks and beyond that, drawn up on the sand, were some flat rowing boats and dinghies. Some of them were receiving attention from their owners – tanned, bare-chested young men with their trousers rolled up to their knees. One or two looked at Oriel as she passed, and they straightened their backs to watch her, hands on hips. They were handsome, she reflected, but she had to admit that they left her cold. For a moment she was troubled by the thought that, after Damian, no man seemed able to set her blood afire.

Oriel walked a few more yards along the beach to the quay, with its line of *caiques* in different sizes and colours, blossoming red, blue and green, rocking at their moorings. As she approached the main jetty she noticed that Damian's boat was not among them. She wondered if he had gone diving but it was more likely, she thought, with a little catch in her throat, that he had taken Yolanda to some other island for lunch, or was swimming in a deserted cove with her, away from prying eyes.

The port, unlike the cobbled streets on its outskirts, was teeming. The air was heavy with the smell of tar and paint, fish and bilgewater. Drying octopus hung on poles next to nets in need of mending, while larger netting was draped on tall wooden posts, graceful as any stage scene. Seagulls wheeled and screamed in the sapphire-blue sky, annoyed because there was no catch from which they could scavenge. Oriel watched their flight, fascinated, for a while. She had always found gulls on land to be greedy, predatory beasts. Airborne, they appeared to her miracles of power and grace, their plumage looking as though freshly laundered.

She found her gaze following one of the birds as it flew from the azure sky above the sea to the steps of the little white chapel, a short distance up from the seafront. Oriel remembered seeing it on her way to Heliades that first day. On impulse, she followed in the same direction as the bird, and paused a moment in front of a pair of blue wooden doors. They were open, allowing the church to air, and inside an old woman in a headscarf and apron was sweeping the nave with a broom. She smiled at Oriel, but left her to her own devices, not seeking to ply her with the usual string of personal questions with which she was so often met. The air was suffused with the scent of roses, many of which adorned a shrine to St Nicholas. She stopped to look more closely and saw that it was surrounded by crude miniature paintings: images, she realized, that told the story of the sponge divers and the perils involved with this ancient tradition. She thought of the poet Oppian who, in the third century AD, wrote of the *spongotomos*, saying: 'No ordeal is more terrifying than that of the sponge divers and no labour more arduous for men.'

So many offerings, such devotion, she thought to herself. *Surely, here on Helios, they don't put their men in such danger still?*

At the end of the church was an unpainted wooden confessional box and, for a brief moment, the atmosphere of the place and her own intense emotions overwhelmed her. Oriel's senses quailed as she thought of the weakness of her own flesh whenever she came near Damian. The feverish images of last night's dream – of his hard body and piercing gaze – flashed into her head. Her stomach gave an odd lurch, like a tilting car at a fairground, and heat moved in a wave to the core of her being, at the same time making her suddenly lightheaded. She clasped the wooden pew next to her for balance and remonstrated with herself inwardly for this alarming loss of control.

After a moment, Oriel glanced at her watch: it was already five o'clock. She had hardly eaten that day and, with her long walk and the sea air, she had worked up an appetite. She wasn't the only one contemplating a late lunch – the taverna was busy. Under an olive tree sat three musicians, surrounded by a group of young men and women in jeans and T-shirts, playing and singing without a care in the world, it seemed. It was a scene similar to many she had seen on other Greek islands, although here there was a subtle difference. There wasn't a foreign face in sight, except for hers.

Tables were set out under a wire trellis, over which creepers had been trained to give protection from the sun, and the whole place, with its white walls and green-painted woodwork, looked cheerful. Oriel found an empty table in the shade and sat at it. She looked around; the chirping of the cicadas had reached its peak, punctuating the merry chatter of the clientele, who were a mixed group of fishermen, labourers and clerks. People were staring – especially the men, but the women too. It was no good trying to be inconspicuous: with her fair hair and skin – despite her freshly acquired golden tan – she stood out like a sore thumb. Shorts, while cool and practical, were clearly not de rigueur on Helios, she realized with a twinge of self-consciousness.

The waiter hurried to take her order and was surprised when she responded in Greek, asking for a glass of ouzo and a *dakos* salad: tomatoes, red onion and feta served on a slice of dried bread drizzled with olive oil. The waiter apologized, telling her that they didn't have any feta, but they used a fresh goat's cheese made from milk and whey called *mizithra*. Much superior, he noted with a wink. He also recommended their *souvlakia*: apparently the spit-roasted lamb – marinated in lemon juice and skewered with tomatoes, onions and green peppers – came from the Tchakos farm, which was the finest on the island.

As at Manoli's, the people were friendly. She noticed that a couple of them had the unusual slate-grey eyes that seemed rather prevalent on the island. A few smiled at her shyly; others, a little bolder, exchanged some words with her. They assumed that Oriel was working for *Kyrios* Lekkas, and one woman told her that the only fair-skinned women they had ever seen on the island had been employed by him, one of whom had eaten here quite a bit lately, although they hadn't seen her for a week or so. Oriel guessed that they must be referring to the French student, Chantal, who had left in such a hurry.

Had the young woman really got involved with one of the locals? Or was it Damian who'd brought Chantal here, before he'd tired of her? Oriel recalled her conversation with Damian on Santorini, when he had insisted he hadn't been in any sort of relationship with the girl, and at the time she had never thought to question that he might not be telling the truth. But after last night's encounter with Yolanda, she didn't feel sure of anything. Then she hastily chastised herself for these obsessive thoughts. The diner had only made the comment that the girl had eaten here, why did she have to bring Damian into it?

By the time Oriel had finished eating and had ordered her coffee it was already six o'clock. The taverna, as well as the beach, was emptying now, although the sun was still warm. Overhead the canopy remained a vivid azure, and the sea lay peacock blue in patches. It seemed to be dancing with happiness and little rills of foam were being tossed gently from the wave crests on to the sandy beach. Once Oriel had drained her coffee cup and paid the bill, she took off her sandals and walked close to the lapping water, feeling the fresh caress on her skin as it flowed past her, its frothy wake breaking easily at her feet. A slight breeze wafted in from the sea.

A figure standing on a flat rock at the other end of the beach caught her attention. A native fisherman, he looked as if he were carved from the same grey boulders that surrounded him. She could see that he was bearded and, although not a young man, he was strongly built, and the sleeves of his shirt rolled up to his elbows revealed the sinewy muscles of his brown forearms. Like a sculpture of Poseidon, he stood still, trident at the ready, the bright iron of its prongs scintillating above the dark water that curled at the base of the rock. As Oriel came closer, the trident flashed down at lightning speed, then the man stooped over. He had skewered a large fish and the water cascaded in a rainbow trail as the creature writhed, its polished gills fluttering frantically beneath a pair of bloodshot eyes. The fisherman threw it, still wriggling, into his basket and slid the trident into the belt around his waist. He then looped the strap of the basket across his chest and stepped down from his rock.

At Oriel's approach, the fisherman turned. He was leaning heavily on a stick as he limped across the sand towards her, no longer the powerful Neptune-like figure of a moment ago. She smiled at him. 'It's a beautiful catch you've got there,' she said.

'Yes, dinner for my children and grandchildren. You are here for the Lekkas diving project, eh?' His dark face crinkled in a smile.

Oriel was astonished. Everybody seemed to know about it. 'Yes, I arrived this week. My name's Oriel, by the way.' She reached out and shook the man's hand and he introduced himself as Mattias.

Now he was close, she noticed that he, too, had the same grey eyes as Stavros, Damian and several of the guests at the taverna, although none of them shared the brilliance of Damian's, she had noticed. The fisherman seemed to read her mind, because he chuckled. 'You have seen many of these strange-coloured eyes on the island, eh? And you're wondering if we are all part of the same family.'

'You're right, I have been puzzled. Not so much because they're grey but because of the brilliance of the iris. It seems almost silver.'

He laughed a hoarse, smoker's laugh. 'My good friend *Kyrios* Lekkas's ancestor was obviously a very virile man. He distributed his attentions freely with women, shall we say. I think, at the time, maybe a hundred years ago, maybe more, quite a few babies were born with these silver eyes.'

Oriel laughed. He had an air about him that was unlike the usual fishermen she'd met. 'I see, that makes sense.'

The man fixed her steadily with his gaze, the grey of his irises suddenly more brilliant. 'We call it *O Lekkas stigma*.'

'Why "stigma"? I find it rather arresting in your dark faces.'

'Every single person, male or female, who is born with this colour eyes is marked to have something tragic happen to them. As you can see,' he pointed to his leg.

Oriel's eyes widened. 'Stavros, *Kyrios* Lekkas's head of works, seems happy enough.'

'He is young, and life is long, *Despinis*. Look at me. I have had a happy life, *Dohksa toh Theh-oh*, thank God.' At this, he touched the tiny wooden cross that hung on a string around his neck. 'But still, fate's long arm caught hold of me. It could have been worse, I could have died. Even so, I am now a cripple for life.'

Oriel thought of Damian and his scarred face, blighted by the deaths of Pericles and Cassandra, and she gave a shiver. She had never liked superstition and now she liked it even less. How terrible that all these grey-eyed islanders might go about their daily business feeling as if there was a gun pointed at their backs.

Oriel could see that Mattias was eager to tell her about his accident but time was marching on and she needed to get back to Heliades before dark. Still, she didn't want to hurt his feelings, and a few more minutes spent lending a friendly ear could do no harm.

'What happened?'

The fisherman bent down and sat on one of the low boulders. He took out a packet of Karelia Greek cigarettes from his shirt pocket, silently offering one to Oriel. When she shook her head, he lit one up.

'It was a shark attack. A great white, would you believe it?' Mattias's large brown hand once again fingered the wooden cross around his neck. 'Every year after Easter, *Kyrios* Lekkas used to take me and Stavros deep-sea spearfishing. You see, I'm the one who taught them how to dive. Anyway, we would travel all over the world on these trips. As a lad, I went with my father to the Red Sea, off the coast of Egypt. He and his father before him dived for big fish to sell to restaurants on the Greek islands.'

At this Oriel forgot all about needing to set off back to Heliades. The diver in her was hooked – like one of his fish – by the opening to Mattias's narrative. She also knew that the story involved Damian, and that made her all the more keen to listen. 'So how did you get hurt? What happened?' she couldn't help interjecting.

'It was in the Red Sea, a bigger expedition than usual. We had some Egyptian divers with us. The three of us went first, swimming down through corridors of coral. Then we found a shoal of green rhinoceros fish. They swam right up to us and I ran my harpoon through one. That fish wriggled like mad, you should have seen it. By Zeus, he was strong! The beast dragged me through the coral, then a branch caught my right fin, and I was thrown on my back.' He paused for dramatic effect and gave a short cough.

'Now I was in open water. There was a current like you wouldn't believe. I tried to get up but the water pulled me one way, the fish the other. My mask was leaking and I was panicking – how was I to see the dark shadow coming up behind me?'

Oriel's two hands flew to her mouth. 'The shark!'

The fisherman paused only to blow out a plume of smoke from his cigarette and carried on, so engrossed was he in his story. He almost seemed to be enjoying reliving the horrible adventure. 'The first thing I knew, it had found its target and torn into my leg. But d'you know what? I didn't feel a thing. That's what your body does to survive, it shuts down pain.'

'But you wouldn't have stood a chance. Not against a great white,' insisted Oriel.

'I knew that, but it doesn't stop you fighting. Luckily for me, the *Kyrios* got to it. Tackled the giant from behind. Stuck him through the gills as he would any other fish. The shark let go of me. Thank God, I thought. But then it turned on him. I couldn't do a thing. I had to watch the *Kyrios* have a wrestling match with the brute, trying to stick him in the eyes and get to his brain. As big as a car that shark was, you had to see it. And the water all red and churning.'

Oriel's eyes were wide. 'And did he finish the shark off?'

'I thought things couldn't get worse but then they did. A group of other sharks came along, smaller than the first one, though that's not saying a lot. Drawn by the blood. Wanted to see what the rumpus was about. Then they started thrashing and snapping at each other. Circling us all the time, you know how they do.' He shook his head. 'We didn't stand a chance in Hades.'

'What about Stavros?'

'He'd gone up to get help, the most sensible thing he could do. He had a couple of sharks tailing him all the way back to the dive boat. Then, I don't know how he did it, but the *Kyrios* stuck the shark four or five times in the head with his spear. I could see the beast was beginning to wobble. But even then the damned thing wouldn't give up. Before keeling over, it bit a chunk out of the *Kyrios*'s chest. And then, if that wasn't bad enough, the *Kyrios* rolled over into the coral. That's how his face was slashed.'

'What happened with the other sharks, or did the divers get there first?' Oriel wanted to know.

Mattias threw away his cigarette. 'Well, a strange thing happened. Just before Stavros got back with the others – one of them, thankfully, a doctor – a school of dolphins suddenly appeared. They circled slowly and beat the sharks into a retreat, butting them and heading them off.'

'I've heard of such things happening. They're amazing creatures,' said Oriel. 'And that is quite a story. You were so lucky.'

'I owe *Kyrios* Damian my life,' said Mattias fervently. 'The damage done to his face … and his chest was even worse. You should see it, a great trench of a scar. They took us to an army hospital in Cairo. I can't remember much about those next few days.'

Oriel fell silent now that the story had ended. Of course, she had seen that terrible scar. And to think that she had thought Damian's scarred face might be the result of a fight over a woman! She felt suddenly felt ashamed. How petty her thoughts about him and Yolanda seemed now. What bravery he had showed! To take on a great white shark, and not to swim away as fast as he could, that took real courage. Her heart warmed at the thought.

'So you see,' said Mattias, pushing himself up from the rock on which he had been perched, 'those grey eyes of his may have been his undoing, but they sure as hell saved me. The *Kyrios* is a good man … a courageous one, too.'

'Yes, I see that,' murmured Oriel. 'That kind of traumatic experience must haunt you.'

Mattias squinted into the sun. 'You learn to live with it. There are more years behind me than in front. I've had a good life, but the *Kyrios* is in his prime.'

Her heart went out to Damian. The consequences of his bravery had indeed been grave.

The fisherman turned his enigmatic gaze on Oriel, once more

seeming to read her thoughts. 'He has more to live with than I ever will.'

Oriel stood next to Mattias a moment longer, looking across the beach and out to sea. Suddenly she was reminded of how late it was getting. The shadows had lengthened; a couple of fishing boats, leaving the port for their night work, steered darkly across the luminous sea. Those jewel-like tints of blue and green had faded from the water, and the cliff scenery had caught a fiery glare. She noticed, too, that Damian's *caique* was back at its mooring. She no longer felt a pang of jealousy, she realized. Her speculations over Damian and Yolanda seemed almost trivial now, compared with what she had just heard.

Oriel said goodbye to Mattias. 'I'd better be going. I've a long walk back to Heliades. It'll be dark, I expect, by the time I get back.'

'I'm sorry if I let my tongue run away with itself. You're a good listener, you know.' He peered up at the skies before fixing his kindly gaze on her. 'My cottage is not far from here, I can ask my son to accompany you. He must have already arrived with the children for supper.'

Oriel smiled. 'No, no, thank you. That's very kind but if I walk briskly I'm sure to get back before nightfall.'

'As you wish. Well, it was nice meeting you, *Despinis*.' The fisherman took her hand and pressed it in his. 'Helios can be a hard place for foreigners. If you ever feel lonely or need to speak to somebody, I'm usually here or in the taverna.'

'Thanks, Mattias, I'll bear that in mind,' said Oriel. 'I hope to see you again sometime soon. Maybe, next time, you can teach me how to spear a fish.'

As she turned to go, Mattias stopped her. 'I don't know if you have plans, but it's the Epiklisi parade tomorrow. If you aren't bored of hearing an old fisherman's stories, why don't you meet me in the main town square?'

Oriel thanked him and arranged a meeting time, grateful for the hand of friendship he had offered so freely. She shot a last look at the sea before walking up the narrow path to the road. The sky was an arc of crimson, reflected in the water as the sun sank slowly down towards the horizon, and suddenly the scissoring of cicadas, the shimmer of sea and rock were absent, as if short-circuited. Oriel took out the long-sleeved shirt she had packed in her bag that morning and put it on. Head down, she walked in the evening coolness, her mind preoccupied with the tale Mattias had just told her. Vassilis had said that Damian had changed since his accident. Had Cassandra been repelled by him? Maybe Yolanda too? Human nature could be cruel and women – like men – could be callous and uncaring.

Somehow, Oriel was not surprised by Damian's bravery. It wasn't just his litheness and his god-like looks that were impressive, he had immediately struck her as someone strong, invincible – a giant mountain that could face the fiercest winds. She felt more admiration than pity for him, she was sure. Still, she was puzzled. On her arrival, Yorgos had described Damian as hard, with a heart of stone. That wasn't the way the fisherman had spoken about him. *The Kyrios is a good man … a courageous one too*, he had said, but of course he would be biased.

In the past two days, she'd learnt there were many facets to Damian's personality but how much did she really know him? A frown crinkled her brow. Perhaps his childhood sweetheart, Yolanda, knew him far better than she ever would. Jealousy pricked at her emotions again and she berated herself for her weakness over this man, who was still such an enigma.

It was the hour of the evening star, before the moon flooded the island with silver radiance and sharp shadows. Oriel walked quickly through the eerie darkness. It was beginning to get misty. Silence had descended over this ancient land. From time to time a dog barked in the distance. The few cottages that she had passed in the arid part of her walk that morning were dark, except for a few sparse dots of light and spirals of smoke curling into the air. Here, the countryside was almost savage in its harshness. The branches of the wild carob trees creaked in the breeze as if some tormented soul was struggling to get out and the rustle of the leaves seemed to whisper, like a multitude of strangers watching her curiously. Bats were whirling in the sky, quite low over her head, catching invisible moths, and from out of the night came a sound like a wolf howling.

Why hadn't she taken the car down to the port? From there she could have explored the countryside at leisure. This wasn't England; she must always remind herself of that in the future. She should have taken a pair of jeans with her but she hadn't expected to be heading back in the dark.

That was reckless of you, Oriel chided.

This was a remote island in Greece, a strange land with people who had alien customs, and now there were mysterious noises stirring near to her and, in the descending mist, they took on a threatening aspect. Again, the sound of a wild animal howling carried on the night air. Oriel drew her shirt closer and hurried on, telling herself that she'd soon reach Heliades.

She had almost arrived at the end of the wild expanse when she heard a different noise. Was the darkness getting to her? Was her imagination running away with her? It was a kind of muffled padding on the dirt road – four-footed maybe? She couldn't make it out, but something was definitely following her, she was sure of it now. Oriel felt an icy chill run down her spine but she didn't want to stop or look behind her. The noise was nearer now, a slow and inexorable pacing at her back. Soon it would be catching up with her. There was the sound of animals panting. Was it wolves? She wanted to run but her legs felt like lead. Then a strong, harsh light flashed upon her face. Dimly, she saw that the dark bulk bearing down on her was a black horse and that it had a rider. Two large dogs trotted at its side.

'Calypso? What the hell are you doing here?' It was Damian's voice.

She heaved a sigh of relief. His great hounds, Heracles and Peleus, approached and sniffed the ground around her and Damian called them back to him with a single word. Oriel realized that it must have been them she had heard howling.

'I'm walking back to Heliades.' She tried to sound composed, but there was a betraying break in her voice.

'How did you get here? Has the car broken down?' Damian sounded anxious.

'No, no, nothing like that, I just didn't take it.'

Damian muttered some Greek oath, which she didn't quite hear but knew was not complimentary to her. He jumped down from his horse. The powerful torch shone on her lightweight gold sandals and bare legs.

'You're hardly equipped for walking, and at night too,' he growled, slowly moving the torch beam up and down her body. His tone left no doubt of his low opinion of her conduct and it spurred her rebellious nature, even though she knew he was right.

She laughed a little unsteadily.

'Oh, Damian, how ridiculous! In England I go for long country walks at night alone.'

Damian's eyes gleamed. 'Your Englishmen might be dead from their thighs up or is it, perhaps, that they are born blind?' His voice was low and hoarse.

The colour rushed to Oriel's face – she hadn't anticipated his response and it left her lost for words

Damian whistled to the dogs to walk on and they scampered ahead, up the road. He took her arm. 'It's a good thing that I came along before some animal happened upon you and mauled you,' he said gruffly and, before Oriel had properly grasped what he intended, he had picked her up with shocking ease and swung her on to the broad back of his big black horse. Clearly left with no choice, she grasped the pommel of the saddle, fighting for balance but then Damian sprang up behind her, holding her tight. The horse swayed and pranced, calming quickly at his command.

Not having been on a horse often before, and certainly not like this, Oriel instinctively leaned forward to steady herself but Damian pulled her back. 'Easy, I have you,' he murmured, his voice softer now.

As his arms clasped her further to him, her head was pushed back against the strong wall of his broad chest where it rested, the muscles of his arms pressing the curves of her breasts with supportive pressure. His body felt warm, firm and reassuring, and together they quickly settled into the cadence of the horse's motion. Above the dull sound of the horse's hooves she could hear the steady beat of Damian's heart. It seemed to vibrate right through her as if it were the throb of her own. It had felt the same when they'd danced, clasped in each other's arms in Santorini, and she'd wished that time had stopped, right then, on the dancefloor.

The strong muscles of his thighs bracketed Oriel's bare ones and she could feel them flex rhythmically, filling her with a crude, undeniable longing. A slow wave of heat curled through her body and the shock of her own need ricocheted through her, frightening in its intensity, bringing back the old memories in a dizzy flood.

When he had made love to her that night in Aegina she had felt the power of him through each sensual caress. His possession of her, at moments, had been almost savage. It was partly because of the dominance radiating from him that she had been able to let herself go, without shame at her wanton behaviour and without restraint. Oriel knew that she could never belong to anyone else after Damian. How could she? Nobody would ever match up to him. During those years afterwards, his face, his voice, his touch had lingered in her memory. Now, after their uncanny reunion, she felt the fire and passion rekindle between them every time they touched. How long would she be able to resist?

The scent of Damian's skin, fragrant with sunlight and the sea, seemed to invade Oriel's senses. His large palms holding the reins covered hers and now, as they came to a bend in the road, his hands moved up with the reins, the backs of his fingers brushing against her nipples which tightened even more under the warmth of his touch that seeped through the fine fabric of her blouse.

'*Se thélo pára poli, omorfi Oriel mou,* I want you so much, my beautiful Oriel,' his lips whispered hoarsely against her ear, triggering a fresh wave of desire melting down through her stomach and thighs. Everything in her wanted to cry out: '*And I want you too, Damian, oh, so much.*' But she was not *his* Calypso, any more than he was *her* Damian. His words only described a physical need; no tender emotion, no love. Perhaps that was a stronger bond reserved for Yolanda. The thought struck her with cold reality and she stiffened in his arms. She would conquer this frantic commotion that was fogging up her brain and torturing her body; she would not be his 'thing', used to purge his frustrated desire like some sensual exorcism.

Oriel didn't answer him. She was rigid like a statue in Damian's arms and didn't dare to move in case her body gave itself away. Until they reached Heliades he made no further attempt to speak to her either.

'We'll go via the stables,' he told her as they clattered under an arched gateway and across a flagged courtyard, an area that she had not yet seen. The stable block was set at the far end of the wing that belonged to Damian. A large cloud had covered the moon, and in the semi-darkness she could only distinguish the outlines of a few different-sized buildings around a large sandy *manège,* enclosed by a fence made of thick logs. The dogs were already there and had gone to lie down next to some sacks on the ground.

Damian stopped in front of one of the buildings, leapt down from the saddle and held up his arms to help Oriel dismount. The cloud glided away and their gazes collided in the moonlight. There was an expression in his that tugged, quite unexpectedly, at Oriel's heartstrings; a haunted look, she thought. A nerve pulsed at the side of his mouth as she slid to the ground, brushing against the length of him, his arms closing around her. Damian held her close, with a sense of urgency, steadying her trembling body. His breathing was laboured and she could feel the thudding of his heart next to her own.

Oriel didn't even try to get away as she felt the hard ridge of Damian's maleness pressing gently into her: she wanted nothing more than to be held, kissed and caressed by him. But then suddenly he let go of her with a low kind of growl that seemed to erupt from deep in his throat. 'I'm only a man, Calypso. What d'you expect when you show so much enticing bare skin? If you know what's good for you, you'll keep that in mind from now on.'

Oriel didn't answer, too stunned to find her words. The torrent of magnificent sensations she'd felt in his arms had brought a rush of heat to her face. Now it was followed by a flood of cold that hit her so hard her teeth chattered as though he had doused her with a bucket of iced water. So this was Damian's way of getting back at her for trying to resist him.

A groom appeared from the yard to take the horse, and Damian gave him an instruction while Oriel tried to gather her wits. As the man led the horse away, Damian tossed her a brief, dark look and then turned his back on her for a few moments, pushing a hand through his hair as though composing himself. Turning round again, he regarded her pensively now. 'I hope you aren't too tired to have dinner with me tonight. I have a suggestion for how you could spend your time tomorrow,' he said, somewhat contritely.

'If you don't mind, I'll skip dinner,' said Oriel. 'I had a late lunch and don't have much of an appetite now.' She didn't mention that there were also uncomfortable butterflies in her stomach after experiencing such close contact with him.

'Then join me for a drink on the terrace.' His mouth quirked. 'For me it'll be an aperitif. For you, an early nightcap.'

One drink couldn't hurt; it might steady her jittery nerves. She nodded. 'That sounds like a good idea.'

'We'll go round the back then. It's this way.'

He walked ahead to open a gate in the wall surrounding the stableyard. Oriel watched his lithe body as it moved, tapering down from broad shoulders to a narrow waist and slim hips. She tried not to speculate on Damian's reasons for refraining from kissing her, but it was difficult to think of anything else when her pulse raced at the mere thought of his mouth on hers.

Still, she wondered at his restraint. Damian was a man with great experience of women, surely he'd known that she wanted him to kiss her? Was he giving her a taste of her own medicine, enflaming her senses and then pulling back? She wouldn't put it past him. Or was he teaching her lesson? His punishing words as he let go of her had sounded very much like a threat. Oriel had to admit it: she had been walking on a deserted road in shorts, which was rather reckless. Her eyes, still lingering on his outline, snapped back up to his face as he turned to hold the gate open.

'I met a friend of yours today,' she announced hurriedly. 'That's why I was late getting back.'

He looked at her sceptically. 'Oh yes?'

She waited as he closed the gate behind them. 'A fisherman called Mattias.'

For the first time a smile appeared on his face. 'Ah, Mattias! Yes, he's a good friend.'

'He invited me to the Epiklisi festival tomorrow.'

'Did he now?' Damian's tone was mocking but he looked pleased. 'You must have made a good impression on him, eh? If you hadn't stayed out so late, I would have told you all about the festival myself. That's what I wanted to talk to you about. I was going to invite you.' He gestured that they should follow the edge of the house, through the gardens.

'You were?'

'The Epiklisi parade is an important day for Helios, an invocation to Typhoeus to protect the island. I thought you would be interested to witness it. There's a procession to Mount Helios, with everyone dressed in costume, then feasting and dancing.'

'But I don't have a costume.'

'Don't worry, Calypso. I will provide you with one.' He glanced at her, his eyes skimming her contours briefly. He then added in a low, suggestive voice, 'I think by now I can guess your size.'

Heat prickled along her skin and she looked away. She had to try and curb this ridiculous infatuation of hers that turned her into a tongue-tied simpleton whenever she was in close proximity to him.

'So you met Mattias …' Damian said pensively as they mounted the steps to his terrace. 'I was going to suggest that Stavros and his family accompany you.' He caught her quizzical look. 'I'm involved in the procession, you see. I'll be tied up for a good part of the day. But that's lucky, Mattias can take you instead.'

'Yes, I'll enjoy getting to know him better. He's an interesting man.'

'That he is,' replied Damian. 'What will you have to drink? I have some excellent Metaxa. Would you like some?'

'Thank you, yes. It's a brandy, isn't it?'

He nodded. 'A blend of brandy and spices.'

'I've never actually had it before.'

'Well, then tonight you will, and the best Metaxa Greece has to offer.' He spoke with a sort of pride, as if he were initiating her to some wonderful ritual, yet there was a pent-up quality to his voice as though he was talking to distract himself. 'The best Metaxa is difficult to find here because we export almost all of it.'

Damian went to a small table standing in a corner on the terrace. It was stacked with various well known brands of spirits and fine crystal glasses, and he picked up a beautiful *Cristal de Sèvres* decanter with a gold-painted stopper. 'This is one of my favourites. Here,' he said, as he poured the clear, deep mahogany-coloured liquid into two heavy crystal glasses and passed one of them to Oriel. 'Breathe in the aroma first, take a small sip and then tell me what you think.'

Silently they moved to the balustrade with their drinks and looked into the night. The stillness quivered from time to time with the low-pitched call of breeding frogs from the pond and ditches, and the sharp, querulous barking of dogs somewhere in the distant neighbourhood. The garden, the sea beyond and the far-off pinpoints of light seemed to belong to a different world. It was as if they were suspended in a motionless bubble of time, so inert it was.

Oriel shot a glance at the tall, proud-faced figure standing beside her and lifted the glass of Metaxa to her nose, breathing in the heavy, spiced fragrance that filled her lungs with warmth. She ventured a sip, then another. Dried raisins and figs, citrus peel, honey, pine, vanilla and sweet spices were released, one after the other, on to her palate. You could almost taste the Attica sunshine in every drop, she thought; a magic potion made for Aphrodite, the goddess of love.

Damian's grey gaze flickered softly over her. 'Verdict?' he asked.

They were standing close enough for her to catch the enticing, masculine scent of him. 'It's intoxicating,' she murmured as she took another mouthful of the caramel liquid, looking down into its bronze reflections. He smiled a slow smile, watching her face, his eyes sparkling as though lit from within. 'Sunshine in a bottle, a love philtre, eh? It should have been named *Charme d'Amour*.'

God help her, his gaze felt as if it were touching her. But Damian had also read her mind.

'I was just thinking along those lines a moment ago,' she said huskily, a strange emotion strangling her voice.

His eyes revealed to her some unknown shade of silver, like a precious metal yet to be discovered. 'That's the way soulmates feel,' he said. 'They're constantly in each other's thoughts and so instinctively read one another's minds.' There was a disturbingly caressing note in his deep, rich voice, making her skin tingle. She found she couldn't answer.

He leaned away from her on one arm, his intense gaze skimming down her body. 'Calypso, you know I only had your best interests at heart this evening. You could have got into all sorts of danger walking in the dark. And not just from our island lotharios.'

Oriel was at once acutely aware of her bare legs. 'I suppose you're right,' she conceded, taking another sip of her drink. The Metaxa was heating her insides with a delicious sensation, but not nearly so much as his overtly masculine scrutiny.

'There are all sorts of wild animals that roam at night here.'

She raised an eyebrow, looking him directly in the eye. 'You mean on Helios or at Heliades?'

His laughter was a low growl. 'Calypso, every man could turn into an animal when faced with the sight of you.'

She cleared her throat, her pulse quickening like a rabbit caught in a trap, and stared into her glass. 'Perhaps I've had enough of this.' She put her drink down on the wide surface of the balustrade.

With quiet consideration, Damian picked up both their glasses and walked over to the table. When he turned back towards Oriel, she had to draw in a breath. Even in the shadows of the evening, he was magnificent. His hair was untamed in a way that managed to be both boyish and provocative. And most affecting was the way he looked at her, with the hungry glint of a predator sizing up its prey.

'Your legs are very long, did you know that?' His voice was a low murmur. He sauntered back towards her with deliberate purpose, his eyes snaking up her body to her face and lingering there.

Oriel inhaled slowly. Things were beginning to spiral out of her control but she had to stand up to him. 'What is it you want from me, Damian?'

He came close to her and a spark, intense as diamonds, flared deep in his gaze. 'You really want to know?'

'Yes, I really want to know,' she assured him determinedly.

For a split second he didn't answer, then his eyes lit up again with a reckless flame. 'I want more than anything to strip you naked and take you to my bed, and feel your body trembling beneath mine. To caress the silky skin of your beautiful breasts and stomach with my hands, my mouth, my tongue, and then lick you until your honeyed juice explodes in my mouth and you cry out with the same frenzied abandonment you did all those years back …'

Oriel drew a shaky breath, her face like hot coals as a tide of fire swept over her. She had walked straight into that. His words brought an insistent throb deep down in her belly … but somewhere a deeper yearning remained. There was no mention of love. Was she so foolish to hope for something more? Could he ever care for her, beyond this lust that flashed between them like a lightning storm? Would she ever be enough for him?

He stood inches away. 'I can't get you out of my mind, Calypso. God only knows I've tried.' He muttered an oath. 'Why shouldn't we give in to this passion? It's burning us both to a cinder. You feel it too, I know you do.'

Her emotions were swinging chaotically between caution and desire and she couldn't keep her eyes from him. 'That's exactly it. I don't know how you really feel.'

With that, Damian pushed her gently but firmly back against the balustrade, his two powerful arms pinning her on either side. 'This is how I feel, Calypso.' His hips pressed against her stomach, his arousal stiff and strong.

Oriel's body flamed once more and wet heat pooled between her legs at his blatant crudeness. There was no escape. Yet having his broad shoulders looming over her, his desire so brazenly evident, was dangerously thrilling. Instinctively she put her hand to his chest, not knowing if she meant to push him away or draw him closer, and felt the pounding of his heart.

His gaze was penetrating as he leaned his head closer. 'I can play your body like a harp, *agápi mou*.'

She stared helplessly at him, the breath catching in her throat, trying to find a reason to refute his arousing words.

'You know I'm right,' he murmured again, bending a little further towards her as he spoke. 'We just have to brush against each other for our bodies to come alive. Can you deny what we felt on the dancefloor at Santorini?'

Oriel swallowed. Her pulses hammered alarmingly; she was mesmerized by his voice and the feel of his hard body; his persona was like a drug submerging her, stimulating those helpless feelings of desire and hunger that had been suppressed deep inside her, until Damian had triggered them once more. There was a dull ache in her solar plexus burgeoning and building up, and she felt that it would soon burst with the pain of her bottled-up emotions.

One of his hands lifted, brushing against her breast, discovering the fullness of it beneath her blouse and sending heat shooting down between her thighs. This wasn't supposed to be happening, she told herself, but Oriel's head dropped back in a position of surrender as his thumb passed over her nipple, making it bud and tighten with exquisite torture.

She let out a breathy sigh. His touch made her burn with longing, starting an empty ache pulsating in her core that cried out to be filled. He was holding her waist against him, his arousal hard, and she almost wished that he would force himself on her. Oriel gazed up at Damian and saw a nerve beating hard beside his lips so near to hers, his look smouldering beneath the line of his brows.

As if reading her mind, his hand slid down between her legs, touching her mound over the denim of her shorts. His hand moved backwards and forwards, tormenting her in ways she had never imagined possible.

'You see, Calypso?' he murmured hotly in her ear. 'It would be so easy for me to have you here, right now … to make you mine again.'

She could barely think, as another turbulent wave of heat coursed down between her thighs as if some white-hot catalyst had been ignited inside her, transferring the fire of his lust to her most sensitive core.

He pulled back to look at her face. Their gazes held and deepened as, with one hand, he deftly unzipped the front of her denim shorts. Oriel knew she could have stopped him but she was entranced by his molten, silver stare.

A sharp gasp of pleasure escaped her parted lips as his hand found where she was naked and wet with longing.

'You're mine, no other man's,' he growled.

Compelled by her own powerful yearning, she moved one knee aside with an instinctive invitation as old as Eve, opening her legs to give him full access. Sensuously, his fingers began to stroke the insides of her thighs. She trembled as they inched their way towards that part of her that was begging for release. His hand now had free rein between her thighs, which became ever more slick with the wetness of her desire, embarrassing her with the wantonness of her response. Yet she saw only raw hunger in his eyes as their gazes remained locked together.

'Yes, *méli mou*, let yourself go.'

His stroking hand parted her tender female flesh, the ridge of his fingers moving against her hot, wet core. A moment later, he slid two fingers inside her and she let out a groan, her hands clutching at his shoulders. Her eyes finally fluttered shut, enraptured by the feel of him relentlessly moving within her. He had complete domination over her body, playing it with expert finesse, like a magician conjuring up wondrous sensations that made every part of her reel with pleasure.

'You want this, don't you, *matia mou*? Just like I burn for you. This is what you can't deny.'

'Damian.' His name hissed through her teeth.

'Feel it, Calypso. Give in to me.'

His mouth took hers suddenly in a carnal sensuality, his tongue invading her with savage purpose, as though meting out some punishment. He plundered her in a torrent of erotic demand, in a way that insisted on her total surrender, which she willingly gave, luxuriating in the skill of his touch, wanting the delicious, intimate invasion never to stop …

Melting in a warm, honeyed tide of response, her mouth responded to his ardour with sensual heat, drinking in his urge to possess her just as every part of her cried out to be possessed by him, the hunger he was arousing making her a stranger to herself. Her body was so awash with all-consuming need that her breathing became faster; her stomach muscles tightened as an exquisite torturing ache pulsed between her legs and she whimpered and trembled with anticipation.

Just when she thought she couldn't bear it any longer, Damian's fingers began to stroke her faster and faster. 'You feel so warm and wet, so deliciously silky and soft,' he whispered huskily in her ear, pinching the excited bud between his finger and thumb and making her moan loudly. 'Do you want more, *méli mou*?'

'Yes, yes, don't stop! Damian, please …'

Oriel gripped his shoulders hard.

He couldn't stop now. She had years to make up for. He'd brought it all to the surface and now he was taking her to the brink of surrender.

'You want me inside you, don't you? I want to feel you tight and clasping me, calling out my name,' he continued to whisper, his voice soft and seductive as his skilful fingers went on teasing, stroking, pinching, rubbing.

Oh, that voice … those words … that touch … how she had missed them …

Her back arched and she moved now in cadence with his caresses as that sweet and terrible rhythm flowed like hot quicksilver between her thighs. Her inner muscles contracted, her release coming with a shattering climax around his fingers and she gave a strangled cry of relief, leaving her weak and shuddering.

Reeling, Oriel clung to him for a few moments, both of them breathing hard. The wave of bliss washed over her …

… which was then replaced by self-awareness.

What had she just done?

When Oriel lifted her eyes to his face, Damian seemed almost as shocked and disorientated as she herself felt. The colour was high in his cheeks and his grey eyes were smoky and almost stormy, searching her features as though looking for answers to a question he hadn't yet formulated.

Oriel was too overwhelmed to speak. The passion he had released in her brought back too many memories, and now she stood before him, more vulnerable than she had ever felt in her life. She stared at him; then, with trembling fingers, fastened her shorts and stepped slowly away without a word.

'*Agápi mou*, talk to me.'

She numbly shook her head. They had agreed to keep their distance from one another and now they had stepped over a line. This was too much.

He wasn't hers.

He ran a trembling hand through his hair. 'I lost control, I'm sorry.'

'So am I.' It was all she could manage before she turned and ran down the steps of the terrace. Her breath came quick and uneven as she half stumbled round to the front of the house and into the hall, her knees still weak, her mind echoing with Damian's hypnotic voice, so low and urgent in her ear, and the heat of his touch.

Self-recriminations spun and swooped in her mind like dark, angry crows. Why had she let him touch her when it was just a cruel reminder that he was wrong for her in so many ways? And they had done this out in the open, like two ravenous beasts, where anyone could see.

Oriel had not yet reached the top of the staircase when she looked up and the chaos of her thoughts came to an abrupt halt. Helena was sitting in her wheelchair behind the banister. This time, she was not alone. There was an older woman standing by her side and Beshir, the eunuch. The woman was tall and thin, with an untidy halo of crinkly grey hair. She had a large, sallow face with sullen features and small soot-black eyes that glittered like those of a raptor as they surveyed Oriel with a hard, unsmiling stare. That was not the only feature that reminded Oriel of an eagle; she had a prominent hooked nose and her mouth, with projecting front teeth, was thin and lightly twisted, giving her a sinister aspect.

Helena gave a spiteful laugh. 'Well, well, well, see what the cat's dragged in! Good evening, *Despinis* Anderson. Still flaunting your pound of flesh, I see. Has it worked with my cousin?' Her tone was mocking and Oriel looked at her sharply, wondering with shame and horror if what had gone on between her and Damian had indeed been witnessed just now. Helena's head inclined towards the woman standing behind her. 'Marika, just look at those bare legs!' Her eyes darting back to Oriel, she sneered, 'These foreigners have no shame.'

Oriel walked up the last three steps, biting back the retort that quivered on the edge of her tongue; she didn't want to be openly rude to Damian's cousin, no matter how much she was baited. Even in her flustered state she caught the strange gleam in Helena's gaze as she walked past – was it jealousy? And yet was that now a faint smile playing on those beautiful lips? She reminded herself that the woman was unstable, to be pitied. Staring straight ahead, she went directly to her apartment.

Once in her room, Oriel closed the door behind her and leaned back against it. Her heart was pounding. She tried to steady her breathing but Damian's effect on her made it impossible to easily calm herself. Not only that, she could still see Marika's malevolent coal-black eyes imprinted in her mind's eye. It was as if they were searing her back, even now. She gave a shiver. *Was she there,* she wondered, *just the other side of the door? Another of Helena's lackeys, doing her mistress's bidding like some witch's familiar?* She held her breath a moment to listen, but all she could hear was the uneven patter of her own heart.

Oriel felt fractured and confused. Every nerve-end in her body was still quivering with the passion she had felt for Damian, a passion that drew her so forcefully to him, almost in spite of herself. She was like a tumultuous spring tide after a full moon, pulled by his magnetic influence, and waves of longing were still shuddering through her, even now.

Was this what people called love? No, she was sure that something so barbarically sensual bore no relation to it. Love was surely a sentiment born out of tenderness, companionship, respect and admiration for the person desired. What did she know about Damian to label these basic untamed emotions with a feeling so much more superior? No, this abject ravishment of the senses could only be called lust, as Helena had so crudely put it.

It must have been so obvious, she thought with a pang of humiliation. Damian's cousin could easily have intuited, by Oriel's dishevelled appearance and heightened colour, what had been going on out on the terrace. The woman had been her usual vituperative self and, as she thought of Helena and her strangely smiling countenance, she started to feel even more unnerved. *What's she up to?* she wondered uneasily. *Is she plotting something vile?* Incarcerated all day in her room, Helena most likely had nothing better to do than fuel her obsessions.

Oriel gave a sigh and opened her eyes. Now look who was being the obsessive one! Anyway, it was absolutely none of Helena's business and she wasn't about to be intimidated by her – or Damian, for that matter.

Everything was so intense here – feelings resembled hot molten lava gently simmering at the heart of a volcano and waiting to erupt. Damian, the tragic scarface; his cousin Helena, the beautiful invalid; the scary-looking Marika; Hassan, the mute servant; Beshir, the eunuch; the old fisherman, Mattias, who had almost been killed by a shark; Yolanda, the bewitching diva pining for her lover … they all seemed to be characters taking part in a Greek tragedy. She shivered.

Oriel placed her canvas bag on the table and was about to head to the bathroom when something caught her eye: a wavering white line on the terracotta floor tiles snaked its way along the side of her bed. At first she thought it was white sand and she bent to touch the fine grains. Salt, she realized, and her forehead creased for a moment in puzzlement.

It was only when she followed the trail around the side of her bed that she took in its significance. There, the white line became a series of whorls, almost like the rings of a dartboard. She stood there a moment, hypnotized by the pattern on the floor. Then she realized with a sickening lurch what it was: the evil eye. She had seen *mati* often enough, the Greek blue-eyed charms – the Greeks, it seemed, couldn't get enough of the bright-blue glass talismans that originated in Ancient Egypt. They hung them over their thresholds and wore them as jewellery, using them to ward off any malign *matiasma*: the curse of the evil eye laid on a person by jealous enemies.

Oriel slumped on the end of her bed, shock and dread coursing through her veins. Now she was a *matiasmenos* in their eyes, she supposed – one who has had the evil eye cast upon them – and although she didn't believe in the power of the curse, she was still shaken by the fact that someone bore her such ill-will that they wanted to hurt her, even destroy her. Added to that, she knew enough about Greek traditions to realize that salt was used to rudely send away an unwelcome guest. So this person, whoever they were, had doubly cursed her. *But I didn't even want to stay in this godforsaken house*, she thought bitterly.

Oriel guessed who it was, of course. Helena had shown her hand, that much was plain. Most probably she would have used Beshir to do her dirty work. Oriel covered her face with shaking hands. Suddenly she felt more alone than ever, which cut more deeply considering the intimate moment she had just shared with Damian. She couldn't go to him now, not after the way they had parted.

Anger took over, like a clean, bright flame. Oriel sat up and squared her shoulders. When she brushed the salt under her bed her hands were still trembling, but now it was with righteous indignation, not fear. She stood up and walked towards the bathroom and, as she did so, she noticed a blue envelope on her chest of drawers. Oriel frowned. It had obviously been hand-delivered as it had no postage stamps attached to it. She tore it open and her eyes went immediately to the signature that was at the bottom of the neat handwritten note. It was an invitation from Vassilis to dine at the Limenarkhees Taverna, the little restaurant where she'd had lunch that afternoon. It should be fun, he wrote, with live music and dancing. He would call for her at nine.

Oriel instantly felt a lot better. It sounded fun. Maybe she wasn't quite so alone after all. Vassilis was an attractive man, with the natural charm of a womanizer. He posed no threat to Oriel and was harmless enough – she'd met plenty of charming men of his ilk before – and he had been quite entertaining at Manoli's. It wasn't his fault if she had been preoccupied by Damian's dark mood and the presence of the beautiful diva, Yolanda. Perhaps dinner with him would be a good diversion from the undesirable attraction she felt for Damian.

Tomorrow, she would see Damian again at the Epiklisi festival and, although the prospect filled her with trepidation, Oriel was glad that she would see Mattias again. One thing was for certain: she could do with a friend right now.

* * *

The sun beamed down from a cloudless sky, bathing the island of Helios in all its splendour, when Oriel started off that morning for the *agora*, the public square, where she had arranged to meet Mattias to watch the Epiklisi procession. Her mood had been lifted by the glowing Greek light but, deep down, her emotions were still in a state of flux and the disturbing thought of whether or not she would speak to Damian at the festival picked at the frayed edge of her mind.

After Irini had brought in her breakfast tray earlier that morning, the maid had returned a few moments later, bearing a dress wrapped in tissue. Oriel had been a little reticent with her, convinced that Irini might somehow have known what had happened between her and Damian last night. Wasn't it true that the servants seemed to know everything that went on in the house? *Don't be so absurd,* she chided, watching the *kamariera* cross the room. Then, seeing that there was nothing different in her demeanour, she relaxed.

'The Master asked the *Kyria*'s dressmaker to make a *chitón* for you,' Irini said, laying out the ancient-styled Greek dress on the bed. It was a long, wide rectangle of linen, sewn up at the sides, designed to be girdled by a golden belt. Irini explained that the *chitón* should be pinned at the shoulders, and she handed Oriel a heavy gold brooch for the purpose. 'It belonged to the Master's mother. It is Helios, see?'

Oriel held the brooch in the palm of her hand and realized that, indeed, its delicate knotwork formed the shape of the island. She was honoured, as well as a little unnerved, that Damian should have entrusted her with a family heirloom that must clearly be precious to him.

Later, as Oriel put on the dress, she marvelled at how beautifully the warm sunshine yellow of the fabric suited her complexion and brought out the deep tan she had acquired during the past few days. She wondered whether Damian had any part in choosing the colour and the intimacy of that idea made her blush. He had even ensured she was supplied with a pair of flat leather sandals in a light-sand hue, with laces that crossed over her slim ankles. They fitted perfectly and added the final touch to her ancient Grecian outfit.

As Oriel walked through the town she could sense an air of celebration and festivity permeating the island. Doorsteps had been swept spotless and the glass in the windows shone like mirrors. There were flowers on balustrades, and garlands were hung upon the columns and pillars of some of the grander houses, as well as on gates and balconies. Even the trunks of trees had been embellished with colourful ribbons, and everything seemed to shine under the morning sun.

The streets were already lively and bustling with people, rich and poor rubbing shoulders. They moved like a shoal of fish, inexorably making for the same destination. Oriel was glad that Damian had thought to make sure she had an outfit for the occasion, as everyone, it seemed, was clothed in fancy dress. Some of the islanders wore the brown raggedy tunics of the slaves of ancient times; others were disguised as wealthy aristocrats, wearing robes, undergarments and shawls in bright colours of indigo, red, green and purple.

Mattias was waiting for her outside the bakery in the square, as they had arranged. Seeing him, Oriel smiled, registering in that instant how exactly he resembled the classical statues of Poseidon. The robe, the beard, the beetling brows over eyes that twinkled alternately with a fierceness and a warmth – all he needed to complete the picture was a trident but instead he was sensibly furnished with his stick, on which he was leaning as he waited for her.

'You look exactly like Aphrodite,' Mattias said with some aplomb. 'Ah, I see you're wearing the Helios brooch.' He made no other comment about the fact that Damian had lent it to her but Oriel knew the implication wasn't lost on him.

Oriel thanked him for offering to look after her at the festival and he raised his hand to halt her protestations. 'I should be thanking you, *Despinis*,' he said. 'My wife is tied up all day preparing the food for the evening bonfire, and my children and grandchildren have their friends here. They don't want an lame old man like me tagging along.' Oriel sensed this wasn't the exact truth, but was grateful for his gallantry.

'Please, do call me Oriel,' she said, smiling.

He nodded, his eyes twinkling kindly. 'Oriel it is then. I take it you got back all right, last night?' he added. 'I felt a little guilty when I realized how late it was. I had been talking and kept you, and you didn't even have a car.'

'*Kyrios* Lekkas picked me up halfway, he was coming back with his horse.'

'I am sure he scolded you for walking alone after dark. In some ways, he's a very conservative man.'

There was nothing conservative about the way he touched me later that evening, Oriel recalled, her face heating at the memory, but she kept her thoughts to herself and said: 'Yes, he wasn't very happy.'

Mattias laughed and took her elbow. Just then Oriel heard in the distance the sound of sporadic cheering. She looked enquiringly at him.

'That's up at the warehouse, where they keep the chariots. Those who have family in the procession are up there, hanging around to watch the start,' he explained. 'Come, it's just a few streets away on the edge of town. That's where we want to be, too.'

The shouts were now mingling with the sound of *salpigges* blaring, ancient Greek trumpets whose sound echoed through the streets, triumphant tunes joining in the buoyant hurrahs of the masses. By now the sidewalks of the square were crowded with people and Oriel felt whipped up in the tempest of their excitement.

They threaded their way through the throng as the sidewalks began to incline upwards, Mattias leading the way. Oriel noticed that his gait was surprisingly brisk despite his limp. The street widened here to little more than an earth track with compacted stones; houses were on one side, and what looked like stables on the other. People were packed in on both sides and leaning out of windows. A wooden construction akin to a large barn stood to the left, its wide doors open, and Mattias ushered Oriel as close as they could manage.

The fisherman pointed. 'Ah, there we go!'

The first chariots began to appear, drawn by horses that looked like great carvings of burnished copper, as if equine statues had been endowed with a fiery life by the mighty sun god, Helios. Neither the chariots nor their bearers had been embellished with flowers, ribbons and bells, as seemed the norm at other southern-European festivals Oriel had attended. Here, in Helios, the two-wheeled carriages and their beautiful bay horses were elegant – positively classical – in their simplicity. A triumphant cheer went up. To Oriel it seemed as though the illustrated Greek myths, on which she had feasted her eyes as a child, had come to life in front of her. It was a procession, she could easily imagine, that might have set off from Mount Olympus itself.

'Ah, that's Kosta's boy,' Mattias gave Oriel a nudge and pointed to the armed warrior standing in the first of the two-wheeled chariots. 'Ares, the god of war, always comes first.'

Oriel looked at the youth, whose striking black eyes and angry expression so befitted his role as the moody and chaotic god. He glared and scowled at the crowd as he passed by. Surrounding him were creatures formed out of clay: a vulture, a snake, a dog and a boar, whose tusks lent even more ferocity to the tableau.

'He's a fine actor,' observed Oriel. 'He really takes his role seriously.'

'It's a serious business placating Typhoeus,' explained Mattias. 'These fifteen gods and goddesses know what's good for them. At any time their houses, their streets, their families could be lost in rivers of lava.'

Oriel realized as he spoke the words that Mattias, too, shared these age-old superstitions, and she quelled the ironic quip poised on her lips.

Athena's chariot was next, at the helm of which was a woman in her forties. She was crowned with a crested helmet and armed with a shield and spear. 'That's Eleni, the schoolmistress,' said Mattias. 'Who better for the goddess of wisdom? She's always given the role.'

Oriel could see why. The woman, bearing a goatskin shield, the *aegis*, over a long golden dress, surveyed the crowd calmly with large shining grey eyes, with just the shadow of a smile floating on her tanned face. She held an olive branch in her right hand and her sacred owl, crafted this time out of papier mâché, was perched on her shoulder.

As if on cue – just as Aphrodite, the goddess of beauty, love and pleasure came past, smiling charmingly to the crowd – Oriel spotted Yolanda making her way through the islanders on the sidewalk, parting the way as if it were the Red Sea.

As usual the singer was dressed with simple elegance, in the softest midnight-blue tunic dress that fell in statuesque folds. At her waist was a thin gold chain, and a diamante hair-clip in the shape of a half moon – such as Artemis the huntress was often depicted as wearing – was the only other adornment. The eyes of Yolanda's fans momentarily left the pageant and moved to gaze at their own nightingale. Oriel, too, was transfixed. The raven-haired girl in the chariot, who had previously been enjoying herself immensely, could in no way compete with the luscious, dramatically sensual figure of the singer as she swung her hips with an exotic grace completely her own. Behind Yolanda walked her brother, Yorgos, and it was as if he were there only as her manservant, for all the attention she was giving him.

Oriel fixed her gaze back on Aphrodite's chariot but she could see that the girl was playing her role with a little less assurance now. She was holding a scallop shell in one hand, which was posed against her breast, and a myrtle wreath in the other, but the statuesque stillness was spoilt somewhat by the darting looks she gave the figure of Yolanda as the singer cut a swathe through the crowd. *If I didn't know better*, thought Oriel, *I could swear Yolanda is trying to upstage the poor girl.*

Just then her thoughts were cut short by Yorgos's voice. He had grabbed Yolanda's arm and had brought her to where Oriel and Mattias were standing. 'Ah, *Despinis* Anderson, it's easy to pick out your fair hair in the crowd! Let me introduce my sister, Yolanda,' he said unctuously. He was dressed in an expensive-looking merchant's costume, dark green with an excess of gold detail. His gold Rolex and the thick gold chain around his neck completed the picture of a man determined to be noticed. Oriel saw that he didn't bother to address Mattias, whom he must have known. She sensed that Yorgos regarded the fisherman as beneath him.

'*Kaliméra.*' Yolanda's voice was melodious, sweet and rich as treacle. She held out a hand to Oriel and the gesture was regal, as if she expected her to kiss it. Then the singer froze. For a moment Oriel wondered what had happened, and then she saw that Yolanda's gaze had been caught by the golden Helios brooch. 'I think we may have met,' the singer added vaguely.

Oriel lifted her chin and smiled sweetly. 'Yes, I believe we might have.'

Yolanda stared straight at her. 'I hope you enjoy the day.' She had mustered a smile but her eyes were chips of ice. 'Yorgos, we'd better not stop. Come, we need to hurry.'

Yorgos shot her a testy look but said evenly: 'Yes, I'm sure he'll want you to be the first one he sees when he gets to the plateau.'

Oriel couldn't help the flush that rose in her cheeks and Mattias, she was sure, was perfectly aware of the undercurrents in the exchange. He clasped Oriel's arm in a supportive grip. 'Yes, we must be going too, Oriel. These legs of mine will need more time to get up Mount Helios.'

Yorgos, clearly annoyed at having been chivvied away by his sister, had just enough time to say to Oriel that they would hopefully catch her later before he was brusquely hustled off. As they walked away, Oriel noticed with some satisfaction that the sultry swing of Yolanda's hips was now more akin to a stalk, the singer's brisk steps conveying quite clearly the change in her state of mind. A few yards off the diva turned to her brother and a cross exchange took place, Yolanda wagging her finger and Yorgos looking no less irritated, though for different reasons.

'I think, perhaps, our nightingale is not happy,' said Mattias sagaciously. 'I wonder what could have caused that?'

The diva had occupied Oriel's thoughts for so long now that she was unable to resist trying to glean more information about her hold on Damian. 'We met the other night at Manoli's. She was clearly put out when she discovered I was staying at Heliades.'

Mattias's grey eyes regarded Oriel pensively. 'Only to be expected,' he said, after a pause. 'For some time now, our nightingale has flitted from tree to tree and has always expected attention on her return. Maybe she wonders if her place in the nest has been taken. Men can never resist our songbird, but what if her charms no longer hold that allure? That's what she is afraid of, like many a captivating woman.'

He broke off to scan the parade, adding on a quieter note, 'Just watch out. Her voice may be sweet but her beak is sharp. That one could peck out your eyes as soon as look at you.'

This was said with a lightness of tone and laughter in his voice but, still, Oriel fancied there was a warning contained in Mattias's words.

'I have to say, I'm not sure I trust her brother either,' she confessed wryly.

'Ah yes, Yorgos Christodolou. I've known him since he was a boy and he was a sly one even then. As the Greek saying goes: "Even though the wolf got old and his fur is white, he neither changed his skin nor his head."' He patted her arm reassuringly. 'I don't trust him either, though the *Kyrios* has his reasons for employing him.'

Mattias looked up just then and waved at Demeter, who returned a dazzling smile. The goddess of the harvest, a middle-aged woman and obviously a friend of his, held a sheaf of wheat in one hand and a torch in the other. A snake was draped like a boa around her neck and at her feet was her other sacred animal, a clay pig.

'Anastasia is a pillar of the community,' he told Oriel. 'One of the main organizers, now we no longer have Cassandra.'

'What was she like?' asked Oriel. 'Cassandra, I mean.' Curiosity had got the better of her; the mystery and scandal surrounding Damian's dead wife seemed so inextricably bound to the strangeness of this island.

Mattias shifted uneasily and Oriel could sense that the shutters had come down. It wasn't like her to gossip and she regretted it instantly.

'I'm not one to speak ill of the dead,' he said shortly. 'She had her faults, like any of us.' He paused, as if trying to pick the right words. 'An energetic young lady, I can say that for her, beautiful and passionate. God rest her soul.'

Oriel could tell by the firm set of Mattias's jaw that he had said all he was prepared to say. She turned her head back to the procession, where Zeus, the king of the gods and ruler of Mount Olympus, was passing. They had chosen a regal-looking giant of a man for the role, with a dark beard covering a jutting jaw. He held the royal sceptre in his hand and had a papier mâché eagle perched on his shoulder. At his feet lay the head of a bull. He was everything Oriel would have imagined the son of Cronus to be and yet Oriel couldn't help thinking that Damian possessed more charisma and potency than this man had in his little finger. Then she berated herself: *Oh, why does it always have to come back to Damian? I'm behaving like a woman possessed!*

'That's Diocles, Anastasia's husband. He's a judge. Very fierce, just as he looks. He's a good friend of the *Kyrios*.'

'Speaking of the *Kyrios*,' observed Oriel nonchalantly, 'I thought he was part of this procession.' Mattias glanced at her, his eyes twinkling with wry amusement. 'Patience, my dear. You've heard the Greek saying, *káthe prágma ston kairó tou, ki o koliós ton Ávgousto*, everything in its time and mackerel in August? Things must be done in their proper time, not before. The *Kyrios* always makes his entrance after the other chariots have passed, it's part of the tradition.'

With nothing else to do but look around, Oriel noticed that some of the islanders were staring at her and then talking among themselves. A few seemed wary, others only curious. She smiled at an old lady standing next to her, who returned her smile shyly and silently offered Oriel a boiled sweet from a packet she was clutching in her hand.

Oriel graciously accepted the sweet, and thanked her.

'You are Greek?' the old lady asked, sounding puzzled.

'No, but I've studied Greek and I've visited your beautiful country many times.'

Their conversation was interrupted, just then, by the sight of Damian's chariot being wheeled out, framed by two stable hands. The crowd went wild. A storm of hailing cheers and applause erupted from the islanders standing on the sidewalk as Damian appeared in all his splendour.

Unlike the fifteen men and women who had preceded him, he wasn't dressed as a god but was still in ancient Greek attire, a deep purple cloak thrown about his shoulders. Beneath it, he was wearing a breastplate and dark-red tunic with a light-kilted loin band over boots of soft hide, strapped up the front with criss-cross ties. His helmet was of bronze, rich with gold, and held under his chin by a chain of wide golden mesh. He settled it more securely on his head and tested the tightness and strength of the chinstrap. Then he reached out and took the whip from the stable hands standing by. The sun shone brightly, casting his proud face in sharp relief. He looked regal, standing in a lightly braced stance in the chariot, his legs slightly apart, knees just relaxed.

The beaming rays set the gold buckles of the horses' bridles, the burnished rail of the chariot, the golden ridge and strap of Damian's helmet flashing as if they were ablaze. The polished harness looked as if light were flowing through it, and the satin glossiness of the horses' coats seemed to reflect the intense glow of fiery strength within them. Damian lifted his hand to salute the crowd on his right and then his left. All could determine on sight that he was the scion of a great house, an aristocrat and, for some of the ignorant people, a figure approaching the status of deity. Still, for all the instinctive authority in his appearance and bearing, his countenance was rich with sensitive feeling.

'Stand back!' he commanded, while the chariot tilted and dropped slightly as Damian settled himself firmly again. The horses reared on to their hind legs, pawing the air, and a loud exclamation of concern lifted from the crowd. A sharp tug of the reins from Damian and the animals came thudding four-hoofed to the ground, only to use the striking of their hooves upon the earth as impetus for a great lifting leap forward. For a fearful moment, Oriel thought that the chariot would jerk away from beneath Damian's feet but, lightly bracing his body and instinctively leaning forward, he met the pull of the vehicle. His masterly manoeuvring was met with shouts of admiration and clapping from the crowd.

Damian gave a tug on the reins, which set the great horses in motion, and the chariot sped off. Oriel saw him lift his free hand in salute as he passed her, his burning gaze fixing on hers for a brief second, but she had no time to respond. Still, she looked at him as he hurtled away and, in that instant, it was as if the whole of her body had sight – she was enveloping the magnificent picture of him standing proudly there in the chariot, the reins held lightly between his fingers, driving those two splendid great creatures on and on.

She leaned out to watch him sweeping down the street at a much speedier pace than had the others. Her heart was thumping and her emotion was such that tears welled up in her eyes as she stared after him. It seemed only a moment or two before the chariot was no more than a vague outline in the distance. A long, whirling, curved line of dust trailed out behind it as though it were indeed a thing charged with fire, sending smoke billowing away as it raced on, lifting and tilting over the unevenness of the ground. Then it was almost obscured by its trail of dust, and the thudding of the hooves and the rumble of the wheels grew slowly fainter and into nothingness, until the chariot vanished from Oriel's view entirely.

The looming bulk of Typhoeus towered over the motley hordes of people as the parade of colourful chariots danced its way down the streets, musicians playing the exotic Thracian lyre and drum, creating a majestic, merry atmosphere. It was the grand party of the year, the one in which all the islanders participated. Looking around her as she and Mattias followed the parade down through the town, Oriel saw that it was a day when the gods blessed the island's streets; it was the locals' day of vacation from reality, when the extraordinary was the norm and just being alive was a riot.

Damian's people were happy and that thought warmed Oriel's heart. She felt the culture of the island soak into her skin. It was a place that breathed the continuity of generations, each family living out their lives in the cradle of tradition. Oriel's pulse responded to the adventure of it all, beating with a thrilling rhythm. There was something magical about being one of the crowd, an easing of the loneliness within, she thought. This sandy-hued island of eternal azure skies, ever-changing blue sea, beaming sunshine and ancient stone temples was beginning to bewitch her.

They started for Mount Helios after a lunch of chicken and flatbread picked up from the village taverna. She and Mattias had waited until the worst of the heat had gone from the day and it was late afternoon when they finally set out for the plateau, where the evening's celebrations were to take place. They climbed the mountain slowly, pausing every now and again for the limping fisherman to take short breaks along the way and to drink from the bottles of water they had brought with them. Happily, there was an easier path than the one taken by the young and agile: an old drover's track that that had been improved by Damian to accommodate wheelchairs, the old and the infirm.

'We can take our time,' said Mattias, wheezing a little as he stopped for breath and leaned on his stick. 'The fire-walking won't start yet awhile.' Oriel was a little alarmed by the idea of the gods and goddesses walking on hot coals – it seemed like a sacred ritual that could easily go wrong. Yet, like the procession itself, it also seemed a fiercely guarded imperative if the islanders were to keep their volcano appeased.

They continued up the track, which snaked its way around ancient, withering trees. Below them, the vivid sea splashed uneasily against a jagged wall of rock. There was a beauty to it, raw and barren though it was. The people around them on all sides were rushing up the escarpment in a frenzy – carrying torches, goaded on by the wild music of the deep-throated flutes and thundering drums that followed them. Dun-coloured earth whirled around the revellers in dusty clouds as they made their way to the final flight of rough stone steps that led to the plateau.

When at last Oriel and Mattias reached the top of the rock the view was breathtaking. The day was ending and settling to rest, the sun dying on the horizon, setting on fire the lively waves of a now purple sea and the countryside aglow with the last orange rays before twilight beckoned the stars – a marine dream scene with a sky dyed pomegranate pink. The atmosphere was surreal.

The journey hadn't been easy and Oriel could not help but admire Mattias's resilience and courage. Now she looked down and the fabulous sight played on her imagination. At her feet the soaring cliff – those noble walls carved by nature that seemed to dominate the island – sloped suddenly away. She visualized herself leaping off, falcon-winged, to glide over the Mediterranean, following the setting sun into its warm, painted seabed. Scarlet, then amethyst, emblazoned the enormous sky before it darkened to obsidian.

There was already a great crowd assembled at the plateau. Ancient trees formed an arc around three sides of it; they rose upwards, seemingly without end, the canopy above distant, like clouds of green. Their gnarly trunks resembled living walls and seemed to turn the place into an outdoor temple. It was as if they were ancient beings providing sanctuary, casting their protective shadow on those who came to worship at the feet of the great beast Typhoeus.

At the far end of the plateau, at the foot of the volcano, stood a black granite altar. A profusion of votive offerings had been deposited there by devout islanders: bunches of flowers, amphorae filled with grain, perfumes, wine and oil, as well as produce from the fields, orchards and olive groves of the island.

With its back to the altar, a beautiful golden throne with red velvet lining stood on a dais. The fifteen islanders portraying gods and goddesses had assembled around it in a semicircle, turned towards Typhoeus, as if worshipping the great volcano.

'That is where the *Kyrios* will sit,' Mattias told Oriel. 'He'll give a speech later.'

'Will he be walking on the hot coals too?' she asked, a little nervously.

'Yes,' said Mattias. 'But don't worry, Oriel, Damian will be fine, you'll see.'

Close by, beside the roots of a tree, a heap of glowing embers lay in a shallow pit. On one side of it candles were burning while, on the other, stood pots of smoking incense.

'The pit was dug yesterday night for the sacrifice of a young boar,' Mattias explained.

'Please don't say they'll be killing it in front of us. I'm not at all sure I want to witness that,' said Oriel, her eyes widening with consternation.

Mattias laughed. 'No, no, don't worry. The sacrifice was carried out at dawn by the *Kyrios* and the chosen fifteen. Shall I tell you how it is done? It isn't cruel.'

Oriel laughed. 'I see you're dying to tell me so go ahead, on the condition that I can stop you if it all becomes too gory.'

Mattias looked gravely at her. 'How can you hope to understand the *Kyrios* and the people of this island if you don't understand their customs?'

She nodded, feeling suddenly contrite. 'You're right, I'm all ears.'

'As the sun appears on the horizon, the beast, which has been attached all night to a tree, is brought to the edge of the pit. He is then turned upside down. His throat is slashed by a sword with a single blow so he doesn't suffer and so that the blood soaks into the earth.'

'At least the blood of the poor animal isn't left in the road to gather flies and vermin. I've seen that happen before.'

'You need to remember, Oriel, that the blood flowing from the animal is said to be the share of the trees and the earth.'

'That almost sounds romantic,' she had to admit.

'The carcass is then hung and skinned to the accompaniment of music, and the raw flesh and hide cut up and put into baskets to be distributed among the families of the islanders who have taken part in the procession.' Mattias sat down on a rock step and placed his stick beside him. 'You must understand, Oriel, it is an honour for the boar,' the fisherman added earnestly. 'The chosen one is picked carefully. He must be over one year old, unmarked and not castrated.'

'I'm still not sure I'd want to see a sacrifice, honour or not,' she said.

'Well, the boar's sacrifice will be commemorated tomorrow when they plant a new tree on the plateau. That way, Typhoeus knows we remember him and pay tribute to his power.'

Now their attention was drawn to the seven male gods, who had rid themselves of their elaborate costumes and exchanged them for simple white tunics. They were swaying and spinning, working themselves into a trance-like state, dancing hypnotically to the beat of the goatskin drums. The dancers whirled round the fire pit, where a group of islanders was spreading out the coals with long poles. Slowly, a glowing oval space was taking shape, ready for the fire walk. The spinning men reminded Oriel of a group of whirling dervishes she had seen in Sufi ceremonies in Egypt, and watching them made her feel almost dizzy.

'The fire was lit early this afternoon. They've been dancing for most of the time since then,' Mattias commented.

'It must be dangerous, surely, in this heat?'

'Only the fittest are chosen,' explained Mattias. 'And even they must have a six-month retreat and a full medical check-up to qualify. There must be no smoking, drinking or sexual intercourse during that period. Besides, they are protected by the gods they honour and are seized by the spirit of Typhoeus, so nothing can harm them.'

Oriel spoke her next words without thinking, then felt a blush creep up her cheeks as she realized what they might imply: 'Damian is participating in the fire walk and he doesn't seem to have abstained from anything, as far as I can gather.'

Mattias gave a chuckle. 'The *Kyrios* has been a firewalker ever since he took over leadership of the island. The soles of his feet are immune to pain by now.'

Then, suddenly, the sound of a *salpigga* was heard, a long copper horn that had been used from the time of the Ancients to signal the start of the athletic games, and the crowd fell silent under its penetrating blast. The islander representing Hephaestus, the god of fire, blacksmiths and volcanoes, came forward – a crippled, bearded man with a hammer, tongs and anvil slung on a strap around his body – and blew into the *salpigga* three times. The coals were ready and the sacred fire-walking ritual was about to begin.

It was then that Oriel spotted Damian, a head taller than the other firewalkers, and her heart lurched in her chest. His face was a mask of concentration and she found it impossible to tear her gaze away from him.

One after the other, barefoot and bearing the statue of the god they represented, the seven male firewalkers approached the bed of scorching coals. Some stepped across it in an unhurried and deliberate fashion, while others took it at a frenzied dash. It wasn't that the hot embers were burning them, more that they were afraid of being burnt. A number of devotees were kneeling down beside the pit and pounding the ash with the palms of their hands to demonstrate their power over the fire.

Finally, it was Damian's turn to walk the fire. His tall, athletic frame, now clothed in the traditional white Grecian tunic, strode with a lithe energy towards the glowing apron of scorching coals. With outstretched arms, he stepped on to the incandescent embers. As striking as a timber wolf, he took light strides, calmly tackling the red-hot oval stretch, which shone in the darkness as if spread with rutilant gems. With his glistening dark hair, his tanned complexion and his white tunic silvered by moonbeams, he was magnificent. Oriel stood there transfixed, breathless. It wasn't just his imposing frame and perfect bone structure that made him so charismatic, an inner beauty shone from his trance-like expression. There was a softness in his eyes, a gentleness in his smile, as he advanced with confidence – a leader for his people who were gathered there to bear witness, while above them glowered the mighty, sacred bulk of Typhoeus.

Silence hung in the air like the suspended moment before a falling glass shatters on the ground. Looking around at the islanders, who were watching their leader breathlessly, Oriel once again witnessed that, although feared, this man was also admired and dearly loved. Was he playing the role for the sole benefit of the islanders or did he share their superstitions? Did he believe in the myths surrounding the volcano?

Then it was over and, with the end of the firewalking, the white shafts of daylight had passed, too. As night approached, devouring the magic light, random twinkles of fireflies could be seen, until the space below the cliff, billowing in dark waves, sparked with benign green embers under a star-speckled sky.

Oriel watched Damian for a moment as people gathered round him. She could see that he was scanning the sea of faces – or fancied she could – and hoped for a brief moment that he might be looking for her; but then Yolanda came up to him and laid a hand on his shoulder. The high-pitched sound of the diva's laughter made its way to Oriel's ears through the noisy chatter of the crowd, like glass shattering in the distance. She turned away, not wanting to see his response. Luckily, Mattias steered her away, saving her from further heartache. 'Come, *Kyria*, let's make our way to where the food is being laid out. I want to introduce you to my wife, Anna. She'll be pleased to meet you.'

As the people dispersed, Damian sat down at the far end of the plateau on the throne, which had been set up at the foot of Typhoeus in front of an altar of offerings. The islanders had been depositing these gifts since the early morning. The light diffused by the profusion of candles, which had now been lit, surrounded the throne with an arc of brilliant gold in the blackness.

Oriel and Mattias paused to turn round as Damian addressed the crowd in a clear voice. 'We must all drink now to Typhoeus who guards our island, and to you, my people, who help me sustain it.

We are as one, marching in one direction, working to one aim. To keep this island and our loved ones safe.'

There was a spontaneous outpouring of emotion and a great shout rose from the crowd as Damian, leading his people in a toast, snatched up a cup of wine and drank to Typhoeus and the islanders' safety.

By now the great bonfire, assembled from timber collected earlier that afternoon, had been lit and a red-and-orange ball of flames roared upwards. Plumes of grey smoke and ash floated by the throng of excited children, who by now were chasing each other with screams of delight. Talkative adults, discussing the sacred ritual that had just taken place, paused to watch the great fiery beast before them in awe, their eyes transformed as each flickering flame played a light show on their pupils. The air was filled with the woody fragrance of smoke and the tantalizing smells of spit-roasting meats, which wafted on the breeze.

The plateau was teaming with chattering, swirling islanders, whirlpools of life, their figures lit up by the golden blaze of the fire. Some of them had seen Oriel at the beach taverna and, recognizing her, smiled shyly or nodded their heads in greeting as she and Mattias resumed their slow progress through the crowd.

'Some of the islanders will stay here until the glowing embers die. The memories of this day will remain with them all through the difficult and harsh winter months, until the Epiklisi next year,' Mattias explained.

Oriel realized that this was a festival like no other in which she had ever participated. There was a sanctity here that transcended everyday concerns – she could feel it – and it was timeless, like the forests, the ocean and the mountains.

Then Mattias spied a large, smiling woman in an apron, who was putting out plates of stuffed eggplant on a trestle. 'Ah, here she is. Anna, my love, I told you about the archaeologist who is working for the *Kyrios*, the one I met yesterday on the beach.'

The woman had coarse dark skin and an engaging smile that showed off a set of brilliant white teeth. Her hair was grey, but still thick, and she had arranged it in a topknot on the crown of her head. She was wearing a simple white tunic, like many of the islanders. Smilingly, she held both of Oriel's hands in hers. '*Kalispera, Despi-*

nis. I hope you have enjoyed the day? Epiklisi is very special to us.'

'Yes, it's been wonderful. Thanks to Mattias, who has looked after me right from the start,' said Oriel.

'Ah, he's not such a bad fellow,' said Anna, her eyes twinkling at her husband lovingly. 'I've trained him well.'

Oriel laughed. 'Indeed you have.'

'You must come to dinner at our house soon. I make the best moussaka on the island, everybody says so.' The Greek woman winked and released Oriel's hands.

'You're very kind.'

Then Anna looked around the sea of faces, her hands on her hips. 'Have you seen the children?' she asked Mattias. 'They need to pay their respects.'

'*Agápi mou*, they're hardly children, you know. Let them have their fun,' he said laughingly. 'We'll catch up with them later. The night is still young.'

Just then, Damian appeared – without Yolanda at his side, Oriel was relieved to see, although her relief was quickly replaced by a wildly nervous fluttering in her stomach. She tried not to think about the passionate encounter with him the previous night. Her whole body still vibrated with the dangerous thrill of it.

'Mattias, my friend.' Damian slapped the fisherman heartily on the back and they embraced warmly. He kissed his wife on both cheeks. 'Anna, how are you? I see you are doing a fine job fattening us all up with your excellent food, as usual.'

'There are many mouths to feed, *Kyrios*,' she answered, chuckling with pleasure at this compliment.

Damian turned his silver gaze to Oriel. A slow, lazy smile swept across his face as he regarded her, and his eyes smouldered for a brief moment before he said: 'You look like a true goddess, Calypso. I trust the costume fits you comfortably?' He stood back and looked her up and down, apparently satisfied that the *chitón* was indeed exactly the right size.

Oriel's mind went blank. She felt as though her emotions might erupt, like the volcano looming above them, but she mustered her disjointed thoughts enough to say: 'It's perfect, thank you, Damian. So very thoughtful of you to have it made for me.' Then, feeling as though she was staring at him, she added as brightly as she could:

'I wasn't expecting to see you as one of the firewalkers. Is there no end to your talents?'

His smile was enigmatic. 'As I've told you before, you should always expect the unexpected with me.' Something in his knowing look brought a glow to her cheeks that had nothing to do with the heat of the bonfire.

Both Mattias and his wife were looking from her to Damian. They exchanged glances and Mattias cleared his throat. 'And you look like Helios himself,' he said, patting Damian's arm. 'The way you tore off in that chariot, I thought you would make flames sprout beneath you.'

Anna nudged her husband in the ribs. 'Come, Mattias, help me with this bread. While you talk, it won't cut itself.' She stared at him meaningfully and, after a quizzical look, he nodded and grinned widely, following her over to a large basket of loaves.

Damian leaned against the trestle and crossed his arms. Oriel felt suddenly tongue-tied as his gaze skimmed over her dress and wandered languidly up to her eyes. There they stopped. In the light of the bonfire, one side of his face was illuminated and he looked half man, half infernal deity.

'Such an amazing array of gods and goddesses you have here,' she said finally, her voice smoky with warmth.

'I knew you'd love all of this,' he said softly.

'You were impressive on that chariot.'

He grinned, the scar on his cheek hitching up as he did so. 'You're positively brimming with compliments today, Calypso. I could get used to this. And may I say how impressive *you* are in that outfit.' His gaze held hers. 'The colour looks exactly as I thought it would against your skin.'

A pulse pounded in her ears. *Damn him!* He had removed his cloak and helmet, and with his hair so touchably tousled, his gleaming breastplate and long muscular legs clad in soft leather boots, he was every bit the mythical warrior hero. An involuntary warmth swirled low in her belly. Oriel's gaze flitted away for a moment, as she tried and failed to find something to say. Among the islanders closest to them, she noticed that people were murmuring and looking in their direction. But Damian chose to ignore them and instead seemed to go out of his way to look only at her.

'Damian, Oriel!'

Stavros suddenly emerged from a group of islanders and came towards them. At his side was a small, pretty woman with dark brown hair curled into a loose bun at the nape of her neck.

Damian pushed off from the trestle and embraced them both. 'I thought I'd lost you in the crowd. Mattias brought Oriel here, I think she approves of Epiklisi.'

Stavros smiled at Oriel and laughed. 'How could you not?' He touched the elbow of the woman who was regarding Oriel with kind curiosity. 'Please, let me introduce you to my wife, Rhea.'

The petite woman shook Oriel's hand warmly. 'What a beautiful *chitón*,' she said, admiringly. 'You fit in very well here, *Despinis*.'

'Thank you,' murmured Oriel, glancing self-consciously at Damian, who was grinning like a schoolboy. His mood was infectious and she smiled brightly at Rhea. 'Are you both here alone?'

'Alone?' Damian laughed heartily. 'Stavros is one of five sons and has twelve cousins, so highly unlikely.'

Stavros grinned sheepishly. 'Yes, the whole family is here.' He motioned behind him to a large group of islanders clustered together, laughing with their children, who were running in and out of their legs and seemed to be falling on top of each other at every opportunity.

'Ah, the starving hordes!' Anna returned with Mattias, carrying a large basket of food, and proceeded to dish out warm pita breads filled with delicious-smelling *souvlaki*.

'If you don't eat, you'll have my wife to answer to,' said Mattias, addressing them all with a wry grin. As everyone laughed, the fisherman's wife came to stand in front of Oriel, her teeth gleaming in a broad smile as she held out the basket. '*Despinis*, come taste one. You're thin as a reed, you need strengthening.'

Standing at Anna's shoulder, Damian leaned in slightly and said in a conspicuously loud voice: 'Don't underestimate this one, Anna. She's as strong as they come.' His gaze shone so sincerely at Oriel that it rivalled the glow of the full moon above. Oriel's insides gave a somersault of pleasure.

The aroma was so enticing that Oriel gratefully accepted the traditional fare. The walk up to the plateau had made her quite hungry and, besides, there was so much wine and ouzo flowing by now that she knew it would be unwise to drink on an empty stomach. As she gazed around the throng laughing and talking with Damian, she found it now almost impossible to believe that this was the same person who had greeted her so cynically when she had first arrived on Helios, and had seemed so forbidding. Here was a glimpse of the old Damian, the man she had met all those years ago in Aegina.

Damian was standing a few feet away and she caught his eye. A smile lingered on his lips as he stared at her. Silent communication fluttered between them, filled with an excited awareness of each other. At that moment, somewhere beyond the bonfire, a young islander took up a lyre and began to sing a hymn to the volcano that towered menacingly over their island yet also protected the people from outside invasion – after all, the lyrics went, who would want to conquer a land that was threatened to be burned to ashes at any moment?

One after the other, a handful of men borrowed the lyre and sang. The hymn merged into a wild drinking song one of the islanders had learnt among the people of the mountains to the north, before moving on to a song of Lesbos, where the poet Sappho had lived, until, finally, it became a martial chorus of the Spartans, which all the islanders joined in until it seemed as if the whole of Helios was echoing with song.

Among the sea of faces, Oriel suddenly saw Yolanda surrounded by a group of besotted-looking young men, all vying for her attention. The singer was throwing back her mane of dark hair, the diamante clip glinting in the firelight, and laughing as though she was enjoying the adulation. Oriel sighed. She had never allowed herself to think too hard about Damian and Yolanda together, but now images flowed into her mind that she tried desperately to banish: of the beautiful singer wrapping her nymph-like body around his, tasting the warm sweetness of his mouth, fulfilling his needs. It was too much to bear.

'You seem miles away.'

She jumped and span around at the familiar deep rumble of his voice.

'You nearly frightened me half to death!' Oriel glared at Damian, her green eyes still flaming with the jealousy that was weighing on her so heavily.

Damian's eyes followed the direction in which she'd been looking. When they returned to her face, he studied her intently.

Rather than give away that she had been brooding about the diva, Oriel quickly said: 'I'm surprised that Yolanda hasn't sung this evening. She has quite a voice.'

He shrugged. 'She may do, who knows?' He continued to look at her as though he had guessed the reason for her interest. 'Would it bother you if she did?'

'Bother me?' Oriel shot back. 'Why would it bother me?'

A faintly amused smile twitched at his mouth. 'Yolanda may be the island's darling but I'm guessing she isn't yours.'

'I have nothing against her,' Oriel lied. She instantly regretted bringing up the subject of Yolanda, determined not to spoil what was still a magical evening. After sipping her wine she gazed around. 'The atmosphere is incredible here. I've never experienced anything like it. Such *joie de vivre*.'

Once more, Damian followed her gaze. 'We call it *képhi* in Greece, the spirit of joy and passion. It's not given to everybody and is totally spontaneous. It comes when the soul and body are overwhelmed with an exuberance that must find an outlet.'

'I remember it from my Ovid. *Képhi* is turned on by Dionysus, isn't it?'

'That's right. The god of wine and debauchery, who inspires music and poetry. In ancient times, the raving maenads, the frenzied women who followed Dionysus, were probably expressing a variety of *képhi*. We Greeks cannot help but express what is within us, Calypso.' He looked around at the laughing dancers as they gave great shouts of exuberance, then turned to her with a grin. There was such simple joy in his eyes that it made her heart lurch. She couldn't help but return his smile, forgetting everything except Damian's being there with her and the electric feeling that resonated between them, tangible as the air they breathed.

As the hours passed and the night grew darker, with the moonlight glittering on the surface of the sea in vast yellow pools, the revelry grew louder and jollier as though Dionysus himself had been summoned by their conversation. More spit-roasted meats and vegetables, barbecued on skewers, appeared, as well as cakes and sweetmeats. Wine cups were being filled continuously as a wave of songs of thanks echoed in the night around the volcano.

For the rest of the evening, Oriel's gaze was often drawn to Damian. His mood was light, almost effervescent tonight; there was a boyish air about him, so different from that of masterful dictator she had witnessed on other occasions. She went along with his light-heartedness happily, sipping at the glasses of ouzo Mattias handed to her, and laughing at the joking banter that batted back and forth between the old friends. She chatted to Anna and Rhea, both of whom were charmingly voluble, and they asked Oriel all about her-self, between making affectionately mocking comments about their men. Damian, she could see, was glancing at her approvingly. In fact, he hardly seemed able to take his eyes off her. At one point, Oriel had to turn her head away to avoid his gaze – there was such a naked blaze in his dark irises that she was almost afraid she might get scorched.

At one point, as she was laughing at something he'd said to Mattias, she glanced up. It was then that she caught sight of Yolanda, standing on the other side of the bonfire. The singer's eyes were glittering in the light of the flames as they watched Oriel's and Damian's every move.

CHAPTER 7

When Oriel woke she didn't lie in bed for long. It was Monday and, even though she'd only had a few hours' sleep after returning from the Epiklisi festival, she had work to do. Nonetheless, images of the day before had crept into her dreams – of the spectacular procession to Mount Helios, of Damian's fiery gaze on her throughout the evening – and a pink hue warmed her cheeks at the memory.

She pushed back the covers and went to her bedroom window, where she drew back the curtains. The day was bright, but there was a brisk breeze outside; she could see it fluttering the little green leaves of the olive trees so that they glinted silvery in the light. For a moment her heart sank. Damian had explained how tide, wind and current could dash their chances of diving the wreck again today, and she wondered if he might call their expedition off.

Her fears, it turned out, were well founded. When Irini came in with her breakfast tray, the maid confirmed that there would indeed be no diving and that Damian had flown to Corfu instead. He would be back later that afternoon and had asked if Oriel could be ready at four o'clock to accompany him on an outing to see the sponge divers at the harbour.

'Oh, and *Despinis* Anderson,' Irini added. 'There was a telephone call for you, an English lady. She left this number.'

Oriel took the piece of paper from the maid. Her face lit up. 'Thank you, Irini. I'll be down shortly. I'll use the phone in the study, if I may.'

After a quick breakfast of freshly baked bread rolls and a bowl of Greek yoghurt and peaches, she dressed quickly in a light-blue short-sleeved linen shirt and stone-coloured capris and made her way along the wing to Damian's study.

So what if they couldn't dive today? That didn't mean she had to be idle. The island was a treasure trove of historical ruins and, for a moment, Oriel felt like a child in a sweetshop, amazed by the array of colourful choices. She decided she would take the Volkswagen and drive to the ruins that lay around Manoli's. She had only seen the acropolis by moonlight, and Damian had already suggested she assess the site, so now was her chance to take a closer look at what had seemed like the remains of a small settlement.

'You sound chirpy,' Cynthia Albright's voice was warm on the other end of the line. 'The Greek air must be suiting you.'

'You wouldn't believe the wealth of unexcavated ruins on this island, above ground and underwater,' said Oriel. 'It's like every archaeologist's dream.'

'Lucky you. Just think of me here in this dark room full of dusty tomes.'

'Oh really, Cynthia! You wouldn't have it any other way.'

Her friend from the Bodleian gave a wry laugh. 'I suppose not. Anyway, I've got the information you wanted about the seal on that amphora you found. Have you got a pen?'

'Yes, hold on.' Oriel opened her notebook. 'Go ahead.'

'Your Roman is called Marcus Sestius. That's what the SES stands for, and I've checked out his trader's insignia and that fits, too. A trident with sea serpent. So that makes your ship third century BC.'

'That's exciting. We knew it was Roman, but somehow it doesn't seem real until you've established provenance. Thank you so much for looking into it for me.'

'Wait, that's not all. I did a bit more digging around. He's quite an interesting chap, this Sestius. He built up a sizeable shipping business in Greece and was as rich as Croesus according to one account I found. He collected works of art, including some of the finest bronzes ever made. Then everything went pear-shaped for the poor man after an earthquake destroyed his home, and records show him retiring to Delos. And guess what? When his business was thriving, he was living in Helice.'

'The lost seaport! We were only discussing it the other night. Fascinating …' Oriel's eyes shone with excitement. It was as if a whole narrative landscape was unfurling in her mind's eye. Now the wreck of Damian's argosy was connected to the lost city of Helice. Had it been on a voyage from there to Helios on one of the great Roman trading routes, and sunk in a storm off the treacherous coast of the island? And Sestius being a collector of bronzes … that, surely, was a significant detail.

Oriel thanked her friend and hung up, promising to keep in touch. As she replaced her notebook and pen in her bag she looked thoughtful. It was like following a treasure trail, laid thousands of years ago, and now that the first clue was solved she couldn't wait to revisit the wreck. Undoubtedly there were a lot more mysteries hidden in the argosy's watery grave.

She ran upstairs to pack a knapsack and grab her straw hat. Ten minutes later she was at the wheel of the Volkswagen. The road to Manoli's looked different in daylight. The coastline was rugged, with rocks of all shapes and colours, awe-inspiring in their majesty. Some formed natural arches, and she could see that in places the cliffs had been hollowed into tunnels and caves by the action of waves. Every so often there was a sheltered cove fringed by sea pines. She made a note to come and explore these little bays one day, as they would be perfect for bathing. On the other side of the road, pine forests and sand dunes stretched monotonously for a couple of miles without a break.

Oriel drove past Manoli's taverna, which was quiet now, and parked the car a mile or so further along the road in the shade of a crumbling barn. There was a dilapidated hut next to it, at the door of which a goat was tethered. She could see an outdoor bread oven and, from the lower branches of an olive tree, cheeses in goat bladders were hanging in the warm air to dry. Two children were playing under the tree, although it offered little shade, and a rotund woman was standing on a ladder, trimming a huge carob. They stopped and waved to Oriel as she passed by.

The ruined acropolis was sprawled a few metres away under the baking sun. Whoever had been in charge of the excavation here had wrecked the place – that much was clear. There was something sad about the tumbled stones in the bright light of day, she reflected. It had looked much more impressive by moonlight. Damian had explained that the island's ruins had been picked over long before his family had taken over the place. Oriel sighed. Just think what might have been recovered in the right hands, careful hands like hers.

Part of the ground was covered with a sheath of stiff blue-and-purple spikes, a shrub that looked just like porcupine quills. Here and there, amid the tumbled stones, were bald patches of red clay, streaks of shale and areas of dune. In among the wild barley grass that had grown all over the ruins, the odd architectural gem had endured the hardship of time. As Oriel picked her way carefully around the fallen masonry, she could see tiny mosaic fragments that must once have formed a pavement. These glimpses of the past were tantalizing, yet so frustrating. Now they would never know the designs that had been wrought by the mosaicist. Think, too, what she might have been able to discover about the people who had lived, worked and worshipped here more than two thousand years ago.

Oriel took a sip from her bottle of water. It was amazing how quickly the sun grew in heat. She could see why the inhabitants of the island all those centuries ago believed that Helios, the handsome Titan crowned with the shining aureole of the sun, drove his glittering chariot across the sky each day. Oriel thought it perfectly understandable that they would have personified such a powerful force: after all, they had no scientific explanation for natural phenomena. She glanced at her watch: ten o'clock. By midday there would be a heat haze over the landscape, scintillating and shimmery, and the sun would be bearing down mercilessly.

Standing in the field were two Doric columns, then another three: all that was left of the settlement's age-old temple. Further away, on the grassy margin of the road, was an ancient tomb guarded by a cypress tree, and beside it the remains of a sacrificial altar. The scale of everything was vast: the buildings, now laid low, must have been so tall, so regal in their carved splendour. Oriel looked at the immense girth of the stone columns, lying in fragments on the reddish, baked earth; it was as though some mighty god, looking down upon this island and abominating the overreaching pride of this ancient race of men, had stretched out his great hand and struck the settlement, reducing it to barely more than rubble.

Oriel looked up at the dark bulk of Typhoeus. How many times had it erupted since those ancient days? Had this devastation been all the volcano's work? Was this island doomed? She walked further on and started to ascend the terraced levels. She began to work in earnest now and for the next two hours photographed, measured and sketched, before pausing to rest in the shade of a carob tree. Oriel had climbed steadily, so that now she was looking over the site, seated on a stone step at the side of a ruined amphitheatre. She took a few deep gulps from her water bottle. This was thirsty work. Hungry-making too. She took off her straw hat and sunglasses and wiped her forehead with the back of her hand, then retrieved from her knapsack the bread roll and peach she had purloined from her breakfast tray earlier. As she ate, Oriel looked across at the amphitheatre's raked steps, forced out of kilter by the shifting plates that had caused one or more earthquakes over the centuries.

It was easy to see the scale and layout of the settlement from this vantage point. It was a large site – larger than had been evident from her moonlit view of it that night at Manoli's. Directly below were the foundations of a substantial building: possibly a public edifice but just as likely to be a rich merchant's villa. She stood up, hoisting her pack on her shoulders once more, and walked carefully down to it.

Barely anything of interest remained. A trace of a mosaic floor here and there, a broken amphora and a small shattered section of an architrave carved with acanthus leaves. The only sound she could hear was the gentle soughing of the breeze in the pines. Again, she had that sense of desolation, made even more acute by the fact that she was here alone. In spite of the sun blazing directly overhead, she gave a shiver. This villa would once have been bustling with children and servants, ruled over by a wealthy man ... and now everything had come to this.

She turned to go, having had enough of the maudlin thoughts that had suddenly beset her. As she did so, her foot kicked at a shard of earthenware pottery. She bent down to pick it up, then turned it round in her hand. It was part of a beaker, the side of which was carved in a sort of crest. She rubbed it gently with her thumb, tracing the ridges and indentations. Inside the scrolled edges of the crest was a trident, the sinuous curves of a sea serpent coiled around its shaft.

The insignia of Sestius.

Oriel smothered an exclamation as she stared, motionless, at the reddish fragment. Never had she imagined that the calcified argosy, submerged under more than a hundred feet of seawater, would leave a mystery trail that she would pick up here and now, in the ruins of Manoli's. How strange. The shipwreck wasn't just carrying the trader's cargo, this small shard of pottery placed Sestius on the island of Helios somehow. Suddenly, she couldn't wait to share all of this with Damian.

Settling herself back in the car once again, Oriel decided to drive on. She didn't feel like returning to Heliades just yet, she felt joyous to be driving beside the sea. The terrain was wild and continuously varying as she went along, following the windings of the indented coast. Facing the sea, the countryside was carpeted with flowers and sweet-smelling herbs: marguerites, lilies of the valley, poppies, lavender, rosemary, heather. Everywhere flourished the white gum cistus, those daisy-like flowers with a purple heart, luxuriantly in bloom, the sun drawing forth their rich balsamic fragrance, which wafted through the open window of the Jeep, filling Oriel's lungs with their aroma.

Up ahead was a small group of buildings, creating a harmonious patchwork of white and terracotta against the promontory on which they were perched. She drove slowly past a row of basic two-room stone cottages, beyond which stood a mansion-sized villa with Italianate touches. Oriel marvelled at the view it must command: endless sea and sky on three of its aspects.

It occurred to her that it would be a good idea to refill her water bottle, which she had drained an hour ago, so she parked beside the end cottage, next to the open wrought-iron gates of the villa. Behind them lay an oval lawn of emerald green, so bright it seemed fake. The house was set like a gem in a circle of cypress, pomegranate, citrus and olive trees. Facing the lawn, it was two-storeyed, the whitewash peeling here and there, with fretted stone balconies at the upper windows and a covered veranda running right round the villa on the ground floor. Purple and yellow bougainvillea and violet morning glory climbed the pillars flanking the studded wooden front door and ran riot over the rough stone walls. The villa's name hung in large letters in an arch over the gates: *I Pýli Tou Apóllona*, The Gate of Apollo. A silver-and-black Bugatti was standing in the driveway.

Oriel got out of the Volkswagen, carrying her canvas knapsack, and walked to the end cottage, where a little girl sat sewing by the side of a well in a tiny patch of garden. As she was debating whether or not to knock on the door, a young woman emerged from the side of the house, carrying a little boy on her hip. She smiled at Oriel, who took her empty water bottle from her bag. The woman nodded vigorously and pointed at a bucket beside the well. Oriel thanked her in Greek and the woman took the bottle from her and ladled some water into it. Oriel wondered whether to give the woman some money to thank her for her kindness, but didn't want to offend her. Then, putting the bottle of water back in her canvas bag, she saw a small unopened tube of mints and gave it to the child, whose big black eyes sparkled with joy. The mother tried to protest, but Oriel insisted.

A moment later she was about to climb back into the Jeep when there was the rich purr of an engine and the Bugatti glided up the gravelled driveway of the gated villa. Oriel stood watching, slightly embarrassed to have parked so near to the villa's entrance, like some nosy tourist. Instead of turning down the coast road, however, the driver of the Bugatti seemed to have second thoughts, and the engine gave a final throb before the ignition was switched off. Next, the car door opened and a pair of gleaming, finely tapered tanned legs emerged, and Oriel had just enough time to admire a pair of beautifully manicured feet in silver sandals before she was brought face-to-face with Yolanda.

The singer was wearing a black halter-neck top and floaty, tiered skirt: understated, yet so perfectly emphasizing her leopard-like grace. Oriel could detect the softest hint of Chanel on the breeze and she was uncomfortably aware of her own dishevelled appearance, having spent the day working under the heat of an unforgiving sun.

'You're that intern, aren't you? We met the other night,' said Yolanda with a bright smile that didn't quite reach her eyes. 'Sorry, I can't remember your name.'

Oriel was incensed by the other woman's complete lack of manners but she decided to ignore her obvious malice. 'Yes, we have met before. I'm Oriel Anderson, the archaeologist *Kyrios* Lekkas has brought in to work on his specialist projects.'

'Ah yes, I remember now. Very impressive,' said Yolanda smoothly. 'You're staying at Heliades. Although as an employee, is it really appropriate staying at the boss's house?' Despite the cool smile Yolanda gave her, the singer's eyes glinted with something akin to malevolence and Oriel couldn't help her blood rising. If Yolanda was going to try and score points, she decided two could play at that game.

'It's useful to be at Heliades because we're working together so closely,' Oriel replied sweetly. 'We can discuss our finds after work, sometimes over dinner. It's also been invaluable to have the use of Damian's study. He has an impressive collection of reference books. Academic research is an important part of the job.'

Yolanda's dark eyes sparked but her smile remained fixed, as if in stone. 'Damian is forever with his head in books, but there is more to life than books and old rubble.' She waved an elegant hand dismissively. 'He has always found that going out with a singer, an artist, is a refreshing change from having to hang around with the dull librarian types employed on his digs.' At this, she looked Oriel up and down disdainfully, which made her even more acutely aware of her unkempt appearance.

Oriel couldn't wait to bring this hateful dialogue to a close. What on earth was she thinking, engaging in a sparring match with Damian's girlfriend, if that's what she was? Yolanda would doubt-less like nothing more than a catfight in order to report back to Damian that his new employee was getting above herself and be-having inappropriately. Suddenly Oriel felt angry with him. That she should have been placed in this position at all was hurtful and belittling.

Deciding to adopt a controlled, professional air, she shaded her tone with cool neutrality when she responded. 'Yes, well, it's a great project to be involved with. I'm grateful to Damian for the opportu-nity.'

Yolanda took her cue and moved back towards her Bugatti. As she slid into the car, the diva couldn't resist having the last word. 'Well, mind you don't take up too much of your employer's time. He wants to dedicate more of it to me now that I'm back.'

With that, she turned the key in the ignition, leaving Oriel stand-ing beside her Volkswagen, seething. As she drove off, kicking up a cloud of yellow dust as she hit the accelerator, Oriel could have sworn she meant to leave her with grit in her eyes and the choking stench of exhaust fumes assailing her lungs. *What an absolute bitch!* she exclaimed silently to herself.

As she drove back to Heliades Oriel brooded, her recent happy mood having turned distinctly sour. The sun was still shining bright, the sea glittering with silvery wavelets, the olive leaves continuing to dance in the light breeze, but it was as if a grey pall had settled over the afternoon. She felt foolish and vulnerable once more, and fought to re-establish her equilibrium. What had happened to the self-confident, relaxed person she used to be, the girl who viewed life as an adventure and had already learnt – albeit the hard way – not to rely on men for her happiness but to put her trust in herself? Where had that Oriel gone?

Pull yourself together, my girl.

She would once again try to maintain a more formal relationship with Damian. It would be the only way this job would work and, after today's new finds, she really wanted to see this project through to the end.

She sighed. How many times already had she vowed she would keep her distance? Then all Damian had to do was come close to her and she would go weak at the knees. This intrigue between them was a dangerous situation, drawing her in like quicksand and, if she wasn't careful, she would be pulled into its suffocating depths. It wasn't just that Damian's childhood sweetheart had returned to lay claim to the man who, in turn, was clearly still obsessed with her: the truth was more complicated. Damian had come through difficult times and, on top of that, he was still preoccupied with island responsibilities and familial duties. Oriel only had to think of his cousin Helena and she'd shiver. Did she really want to be embroiled in all of that?

In a few hours she would meet him at the harbour and tell him about the Sestius find. Everything, she determined, would be focused on work. Still, a part of her knew that the thrum of excitement buzzing through her at the prospect of seeing him again could not be explained entirely by professional zeal.

* * *

When Oriel reached Heliades, she went straight up to her bathroom to shower. As she felt the warm rush of water beating down on her, rinsing the reddish streaks of dust from her limbs, she also found her anger and frustration melting away with it, almost as if the steady fall of water had cleansed the singer's words from the front of her mind, words that had stung with vitriol, the strength of which she had been quite unprepared for. As she stood, face raised, eyes closed, letting the liquid torrents run down her hair and over the soft curves of her pale-gold body, her resentment towards Damian for putting her in such an invidious and humiliating position shifted. Her mind began to wander over the events of the morning and, as they did so, a tingling excitement welled up inside her. Suddenly all Oriel wanted was to talk to him.

Well, that's all right, she thought to herself. *It'll be an entirely professional conversation.*

She had dressed in a pale-blue linen sundress and was applying the merest touch of rose lip balm when she heard the dogs bark and, a moment later, in response, the deep, commanding voice of Damian echoed through the house as he greeted his hounds. A few moments later, Irini tapped at Oriel's door.

'The *Kyrios* is ready, if you want to join him?' the maid asked.

'I'll be down in a moment,' replied Oriel, moving from the mirror, where she had just finished coiling her hair into a neat chignon, to fetch her bag and a soft white mohair cardigan in case it grew chilly later on. It was still only May, although the weather had been unseasonably scorching these past few days.

'Are you ready to go?' Damian was standing in the hall as she descended the stairs, his grey eyes smiling a welcome that belied the peremptory tone of his voice. Oriel reflected for an instant that he must be so used to being master of all he surveyed that he simply wasn't aware that his voice carried such a tone of authority; it had become almost innate. 'This farewell ritual we have every May when the sponge divers head off for North Africa is something you have to see,' he added. 'We should hurry, I can't afford to be late.'

Oriel gave him an offhand smile. 'I'm grateful to have the opportunity, I've read a bit about it. Do you have some role in the proceedings?' she asked, following Damian through the front door and out to his Jeep.

'In a way, yes,' he replied, 'although I have mixed feelings about the whole thing, if I'm honest. I support the islanders in their heritage and traditions where I can, but it's hard when the whole sponge-diving industry is so rife with injury and danger.'

'Yes, I can see that,' she agreed, as they walked down the terrace steps. 'Just to hear Spyros the other day boasting about sponge divers and their own rather dubious methods of warding off the bends made me realize how much pride and bravado must be wrapped up in the tradition.'

'Exactly. It's one of the reasons I wanted you to come today, to observe something so essential to the character of this island and its people. I think you'll find it worth witnessing. I'm sure some of the divers you've worked with before in the Mediterranean might well have come from similar sponge-diving families.'

Oriel glanced at him. Despite the usual intensity in Damian's gaze as he looked at her, gone was that particular carefree look she had seen the day before at the Epiklisi festival. She found herself wondering if he had forgotten the magic that had surrounded them last night. He appeared more reserved today and she could see that his demeanour of serious leader of Helios had returned. At least it might make it easier for her to maintain her own distance, she thought ruefully.

Keeping to her resolve, as soon as they were both in the car and Damian had pulled out of the drive on to the road, she raised the subject of her day's recce to see the ruins around Manoli's. She started from the beginning, filling him in on her phone conversation with Cynthia, and finished with a description of the shard of pottery she had found at the site of the villa. Oriel was maintaining a cool, scientific tone, but she could see Damian's eyes had kindled with excitement. He started to fire questions at her, which she answered in the same deliberately methodical and measured way. Very soon, however, she was caught up in his adventurer's zeal.

'So you think this villa could have belonged to our shipowner?' he asked.

'Well, it's not such a stretch to believe so …' her voice trailed away, and Damian picked up the thread that she hadn't yet expressed.

'And the conclusion you're coming to is that if he lived here, then his business was no doubt here as well …'

'Perhaps ...' said Oriel tentatively.

'Leading us to suppose that the lost port of Helice was a thriving harbour that once belonged to this very island, before it was shattered by earthquakes and engulfed by tidal waves.' He glanced at her. 'I presume that also occurred to you?'

'Well, yes, it did,' admitted Oriel, and she couldn't help smiling.

Damian gave a slow whistle and wide grin in response.

'The piece I found at the ruins ... it's only a piece of one beaker, of course,' she said quickly. 'But it did occur to me that our argosy might not have been lost in a storm en route to its destination after all. Perhaps it was simply lying at anchor in its home harbour.'

'And that might account for there being evidence of more than one cargo, more than one ship,' added Damian.

'Exactly,' said Oriel, thinking for a moment just how well their minds fitted, so that each followed the other's train of thought without any apparent effort, it came so naturally.

'Well, there's only one way to find out,' Damian said after a brief pause, during which Oriel could almost sense his mind working with laser speed. 'The next time we dive, we'll make sure we look for evidence of the argosy's location having been a harbour.' He took one hand off the wheel and ran it through his hair, his eyes alight. 'You never know, if we're very lucky we might actually find the massive statue of Poseidon.'

'Now that's wishful thinking indeed!' laughed Oriel, although she had to admit to herself that a tiny flicker of the same hope had been lit in her as he spoke. 'Just remember, we only have a broken beaker and an amphora seal at this stage. Don't let your imagination run away with itself.'

'Always the scientist,' chuckled Damian. 'All right, you win. We'll go about this in the most methodical way imaginable.' He broke off for a moment as they had just turned off the main road leading to the marina, the central part of which had been roped off. He slowed the car then parked behind the warehouse near the taverna. 'Excellent. We haven't far to walk.'

A big crowd had assembled near the waterside. Among the mothers, wives and children who were gathered there to wave their relatives and loved ones goodbye, Oriel couldn't help seeing various men among them who had twisted legs that dragged as they walked, while others were leaning on sticks. One man was sitting on something that looked a little like a go-kart, fashioned from part of a door with old trolley wheels attached, which he moved along with his hands.

Oriel thought back to the other day when she had briefly entered the church at the harbour. Her attention had been attracted by the shrine of St Nicholas, with the unusual amount of flowers and gifts laid at his feet. It was here that the women of the sponge-diving families made their requests for favours, as well as giving thanks for miracles received. Until then, she'd had no idea that the islanders of Helios were taking part in such a dangerous exploit. She knew it was the tradition on Kalymnos, but thought it had largely died out elsewhere. True, no longer did one see a diver enter the sea holding a *skandalopetra*, the thirty-pound slab of marble the free-divers once used to take them to depths of a hundred feet. Still, the fact remained, despite the modern diving suit with breathing equipment, the *skáfandro*, diving for sponges, was a hazardous escapade. Oriel had been on a couple of dives where one of her team had had decompression sickness – the 'bends' – and she would never forget their shrieks of pain, torsos writhing as if red-hot scorpions, rather than nitrogen bubbles, were coursing through their veins.

Damian walked beside her, his tall figure drawing the eyes of the islanders as he passed by. Oriel wondered, a little ruefully, if they were speculating on who his companion might be. He didn't seem to care or notice the looks that passed among them, intensely engaged as he was in conversation with her – so much so that he responded with the barest gesture of a nod to their greetings.

'When my father was a child,' he told Oriel, 'one of the great industries of Helios was sponge fishing. It helped with the economy. About a third of the island's men and boys were absent all the summer, fishing or diving off the shores of Tripoli and Malta. In those days, one man in three was either dead or crippled from the bends before he reached marriageable age.'

'That's terrible,' interjected Oriel, looking around her at the stoical, weatherbeaten faces of the islanders. She gave a small shiver: they may have gathered for a festival but it might as well be a funeral wake if what Damian said was true.

'There are far fewer now that go, thankfully. In those days they would leave in a sizeable group in May, but when they returned during the autumn it was in a much reduced number. The summers on Helios were bleak. It was as if all the able-bodied men of this harbour town were away at war. The islanders carried on as best they could but never knew how many would come back.'

'Did that mean that everything stopped for the summer?'

'No. The island was still active as a commercial centre, and many women worked in the fields, taking on whatever jobs their husbands or sons held in winter and, of course, they were the main harvesting hands. But I remember the atmosphere, even when I was a boy. There was less bustle and merriment. The people were heavy-hearted. While other islands prospered during the summer, bringing in money via their cafés and tavernas by the sea, life here was rather grim.'

'Surely, nowadays, with the advancement of diving technology, there are far fewer accidents?'

'Yes, sure. But every year there are still two or three casualties, which is still too many. And you have to wonder if it is really worth the pain. Before the war, the sponge industry was booming and the island needed it, but today, with synthetic sponges flooding the market, it's nothing like as lucrative as it used to be.'

'Have you tried to change their minds? Encourage them to do something different, train for other jobs?' asked Oriel.

'Yes, of course, but to little avail. Traditions like these are almost indelible.' Damian shook his head and gave a sigh. 'To the romantic young, it naturally seems a grand thing to sail away every summer to the shores of Africa and to come back, pockets full of money, hailed a hero. They get a six-month holiday, after all, and have earned ample pay to keep their glasses topped up at the tavernas every night of the week. And so the custom continues …

'I have seen young boys playing at sponge fishing: swimming underwater, wearing the sponge-fisher's mask and carrying their spear, pretending to detach sponges from the bottom of the sea. An aura of heroism surrounds the profession, which for generations has been handed down from father to son.'

Just then Oriel spotted Mattias, who was sitting against a low wall next to the steps leading up to the quay. He was talking to a man who was leaning on a stick, his weight on one leg. Damian and

Oriel went over to the pair and Mattias made the introductions.

'Tadeas has been telling me you might hire his son, Panayotis, is that so?' the fisherman asked. Damian nodded and shook the man's hand.

'Have you been diving for sponges a long time?' Oriel asked the man.

Tadeas gave a brief nod. 'My family's been doing it for generations, *Despinis*. I lost my eldest brother ten years ago while he was fishing sponges on the shores of Malta. I've had some near misses myself, of course. My legs aren't what they were. Sometimes the pain makes working difficult but I have a family so you do what you have to do. I dive where it's not so deep.'

At this Mattias clapped the man on the back. 'You're an addict for it, admit it, Tadeas,' he said.

Tadeas grinned at him, uncovering two rows of pearl-white teeth, and gave a shrug. 'The sea is my second home.' His expression then became more serious. 'Ah, maybe you're right, Mattias, but that doesn't mean I don't want something different for my son. When you, my friend, said that the *Kyrios* might be willing to hire Panayotis, I figured that might be the best thing for the lad. And anyway, the sponge business is not what it was. There's little future in it now.'

'Well,' said Mattias, clasping the shoulder of his friend, 'now's your chance. If the *Kyrios* has time, he could have a word with the lad. He's a fine boy.'

Damian glanced at his watch and said he had just enough time to meet Tadeas's son before he needed to join the procession, if they were quick about it. Oriel elected to stay with Mattias and perched next to him on the wall. Although she would have liked to discuss how reckless his friend's attitude was, especially given the market for sponges was in steep decline, she refrained from giving her opinion. By the looks of it, Mattias seemed to approve of the tradition and the last thing she wanted was to offend him by undermining the sponge divers' courage and achievements so, instead, she sat enjoying the late afternoon sun on her face. They had an excellent view of the proceedings from where they were positioned.

About fifty brightly coloured *achtarmádes*, the boats used for sponge diving, bobbed and glinted in the sun, painted brightly in various combinations: orange and black; blue or carmine; blue and yellow and black; or just white, grey, purple and green. They formed the fleet that would be setting sail for North Africa, for its seven-month summer season, to bring back what they called 'the golden fleece' of the sea.

Some last-minute supplies were being loaded on to the nearest *achtarmádes*, and Oriel watched the men carry heavy wooden breadbins aboard. Mattias explained that they would be full of the dry biscuits, hard as rock, called *paximadi*, which would be the divers' main source of nourishment on the voyage.

'Apart from *paximadi*, the basic shipboard food is chunks of pig fat, which are laid up in the locker with a few onions and potatoes. They live on next to nothing, these sponge fleets. They are men who suck their living from sponges as the sponges suck theirs from the tide,' Mattias explained with that sense of the dramatic that always made Oriel smile inwardly.

The taverna was open. A few men and women were drinking, but no one was celebrating. Oriel could feel the tension and sadness in the air, and the few bantering exchanges by the divers could not dissipate the cloak of sorrow and anxiety that had fallen over the island.

A moment later, she felt a sudden change in the atmosphere – a flurry of festival spirit – as the divers began to be ferried out to their boats, lying at anchor in the middle of the harbour. Very soon, these wooden craft began to race up and down at full speed, sometimes coming directly at each other head-on, sometimes broadside, the boats missing each other by inches. This display of daring went on for more than an hour in full view of the quay, with the crowd whooping and yelling from the docks, cheering on the sponge gladiators.

Then, just as abruptly, the show stopped and the divers came back to shore. Now the crowd turned its attention towards the top of the cliff behind them, from where music could be heard, and where a procession had just started making its way down to the port. It was led by the island's police force – of three – on motorcycles, along with Helios's coastguards. Bringing up the rear came a group of young choristers carrying banners, dressed in blue satin cassocks, with a large white cross embroidered in the middle of their chests.

These were followed by a youth orchestra in Greek soldier *evzone* costumes. The sound of the clear young voices rising above the hollow beat of the goatskin drums, the strident noise of the trumpets and the squawks of the bagpipe-like *tsabounas* thrilled Oriel. There was something so archaic about the procession. She would hazard a bet that it must have been just the same two thousand years ago.

The black-robed priest with his long white beard and quaint *kalimafi* stovepipe hat followed with Damian, who was surrounded by six young girls – the dove bearers – in long white tunics. It would be their task, Mattias told Oriel, to release the birds just as the flotilla of boats carrying the sponge divers headed out to sea.

'Only the pure of heart, the young innocents, can be dove bearers,' he told her. Then he gave a chuckle. 'I heard that the one who calls herself the nightingale of Helios wanted to sing with them. Thought she'd stand next to the *Kyrios*, no doubt.' He gave Oriel a nudge and another wheezing laugh. 'She hadn't reckoned on the priest thwarting her, eh? I don't know what the Father said, but I can guess. *Ha!* Our nightingale was furious. She drove off in that fancy car of hers like some mad harpy. Nearly ran into Xander's goats, that's what I heard.'

Mattias realized that Oriel wasn't fully sharing in the joke and he paused, looking kindly at her. 'Has that minx been giving you trouble?' She gave a weak smile and shrugged. 'Ah well, that's how it goes. But you mustn't mind her. She'll be off again before you know it. The girl never stays long in one place, that's for sure.'

It seemed to Oriel that Yolanda didn't look as if she wanted to go anywhere, not until she had secured her position as mistress of Damian's household – and the island, of course. She gazed at Damian's tall figure at the back of the procession, which had just reached the quay. As she did so, he glanced over to where she and Mattias were sitting and his eyes met hers with an almost burning intensity. Oriel gave a little shiver and her heart fluttered for a moment like the wings of the doves held captive in the hands of the white-robed girls.

At the quay it was now time for goodbyes and the mood shifted again, almost as if a cloud had suddenly veiled the sun. The pain of leave-taking, the heavy weight of absence to be borne, the apprehension of dangers to be encountered … the uncertainty … was imprinted on each of the swarthy features of the women. Mothers, wives, sisters, sweethearts – every one of them dressed in black – now stood as still and undemonstrative as statues. From time to time, children holding the hands of their mothers or grandmothers would look up at them with troubled eyes, trying to guess at their emotions as if they wanted to make sure they knew how to copy the adults' behaviour. Oriel felt the strings of her heart wrench for them in their silent despair.

After the youths were all settled in their boats, the priest boarded a *caique* that took him to the centre of the bay.

'What's he doing now?' asked Oriel, as she watched the old man dip his hand into some sort of dish and swing his right arm from left to right.

'He's holding basil leaves, and that's holy water. See, he's sprinkling the boats. Blessing them,' Mattias told her.

Then a bell tolled and all was silent. A moment later there was a flurry of white, and the doves took to the air and swooped above the ocean. This was the sign the sponge divers had been waiting for, and now a shout rang out and the lead boat started to churn and sway as its engine throbbed into life.

The boats traced the sign of the cross in the harbour three times, then, one after the other, headed out to the open sea. As they did so, the whole quay filled up with song:

The time to part and sail away is here,
Our brave, courageous men stand jointly without fear.
They sail away from Helios, these branches of the olive tree.
You've burnt this heart of mine, oh cruel, stormy sea.

It was sunset. The fiery red orb of light slowly sank beneath the horizon and threads of light lingered in the sky, mingling with the rolling clouds, dyeing the heavens first orange, then red, then dark blue, until all that was left was a chalky mauve. Like a Greek chorus, the islanders watched the boats slide gently away on the water with an unwavering gaze. Occasionally, a sponge diver turned back to wave, but not a soul moved in the group of figures standing on the quay; each one seemed as if he were already mourning.

A few sobs were heard. Oriel caught a mother murmuring to her child as she pointed to the flotilla of boats outlined against the setting sun: '*I thálassa ta dínei ki i thálassa ta paírnei*, the sea gives them and the sea takes them back. You must promise never to become one of those sponge divers, my son. Money is not everything.'

Now, as the last boat rounded the corner of the bay, a tall, white-haired old man stretched out his arm and waved. Immediately, in silence, all hands went up in a hieratic farewell and then all the islanders crossed themselves. The sun blazed out and melted away and a bluish light fell over the harbour as a stygian darkness took over the sky. A hush – such as might greet the ending of some great tragedy – enveloped the island. The long months of waiting had begun.

Gradually, people began to move. Oriel remained with Mattias on the wall by the steps, while down on the beach, as the taverna slowly filled up with those who had been left behind, a group of men and women had assembled around five dancers. Damian joined Oriel and Mattias on the now empty quay.

Mattias stood up. 'Well, after all that, I, for one, need a drink,' he said. 'If that lot are all watching the *Mihanikos*, I might have a chance of getting served.'

Damian told his old friend that they would join him shortly. 'Oriel will want to watch the *Mihanikos* first.'

Mattias nodded and wandered towards the taverna.

'What is it?' she asked.

'The bends dance. It tells the story of a proud, handsome man who goes to sea, dives for sponges and becomes crippled after an attack of the bends. It's also about his will to live, despite his disability.'

'I can't believe they've actually come up with a dance about it,' said Oriel.

'They're keeping the myth alive.' Damian gave a heavy sigh. 'So you can see what I mean about it being at the heart of the islanders' identity. Stavros thinks I should ban sponge diving, but it's easier said than done.'

'You could refuse to take part in the parade, at the very least.'

'Greeks, and especially the ones from Helios, are a proud people. Their inherited skills, their traditions, mean everything to them.

It would be a slight to everything they represent if I wasn't there.'

'Yes, but perhaps it's up to you to show them a different way. It would be harsh at first, I suppose, but on the other hand …'

'No! I could never do something like that.' His tone brooked no argument and Oriel decided she would be wasting her breath if she tried. Perhaps she'd been a little too hasty to voice her opinion. She sensed, quite keenly, that a barrier had come up between them and she could almost hear his unspoken words: *You're not from Helios, you aren't even Greek. You wouldn't understand.*

The five men had begun to dance now, circling, swirling and kicking in the traditional Greek fashion. At first Oriel was drawn into the lively blur of sound, colour and rhythmic movement as they moved faster and faster. But then – like the whole strange event, it seemed to her – quite suddenly the mood changed. One of the dancers fell to the ground. Then, in a macabre and jerky mime sequence, he dragged his unresponsive, shaking and impotent legs along the ground, slowly and painfully struggling to lift himself up with the aid of a stick. Oriel watched as a host of exaggerated expressions passed over the man's face: determination and willpower were replaced by anger, frustration and despair as his hopeless limbs refused to cooperate.

Goosebumps rose all over her body as she listened to the desolate strings of the weeping violin, all the while watching the tragic progress of the grotesque dance. At this point Damian, sensing her discomfort, took Oriel's arm.

'Come, let's go down to the taverna and join Mattias,' he urged, and Oriel didn't resist him.

They spent an hour sitting at a table with Mattias. Damian began to look more relaxed, his legs stretched out in front of him, crossed easily at the ankles, while he smoked his Gitanes and drank ouzo. The sombre mood of before melted away and he even began to laugh, his eyes crinkling at the corners every time Mattias said something that amused him. Now and again, he would glance at Oriel to share the joke, a contented warmth flowing between them, and she wished it could always be like this … that he could always be like this.

Mattias was in full party spirit too, his eyes twinkling mischievously in his nut-brown face. 'So, that's it then. Off they go to North

Africa, leaving their womenfolk undefended from Algerian pirates sailing the other way,' he joked.

'Did the island suffer much from pirate raids in the past?' asked Oriel.

'Hasn't the *Kyrios* told you about the island's holy icons – the *Martiatissa* and the *Mayitissa*?' Mattias asked her. 'Our Lady of March and our Lady of May, the Virgins of Chora.'

'No, he hasn't,' replied Oriel. 'What did they have to do with pirates?'

Damian settled back in his chair, the warmth of the taverna and the spirits he had drunk making him expansive. 'Well, they're two good stories, dearly loved by the islanders. The first happened at the end of the eighteenth century when Capitan Zacharias, a fearsome Spartan pirate, came in a galleon that sank at Lygaria, on the north-west shore. Forty pirates escaped. A farmer saw them from a distance, as they were drying their powder in the sun. The man ran to Chora and very soon the bell was sounding a warning from the church. Everyone retreated to the *castro* just in time. From the battlements, they held aloft the icon of the *Martiatissa* before firing at the Spartan pirates. And that was the end of them.'

'The second story is even better,' said Mattias, reaching for his tobacco. 'This time it was a massive great fleet of Algerians.'

'Indeed,' agreed Damian. 'It happened on the first of May, some time before the raid of Capitan Zacharias. Eighteen Algerian pirate vessels were seen off the north-east point of the island, bearing for the shore. This time, the villagers took refuge in the church of the Panayia, while one brave islander stood on the cliff and held up the *Mayitissa* icon.'

'And that was the end of the Algerians?' laughed Oriel.

Damian grinned. 'Of course, what did you expect? A miraculous storm broke out and that was the end of their ships. Only one man survived, a Christian captive who had been held on one of the Algerian vessels. He told the islanders that a flash of lightning from the Panayia's cliff had sunk the entire pirate fleet.'

'It was a shame you weren't here a few weeks ago, *Despinis* Anderson,' said Mattias. 'On Easter Day, the icons of *Martiatissa* and *Mayitissa* are taken from the church in a great procession and visit every house in the village.'

'I would have loved to have seen that,' agreed Oriel.

Then the conversation moved to more serious matters. The business of running the island was never far from Damian's consciousness, and now he and Mattias were talking about the harbour master and the coastguards, and whether they were doing a competent enough job. Damian drained his glass. 'With work starting on the wreck, we certainly don't want any smugglers or traffickers on our coastline.'

'I think the men are working in much the same way as they always have,' said Mattias comfortably.

Damian looked thoughtful. 'I saw a ship without its lights the other night. It didn't bother me at the time but I wonder now if it was up to something. Have you seen anything going on?' he asked. 'You know I always rely on your eyes, Mattias.'

'Can't say that I have, but I'll keep a look out for you, my friend,' said the fisherman. 'Has anything happened further with that business of Yorgos?'

Damian glanced in Oriel's direction, as if to tell Mattias to watch what he said. 'I've taken it to the mainland police,' was all he revealed. 'They'll proceed with discretion.'

Mattias gave a brief nod, and nothing more was said. Oriel wondered for a moment what business they might have that could involve the police but she very soon forgot all about it because, at that moment, Damian stood up to signal that they were leaving. They were quiet in the car on the way back to Heliades, but it was an easy silence.

When they got back to the house, Oriel was both relieved and a little disappointed that Damian played the perfect gentleman, as he had the whole afternoon. The frisson between them was as strong as ever and, as they stood in the hallway, his smile lingered as he looked into her eyes.

'A long day, eh?'

'Yes, I think I'm ready for bed.'

His gaze sparked with a glitter of mischief. 'An excellent idea.'

'I meant—'

'Of course you should go to bed, Calypso,' he added with a wide grin, enjoying her flustered response. 'You need your rest. Tomorrow we dive. You did well today, discovering the Sestius connection to the wreck. Who knows what we'll find when we go down this time.'

Oriel visibly relaxed. 'Yes, but remember, let's not get our hopes up too soon.'

His silver eyes glittered. 'But hope is not a dream, so they say, but a way of dreams becoming reality. Now, I've got some papers to look over before I go to bed. I'll see you in the morning, Calypso. Sleep well.'

Oriel watched him as he sauntered off down the wing in the direction of his study, and let out a quiet sigh. He had such a masculine, confident way of walking that never failed to assault her sense of self-possession. Slowly, she made her way back to her room, eager for the softness of her bed.

But the moment Oriel set foot in her bathroom upstairs, the pleasant feeling of sleepiness that had assailed her limbs with such glorious lassitude was abruptly jolted from her as one hand froze on the open door. She gave a start, uttering a little cry. There, on the bathroom mirror, marked out in a greasy substance that she supposed must be soap, was an evil eye – another *mati* – exactly like the one that had been drawn in salt on her bedroom floor.

She took a shaky breath to steady her nerves and caught sight of her ashen face in the mirror. Her eyes were round pools of fear. Seeing herself like that – terrified and poised for flight – only managed to alarm her even more. Unlike before, instead of anger offering her a line of defence, she felt nothing but blind panic. It felt as though now she was tired and contented, her guard had been lowered and she was wholly unprepared for this latest attack by her unseen enemy. This time, however, she didn't hesitate: all she could think of was flying to the sanctity of Damian's protective arms.

She ran down the stairs and headed along the wing for his study. He was there, smoking at his desk, head bent over some papers in the orange glow of his lamp. When he raised his eyes, she saw some emotion flicker in their depths and then he pushed his chair back and rushed to her side.

'What is it? What's the matter?' he asked quickly. 'Your face looks as if you've seen a ghost! What's happened, *agápi mou*?'

Oriel barely registered the endearment, fearful as she was, but she moved reflexively into the circle of his strong arms. 'It's on my bathroom mirror …'

'What is?'

'The *mati* …'

Damian's jaw tightened and his hands gripped her shoulders harder. 'Come, show me.'

He led the way upstairs to her apartment, letting Oriel open the door, still instinctively respecting her privacy. She led him to the bathroom and stood in the doorway: there was nothing – not even a smear – on the mirror.

'It was there! Y-you must believe me …' she stammered. 'I'm not out of my mind!'

Damian was soothing now, asking questions gently but firmly. She confessed to there having been a similar instance, a salt *mati*, on the Saturday evening.

He muttered an oath. Then after a pause, he said: 'This is He-lena's work.' His eyes were unreadable but Oriel sensed a lowering of his spirits, a return of that almost habitual crease between his brows. For a moment she was taken over by fury at Helena, and the fear she had felt for herself melted away. Just to think! He had seemed so relaxed, so happy today – and now Helena had managed to spoil it all. Couldn't she just let him be?

'Why didn't you tell me the other night when it happened?' Damian asked eventually, his eyes studying her face.

'It was that night you came to find me on your horse and we drank Metaxa on your terrace. When we … I couldn't go back down to you. Not after …' Her voice trailed away and for a moment both were silent.

'Look, I'll speak to her tomorrow,' he said, gently. 'It won't happen again, I promise. You're a guest in this house. I will see to it that Helena respects that.'

Oriel stared at him for a moment, thoughts clamouring in her head. One thing was for certain, she was right to think that life with Damian would be unsettling, impossible even. She turned to walk across her bedroom, through to the sitting room. Holding the apart-ment door open for him, all the while she yearned to have him stay the night and sleep beside her – to feel the sheltering comfort of his arms. But she said nothing.

As he left, Damian touched her arm, leaving a warm imprint on her skin that made Oriel almost weaken. 'Try and get some sleep,' he said. 'We have a big day tomorrow, I want you to be fit for the dive.'

She nodded briefly and gave a washed-out smile, before bidding him goodnight.

* * *

The afternoon sky around Helios was a pure, uninterrupted blue that stretched seamlessly across Oriel's field of vision. The sun was at full blast and the heat rained down on Damian and his crew like the breath of hell, sparkling off the water in a sort of dreamy haze. Summer was only just arriving and yet the Ionian Sea was like a semi-molten mirror. Around them the scorched cliffs and sand shimmered almost silver under the blinding glare.

They had spent the morning diving the wreck of the Roman argosy, Stavros patiently winching up basket after basket of earthenware pots and other artefacts. There was nothing on this trip to equal the excitement of Alexis finding the Alexander bronze but, little by little, they were starting to find their way around Marcus Sestius's wreck and their knowledge was growing hour by hour. There had been no sign of anything that could be the remains of Helice underwater, and both Damian and Oriel tried to stifle their feelings of disappointment. After lunch, Damian suggested he and Oriel took a break to do some purely recreational diving.

'You've done two thirty-metre dives and that's enough for one day,' he noted. 'We can search again tomorrow, there's still a lot of ground to cover. For now, let's have some time in the shallower water of the reef. The islanders are very proud of it, for good reason. It's totally unspoilt and there's a magical quality to it. You'll see.'

Stavros took up the anchor and headed north before bringing the boat towards shore once again. Ahead of them was a small island that consisted of two conical peaks joined by a saddle of treeless land. The earth had a look of redness, glowing in the reflected light of the sun. They entered a crescent-shaped bay enclosed by dark cliffs that rose at the edge of a stony beach, about twenty metres wide. Stavros weighed anchor at a spot in shallow water where corals growing from the gently shelving bottom gleamed right up to the surface, showing a kaleidoscope of rainbow colours. Beyond the rocks Oriel could see a lagoon, about four hundred metres end to end, she estimated, its shallowness causing it to glisten in green and yellow hues.

Damian and Oriel put on their fins and were overboard in no time. The visibility was good, so they began their dive with a slow descent, taking time to admire the myriad soft corals, fish and small creatures around them. There were large areas of plate coral, stacked in layers, interwoven with the more precious red coral. The huge rock formations gave the place a prehistoric aura, redolent of the beginning of time. Shoals of bream passed by and large groupers emerged from behind rocks to greet them, a majestic sight with their bloated body mass and huge eyes.

As Damian and Oriel descended further, an octopus that was hiding in one of the small crevices ventured out to inspect them. Damian kept very close to her. He lit up his torch and pointed out a forest of gorgonian sea fans, a rare species in these waters, glowing red under his beam. Oriel had come across the colourful fan-shaped branches before, bent by the current at Secca del Papa, when she'd been on a dive in Sardinia. There was also a profusion of black-and-white spotted sea cows that were resting on a colourful blanket of sponges, their external lungs and small horns clearly visible as Damian shone his light towards them. Oriel laughed; she loved this weird and wonderful three-dimensional world under the waves. All of a sudden she felt free and light as a butterfly floating in an azure sky.

Now they were following a gentle slope of sand towards a dark, isolated expanse that proved to be a small platform marked by scattered posidonia, and she paused a moment to watch the delicate marine plants waving in the current, like wide blades of grass in the wind. Diving a little deeper still, they struggled against the current, which hampered their progress and, even though Oriel was fighting it as hard as she could, it seemed to be dragging her in a direction away from Damian. Deep inlets had been formed here by the vigorous agitation of the water and in some places she could see they had made lagoons in pockets of the reef.

A shoal of silver fish obscured Oriel's vision for a moment and she lost sight of Damian completely. Suddenly a huge Mediterranean eel slithered out of a cavity in a rock, its spotted, elongated brown body swaying backwards and forwards as it wriggled straight towards her. She was transfixed like a mouse before a snake, her eyes locked on the open pharyngeal jaw, which would bite into its prey with the first set of teeth before using the second jaw to grab and swallow its victim. As she started to back away from the creature, it was still locked on to her and closing fast. She froze again. Her muscles were tensed, poised for flight but somehow unable to react.

Then she felt the clasp of Damian's hand as he pulled her forcefully from the path of the eel. There was such strength in the adamantine grip of his fingers and, as she turned to him in relief, she took in the sheer power of his muscular frame, the breadth of his rock-like shoulders and, not for the first time, felt a sense of safety in his presence that she had never felt before with a man.

Damian used dive signals to ask if she needed to surface but she shook her head. Although a little shaken, she had recovered her self-confidence quickly, and she certainly didn't want to be branded a wimp by him. Damian seemed happy by her decision and now didn't let go of her hand. It was clear that he knew where he was going and Oriel felt secure in his care.

They swam along a wide crevice in the reef now, following the current in the wake of a school of golden fish whose movements caused intermittent flashes of light. Ahead of them was a natural archway at the edge of the reef, through which, Oriel knew, lay the deeper water beyond. She felt suspended for a moment, seeing the vacant blueness ahead, and a strange feeling came over her as her instincts became attuned to something. The archway felt almost mythological to her alert imagination, as if she and Damian were about to enter an ancient land of legend, where, if they passed through, nothing would ever be the same. They would find themselves moving through time, into another world altogether perhaps. Damian glanced at her and she read the question in his eyes, and together they continued swimming in the direction of the reef-edge. As they did so, part of her felt as if she were headed for a high precipice, destined to hurtle into nothingness.

As they passed through the archway into the deep and open water, Oriel's eyes had to adjust to the change in perspective and light. They trod water for a moment, suspended upright in the lapis blue of the ocean, and then – as one – they saw it. Damian's hand gripped hers hard. About a hundred feet away, the head of a great bronze statue loomed, encrusted with algae and lying on its side, one of its vacant eyes gazing fixedly upon them. Oriel gasped, her heart beating faster all of a sudden. She couldn't tell if it was fear or excitement but she felt slightly giddy and a little sick, as if she had suddenly been transported to a mountain peak at high altitude. She knew by instinct exactly which of the gods was staring at her with his baleful and tyrannical gaze. He was colossal, each of the sculpted curls of his beard almost as big as Oriel herself. The creases of his tall, patriarchal forehead seemed to be frowning a ferocious message at her, rebuking her for having dared to enter a watery world that didn't belong to her or her kind.

As if in a dream, Damian and Oriel swam, hand in hand, towards the gargantuan prone figure. The muscles of its torso seemed like a great range of hills to her as she passed wonderingly along its length. Damian pointed to the fist at the end of the massive, rope-veined, muscular forearm, clenched around a now broken trident, its three-tined head lying a few metres away on the seabed.

One thought and one thought alone passed through Oriel's mind: the Poseidon of Helice. And although she later found all sorts of reasons why this colossus couldn't possibly be that statue of legend, nonetheless she couldn't rid herself of the idea, which had come into her head by a natural reflex, knowing this was what they had been hoping for against all the odds. She glanced up to see Damian treading water beside her and, even through his mask, she could see reflected in his eyes the same stunned awe and incredulity that was overwhelming her, as the two of them stared over what remained of the fallen mammoth sentinel of the deep.

* * *

Later that evening, as Oriel showered, she realized that her excitement about their discovery had barely died down in the preceding hours. Even Damian had found it hard to conceal his emotions, and his elation about the find had been almost tangible as they'd hauled themselves aboard the *Ariadne*.

'This *has* to be proof that Helios is the site of the lost city of Helice,' he'd murmured, keeping his voice low as the rest of the crew milled about on the other side of the *caique*. He looked feverish as he ripped off his mask, his grey irises glittering so brilliantly that if she didn't know him, she would have sworn he was under the effect of some drug. 'You were right, Oriel. None of the ships down there crashed on to the reef and were then blown into the lee of the island. They were moored there to start with, in the thriving port of Helice. We have to keep this from the others. For now, at least.'

Oriel unbuckled her air cylinder and shrugged off her diving gear. 'I agree. This … this is unbelievable. This project is now of global significance and we need to shut down the site. We'll need a licence to bring this up and so the site must be secured.'

Damian nodded. 'No diving until I have all the right documentation and specialists assigned to the project.'

'What will we tell the crew then?'

He slicked back his wet hair with his hand. 'Leave that to me, I'll think of something.'

They'd returned to shore as planned but had then holed themselves up in his study, poring over books and maps. Neither could get away from the idea that their statue was the legendary bronze of Helice, a thought that had occurred to each of them quite independently. In Oriel's mind's eye she could see the great statue standing proud, the sun glinting on the reddish metal, tall as an ancient redwood tree. It must have guarded the warlike Ionians faithfully at their harbour's mouth, trident held aloft, glaring at every ship that dared to venture close … little realizing that it wouldn't be the hand of man that brought about the port's ruin but a great tidal wave, obliterating everything that stood in its path. She thought of the implacable and flint-like man beside her, he too standing proudly guarding his own island and its people, quick to defend or to flare up in fury if one of his islanders failed to do his bidding.

The electric energy between them had been magnified by the shared thrill of their monumental discovery and longing rippled through Oriel, coursing down her body to her core. She was feeling his nearness in every fibre of her being and it was unsettling, almost maddening.

Finally they had noticed the time as the light through the tall windows deepened to sunset, an incandescent glow visible in all parts of the sky, drenching it with an aureate light. Damian had told her that tonight they would celebrate with champagne and that she should rest first; Hassan would come for her at nine-thirty. Oriel's pulse had raced with anticipation, so caught up was she in the moment and Damian's glittering gaze as it had fallen on her smiling lips.

And now there was the problem of deciding what to wear. She looked through her wardrobe with a critical eye, trying to anticipate Damian's reaction to each dress. She was thankful for her usual extensive wardrobe, not knowing what to expect. From experience, she had learnt that Greeks, like most Mediterranean people, took great care and pride in their appearance and consequently didn't hesitate to dress up, rather than down like the English, who branded that sort of behaviour vulgar. It was a trait that she loved, giving her the excuse to indulge her own love of clothes.

Eventually she chose a Malcolm Starr dress in fuchsia silk with a low V cut front and back, which revealed just enough skin to be sexy without being outrageous. Although Oriel had a beautiful figure, she had never had the stick look to which so many women of her generation aspired. Her soft rounded curves were in all the right places, with a bust and hips of roughly equal size and a narrow waist. The only jewel she wore was a hammered gold brooch representing the head of a horse, with an emerald eye that made it seem almost alive, designed by the sculptor Georges Braque and the well known goldsmith Baron Héger de Lowenfeld. A graduation gift from her parents after she'd been awarded a first in Classics, it was one of a few pieces of jewellery that Oriel held dear to her heart.

She pinned her hair back into a thick twisted knot at the nape of her neck, which brought into relief her high cheekbones and accentuated the depth of her green eyes. Rimmed with dark lashes that were in dramatic contrast to her pale hair, they shone like large peridots in her newly tanned face. No make-up was needed except for a small amount of tinted gloss on her lips. Oriel had just slipped into a pair of delicate fuchsia stiletto sandals when there was a knock at the door: nine-thirty on the dot. She flashed a last glance at the mirror before leaving the room.

Hassan took Oriel through the house to Damian's terrace. Tonight, the place was not in darkness. Lanterns shone here and there, lighting mysteriously the few remnants of Greek statuary and the big terracotta pots against the balustrade, over the sides of which flowers of various hues spilled. She found Damian leaning with one shoulder propped against a trellis of roses, his head tipped backwards as he seemed to be studying the star-studded sky; a tall figure, stranded in the shadows beyond the perimeter of light being cast by the low-slung lamps. The air hung still and heavily scented, with night-time rustlings in the hedges and undergrowth. When he remained unaware of Oriel's soft-footed approach, she paused to inhale deeply the sweet, fresh aroma of exotic flowers and greenery rising from the garden that lay in the moonlight below.

As if becoming suddenly conscious of her presence, Damian swung round. '*Kalispera*, Calypso. I hope you had some time to rest after all the excitement of earlier.' He looked utterly relaxed in his white silk pinstripe suit and thin, open-necked cotton shirt that showed the swing of the gleaming golden medallion she had noticed previously.

Despite his casual words and demeanour, Oriel saw the intensity in his eyes as they dwelt on her. The truth was she'd had little inclination to keep still, let alone lie down, since they had parted but she smiled and answered: '*Kahlee sphera*. Yes, I feel very refreshed, thank you.'

As she approached him, Damian picked up a small glass of mahogany-coloured liquid from the table next to him and held it out to her. 'I took the liberty of pouring you some of this.' Devilment sparked in his eyes as Oriel took it from him: Metaxa.

She raised an eyebrow. '*Charme d'Amour* again, *Kyrios* Lekkas?' Yet she couldn't help smiling shyly into her glass as she tipped it back to sip the warming, spicy brandy.

'What else, *Despinis* Anderson?' His cool, shuttered gaze dropped slowly to the deep V of her neckline and, suddenly tingling with self-consciousness, Oriel lifted a casual hand to her throat, where she knew a telltale vein was throbbing, her skin warming under that overtly masculine scrutiny.

There was a disturbingly caressing note in the deep voice, which made the perfectly respectable dress she was wearing feel transparent, and once again he left her lost for words. He took her arm, the grip of his fingers firm but gentle. 'Come, let's sit down to dinner. I thought it might be cooler out here, it will be a hot night. What do you think?'

'Lovely,' Oriel whispered.

'I've ordered a cold supper of seafood and salads, so we're not disturbed.' He gave the words a sensual meaning and warmth ran over Oriel's skin as she wondered what he had in mind.

The table was beautifully set, as on the night of her arrival. This time it was rectangular, a solid slab of cream-coloured marble sitting on delicately carved wrought-iron legs. Creamy candles were set in finely etched hurricane lamps and, under their flickering flames, silverware and crystal shone with rainbow lights that made the velvet petals of the spray of white tuberoses in the middle of the table seem made of gold. Beside the table stood a trolley with a huge dish piled up with shellfish of all sorts, surrounded by an array of smaller plates of delectable-looking salads. A bottle of pink champagne stood in a silver ice bucket with two flutes beside it.

Damian pulled out a chair for Oriel and she sat down. He stood over the pale shine of her hair. She could feel him looking down on her for a moment before taking his place opposite her. His eyes held glints of moonlight that added to their brilliance in his lean face and her heart skipped a beat.

He filled both glasses with the rosy-coloured bubbles and passed one to her. 'What a day, eh? Here's to our very good health and to our unique teamwork, Calypso. *Yamas!*' He raised his flute to Oriel's and she beamed back at him as their glasses clinked together.

'I'll fly to Athens as soon as I can in the morning and speak to the Minster of Culture. I may need to stay overnight as there'll be a lot of people to talk to. Whatever this statue turns out to be, it's big news.'

'We'd best not drink too much of this, then,' she said with a wry smile.

'I'm too wired for it to make any difference. Aren't you?' He grinned at her and Oriel wanted to curl up in his lap and never leave. 'I've given orders to close the wreck site for a while.'

Maybe this will be the end of my work here, she thought quite suddenly, feeling as if a cold blanket had been thrown over her. She tried to ignore the prospect that her time with Damian might be running out. 'I imagine you'll have to bring in extra security,' she said, picturing the mayhem news of their find would undoubtedly bring.

'As I said, for the moment we'll keep the news to ourselves,' Damian replied. 'That'll be the safest thing. Otherwise we'll be sitting ducks for every treasure hunter around.'

'Yes, and if we're right and this is a submerged seaport of some importance, then there will be a great deal more than just one wrecked ship to excavate.'

'And you, Calypso, will be the one to excavate it,' he said, his silver gaze gleaming.

Oriel was unable to suppress the smile that flooded through her whole body at his words. She traced the rim of her glass. 'It would be like my own personal golden apple.'

He looked at her quizzically. 'Golden apple?'

She looked up. 'Yes, you know, the Twelve Labours of Heracles. The near-impossible feats that he had to perform for Eurystheus, the king of Tiryns, I think it was. Including bringing him the golden apples that belonged to Zeus himself.'

'Yes, I remember the story. The apples were kept in the garden of the Hesperides, no?'

She nodded. 'That's right. They were guarded by the Hesperides, nymphs who were the daughters of Atlas. The trouble was, Heracles didn't even know where the garden was at first.' Her eyes shone with enthusiasm. 'A bit like us and our search for the lost port of Helice.'

'Ah yes, and Heracles was challenged by the sons of Poseidon.'

'Not unlike our own struggles with those treacherous waters around Helios,' she affirmed, warming to her theme. 'Then he killed the eagle that tormented Prometheus, bound in chains on his rock on Mount Caucasus, in exchange for the secret of how to get the apples … which was using Atlas, the Titan, to fetch his prize.' She gave a light shrug. 'For me, finding Helice would be a little like Heracles completing his labours.' Oriel paused before laughing. 'A golden archaeological feat, don't you think?'

Damian grinned, his eyes roaming with enjoyment over her face. He raised his glass. 'I'll drink to that too. Though you are far prettier than Heracles.'

Oriel couldn't help smiling back shyly as she took another sip of the deliciously cool champagne.

'Besides,' Damian continued, 'Heracles became the perfect embodiment of the Greek idea of *pathos*. Virtuous struggle and suffering resulting in fame and, for Heracles, immortality. I think discoveries like this are a way for us to live on, in some tiny part, by leaving our mark.' He cocked an eyebrow. 'But let's hope we don't have the struggle and suffering, eh?'

She laughed again. 'I agree, let's just make sure we're careful.'

His expression became animated. 'Isn't this why we go down there? Just seeing that magnificent bronze figure lying there waiting for us to discover him … Tell me, Calypso, is there anything to rival this feeling?'

Oriel recognized Damian's mercurial mood. He was excited and on edge; it made him talkative and lyrical. She laughed. 'We do it because of our love and admiration for those ancient civilizations that taught us and left us so much, and also our reluctance to see their work disappear. In your own words, Damian: you Greeks were the cradle of civilization. Now that instinct, to seek out the secrets of history, has been vindicated. This find doesn't get any better.'

He gave her a penetrating look of raw interest. 'So wise, Calypso …'

She shrugged.

'I want to get to know you.'

'Do you?' She thought her voice sounded stunned.

'Well, you're a fabulous-looking creature. Perhaps a bit tall …' He smiled and leaned back in his chair.

'I'm not *that* tall,' she started to protest, and then saw he was teasing.

Damian's brilliant eyes raked over her vivid face. 'How old are you, Calypso? You omitted that information on your résumé.'

'I was born in 1512,' she returned lightly. 'This is my forth reincarnation.'

'I suppose the first time they burnt you as a witch.'

She forgot that she was supposed to remain cool and stared into the orange candle flames. 'Throughout history, women have been persecuted, more harshly judged than men.'

'I won't deny it,' he replied in an unexpectedly sympathetic voice. 'No need to get so het up, we're just having a conversation. Besides, I already know that.'

'Well, you could have fooled me. You might be aware of it in theory, but not in practice,' she told him in a voice that she hoped would sound dispassionate. 'A woman would only have to look at you to realize you would quickly reduce her to a slave.'

'On the basis of my general appearance?' He sounded more sceptical than offended.

'You're the quintessential male, a conqueror by your very nature.'

'Is that how you see me, *agápi mou*? You flatter me.'

Once again, Oriel knew that he was trying to bait her and even though his arrogance was insufferable on occasion, part of her was starting to enjoy the challenge of their sparring: male against female. 'I'm not your *agápi*,' she retorted. 'Actually, I could equally well say, I'm no man's *agápi*.'

'No man's love? A woman like you? You must be!' Damian leaned back in his chair again, staring with amused mockery into her eyes. 'All the men here are mad about you, haven't you noticed?'

It was hard to keep her composure in the face of such a comment. 'Oh, for goodness' sake, Damian, what are you talking about?'

'Forgive me, Calypso.' His eyes flickered as he regarded her speculatively. 'Perhaps I'm trying to unravel you too quickly.'

There was a moment's silence as he paused to look up, watching the fireflies make little sparks in the air. 'What a beautiful night,' he murmured.

Their gazes caught and Oriel swiftly glanced at the vase of tuberoses, her heartbeat beginning to pick up inexplicably. She took another sip of champagne, enjoying the feeling of the icy bubbles in her throat. 'I love those flowers.'

'Tuberoses are like most women,' he said, his eyes still fixed upon her. 'They change with the hours and are lovelier by candle-light than in the glare of sunshine.'

'Most things look better by night than in the daytime, I suppose.'

'Perhaps, but I said *most* women. You, Calypso, are not most women. Your beauty is as exceptional in daylight as it is by candle-light.'

Oriel gave him a speaking glance and his dark brows lifted in amusement. 'Just an honest observation.'

She ignored the warmth that had reflexively crept up her cheeks and cleared her throat. 'I see oysters are on the menu.'

'Here, have one,' he said, placing a few of the shellfish on a plate with a wedge of lemon. 'They're freshly caught today.'

Oriel loved oysters and these were particularly plump, with a fresh delicate flavour of sea and seaweed. 'They're delicious,' she said as she held the last one between her thumb and first finger and tipped the narrow side of the shell into her mouth.

He gave a satisfied smile. 'They taste of heaven, eh? Have some more.' He chose another six and placed them on her plate.

'That's too much,' she protested.

'Do you know the legend attached to these delicious little mol-luscs, known to be a potent aphrodisiac?' Oriel saw his eyebrows quirk as he studied her face.

'You mean Aphrodite being born from the ocean waves on a shell?'

'That was a scallop, not an oyster. Actually, Hesiod tells a much gorier story in his book, *Theogony*, about the birth of Aphrodite.'

'I should have known you would have another gruesome take on Greek mythology to share,' she said wryly, squeezing a wedge of lemon over another of the oysters.

Damian grinned and continued. 'According to his tale, Uranus and Gaea bore a race of deities that were hideous to look at. Uranus did not care for these children due to their monstrous appearance and banished them to the abyss beneath the underworld, known as Tartarus, the Greek equivalent of the dungeon of Hades. Gaea be-came angry and conspired with her children to depose their father. Then, while Uranus was bedding her, Cronus, their son, escaped from Tartarus and then castrated his father with a sickle of his mother's creation. The testicles were thrown into the sea and they foamed into the ravishing Aphrodite.'

'I knew it. Gruesome,' responded Oriel, though it didn't stop her defiantly eating another of the shellfish while Damian looked on, his mouth twitching with contained laughter. She added casually: 'I didn't know that version of the legend but I've heard of the oyster's reputation as a strong aphrodisiac, of course, though I can't say I've ever experienced the effect.'

'Then I'm afraid the man who was with you at the time failed you.'

Oriel read the allusion in his gaze and in his words, a message there for her if she just cared to acknowledge it. 'Must you bring everything back to that?'

'Isn't *that*, as you say, what it's been all about since the beginning of time? Adam and Eve and the sinful apple?'

Oriel shrugged. 'What's the use of discussing anything with someone who's so one-track minded?'

His eyes flashed again and flirted. 'How can I do otherwise in the presence of a woman that delights my eyes, makes my heart sing and fires my blood as no woman has before?'

She gave him a cool-eyed look that belied the way she was feeling. 'It's not your plan to seduce me, is it?'

To her annoyance he just laughed. 'Why? Because I'm drawn to your beauty and your spirit? No ...' And although Damian left his negation unfinished, the look in his eyes told her he was thinking, *I did that a long time ago.*

Oriel shrugged and turned her head away. 'Just as well,' she whispered, 'because here's one radical female who doesn't care to get her wings singed.'

He ignored the answer. 'You're an elusive girl, Calypso. How would you describe yourself? Yes, radical, perhaps. Gentle, tolerant ... submissive? In certain situations, I'd guess.' Damian leaned his forearms on the table and a gleam of predatory interest lit his grey eyes. He seemed mesmerized by whatever he saw in her face. 'I think you're the reverse of all that and it's what attracts me to you. I'd guess you're even more of a challenge to a man in many ways now.'

She shot him a scathing look. 'And I think you're sexist and a womanizer.'

Damian laughed. 'I never thought that I'd enjoy having a woman call me sexist and a womanizer. Instead, I'm finding it most entertaining.' He stood to clear away her plate of shells and served her with half a lobster and a dollop of mayonnaise. 'What has made you so cynical, eh, *koritsee mou*?'

Oriel frowned at him as she took her plate. 'I'm not your girl,' she said, trying to conceal the way her emotions were gradually rising as the evening progressed. She was enjoying her meal. The Metaxa had already had an effect earlier on, and now the champagne she had been sipping quite liberally made her insides feel warm and languorous. She was aware of a stirring, a vague bubble of elation.

No one had ever talked to her with the direct audacity Damian had been doing since her arrival, and she took pleasure in the curious prickling his words created under her skin, a tingling all the way up and down her spine as the beauty of the night, the soft indolent charm of the island and the personality of the man sitting opposite her soaked into her senses. She felt trapped inside a strange dream: Damian captured her imagination even if he eluded her understanding.

Still, that small voice at the back of her mind appeared again: Damian didn't love her, his hormones were the ones pulling the strings where she was concerned. His heart belonged to his childhood sweetheart, a passionate woman with the voice of a songbird and the physique of a goddess – Yolanda, the beautiful singer.

Damian ignored Oriel's rebellious retort and passed her another dish.

They ate in silence for a while, finishing their main course. The night was very warm, the air a caress, the moon a slice of cantaloupe suspended high in an ebony velvet expanse of sky. Oriel loved Helios's nights, the fragrances and sounds. The aroma of seaweed and salt surrounded them, mixed with the tang of ozone and eelgrass that mingled with the scented breath of exotic flowers – the smell was invigorating and the breeze glorious. She could hear little scuttling creatures that twittered and whispered in the flowerbeds beneath the terrace. Away down on the shore the sea sighed rhythmically. The birds were silenced, while the incessant chatter of cicadas in the tall grasses formed a backdrop to Damian and Oriel's conversation.

Oriel was glad that, for a while, their talk moved easily back to the Poseidon discovery, moving on to the Alexander bronze and the likelihood of its having been sculpted by the legendary Lysip-pos. Damian served them both with a light fruit salad and, as they finished their dessert and he was pouring them coffee from a per-colator that had been slowly brewing during supper, he produced a packet of Gitanes.

'I know that you don't smoke, but may I?' he asked.

'Yes, of course, go ahead.'

Damian flicked his lighter, lit a cigarette and settled back in his chair. For a short moment he watched Oriel from under his eye-lids, lightly blue-tinged smoke playing over his head. He shot her an enigmatic glance.

'We need to talk.'

Somehow, she knew he was not referring to work any more. 'Do we? What about?' To her own ears, Oriel sounded breathless.

'About what happened on Aegina six years ago.'

Her eyes darted back to his. 'Why do we need to talk about that? It's all in the past and forgotten.'

'Is it forgotten, Calypso?' His lips quirked at the edges and his voice became soft. 'Is that what you think? Is that how you feel?'

'I thought we'd both decided to ignore it,' she tried to retort haughtily, willing her heart to stop its idiotic racing.

Damian drained his coffee cup and poured himself another be-fore answering. 'I don't see how we can.'

'We've managed so far.'

'We've managed so far.' He repeated the phrase and his deep voice held a hint of buried laughter as if giving it due consideration.

'Yes, we have,' Oriel said emphatically, endeavouring to steady her gaze as she met Damian's moonlit irises, but she flinched and looked away.

'Your eyes do the speaking for you. They always did.'

'I don't deny your attractiveness, Damian … even with that scar you're the best-looking man I've met, or am ever likely to meet. You've probably always known that you can have your way with women. Let's face it, you had your way with me, but then I was younger and naïve, with no experience of men, and you seduced me.'

'Seduced?' Damian's eyes flashed with sudden anger through the smoke of his cigarette. 'That's an unpleasant word to qualify what happened between us. Besides, it suggests that I was the first man who ever touched you.'

Her eyes widened. 'Of course you were.'

A smile came and went about his lips. 'There is no "of course" about it, *agápi mou*.' Although his expression didn't show it, Oriel sensed that he had suddenly become angry and was struggling to conceal it.

'How *dare* you! Y-You know full well that I was a virgin.'

'Ah yes, I admit I could tell that, but there are other ways of making love without allowing the treasure trove to be ravaged. You want me to believe that no man ever enjoyed that delectable body of yours in some way?'

Oriel's head snapped up and she glared frostily into his glittering eyes. 'I never …' Her voice came out in an anguished croak.

Damian reached a hand towards the spray of white tuberoses on the table and Oriel watched as his fingers seemed about to crush the delicate petals. Instead, they fondled with slow deliberation, his skin dark against the snow-like petals, and his gaze swept hers with its outraged look, lingering on her lips and very slowly moving down to her throat, and again to the darker place where the soft curve of her breasts were barely concealed by the cleavage of her dress. His insolent scrutiny sent a flame of colour flooding her cheeks.

'You never …?'

'Until I met you, I'd never let a man be anything like that intimate with me.'

The candle flame reflected in Damian's silver irises, intensifying their dangerous beauty, and the flickering light made a frame of shadows around his face. 'Really?' his tone was mocking. He narrowed his eyes then stubbed out his cigarette with a gesture of finality. Pushing his chair back, he stood up. 'If you'll excuse me a moment.'

Oriel also stood up. 'I think I should be going back to my room.'

'Not until I've shown you something that you might find very interesting. I won't be a second.' He left, the quiet hardness of his tone indicating that he expected her to wait for him and, though Oriel did not feel that she had to bow instantly to this man's orders, she remained on the terrace and walked to the balustrade.

She looked up at the moon. A missing piece on one side of it showed that its course was almost half run. Down below in the garden, haunted by bats and white moths, the heavy shadows of cypress, ilex and other great trees broke through the darkness, the pattern of leaves printed upon the moonlit walls. She jumped as a long-fingered hand trailed tantalizingly down her bare back; the movement sent a tremor shuddering through her.

'Is that what you felt when Rob touched you?'

'Rob?' Oriel turned abruptly. Her mind went on alert. 'Who told you about Rob?'

'I didn't need anybody to tell me, *kouklitsa mou*,' Damian held out his hand. In it was the photograph of Rob and herself in Venice. 'You look rather cosy, eh?'

Oriel swallowed on dryness. 'Where did you get that?'

'You left it on the beach.'

'And you took it.'

'Yes, to remind me that women are all alike.'

'Rob and I never …'

'You'll tell me next that the relationship was platonic.' His tone was taunting, his icy silver eyes cutting into hers. 'From the way you were looking at each other in the photograph you were just warming up for a playful night.'

Oriel fixed her gaze on the buttons of his shirt, her body tense. 'The relationship wasn't platonic. Rob was my fiancé, it's true, but we … I had decided that I wanted to remain chaste until my wedding night. That night you and I met in Aegina, I had just learnt that he was marrying my best friend, who was pregnant by him.'

Damian was silent for a moment, as if digesting this information, and placed the photo slowly down on the balustrade in front of her. He gave her a hard stare. 'In other words, he dumped you.'

'You could have put it in a more elegant way but, yes, he left me.'

'And you still haven't learnt that the thirst of desire cannot be quenched by the cold wine of chastity. I despise that word. It is an insult to the Creator and an abomination to man and beast.'

She raised an eyebrow at this dramatic turn of phrase. 'Well, if it's chastity that offends you so much, you shouldn't have a problem. I gave myself to *you* that night, and I don't feel that I have been denying you much since my arrival here.'

Damian ignored her dry remark and lit another cigarette. 'So you came to me on the rebound, as you say in English, eh?'

'I really don't know why I'm answering all your questions. Who are you to judge me? We had a one-night stand a very long time ago and, anyhow, you went off next morning without a second look.'

He glanced at her, running a hand through his hair. 'I was going to stay on a few more days so we would have a chance to get to know each other, but then I found the photograph and so I left.'

'Fine, you left, and we've each lived our life. What's your problem?'

'*You* are my problem, *zoi mou*. Purity and passion.'

'Meaning?' Oriel stared at Damian as the smoke played over his face in a sort of thin haze that made his eyes seem more mysterious than ever. She sensed the tension coiled in him like a quivering spring as he towered over her.

'*Theé mou!* A woman of your beauty and intelligence and passion. What good are your conventional notions if you aren't being true to yourself?'

'Would you be saying such things if I were your daughter, or your sister?'

'Maybe not if they were part of this island. It's harder for women here. Emancipation has not yet touched Helios, but the day will come when there'll be an end to this chastity-worship and everyone will realize the stupidity of such unhealthy repression of natural human drives.'

'This might be your philosophy, but what you really mean is a hedonism that serves only you, isn't it?' Oriel fought her emotions, wanting to believe there was something deeper than Damian's libido that drove him to pursue her in this relentless way. 'But since that's the way you think, why me? I'm sure there must be hundreds of women out there who would be only too pleased to satisfy your needs.'

He didn't answer her immediately. 'You've understood me wrongly, Oriel. I'm not promoting promiscuity, no, quite the reverse. But a woman's body, like a man's, needs warmth and care to bloom and flourish. If not, it shrivels up like a wintry tree, alive but stripped of its splendour.'

Oriel gazed at him, unable to summon the words she knew she should be saying to parry his.

'What are you thinking, *agápi mou*? Those innocent eyes of yours are like a pool that hides things beneath a cool surface.'

'You make me sound secretive, Damian. What have I got to hide?'

'I wonder ...' He remained silent a few moments. Then again he stirred. 'Don't you find it strange we should meet again, eh? What happened between us was special, though incomplete ... unfinished business. And being Greek, I believe in the unsuspected manoeuvres of the Moirae.'

'Well, being English, I don't.' Oriel was trying to ignore the frantic thud of her heart. 'As I've told you before, this doesn't mean that I'm not attracted to you and I'm not saying I regret that night, because I don't ... not in the least.'

'You've made my day.' A mocking inflexion edged his voice.

Oriel went on the defensive. 'Believe it or not, one-night stands are not my style. After that night I didn't make it a habit.'

He lifted a dark brow sceptically. 'Really? So tell me, Calypso, what *is* your style? Maybe I'll be able to accommodate.'

'I believe that making love is something sacred, to be cherished.'

He leaned closer to her. 'And I don't dispute that. The body is a subtle instrument to be played upon in every conceivable way. It's made to be sensitive to pleasurable impressions ... like a harp.'

A husky sensuality had crept into Damian's tone as he whispered the last three words. Oriel stared at him, remembering instantly the last time he had said that to her in this very same spot and an erotic urgency sang through her blood. The smouldering blaze of his eyes was dwelling with open passion on her face. Their magnetic grey held her, though she wanted more than ever to run away. Still, she could not bear to move away from him even as she knew that she was playing with fire.

With each minute that passed, the need to touch grew stronger. It wasn't enough to talk or to look as it only fed the desire for greater intimacy. Now, as they couldn't tear their eyes from each other, silence fell between them, a silence that grew tense with unfulfilled passion.

'How much longer will you live in denial, *agápi mou*?' Damian's voice stroked over Oriel like silk. His face was so close that she collided with the icy fire of his irises as it glittered over her. Clutched by the nettling vibrations from his powerful frame, his potent sexuality and the disturbing intimations of desire she'd read in his gaze, the base of her spine dissolved. Although she knew he was trying to keep a check on his libido, he looked saturnine, very much a fallen angel, all pride and arrogance.

Damian turned away and faced the darkness of the starlit sky. He raked a tanned hand through his inky hair. His expression became unfathomable. Still, the closed mask of his features was hard, his mouth tightly controlled, only the irregularity of his breathing hinting at the depth of passion he kept leashed. They stood close to each other, still sharing a silence pregnant with unspoken words, tasting the absolute serenity that enveloped the atmosphere. The whole night felt as if it were simmering with hidden intensity, like Oriel herself: a tranquil, sweet, languid night with its scented air, its heart throbbing imperceptibly with hushed undercurrents. Every now and then, a toad calling to its mate uttered its treble love note, and the dry cicadas kept up their endless rasping. The breeze held a caressing quality, sighing with anticipation.

Damian smoked his eternal Gitanes; Oriel's eyes followed the line of his white cuff for a few moments, the lift and fall of the glowing cigarette end and the blue smoke that spiralled into the darkness. She could only see his profile, his good side. She wondered what he was thinking – he seemed so far away, as if he had forgotten her presence, and yet she knew he had not because of the electric awareness that rippled between them.

A shooting star with a long tail, in the shape of a tadpole, left its place in the heavens and shot across the canopy of stars to find a new dwelling.

'A shooting star again. It's said they only appear to lovers.' Damian pointed it out, his arm brushing against her cheek. 'Did you see it?'

'Yes,' she breathed.

He turned towards her. 'How swiftly it fell, and how quickly it died. Is the spark that flared between us that night as transient, do you think?'

Oriel met the regret in Damian's eyes but couldn't find the right words to answer him.

His gaze intensified. 'Are there only black ashes left of the fire that burned so strongly between us, or are the embers still glowing, waiting for the right moment to burst into flame again?'

He fell silent a moment and stood, studying her face in the moonlight. 'I went away at dawn that morning, as though I'd left an enchanted girl lying on the bare rock in a cave, her beautiful wheat-coloured hair cloaking her naked body, who would stay there forever until I returned to kiss her awake.'

'But you didn't return,' Oriel murmured huskily. Her face was raised to him, gravely intent.

'Circumstances, a misunderstanding, tried to part us but we met again. Why is that, my beautiful, doubting Calypso? Because an unbreakable cord of love binds some people from birth, and a mysterious force exists to ensure that nothing, not time, distance nor anyone, can keep them from finding each other and uniting.'

Oriel's heart nearly leapt out of her chest. She struggled to believe what he was saying, her eyes dwelling wide on his lean, powerful face, but still she didn't answer.

'You feel the same as I, *agápi mou*, I know you do. You have eyes that speak and an expressive body, and they reveal rather more than you would wish, perhaps.'

At once she dropped her lashes, unable to look at him, but Damian took her chin between forefinger and thumb and lifted her face, forcing her to meet his burning gaze. She was lost for words – they seemed locked in her throat; the soft night breeze could not cool her cheeks as the silver irises appraised her, and her body appeared gripped by a strange and helpless feeling. It was like a dream ...

How much longer could she resist this overwhelming desire to give in to everything that she felt for this man? This longing to stroke his coppery satin skin, to press her lips to his muscled body. It was sheer hell pretending she didn't want him when every molecule of her being was longing for his touch. It had been building up all evening, this need for him. She had known it, even though she had pretended it wasn't there. And so, after the first struggling moment, she couldn't deny herself the relief of pressing her face to his shoulder and breathing in his masculine scent of clean, sun-heated skin, and the smoke of the Gitanes that clung to him.

Damian threw away his cigarette. Then all at once, with a growled oath, he gathered Oriel in his arms and lifted her to him, clasping her body so tightly that she thought her ribs would break.

Oriel gasped, flooded with riotous heat. She should stop him; she should *want* to stop him! She should push him away, not spread her hands caressingly across his powerful chest. His breath was warm against her forehead. She could feel his heart hammering beneath her fingertips through the thin material of his shirt, pulsing its intimate message to her, holding her captive; igniting her with the same fire that was burning inside him.

CHAPTER 8

Damian carried Oriel to the far end of the terrace through the archway of tall double doors into an airy white-walled room. It was lit by two large candelabra, placed on each side of the only piece of furniture that adorned it: a queen-sized carved-oak bed with a mirror set in the ceiling above it. An explicit nineteenth-century engraving by Félicien Rops, *Le Diable au Corps*, was hanging over the headboard, featuring a man and woman entwined naked, simultaneously performing oral sex on one another. Carpeted in tawny oriental colours, the rest of the room had a warm, sensual glow and an unreal dreamlike feel.

Oriel stared at the striking face above hers as Damian's powerful arms flexed beneath her and she linked her hands around his neck, her heart racing. 'You're the most perfect creature, with a lovelier, more graceful body than any other woman alive!' he murmured. His eyes were like pewter now, his pupils expanded and dark with desire as they swept over her. 'I know how soft and warm and sweet it can feel. Even though I can remember it in every little detail, there's a terrible ache inside me to see how lovely it can look, and not with this around it.'

With these few words, Damian was exciting her to such a dizzying peak of longing that Oriel was becoming lost, a prisoner of his passions. Wings seemed to be fluttering inside her; more than ever she felt that her body needed to be warmed, needed to be desired, needed to be appeased – by him and him alone. Her eyes flickered to the enamoured couple in the engraving over the bed, their limbs entangled, leaving nothing to the imagination, which served only to enflame her further with pulsating lust.

Damian laid her down slowly on the ruby damask eiderdown and in the confusion of the next few minutes of touching and breathing and pulling, they were both naked: her willowy, fair frame and his muscular golden body two contrasting beautiful sculpted figures reflected in the glass above them. Her eyes took in the proud arousal piercing the curly black hair that formed a glistening dark nest between his lean, toned thighs, mirroring the hunger and frantic need that raged in her core.

Oriel looked up again and saw her eyes shining with desire, wider and greener than she had ever seen them; her pink tongue passing over her parched lips, asking to be kissed; her swollen, firm breasts with their dusky rose areolae and hard twin peaks clamouring to be touched, and her parted thighs so wantonly inviting an erotic invasion. This unexpected confrontation with an image of her unashamed desire was a total shock to her but, strangely enough, seeing herself as Damian saw her only strengthened her need for him to touch her intimately. Oriel's pulse rate tripped into a quickening beat and her gaze turned to the silver irises surveying her with slow deliberation.

Damian's expression lingered on her, now edged with amusement: 'Not so innocent, Calypso, eh? It excites you already to see, to watch. A bit of an exhibitionist, maybe?' he taunted softly. 'The way you made me feel that night, I always knew you had the imagination to match a natural appetite.' His voice was low and husky.

He looked vaguely satanic with his scar standing out in jagged detail against his swarthy skin in the penumbra … dangerous, indomitable … displaying also, quite openly and almost defiantly, the terrible marks on his chest. Surgery, extensive physiotherapy and exercise had built the muscles back to normality, but only one nipple remained, which gave his front a lopsided, barbaric look that Oriel found oddly arousing.

'But your experience is vastly superior to mine,' she opined quietly.

'Oh, I wouldn't worry about that,' he murmured, gathering her more closely so that his fully aroused manhood nudged against her thigh. Despite the damage to his torso, his muscled body was magnificent, like steel encased in hot skin, his voice deep and husky. 'Just watching you lying there naked and beautiful, like a goddess, with your satiny alabaster skin and your moonspun hair, sends my blood pounding.'

If he wanted her so, why wasn't he touching her? What was he waiting for? Why was he prolonging her agony?

Damian's head bent, his gaze never leaving hers, his mouth in reach of her lips. His hands now moved slowly, hovering just an inch above her body, following her curves, evocative, arousing; so close that she could feel the heat of his flesh almost brushing hers. His movements were tantalizing, daring her to stretch out and pull his hands down on to her breasts, her stomach and the place between her thighs that was crying out to be explored and plundered; but she managed not to do so, trusting him and knowing by instinct that anticipation would only make the surrender more ecstatic.

Damian smiled as though he had read her thoughts. 'I'm not a sadist. Really. I'm like an artist surveying the canvas you're giving me to work on. Where will I begin? Here?' He brushed a finger against her lips. 'Or here,' he murmured, stroking her throat. 'But maybe you'd prefer to feel me here ...' He placed a hand lightly on one of Oriel's breasts, then slid it down to her stomach. 'Or here.'

The caress of his eyes, more than anything else, was driving her wild. Her naked flesh was vulnerable and feverish, awaiting his next move, wanting him to touch her where the ache for him was becoming almost unbearable. Her lips parted, longing and desire flashing through her, pulsing beats that desperately sought release.

Damian's hand slipped down further and rested on the neat triangle of hair between her slender creamy thighs. She parted them automatically, waiting breathlessly for his next move, her eyes wide and dark with need. The narrow-eyed look of frank and unhurried assessment he gave when she did this told her he knew exactly how she felt; the slow, lazy burn deep in his pupils conveying that he was attuned to each tremor of her skin.

'Is this what you want?' There was a soft sensuality to his voice as, with one finger, he parted the delicate petals covering the moist, throbbing core of her desire. Oriel gasped when the tip of his middle finger teased the swollen bud and then retreated immediately; she was actually trembling she needed him so badly. The temptation to pull him down on top of her, to feel his virility press hard against her and await the delicious consequences was excruciating.

'I want you,' she breathed. 'I've wanted you for so long, Damian. Please ...'

Damian looked at Oriel for several long, lingering moments without moving, seeming to take in everything about her appearance: her pleading eyes, the little vein that throbbed rhythmically in the middle of her throat, the globes of her breasts brazenly inviting his attention, her whole body offered to him in flagrant submission for him to take – a sort of a sacrifice to her pagan Greek god.

And at long last, those silver eyes lifted to Oriel's full lips, glittering like diamonds beneath his heavy lids. With his hand Damian smoothed a strand of hair from her face before lowering himself down slowly beside her. 'Your mouth is made to be kissed,' he said as he covered it with his, teasing it with the tip of his tongue, forcing his way in and delving deep. She didn't resist, opening it for him, her lips warm and generous as they met his, accepting him, devouring him, feeding her own appetite.

Fires seared through Oriel; she was ablaze, already a mass of tension and desire, prepared by the fantasy Damian had created in his tormenting foreplay. His palms cupped her breasts, his thumbs pressing into the fleshy sides, circling first one, then the other. The caress of his strong wide hands was tender and loving as they rubbed in slow, incredibly sweet circles until the hardening tips showed him just where to concentrate his attention. Leaving her lips, his hunting mouth took into its warm depths one peak and then the other, biting and licking, a sweet delicious torture, making her whimper and moan softly as she felt everything inside her go haywire.

Oriel undulated against him and reached down to the compelling length of his hardness, but Damian pushed her hand away. 'Patience, *ómorfi seirina mou*. This is just the *mezedes*. I haven't finished with you yet. Relax, *agápi mou*, let me feed you the food of our Greek gods.'

The glitter in Damian's eyes intensified before he dipped his head again. 'So, where did we get to …' he said as he skimmed over her midriff and smooth belly, moving to the indentation of her navel and licking it, oh-so-erotically with the tip of his tongue. 'Where do you want me to go next, eh?' he asked, his eyes searing hers with his question, and he smiled that slow, secretive smile she was beginning to know so well, which lifted one side of his mouth a fraction.

'Let me see,' he whispered again, kissing a trail over her smooth skin, continuing his slow journey down her body, lingeringly, loving every inch of her as she shook with passion beneath his fingertips and the exploring hardness of his lips.

Damian brushed two inquisitive fingers against the soft petals of her womanhood, a butterfly's wing of a touch that drew a moan from her and made Oriel's legs automatically edge apart in silent invitation, signalling she wanted more ... oh, so much more! 'Yes, I can see, you are so swollen, so moist, so hot, so delicious ... is this for me?'

Oriel didn't think she could speak without crying. The heat flooded her face as she lifted her gaze, searing him with the naked lust she knew was evident in her green eyes. She was not ashamed to show him that his power over her senses had taken over her mind; she was not ashamed any more of this overwhelming emotion flooding every secret part of her. She wanted him to know it. That she – who had always been modest to the point of prudery about her body – should be filled with this desire to have him look at her while in the throes of pleasure was a startling experience but it thrilled her in a way she never thought possible.

Damian seemed to sense Oriel's silent message, spurring on his arousal. He was trembling and the tip of his manhood was engorged and moist. With a groan he cupped the curved cheeks of her bottom and drew her closer to him. Nudging her thighs even wider apart, his lips found her core, sucking it into the moisture of his hot mouth, wrenching a cry of ecstasy from her throat. He held her hips, murmuring her name as he licked and teased, feasting on the swollen silken bud as he flicked his tongue back and forth across it. Stroking delicately at first, he explored this territory that she was so openly laying in front of him, skilfully applying pressure, responding to each sound she made while massaging the inside of her thighs.

Oriel reeled and moaned, her skin on fire, urging him on, asking for more – always more – wanting the rapture never to stop; and Damian gave, and gave without respite, as though he couldn't get enough of her taste and texture. More than once he brought her to a cliff-edge before starting all over again.

'You smell so sweet, so good. You're driving me crazy,' he said, his voice dropping to a velvet purr.

Oriel could see his eyes had darkened, his breathing was ragged, his control had reached its limit. 'I want to be inside you, Calypso, all the way inside you,' he whispered, his voice husky and slurred, giving each word a sensual caress. 'You are so voluptuous, so exciting and warm … Let me in, *agápi mou*,' he continued, as his hands slipped down her spine, encircling her waist. Then he pulled her up on top of him, parting her thighs so that she straddled him.

As the hard, satin-skinned tip of his shaft brushed against the crest of her own desire a deep almost animalistic groan was ripped from Damian's throat and she felt him stiffen, his hands squeezing her waist, summoning all his control.

Following his lead, Oriel reached a hand down to the heated nest of his lower belly, between his muscular thighs; she found his virile force awesome, swollen as it was to its fullest extent and so tremendously beautiful.

'Let me show you how I love *you*,' she murmured, encircling it with her long fingers and brushing it against her warm, soft moisture, moving back and forth. 'You feel so hard, so strong against me. It's so good …'

She moved slowly on top of him, abandoning herself to sensuality, telling him how he made her feel, what his maleness was doing to her, her explicit words stimulating his desire as much as her own. The longing to taste him the way he had tasted her overrode any remaining shadow of inhibition. Her hands glided swiftly over the length of him, exploring his body with an innocently absorbed fascination, caressing and stroking his deeply muscled chest.

Leaning forwards, Oriel slid her mouth along Damian's smooth shoulders, following every curve of bone, every hollow in the flesh before teasing his nipple; kissing, biting and squeezing, grazing with her teeth and then soothing with her tongue. All the while she could feel the velvet tip of him growing harder and harder against the silky-smooth wetness of her apex. He groaned with pleasure beneath her, moving to her rhythm, his muscles tensing every time her long flowing hair brushed against him.

Catching Oriel's chin between his fingers, he tilted her face upwards. 'Look in the mirror, Calypso, see how beautiful you are.' Lifting her silken platinum mane away from her face, he pushed it to the back of her shoulders, exhibiting the erotic image of their naked, aroused bodies to her own view.

And as she leaned back and raised her head up to the looking glass, Damian arched up towards her and, cupping her breasts, he penetrated her with one sharp thrust, driving into her with almost frightening intensity. A soft cry escaped from her lips at his abrupt invasion and a deep shuddering seized her, followed by a feral groan that came from deep inside as her muscles began to spasm. She opened herself up for him, bloomed warm and wet, urging him to go deeper as he moved into her with a circling motion, pressing the swollen bud of her pleasure against the base of his hardness with every possessive thrust of his body. She marvelled at how he was stretching her, filling her, and she moaned his name voluptuously, cresting a magic, ecstatic wave of passion, never wanting this journey to stop.

Damian was looking up into the mirror and, through her own erotic haze, Oriel could see and understand the pleasure he derived from watching while touching her. She knew that, aroused in the way she was, she couldn't help but appear seductive to him; and she drew just as much delight in seeing the effect her caresses had on him – his body glorious in his shameless exposure.

Watching their writhing reflections in the mirror was exciting them both, sending the raw edge of desire flaming within them, inciting them to go further into their carnal adventure. Their eyes glazed with lust, their lips swollen, skin laced with glistening sweat, they revelled in every second of their frenzied lovemaking, stripped of all inhibitions. Oriel let Damian take her in every way imaginable, surrendering to her deepest secret cravings, primitive, dark and wild.

As he pulled back her hair, she tightened her thighs around his waist, urging him on, deeper and harder, while she rasped in his ear, 'Please, Damian, I want your hot milk to flood me.' He growled low in response, his muscular shoulders flexing above her. They were building towards shattering peaks of pleasure now, soaring into a world of blinding light, until their torturous tension finally exploded again and again into a sunburst of glorious ecstasy.

And afterwards, when they had kissed, licked, touched, caressed and explored their way over every inch of each other's bodies, they lay trembling and satiated, trying to breathe again at a steadier pace in each other's arms as the thunder of their heartbeats dropped to a slow pulse.

Oriel lay nestled in the hollow of Damian's strong shoulder, drowsy and boneless. The white room with its flickering candles, which minutes ago had been full of their cries of pleasure-pain, was now filled with a silent languor, broken only by the breeze whispering through the open windows, the night sounds beyond and the sigh of the sea.

Oriel's feelings for the man who lay relaxed and sleeping beside her were both primitive and shameless. Although Damian had made her feel loved, with his lavish lovemaking tender and caring as well as passionate, he hadn't said he loved her. Those three unambiguous words would have left her in no doubt about his true feelings. He'd spoken of *an unbreakable cord of love* – was that the same thing as declaring that he loved her or just a figure of speech, uttered spontaneously in the throes of passionate seduction? How far beyond lust for her did his emotional involvement go? How soon would he tire of her? Did it matter, she wondered sleepily.

She turned to look at him, sprawled on his back with outflung arms, unmoving except for the slow flex of his naked chest as he breathed. He appeared peaceful, almost innocent, in repose. Oriel read the vulnerability in his features, but also the strength of him, the pride and willpower. Magnificent …

Was she falling in love? She certainly didn't think that she would be able to welcome another man into her bed, let alone bare herself to him so candidly. She had only ever been touched by him, she belonged to him completely. Damian had initiated her into womanhood all those years back, but tonight they had travelled a long way beyond that first horizon, lifting them both to a new plane of sensual excitement.

Her mind began to freefall, once again falling prey to her own vulnerability that only he could produce in her. Was this all just rampaging lust? Did he play these erotic games with every woman he bedded? She shivered at the thought. The mirror in the ceiling, the mellow candlelight, the graphic lithograph above the bed, even the bareness of the room itself certainly suggested it. Had Yolanda been able to make him shudder and tremble and sob with pleasure? Had his body come alive in the way it had done in *her* arms tonight? And his wife, Cassandra? Others? The images of Damian in the embrace of woman after woman burned like acid in Oriel's brain, bringing tears to her eyes. A faint hollow feeling settled in the region of her heart. She couldn't bear to think of that …

Moving quietly, she slid from the bed and picked up the pile of clothes that had been thrown haphazardly at the foot of it. She blushed at the memory of the fierce haste in which they had cast them aside, urgent and frantic, the compulsion to be rid of everything that came between them almost violent.

Oriel remembered the stab of lustful heat that snaked through her body as her gaze had fallen on Damian's nakedness. There wasn't an ounce of surplus flesh on his body to blur the rippling muscle definition on display beneath his golden skin, gleaming like oiled satin. Her heart thundering, all she had thought of then was to be mated with this beautiful Greek god; but somehow now she wanted more and it tormented her unbearably.

Oriel dressed noiselessly … the last thing she needed was to wake Damian; she was too vulnerable – still under the spell of what had passed between them. She needed to put some order into her thoughts before she saw him again.

She stole away through the arched open window, down the veranda. A draught of pure sea air greeted her, bearing with it the scent of flowers and the smell of darkness, which stretched away over the garden and across the sea towards the looming hump of Typhoeus, the silent volcano. Heliades was sound asleep but for Oriel sleep had never been more elusive.

She walked noiselessly to her apartment and closed the door behind her, but didn't turn on the light. The moon was all but gone yet the light rimmed the whole of the room with its aluminium glow. In the heavy silence, the only sound she could hear was the enduring murmur of the water down below on the beach. Strange … it was almost too silent. It seemed to her that some other noise was missing, but she was too tired to think.

Her body was still half drugged with Damian's lovemaking – her senses still alive with the thrill of his caresses, his kisses, and her mind full of his sensuous words. It was too much … she needed to cool down.

The night outside had the peculiar velvet quality of darkness over water, the sea smooth like an ornamental lake, with curling wavelets at the edge, their gentle foaming crests lapping serenely at the golden sand; so harmless at this moment, yet she had known seemingly quiet seas swell to great choppy waves, smashing violently on to the shore. Such maritime moods echoed Damian's lovemaking with her, and perhaps even their feelings: wild passion laced with tenderness.

Oriel wrenched her clothes off for the second time that night and scrambled down the few steps to the beach, plunging into the water, clear and cold as chilled wine. Cool though the water was, she lingered awhile, soaking her burning skin and her aching body, washing away the tension that was suffocating her, the sky above all diamonds and black velvet, the air spicy from the pines that grew on the island and surrounded the house. She swam for a few minutes, feeling the pressure in her chest seep gently away. Only then did she wade out of the sea and go back to her room.

Exhausted, she lay on the bed naked, her skin still salty and cold, trying to blot from her mind the rapturous lovemaking she had experienced in Damian's arms. She gave a contented sigh as sleep began to overtake her, and slipped immediately into a dream where strong, golden-brown arms were sliding around her languid body … arms she no longer resisted but welcomed.

* * *

Oriel awoke in the fresh morning, her bedroom splashed with sunshine. The birds were singing with what seemed to her an almost Edenic rapture. She was still lying naked on the bed, where she had fallen asleep after her nocturnal swim. The view from the open window was sparkling, the sea and sky bluer than any metaphor could express. Her half-opened eyes lingered a moment on a green lizard that had crawled up the shutter and was warming itself in the indirect light of the sun. Its satin throat quivered as if with song and she turned reflexively to the golden canary cage. Her still drowsy mind registered that he wasn't chirping or hopping about this morning – had he also slept in?

She slid off the bed and reached for her dressing gown, putting it on as she walked across the terracotta tiled floor to the cage. There, the sight that met her gaze made her gasp and for a few seconds she stood transfixed, her hands at her mouth, wide-eyed in horror. The little bird was lying on its back, tiny claws spread limply against the bars, eyes glazed. A few drops of blood had trickled down the side of the cage, leaving a minute red splash on the floor. Oriel's hands, spread over her mouth, held back the scream that froze in her throat.

The first moment of shock past, she forced herself to examine the bird more closely. She didn't need to open the cage or handle the body to see that its neck had been deliberately slit. She shivered. Who could have done such a cruel thing, and why? What should she do now? Maybe she should just bury it in the sand on the beach and try to erase the whole incident from her mind? After such a wondrous night, it seemed like something sacrilegious, a desecration almost. Irini would surely miss the creature when she tidied the room and would ask questions.

Oriel didn't need to ponder for long; there was a knock at the door and Irini came in, carrying her breakfast.

'*Kaliméra, Despinis,*' she said, with a smile that froze as her eyes fell on the tiny body of the slain bird. The *kamariera* put down her tray and joined Oriel next to the cage. To her amazement, the maid seemed neither surprised nor particularly shocked.

'I found him like this when I woke up this morning.'

'He was all right last night?'

'When I went out, he was fine.'

'And when you came back, he was still alive?'

Oriel shot her a furtive glance, feeling as guilty as a schoolgirl about to be caught on one of her secret escapades. 'Well, I came back quite late. I was tired and did not turn on the light, I went straight to bed.'

If Irini had guessed where Oriel had been, her eyes didn't flicker. Her voice was expressionless when she spoke: 'It is the work of Beshir.'

'Beshir?'

'You know … the eunuch.'

'But I don't understand.'

Although Oriel *did* understand: her mind conjured the imposing, silent figure of Beshir, obeying Helena's every command. After the two evil-eye incidents, she could imagine Beshir killing the canary only too well. She almost felt relief that Irini had voiced her suspicions – it made things a whole lot plainer in her head.

Helena hated her and wanted to keep her well away from

Damian, that much was clear. Yet was it because she couldn't bear the idea of a potential threat to her status as queen bee in the hierarchy of the island? Or did she think that Oriel, as a blonde foreigner, might taint the blood of her precious, noble family if she became involved with her cousin? This place was like something from the last century. The Lekkas family was obviously proud of its family name and in a narrow-minded, conservative community like Helios the rumour that the head of the island was fornicating with the hired help under his own roof could create the sort of scandal that brought discredit on everyone in the house.

To Oriel it was no surprise that Helena was mentally unstable but this was madness with such cruel intent, she mused. Could Damian's cousin actually be dangerous? Especially with Beshir only too willing to do his mistress's bidding …

Irini looked as if she had said too much already. She hesitated before lowering her voice. 'Maybe it is a warning, *Despinis*.'

'What are you telling me?'

'I don't know, I don't know,' the maid said hurriedly. She looked nervous, almost afraid. 'I am accusing no one. It might not be him. Maybe someone is trying to frighten you, or give you to *kakó máti*.'

'I don't believe in the evil eye,' Oriel returned sharply.

Irini looked at the young Englishwoman standing in front of her as if she had said something totally absurd. 'You are wrong to think like that, *Despinis*,' she said fervently. Then she crossed herself. 'You know, I saw the salt on your floor, under your bed. Someone wishes you ill. You need to believe it. *Pou pas xypólitos st' ankáthia?* Why do you walk barefoot on the thorns? This is a troubled house. You would be wise to remember that, *Despinis*. There is a lot of *kakóvoulo koutsompoliá*, malicious gossip, going around here. Heliades' walls have keen ears and sharp eyes that never sleep.' She gave her a look charged with innuendo.

'Why? What do you mean?'

'Because the *Kyrios* insisted that you should stay here instead of the staff house … there is talk, jealousy and … evil. You are a kind *Kyria*, and I would be very sad if any harm came to you.'

Oriel gave a shaky laugh and assured Irini she would be absolutely fine. But all the while she was imagining the dark, panther-like shadow of Beshir coming in from the sea into her room, through the windows, which she never thought to close when she went out. What if she had been in her room? Would it have been her throat he'd have cut? She suppressed a shiver. No, that was a step too far. They had only wanted to frighten her and they'd succeeded in doing so remarkably well, she admitted to herself ruefully.

Irini, who had said all she would say, busied herself with taking down the cage. 'I will take it away, but you need to tell the *Kyrios* when he gets back from Athens tomorrow. He will want to know, I am sure.'

Oriel's heart gave a little jolt. She had forgotten that Damian was planning to visit the Minister for Culture to report the news of their latest find in person. Despite this knowledge, she still felt a wave of insecurity. Why hadn't he sent a note or come to see her to say goodbye? Had he regretted their night of passion? They had both been so uninhibited, so intimate in every way … perhaps he didn't want to face her this morning. She could understand that; she felt a little that way herself, remembering some of the things they had said and done to each other.

'I will go now, *Despinis*,' the *kamariera*'s voice drew Oriel from her momentary distraction and she watched her pick up the cage and the dead bird that she'd wrapped in a teacloth. 'Remember, please, you must be careful.'

'I will talk to *Kyrios* Lekkas about the canary on his return,' Oriel said to her shortly, suddenly desperate to be on her own, away from Heliades. 'Thank you for your concern.'

When Irini had left the room, Oriel drank her coffee without really tasting it. Though still hot, it didn't melt away the ice that had formed in her stomach, sending waves of coldness through her body. She pushed away the breakfast tray, unable to stomach any food. Again, she felt uneasy thinking about the night before. What if the servants had overheard their rapturous groans when she and Damian had been in the throes of lovemaking? She remembered now that the windows of the room had been open as she left the veranda and headed for the beach. True, the candles had long gone out and the terrace was in darkness, but she couldn't remember noticing the remains of the dinner they had shared. Had someone cleared the table while all this was going on? Had a servant heard them, seen them even? The thought made her blush to the roots of her hair.

Anyway, what that had to do with the dead canary she didn't know, except that perhaps a witness to her night of passion could have reported it to Helena and then … Anyway, whatever the truth, someone – or several people – were very keen to see her out of Heliades, even off the island. Oriel's thoughts drifted to the French-woman, Chantal, who had left so abruptly, and, before her, the Dutch student. She recalled Irini's strange words on the day of her arrival: *It's happening all over again. What do you expect with these loose foreign women? They must have excited the anger of Hades.* And again: *Chantal looked afraid.*

It was no good going round and round in circles, she would have to talk to Damian about it all tomorrow. In the meantime, she needed to get out of this house. She would go down to the marina, she decided and, with that in mind, Oriel put her bikini on under a long sundress and collected her things together, packing her ruck-sack with some sun lotion, a towel and a bottle of water. She wanted to spend as much of the day as possible away from Heliades. That way, at least, she wouldn't chance running into Helena and her two sinister servants.

Fate, Oriel thought to herself wryly, had no intention of letting her off so lightly. As she was about to cross the hall to the front door, Damian's cousin appeared from the direction of the dining room, blocking her way. She had a newspaper in her lap and was flanked by the sullen-looking Marika and Bashir, the latter resting a large dark hand on the handle of his mistress's wheelchair. For a moment Oriel marvelled at what a strange sight they presented: Bashir as black as night and Marika with her sallow skin and dry ashen curls while, between them, the lustrous raven-haired Helena stared at her with glittering slate-coloured eyes. How Oriel ever could have thought that she and Damian's cousin might become friends was beyond her – or that she should ever have had any fel-low feeling for the woman at all. Noticing the vicious, manic glint in Helena's eye, she thought with a degree of alarm it was so very clear that she was completely unhinged.

'I'm surprised you have the nerve to show your face this morn-ing,' Helena said, getting straight to the point.

Oriel turned a little pale. 'I don't know what you mean,' she answered stiffly.

'You had dinner with the *Kyrios,* yes?'

Oriel swallowed the dryness from her throat. 'The *Kyrios* and I had some business to discuss.'

'It must have been very private business.' The Greek woman regarded Oriel sardonically. Then something flickered in her fevered gaze, like a scorpion deliberating its next venomous strike, and she narrowed her eyes. '*To mystikó domátio,* the Room of Secrets, has been closed for a long time, ever since the *Kyrios*'s accident. I should have known when my cousin ordered for it to be cleaned and aired only a few days ago that he was preparing a special treatment for his latest conquest.'

Helena gave a twisted smile and wrinkled her nose as if at something distasteful. 'I'm sure you won't be surprised to know that it has been the main topic of conversation in the servants' quarters.'

Oriel felt too angry and mortified to speak. She wanted the ground to open up and swallow her. So the entire household had been aware that 'the *Kyrios*' was intending to take her to his bed – everyone, that was, except her – and now they knew that he had actually succeeded. How could Damian do something so public, so utterly humiliating? She had thought that he'd acted spontaneously last night but, come to think of it, candles were already lit in the room. She had naïvely taken it to be his bedroom, even though it had been rather bare for a room that was lived in. How blind could she have been?

But Helena had only just begun. 'He brought that Yolanda woman there, of course, in the beginning, although now I doubt he'd bother. It's a bit of a ritual with Damian, you see.' She held up a hand. 'Not one I approve of, I assure you. It is vexing, after all, when he ends up losing members of his staff because he can't control himself.'

Her eyes were glittering wildly as she spoke and there were flecks of spittle on her lips. Marika bent down to try to intervene – to soothe her mistress – but Helena batted her away. By now she was one hissing shriek of bitterness. 'All men are the same, slave to their lusts! They don't stand a chance against you sluttish gold-diggers. Pericles was ensnared, I know it was against his will. Now Damian has succumbed too … Who else can protect him except me, eh? Protect the island. … I have to!' Her breast was heaving now, her eyes bulging alarmingly.

Oriel made a dash for the front door. She had to get away from this madwoman … from her poison … from the things she was saying about Damian … from the things she was saying about her. As she pushed past the wheelchair, Helena bent forward, darting like a snake, and lashed out at her, hitting Oriel as hard as she could with the rolled-up newspaper she was holding in her elegantly manicured hands. Oriel gave a shocked cry that was half a sob as the newspaper caught the back of her leg but she kept going, wrenching open the front door and running outside. Without looking back, she headed for her Volkswagen, parked in the drive, and jumped in, fumbling to turn the key in the ignition before the engine roared into life.

She took off down the driveway and drove towards the port, breathing rapidly. Her mind was in chaos. The woman was insane. Yet Helena must have been right about the servants knowing about the room. To think Damian had planned to bed her in advance, as if she were simply his next concubine – just one in a string of conquests. How utterly humiliating!

Oriel glanced in her mirror: the road was empty. Abruptly, she pulled the car over on to the dry, dusty verge in an effort to calm down. She took a sip from her bottle of water and closed her eyes. This whole situation was becoming unbearable but she refused to be cowed, she promised herself with grim determination. She was made of sterner stuff than that, capable of withstanding anything that Helena could throw at her, or Damian for that matter …

After a few minutes she started driving again. The further she got from Heliades, the calmer she became. Oriel couldn't help taking in the unearthly beauty of Helios and it restored her spirits like a soothing, magical balm. The sun had climbed into the heavens and was now high in the sky. Its beams diffused over everything with a dense coppery hue, turning the water to lead far below her.

Oriel parked her car at the top of the cliff under a plane tree and got out to stand a moment, feasting her eyes on the view, watching the light playing upon the scene. The air quivered above her; it was hot. The beach at the marina was busy although it was midweek. A procession of sailing boats moved slowly out of the harbour with the gait of queens; three little girls in one-piece bathing suits of blue, red and yellow stood arm in arm, watching them. Further along the sand some fishermen were pushing a catamaran into the water; they spread its russet sail, one man squatting on the large outriggers as it bobbed about on the sparkling waves. A boy, clothed only in a loincloth, sauntered by, swinging a bundle of dried fish. He stared at Oriel with his jet-black eyes, obviously curious to see a foreigner. By now she was used to being noticed: an English rose among the dark Ariadnes and Iphigenias on Helios. Some of the more insular islanders couldn't help but gape at what appeared to them an outlandish stranger.

Oriel grabbed her rucksack from the car and made her way down to the marina. She bought herself a feta and tomato sandwich and a bottle of *Avra* mineral water at the taverna, which was packed with customers and employees busily carrying crates to and fro, and walked down to a shady part of the beach. Preparations for the evening's entertainment were in progress; the bustle was on. Men were walking up and down the steep path, laden with chairs and benches, which had been brought over by big trucks that were parked at the top of the cliffs. Hordes of workmen were erecting posts and hanging up coloured lamps in the trees. Waiters were already laying tables along the front of the beach. Some were trestles, others long planks placed on large plastic olive barrels and cinder blocks.

Seeing the festive preparations made Oriel remember that she had phoned Vassilis at the weekend, agreeing to accompany him to this party at the beach taverna. She had completely forgotten. Now, for a split second, the thought of putting him off crossed her mind. She seriously doubted she would feel up to going out tonight, not after everything that had happened in the last twelve hours. Still, she sensed an evening spent in his company would be a refreshing change from Damian's intensity and the confusion of her own feelings. Anyhow, Damian was away this evening, and anything would be better than being alone at Heliades.

Oriel walked along the edge of the sea, next to the breaking waves and foam. The brilliant glare flooded the seashore, glancing off shells and shining stones. The beach's loveliness, she thought, held within itself all the transient beauty she was now used to seeing and hearing: the tide and light, the sound of the waves and the crying of the gulls. How strange that on Helios there was such magic and enchantment – so much so that the island seemed to reach out to her very soul – but at the same time, so many dark emotions. It seemed to her that the ungovernable passions of these strange silver-eyed islanders had haunted her the whole time she had been a guest on the island. She had always considered herself a positive, happy, stable person but now she could barely remember how that felt.

Her gaze meandered as the melancholy edge to her thoughts melted into wonderment at the exquisite natural world lit up in front of her. One shell in particular caught Oriel's attention: thin and rather fragile, it was elongated and pear-shaped, measuring about three inches from end to end. It had a low spire with a large whorl, whitish in colour, with darker axial lines running over it. A painter makes his sketch, a poet writes his line, but what can an ordinary person do at such a moment to capture such beauty? Oriel picked up the shell. It was so smooth and there was a tactile and sensuous satisfaction in just holding it. She put it in her pocket, subconsciously wishing that, this way, she could hold on to the purity of its perfection like a magic talisman, and keep at bay the unsettled thoughts that assailed her.

She sat down on a band of red rocks sheltered by a mantle of sea pines. For the last hour or two she had tried not to think about Damian, the dead canary or Helena but it hadn't been easy. Far from the noisy crowd at the marina, the only sounds were those of the orchestra of cicadas filling the afternoon with their deep humming and the roar of the surf hitting the rocks a little further down the beach. Now she was alone, the undesirable thoughts rushed back to haunt her.

In daylight, the memory of her night of passion shocked Oriel's sensibilities. In Damian's arms she had rediscovered strange paths of sensuality, and she would never have believed herself capable of being so crudely wanton. How could she now stay on Helios and work with him? Yet how could she not? The pain of shame caused her whole body to ache but the desire for him made it burn.

Some of the phrases they had exchanged rushed back to her, stealing her breath again and squeezing her heart, knotting her stomach and making her blush.

'I want to ravish every part of your body, to know all its dark, inner secrets. Entwine it around mine,' he had said as he lifted her slender frame and straddled her from behind. 'This is the way our ancestors made love,' he told her when, looking up into the mirror, she had hesitated, aghast at the earthy and primitive image of their bodies so wantonly displayed – more like animals mating. But he had promised to take her where she had never been before. What woman, aroused as she had been at the time, could resist such an offer?

Damian had kept his promise. Waves of excitement, explosions of passion, new crescendos of sensation had flooded through each part of her as he had bored into her with an almost savage, plundering drive for total possession and a ravishing stream of entrancing caresses – using his hands, his lips and his tongue in addition to the masculine part of him – and she could still hear her trembling voice crying out her desire and urging him on as the full, heavy surge of him moved inside her. How could she have said such things? Yet she knew with a throbbing certainty that, no matter how many women Damian had seduced before her, she would be wantonly prey to his lure all over again if he beckoned.

Despite the cooling sea breezes mitigating the sun's heat, Oriel suddenly felt terribly hot. She was wearing her bikini underneath her sundress and, without a second thought, discarded the offending garment and slipped into the sea. The rocks were sharp and cut her feet, and there were tiresome drifts of seaweed to negotiate before getting to the sandy part, but she didn't care. She lay on her back, cradled in the clear, sparkling water as it undulated beneath her, watching the sun glittering on the white foam and dancing waves, and looking up at the seabirds drawing big circles in the limitless blue expanse. For a moment, Damian, the poor little canary, Beshir, Helena, Chantal, Yolanda – all the trials and afflictions of this mortal life – were simply washed from her memory, her heart singing inside her in sheer thankfulness for this harmless rapture of the senses, one which posed no threat to her, only joy.

Suddenly, over the eternal boom of the breakers on the boulders, Oriel heard a voice calling: 'Hello, Oriel! *Kalispera.*'

She turned her head towards the shore. Mattias was standing on the rocks, waving at her. Oriel waved back.

'Be careful, haven't you read the sign? *Kíndyno*, Danger!' he shouted, cupping his hands to his mouth. 'The sea currents are treacherous here.'

Oriel hadn't noticed a sign. She had assumed it was safe on this part of the beach since it was only fifty yards from where a large group was swimming, further towards the quay. However, as she tried to swim back to shore she realized that the current was working against her and that, despite being an excellent swimmer, she was having some difficulty in fighting the tide that was pulling her back towards the rocks. Thrashing frantically, beating the water with her hands, she battled the sea … but she knew she was losing ground.

Oriel suddenly recognized that she had been foolhardy and a coldness closed like an unfamiliar hand about her heart as the first prick of fear assailed her. She began to gasp and splutter and, as if that was not enough, an excruciating pain shot up her leg, almost paralysing her. *Cramp!* A wave broke over her face and then another; she was taking in water … choking. Panic flooded her now, robbing her of her last ounce of control – *I'm going to die*, she thought.

'It's all right, I'm here. I'll get you back safe and sound.' At the reassuring voice of Mattias, Oriel's fear instantly ebbed. She had been too busy fighting the current to notice that he had plunged into the water to come to her rescue. 'Just let yourself go limp,' he told her. 'Leave the rest to me.'

Oriel obeyed and, after a few seconds, she relaxed fully in Mattias's grasp. Despite his disability, the fisherman was a powerful swimmer and it wasn't long before they were safely back on the sand. She still felt a little shaken; she was shivering but the cramp in her leg had subsided as suddenly as it had struck.

'You shouldn't have ventured out so far,' Mattias reproved. 'It is not so sheltered this far down the beach, you can see it in the pattern of the waves.' He pointed his finger. 'Look how the sea slaps on to the rocks there.'

'I hadn't seen any sign,' said Oriel, 'So silly of me, I'm sorry. As a diver, it's my job to be aware of hazards.'

'Well, no harm done this time. I will talk to the harbour master. He needs to move the sign and red flag to a more obvious place.

They've put them over there behind that pine, out of the wind.' He gestured to a large sea pine some twenty yards away before frowning at Oriel. 'You're shivering, you'd better get dry and dressed quickly.'

Oriel was deeply touched by his fatherly concern. 'I'll be fine now. Thank you, Mattias.' She took the towel out of her bag and dried herself, before putting on her sundress. While she dressed, Mattias had turned his back considerately and was sorting out his fishing gear.

'If you don't mind my saying, Oriel, you should not be wearing that sort of bathing costume around here,' he told her, still with his back to her. 'Men are not used to it and you are so fair …'

'I thought no one was around to see but, yes, you're right, I'll bear that in mind. I think I brought a one-piece with me. I'll make sure to dig it out for my next swim. That was very courageous of you to jump in after me.'

'I'm used to these waters. I swim in them all year round, in all weathers,' he explained. 'If you want to have a swim, you could have it down on the beach, outside the taverna, although the water is not so clean there. You're better off going to one of the little coves, though. There are some narrow paths that lead down from the cliffs.'

'Yes, I saw a few of them when I went for a drive on Monday, past Manoli's on the coast road to the north of the island.' She came to stand beside him.

'Here, have some of this. It's good brandy,' he said, removing a flask from his canvas bag.

'Thanks,' Oriel murmured, and she swallowed a small quantity of the neat spirit. She smiled warmly at him. 'I already feel better.'

'If you drove on past Manoli's on Monday, you must have come across the four villas that belong to the richest families on the island … after the Lekkas family, that is.'

'Yes.' She coloured slightly as the memory gave her momentary unease.

Her discomfiture wasn't lost on Mattias. 'Ah … Yolanda,' he said, giving a small shrug. 'She's headstrong, that one. It has helped her career, no doubt. But love for the *Kyrios*? I don't think so.'

'Why?'

'She threw it all away in order to pursue her ambitions.'

'You mean with Damian?'

'*Kyrios* Lekkas cared deeply for her. They were childhood sweethearts.'

'I heard that, but I was also told he couldn't marry her because she comes from a different social class, and the family objected.'

Mattias scoffed. 'Wagging tongues! People gossip, often without knowing the whole story. They spin a thread from what they hear with their ears and fill the gaps with tales from their imagination, and so the web grows.'

'So what is the truth?' Oriel asked hesitantly.

Mattias appraised her silently before replying. 'I am in no position to tell you that, Oriel. But believe me, the *Kyrios* tried his best. He went against everybody … Yolanda threw it all away and now she cries. As we say: *Ap' éxo koúkla ki apó mésa panoúkla*, outside a doll, inside the plague. I never thought he should have trusted her.'

Oriel faltered slightly. 'Are they … are they not together any more? Even now that he is widowed?'

The fisherman dealt her a wistful smile. 'Who can tell what the unknown holds for each of us? *Móno O Theh-óhs kséri*, only God knows, but I don't think that a glass that has been shattered can be mended.'

'Damian seems quite balanced for a person whose life has dealt more than one knock.'

'You can say that again.'

'What was his wife like?'

Oriel realized, as soon as she had asked the question, that Mattias had refused to open up about Cassandra before, at the Epiklisi festival, and she felt wrong to have brought up the subject again. But this time he seemed willing to take her into his confidence. She sensed he trusted her.

'Cassandra? What can I say? She was frivolous and a little spiteful, in the way young kittens are. She was very beautiful. Rich, too. But she didn't love him. She married him because he was a Lekkas.' Mattias sat down on a rock and Oriel perched beside him while he continued: 'At the beginning of their marriage, the *Kyrios* tried to make it work, but I think his heart was still hurting over Yolanda. Anyway, he didn't deserve Zeus's thunderbolts when they came hurtling at him, one after the other.'

'Cassandra dying,' stated Oriel, gazing across to the horizon. 'And losing his brother.'

'Exactly. But it's one thing losing your family to illness or an accident but to find the pair of them stretched out on the sand together … murdered.' Mattias's voice hushed as he spoke the word, and he crossed himself.

Oriel flinched. *The pair of them* … She spoke tentatively. 'So Pericles and Cassandra, were they having an affair?' She thought of the shark attack and the damage to Damian's body. So his wife had shied away from him and taken a lover … his own brother?

Mattias looked closely at Oriel, seeing her stunned reaction. 'I'm sorry, I thought you knew, seeing as you mentioned them dying.' There was an awkward silence then he spoke again quietly. 'It was just around the headland, there.' He pointed towards a spit of land on the far side of the harbour. 'Poor devils, they didn't deserve that. No one does.'

Her eyes widened with shock. 'Did they ever find out who did it?'

'The police tried. The *Kyrios* made sure they brought in a top man from Athens to investigate … but nothing.' He paused. 'The islanders always protect their own. Other than the murderer I'm sure someone knew the truth, but the secret will go to the grave with them, most likely.'

Oriel had to ask her next question. 'Did the police think it was Damian? He must have been a suspect, surely?'

'He was away in Paris at the time, *dóxa to Theó*,' said Mattias.

He took out a pipe from his canvas bag, tapped it on the rock and stuffed the bowl with tobacco, tamping it down before lighting it. Then he stretched out his injured leg gingerly, comfortably settling himself for a more lengthy conversation. While Mattias was doing this, Oriel gazed at the whole world at her feet, lost in thought. The rocks were fringed with little foamy waves breaking softly on the sand; the beach-shallows picked out in lime-green and yellow against the reddish, deckle-edged surfaces of stone. The curled green, brown and maroon branches of seaweed wavered gracefully in the current, with small fish travelling in and out of the tangle in phosphorescent sparks of light. The scene was luminous … harmonious – so different from the bleak and gory events of Damian's past. *No wonder he has scars*, she thought to herself, her heart suddenly contracting with pity.

Aloud, she said: 'It seems like a lot for one person to bear. An avalanche of misfortune, something that might have destroyed a weaker man.'

'Never a truer word said.' Mattias nodded, puffing on his pipe. 'And it started way back, in his childhood. It's as if the whole family was cursed. Of the two brothers and their cousin, only the *Kyrios* came out unscathed. He was the only sane one.'

'What happened?' Oriel's eyes fixed on Mattias, needing to know the whole story and yet fearing what he might reveal.

Mattias was silent, as if mulling over whether or not to answer the silent questions reflected in her luminous green gaze.

'You must on no account bring it up in front of the *Kyrios*,' he said eventually. 'As far as I know, he has never talked about it to anyone.' Then he paused for a moment, before adding: 'I'm telling you this, Oriel, because I sense it is right for you to know …'

Oriel looked away again, fearing her fascination would be betrayed in her expression. 'You can count on my discretion,' she murmured.

'The Lekkas family, especially Damian, has been touched by tragedy again and again. There is in the soul of this man a penetrating pain that lingers. He is still young and handsome, despite his scars. Women queue up in the hope that he will surrender his heart … but only a very special love will be able to chase away the demons that haunt him. I hope and believe this person will mend the deep, internal wounds that scar him in other ways, teach him to trust again.'

Oriel's heart gave a flutter but she urged him to continue. 'Were these incidents so terrible?'

He regarded her steadily for a few moments – she could sense those disturbing grey eyes probing hers, weighing the pros and the cons of giving her his trust. 'You are an archaeologist who speaks our language as well as a native, so I'm sure you are familiar with our Greek mythology.'

'Of course. As a child the tales fascinated me, they still do.'

'Greek men know the many wonderful differences that exist between them and the fairer sex, but they have a passionate streak for vendetta in their psyches, should a woman be the cause of a tragedy in their life,' Mattias said, searching Oriel's face, his gaze holding hers.

'The story of Damian Lekkas's parents mirrors one of our Greek tragedies in an uncanny way. His mother was actually named after Aphrodite, and she was very beautiful and charming. Her husband, Hephaestus, the *Kyrios*'s father, was ugly and dull, though hard-working. Hephaestus had two brothers, Cyrus and Ares. The younger brother, Ares, a widower, was strong and handsome and something of a playboy. They all lived at Heliades. *Den vázoun mia asfáleia pára polý kontá sti fotiá,* don't put a fuse too near a fire, says our Greek proverb, because from a little spark a mighty flame might burst. And as the devil always does everything well, that's exactly what happened.'

'I can imagine the next bit,' said Oriel.

'You guessed right. Aphrodite and Ares fell passionately in love.'

'That must have shocked the islanders,' said Oriel thoughtfully. She could only imagine the horror and scandal that must have ensued.

The fisherman nodded. 'It may be different elsewhere, but here on Helios people regard marriage as sacred. Fornication outside of it is a mortal sin.'

Oriel blushed a little, as a picture of the night before with Damian flashed into her head. But Mattias didn't seem to notice her discomfort and continued with his story.

'Well, after that Hephaestus set a trap for the lovers during one of their rendezvous, surprising them in bed. He shot his brother and wife, then turned the gun on himself afterwards.' Mattias brooded a moment after this bombshell, distress etched in each crease of his tanned and weathered skin.

Oriel gasped, her hands flying to her mouth. 'How dreadful!'

'That is not the worst of it.'

'What could be worse?'

Mattias hesitated as though he found it difficult to continue. His features contorted with something that looked akin to anger mingled with misery, and he added in an almost imperceptible voice:

'The three children witnessed it all. Damian was nine, Pericles was seven, while Helena, Ares's daughter, was five.'

Oriel paled, aghast at what she had just heard. And in the silence that followed this shocking and gory revelation, a dove flew down from a pine tree, its beautiful white throat palpitating like a living torn-out heart as it stood a moment on the sun-struck rocks before flying away. The sadness was sculpted even deeper into the lines of Mattias's face. For a few seconds Oriel buried her face in her hands and fought to control her emotions. 'How dreadful,' she murmured again. 'How utterly dreadful.'

'From that day Helena never walked again. She lost her speech for a few months.'

'Oh, that poor girl!' Oriel's eyes were gentle green pools of sympathy. For the first time, despite Helena's malevolent actions of earlier, she could see why Damian's cousin had become the way she was.

'She was never the same again. It was as if the laughing, dancing five-year-old had died along with the three adults. The girl that remained was so damaged inside that she became quite unbalanced. The *Kyrios* was very protective of her after that.' He sucked on his pipe and sighed. 'She was obsessed by her cousin Pericles, and now the poor woman has lost him, too.'

'She does seem sometimes to have forgotten he's gone,' agreed Oriel. 'Her apartment is a shrine to him.'

'And the pitiful thing is that her affections were wasted on Pericles. The lad was handsome, that's for sure, but he was a waster in every other way. Women, drugs, alcohol … they were all he ever thought of. Very different from the *Kyrios*.'

'You can't entirely blame Pericles, surely? How could anyone, let alone a child, get over the trauma of such a tragedy?'

Mattias shook his head. 'His brother did. No, Pericles was a bad egg. Always was a selfish boy, never showed a grain of loyalty. After the accident with the shark, Cassandra couldn't bear to look at the *Kyrios*. She turned to Pericles and well, you know now how that ended.'

'I'm not a superstitious person,' said Oriel cautiously, 'but the family does seem to be jinxed, struck by one disaster after another.'

'People say on rainy nights in winter, if you listen carefully, you will hear Aphrodite sobbing, the sound trembling on the wind. They say when it rains that it's tears for her children pouring down on to the island.'

'How desperately sad! I'm glad you told me, though,' said Oriel quietly. 'I love your beautiful island but it hasn't been easy at Heliades. This will really help me understand the family and make allowances.'

'That is what I hoped or I wouldn't have talked about them in this way.' Mattias shook a sad head. 'You see, after the way Yolanda and Cassandra behaved, the *Kyrios* could only see love as unbearable pain. Each time it shows the tip of its flame, he snuffs it out. He only ever allows himself short-lived passions. Here today, gone tomorrow. And all the while a shell hardens around his heart. This is not good, and it makes my own heart ache.'

Oriel's eyes filled with tears. She blinked them away fiercely, hoping the fisherman would not guess the tumult of her thoughts. Only last night she'd been the victim of those short-lived passions. After what Mattias had just said, and after Helena had told her that she was just one in a string of conquests in the Room of Secrets, how could she ever see her and Damian's lovemaking as anything more elevated than a fling? She knew his story – why he was too cynical and wounded to love her – and the unveiled truth, as she saw it now, echoed again and again in the frozen wasteland of her mind. The dream was over. Instead of sweet memories – something to hold and cherish – they would always be mixed with the bitterness of regret. How that hurt!

Mattias patted Oriel's hand. 'I'm sorry if I've caused you distress, *Kyria*, but I told you all this for the best reasons.' He puffed on his pipe a moment, his eyes fixed on a point far out to sea. 'You see, with your bright hair like an angel, you have come to us for a reason. I sensed it when I first saw you and the feeling is only growing stronger by the day. I'll say no more but … please don't run away. Be brave, Oriel.'

There was a wisdom in his eyes as if his habit of always scanning the horizon had allowed him to view the past, the present, and the future in one big picture. Oriel's heart squeezed painfully but she took some comfort from his words and dried her eyes.

'Now I don't want to keep you. Last time we spoke like this I talked so much the sun went down and you had to walk home,' Mattias told her.

Oriel laughed shakily. 'I've brought the car this time. I'll give you a lift home if you like?' she offered, standing up and slinging her rucksack over her shoulder.

'Thank you, but my home is not far and I'll be staying here a little longer. One day, though, you must come by the cottage. Anna took a great shine to you at Epiklisi. She would be so happy to see you again. You must try her *loukoumades*. She makes the sweetest, softest doughnuts of anyone on the island.'

'I'd like that. But you're right, I'd better be going,' said Oriel, although the thought of returning to Heliades held little charm. 'I need to get back as I'm going out tonight.'

'Another time maybe you can come and eat pastries with us, any time indeed. You will always be welcome in my house. And if you ever need me, I'm on that rock fishing almost every day, and I'm often to be found at the taverna in the evening.'

Oriel nodded and smiled. '*Kalispera*, Mattias.'

'*Kalispera*, Oriel.' He raised a hand in salute and wandered off with his fishing gear.

Now the sun had become a yellow inferno as it slid into late afternoon, still a cruel mistress, beating down on Helios in her relentless way. Somehow the scorching weather mirrored the inferno that had been Damian's life, Oriel thought as she lifted her face to the dazzling beams. She made her way back to the car and, despite the heat, shivered.

CHAPTER 9

Damian's car sped across the island from the airstrip where his plane had touched down. The sun had been setting when he arrived, streaking the sky with rose and gold and angry red as it slid down towards the sea. Now the night was moving in gradually. This was usually the time when the demons residing within him came out to play, bringing out the worst in him.

Yet, tonight was different.

The angels, it seemed, had decided to shield him from the darkness, pain and agony. His heart throbbed with hope, not torment; his soul soared like a bird in the sky and his mind was a frenzy of sparks. With every moment came wonder and with every breath anticipation as he reached the final road home and images of Oriel crowded his mind like a hypnotic dream. In a few minutes he would be seeing her again and would be able to take her in his arms. The medicine she brought healed him and, although Damian was addicted to her, somehow he felt safe because he knew since last night that she was equally hooked on him.

Earlier that day his whole being was still reeling in chaos. When he had woken at five o'clock in the morning he'd been surprised to find that she had already left. He had brooded on her absence, his mind filled with the memory of the taste of her lips, her skin, her exquisite heat wrapped around him – and his body already ached and burned for her again.

He had never done to a woman – and had never let a woman do to him – what Oriel and he had enjoyed with each other: Adam and Eve, exploring their bodies without restraint and discovering all the pleasures the sinful apple could offer. A shiver slipped up his spine at the thought of her arched body, a pagan offering that had stirred him like no woman ever had, and no other woman would ... In the past he had always been driven by animalistic needs but, with Oriel, somehow, his need went much further ... Damian wanted to

325

be close to her body, to her heart, to her soul; and he had used their bodies to create a blazing fire that had melded them together to the extent that they hadn't known where the one ended and the other began.

What was happening to him? An uneasy feeling stirred somewhere deep inside him about what it all meant. Vexing thoughts were tangling themselves up with his heightened sexual urges, weaving an intricate pattern whose picture he could not – or would not – see. His mind became one large knot, making him almost growl out loud with frustration.

Damian would have gone to look for her, even to make love to her once more before he left, but the voice of self-control battled with his hungry desire, and he forced himself to leave the house rather than go to Oriel's room. He was due at an urgent meeting with the Minister of Culture and if he didn't leave immediately, he would be late.

However, once he'd arrived in Athens, and despite a keen interest in relaying the specifics of their discovery to his excited colleagues at the Ministry, Damian had found it almost impossible to prevent thoughts of Oriel from occupying his mind. Their steaming, intimate encounter had obsessed him all day, to the point where he declined to stay on after the meeting to discuss things further, cutting short his visit and coming back now, rather than the following morning, to be with her.

He needed Oriel … needed her badly.

Now the gates of Heliades were in view and soon Damian was pulling up sharply in front of the house. Striding impatiently through the front door, he went straight up to Oriel's room. There he was met by Beshir, who informed him that the *Kyria* needed to speak to him urgently.

He found Helena waiting for him and immediately realized that she was suffering one of her crises. As soon as he entered the room she gave a shrill laugh and her mouth curved scornfully. 'Ah, the stud has come home! I was told you weren't coming back until tomorrow, but I suppose you couldn't stay away … eh?'

Resentment distorted her beautiful face. 'You've opened that room of debauchery … playing your raunchy games with this girl, this foreigner, this slut that you've brought to live under our roof.'

'Calm down, Helena, there's no need to put yourself in this state. Besides, *Despinis* Anderson isn't a slut.' Damian was used to Helena's outbursts but, still, hearing her talk that way about Oriel made his blood simmer dangerously.

'*Calm down, Helena*, he says … *Despinis Anderson isn't a slut,*' she mimicked, her grey eyes cat-cruel. 'The girl came here to work, not to provide you and my staff with some live pornographic diversion, here in our home.'

His eyes narrowed to angry slits but he kept his voice even. 'Helena, I have told you before never to interfere in my private life. What I do in the privacy of my apartment is my business and mine alone.'

'*In the privacy of my apartment*, he says … *Uch!*' Helena scoffed. 'Your disgusting groans and cries were so loud, I'm quite sure they could be heard as far as Typhoeus. How do you think I learnt what you were up to?'

Damian tried to keep calm. 'Because one of your spies told you about it. I noticed our supper had been cleared away when I had given strict orders for it to be left there until the following day, after I'd gone.'

Helena sneered. Again there was that savage light in her eyes. 'Beshir saw you … he said you were copulating like animals. Filthy, disgusting animals. But let me tell you the news. She's gone off … your little angel has gone away.'

Damian tried to control the mixture of anxiety and anger in his voice. 'What do you mean? If you've upset her, Helena, I swear …'

His cousin sighed deeply, looking up at him with an expression where hatred had suddenly been replaced by self-pity. 'How could I? Stuck in this wheelchair, a helpless invalid, forced to spend the rest of my days in this contraption … being wholly dependent upon other people … Tell me, how could I?' She shook her head.

'Oh, you might think I'm selfish and possessive, perhaps, but that's the way I'm made, dear cousin. I have no one else but you on this earth and you don't understand me. Pericles, he knew how I felt, but that bitch Cassandra had to go and spoil it all …' Helena's eyes filled with tears.

Damian's tone hardened. 'Enough theatricals! Where is *Despinis* Anderson?'

Helena's tone changed again and she flashed her cousin a triumphant smile. 'Oh, didn't I tell you? She's gone off to find greener pastures. Vassilis Markopoulos picked her up just a few minutes ago. … I told you she's a slut in disguise … a harlot dressed up as a saint, with her bright blonde hair. It's written all over her goody-goody face … the only thing missing is the halo! But you men are guided by your libidos, you—'

Damian left the room, unable to bear any more of Helena's poisonous words. They were like a bucket of icy water in his face. How could Oriel have gone off with someone else after what had passed between them only the night before? Guessing that Vassilis had taken her to Limenarkhees Taverna, he drove like a madman down to the marina.

* * *

Damian only narrowly missed seeing Oriel. Only half an hour earlier she had slipped out of Heliades, praying that Helena wouldn't emerge from her apartment as she soundlessly tiptoed down the passageway, holding her white stiletto sandals and thin cashmere wrap in her hand. The house was quiet. She ran down the staircase as though followed by shadows, Irini's disturbing phrase resounding in her head: *Heliades walls have keen ears and sharp eyes that never sleep.* She could well believe it.

Oriel had thought carefully about what to wear that night and had selected a sleeveless dress in white broderie anglaise, so simple to look at but, when she put it on, it looked stunning against her lightly sea-tanned skin. Its classic lines suited her and it was just right for an evening at Limenarkhees Taverna. Furthermore, nothing about the dress could possibly shock the sensitivities of even the most conservative Greek islanders. Her hair was looped at the nape of her neck and secured with a tortoiseshell slide. There wasn't anything about her make-up that could cause offence either: she had applied only a whisper of shadow on her eyelids and a little gloss to her lips.

She had waited outside for Vassilis, having decided to come down from her room ten minutes before he was due. That way, she hoped she could slip away surreptitiously in his car without anyone being the wiser. Oriel breathed deeply. What a relief! The freshness of the night, cooled by the salty whiffs of the sea, was intoxicating, the island breathing richness and earthy airs. The hush was intense. It was hard to imagine a more peaceful setting, a greater harmony between the natural and architectural elements … yet, she recalled, so much pain and hurt lingered behind those ancestral walls.

As she stood in the shadows, her back against one of the pillars of the portico, Oriel let her mind wander over the events of the past twenty-four hours and the words of Mattias. Damian, it transpired, had had more than his share of gruesome experiences to harden his mind. He was a man not only with a scarred face but also a scarred heart. Had Yolanda or Cassandra ever possessed the tenderness to ease the pain of his memories? *Yolanda threw it all away*, Mattias had told her, while Cassandra had shunned his bed and turned to Pericles, his degenerate brother, just when Damian must have needed her most.

The sad words of the fisherman rushed back to Oriel: *Each time love shows the tip of its flame, he snuffs it out determinedly and replaces it with short-lived passions …* Who could blame Damian? Even if she had been naïve enough to momentarily become one of his passing flings, how could she condemn him? She had only herself and her wantonness to hold responsible for any heartache she was going through now.

The sensible thing to do was to give in her resignation but Oriel was not a quitter – and besides, she knew she would never have another career opportunity like this. She and Damian had discovered the giant bronze statue of Poseidon, lost to the waters of the Ionian for more than two thousand years. Their find, and this site – one that would make history, surely – was almost impossible to walk away from. Anyway, she had nothing with which to reproach herself, really, apart from indulging in some sex with her employer. Could she really be blamed for her naïvety, or being somewhat under the influence of alcohol? Was it so bad that the history that linked her to this charismatic man and the romance of the setting had led her to mistake sex for true 'lovemaking'? Yet, then again, surely she couldn't remain at Heliades in these circumstances? She would talk to Damian. She *had* to talk to Damian … but at least it wouldn't be tonight. In the meantime, Vassilis's invitation was a godsend. Oriel realized she needed, above all, to go out – to see people, and maybe dance the night away until she was exhausted.

At the sound of a car, she looked up: Vassilis was on time. The elegant red Porsche drew to a halt beside her and he leapt out of the car, beaming. 'I'm not late for you, am I?' he said, coming round to open the door for her. He bent over and gave her a friendly kiss on both cheeks.

'No, no, I've just come down.' Oriel smiled, taking in the young man's casual but smart chinos and shirt, and the wine-coloured paisley cravat, which gave him a chic look. There was something about the way Mediterranean men wore their clothes – a carefree sophistication, as though once they had put them on they never gave their appearance another thought.

'You look stunning. The sun suits you, for sure. With us Greeks, it can only ever accentuate our natural tan, but it gives your white skin a lovely pale-gold colour. I'll be the envy of every man at the party,' he said laughing as he slid in next to her.

Within seconds the powerful car had traversed the drive and was picking up speed on the open road heading towards the harbour, the wind blowing wisps of hair out of the loosely looped style Oriel had created.

'Are you cold? Would you like me to put the hood up?'

'No, please, it's a lovely night. The air smells so wonderful here.' She inhaled the warm scents. 'Pines and wild herbs, it's one of the things I love about Mediterranean countries.' Oriel relaxed and tried to force herself into a cheerful frame of mind, determined to have fun and forget all about her apprehensions and doubts.

Vassilis drove with skill, yet at breakneck speed, steering most of the time with only one hand on the wheel. Oriel had been briefly wooed by a French racing-car driver so not only was she used to this sort of dangerous driving but it had always given her a sense of exhilaration, bringing out the adventurous, slightly reckless side to her nature. She often wondered if that wasn't an internal mechanism to compensate for her wariness and control where her emotions were concerned.

Though playful and easy-going, Vassilis neither had the charisma nor the electric *je ne sais quoi* that made heads turn whenever Damian entered a room. Oriel had witnessed this phenomenon the night he had taken her to Manoli's and again at Santorini. But she felt comfortable with Vassilis. It helped not being attracted to him in the least, and his playful, boyish charm was exactly what she needed right now.

'I thought you wouldn't want to miss the special celebration tonight at Limenarkhees Taverna,' he said. 'It's for the diva's birthday. This is the first time for a while that she's on Helios to celebrate it with her people. She will be singing, of course.'

Oriel hadn't realized that the beach party had anything to do with Yolanda; if she had known, she probably wouldn't have come. However, she'd promised herself a night out and hopefully their paths would not need to cross. 'I look forward to it, she has a wonderful voice,' was all she said.

They were silent for a moment as Vassilis negotiated a tricky stretch of road, and her thoughts automatically drifted back to Mattias's words that afternoon: 'The Kyrios tried his best. He went against everybody ... Yolanda threw it all away, and now she weeps.' She wondered at those words ... Was Yolanda the real reason why Damian had absented himself tonight from the island? If he really wanted to, he could have come back from the Athens meeting in time for the party, surely? Mattias mentioned that Damian's heart hurt over the diva, his childhood sweetheart. Maybe it still did? Perhaps he had never quite been able to break free.

As if aware of her withdrawal, Vassilis glanced her way. 'You're very silent,' he remarked, jogging Oriel out of her thoughts.

Her colour rose. 'I'm enjoying the drive, you're a good driver.'

'Thank you. Driving is my hobby. Last year I took part in the Tuareg rally in Morocco. It was amazing racing through the desert.'

'That sounds fun. Are you going to drive in any rallies this year?' Oriel asked.

'Not sure. There's a lot of work on, including Damian's site and everything else I oversee with my company. My dream is to pilot one of my cars in the 24-hour Le Mans.'

'Dreams come true when you believe in them, you know,' said Oriel with a smile. 'You just have to do something about it, turn them into realities.'

'So I keep telling myself. When I can, I spend Saturdays on a circuit in Athens, practising.'

'It's a dangerous hobby.'

'What is life for, if it isn't to be lived to the full?'

'True.'

Images of herself and Damian in the throes of lovemaking, reflected in the ceiling mirror, danced in front of Oriel's eyes.

They had arrived at the marina. Vassilis parked the car at the top of the cliffs and turned off the headlamps. He climbed out and came round to the passenger side, opening Oriel's door for her. It was dark by now and the stars were noticeably bright in the amethyst glow of the sky. Night birds swooped across the beach, speeding black shapes of chattering sound.

Vassilis guided her along the path, a hand on her arm, but Oriel felt no hammering heartbeats in her ribcage or butterflies in her stomach and, for a split second, she missed those delicious sensations that only Damian's touch was able to arouse. Still, she didn't want to think about that and she tried to stem her thoughts by concentrating on the scenery as they made their way down to the taverna.

The bay was unusually full of boats on the flat sea: it was clear that there had been an influx of visitors for the occasion. Beyond the rocks the chromium waters glittered and the sky was hazy with stars and a half moon. The cliffs behind were dark smudges and, further away to the left, in the distance, the forbidding black mass of Typhoeus loomed.

As they walked down the winding track, they could see below them the beach packed with partygoers. People from all over the island, it seemed, had converged outside the taverna to wish their diva a happy birthday. It was as if a modern-day Bacchanalia were in progress. Coloured light bulbs had been strung from tree to tree on the beach and around the bar, and they twinkled from wooden posts on the waterfront, too. A rudimentary speaker system, turned up to its highest possible level, had been set up to pipe out recorded tunes while the crowd awaited the live music of Yolanda and her band.

Still, this was not a crowd awaiting a show in silence; it was as if they were infused with joy. Some were singing at the tops of their voices, clapping their hands; others danced on a square stage made from blocks of wood and a few danced on tables. Still more were seated at long trestle tables covered with brightly patterned cloths, helping themselves from huge plates of *mezedes* and bottles of drink set in front of them, like spectators at a football match. Customers were queuing up at the bar and empty bottles of ouzo, *Fix Hellas* Greek beer, retsina and a rosé known as *kokkineli* were already littering the sand.

The noise was horrendous. As they drew even closer to the taverna, Oriel realized that it would be almost impossible to communicate without shouting over the nerve-jangling, electrified thudding of the *bouzoúki*. It was a time for singing and laughter, and the guests could no more have stopped their hedonistic partying than the birds in the trees their singing.

The carcass of a goat was roasting on a crude spit set over an open fire in one corner of the beach, its reddish-brown skin glistening. Two women, one squatting at each end of the beast, wide cotton skirts lifted up around their tanned knees, turned the spit and brushed the goat with a bunch of fresh wild herbs, which they dipped in a large earthenware bowl full of some sort of marinade. A huge, heavy, cast-iron cauldron had been placed under the charred carcass to catch the drops of fat running down its sides. The delicious, pungent aroma of the sizzling meat mingled with the fragrance of salt, iodine, seaweed and pine.

There was a remote and primitive air hanging over the entire scene that some might have found outlandish and somewhat barbaric, but it excited Oriel in the same way Damian excited her. While watching the revellers and listening to their cheers, laughter and raucous songs, she had been thinking of the man who ruled them. In that moment Oriel wished she had been a writer or a painter so she could transfer to paper or canvas this incredible sight that opened her mind, giving wings to her imagination, her soul almost becoming one with this place.

They had almost arrived at the beach now and the noise was getting louder. Vassilis guided her down a side path that she could see led to a quieter part of the bay, about fifty feet away from the throbbing heart of the celebrations. There were a few tables set up here, with a counter where you could buy drinks. A couple of waiters were standing around but Oriel could see from their faces that, stuck at this end of the party, they felt like they were missing out on the fun. Although the masses were gathered where the music, the food and the merrymaking were taking place, some guests had discovered this more intimate corner; they were mostly couples and bevies of women on their own who, without an escort, perhaps felt a little uncomfortable among the raucous rabble.

'You find us loud and vulgar, eh?' Vassilis's voice drew Oriel out of her contemplation.

'Not at all, quite the reverse. I was admiring the way the islanders are able to give themselves up to such *joie de vivre*.' Her mind flashed back to the scenes of uninhibited joy at the Epiklisi festival. The spirit of *képhi*, as Damian had called it. 'I do love the way the islanders celebrate so wholeheartedly,' she exclaimed, turning to him, her eyes sparkling with the exuberance of it all. 'They dance, they sing, they carouse as if there's no tomorrow.'

'We Greeks know how to have fun, that's for sure,' said Vassilis, grinning. Oriel smiled back, thinking how endearing he was, with his hair falling over his forehead like a playground scamp. What a strange mix of a man: with his love of cars and having fun, combined with the careful diligence of the trained archaeologist. In some ways, the perfect man for her, she had to admit – it was just a shame she couldn't find him attractive. It didn't help that the powerful, broad-shouldered figure of Damian got in the way, his intense eyes and somewhat forbidding expression filling her mind.

A waiter came to take their order for drinks and appetizers. Despite Vassilis's coaxing, Oriel declined the various alcohols on offer. She had indulged the night before as well as the night before that and, after her conversation with Mattias that afternoon, she was ashamed of the consequences. She ordered carob juice, which she had discovered during one of her trips to Greece: a chocolate-like flavoured drink native to the Mediterranean. Vassilis ordered Metaxa and an array of *mezedes*. Drinks and food were brought to the table without delay and Oriel, who had eaten nothing for breakfast and only a sandwich for lunch, tucked in heartily to the numerous little dishes that were placed on the table in front of them.

Still the crowds were arriving. The place was heaving and soon they would overflow to this quieter part of the venue. 'I didn't realize that there would be so many people.'

'Yolanda always draws a crowd. After all, she is the beloved superstar of the island, a celebrity acclaimed all over Greece and now the world, too.'

'Do she and her brother get on?' asked Oriel. She didn't know Vassilis well enough to voice her instinctive dislike of Yorgos, who had always seemed sly and ingratiating whenever she had met him. She had to wonder why Damian had chosen him as estate manager, a responsibility that would require a great deal of trust.

Vassilis seemed to intuit her feelings and was rather more blunt. 'She and Yorgos are a team, they only have one another. I'm not sure if they actually *like* each other, but they do have one major thing in common, other than their parentage, of course ...'

'What's that?' asked Oriel.

'Their ambition. She wants to be the proper queen of the island. He, of course, wants it for her so she can elevate him, too. They share a plan, it seems to me. Yolanda Christodoulou is determined to bear the name Lekkas one day and, with her brother keeping close to Damian, she stands a far better chance than all the other women who have tried fighting for his affections.'

'How awkward for Damian to have so many women throwing themselves at him.' Oriel found it hard to keep the bitterness out of her voice and hoped her words merely sounded ironic.

Vassilis nodded his thanks as the waiter returned with a bottle of water. 'As I said before, no one else has managed to get closer to Damian than our diva here. Let's face it, who could possibly hope to compete with her? She wants it all: Damian, fame, the island, everything. You have to admire her,' said Vassilis, twinkling. '*Yassas!*'

Oriel didn't respond to this comment and instead raised her glass to his and gave a half smile, taking a sip of carob juice. Instead, she said: 'I was surprised to find that Damian owns everything. I imagined his cousin would share the inheritance.'

'Ah, poor Helena. *Eínai trelíi*, the crazy invalid. Of course, you must have met her if you live at Heliades.'

'Yes.' *And how I wish I hadn't*, Oriel said to herself silently.

'You see, girls on Helios don't inherit. They receive an annuity instead. That way, capital remains intact in one family.'

'Yes, Yorgos told me about that particular island rule. Not a very nice prospect for the women, I thought.'

'I know what you mean but, from what I can see, the women on Helios are quite happy with this arrangement. I'm not saying it's right, but it secures them an income so they can tend to their families' needs.'

'I could never bend to such laws.'

'Trust me, they save a lot of grief. Have you had much to do with Helena?'

Oriel tensed slightly and looked down at her glass. 'I have only met her briefly.'

'They're a crazy family, all of them.'

'Damian doesn't seem crazy to me, quite the reverse, in fact. As far as I can see, he's hardworking, organized and knowledgeable in his field.' Why did she resent Vassilis's criticism of Damian? Oriel wondered. Why was she defending him?

He gave her a sidelong glance. 'Don't tell me that you've also fallen for *Drákon* Damian's hidden charms.'

'Of course not.' The answer snapped out sharp and instinctive. 'But he comes across as a confident man who knows clearly and surely, right back through the generations, who he is and where he comes from.'

'You're right, he has many good qualities. I wouldn't call him my friend otherwise,' acknowledged Vassilis. 'You must admit, though, he can be boorish sometimes.'

A boor but never a bore, she thought to herself but, before she could answer, Vassilis interrupted with a smile laden with impish charm. 'But I haven't invited you here tonight to talk about Damian Lekkas.' His eyes gleamed appreciatively. 'I'd like to know more about you. Tell me about yourself.'

Oriel knew that tone and she froze a little, her defences up. An involuntary shiver of alarm feathered the length of her spine. *Oh God, not Vassilis, not tonight … what was it with men?* He had managed to inject an intimacy and a caress into his voice that she would be naïve to wilfully misunderstand.

She sighed inwardly and felt a fool for having supposed his attentions to be purely the innocent ones of a friendly colleague. He had asked her to the party, after all – he probably thought he had made his intentions perfectly clear. She had to admit that it was her own need for a friend's shoulder to lean on just now that had led her here. Now it was up to her to tactfully extricate herself and spare him any embarrassment. If they were going to work together then this was an imperative.

'My life history is very dull,' she declared, trying to inject a little coolness into her tone and demeanour.

'Where do you live?'

'In London.'

'Alone?' Vassilis raised an eyebrow, leaving no doubt as to his meaning.

'I share a house with friends. Your next question is do I have a boyfriend?' There was no hint of flirtation in Oriel's voice as she said this.

But Vassilis didn't notice – he was on a mission, determined to deliver his lines. 'With looks like yours I imagine men beat a pathway to your door.'

Oriel uttered a brief sardonic laugh. 'Yes, they fall over each other in their race to get to me. My doorstep is a real battlefield.'

'Like bees, the men flit around the honey pot.'

'Trust me, I'm no honey pot.'

'No wedding ring that I can see on your finger.'

'Not yet.'

'Do you have someone in mind? Or are you one of those women who aren't interested in marriage and children?'

Oriel gave Vassilis her sweetest smile. 'Is this inquisition into my private life going to continue for long?'

'Oh dear, have you had enough of me already?' Vassilis had sufficient tact to realize his flirtation wasn't being received with quite the wholeheartedness he had hoped for.

'I'd rather we just concentrated on having fun,' Oriel said, tactfully. 'Shall we go and join the crowd? I find people and their customs fascinating.'

Vassilis's eyes regarded her solemnly. 'Like animals in a zoo?'

'Sarcasm, *Kyrios* Markopoulos?'

He shook his head and laughed. 'No, no, just a little peeved at your rebuff,' he said good-humouredly. 'Still, as you say, let's go and join the crowd and have some of that delicious roasted goat. It smells amazing.' He lifted his glass in a casual salute, inviting her to join him in a toast. 'To a successful evening, and to many future ones!'

Feeling light-hearted again, Oriel lifted her glass. 'Thank you.'

When he helped her with her wrap she was relieved that he was merely courteous, and there wasn't a trace of lasciviousness. She felt a tacit mutual awareness that a line had been drawn, and she felt comfortable after that to walk to the opposite side of the beach with Vassilis holding her arm lightly.

The dancing had already started. Couples shuffled around the raised wooden dancefloor, arms around each other, bodies touching because there were so many people on it.

'Shall we dance before dinner, before the stage becomes even more crowded?' Vassilis asked as they were led by a curvy waitress to the table he had reserved. 'We can eat during the performance.'

'Good idea! I'm not really hungry after all those delicious *mezedes* you ordered. That was a dinner in itself.' Oriel looked at the crowd, hesitating a moment. 'Is it safe for me to leave my wrap and bag at the table, do you think?'

'Don't worry, Nitsa will keep an eye on them. Let's give her our order now. She'll bring it to us when we come back.'

He slipped a note to the waitress, who giggled and thanked him. Then Nitsa led them to a small table, on which was a reserved sign, and she pulled out her notebook to take Vassilis's order.

'When we come back to the table we'd like you to bring us some of that roasted kid, a selection of *dolmadakia*, some *tsatziki* and warm bread,' Nikos turned to Oriel. 'Is that okay for you?'

'Sounds perfect.'

'Will you join me in a glass of wine? Or maybe you would prefer something else?'

'I'll just have one,' said Oriel. 'I've got work tomorrow and I want a clear head.'

Vassilis ordered a bottle of *Kratistos Nemea*. 'It's an excellent red wine, made from *agiorgitiko*, St George's grapes. It'll go very well with the goat.'

'It's a good choice. I love its dark colour, it reminds me of our Victoria plums.'

'Not many people know about Greek wines. It's an interest of mine too. I love the fact that their history goes back six-and-a-half thousand years.'

'Me too. The Minoans learnt winemaking from the ancient Egyptians and, thousands of years later, producers are probably doing things in much the same way,' she agreed, happy to be on safe territory again. 'Did you hear about the wine amphora we brought up? Its seal is intact. Damian suggested we try the wine.'

'Urgh! I'm not sure drinking a toast to your health with it would be such a good idea. It would probably poison you.' Vassilis laughed. 'Come, let's dance.' He stood and held out his hand to Oriel. 'Though I could sit here talking to you for hours ...'

They snaked their way to the dancefloor. Oriel was thankful that the music was typical Greek pop music, noisy and full of rhythm, not slow and languorous as it was in Santorini. The idea of being held by any man other than Damian filled her with distaste. She had always loved dancing and happily Vassilis seemed to share her delight in the music. She forgot about the canary, her anxiety over Damian, Helena's violent outburst and the disquieting words of Irini, then Mattias ... she forgot everything but the sheer pleasure of the music, the warmth, the bright lights and the celebratory atmosphere.

Suddenly the lights dimmed and the cadence of the music became slow and dreamy. Oriel hadn't time to withdraw before Vassilis had pulled her into his arms. *People will say we're in love ...* crooned the singer with laughter in his voice, and Vassilis held her a little closer. As more couples invaded the stage, she found herself sandwiched in the middle of the crush with nowhere to escape. She couldn't bear being held like this ... every cell in her body was rebelling against the warmth of the man clasping her to him. It wasn't his fault, it was just a slow dance ... nevertheless it felt wrong. The thoughts in her brain were racing at one hundred miles an hour, trying to conjure up an excuse to go back to the table.

And then, suddenly, Oriel's heart contracted sharply, her eyes widened and she caught a quick inaudible breath. *Damian was there!* Across the expanse of the dancefloor, over the heads of the throng, she saw him. He was dancing with Yolanda on the far side of the stage and the singer was gazing up at him with the entranced look of a woman in love. Oriel's body stiffened in Vassilis's hold with an involuntary startled movement she could not control.

So Damian had come back especially to celebrate Yolanda's birthday, despite the night of passion he and Oriel had shared less than twenty-four hours ago! Disillusionment rose in her throat, bitter as gall. Suddenly, all the enjoyment of the evening was tumbling down like a toppled house of cards. She felt crushed, humiliated.

In the same instant, as if drawn beyond the crowd by the power of Oriel's thoughts, Damian's eyes met hers. There was an odd flicker in his eyes but no surprise, no reproach – not even a sign of recognition in the steel irises, yet she was sure he had seen her. That stark, empty look gave her a strange, cold feeling down her spine, in spite of the warmth of the atmosphere. She saw Yolanda's mani-cured hand slide over his arm possessively, saw the undulating way her body swayed and rubbed itself against his, and saw Damian look down into her eyes with absorbed attention. The bleakness Oriel had thought she had seen when she had met his gaze that second before had been wiped entirely from his face.

He then stooped slightly to answer some remark of Yolanda's, something that was obviously both intimate and mischievous. And they laughed, Damian and this young woman who was utterly at home on the island, among these people – a diva adored by a world-wide public, who was more beautiful, more sophisticated than Oriel could ever hope to be. She wasn't sure whether Vassilis was watch-ing her and she tried as hard as she could to keep her expression impassive. Meanwhile, pain tore at her with sharp, lance-like fin-gers.

'She enjoys dancing too,' Vassilis said. He had turned his head, probably because he had sensed Oriel stiffening in his arms. 'Come, let's return to our table.'

Dry-eyed yet torn apart by a storm of emotion she had never known before, Oriel allowed Vassilis to lead her through the crowd, relieved that the suggestion had come from him because she wouldn't have been able to muster the presence of mind to ask him to take her away. She moved like a woman in a dream, listless, with-out volition. She only knew that seeing Damian like that, across the crowded stage, had stabbed her to the core. She was ashamed, too, of her wild desire to be dancing with him instead of with Vassilis: to be in Yolanda's place.

You fool! You damned idiot! Oriel cried to herself. Hadn't she learnt her lesson?

Oriel turned the knife in her own heart; she couldn't take her eyes off the couple, wondering how happy they were really. She could hear Mattias's words, intimating that Yolanda had thrown away Damian's love, and that he had continued to hurt at having lost her. Maybe Damian didn't want to commit to a deeper and more serious relationship after all the pain he had been through, but it seemed clear to Oriel, watching them now, that they were lovers.

Her thoughts kept her silent, more subdued than she had been during the earlier part of the evening. She couldn't see her own eyes, but she knew they must have appeared troubled because Vassilis's expression appeared crestfallen. Had she hurt him?

As soon as they were back at their table, Nitsa brought over their order. Oriel felt the beginning of a headache probing her temples. She would have difficulty swallowing anything and instead toyed with the food on her plate, wishing she had not allowed discord to spoil what had promised to be an excellent evening.

A crease deepened between Vassilis's dark eyebrows and he looked at Oriel in a puzzled way. 'Are you okay? We don't need to stay for Yolanda's performance if you don't want to.'

Oriel felt a burning at the back of her eyes. 'No, no. I'm fine really. Thank you. It's been a long day and weariness has just caught up with me. I'll be all right after a good night's sleep.'

Once Damian and Yolanda had left the dancefloor, Oriel couldn't see them: the place was too crowded. She tried to catch sight of Damian in the sea of people but to no avail. The meal staggered painfully to its conclusion. There was the cutting of the birthday cake and the distribution of free champagne for everybody in honour of the diva's birthday, during which Oriel excused herself and went to the cloakroom.

Just as she was coming back to her table she spotted Damian. He was walking towards her with the easy assurance of a man who was accustomed to getting his own way. He was dressed less formally tonight, with a sky-blue polo shirt and pale, faded jeans, which moulded themselves to him like a second skin.

Oriel's nails curled into the palms of her hands. Her legs felt weak and there was an agonizing hollow feeling in the pit of her stomach. Damian stopped a moment to say a few words to a group of people who had called out to him. She tried to deviate from her path so she wouldn't have to go past him but in no time he was next to her, blocking her escape in the same obstructive way he had done six years ago on Aegina.

Something flashed in Damian's eyes as he looked down at her, then his dark lashes cut across his gaze, concealing it. 'Tomorrow we have a heavy day in front of us so I hope you haven't indulged in too much wine,' he said softly, icily. 'We'll be leaving before seven.'

'I'll be at the quay on time.'

'There's been a slight change of plan.' And before she could ask any questions, he added: 'I'll explain tomorrow.'

'Fine.' Oriel tried to pass, but he barred her route and gave her an insolent look, his mouth pressed into a hard line. 'Frankly, I'm surprised you have the energy after last night. I hope you're not leading my friend astray. Maybe later you can tell me how Vassilis compares in the bedroom, eh?' His eyes were luminous with silent wrath.

Oriel bit her lip until she could taste blood and her face became tinged with self-conscious colour. She should have known that he would not react well to seeing her at the taverna with Vassilis, however innocent her motives. No matter that Damian was the worldly, educated leader of Helios. He was still as Greek as the next man: hot-blooded, passionate and with an easily wounded pride to match.

She looked up at him steadily. 'Can we stop right there, please? I find this conversation thoroughly abhorrent.'

'Is that so?' Damian's voice was like tempered steel. 'And I find the thought of you with Markopoulos equally so.' He gave her a derisive look. 'There's something to think about next time you're in his arms. Maybe it'll spice things up for you.'

Oriel glowered at him, loathing him for his unfounded and hurtful insinuations, particularly when he had the gall to be there with Yolanda. 'I'd rather you didn't say anything else,' she replied raggedly. 'I see you're not—'

Vassilis didn't let her finish her phrase. Neither of them had seen his approach but it was clear he had heard some, if not all, of Damian's distasteful words. He stepped forward and interposed himself between them.

'That's no way to speak to a lady.' His manner was politeness itself, but there was no misunderstanding the veiled anger behind his words.

An amused, half-mocking smile played round the corner of Damian's mouth. 'Just like you to come to the rescue, Vassilis,' he said. 'You've always managed to charm women with your knight in shining armour act. Don't think I don't know what you're up to.'

'You arrogant *kátham*, son of a bitch.'

Now they were standing opposite each other, Vassilis seemed much shorter than Damian and was having to stare up at him, although it didn't stop him from looking as if he was about to lose control, his temper and recklessness fuelled by Metaxa. Oriel licked dry lips. The last thing she wanted was to cause a quarrel. Among Greek men, this didn't take much. Insults poured out of them without restraint when they were angry, even between friends. She was aware of the curious scrutiny of some of the guests and guessed that they were wondering what part she had played in this heated argument.

'You're a lout. She may be your employee but you've no right to speak to Oriel that way.'

People had started to gather around them, whispering, obviously looking forward to the addition of a juicy spectacle to the evening.

'And what are you going to do about it, eh?' Damian taunted, an unpleasant smile twisting his lips.

Vassilis answered him by putting the flat of his hand against Damian's face and giving it a shove. Then as Damian staggered back, he waited, fists up. Damian, who had been taken by surprise, recovered his balance immediately.

'Ah, you want a fight, do you?' He raised his fists likewise, dark fury etched on his face in a way that Oriel had never seen before.

They danced round each other, then Damian led with a left hook and brought his right fist round in a heavy swinging blow that landed on the side of his opponent's head. Vassilis grunted but bore in on him. Damian took another swipe and, but for a last-minute dropping of his head by a fraction, Vassilis would have taken the blow between the eyes. Instead, it landed on his forehead. His head went back. That gave Damian another opening and he took advantage of it: his right connected with Vassilis's jaw. It was a heavy blow and it shook him.

Some of the guests tried to separate them now, but the enraged pair were having none of it. Oriel was shouting, 'Stop it, both of you! Please, stop!' but her voice was lost in the noise of the melee. Yolanda was nowhere to be seen, she noticed, probably not wishing to be tainted by this unsavoury brush.

Vassilis had now brought his forearms and fists closer to his face but he wasn't giving up. Damian drove a punch to his stomach that made him gasp but, in striking the blow, he left himself open for a moment. Vassilis saw his opportunity and put the whole weight of his shoulders into a solid punch that caught Damian full on the nose. Immediately, blood poured down over his mouth and chin.

Furious, and obviously in pain, Damian came in with a quick, springing lunge. Pushing Vassilis back towards the wall, he pinned him against it and, as though a mad fury had suddenly taken possession of him, smashed home punch after punch, without ever troubling to guard himself. Hopelessly cornered, with blood streaming down his face, Vassilis continued to fight back like a trapped and maddened wolf.

It was too much. The next thing, Vassilis's arms came down to shield his torso and, as he did so, Damian struck his opponent's jaw with a terrific punch, sending him spinning half round, leaving him for a moment wobbling on his feet, hands at his side. Then Vassilis crumpled to his knees.

Sirens were heard and someone was crying out, '*Ee ahstinomeea, ee ashtinomeea,* the police!' and within minutes two policemen had made their way through the crowd. By now Vassilis had staggered to his feet and both men were breathing heavily. The lower part of Vassilis's face was covered in blood and his right eye was closing fast. The skin on Damian's forehead had split and there was a swelling at the side of his mouth. When the police glanced nervously at him before asking if either wanted to press charges, both men shook their heads and, as there had been no damage to the taverna, the police merely told them to stop brawling and go and patch themselves up.

The owner of the taverna clapped his hands a few times. 'Look, folks, the cabaret is over,' he shouted at the top of his voice. 'Everybody go back to what you were doing and enjoy the evening.'

As the onlookers dispersed, Yolanda suddenly appeared, rushing to Damian's side, the picture of tender sympathy. 'Damian, *agápi mou,* are you hurt?' she simpered. 'My poor *glyké mou,* sweetheart. Your head, so much blood … let me look after you.'

Oriel turned her back on them both, not wanting to witness Yolanda's sudden fawnings, and helped Vassilis back to the table. 'You need compresses of ice to stem the bleeding and the swelling,' she said. She took out of her bag a small white handkerchief and, pouring some cold water over it from the jug on the table, she dabbed at the eye that was swelling fast. 'I'm sorry, this is all my fault.'

'Damian is arrogant. He should never have spoken to you like that. A boorish lout, as I said.'

'I feel so guilty.'

Lifting his sleeve, Vassilis tried to wipe away some of the blood trickling down his face. 'Please, don't feel bad. I'm fine. For once it gave me great pleasure to stand up to that conceited *pagoni*, peacock, friend or not. Sometimes he just goes too far. I just wish the police hadn't turned up, I would have knocked him out.' Vassilis took Oriel's hand, which was lying on the table, and turned it over, brushing his lips to her palms. 'No one has the right to talk to you the way that *bástardos* did.'

The musicians were taking their place on the stage for Yolanda's performance. By now, Vassilis was looking very pale. Oriel could see that he was suffering although making a valiant attempt to put on a brave face. His nose was still bleeding slightly, and he had placed his own handkerchief against it to stop the dribbling. His right eye was all but closed, the swelling extending to his cheekbone. Oriel tried to order some ice from a waiter but there wasn't any left.

'You need a doctor, you can't leave these wounds unattended. Is there a hospital we can go to?'

'Don't worry, I'll call the doctor when I get home. I'll be fine.' He tried to smile at her and winced. The sight of his white teeth in his tanned and bloodied face looked almost gruesome.

'I think we should leave now before the beginning of the show. It'll probably go on for another two or three hours. That's too long, with the state you're in.'

'You're a sweet girl, Oriel. Look, I've been irresponsible. I should have handled Lekkas differently. Settled our scores somewhere else. I'm fine. I promise I won't spoil your evening further.'

'Well, then, do as I say and be wise. There'll always be another party, another show … We've just started on the excavations. I'll be around for another month at least.'

'Are you sure?'

'Quite sure. Anyhow, I'm tired and *Kyrios* Lekkas has just told me that we have an early start tomorrow.'

'Thank you, Oriel. I promise to make it up to you.'

'Don't worry about that. Are you all right to drive?'

'Yes, yes, it's nothing. My cuts are not very deep, but I should get cleaned up.'

Oriel picked up her shawl and bag, and together they left the taverna.

* * *

It seemed that the day was destined to provide Oriel with one disturbance after another. Even before putting her key in the lock, as she stood outside her apartment, she drew a startled breath, alarmed by a noise she could hear behind the door and aware of a flurry of sound that rose in volume as she listened. She hesitated, knowing that someone had once again violated her space. What was she to do? Go in search of Irini and ask for her help? Let everyone know she was afraid? She could always say she'd lost her key, but Oriel thought that sort of cowardice beneath her.

Taking the bull by the horns, she turned the key in the lock and pushed the door open. The noise was coming from her bedroom. She walked across the sitting room and opened the door. The chirping, chattering and shrilling that filled the darkness was deafening; it sounded as if she had entered an aviary. When she switched on her bedroom light she saw, hanging over her bed, an ornamental cage like the ones she had seen swinging from the ceiling on Helena's veranda the night she'd had dinner with her. Now Oriel had no doubt that the dead canary was Beshir's work too, performed on the sick orders of Damian's cousin.

Fear and fury mingled in Oriel's mind. They washed over her: wave after wave of violent emotion. For a few shocked seconds she stared with huge eyes in frozen horror at the golden jail full of small birds. The screeching was unbearable. She paused, pondering her

346

next move. All she could think of was her own sharp aversion to going near the cage but she knew that setting free the poor captive creatures was the only sensible thing to do.

Oriel shut the door behind her and, heart thudding, made her way to the small aviary. Dread gathered about her like shadows, paralyzing her body so that she could barely move. She managed to extend an arm towards the cage and, with shaking hands, seized the loop at the top and took it down. It was heavy and swung from side to side, the birds going berserk, twittering in terror, fluttering their wings as they beat frantically against the bars of their prison, injuring themselves as they did so.

Oriel was just as terrified; fear was burning a hole in her. Still, her determination to release those tiny frightened souls from their golden prison gave her the courage to carry the cage to the terrace outside her bedroom. She stumbled over the threshold, almost letting it slip from her hand, but righted herself immediately. Then she laid it on top of the stone balustrade.

The birds had become frantic now and she waited, uncertain. What if, when she opened the door, in their panic they flew at her? A few minutes passed. The birds calmed down. They had stopped twittering but were still quivering, huddled against each other, their beautiful feathers ruffled, pupils shining as they darted here and there, desperate for escape.

Taking a deep breath, Oriel pushed up the catch and the little door swung open. Nothing happened at first then suddenly away they flew towards the sea, one after the other, and into the sheltering trees. Oriel went back inside and closed the French windows. As she did so, Irini's ominous words played in her head like the maddening refrain of a popular song. *Someone wishes you ill. You need to believe it. This is a troubled house ...* So much for Damian warning his cousin off. If Helena was now defying Damian himself, what lengths would she go to? Suddenly she was afraid for her safety. Afraid for her life, perhaps! The whole dark, looming house seemed like a cage about her, shutting her in, stifling her ... She felt like a piece of thin crystal, which the barest touch would shatter; she wouldn't stay one minute more under this roof.

Grabbing her handbag, Oriel ran down the stairs and out of the cursed house. This time she made no effort to be quiet and, in her

347

haste, slammed the heavy front door behind her, little caring if she woke Helena and the other strange inhabitants of Heliades. She ran and ran, heedless of the darkness about her … down the drive, down the hill, running as if the devil himself were at her heels. She didn't know where she was going, and she didn't care.

* * *

As he drove back to Heliades, Damian's muscles were tense, his head aching and his jaw was stiff. He felt it gingerly, wondering if Vassilis's driving right fist had broken it. His cheek felt hard and swollen. He worked his jaw gently, as though eating tough meat or tackling one of those hard *paximadakia* Lent biscuits. He welcomed the feel of the cool night wind as it played on his bruised forehead and soothed his brain, which was full of confused thoughts, making him feel hot and bothered.

He had wanted to leave the taverna immediately so as to be at Heliades when Oriel returned but he needed to speak briefly to the two police officers, Stelios and Pantelis, as well as Thanos, the owner of Limenarkhees. Damian did not tolerate corruption of any kind and so he had instilled a cardinal rule in the island's local force that everyone, no matter their background, should be treated in the same way if they caused a disturbance – and that included him. He'd apologised for his outburst and then cursed himself for displaying such a lack of self-control in public.

Yolanda hadn't let him go easily, and had insisted on trying to apply some arnica, plus the last of the taverna's ice, to minimize the damage. She had wanted to take him back to her house, 'so I can nurse you, *agápi mou*.' He'd let her know in no uncertain terms that he didn't need her nursing and would be fine. Yolanda nursing anybody … *O, Theé mou!* Damian's mouth twisted in a sceptical grimace. *That would be the day!*

Stavros had always said that he was far too tolerant of Yolanda. 'You need to be careful, my friend,' he'd told him one day when they were drinking late into the night at Manoli's. 'She thinks she has you and will only ever be trouble.'

Damian had shrugged. 'Don't you think I know that, Stavros? Besides, what do I care what she thinks as long as the islanders are happy with her and she brings money to Helios?'

Yolanda wounded him once, more deeply than Stavros would ever know, but Damian was a cautious man now. The saying was true, he thought ruefully: *Ópoios káike sti soúpa fysáei kai to giaoúrti*, whoever gets burnt by the hot soup blows on the cool yoghurt. He was being watchful. Yolanda was quick to harbour jealous resentment and was spiteful as a monkey, and he was in no doubt that she had sniffed out the threat that Oriel posed to her now. The thought brought him some disquiet: what might she try to do to ruin his chances with Oriel?

Still, hadn't he done as much damage himself now?

When he arrived at Limenarkhees, it had been just in time to see Vassilis taking Oriel down the path leading to the more intimate side of the beach. He had wanted to break Vassilis's face right there and then but Yolanda chose that moment to appear and then hadn't let go of him the whole evening.

Damian was not normally violent, despite his reputation. On the contrary he thought of himself as an even-tempered man, fair but uncompromising. He was feared by people who didn't know him well and by those who broke the rules. After all, he was head of this island and had to maintain law and order – but it was better to enforce law using firm persuasion first, before ever thinking to use force, that was his motto. His friends said he governed with an iron fist in a velvet glove, but it was his enemies who had named him *Drákon* Damian, an epithet he welcomed because it stopped people becoming too complacent.

Seeing Oriel with Vassilis on the dancefloor later had exposed a raw nerve. Oriel in the arms of another man … The simmering rage that had gripped him at the sight of the two of them together had eaten away at his iron self-control; he had waited as long as he could for the opportunity to talk to her before he'd snapped. He couldn't remember the exact words he had said to her, it was as if another person had been talking; all he knew was that he had behaved like a snarling animal and he deeply regretted it.

Still, possessiveness boiled in Damian's gut. He fought the selfish part of him that desperately needed Oriel's light in his life, that wanted to hide her away from the eyes of others – wanting to grab her and roar: *she's mine*. Something like panic had edged up his spine as he had watched Oriel and Vassilis on the dancefloor together. Panic born from anger, from jealousy, and from a sudden self-doubt as some of the malicious words Cassandra had said to him after his accident flooded his mind.

He had never felt diminished by his scars: on the contrary, he was proud of them because they were the proof that he had saved a life. Sure, he had lost his looks, but that hadn't bothered him, even when Cassandra had refused to share his bed, turning away from him in disgust. He had accepted it from his wife; there had never been any real love there, it had been a marriage of convenience on both sides. It was Pericles that she always wanted anyway. He shook his head. None of that mattered now.

What tormented him was that suddenly he was afraid that he wasn't good enough for Oriel, that given the choice between the Americanized Vassilis and the battered man he felt like tonight, she would choose the smooth-talking driver of fast cars, the knowledgeable archaeologist with more than one grand villa to his name.

Damian's emotions had never ruled him before, but he had let them do so tonight. This reaction at seeing Oriel with Vassilis was making him face up to his feelings about her. It gave him the realization, as perhaps nothing else could have done, of how deeply he … he couldn't even bring himself to utter the word silently in his head. It had been deleted from his vocabulary such a long time ago.

Damian's knuckles went white on the steering wheel. He suddenly grasped that what he had been doing was not far removed from playing about with Oriel. It had never been a conscious decision; as far as he was concerned, up until now, he simply had to have her. He would go to any lengths to pursue her and wear down her resistance. The chemistry between them was so strong that it had coloured all his thoughts and actions, cloaking the truth of his real feelings.

There had been that small glimmer of awareness, of course, when Stavros had brought him Oriel's résumé and photograph and he had discovered that she was his one-night stand. That beautiful stranger who, through these years of ups and downs, had often visited his thoughts by day and his dreams at night. Always carnal dreams where love had no place. Yet the joy that had overwhelmed him when she had accepted the job, the warmth that inundated his heart, he now knew could have only meant that he loved her. At the time Damian hadn't recognized the feeling as such and, when he had seen her again, his lust for her had bubbled to the surface with a power so strong that it had obliterated any other thought.

Last night in the Room of Secrets they had made love – there could be no other word to describe what had passed between them, he knew it now … only now. What a blind fool! Finally, he understood what that need was that drove him to want to wrap Oriel inside and outside of him, body and soul; the need for her that was as elemental as drawing breath, which made his heart pound inside his chest.

After Yolanda's betrayal he had thought that he would never love again or, at least, that he would never find the person who would make him trust once more. But tonight, reality slammed into Damian. Now he saw that there were moments in life – ecstatic moments – which could banish sorrow and heal gaping wounds. Miraculously, the darkness of the soul could be illumined by a light that soothed a wounded heart and created the natural human desire to love. To live joyously – that was the secret of earthly happiness, he saw that now – and what better way to enjoy this earthly happiness than to share it with someone who was the extension of yourself?

When he had seen Oriel sitting in the moonlight on Aegina, reminiscent of a moonbeam, she appeared to him so unearthly with her pale hair and wistful green eyes that looked up at him with such innocent candour, it seemed as though he were dreaming. That moment when she ran and he'd wrestled her to the sand … her luscious body lying warm and soft beneath him, her breasts full, taut and firm against his chest, her slim waist flaring gently out to perfectly proportioned hips and down to her slender legs … he'd thought he was in heaven right there and then. A protest had fallen from her lips but they had parted in a small smile as if she were stating something more out of bravado than anything else. And then she had given herself up to him totally, generously, without hesitation, and she became for him an angel of mercy. But his hopes had been dashed because of a misunderstanding. A simple scrap of paper with a picture on it had sent him away that same night.

Fate, life, God, whatever, had given him a second chance … and now cold dread filled him. Had what he had seen tonight been another misunderstanding? Had he become too cautious a man … too quick to jump to conclusions, to judge?

A dozen scenarios flooded his mind and none was good. He shouldn't have reacted in that brutish way. True, it had been a shock to see Oriel with another man, but he should have handled the situation differently. Making a spectacle of himself in public diminished him and the love he felt for her. Still, questions that needed answers clamoured in his tired mind. Why had she agreed to go out with Vassilis? How could she dance in the arms of another man after yesterday? She sounded cool, aloof even, when Damian had approached her – not like someone who had shared a night of passion with him only hours before. Maybe she had qualms about what had happened between them; the idea had sent a bleak fury coursing through him as he'd stood close to her, watching her lift her beautiful chin in defiance. At the time he had wanted to bait her, to get some sort of reaction out of her, but he had gone too far.

He would go and see her now – she should still be awake and, even if he had to wake her up, he needed to talk to her, to explain. He wanted to apologize for his outrageous behaviour and put things right. If Damian could just try to curb his jealousy and have a quiet conversation, maybe that would be the opportunity to tell her how he felt about her, that last night he hadn't just been passing the time or using her to gratify his needs. He loved her deeply – deeply enough to want to spend the rest of his life with her. Perhaps he was arrogant enough to think that what was between them could see them through any storm, and that he had plenty to offer her – and that even if she didn't love him today, she could learn to love him in time. He had to try.

Once at Heliades, Damian parked his car and took the stairs two at a time, suppressing the instinct that told him what he was about to do was not only foolish but downright rash. The house was silent. *Good*, he thought, *everybody is asleep*. He walked to Oriel's apartment and, without giving himself time to have second thoughts, knocked firmly on the door, his heart racing as never before. He tried it once, twice … and the third time he knocked a little harder and the door pushed open easily. Damian crossed the apartment and rapped on her bedroom door. When there was still no answer, he turned the handle and switched on the light. The room was empty and the bed hadn't been slept in, confirming his most painful fears. Oriel had not come home, she was obviously spending the night with Vassilis.

In a bitterness of spirit such as he had never known, he flung himself out of the house and into the deep-blue darkness of night.

* * *

Oriel had no idea for how long she had been running on the deserted road. She had instinctively made for the harbour: it was a route she knew, and it wasn't the first time she had headed blindly for the beach after a frightening episode at Heliades. It was still dark. A wan, moth-eaten-looking moon dangled over the black placid waters and the white lonely beach; it seemed to her a sickly thing, out of condition, as if it had been on duty for weeks on end.

No one was about. A smell of woodsmoke lingered in the air, mixed with a slightly acrid scent of burnt grease and charred goat. The taverna was closed; gone were the chairs, tables, dancefloor ... everything had been cleared away, even the lights from the trees. The only things that remained were the piles of rubbish littered here and there in tragic desolation on the shore. In the semi-darkness the slabs of broken rock, stacked one over the other in ruthless confusion, looked to her eerie, like a scaled-down scene of some prehistoric land, where monstrous beasts roamed. One particularly large slab – Mattias's favourite fishing spot – appeared particularly menacing.

A row of seagulls were resting in the softness of the night on the edge of a large empty *caique* moored close to the shore. And in the silence, broken only by the gentle sound of tiny waves frilling along the flat, an owl's melancholy cry reached out to Oriel from the dark trees that skirted the bay, making her jump. Athena's messenger, she thought to herself, as she stood on the cold sand, dazed and broken. If the bird was crying out a warning, it had come too late.

Oriel felt physically sick, with an inward suffering that was like a burning pain. Conscious of an aching void in her heart, she kept replaying her last scene with Damian. How could he have behaved like that? How dare he assume that she and Vassilis were ... Then a

353

desperate longing for him would sweep over her like a wave, which felt as though it would drown her. Each time it threatened to engulf her, she caught herself up sharply. It was no use fretting over Damian, she told herself; he didn't love her, he belonged to someone else.

The lonely beach and the rocks, the sea whispering and sobbing, seemed an evocative reflection of her mood as she settled down on the damp sand under a tree. That's when the first rush of pent-up emotion broke. Her throat ached; her eyes smarted with tears that streamed down her cheeks: tears of fatigue, hurt ... and anger.

Oriel fell asleep with hair tousled and eyes swollen. When she woke hours later, just before dawn, she was stiff and cold. Her limbs pained her so much she had almost forgotten her heartache. She sighed. Everything was in a terrible mess. She would have liked to talk to someone, to unburden herself – it would be so much easier if she could share her troubles with a real friend, a sympathetic ear, to help clarify things in her mind. Still, that wasn't an option. There was no one on the island she could confide in; she had no family, no friends here. Yet there was always Mattias. He was such a kind and wise man. Another time ...

She needed to think but she was tired, feverish and weak, so much so that she felt as if she had been physically battered. The future rose like a black curtain in front of her. She felt sick inside and shaky, as though she had just suffered a major trauma. Part of her craved a hot bath and a steaming cup of coffee; the other was dogged by a desire to simply curl up and go to sleep, and let the rest of the world go on without her.

Chapter 10

Leaning against the trunk of the pine tree, under which she had spent the night, Oriel watched the whiteness of the daylight slowly leak into the sky. In the shadowy half light, between the paling of the brilliant stars in their dark-blue setting and the first hint of glorious colour heralding the sunrise, a flight of wild geese skimmed past, their long necks outstretched in perfect formation – like an enormous squadron of aeroplanes. For a few seconds, the pattern they made against the dusky mother-of-pearl sky turned her thoughts away from her troubles to the beauty of the dawn.

A gull swooped down and then winged away again. A solitary fisherman was trudging along in the distance. A fishing *caique* had just pulled up on the shore, not far from where Oriel was sitting, and suddenly there was considerable excitement on the beach, with people appearing from nowhere and surrounding the boat.

Welcoming the diversion, Oriel stood up and joined the group. A large octopus had been caught during the night. It had been placed in a huge tank of seawater, which six men were in the process of carrying on to the sand. The octopus swam slowly to and fro, its tentacles, like films of soft soap, weaving about the bulbous head. Eyes, which were fixed on its captors with a malevolent intensity, seemed to take up most of the pouch-like head, which moved from side to side with the acute lateral movement of an Indian dancer, as if wishing to get a better look at those peering at him. On the sandy floor of the tank lay the remains of very small crabs.

The crew of the *caique* were in high spirits, fielding question after question as they stood, hands on hips, gazing at the octopus as it writhed in the tank. Oriel gathered, from what was being said, that it would fetch a tidy sum from the owner of a new aquarium on the mainland.

'You are an early riser, Oriel, eh?'

She turned abruptly and met Mattias's laughing eyes. But his smile vanished as soon as he saw her pale face and tired features.

He gave her a worried look. '*Ti eínai láthos*, what's wrong?'

Oriel's eyes moistened slightly at the sight of Mattias, so relieved it was he who had appeared just then; but the world felt too much of a tumultuous hub, whirling her round and round, for her to answer. So she said nothing, only managing a wan smile.

The pale, bold eyes of the fisherman looked searchingly into hers. '*Po! Po! Po!* Something is very wrong this morning! You look as though you haven't had any sleep for a week.'

'I haven't, it's true. I left Heliades yesterday and spent the night on the beach,' she admitted in a small voice.

Mattias's brows rose fractionally and he stared at her in disbelief. 'And *Kyrios* Damian let you leave just like that?'

'He doesn't know. I left before he came back,' she explained quietly. 'I simply couldn't stay at that house a minute longer … the dead canary … and then those dreadful birds …' She gave a shudder as she recalled the incident. Oriel was talking all at once, her words tumbling over each other, and it was as if it were someone else's voice, incoherent and all in a muddle. 'I really don't know what to do now.'

He looked calmly at her. 'I don't quite understand what you're saying. Come, let's sit down on the rocks and you can tell me slowly all about your troubles. Not that I want to pry into your affairs, it's just that there might be something I could do to help.'

Oriel nodded, her eyes bright with unshed tears. 'Of course you aren't prying, Mattias,' she said shakily. 'I really need to talk to someone. You've had your share of suffering in life, and you're a kind, wise man.'

Together they walked in silence to the rocks that had borne witness to their earlier conversations, and sat down on a boulder, facing the myriad colours of the dawn sky. Seabirds flew fearlessly over the water, uttering their peculiar, harsh cries that resounded loudly in the hush of the morning. It was that brief quiet time before the dogs started their barking and the goats were led by their herders, bells tinkling, to the greener pastures at the top of the cliffs.

Oriel felt as though she had always known Mattias. She had swiftly grown to admire his strength and trust his judgement, and then … of course he knew Damian and the history of his friend's disturbed family. Slowly, she told him all about what had happened with Damian six years ago, and everything that had taken place since her arrival on the island. She was almost unable to finish her story, she was crying so much. Oriel could not remember having cried like that for years and years. She tasted salt on her lips as the tears streamed down her cheeks, somehow or other bringing relief in their wake. It was as if something that had been frozen inside her for so long had suddenly thawed. And Mattias, understanding that, let her weep and made no attempt to check her.

When she had finished, he said nothing for a moment, but there was a knowing look in his gaze and sympathy trembled at the corners of his mouth. 'You have done right in your own eyes in leaving, but I'm not so sure you'll have done right in the *Kyrios*'s, whatever your excuse.'

'Can't you see I had to leave? Helena wanted me out of there. And I couldn't stay, not after Damian humiliated me in public.'

'And so you decided to run away,' Mattias said slowly.

'I had little choice,' Oriel replied simply.

'You have not asked yourself why the *Kyrios* acted in such an ungentlemanly way. It is not like him at all.'

'Perhaps he has never shown you that facet of his personality.'

'No, Oriel. I know *Kyrios* Damian well, he is a sensitive man.' He paused, stroking his beard a moment. 'No, I have an idea that he has fallen in love with you. It's the only explanation.'

Oriel inhaled sharply as if to speak, her heart leaping in the hope that it were true, but all she could manage was, 'Oh.'

Mattias saw her stunned expression. 'Seeing you in the arms of another man must have made his blood boil. Like Typhoeus over there, erupting out of his control.' He cleared his throat and continued gently: 'If you don't mind my saying so, Oriel, from what you have told me, I think that you reciprocate his feelings, no?'

She blushed and let her eyes drift towards the blue water that stretched out towards the horizon, merging into the azure sky. Did she love Damian? Was that why she had been so upset to see him in Yolanda's company, or was that just her pride?

Still, it was a relief to share her secret, to feel her taut nerves slackening under the comfort of being able to confide in someone whose views she respected, and who knew Damian and his family well. 'I'm not proud of the way I've behaved but I'm really confused.'

'Well, there's one way to sort out this confusion. I will ask him to come down here now, he needs to know where you are.'

There was a catch in Oriel's breath and a look of panic flashed across her eyes. '*Ochi!* No!' she cried vehemently.

'*To paidi mou,* my child, why ever not? You need to thrash this out. Don't let misunderstandings settle between you. *Tha ítan tóso kríma*, it would be such a pity to let pride get in the way of your chance of happiness.'

'Anyhow, he belongs to someone else.'

'You are wrong to think there is still love left in the *Kyrios*'s heart for Yolanda Christodoulou. She killed that love a long time ago.'

'How do you know? What are you saying?'

'I don't know all the facts but I *do* know *Kyrios* Damian as if he were my own son.' The fisherman seemed to be pondering awhile and Oriel waited patiently as he picked his words.

'As you already know, the *Kyrios* and Yolanda were childhood playmates. They were inseparable even before they became sweethearts but his family, among them his uncle Cyrus, the eldest brother of his father and the *Kyrios*'s guardian, who violently opposed this relationship, were never happy that they were so close. Yolanda doesn't only come from a different background, you could say it wasn't the best household to grow up in. Her mother was a drunk, her father was old and ignorant … doted on his daughter, giving her no guidance or discipline at all. So the child was left pretty much to her own devices. Besides, it has been a tradition in the Lekkas family to marry into one of the rich families on the island.

'In some ways, I don't blame the girl for wanting out,' he continued. 'It must have been unbearable for her in that squalid house, with her mother lying in a drunken stupor half the time. Yolanda's ambition to become famous was just her way of clawing her way out of that life. And Yorgos, without any particular talents at all, rode on her coattails. He got taken on by the *Kyrios* to help run the Lekkas businesses.' He snorted. 'Heh! *Évalan to lýko na fyláxei ta próvata*, they got the wolf to guard the sheep with that one.'

'Anyway, the *Kyrios* hadn't been given his inheritance at that stage. He was in his mid-twenties but Cyrus was still the head of the family. Who knows what happened but Yolanda refused to wait. It wasn't as if he hadn't asked her to marry him, he had. Even though it had caused a huge fight with the family, including with his brother and cousin.'

'So why didn't they marry?' Oriel asked faintly.

'Something happened, which is not my place to tell. But I saw the *Kyrios* curl into himself, cut himself off from his feelings. It was a hurt as deep as if the diva had stabbed him in the heart. Then off she went to America without so much as a glance over her shoulder. She had a recording contract, apparently, and an offer to sing in Las Vegas. There was talk of a Hollywood film, too.'

'But surely they could have maintained some sort of long-distance relationship?' persisted Oriel.

'If things had worked out differently, then perhaps. They were only young, after all. No harm in getting out there, seeing the world. Many young islanders do,' answered Mattias. 'No, that's why I said something happened. That woman dealt him a blow, from which even Damian couldn't recover. You see the scars on his face? They're nothing to the wounds he bears inside.'

Oriel listened in sombre silence, wondering what had occurred with Yolanda to make Damian so hurt inside. Perhaps he loved her too deeply to recover, she thought, with a pang of anguish in her heart. Mattias drew a deep sigh and the lines were deeply etched in his face.

'The *Kyrios* then took his *caique* and went far away from Helios, for a year or so, like some roaming gypsy, touring the waters of the world. I think that must have been when he met you. When he came back, he married Cassandra. And, of course, you know how that turned out. If only he had met a girl who had the sensitivity and kindness to salve his wounds. Cassandra may have been rich and beautiful but she never understood him. She was never the soul of kindness and she finally betrayed him.'

Oriel's heart filled with pain for Damian, for whom she had such confused feelings. 'Poor Damian,' she said, whispering his name with such emotion that Mattias gave her a speculative look.

'Listening to you talk to me about him, looking at you now that you know his whole story, there is no doubt in my heart at all that the *Kyrios* has met in you his saviour, with your bright hair like an angel, and that you reciprocate his feelings.'

Oriel swallowed a little lump in her throat. Such a sad story, but one upon which it hurt her so much to dwell. She didn't want to imagine another woman in Damian's arms. That oh-so-powerful love that had its roots in childhood. How could she possibly compete with that? She could imagine him and Yolanda as carefree young children, running right here on the beach, in and out of the waves, laughing and wrestling with each other, throwing seaweed, burying one another in sand, sharing secrets, feeling that intense closeness children sometimes share when they have suffered greatly in their short lives, as indeed both, in their different ways, had. It was undoubtedly a deep love Yolanda and Damian shared, and a deep hurt for Damian when it all went wrong. And now? Yolanda was certainly determined to rekindle their earlier passion. How could Damian possibly resist?

Mattias with his usual uncanny powers of perception seemed to intuit which way her thoughts were running. 'Their time is past, believe me. She dealt him a blow, one that has taken him a long time to recover from. Do you honestly think he would want to reopen that wound? Anyway, time is like a strong runner, swift but sure. And though he is a cruel master, a thief that robs us of our years, trust me when I tell you that he is also a generous friend that heals our wounds.'

Oriel shook her head sadly. 'You told me yourself that every time love shows up, Damian kills it in his heart and replaces it with short-lived passions. What he feels for me is pure lust and I'm afraid it'll never be anything else.'

'What I do know is that timing is everything. Many years have passed since Yolanda hurt him, and as for Cassandra's slight, it affected his pride more than his heart. Theirs was a marriage of convenience. Maybe *Kyrios* Damian thought he would never love again, but it is often when one has plumbed the depths of despair and drained the cup of sorrow, when hope is dead in our soul, that the sun rises and shows us a bright new day.'

Oriel smiled at him. This simple man of the sea had such a

beautiful way with words. 'You speak like a poet philosopher, not a fisherman.'

The old man nodded slowly. 'The wide horizons of the sea and the sky are the best teachers, I always think. Faced with the immensity and beauty of nature, you cannot but hope for a better future. Give the *Kyrios* and yourself a chance.'

'Damian frightens me. He's too extreme … too passionate. The way he reacted to seeing me with Vassilis wasn't balanced, wasn't fair.'

'Love isn't always fair. I would say it is more like a pleasant potion that whips the emotions into a sort of *ékstasi*. Sometimes it is an elusive *fántasma* that leads the feet of men into chill caverns of despair and across burning deserts of unsatisfied desire. In that state, how could a man's reactions be balanced?'

'He was hurtful. How could he … how could he think I was …?'

'Love is not always kind. Hurtful as a double-edged sword, it lacerates, it blinds the eyes. It is sometimes an intolerable *emmon*, an obsession which gives neither *eiríni*, peace, nor *chará*, joy …'

Oriel sighed. 'I don't know if I can bear it. My life was so orderly before, now it's all topsy-turvy. It really scares me.'

He turned to her and patted her arm. 'Let fate play its role, child … don't fight it. Come, I'll take you to my cottage. Everything will look better after a wash and some breakfast. Then you can decide what you're going to do next.'

'Are you sure? What will your wife say?'

'Anna will be delighted. She's been looking forward to seeing you again since the festival. Besides, with our boys married now and in their own homes, you will give her someone to fuss over.'

Óasi Cottage was, as its name indicated, a little oasis amid an arid expanse of land, its flat roof crowned with the tumbling red of bougainvillea. In its little garden, splashed with sunshine, were two olive trees and a lemon tree, to the trunk of which a goat was tethered.

'After my accident, we had to move because our old cottage was on two floors. The *Kyrios*, very kindly, had this bungalow built for us. It is so much more comfortable than the other place, with running hot and cold water and electricity that never cuts out. He's done much to modernize Helios, you know. Even though he faces many difficulties here, he never tires of trying to make things easier for the islanders,' Mattias explained.

They arrived to find Anna setting the table for breakfast under one of the olive trees. She was humming a little tune to herself and her round, tanned faced broke into a wide smile when Mattias and Oriel appeared. As they came closer and the woman saw the sorry state Oriel was in, she frowned, turning enquiring eyes towards her husband. The fisherman shook his head and gave her a meaningful look, which didn't escape Oriel's observant eye.

'Anna, you remember *Despinis* Anderson. She has had a small accident on the beach so I thought to bring her back here for a wash and a glass of fresh milk and one of your delicious *milópita*, apple turnovers.'

'Of course. *Kaliméra, Despinis,* how good it is to see you again. Welcome to our home. Please, come in.' She scurried forward and gripped Oriel's shoulders, giving her an enthusiastic kiss on each cheek.

Oriel almost laughed out loud at the uninhibited warmth of Anna's greeting and she smiled into the woman's eyes, which were so keen and bright amid the wrinkles. 'I ought to apologize for descending on you like this but Mattias very kindly insisted.'

'Apologize?' Anna waved her hand dismissively. '*Amésos*, I will bring you some clean towels. When you've had your wash, you must have some milk. It's come straight from our goat this morning,' she said and disappeared through a door into the back of the house.

Inside, the cottage felt warm and welcoming. The square entrance was flagged, its stone well polished. A flimsy voile panel was pulled across an archway leading into the living area. Oriel assumed it was there to preserve the intimacy of the household while letting the breeze in through the open front door during the hot summer months.

They walked through to find a sunny room, divided into two halves: the first contained a sofa and two armchairs covered in durable terracotta-coloured cotton; the other, a polished dining table, on which sat a salt-glazed jug of bleached-out dried seed heads and bright-hued flowers. The furniture was artisanal, old and well polished. Pewter wall-lights, cheap but in good taste, adorned the plastered walls, which were decorated in soft shades of peach and yellow.

The first thing that attracted Oriel's attention was a small bookcase that contained a collection of beautifully bound books. Mattias had followed her eyes. 'I have always been interested in the classics and our Greek myths, a passion I share with the *Kyrios*. He's brought all these books back for me from antique dealers on the mainland.'

Oriel drew nearer to the shelf and looked at the spines more closely. 'You've got quite a collection here.'

'While we were both convalescing from our wounds, the *Kyrios* and I spent many happy days reading Homer and the tragedies of Sophocles and Euripides.'

What had, at first, seemed a relationship that existed primarily because of their shared interest in diving – cemented further when one man saved the life of the other – now seemed to Oriel a bond that was even more multi-faceted and profound. No wonder Damian had confided in the fisherman: a strong friendship united the pair and she felt happy at that idea.

Now her eyes wandered to the wall beside the bookcase, on which hung a number of different-sized framed photographs of a younger Mattias, proudly holding the great sea monsters he had hunted over the years. Among them was a snapshot of him, Damian and Stavros: a beaming, happy Damian, before the accident. She thought back to the photo she'd spied in his study, showing him with his brother Pericles, and once again was struck by how much the young man had aged since their night in Aegina.

'That photograph was taken on the last trip we made to the Red Sea, before the accident. As you can see, we all look like we've put on some years since then.' Mattias sighed. 'But it could have been worse and I am thankful to God that we came out of it alive.'

'He looked so happy then. Life hasn't been kind to Damian.'

Mattias came to stand beside her. 'Yes, and that is why I think that you must talk with him and clear the air.'

She turned to look at him and gave a half smile. 'Let me think about it.'

'Very well, Oriel,' he agreed, but there was a determined gleam in Mattias's eyes as he fingered his beard pensively.

Anna was soon back, carrying a pile of fluffy towels. She handed a glass of water to Oriel, along with a fruit sweet in a crystal dish. 'It's our tradition in Greece to offer a visitor a glass of our delicious water and *koutalyú*.'

'Thank you, how very welcoming,' Oriel said as she popped a teaspoon of the gluey confectionery into her mouth. 'Umm … lovely! What is it?'

'Date and clove conserve.'

Grateful for the glass of cold water, she drank it in one go. She remembered how Damian had described the special taste of Greek water and it made her smile. 'Yes, this does taste exactly like your Greek air and light. So fresh and, as you say, delicious. *Efharisto*.'

'*To theó*.' Anna beamed at the compliment. '*Éla mazi mou*, come with me, I'll show you to the bathroom. Give me your dress. I will iron it for you and brush off the sand. It's so fine, here in Helios, it clings to everything.'

'Are you sure?'

'*Né, né fysiká se*, yes, yes, of course! It will only take a few minutes.'

Oriel thanked Anna, who bustled off with the dress on her arm, seeming to relish the task.

The bathroom at the back of the house was simple but functional and spotless. It smelt of the sweet, subtle fragrance of the roses that grew outside the window. Oriel caught a glimpse of herself in the wall mirror. Her face seemed longer, as though a weight was drawing it down. There was a minute trembling at the corners of her mouth and her eyes had an unnatural brightness to them, as though she were running a fever.

She had a quick wash using the hand shower in the bath and rubbed herself down briskly with one of the thick towels that Anna had given her, leaving her skin tingling and fresh. The hot water had loosened her limbs and her mind was beginning to stir actively once more. She took a comb from her canvas bag and ran it through her hair so that it gleamed like a long, pale-gold river, massing into curling sweeps at the sides and back. She examined herself in the mirror. Her face without make-up was a little pink after the stimulation of the shower, which had brought much-needed colour to her pale cheeks. Her body, too, held a roseate glow from the hot water and the brisk towelling afterwards.

Suddenly she couldn't help thinking of Damian's nakedness. And as the memory swept through her, she wrapped her arms around herself, feeling in those pleasure centres of her body the glow that had not yet waned. Her heart beat fast and her senses swam just to think of the intimate secrets she had shared with him. Oriel was swept from head to toe by a longing to see him – to feel him … love him … and be loved by him – a torrent of strong, sensual feeling over which she had no control. Then she berated herself for her reckless wantonness.

How can I protect myself from getting hurt if I continue to follow the call of my body and my heart?

Oriel turned sharply away from the mirror and quickly put on her dress, which Anna had left just outside the door, refreshed and ironed. Now that she was presentable again there was no longer a trace of self-pity in her thinking. That was over, she had regained her outward poise.

'You look like a different person,' Mattias beamed when she joined them at the breakfast table in the garden.

She laughed. 'I feel like a different person. Thank you so much.'

'And now you must have some of our own goat's milk, none of this homogenized stuff they sell you in Athens,' Anna told her, pouring Oriel a large glass and setting it in front of her.

'Is it safe to drink raw milk?'

Anna laughed. 'Yes, of course, so long as it's boiled before you drink it. Most of the islanders drink milk from their animals. Our goats are fed on pasture.'

Oriel ventured a sip. It had an odd, distinctive flavour and was much creamier than the milk she was used to drinking.

Mattias smiled at her. 'You don't need to drink it if you're afraid, or don't like it.'

'It's definitely different, but I like it. I could get quite addicted to the taste.'

'Some have cow's milk, which is delivered every week from the mainland to the few fancy villas on the island, but they're missing out. I can vouch that raw goat's milk is a cure for all sorts of ailments. Ear infections, asthma, allergies … you name it.'

Oriel took a few more sips. 'So Helios does have some modern help from the mainland?'

'Some.' Mattias nodded. 'But we like to be as self-sufficient as possible. The old ways were fine up to a point.'

Anna poured some more milk into Oriel's glass. 'Our fridge used to be the nearest well, or the sea even, into which we lowered bottles and perishables. Our grannies were our washing machine, in some ways better than today's electric ones and glad for the money, too,' she chuckled before moving away to the oven.

'But that sometimes proved unhealthy with children,' qualified Mattias. 'They could catch illnesses like ringworm or dhobi's itch from badly washed clothes.'

Anna returned with a tray, which she set down on the table, and emptied fresh hot pastries on to a wooden board. 'I can tell you, the housewives of Helios today bless the *Kyrios*, who has brought in modern amenities like butane gas, insect spray and washing soap. And of course the island's telephone system … a real godsend.'

Seated in his chair, Mattias looked up at his wife affectionately. 'Here, taste one of Anna's *milópita*, the best on the island.'

Oriel hadn't really eaten since the few *mezedes* she had shared with Vassilis at Limenarkhees. She had hardly touched the food that had been served up to them at dinner, her appetite having been dampened by the appearance of Damian. So it was with relish that she ate Anna's delicious, warm apple turnovers.

Once she had finished, Anna started to clear the table, refusing Oriel's help, and then she and Mattias were alone again. Mattias lit a cigarette and leaned back in his chair.

'What do you intend to do now?'

'I don't know. I can't go back to Heliades, that's for sure, but at the same time I'm bound by contract to finish the job, which means that I have to stay on the island. Anyway, I want to see it through. I'll never have another opportunity like this. It's every archaeologist's dream site.'

Mattias nodded and brought out his pipe. 'Indeed. *Tóra éfages to vódi, tha afíseis tin ourá*, now you've eaten the ox, you cannot leave the tail.' He pushed some tobacco into the bowl of the pipe. 'Well, I hope you will not be upset with me when I tell you that I have taken the liberty of ringing the *Kyrios*. He was very relieved to know that you're safe with me here. He will be coming over at midday.'

Oriel felt her throat go suddenly dry and her pulse quickened. 'Why did you do that, Mattias?' She sighed and then quickly pulled herself together. 'I suppose one way or another I had to see him and it's probably better to see him here rather than at Heliades. I really cannot bear to go back there again.'

'He sounded very upset on the phone.'

'Well, it's all of his own making.'

'Maybe, but we Greeks always say: a heart that loves is often unreasonable.'

'Damian doesn't love me, we hardly know each other. He lusts after me. That's more the truth of it.'

Little devils danced in Mattias's grey eyes. 'And is that the way you feel about him too?'

Oriel evaded his gaze and shifted uncomfortably in her chair. 'I don't know how I feel about Damian.' She shrugged. 'All I know is that I was foolish enough to give in to the chemistry between us and I got myself burnt. It serves me right. You say he's finished with Yolanda but, I'm telling you, the way they were together yesterday demonstrated the reverse.'

Mattias shook his head and grinned as he lit his pipe. '*Aman!* You and Damian are as stubborn as each other. I've already told you, I'm sure Damian loves you. I think that it was love at first sight for you both all those years ago and you just need to recognize it.'

Nevertheless, Oriel stuck to her guns doggedly. 'I don't believe in love at first sight and, anyhow, that can't be real love because it means you're falling in love with someone's appearance, not their character. And that is exactly what happened with me on Aegina. He looked like a Greek god appearing from the depths of the sea in the moonlight, at a time when I was hurting. What do you expect?' She sighed hopelessly. 'And he still looks like a Greek god, despite the shark's best efforts.'

Mattias eyed her sideways through a wisp of smoke. 'No one believes in love at first sight … until that special person comes along and steals your heart.'

'Maybe, but then you must be sure that you're seeing that person clearly and not with blinkers.'

'Just give him a chance, Oriel, give him a chance. You wouldn't be talking like this if you hadn't seen him with Yolanda yesterday, and he wouldn't have been so hurtful if he hadn't been jealous of Vassilis Markopoulos.'

'Maybe,' Oriel said pensively, wondering where this tangle would end, then adding to herself, *And what about his crazy cousin? I could never cope with that.* She felt her panic only rising at the thought of meeting Damian again, and part of her wanted desperately to run away. But she wasn't a quitter and there was nowhere to hide on this island, where she was a stranger. Still, something more powerful than panic held her there – something that was in her heart, clamouring for recognition. And it would not be quietened …

* * *

When Damian walked through the gate, Mattias and Oriel were still sitting at the breakfast table and Anna had gone into the house. That morning he looked something of a brigand, lean and fit in his well washed shabby jeans and open-necked shirt; his thick dark hair ruffled by the morning breeze. However, his grey eyes were sunken and she could see the new ravages in his face from the fight. It was a strange colour, as though a deathly paleness lay under skin that was usually almost as brown as that of a field worker, and the right side of his jaw was swollen under the dark shadow of a nasty bruise.

'*Yassou,*' Mattias called out to him.

Damian smiled lopsidedly and waved. '*Yassou,* Mattias.'

Oriel was intensely aware of the resolute power in his tall figure as he walked towards them and she rose automatically.

'You look terrible, Calypso,' he said, coming up to her. His grey pupils seemed even paler today in his saturnine face as they slipped caressingly over her.

'So do you,' she replied in a flash, green eyes lifting up to the frowning face and glaring at him.

Damian took Oriel's hand and covered it with both of his for a moment, holding her gaze as firmly as he held her hand. His old charming smile was back. 'Shall we go for a walk?'

Mattias pulled himself out of his chair slowly and grabbed his stick. 'You can stay here, if you like. I'm going fishing and Anna is inside, cooking tonight's supper. You'll be quite private,' he told them.

Picking up her bag, Oriel turned to the fisherman. '*Efharisto*, Mattias, but we'll go for a walk. I need to stretch my legs.'

'*Parakaló*.' Mattias gave a short nod and went off to collect his fishing gear, leaning on his stick.

Damian made a move to take Oriel's arm but she drew away from him determinedly and took the lead. He strolled nonchalantly behind her and, as they came to the gate, he asked: 'Would you like some lunch?'

'I've just finished breakfast, thank you.'

'The Jeep's parked outside. I brought a picnic in case you were hungry.' He hesitated. 'I know a sandy beach sheltered by pines, which goes on for a mile or so. It's a pleasant walk. Not many people go there because the sea is quite rough and it's not advisable to bathe there.'

They walked towards the Jeep. Damian held the door open for her but Oriel hesitated. Her heart felt as if it were beating in her throat. Did she really want to go to an isolated place with Damian? Could she trust being alone with him?

'What's wrong, Calypso, don't you trust me?' There was a sudden steely note in his voice as though he had read her thoughts. Oriel gazed up at him. His mien had grown stern and she was aware that, despite what had gone on between them, he was still almost a stranger to her and the breadth of his shoulders and the bold strength of his features held the power to unnerve her.

She stifled a bitter laugh. 'Trust, Damian? You have the nerve to speak about trust?' Her eyes were charged with hurt and disdain. 'What is trust to you when it only takes suspicion, not proof, to destroy it?'

Damian stood there a moment considering her question, a nerve moving in his cheek like a tic. Then he spread his hands in a gesture of appeal, a tortured expression on his face. 'We can't discuss this here. Let's go somewhere quiet where I can explain.'

No matter what Mattias had advised, Oriel wanted to delay the discussion, delay the moment when she would be alone with Damian; escape the feelings, the sensations now rising in her, despite the anger, despite the hurt, all frightening in their implication. She didn't know whether she had the strength or the will to resist him, but one thing was certain: she had to try.

Closing her eyes against the undeniable attraction of his sensuality, she turned away. 'I'm sorry, I shouldn't have agreed to see you,' she said, biting her lip. She took a few steps to the edge of the cliffs, trying to put some distance between them, silently concentrating on the view. The scenery was painted in vivid colours. The midday sun was high, the splendour of the light defying all comparison. A salty breeze blew off a sea studded with little, white-sailed *caiques* and motor boats, and the tufts of the isolated pines that indented the rocks stood out against the same azure-blue, soaked in a golden clarity so unlike the confusion of her own thoughts.

'Calypso, please let me to speak to you.'

Oriel turned back to face him and, adopting a defiant countenance that she was far from feeling, she replied: 'I have nothing to say to you.'

If that were the case, why didn't she feel anger or contempt towards this man? Why, instead, did she feel this disturbing sense of compassion? Compassion? Sympathy? Or was it something else entirely; something she wanted to ignore, to smother, to eradicate from her heart?

Damian came towards her slowly, his gaze so hot and intense that Oriel was filled with conflicting sensations. On the one hand she was rooted to the spot, a prisoner of those searing molten eyes that were turning her inside out and, on the other, she wanted to turn and run as fast as she could. His hands moved down to her shoulders, drawing her towards him.

She felt the heat flood her face as she finally gave in to her outrage. 'Let me go, Damian Lekkas, let me go!' she cried out, wrenching herself away.

His hands slipped gently down her arms, his voice soft and low. 'But I must speak to you. Can't you grant me one last favour? Come, let's go for a walk on the beach, it's such a lovely day.'

'You're insane to think that I will go anywhere with you after your incredible behaviour.'

Damian's air of tender pleading gave way to the old arrogance; he smiled with a flash of strong white teeth. 'Then I shall carry you. Take your choice, Calypso, for I mean what I say. I intend to have a talk with you, one way or another.'

She flushed again, those words sending a sprinkle of awareness skittering through her and, in spite of her deep anger and passionate resentment, her heart stirred, pounding so loudly at this familiar audacity that excited her so, she thought he must hear it. Her breast rose and fell on a sharp breath and she felt herself wavering. His hand tightened on her arm.

'Come, Calypso.'

Oriel dropped her gaze to his chest, unable to look at him any more. He was making this so hard for her: she loved to be called Calypso, loved the way he looked at her; it filled her with purring warmth. Confused by the wrangle of emotions churning inside her, gently she pulled away from him and returned her attention to the view.

They were silent for a long moment and she sensed that he had retreated. Finally, she turned back to look at him and her heart gave a painful squeeze. Damian was leaning against the Jeep smoking, his wide shoulders hunched, jet-black head lowered in contemplation of his shoes. He looked oddly vulnerable, standing there alone, as perhaps, she realized, strong men had to be if they were to maintain an appearance of strength.

'Well,' she said, speaking as evenly as she could, trying to subdue the tumult within her. 'What is it you want to say?'

Damian lifted his head slowly; Oriel had never seen his grey eyes so dark – they looked almost charcoal, like tarnished silver. 'Simply that I wish I'd bitten my tongue before saying the things I said to you yesterday.'

Her eyes widened and she caught her breath again, but answered bitterly, 'It's rather late to think of that.'

'Is it too late? If I ask your forgiveness …'

'Forgiveness? I don't understand you. You said the most vile, horrible things to me.'

'I admit it. But you don't understand. I was not myself … I was all worked up …'

'What about?' Oriel knew the answer but she wanted him to explain himself properly.

He gave her a defensive glance. 'I was half mad with jealousy when I saw you in Vassilis's arms after … after you'd let me make love to you the night before.' His jaw hardened and a muscle in his scarred cheek twitched. 'That wasn't me.'

She raised an eyebrow coolly. 'You were jealous of Vassilis, yet you were there with Yolanda,' she stated. 'Why is it that Greek men find it so easy to adopt double standards?'

Damian ignored her jibe and gave her a long hard stare. 'I wasn't there with Yolanda, I came there looking for *you*.' He muttered an oath under his breath. 'Is that what you thought? Is that why you were so distant with me? I see ...'

Oriel digested this for a moment, wondering if it were true. Even if it were, it still didn't prove that he was finished with the singer. She looked at him with green eyes that held an inscrutable expression. 'You accused me of ... of ...' She couldn't bear to think of what he had insinuated, let alone repeat what he had said to her.

'Yes, yes,' he interrupted, running a hand through his hair. 'I said some cruel things. I lashed out at you because I was so miserable. I wanted to hurt you, to ease my own pain. Humans are like that, Calypso. God forgive them.'

He sounded as if that explained everything, and it did, of course ... if he loved her. Oriel went very still, every sense on red alert. Did Damian love her? Was Mattias right about his friend? She didn't want to ask herself that question really – she didn't want to know. It would be too easy, far too easy. Perhaps he could love her, but he wouldn't let himself ... Or was that just her hopeful imagination? No, she preferred to think the worst of Damian; that way, her pride would protect her from being hurt, keep her away from this man who just had to look at her for her bones to turn to water and her brain to mush so that, flooded with a chaos of irrational feelings, she became blind, wanton and weak.

'I will naturally honour my contract,' Oriel told him, her voice a little unsteady, 'but on one condition.'

Damian puffed on his cigarette and his eyes narrowed. 'Which is?'

'I will not live at Heliades, I'll move into the staff house today.'

Damian lifted his eyes to the sky. '*I mitéra tou Theoú na me voithísei!* Mother of God, help me! I have already told you that it is not a place for you.' He spread out his hands in an emphatic gesture. 'It is very primitive.'

Oriel looked at him apprehensively. 'I don't care. There's *no* way I'm going to spend another night at Heliades. Anything is better than that.'

His eyes glinted darkly in the sunlight while he scrutinized her face for a few seconds. 'Will you at least come with me to visit the staff house before making up your mind?' he asked quietly.

'It'll make no difference.'

Damian sighed. 'Mattias told me about the cage of birds. I'm sorry I didn't get the chance to speak with Helena. My cousin is an invalid, confined to a wheelchair with not much else to do, or think about, than play harmless tricks on the people she's jealous of.'

Oriel's mouth tightened. 'Harmless tricks? You mean sick ones.'

'Sick, if you prefer, but that is what she is: a sick woman,' Damian persisted grimly, ignoring her pointed remark. 'But these actions of hers are still harmless if you accept them for what they are: unpleasant but not dangerous. Helena is not wicked, just a very unhappy woman whose mind sometimes goes off-balance. At the end of the day, restricted as she is, she's powerless.'

'She gets Beshir to do all her dirty work,' Oriel shot back, her green eyes hot and bitter.

Damian winced but didn't try to defend him. 'I will keep an eye on Beshir in the future.'

'It still won't make a difference. I'm not going back there, full stop.'

'All right, we'll visit the staff house. But I'm warning you, when you see how basic it is, you may well want to reconsider your decision. Maybe I can come up with another solution. Let me think about it.'

Suddenly, as they were talking, a silver-and-black Bugatti came tearing along the road, then stopped abruptly with screeching brakes a few metres away. Oriel tensed as she watched Yolanda alight, her gleaming brown legs and dazzling white smile in themselves seeming to proclaim her international stardom. But the singer only had eyes for Damian and was apparently oblivious to Oriel's presence.

She was wearing a white halter-neck jumpsuit that set off her tan and figure to perfection. Her shiny black hair was loose and it flowed like a glossy river down her half-naked back. In the bright sunshine she looked like a luscious velvety rose: dark crimson, heady with fragrance. She took one's breath away, thought Oriel – the flush of her flawless skin, the perfection of her make-up, the enormous sultry eyes, glowing with a million secrets. The diva seemed like the very embodiment of the perfect woman: incredibly sexy, vibrating with exquisite passions denied to ordinary mortals. No wonder men lost their minds over her.

As Yolanda reached them, Oriel realized that the singer wasn't so oblivious to her presence as she was making out. She could feel hostility radiating from the diva although, if Damian's impassive expression were anything to go by, he seemed unaware of the undercurrents. Or was he? Oriel thought she could detect a slight tightening of his jaw as Yolanda approached.

'*Yassou*, Damian, *tee khanees, agápi mou*?' Yolanda threw a possessive arm about Damian's neck and kissed his cheek lingeringly. He pulled away from her embrace with a little less force than Oriel would have liked, considering she was standing next to them both. By now, the singer's total disregard for her was becoming extremely rude. Couldn't Damian see that?

'I was worried sick, *mathia mou*.' Yolanda's hand was holding Damian's arm, her body still far too close to his. 'I tried to ring several times last night but you weren't picking up. I nearly came over to Heliades but it was so late … and I didn't want to disturb Helena, of course.'

Damian's face was unreadable, guarded, as he smoothly brought Oriel into the conversation, moving stiffly away from Yolanda as he did so. Somehow, however, his cautious demeanour only helped confirm Oriel's fears that he was feeling compromised, that he had something to hide.

'Oriel, you know Yolanda, don't you?' He made no reference to the concern the singer had expressed, clearly not wishing to discuss his fight with Vassilis.

Oriel held out a hand to the exquisite diva but Yolanda ignored it, instead saying acidly: 'Ah yes, you were the reason for that exhibition last night. *Sing-hariteeria*, congratulations! I expect you're proud of yourself.' Her almond-shaped eyes moved over Oriel's face. 'Quite a boost for your ego, I imagine, to have two men fighting over you in public.'

But Damian didn't give Oriel the opportunity to answer.

'Yolanda, that's enough.' His voice was forbidding – the dragon flared in his eyes – although it didn't seem to have the slightest effect on the singer, who continued to glare at Oriel scathingly. 'No one else shares any blame in what happened,' he added gruffly.

Yolanda pouted her scarlet mouth at him. 'Really, *agápi mou*? You men really have no idea at all, do you? You're such lambs! But what a tragedy that two old friends were at each other's throats last night.' She darted a vicious look in Oriel's direction. 'And I know who *I* blame for that, no matter what you say.'

Damian ran a hand over his tired eyes and sighed. '*Gia ónoma tou Theoú*, oh, for God's sake, Yolanda! Let it go, will you?'

'I was only thinking of you. Who's going to look out for you otherwise?' Her eyes, gazing up at him, were now liquid pools of tenderness.

'I'm perfectly capable of looking after myself, as you well know, Yolanda.'

Oriel stood stiffly, feeling humiliated and quietly furious. Why was he even listening to her? Every time the little witch so much as curled a beckoning finger in his direction it was as if he became enslaved all over again. Was this a pattern – a dance – that had controlled their lives since childhood? Would it ever end? She, for one, wanted no part in it.

Yolanda's pink tongue moved over her red lips and she broke into a mischievous smile. 'I think you should drop your little intern back at work and come join me at the beach. We could go to our favourite place. Remember the last time, *agápi mou*? ... What we did there?' Her words held such passionate promise that Oriel found herself blushing with mortification.

'Don't, Yolanda,' said Damian, his voice a blunt warning. 'And *Despinis* Anderson, for your information, is the senior archaeologist on my team. You should show more respect.'

Yolanda shot Oriel a vitriolic glance. 'If you say so, *agápi mou*.' She laid a jewelled hand on Damian's arm. 'Will I see you tonight?'

'Tonight? Where?'

'At the Zervoudakis.'

'No.' Yolanda waited for his explanation, but he didn't offer one.

'Since when have you become such a stick in the mud?' The

singer's eyes snapped, though her tone was still teasing.

Seeing his scowl, she blinked her jet-black eyelashes at him. 'Don't look so cross. I say the truth, *zoi mou*. You know something? I hardly recognize you these days. You need to let go a bit more, have some fun.' As if she sensed her words were getting her nowhere, Yolanda suddenly changed tack, softening as she did so. 'But forgive me … the last thing I want is to anger you, Damian. You upset yourself enough yesterday. Let there always be peace and love between us.' She gazed up at him, her eyes shimmering with a kind of feverish insistence as Damian gripped her arm and said something to her in a low murmur.

But Oriel had had quite enough. She turned away and took a few steps along the road. As she did so, she couldn't help hearing Yolanda purring, 'I won't go to the Zervoudakis' party tonight, I don't care to go alone … Let's have a private party of our own. Stay with me tonight, *agápi mou*. I want you with me. *Mou éleipses*, I miss you.'

She didn't hear Damian's answer but she looked round to see him escorting Yolanda back to the Bugatti, his face unreadable. Then he stood for a moment, watching the convertible moving away into the distance, before slowly retracing his steps towards her.

'Let's go to the staff house,' he said a little brusquely, and Oriel got stiffly into his Jeep. Once seated beside her, he gave her a sideways glance, 'You mustn't take any notice of Yolanda's direct way of talking.' He smiled awkwardly. 'She grew up rather wild, without much guidance, and now she is spoiled by her public. I'm afraid fame has gone to her head a little.'

He was making excuses for her! Oriel swallowed a sharp pang of jealousy that tasted like poison. 'You don't need to apologize for her,' she said curtly. 'I'm quite thick-skinned, you know.'

They drove in silence for a while. Oriel watched Damian's long, elegant hands manipulate the wheel, hands that had caressed her so expertly. Anger and desire collided painfully inside her. Why did he make her feel this way? 'At what time are we starting tomorrow?'

'Early, but we won't be going to the usual place.'

'What do you mean?'

'I've arranged for us to go over to Delos. If your friend at the Bodleian is right, the Roman trader, Marcus Sestius, retired there after his business collapsed, along with the seaport of Helice. So it's a nice piece of the jigsaw, *né*?'

Oriel nodded, relaxing slightly. 'What about the works I was contracted for? Am I not needed at the temple site?'

'Vassilis, Stavros and the boys will still be working on that. I'd rather have your efforts concentrated on the undersea excavation, anyway. That's what you were brought here to do. So, as there's no diving until the site has been inspected by the Ministry, we may as well continue our research on Delos. Vassilis's new equipment needs time to get here from the States anyway.'

'Who's coming with us?'

Damian turned to look at her. 'It'll be just you and me. Is there a problem?'

Oriel shrugged in an effort to be casual, despite the sudden racing of her heart, but the colour in her face deepened. 'No, why should there be?' she replied, meeting his gaze with a defiant lift of her chin. Still, her mind was crying out, *You know what you're doing to me, and you're enjoying it.*

Damian nodded. 'Excellent. *Étsi óste na échei enkatastatheí*, so it's settled.'

'Delos is quite far. Are we going by plane?'

'No, by sea.'

'The dive boat?'

'No, we'll be taking my private yacht.'

Oriel was alarmed. 'So we'll be away at least for a couple of nights? How many nautical miles are we talking about?'

'Almost a hundred and fifty so, yes, it will probably be a little more than that.'

'What do you mean, a little more than that? I won't go then.'

Damian flinched slightly at Oriel's unequivocal answer. 'Are you so afraid of being alone with me, Calypso?'

Afraid? She was terrified. The mere thought of being alone, totally alone with Damian, even for an hour, threw her into turmoil.

'Don't flatter yourself, *Kyrios*,' she retorted, green eyes flashing daggers. 'I'm not afraid of you, I simply don't care to be alone with you. But I'm a professional and this new discovery is important, so you can count on me.' And to herself a scared and defeated voice whispered: *I've just signed my death warrant.*

He gave a brief nod and, at that moment, slowed the Jeep and turned off the coast road, pulling up in front of a roughly built, two-storey grey house that stood in a courtyard on a cliff, overlooking a most spectacular view. There was no garden, only a few scraggy pines and olives.

'We're here,' Damian announced, amusement hovering on his lips. 'Still want to go in?'

'Yes, of course,' Oriel said with conviction but, having seen the exterior, she wondered what the inside of the house would be like.

'Sure?'

'Absolutely.'

'Let's go, then. There'll be no one here at this hour. The men are all still on site,' he told her as he unlocked the front door.

Oriel stood in the hallway and looked around her. The place was clean and functional, denuded of the faintest hint of luxury. The walls were painted white with no adornments and, when she walked into the communal sitting room, the furniture appeared old and shabby. The contrast between this place and Heliades was shocking. Still, she had lived in accommodation that was much more basic than this.

'Having second thoughts?'

'No, not at all but, having seen your beautiful home, I think that a little more thought and effort should have been put into your staff house. After all, these men are your employees and the foreigners who come here are your guests.'

Damian shrugged. 'In Greece we live outside, *agápi mou*, and anyway, most of the men have homes to go to when they're not on duty. As for my guests, as you put it, they are very handsomely paid and this place is kept clean and has good electricity, and hot and cold running water.'

'Is there a kitchen?'

He gave her a look and crossed his arms. 'Of course, through there.' He pointed back towards the hall. 'They can cook their meals, but it's only a short walk into town to the shops and local cafés. They have a car at their disposal, plus the minibus to take them around. What more can anyone ask for?'

Oriel saw his point but refrained from making any other comment.

'The bedrooms are on the upper floor.' Damian led the way up the stairs. Eight doors opened off the landing. He pointed to one at the end of the corridor. 'That's the bathroom, which is shared by everyone.' He was watching her, probably expecting her to be dismayed, she thought, but Oriel just nodded.

Damian opened one of the doors on the landing. 'This is your bedroom. It has a lock on it, which I would advise you to use. Some of these men like to drink. They're rough but they're good men and I wouldn't want ...' The hint of a smile touched his mouth. 'Well, you're a big girl, you know what I mean.'

Oriel glared at him, eyes blazing. Was there no end to his sarcasm?

'I can handle myself,' she said with confidence. 'I've met your men and they're gentlemen. They wouldn't take advantage of me.'

The look he gave her was enigmatic. '*Anarotiémai*, I wonder,' he said softly, his eyes skimming down her with deliberate provocation.

She studiously ignored him, turning away to survey the bedroom. Like the rest of the house, the room was spotless with basic necessities. There was a single bed with a white sheet thrown over it and a blanket folded at its foot, plus a bedside table with a small lamp. In lieu of a cupboard, there was a rail for her clothes and, in the corner, stood a washstand with an old-fashioned jug, a basin and a pile of towels. Oriel's eye was drawn to a quaint rocking chair that stood next to the window looking on to the sea: the only item in the room with some charm, and it made the place oddly appealing. With a bit of colour – some pictures and nice curtains – this bedroom could be transformed into a cosy space.

'It's more than I expected,' she said. 'Thank you, I'll be very comfortable here.'

'Suit yourself, *agápi mou*. All I want is to please you.' A sparkle of amusement flickered in his eyes.

'I'll need my clothes. Could you give me a lift to Heliades so I can pack my case? I'll drive myself back.'

'Yes, of course *agápi*, it'll be my pleasure.' Damian looked at his watch. 'It's already five o'clock. Will you have supper with me?'

'No, no, thank you. I didn't get much sleep last night and if we have a long journey tomorrow, I'd prefer to have an early night.'

'Very well.' Damian smiled. It was a *we have all the time in the world* kind of smile, and Oriel retaliated with one of her own that said, *don't hold your breath,* which made his sardonic features break into a slow grin.

'I'll come and collect you at five-thirty. Pack a mixture of cool and warm clothes. It'll be very hot during the day and we'll be doing a lot of walking, so comfortable shoes, but at night it can be quite cold, especially at Delos. Don't worry about a sleeping bag, I have all that sorted.'

Damian's tall, broad figure passed in front of her out of the room and Oriel followed him, shivers of anticipation coursing through her as they left for Heliades.

She was surely in trouble now.

* * *

It was almost seven o'clock when Oriel got back to the staff house with her suitcase. The men had returned by then and gave her a polite welcome, seemingly on their best behaviour. Had Damian somehow found time to give them a briefing, she wondered. They were going into town for dinner and asked her to join them and, although she thought it would have been a good idea to bond with the crew, she declined their invitation on this occasion. Oriel had already stopped off on the way back from Heliades to buy some fruit, a couple of tomatoes, a loaf of bread and a chunk of feta cheese. In all honesty, she was looking forward to having the place to herself.

The house was very quiet. She unpacked, hanging her clothes on the rail and putting a few casual shorts, tops and jeans into a small case with her more personal belongings to take on the trip to Delos. Damian had insisted on comfortable footwear so she packed her deck shoes.

They had not spoken much on their return to Heliades in the Jeep, or while she gathered her belongings. Damian had waited in the *salóni* of her apartment while she did so, never explaining why he remained there, but Oriel neither cared to ask nor discouraged him. On the contrary, she was relieved that he was there in case Helena or Beshir made an appearance.

He had carried her luggage down to the Volkswagen, put it on the back seat and opened the door for her. Then, just as Oriel was getting into it, Damian's brows knitted together pensively, his large hand clenched on the handle. 'You've found a friend in Mattias. Unusual, because he doesn't take to strangers easily.'

'I like him too, he's an interesting man. He's very fond of you and grateful for everything you've done for him. You saved his life and built him a new house … that's quite something.'

A shadow had passed over Damian's eyes. 'If there is one thing I don't want from you, it's pity,' he said gruffly and before she'd been able to answer, he had shut the car door and stepped back, signalling their conversation was at an end. She had driven off, wondering at how important Damian's pride must be to him and, in response, another strong twinge of emotion jolted her heart.

Oriel went downstairs to make herself a cup of coffee and a sandwich. She was just filling the kettle when she heard a car draw up to the house. When she peeped out of the window she was horrified to see Yolanda, dressed to the hilt in a black chiffon mini dress. A few seconds later, the doorbell rang.

Oriel went to the door and opened it a fraction. '*Kaló vrády*, there's no one here. The men have—'

Without more ado, the singer pushed it open and walked in. 'It's you I have come to see, *Despinis … Despinis …*'

'Anderson,' Oriel supplied coolly, as she tried to curb the electric volts of fury coursing through her.

Yolanda gave her a long, sideways glance and laughed lightly. 'So, Damian Lekkas has lost his head over a piece of pearly fluff, whose great big Little Red Riding Hood eyes look at me as if I were the big bad wolf about to gobble her up.' The tone of her voice matched the cruel sensuality of her mouth.

Oriel marvelled at how dwarfed she couldn't help feeling in the other woman's presence. It was strange – Yolanda had a smaller frame than Oriel but such a strong personality shone from her that it filled the room in which they stood, making the place seem smaller because of the aura she radiated. Yolanda might have stepped from the frame of an El Greco painting; she could easily have hailed from a different time – totally at one with the pagan surroundings of Helios.

'You must be wondering why I've come to see you. Why I'm not scratching your eyes out, since it's obvious Damian is interested in you.'

Oriel opened her mouth to protest but the singer stopped her, raising a peremptory hand. 'Please, don't bother denying it. After all this time I recognize the signs,' she said, nodding her head knowingly. 'A man would have to be blind or emasculated not to notice your pale beauty, and I've been with Damian long enough to know that he has eyes like a hawk and the sensual instincts of a jaguar. He's noticed you, and has probably even bedded you.'

Oriel felt the colour mounting in her cheeks but she stared unblinkingly back at the Greek diva. 'If you really believe Damian is interested in me, I'm surprised you're so calm about it. That is, if you really are in love with him.'

Yolanda laughed, throwing her head back, and the sapphire-and-diamond earrings dangling from her lobes caught the light from the lantern in the hallway and shimmered as dangerously as the diva's eyes. 'At least you get to the point, *Despinis* Anderson. Yes, I'm in love with Damian, and he's in love with me. Our love story goes way back and though we haven't yet tied the knot, we're still lovers. But I'm not blind to his faults. I don't just love him, I know him and, most of all, I know how to handle him.'

'Meaning?'

'Damian is a womanizer. His natural charm and charisma attracts many young ingénues like you. Women have been trying to get their hands on him since we were teenagers.' Yolanda threw her a disdainful grimace. 'You're not the first pretty girl he's thrown his cap at, you know. But he doesn't usually go for insipid foreign blondes … the milk-and-cookies type is too bland for such a passionate man. That ninny-just-out-of-school appeal won't last with him.' She gave a contemptuous laugh. 'What can you give him that he won't soon find boring? You are like syrup when what he needs is pepper …'

This was awful. Oriel stared unblinkingly back at the singer, frozen, unable to find a response.

Yolanda moved closer to her with feline grace. 'But you see, although Damian wanders away from me occasionally to give you or some other blue-eyed woman a whirl, he always comes back.'

A stab of jealousy pierced Oriel but she managed to shrug. 'I don't believe I'd care to have a man like that. Besides, you're wrong about *Kyrios* Lekkas and me. I'm just an employee.'

'Believe me, after all this time I know the signs. Damian wants to take you to bed and that doesn't worry me, you see … we're lovers, *special* lovers.' Yolanda's small pink tongue outlined the full curve of her lips in the same sensual way it had that morning when she had clung close to Damian, and she laughed suddenly. 'He's a terrific lover, the kind of man no woman in her right mind would turn down, if you know what I mean.'

Oh yes, Oriel knew only too well what she meant.

'Damian likes his women hot and tempestuous and I give him all that. You wouldn't be able to hold him. You have no *alahtee*, no salt, as we say in Greek. You can't even begin to understand the Greek woman's capacity for passion.' Yolanda's hands stirred the air with emphatic gestures as she spoke, flames smouldering in her eyes. 'He's all fire, and there's something frosty about you, *Despinis* Anderson. You're all alike, you pale and insipid northern women, you run after our men but have about as much knowledge of their true nature as you have of a lion.'

Although she felt as if a steel door had slammed inside her, Oriel managed to force a smile. 'I don't know why you're telling me this, *Despinis* Christodoulou. I have no interest in *Kyrios* Lekkas and I'm not particularly fond of your island so you have nothing to worry about. As soon as the job is finished, I'll be off.'

Yolanda arched a speculative eyebrow. 'That's good. You're an intelligent lady, I wouldn't want you to get hurt. As I've said, Damian may stray from time to time but he comes back eventually because he is inside here …' She bunched the fingers of her hand together and tapped her heart. '*Eínai orycheío*, he's mine.'

'And what if he falls in love with someone else? I mean, really in love?' Oriel couldn't help saying. Her polite English coolness carried an edge with it – and a meaning Yolanda couldn't fail to understand.

Oriel saw the shock of the implication in her words drill through the dusky woman. The singer's dark eyes narrowed and she gave her a hard, calculating look. 'Then I might have to take more drastic action.' Although the smoky tones of Yolanda's cultured voice hadn't changed, Oriel recognized the almost *mafiosa* quality in her conclusion. She couldn't help noticing how Yolanda's expertly applied make-up concealed harsh lines around her mouth. That was a bald threat, one the diva made no effort to conceal.

Oriel didn't answer, she was too dazed by the whole conversation.

'I must go now. Damian is meeting me for a drink at Manoli's before I go out.' She gave a rueful smile. 'He doesn't like to be kept waiting, and I'm already late.' Yolanda placed a perfectly manicured hand on Oriel's arm. While her voice was saccharine, her eyes held no hint of a smile. 'I'm so glad we've had this little conversation … and that we understand each other.' With that, she was through the door and, before Oriel knew it, she was gone.

Oriel went back to the kitchen. Too angry to eat, she made herself a cup of tea then forced herself to have some fruit. She was aware that her hands were clenched, her nails digging into her palms. She didn't unlock her fists immediately but stretched out her arms and then, very slowly, tried to open one finger after another until she was able to spread them out completely. Then she opened and closed her hands a few times to work off the tension.

Yolanda was, Oriel decided dismally, a finished, polished work of art and she was in love with Damian, there was no mistaking that. She had shamelessly flirted with him that morning and now she had come, claws out, to defend what she thought was hers. There was hate in this woman, she felt, the kind born out of frustrated love. It was eating at her heart like a cancer, and it made her dangerous …

It had been difficult to see what Damian thought of such an open parade of emotions. He'd been as reserved as ever, and certainly annoyed with Yolanda that morning, even offering a sharp rebuke when the singer stepped over the line. But had his irritation not stemmed from the fact that he was feeling compromised? Caught between two lovers, just when he was trying to make up lost ground with Oriel …

If there had been the slightest remains of a voice in Oriel's subconscious clamouring her love for Damian, it was now stifled and it sank, mute, within her. It wasn't enough to love someone, you had to trust them, and the atmosphere between Damian and Yolanda that morning and the words of the diva this evening did not make for a feeling of trust.

It was a long time that night before Oriel found escape from her troubled thoughts in sleep. Too much had happened too soon, she told herself, making her feelings towards Damian such a tangle of emotions that the logical processing of them was impossible. Perhaps, given a few days, she might have been able to rationalize the whole situation. Still, would that be possible now that she was about to spend several days and nights in close proximity with this man, who played havoc not only with every cell in her body but also with her mind?

CHAPTER 11

Damian ran down the cliffs. He could see Oriel ahead of him, laughing and beckoning, but the faster he ran, the faster she did also. It seemed that she could run much more quickly than him, for he panted and sweated as he went, and sometimes lost her altogether.

He called out to her but she wouldn't wait for him. Then at last he caught up with her and she was not alone. Vassilis was there with his arm around her shoulders, laughing at Damian and calling him *énas anóitos*, a fool. Damian struck him and suddenly they were not Oriel and Vassilis but Cassandra and Pericles.

The agony of hurt smote him and he moaned as Cassandra and Pericles moved away from him before, once again, he saw Oriel. Now she was sitting on a rock, gloriously naked, her hair tumbling freely over her bare shoulders and chest in a torrent of moonspun silk. Under the night sky the water at her feet was liquid black, glistening like obsidian.

Oriel stretched out luxuriantly on the mossy rock, her flesh the colour of alabaster, provocatively exposing herself to him. When, with a languorous smile, she signalled him to come closer, Damian obeyed. He stood in front of her as though transfixed, like an artist memorizing each detail, his eyes languidly tracing her form: from her firm, ripe, rounded breasts with their dusky pink areolae, over her slender waist and smooth belly to the pale triangle between her white-skinned, slightly parted thighs. Her body was eloquent, and each feature of her face was beckoning him to explore her.

His appraisal finished, Damian continued to watch her with leaping eyes, knowing things about her, secrets they had shared. He sucked in a breath and his mouth went dry. He'd like nothing more than to kneel beside her and draw every luscious line on this canvas with his tongue. Lightning fires seared through him. He was ablaze, a mass of tension and desire; pulsing beats strained his muscles and his loins throbbed, desperately seeking release. Damian felt himself grow painfully harder, near breaking point, yearning to be a part of Oriel, at one with her.

And then, as he bent down to taste her, they appeared from behind a boulder – Vassilis, Pericles and Rob – and Oriel burst out laughing. Her laugh was so loud, it echoed over the cliffs, awakening the birds sleeping in the trees; they flew out shrieking, joining their eerie cries to the sounds of Oriel's mirth.

Soaking with sweat, Damian jerked awake, his eyes blank and staring, mouth bitter with bile. His ears were still full of the disquieting sounds of his nightmare and blood pounded in his head, while a strange pressure constricted his chest. He couldn't think or move, as if he were locked in a freeze-frame. Glancing at his aching hands he realized that he had curled his fingers into tight fists as if needing to strike someone. Shoulders drooping, he growled inwardly as he looked down at the hard, swollen evidence of his desire, his whole body a sea of pain, the bittersweet ache spreading through him like quicksilver.

The room was still and hot. He glanced at the clock on his bedside table: it was three o'clock. Shaking his head, he wiped the perspiration off his face and ran a trembling hand through his hair and down his unshaven jaw. Pushing himself up, he reached out for his cigarettes, snatched one from the packet and lit it. He inhaled deeply, filling his lungs with the nicotine, his only release for the time being. The most frustrating fact was that, from the first moment he knew Oriel had applied for the archaeologist job, he hadn't been able to take another woman to his bed. Why did she have such a hold over him even though they hardly knew each other? But he knew the answer …

'Oriel …' he whispered, and her name resounded like a soft agonizing sigh in the quiet bedroom, long and tremulous. She was such a contrast: there was a certain shyness about her; something in her eyes that spoke of innocence … until she was in his arms in the throes of passion, when she became a weaver of sensual fantasy. He loved her voice, full of layers, husky and supple with dips and slows. The intonation of her moans excited him even more: low, voluptuous and erotic. He had sensed the magic that first faraway night on Aegina and wouldn't have walked away if fate had not intervened. If only he hadn't seen that one misleading photograph.

A stroke of luck had brought them together again and he couldn't forget their night together in the Room of Secrets; he still trembled at the thought of it and knew he had to hold on to her, as passionately and fiercely as he could, for always.

He smiled grimly to himself. If fate did exist, then the gods must have been jealous of his fortune and had decreed otherwise. They had set the Moirae on him in the shape of Helena and Vassilis, and probably even Yolanda. Damian sighed. Of course he hadn't been blind to his former mistress's open overtures the previous day and knew how it must have looked in front of Oriel. He cursed under his breath.

It's funny how, sometimes, the people you'd take a bullet for are the ones behind the trigger.

Well, at least in the past he'd have felt that way about Yolanda. No longer.

He should have said something at the time, but what? He could read Oriel like a book and it had been neither the time nor the place to open that particularly sensitive subject. He would talk to her during their journey.

Still, he wished that he could set the clock back, wipe the slate clean, and that he and Oriel could start all over again – except he knew only too well that you can never go back. Once the wine is drawn, it must be drunk, goes the proverb. The torments of his past could never be erased, nor could his blindly jealous outburst with Oriel. It was done now.

Would she ever be able to forgive the cruel words he had said to her? Would she ever trust him again enough to surrender herself – her all – to him once more?

He had been mortified when Mattias had rung to tell him why Oriel hadn't spent the night at Heliades; mortified when he realized how unfair he had been towards her, condemning her once again without proof; ashamed at the unfounded thoughts his imagination had conjured up. He had galloped on his horse, Ánemos, all round the island until dawn to relieve the tension cramping every limb in his body. Still, Mattias's words had also been a relief: they signified that Damian had been mistaken and was responsible for all his torment, not Oriel.

He had expected Oriel to look tired when he saw her but had been shocked to see that she looked more than simply fatigued. She was pale, the smooth skin beneath her eyes smudged with purple shadows. Yet to him she still looked the most beautiful woman on earth and he wanted her with a craving that ran much deeper than anything physical; it was soul-deep ... beyond anything and everything he had felt before.

Still, gazing into her dark-green eyes, he'd read that she was nowhere near trusting him – she was afraid of him, he thought, afraid of the animal passion they shared, which she craved as much as he did. It meant that he had to tread carefully, bide his time, be patient, a trait which did not come easily to him; but Oriel was worth waiting for.

Life had suddenly become complicated for Damian. Romance was complex enough without tossing in vexing outside influences to muddy the waters. Already he'd had more than his fair share of pain during his lifetime. He had always dealt with the hurt by burying himself in his work: it had been his escape, his deliverance, his obsession. And now, having admitted to one obsession, he could recognize another.

Damian lay there brooding, lighting up one cigarette after another until finally, cursing again, he stubbed out the last and dragged a hand over his face. It was almost four-thirty – time to get up if he wanted to be on time for Oriel. He needed a shave and a long hot shower to get rid of the frustration, the sweat and the cigarette smoke, although Oriel had told him the other night that the smell of Gitanes, mingled with the fragrance of his aftershave and his maleness, turned her on.

Oriel turned on ... no, he mustn't think of that now ... mustn't think of the hot, erotic, scandalous things they did to each other when she allowed her emotions free rein. Damian swore under his breath. Desire twisted inside him like a hot knife. He was rock hard again ... No, he needed to pull himself together, he chided, as he headed towards the bathroom.

* * *

When Damian arrived at the staff house to collect Oriel, the stars had faded in the sky, leaving it a translucent blue that soon turned to lilac. In the pale light before dawn, Helios had a look of sleep about it; the dominant impression was one of deep abiding peace. It was misty; the birds were just beginning to whisper in the trees. Over the sea came a chill soft wind, sweeping in across the slumbering island.

Oriel had come down to the kitchen to have some breakfast. She was wearing khaki shorts with a striped, tone-on-tone, beige men's-style shirt, tied in a knot at the front, and a pair of comfortable canvas shoes. As the doorbell went, her foolish heart gave that too familiar leap and she looked out of the window to see Damian – handsome as ever – in sea-faded canvas shorts that showed off his lithe, strong thighs, and a red shirt with the sleeves rolled above the elbows of his muscular arms. As far as she could assess, the traces of the fight of two nights ago seemed to have almost vanished. Definitely the swelling had gone down, and the bruise was only a shadow on his jaw. Oriel put down the kettle she was about to fill and went to the door.

'Good morning, Calypso. Up and ready, I see.' Damian beamed as she appeared on the threshold.

'Good morning,' she replied, trying to ignore his smiling voice that seemed to imply so much more than the lightly spoken words.

'Sleep well?' His blinding, charismatic grin was unforgivable.

'Very.' It was a lie, of course. She'd barely closed her eyes through the long eternity of the night but she wasn't about to tell him that and changed the subject quickly. 'I was just going to have something to eat. Would you like to join me?'

'Thank you, but there's a delicious breakfast waiting for us aboard *Alcyone*. You might find that the food tastes better while you're watching the sun come up over the sea, instead of eating it in a dreary staff house kitchen. What do you think, eh?'

'I suppose so,' she conceded.

He pointed at a Havana-coloured backpack. 'Is that your bag?' he asked, picking it up.

'Yes, thank you.'

'Do you have any sun cream? You'll need it. There's barely any shade on Delos other than in the museum or the small cafeteria, where I would feel ashamed to take you. No roofs, hardly any trees.

It's a pretty stark place.'

'Don't worry, I have everything I need.'

'Well, don't forget your sunglasses, whatever you do. The light on Delos has a strange glitter that really dazzles the eyes. You'll understand why it's been described as the "whirling of silver wheels" when we get there. It takes a while to get used to, especially if you've got eyes the colour of yours.'

His gaze lingered on hers and she almost had to clear her throat. 'Thanks, I've got a pair of dark glasses in my bag.'

'Well then, if you're ready, *pahmeh*, let's go.'

Oriel followed Damian to the Jeep. He stowed her case in the back before helping her in, then walked round to slide beside her, his thigh brushing hers as he made himself comfortable. She shivered at this contact, but the early morning air was still cool and she pulled her collar up.

'Are you cold?' he asked and, without waiting for an answer, produced a plaid blanket from underneath his seat. 'Here, put this around you.'

'Thanks.'

They were off and Oriel nestled in the brown tartan throw, sitting quietly on the far side of the seat. As they drove, the darkness in the sky dissolved as though rinsed in light. Dawn was creeping up, and she watched the advancing glow of the rising sun as it illuminated the sky in the east. Damian drove silently, hands relaxed on the wheel. He seemed absorbed in his own thoughts and Oriel found herself wondering what they might be. What kind of a night had he spent? Had he just come from Yolanda's bed that morning? She stole a look. Like the rest of him, his profile was arresting, the lines clear and well defined on his face. She noticed that his complexion was paler than the usual deep suntan, and the scar across his cheek seemed more prominent.

'What are you thinking, beautiful Calypso.' Damian's voice broke through the stillness, taking her by surprise. He'd been so absorbed himself just now that she hadn't felt as if he was even aware of her.

'Oh, nothing.'

He raised his eyes heavenwards. 'Such a typical female answer! Why do women always say that when you ask them a question?'

Oriel shot him a wry look. 'I thought it was usually the other way round. Besides, isn't it better than saying "It's none of your business?"'

Damian didn't answer but his eyes briefly settled on her face. Confused suddenly, Oriel turned her gaze back to the road. She watched the beginning of the sunrise, like a lady's delicate white finger pointing across the sky in the east. Water and countryside, which had been soaked in blue light, were now wrapped in a pinkish glow.

'The dawn of a new day. Enjoy it.' Damian's voice was quietly husky, as though it came from a distance. Was there a double meaning in his words?

As if he'd read Oriel's thoughts, he reached over and took her hand. She pulled it away gently and pushed back a strand of hair that had flown across her face. Then she turned, meeting his gaze full-on. Damian was smiling and, for the first time since their argument she softened, venturing a small smile in return. 'I intend to,' she said slowly.

When they arrived at the marina Damian led the way from the quay on to the wooden jetty. Oriel could see Stavros waiting for them at the far end, on the forty-four-foot yacht, *Alcyone*, which rocked gently on the swell. '*Yassou*, Damian. *Kaliméra*, Oriel,' he said as he took the cases from Damian.

Oriel gave him a warm smile while Damian started issuing instructions.

'*Yassou*, Stavros. The camping gear is still in the Jeep.'

'*Den eínai éna próvlima*, no problem. I'll fetch it.'

Damian swung himself lithely into the cockpit and held out a hand to help Oriel step down to join him. '*Ela tohrah*, come on.'

White and silver, the *Alcyone* was a two-mast craft, small and sleek in comparison to the dive boat, *Ariadne*. This was no *caique* but the final word in compact luxury. Its name was painted in bold, black letters on the hull and it flew the blue-and-white Greek flag. There was plenty of space on the sundeck to stretch out and work up a tan, should one want to, and a canvas bimini sunshade, which could be extended over a table, was half stretched over a stainless-steel frame fastened above the cockpit. Oriel could imagine nothing nicer than relaxing in the shade on one of the orange-cushioned benches while looking out at some wonderful panorama, or dining at the handcrafted, teak folding table. Just now, it had been set for breakfast.

Damian took Oriel below deck, where polished mahogany panelled the living area, concealing an array of sophisticated electronics, including a music centre and a hidden bar. Overhead was a square Art Deco ceiling and on the walls were lamps with brass fittings. Glass-fronted cases of leatherbound books graced the walls behind the built-in sofas, which were set in a semi-horseshoe shape on each side of the saloon. A table stood in front of one of the sofas with two stools tightly fixed to the floor, creating a comfortable dining area for four. There was a kitchen in one corner that seemed, from Oriel's cursory glance, to be equipped with all the facilities required for modern cuisine. The room had been well thought-out, with no waste of space, and it was neat, functional and elegant.

The soft furnishings in shades of brown, gold and beige felt masculine in their conception, and the interior even smelt pleasantly of leather and fresh tobacco – warm and sensual – which she immediately associated with Damian's personality.

Oriel couldn't help smiling. 'It's beautiful. But I thought that we were going on an archaeological expedition, not a luxury cruise.'

'True, but there's no reason why we can't make the journey in comfort, eh?' His grey eyes sparkled with amusement. 'Besides, this boat has a nice shallow draft, which will allow us to explore the waters close to Delos,' he explained. 'That part of the Ionian is full of fascinating sites under the sea. You never know what you might stumble upon.'

There were two cabins, Oriel was relieved to note, each one tastefully furnished in the same neutral, masculine colours, with a double bed, dressing table and an en suite bathroom. It meant that if they had to spend a night on the boat, she would be able to shut herself away from Damian's male scrutiny. Inside, she smiled at the irony: the night before he had told her to lock her door against the men at the staff house and tonight she would be locking her door against *him*.

Stavros returned with the camping equipment, which he handed to Oriel. 'There's freshly baked bread and pastries in the warming oven,' he said as he untied the rope and tossed it to Damian. 'You'll find plenty of figs and apricots in the fridge. Have a good journey. Don't worry about the excavation here, I'll take care of it.'

'The people from the Ministry of Culture are coming to inspect the wreck site some time after the weekend, so we wouldn't have dived it before then anyway,' said Damian. 'But yes, do keep an eye on the team at the temple site. With Vassilis away, they'll need overseeing.'

Stavros raised a hand and nodded as Damian coiled the rope neatly before manoeuvring the yacht away from the shore. '*Efharisto*, Stavros. See you soon.'

The yacht set off, out of Helios's harbour, trailing foam just as the sun was coming up behind the horizon.

'If you'd like to stand next to the mast, you'll need to wear a harness as there are only two of us on board. In open water it's either the cockpit or being tied on, *né*?'

'Yes, of course. I am quite aware of the rudimentaries of sailing,' Oriel replied, a little miffed at his patronizing tone. Her evident irritation was met with a mischievous grin from Damian, as though he enjoyed seeing her nettled. While he went astern to the self-steering device fixed to the rudder, Oriel leaned into the comfortable cushions in the cockpit under the bimini and looked back at Helios as it diminished slowly into the distance.

Once they were out at sea Damian turned round and signalled to her, '*Éla*, Calypso. Come and feel the rays of the early sun on your face and the wind in your hair, *agápi mou*. You'll have a much better view of paradise from here.'

He looked formidable gripping the great wheel of his boat, strong legs braced against the deck, bathed in the glory of the sunrise. Even from the back, with his wide shoulders outlined against the dramatic sky, he appeared to Oriel a striking and masterful figure: haughty, almost unreachable, at one with the grandeur of nature in surroundings that suited him well. Apollo, the audacious god from whom no virgin was safe, came to mind. Oriel hadn't known that the silent physical presence of a man could be so overwhelming. Still, despite this apparent self-sufficiency, Damian carried an aura of loneliness as he stood there guiding his craft through the waters and her heart ached for this man, whom she hardly knew and yet with whom she had enjoyed such rapturous intimacy.

Oriel looked down at the sea, sparkling and dancing around the boat, feeling its restless buoyancy suddenly thrill through her veins. Her pulse quickened at Damian's invitation, although warning lights flashed amber. The idea of standing so close to him right now made her acutely nervous, even though that was the very thing she wanted to do. 'Maybe I should go downstairs and make us a cup of coffee.'

He looked at her speculatively over his shoulder. 'Once we're in open water I'll set up the self-steering and we'll settle down for breakfast. It won't be long now. *Éla matia mou*, come here.'

Oriel went on looking at the water. She didn't want him to perceive the internal battle she was having with herself. 'I'm quite happy where I am, thank you.'

Damian shrugged. 'Suit yourself. Have you ever handled a boat?'

'I've taken the wheel sometimes but I can't say I'm an expert, or that I'd be able to hold my own in a strong wind.'

His eyes glinted. 'I can teach you.'

'That's very kind, but maybe not today.'

Oriel waited for Damian to comment but he didn't. She turned away from him and they didn't talk for a while, soaking in the beauty of the hour, each absorbed in their own thoughts, the silence sympathetic to their mood. The sun was climbing into the heavens, its golden rays shining directly upon the water, beams diffusing themselves over the vista with a dense, coppery hue. The light grew brighter now, glowing on the ancient villages that clung to wooded slopes that clambered their way up into the jagged mountain peaks. It was like a flamboyant painting, with the sparkling Ionian, the olive-groves, a burning sun and a sky of illimitable blue.

Soon the coast became barer and more arid. The last of the islands, which lined the corridor between Helios and Delos like ancestral totems, was now vanishing into the distance. They had left behind all evidence of human habitation and now there was nothing but sea to look upon. They were going swiftly now, the water rushing along the sides of the boat.

Oriel's breath caught in her throat as, suddenly, Damian loomed large beside her. Before she could protest he had put an arm around her shoulder, drawing her to his side. '*Deíte!* Look!' he said, pointing ahead at the water. Two dolphins danced through the wavelets at the bow. They were quite close and she watched, fascinated, as they leapt out of the water in curves of inimitable grace. Dolphins dancing over an azure sea! It was a childhood dream come true.

'How beautiful,' she murmured.

'Shall we have breakfast? I've put the boat on autopilot.'

'Oh yes, please, I'd really welcome a cup of coffee.' She became aware of his hand on her shoulder and through her shirt the heat of his torso next to her breast flooded her with warmth. 'Are you sure you can leave the wheel unattended?'

'Don't worry, the sea's calm and we'll have our breakfast up here where I can keep a weather eye on it. You don't need to come down, stay and enjoy the view. I can manage on my own. I won't be long.' Damian half bent towards her then, seeing Oriel tense suddenly, he drew back. There was a momentary tightening of his jaw then he went below deck.

The air was still bracing and cold but the sun shone from a cloudless sky. The sea was as smooth as an ornamental lake and Oriel's eyes travelled the far horizon from east to west, slowly surveying the limitless expanse of water that glittered like a carpet of diamonds. She tried to concentrate on the view but it was hard to focus on anything when she was so aware of being alone on the vast sea, with an intensely disturbing man who did strange things to her body and mind. All at once she felt helpless: there was only one way this could end. Her head was heavy and yet light, and inside her every nerve quivered, humming with tension. Was that what she wanted? Oriel felt as uncertain as if she were standing at the edge of a high precipice and was being dared by fate to leap off.

Within a few moments Damian returned with a tray laden with a coffee pot, a bowl of fruit and two dishes: one piled high with several varieties of mouth-watering Greek pastries, the other with warm rolls and croissants. He placed everything on the table, where chilled butter and milk, sugar and an array of jams had already been set.

Oriel smiled and gave him a quizzical look. 'Croissants?'

'Just in case you aren't fond of our national pastries. Some people find them too sweet.'

Damian sat down opposite her under the canvas awning and

chose a fig from the fruit bowl. He set about peeling it before offering it to Oriel. 'The fig is a legendary tree. Volumes could be written about the stories and superstitions surrounding it.'

She took the fruit from him and bit into it. 'Thank you, these are really delicious. They taste like honeydew, and they're so much smaller and sweeter than the ones I've had before.'

'I'm glad you like my figs. They're called St Anthony. I brought the seeds back from Italy one year. It's the variety we keep for ourselves at Heliades.'

Oriel helped herself to another. 'I love figs but it's rare to find them in shops in England.'

'Fig trees are everywhere in Greece. Did you know that they're associated with Dionysus? According to Plutarch, a basket of figs was always carried in any procession that honoured him. And I bet you didn't know, the wood of the fig-tree was invariably used for statues of Priapus and his sacred phallus.'

Hearing the amusement in Damian's voice, Oriel steadfastly refused to meet his eye. Typical that he should allude in one breath to a god associated with drunkenness and a satyr who symbolized sexual desire. Eyes down, with a blush rising in her cheeks, she fought the flames Damian was trying to ignite. *He really is one-track minded.*

She felt his eyes intently upon her, as if reading her mind, though his voice was even as he went on. 'The fig tree is a lover of men. That is why we foster it. Besides food, it gives us shade and, when the leaves fall in winter, it allows the sunlight to percolate into our rooms. You'll never find evergreen trees planted near our windows. We know the value of sunshine. *Ópou o ílios baínei o giatrós den títhetai*, where the sun enters, the physician does not, we say in Greece.'

This short lecture had given Oriel time to recover from his mischievous teasing. She decided to change the subject before he had a chance to get on to Adam and Eve covering themselves with fig leaves – she didn't need to be reminded of the foolishness of tasting forbidden fruit.

'What's the plan? Where exactly are we heading?' Oriel asked him.

'We won't be able to make Delos tonight, so I thought we'd

stop for the night at Milos. It's seventy-three nautical miles from here. We'll anchor in the bay of Kleftico. It's beautiful and its sandy beach isn't accessible from land.'

'I've heard it's called Bandit's Lair. Was it a smugglers' den?'

'Yes, in the old days it served as a hideout for the pirates of Capsis and Barbarossa. With any luck, we'll be there by eight or nine tonight.'

'Aren't you being a bit ambitious? There's almost no wind at the moment.'

Damian shrugged. '*Dhen Peerahzee*, never mind. If the worse comes to the worst, we'll use the engine. Not as romantic, I admit. Then the next day we should reach Delos by evening. We'll camp that night. We've got sleeping bags with us. I'm afraid you might have to rough it for a couple of nights.'

'I'm not worried about that, I've roughed it before. I'm more concerned with the sailing part of it. Aren't the waters around the Cycladic Islands meant to be dangerous? Can you handle the boat if it gets really choppy? You'll be pretty much single-handed.'

Damian burst out laughing and shook his head. '*Gynaíka oligopistos*, woman of little faith, you really don't trust me, eh? *Sou eeposkhomay*, I promise that you have nothing to worry about. I've sailed these waters many times, and with smaller and less powerful boats. True, the Cyclades attract their fair share of rough weather now and then, when conditions can be really bad, but that's mostly when the *meltémi* blows, or when we feel the aftereffects of an earth tremor somewhere near Kythira. I've studied the weather forecast and it looks fine.' He arched an eyebrow. 'Reassured now?'

Oriel remembered now that Mattias had told her that after his breakup with Yolanda, Damian had spent a year sailing around the Mediterranean. She laughed, feeling a little foolish. 'That's good. Yes, of course, totally reassured …'

'Look, if I felt for one minute that I was putting your life in danger I would never have suggested you accompany me on this expedition.' His mouth quirked with amusement as he poured himself a second cup of coffee and lit a cigarette. 'There are plenty of other ways I could engineer time alone with you if I so chose.'

Oriel silently took a mouthful of her coffee. All of a sudden she felt like a nervous horse, ready to bolt, but there was nowhere to run to on the sailboat so she would have to stay calm. She returned to safer, more impersonal ground. 'Tell me about Delos. I've always wanted to go but I never got round to it that student year I worked in Greece.'

'Tourists are allowed on the island but where they can go is limited. It's of great value to the entire world, not just to Greece, because of its vast array of archaeological finds. UNESCO has made sure that the sites and ruins are protected from harm.'

'I thought getting permission to stay there overnight was almost impossible, especially as all food and provisions have to be shipped in. No one actually lives there, do they?'

'Only those who work on the sites. As archaeologists, they've issued us with a pass. Don't worry, *agápi mou*,' Damian smiled, eyes twinkling, 'if we're short of food we can always dive for our dinner.'

Oriel shot him a quizzical look. 'I thought you just said you weren't allowed to fish around Delos.'

Damian burst out laughing. '*Touché!* You are too quick for me, *koukla mou*.' He drained his cup and stubbed out his cigarette before rising from the table. 'Right, let me see to the sails. As soon as we're on an even course I'll engage the auto-helm and then we can talk.'

'Can I help at all?'

'*Oyhee efharisto*, no, I don't need help. Technology is so advanced in these boats nowadays that almost everything is done with the press of a button. Come, I'll show you.'

Oriel joined Damian at the wheel and he began to point out the features of the boat's autopilot system. The faintly musky masculine scent of his body and the warm air caressing her neck from his breath as he leaned close to her to explain what he was doing made her feel strangely dizzy, and she shivered involuntarily.

He paused. 'Still cold?'

Their gazes locked and held. All at once the atmosphere seemed to have become highly charged with sexual tension. 'No ... Yes, umm ... I'm fine,' she mumbled, dropping her eyes to the wheel. 'I'll clear the breakfast away.'

'You don't need to do that.'

'I know, but I'd like to make myself useful.' Without waiting for a reply she piled up the tray that Damian had left on the side and hurried below deck.

When she came back up, Oriel found that he had taken off his T-shirt and had laid a chart on the table. As she was about to take her place opposite him he said, without lifting his head: 'Why so far, Calypso?' She recognized the teasing in his voice. 'It'll be much easier for me to explain things if you're sitting here.' He gestured to the empty space next to him.

Maybe it would be easier for Damian but it certainly wasn't going to be easy for her to concentrate on his explanation, having him sitting there next to her, half naked. Oriel could imagine him taking her hands and drawing her against his bare chest. She would be lost, of course; she wouldn't be able to hold out. But she wasn't going to give him the satisfaction of knowing that, even if he already suspected it, and reluctantly she took her place beside him.

'I'm looking at the best way of entering Delos,' he told her, his eyes still fixed on the chart in front him. 'Although it offers a fairly safe harbour once it's reached, the fierce waves of the Aegean break on its northern shore. The island is like a ship in a rough sea.' Damian smiled, as though to himself. 'Perhaps that's how the legend arose that Delos was an aimlessly floating rock in the Aegean.'

'It was to do with one of those females fleeing the advances of Zeus, wasn't it? What was her name, Asteria?' asked Oriel.

Damian leaned back against the cushions with one arm stretched across the back of the seat. 'Exactly. She leapt into the sea, where she became an invisible island. Her sister Leto wasn't so lucky. She was impregnated by Zeus, which of course made his wife, Hera, jealous.'

'Oh yes,' recalled Oriel, her eyes sparkling. 'Hera connived with other gods to prevent Leto from giving birth anywhere in the world, didn't she? So Leto wandered from place to place, followed by the serpent, Python, that Hera had set on her.'

'That's right,' said Damian approvingly. 'Which brings us to Delos. Zeus appealed to his brother, Poseidon, to help Leto find some place where she could give birth to his child. Poseidon then took the floating rock that Asteria had been transformed into, now called Adelos the invisible, and made four granite columns rise out of the sea to anchor it in place. He renamed it Delos, the visible.'

Leto, in the form of a quail, a ruse by Zeus to put Hera off the scent, then came to Delos, where she resumed her original shape.'

'I remember it, yes. It's been so long since I read Ovid's *Metamorphoses*. I really need to refresh my studies now I'm working here,' said Oriel ruefully.

'Ah, but there's more to the legend. Nothing is ever simple in our stories. Adelos was afraid that Hera would take revenge and kick her back under the sea. So Leto swore an oath on the River Styx that her son, when he came into the world, would build a temple there. And from that time onwards Delos became a sacred place. I will tell you the last part when we get to the island.'

'Your history is so rich in myths.'

'*Né*, every part of our land has a myth attached to it. Sometimes I can't help feeling that they repeat themselves in an uncanny way, even today. It makes you wonder if some of us aren't marked by the gods to keep these legends alive.'

Damian sighed heavily and squinted at the horizon. She knew to what he was alluding and wished with all her heart that she could put her arms around him, cradle his dark head against her breast and take away the hurt.

'It has always puzzled me that Delos, being just a rock and one of the smallest islands of the Cyclades, should have been chosen by the Greeks as Apollo's sanctuary, rather than one of the other bigger and more fertile islands.'

He looked back at her with a half smile. 'It cannot be explained in words. Once you get there, *agápi mou*, you will understand. Just bear in mind that in ancient Greece nothing occurred by chance.'

Damian took a cigarette out of the packet of Gitanes that lay next to him on the table, spun the wheel of his lighter and lit it. Leaning forward, he bent over the chart again, drawing deeply on his cigarette, then puffing the smoke away from the table so it eddied over the edge of the boat and out to sea.

Oriel watched him as he cast his eyes over the map and then, all of a sudden, she said: 'How long have you been interested in archaeology?' She was surprised she had never asked the question before. The two of them knew each other's bodies so intimately, yet there was still so much about each other that they didn't know.

'Ever since I was a schoolboy. When I was fifteen, during the summer holidays, I was taken on a tour of the archaeological sites of the islands and I was immediately hooked. After that, I managed to get myself on various French excavation teams as a student and, as soon as I got my degree, set up my own archaeological company, with the purpose of helping our country's museums.'

Oriel found herself smiling into his eyes and she couldn't help but think of the eager young student he must have once been, a world away from the *Drákon* Damian she knew now – hurt by life, closed in on himself – who almost seemed as if he, like Atlas, were holding up the world.

For the rest of the morning she read Homer's account of the fall of Troy, in which she knew Helice was mentioned at some point. She'd found the book in Damian's study after he'd told her to help herself to his extensive library. She found herself enjoying the companionable silence between herself and Damian. During the moments when he wasn't at the wheel he caught up on paperwork, and Oriel stole covert glances over the pages of her book at his expression of focused attention, his eyes burning with an intelligence she found deeply attractive.

They were lucky with the weather; it was perfect. The sun blazed down on them from a sky of cloudless blue and the sparkling sea couldn't have been calmer, with a gentle zephyr favourable for sailing. *Alcyone* rode the swells with effortless grace, her taut white sails capturing the breeze. Gulls swirled in the sky and from time to time schools of tiny silver fish leapt out of the water in unison as they crossed the boat's path.

It had just turned noon when land came into view in the distance and Damian called a halt. 'The land you can see there is Antikythera,' he called over to her, 'one of the smallest and poorest islands in Greece, inhabited by only forty-five people. It's protected, a nature reserve. We're doing well on time. What do you say to a quick swim before lunch?'

Oriel gazed down at the unfathomable depths; the sea had a breathless beauty and seemed to invite her in. Her eyes lit up. 'Why not?'

Damian released the brake on the windlass and the anchor rattled on its chain as it dropped into the clear blue water. 'I've put your case in the bedroom. If you haven't brought a swimsuit, I always keep a couple on the boat for emergencies.'

Oriel tilted her chin slightly. *Emergencies indeed*, she thought, and her green eyes glared at him. He was mad if he thought that she would wear one of his other women's cast-offs.

A smile flickered across Damian's lips and the icy fire of his eyes clashed with hers for a brief moment. 'Don't worry, they've never been worn. They still have their tags on. I like to envisage all conceivable requirements when I kit out a yacht.'

Oriel felt a burning flush sweep over her face. Was she so transparent? 'Thank you for your offer but of course I have my own swimsuit. I'll go down and change.'

As she undressed, it dawned on her that going swimming with Damian was not such a good idea after all. She hadn't heard him come down after her to change. Was he clad in his trunks underneath his shorts or was he primitive enough to swim in the nude? Oh no, she couldn't deal with that! Oriel's knees went weak as the thought of him naked crossed her mind and she sat down on the bed. Had his suggestion that they swim been aimed at getting them both into minimal clothing? *This is turning into paranoia*, she chided herself. She must stop looking for hidden meanings in perfectly innocent remarks and give him at least some benefit of the doubt.

Armed with this resolution, she put on her bright-green, one-piece swimsuit – cut high at the thighs and with a deep V at the front, which cupped her breasts snugly – and went up on deck, her heart pounding with a mixture of awareness and dread.

She almost collided with Damian on the steps and stifled a gasp. He was wearing red briefs, which did little to disguise his masculine shape, and had a white towel slung around his neck. Once again she was conscious of his sheer physical beauty: his wide and muscled shoulders which, despite the shark's mutilation, were in good shape, and his strong chest with its smattering of curly black hair that narrowed to a V on the way to his trim waist.

He wore a boyish grin. 'I was coming to look for you. Any problem?'

Oriel shook her head. 'None at all,' she whispered and Damian moved backwards up the stairs.

'*Éla*, come on, Calypso. It's such a lovely day and we mustn't waste time. I need a swim and so do you,' he said, glancing down at her with a look that sent her senses spinning into chaos. 'I promise to be good and keep my hands off you,' he added with mock solemnity, but she could see the desire lurking in his eyes, telling her that she only needed to murmur a suggestion and she could be in his arms again.

Oriel followed him on deck, a sensual haze holding her in its spell.

'See you,' Damian called out over his shoulder and, before she had time to answer, he dived powerfully into the shimmering sapphire water, his body slicing into it cleanly with almost no splash, before he struck out with a powerful, brisk crawl, quickly leaving the boat and Oriel behind.

Galvanized into action by Damian's somewhat cavalier attitude, and with a little toss of her head, Oriel leapt without hesitating from the side of the boat after him and proceeded to swim quickly and gracefully, as if she had lived in the sea all her life. With firm strokes of her arms she cut through the blue water, which reflected the bright rays of the sun like the facets of some giant gemstone, swimming briskly away from the sail-furled *Alcyone*. The sea was fresh and she revelled in the cool, silky slide of the water as it lapped her skin. She turned over and began a gentle backstroke. Damian was out of sight, having clearly enjoyed racing off, and so she just kept on swimming towards the horizon, paying no real heed to where she was going, her mind empty, only concentrating on the steady rhythm of her strokes. It was bliss!

Suddenly, a pain like a million red-hot needles drove fiercely into her right foot. Oriel let out a strangled cry as a shaft of pure agony shot halfway up her leg.

I've been stung by something vicious, she thought in panic.

The pain seemed to paralyze her, and the numbness prevented her swimming any further. *I need to get back to the boat!* It was essential that she returned as quickly as possible – some of these fish and aquatic insects could be lethal. She could see *Alcyone* in the distance and was afraid that she wouldn't make it. The next thing, a cramp contorted the muscle of her left calf. The pain was excruciating and she hugged her leg in agony. She gulped a mouthful of water helplessly and as she floundered she thought of Mattias, who wasn't here this time to save her.

This time I'm going to drown! she told herself, before panic overtook her and she gasped and went under.

All of a sudden there was a dark shape beside her in the water; the sea churned and strong arms wrapped themselves around her waist, hauling her bodily to the surface again. Oriel heard Damian say something in furious Greek, then: 'Just relax and breathe!' as he held her against him. Now, with a powerful sidestroke, he was towing her backwards towards the boat as she clung to him, gulping in great lungfuls of air, her panic slowly melting away.

'Can you climb the ladder?' Damian asked gruffly when they had reached *Alcyone*.

'Yes,' she breathed.

'I'll help you.' Placing one of Oriel's hands, then the other, on the ladder, he heaved her on to the boat from behind. Clambering into the craft after her, Damian picked her up and carried her below. Oriel felt awkward and weak and hated being carried, helpless, in Damian's arms. She was tired, wishing she could rest her head against his shoulder, but that would be too demeaning so she resisted the temptation, even though she was shivering, her teeth chattering, the pain in her muscles seeming to worsen by the minute.

Damian laid her on one of the built-in sofas. 'Don't move,' he ordered. 'I'll get a blanket, you're in a state of shock.'

'I think I've been stung by something nasty.' She leaned forward shakily to study her foot.

'Here, let me see.' He bent down and inspected the raised red welts of the sting. 'Ah, you'll be okay in no time. Just a moon jellyfish, it's the time of year for them. I'll get some vinegar from the galley. That'll neutralize it and bring the pain down.' He looked at her white face. 'First, let me get you a blanket. You need to keep warm.'

Oriel watched him disappear into one of the cabins. He came back with a blanket and, just as he was about to wrap it around her, she took it from him. 'Thanks, I can do that.'

He didn't argue and instead went to fetch the vinegar. After dousing the painful foot liberally, he sat down on the edge of the sofa. 'So, tell me what happened,' he said.

'First, I was stung and then I was hit with cramp in the other leg.'

'Cramp, eh?'

'Yes, I'm prone to it.'

'Well then, you should know better than to swim out that far.' He cast agitated fingers through his hair, a scowl settling on his face. 'You might have drowned.'

Oriel knew she'd been foolish and had to admit to herself that it was only because she'd been annoyed that Damian had dived in and left her behind that she'd swum out so far. She hadn't been thinking straight.

'I know, I admit that was a little careless.' She was aware of him: his vigour and his proximity; the sheen of his copper-tanned skin studded with shining drops of seawater; the damp tendrils of hair curling on his forehead and at the nape of his neck and, above all, the steel-grey eyes that were watching her with a steady, unreadable glint. In the dappled sunlight of the room, Damian was like a sculpture of tawny light and shade and, although he wasn't touching her, her body was afire under his gaze. It was no use telling herself that he was dangerous, that his heart had frozen over or that he would never love her – what she felt for him was a purely instinctive reaction that conscious thought could not banish. It had become an obsession.

'How's the foot?' Damian's voice was softer now: his anger, born of concern, having fled almost as suddenly as it had arrived.

'A lot better. It was just frightening when it happened,' she said.

'I'm sure it was. The good news is that it's been at least twenty minutes and you haven't developed any shortness of breath. The colour's back in your cheeks, which is good. I hope I didn't hurt your foot when I put vinegar on it.'

Oriel shook her head. He smiled down at her and, as their eyes met, she felt a warm flow of empathy between them. The trusting side of her nature wasn't afraid to be vulnerable. Why wasn't it always like this between them?

No longer shivering, she felt comfortable and cosy in the blanket. She watched Damian's noble head and wide shoulders as he crouched beside her, giving her foot one final check. Oriel's eyes were then riveted to his lean, tanned fingers as he lifted it to inspect her sole and heel.

'I'll apply a plaster to keep it clean. You might find walking a little painful for a while but as we're sailing for most of the next day, you won't need to move about much. By the time we arrive at Delos tomorrow evening you'll be fine.'

'Thank you, I feel much better already.'

Damian stood up. '*Kalós*, right then! You need to get out of your swimsuit. Would you like me to carry you to your cabin?'

'I'm sure I can manage on my own, thanks.'

'Very well then. I'll weigh anchor now and we'll set off before lunch. Give me a shout when you're ready and I'll help you upstairs to eat.'

Oriel hopped to her cabin. She was able to shower and dress without much difficulty and soon she felt the boat moving. She glanced out of the porthole. Yes, indeed, *Alcyone* had set sail and they were on their way again. It was too hot to get back into her shorts and shirt so she put on her spare clean one-piece bathing suit of the palest yellow. She had tanned nicely that morning and her cheeks had a sun-kissed apricot hue. As she stepped out of her room gingerly she found herself face-to-face with Damian again.

He smiled at her. 'You know, you have to be the most self-possessed near-drowning victim I've ever laid eyes on. Is that what you English call a stiff upper lip?'

'I suppose we don't like to make a spectacle of ourselves. We find public displays of emotion rather embarrassing so I suppose we do tend to react with calm self-control when we can,' she murmured.

He chuckled. 'Depending on the circumstance, eh?' He was hinting at the way she had fled from Heliades, Oriel knew that. But before she could answer, he said, 'Come, let's have lunch.'

He made a gesture to carry her but she evaded him with a swing of the hip.

'You plan on hopping up the stairs?'

Oriel's heart shuddered and she shook her head. 'I'm fine now, really.'

'It's rather a long way to hop, eh? Maybe you'd prefer to eat down here,' he suggested.

'Please, no fuss. I can walk and I can't think of anything better than to have lunch on deck, looking out to sea.'

Oriel carefully limped her way up the stairs. Damian had laid out a delicious lunch under the bimini, a white tablecloth covering the teak table. The china, silver and crystal glasses gave a touch of romance to the colourful spread. There was an appetizing-looking seafood salad – a succulent mix of prawns, lobster claws, mussels and scallops – laced with pink Thousand Island dressing; a platter of *gemistá*, small round zucchini, peppers and tomatoes; vine leaves stuffed with rice, herbs and tomatoes, served with *tzatziki*; and a bowl piled high with *patatasalata*, new potatoes in a green herb mayonnaise. A bottle of Greek rosé stood chilled in an ice bucket.

The wonderful mix of colours and aromas made Oriel realize how hungry she was. 'What a spread,' she exclaimed as she sat down at the table.

'Here, drink this first,' Damian ordered in a tone that brooked no arguing.

'Orange juice?'

'Yes, I've pressed it myself. You should really have a glass each morning before breakfast. Not only is it full of vitamin C but it's the best thing to cure cramp if you're prone to it.'

'Where did you learn that?'

'A Swiss doctor prescribed it to Helena a few years ago. She used to get cramp quite often.'

'Thanks.' As she sat down, Oriel noticed a dish with cold baby eggplant cut in half and filled with a tomato mixture.

Damian followed her eyes. 'I can see you're intrigued.'

'I've had many Greek dishes but I don't think I've ever come across this one.'

His eyes crinkled into a smile. 'You wouldn't have because it is essentially a Turkish dish, but some Greeks have adopted it. It's called *imam bayildi*, which in Turkish means "the priest fainted".'

Oriel laughed. 'Strange name.'

'The story goes that the *imam* fainted with pleasure when he was served them by his wife.'

'What are they stuffed with?'

'Onions, garlic, skinned tomatoes, parsley, raisins and a pinch of sugar. Cooked in olive oil. Shall I serve you one to taste?'

'Thank you, yes. I love the story, it's so quaint.'

'A glass of wine?'

'I'd better not. I tend not to drink it at lunch, it only makes me fall asleep and then I feel groggy when I wake up.'

'Greek wines are relatively low in alcohol so that shouldn't be a problem. They're flavourful and refreshing, never heavy. Drunkenness has always been frowned on in Greece. For millennia, in fact, so the wines here have been formulated differently.'

'It looks very tempting so yes, in that case, I'll have a glass, please.'

Oriel was enjoying her lunch, and Damian's company. She was feeling light-hearted and a little light-headed, although not from the wine, he was right.

The long sunlit afternoon flew by. Damian had clearly decided to be circumspect and treat her in a respectful way. Despite the romantic setting – and the deep, attentive look in his eyes – he adopted a platonic behaviour that never wavered. Not an inappropriate glance, nor a word out of place – not so much as a fingertip did he lay on her. He seemed relaxed and carefree and Oriel discovered once more what good company he was. As the sun caressed them, they discussed their work – a safe terrain that always seemed to create a harmonious, mutual rhythm in them both, together with a feeling of natural companionship born of a common interest held by bright and enquiring minds. The world might have belonged only to them.

Oriel felt free and fearless; the here and now was fun and pleasure should be taken in it. And although they never touched on intimate subjects, the pair kept talking all afternoon to the sound of the water splashing softly at the sides of the *Alcyone* as it slipped through the glistening sea.

CHAPTER 12

Damian picked up a set of binoculars and stared at the horizon. 'Kleftico, our next stop. Those rocks just over the horizon. Here, have a look.' He passed the binoculars to Oriel. 'We should be there in less than half an hour.'

The imposing and convoluted white bluffs and archways, which concealed small beaches and caves, were bathed in the afterglow of the dying sun, which made them look as if they had been set on fire. Kleftico loomed on the southern edge of Milos, its jagged cones darkly ominous against the flushed sky. Dazzling spokes of gold were spread out on the expanse of blue fronting the island. The sea gleamed like molten metal as if rays from some great lighthouse were beaming down on it.

'It's magnificent. I've never seen anything like it,' Oriel breathed as she put down the binoculars and glanced around her at the spectacular picture.

Damian looked at his watch. 'We're in good time too.'

'You were right, we were lucky with the weather.'

'Well, let's hope the gods will smile on us for the remainder of the journey.'

'That crimson sunset bodes well for tomorrow.'

They sailed the last part in silence. Damian's tall, lean figure stood a little apart from Oriel's, arms folded against the powerful wall of his chest, legs slightly apart. He was staring out to sea and seemed deep in thought. Oriel looked up at the dark, impassive profile, her glance lingering for a furtive second on the scarred cheek. It was easy enough to tell herself that she was no more than another of Damian's conquests and that he enjoyed a life where love, trust and fidelity held little meaning. Yet, if this were so, what was this electric heart-swelling pervasion of feeling that she was convinced they both shared?

As though he knew that Oriel was looking at him, Damian

turned towards her, his eyes bright and shining like glass. His stare was so brilliant that she was forced to look quickly away. Her fingers gripped the rail and she fixed her attention on the rushing water, knowing that what she felt was showing nakedly in her eyes.

As darkness fell, they arrived at Kleftico. Damian turned the craft into the wind, holding the yacht steady as they headed for the sheltered bay. Then the motor kicked into life and he switched on the autopilot. The next moment, he was quickly rolling the headsail and mainsail; then, with both sails down, he flicked off the autopilot, pushed the throttle forward and the boat picked up speed as he steered it into the bay.

Minutes later, they were safely at anchor, close to a sheltered beach. The boat swung gently, quiet at last. The waning moon had risen in all her splendour. Although in her last quarter, she was large and near enough to shine bright in the midst of the golddust of stars patterning the sapphire sky. All around the boat, the sea shimmered under her iridescent beams like a woman's gown, set with a sweep of diamonds, caressing the pearly shore.

There are times, even in the most uneventful of lives, when one experiences an intense feeling of unreality, whether from delirious joy or crushing sorrow. It comes swiftly like a dream. Such was the sensation that gripped Oriel when she laid eyes on that magical scenery conjured by the moon, where the peaks and cliffs of Milos rose and fell, bathed in patches of light and deepening shadow.

Damian came to stand beside her. She lifted her head to look at him. His eyes seemed suddenly darker now, penetrating, searching hers as though seeking an answer. Damian wanted her – all the more, she knew, because he sensed she wanted him too. Their mutal desire was quickening into still greater proportions and her resistance was swiftly dwindling away. Oh, the fight was so hard!

'A drink?' he asked abruptly, breaking the moment.

'Yes, yes, please,' Oriel answered quietly, reaching for her pale-yellow sarong and tying it around her waist.

'A glass of wine or something stronger?'

'Wine would be great, thank you.'

'We'll have it up here and I'll make us something to eat.'

'Not for me. It was a big lunch, I couldn't eat anything else.'

'Very well, I'll just bring up a few *mezedes*.' As Oriel was about to offer her help, he raised a hand. 'Everything is ready in the fridge. Besides, I want you to rest that foot. You shouldn't be going up and down the stairs unnecessarily.'

'The pain's almost gone.'

Damian gave his quiet and devastating smile. 'That's good, but you might feel that it throbs tonight.'

'I'll be fine tomorrow, don't worry.'

He gave her that look which had so disturbed her earlier. The silence hummed between them and then Damian disappeared down the stairs, leaving Oriel to relax and soak up the atmosphere.

Oh, she was soaking it up all right: she was quite heady with it. Indeed, with all this moonlit beauty, it was a night for romance. She moved to the mast and leaned against it. From this vantage point she could take in the whole mesmerizing view. Still, she couldn't help the thoughts that invaded her mind like a fearful refrain when faced with the pent-up desire she read in Damian's eyes.

He will never love you. His heart is too wounded and, even if warmth and trust find their way back into it, the arms of Yolanda, his childhood love, would be the first he'd seek. Oh why did she have to think of all that now? Why couldn't she just enjoy the moment?

Only when Damian placed a loaded tray on the table was Oriel aware that he had come back up on deck. He was regarding her fixedly, as if he knew every thought that had strayed into her mind. It was almost dreamlike when she heard his voice, quiet yet shattering the silence.

'Well?'

There was a world of meaning in that one word, a meaning she couldn't – wouldn't – face. Tension sprang along Oriel's nerve ends, holding her mute and still. She sighed, then turned fully to face Damian in the moonlight, the light breeze playing with her hair. 'The view is intoxicating,' she murmured.

'It is your beauty, Calypso, that's intoxicating.'

Oriel's senses swam in frightened circles, her leaden limbs forcing her to remain where she didn't want to be … but there was nowhere else to run to except the deserted, dead-calm sea and those giant, precipitous rocks mutely rising from its bosom.

In two strides Damian had joined her at the mast, taking her hand in both of his. Even that slight touch was shocking in its intensity.

His grey eyes scrutinized hers, a stark hurt lingering in their depths. 'What's happened, Calypso?'

The resonance of his voice hit an answering chord somewhere within her and her head tilted back so that his jagged scar came starkly into view.

'Didn't we start to love each other?' He stared down into her eyes, his own feverish, seeking an answer.

Oriel drew a ragged breath. *Love* … yes, if only the intimacy that had passed between them had been prompted by love! For her, maybe … but not for him. How could it be when Yolanda held prime place in his heart?

The flat palms of his hands slid down her arms to her waist, to the curving rise of her hips and he pressed her against the hardness in his thighs, a movement more eloquently provocative than any words would have been.

'*Oh Theó*, Calypso, don't you know what you do to me? Don't you still want me?'

Damn! Oriel didn't need to answer him, every part of her was responding to the potency of his body: her breasts peaking, fire licking her thighs, her mouth drier than a desert.

She heard Damian half sigh, half growl in his throat as he gathered her fully against him. His lips met hers forcefully and she recognized the hunger in him because she shared it – an appetite no kiss alone could satisfy. Oriel clung to him, silently begging to be taken, knowing that later she would probably die of shame remembering it.

Damian's kiss was hard yet soft, aggressive but amazingly sensual. Wedging his thigh between Oriel's legs, he pushed against the sensitive triangle covering her femininity, his tongue in her mouth playing a tantalizing game of advance and retreat, enacting the motion his manhood was begging to make inside her.

Cupping her face in his hand, he kissed his way slowly along her jaw to the hollow in her throat, pushing the straps of her bathing suit off her shoulders. His dark head slid towards the tender swell of her thrusting breasts, slowly, oh-so-erotically circling the pink areolae with his tongue, suckling and moistening the taut peaks before nipping at them lightly, making her moan softly.

Trembling, Oriel's arms slid round Damian's shoulders, her frame moulding itself to his straining hardness, the core of her remembering the magic of his touch and aching to feel it again. The need for him driving her crazy, she arched towards him and lifted a leg, wrapping it around his waist, the better to feel his arousal, the swollen nub between her thighs throbbing painfully, begging to be relieved.

'This is what you want, eh?' he whispered huskily against her ear as his hand slid down, his fingers moving possessively to the junction of her thighs and sliding under the thin material of her bathing suit. Damian's groan was the extension of Oriel's as he parted the soft damp lips and found the slick, pulsing bean. '*Theh mou agapi*, you're so wet, so warm, so soft … I can see how much you want me, eh? Tell me what you need.' He was whispering hoarsely against her lips as he brushed the centre of her desire.

'More, yes …' she managed. Sensations, like an ever-expanding circle, were spreading out from that midpoint within her where the blood pounded hotly, rapturous pleasure accompanying every stroke of Damian's deft fingers, and she couldn't stop herself from moaning his name passionately, her nails digging into his broad shoulders fiercely as she clung to him.

'You like this, eh? You want me to go on? Shall I be cruel, *matia mou*, and stop, like this?' he asked, suspending his caress and making her cry out, begging him to continue. 'I don't only want to touch you. I'm hungry for you … I want to take you in my mouth, lick you, taste you, push myself into you …'

In turn, Oriel's hand slid down Damian's body and pressed against the hard heat of his arousal. Her senses pulsed with the need to touch him closely, intimately, without the barrier of his shorts, remembering how exciting it was to touch his bare flesh.

Her breathing was coming in short rasps. 'I want to feel you, Damian … I want you inside me.' Her soft mewing sounds were becoming urgent.

'Let's go down to—'

His words were abruptly interrupted by the deep blast of a ship's siren and the wash of the passing tourist launch rocked the *Alcyone* with such force it jolted Damian and Oriel out of their passionate embrace. She let out a cry as she lost her balance for a moment, her leg slipping on the slick surface of the boat. But Damian was quick: in one fluid movement he grasped her arm, pulling her back. Encircling her waist, he held her firmly against him, while gripping the mast with his other hand until the rocking of the boat had stopped.

It took a few minutes for the *Alcyone* to settle back to its gentle sway. Oriel felt as if her breath were suspended somewhere in her throat. Damian's face was still dark with desire but his eyes skimmed over her with concern. 'You were almost over the side there. Come, *agápi mou,*' he said, taking her into the cockpit. 'While you're with me, you have nothing to worry about. You'll always be safe, eh?'

But Oriel was now becoming clear-headed again, jolted from the feverish passion that had consumed her only a moment ago. *Keep her safe?* Surely this man presented the most clear and present danger in her life just now.

'Sit down, *agapi*. Let me pour you a glass of wine … unless you'd prefer me to carry you downstairs.'

'I'd love a glass of wine, thank you. I think it'd be too hot in the cabin,' she told him quickly. The last thing she wanted was for Damian to carry her. Although the immediate urgency of her desire had ebbed, it didn't mean that her body was satiated. Far from it, she recognized, as her eyes fell on the strong arms that had kept her from falling and the elegant fingers that had caressed her so intimately and were now uncorking a bottle of rosé.

'It's been a day heavy with excitement, eh?' Damian's lips quirked at the edges and his eyes held glints of moonlight that added to their brilliance in his lean dark face.

'Yes, I hope this isn't typical of what's awaiting me for the rest of our trip. You must think I'm really high maintenance.'

'High maintenance?'

'Yes, an English expression: it means that I'm demanding of a lot of care and attention. I promise you I'm not usually like this. You seem to bring out the worst in me,' she added with an awkward smile.

Damian laughed deep in his throat. 'That's what I'm here for, to lavish care and attention on you.' He poured her a glass of wine. 'Here, drink this, you'll feel better.' He smiled that sort of innocent smile he sometimes gave her, and which made him look much younger.

'Thank you.' She turned to look at the view of Kleftico behind her. She had so enjoyed her afternoon with him, she had almost forgotten that he wasn't hers to want. Still, even now, without looking at him she could feel the hot, self-conscious colour sweeping over her flesh, despite her best efforts to suppress it.

A small silence followed while Oriel sipped her wine pensively, trying to cling to reality, repelling the emotional trap her senses were setting for her. They had behaved like teenagers just now – she must talk to him like the adult she was. Explain that she didn't want an affair, she was happy to be his friend but there would be no more indulging in casual sex.

'What's wrong, *agápi*?'

Oriel struggled to think of something to say – some throwaway remark she might make – but her brain refused to provide one.

Damian moved to the place beside her and offered her a plate of *mezedes*. 'Have some of these.'

Oriel turned to face him. She could feel his warm breath on her face and smell the mingled fragrances of aftershave, cigarettes, salt and male skin so particular to him. This was torture! Maybe if she gave in to these wild instincts of hers, she would eventually get him out of her system.

'I'm not very hungry,' she said lamely.

'You can't drink without eating, you'll make yourself ill.'

'Don't tell me what I can or can't do,' she flared, knowing how unreasonable it must sound as soon as she had uttered the words. 'I'm sorry, Damian, I'm tired. I'd better go to bed. I'm afraid I won't be very good company tonight,' she whispered. Seeing how confused he looked, she only just stopped herself from caressing his face.

'*Né, né,* I'll take you down.'

Automatically, she placed a hand on his arm. 'I know the way, Damian. Stay here. I'll be fine in the morning. It's been a heavy day and I need to be alone.'

His expression became unreadable. 'I quite understand, *agápi mou.* If you need anything, just call out. I'll be either on deck or in the next room.'

Oriel went down to her cabin. She turned on the cold water of the shower in the bathroom and forced herself to step under it. It briefly took her breath away and she shuddered violently but it was the only method she knew to rid herself of the tension that held her so tightly: the grip of a need so savage that it was almost a physical pain. She stood there for a long while, totally still, feeling the pressure seep out of her under the cool drizzle, and willing it to wash away the yearning she felt for him.

When Oriel came out she towelled herself vigorously, bringing back some life and warmth into her numbed body. She studied herself in the mirror with bitter contempt: she was pale and there were dark rings under her eyes. *Your head is in a mess,* she told herself. *Isn't it time you unscrambled whatever brains you have left? Don't look vulnerable. More than that, don't be vulnerable.*

The night was warm, the cabin was hot and although equipped with air-conditioning, she preferred to open the porthole. She slid between cool sheets that felt silky against her naked skin. Her nightdress was at the bottom of her case and she was too tired to go looking for it. Still, when she lay down and closed her eyes an agitated feeling ran like a low hum through her body. Restless, she lay there, willing herself to relax but she knew that whatever he was doing, Damian was close by.

The tap at the door was so soft that she chose to ignore it, thinking it must be the boat creaking. Yet her female intuition – something that seemed to operate on overdrive whenever Damian was near – made her open her eyes wide and she realized that he had come into the cabin and was standing next to her bed. He had a mug in his hands.

Oriel sat up with a jolt, pulling the sheet almost up to her chin. She was quite awake now. 'Don't you ever knock?'

'I knocked but you didn't hear.'

'What … what are you doing here anyway?' she demanded with an uncontrollable tremor in her voice.

'Bringing you some hot milk, I thought it would help you sleep.' Damian set the cup on the small shelf beside her bed. He stood there looking down at her. The moon, through the porthole, shone on his scarred, broad chest, leaving his face in the dark. *Why couldn't she find him repulsive? It would solve all her problems.* He had a towel wrapped around his waist and Oriel guessed that was all that was covering him. A tiny kick of panic in her stomach heightened the excitement that had begun to invade her body. She was trembling, a pulse beating in her throat, afraid of being alone with him in this room while both of them were almost naked. Taking a deep breath, she pulled the sheet up even further.

'Thank you, that's very kind. But you'd better go now,' she told him in a hollow voice.

'You want me to go?' He'd heard but it seemed he couldn't believe his ears, and she didn't blame him. It seemed only minutes since they had been up on deck, clinched in a steamy embrace.

'Yes, I'm very tired.' She gripped the sheet tightly.

He flicked the switch on the night lamp next to her bed. 'Why do you cover yourself, *agápi mou*? Do you have anything to hide that I don't already know about?' His hungry scrutiny roamed up and down her body, starting a throbbing ache between her thighs. His eyes were hot with challenge. 'Tell me you don't want me.'

'You know that's not the point ...'

'You want this, I want this ... that's all that matters.' Damian reached out a hand to touch her face.

'No ... please don't,' she cried out, jerking her head away, summoning the strength to pit her will against his.

'*Mitéra tou Theoú!* Mother of God!' His gaze was wild, lit by the fire of raw possession; the heat between their bodies was smouldering so intensely it could have turned metal to liquid. 'There's only so much a man can take,' he growled, pulling the sheet back and exposing her naked body. Oriel's arms flew automatically to her bare breasts. 'What are you hiding from me, eh? Have you forgotten that I have touched, caressed, licked, loved, every intimate inch of your body? You drive me wild and then you say, "Don't touch!" Do you want me to lose my mind?' He pulled away his towel, exhibiting the effect she had on him.

'Please, Damian, don't ... don't do this.' Oriel's breath was coming in ragged gasps; her body rigid at the display of his potent arousal. She could see he was fighting for control, as was she herself. Lifting her head, she was trapped in the endless liquid silver of Damian's eyes. Her heart was beating so violently against her ribcage that she could hardly breathe, and a pulse was drumming wildly at the core of her, flooding her with a warmth that seemed to find its way through her limbs, all the way to her head. The emotion was such that her eyes welled up with tears. *Oh, how she wanted to feel him inside her!*

Obviously mistaking them for tears of misery, Damian paled and his body relaxed. '*Ochi, agápi mou*, no tears, please.' His frustrated anger was over as quickly as it had flared and his expression suddenly tender. Immediately wrapping the towel back around him, he sat on the edge of the bed.

Oriel couldn't bear to see him like this. Earlier she had left him unsatisfied and now she was doing it again. It was as much her fault as his, she thought bleakly as she watched the struggle in his eyes. All she wanted was to comfort him.

'What's wrong, *matia mou*?'

'What we're doing isn't right.'

'What do you mean it isn't right? So what was the other night, a momentary lapse of moral principles?'

Oriel's cheeks flamed. 'I'm trying very hard to forget that.'

'Why? And what about half an hour ago? We both know what would have happened if that boat hadn't interrupted us.'

She tried to stay calm in the face of his frustration. 'Physically … sexually, you excite me, I'm not denying it. But I don't want to become more involved with you, so I feel that what we are doing is wrong.'

'Making love to you is wrong?'

Oriel shook her head. 'This isn't love, Damian. It's rampaging lust, and you know it. It's a betrayal of all my most private dreams. Yes, you ignite a desire within me with a skill bordering on demonic, but giving in to that is a desecration of everything I hold most dear.'

Damian looked at her, his eyes turning to slate. She could see the muscle angrily tensing in his jaw as he leaned his elbows on his knees and looked back at her. 'Since when has our lovemaking become a betrayal of your private dreams? And what is all this about my demonic skill in arousing you?'

Oriel paused. Her eyes fell to his muscular forearm, thinking about how many women had felt the way she had about those particular skills … how many he'd taken to the Room of Secrets and made love to between those sheets, under that outrageous mirror.

She pushed the hair away from her face and tucked it carefully behind her ear. 'That room we … how many times have you …?' She looked up and read the confusion in his expression. Oriel adjusted the sheet around her impatiently. 'How many other women …?' The words stuck in her throat. She couldn't finish her sentence because of the fear that his answer might make the stab of jealousy she felt in her chest even more agonizing.

Damian shook his head ruefully. 'No, *matia mou*, you have it all wrong.'

'Do I?' Oriel responded, her voice edged with terseness. 'How is that?'

He met her intense gaze, his own bright with frustration. 'The Room of Secrets was built by Gjergj Lekkas. It was a kind of homage to an ancient Greek room dedicated to erotic love. I'd never used it before.'

Oriel blinked. 'Never?'

His silver eyes bored into hers. 'I had an idea that this room was made for us, a room where passion could be unlocked. *Your* passion. So no other woman has been there with me before.'

'But you planned to take me there.'

'Yes. Or at least I wanted to … as long as you were willing.'

'And everyone in the house knew of your intention.'

Damian swore under his breath. 'All right, yes. I realize it wasn't the most tactful thing to do. I'm sorry, *agápi mou*. That doesn't change the way I feel about you and I don't regret what we did. Do you?'

It made a difference that she had been the first, Oriel had to admit it, and with that realization something tightly coiled inside her softened and loosened, giving way to hope. Still, she held his gaze and said quietly: 'I've told you before what I think about this sort of intimacy. It's special, sacred, to be enjoyed by people who love and trust each other.'

Damian's eyes flashed and she could see the effort he was making to keep his cool. It was a hurtful thing to say but it had to be said if she wanted to protect her sanity and not degrade herself any more than she already had.

'So how do you explain that our bodies are so attuned to each other, in such perfect harmony, eh?'

Oriel looked down at the sheet covering her. 'Chemistry and lust, I suppose. We both have strong libidos and find each other attractive.'

'If you really think that then you're lying to yourself. You're not the sort of person who indulges in casual sex, anyone can see that. The proof? You stayed without a man since that first night we spent together, a lifetime ago.'

Her eyes became green pools of emotion. 'Yes, that's true,' she said softly. Admitting it to him was almost painful.

Damian straightened up and ran a hand through his hair. 'God knows, yes, you have a strong libido like me, *agápi mou*. Despite your innocence, you're not shocked by what we do and you show no inhibition, no restraint. And you do and say things to me that I wouldn't dare ask for. You think there's no trust between us? You've let me please you with a wantonness that is totally out of character, openly revelling in my touch. Sure, I'm experienced, I've had many women but, as God is my witness, I have never done or wanted to do with them what you and I have done together.' His gaze became penetrating. 'This total abandonment in our intimacy has only one name: lovemaking. I love you, Oriel, and, whether you accept it or not, you love me too.'

She looked at him, astonished. *I love you, Oriel?* Had she heard him right? She could barely recall his ever having uttered her name before and, in his mouth, it took on another dimension. It sounded liquid, like music or poetry. Dear God, what was she to do?

Damian was scrutinizing her with a quiet intensity that unnerved her. Oriel drew a ragged breath, her mind fighting what her heart wanted to accept. He was ruthless when it came to relationships with women, it was something she must never forget. How could she truly know that he meant it?

She smiled. 'You should have been a lawyer … you argue well.'

'I'm battling for my life … you *are* my life, *agápi*. But I can see that you don't trust me.'

'How can you talk about love, about trust? We know nothing of each other.'

'*Pístis, elpís, agápē*. There are only three things that count in life, we say in Greece: faith, hope and love. You have given me all three. Faith, because I trust you. Hope, because you have restored my belief in humanity, giving me a new reason to start my life again. And love, because in the way you touch me there is all the proof I need of your love, and that is all I want.'

Oriel turned away. 'Oh, Damian … why are you doing this to me?'

'Look at me, meet my eyes,' he said very softly, leaning forward, his hand on the side of the bed. 'Give me a chance, *Ochi*, give *us* a chance. I will prove to you that I love you, and that you love me too.'

Oriel turned back and did as he asked. She met Damian's mesmerizing gaze, boring into her, and looked at him blankly. 'And how will you do that?' She gave a hollow laugh. 'In fairy tales, the prince was given a difficult task to fulfil in order to win the princess's heart.'

'We have a saying in Greek: *Tò dìs examarteîn ouk andròs sophoû*, to commit the same sin twice is not a sign of a wise man. I won't commit the same mistake of letting you go without giving myself enough time to win you first. I've made mistakes with you that I have no intention of repeating.'

'What are you saying?'

He paused. 'The most difficult thing for me is to be near you and not be able to make love to you. From now on I will love you in silence. You'll be locked up inside me, here.' Damian put a hand to his heart. 'But I will keep my feelings to myself.' His eyes were intense, his voice husky. 'As God is my witness, I will not in any way try to seduce you or put pressure on you to make you change your mind … until you come to me, Oriel … and you *will* come to me.'

Her eyes widened at his unshakeable confidence. 'Just like that? How can you be so sure, when I myself have no idea of how I feel about all this?'

'A green fruit ripens slowly, as we say here. I am a patient man, Oriel. *Peprōménon phygeîn adýnaton*, it is impossible to escape from what is destined, and I firmly believe that it is our destiny to be with each other.'

Oriel saw that Damian's eyes, level with hers, were as passionate and determined as his voice had been. A great shivering suddenly seized her. Was she really that valuable to him?

He took the mug of milk and gave it to her. 'Here, drink this, it'll help you sleep. *Kalinýchta agapité mou.*' Then he turned off the bedside lamp and walked to the door.

'*Kalinýchta,*' Oriel whispered.

Damian stopped and looked back at her once again. 'Remember, when you're ready to come to me, I'll be waiting … however long that takes.'

He closed the door softly behind him, leaving Oriel alone and trembling, her hands gripping the mug of milk he had so thoughtfully brought her. Propped against her pillows, she sipped her nightcap thoughtfully. Her eyes were wide open now.

What was happening to her was worthy of a romantic novel – six years apart, and then a few days together, and now they were arguing naked on a boat in the middle of the Aegean. Oriel was more confused than ever. Damian loved her? She had unrealistic dreams – so she'd been told – and she hadn't yet met the man who matched her ideal.

Was Damian the man of her dreams? What did she know of him apart from the fact that he was brave, a hard worker and proud to a fault? Strong and determined, of course – he'd had to be to overcome the tragedies in his life and still be standing – though it had left him with a vulnerability that he hid behind a mask. Still, that was not enough! Everything she knew of his life had been told to her by other people, he had never opened up to her. For all she knew, Mattias's interpretations of the incidents in his life could be just the fisherman indulging in romantic drama. Yet that small tendril of hope was slowly unfurling inside her, reaching for the light.

She finished her milk and settled down to sleep. In her dreams Damian came to her and loved her with all the passion and tenderness of which she knew he was capable, letting the tension seep slowly from her aching body, leaving her calm until dawn.

* * *

Oriel woke as the sun was coming up over the horizon, bathing the cabin in its aureate light. They were under sail.

423

'Damian,' she whispered, remembering her dream. She could hear him moving about on deck. Their conversation of the night before came back to her with a flood of warmth and nervous excitement.

She sat up and pushed the hair back from her face, now fully awake. Damian had said he loved her – she hadn't dreamt it. Was all that talk just a ploy to erase her misgivings so he could give full rein to his desires during the days they were alone together? No! Oriel couldn't believe that of him ... he wasn't so underhand. Any man who put his life in danger to save that of another, as he had done with Mattias, couldn't have such base instincts. She sighed. Tired of analyzing it now, she would leave a little to chance, she decided ... luck, destiny, fate – each person had a different name for it.

Oriel showered rapidly and put on her white shorts and a pink T-shirt. The mirror told her she still looked pale under her tan but her eyes were bright and she didn't look too tired. When she went up on deck, Damian was at the wheel and the sails were billowing in the breeze. He was wearing denim shorts and a white polo shirt. Dark glasses covered his eyes, shielding them from Oriel; they also hid most of his facial scar and he appeared to her almost like the beautiful god she had met long ago. From the shore, she reflected, the boat must look like a painting in the pink morning on the calm blue sea, and he seemed more than ever at one with his idyllic surroundings.

'Ah, Calypso! *Kaliméra*. You're up early. After the eventful day we had yesterday, I would have thought you'd be asleep until noon.'

Oriel smiled at him, marvelling at how bright and full of energy he looked. 'I'm an early riser.'

'I've just brought up a pot of coffee and your orange juice is ready. Which reminds me, how's your foot today?'

'Fine, thanks. It's as if nothing had happened. Can I do anything?'

'There's some fruit in the fridge and pots of homemade *real* Greek yoghurt, if you'd like to bring them up.'

'I'd love some homemade *real* Greek yoghurt,' Oriel responded cheerfully. 'Can I bring you anything?'

'*Ochi efharisto*, I had some breakfast earlier, but I'll have another cup of coffee with you.'

Oriel went down to the fridge. The place was spotless. Everything had been washed, dried and tidied away. To think Damian would be so house trained! She found it surprising in a Mediterranean man who, all his life, had been surrounded by an army of staff. Oriel helped herself to some yoghurt and went back upstairs.

She spent the rest of the morning reading and lying in the sun, getting up only once to make Damian some coffee. He barely took a break from sailing, as the water was slightly choppier that day, so at lunchtime she brought him a plate of food. Considering what had happened the night before, he seemed remarkably cheerful, even when the weather took a wilder turn.

By the early afternoon, the *meltémi* had started up: a wind, he explained, that was very much like the monsoons of Asia. Dark clouds came in from the north and he decided to put down the sails and motor. He gave Oriel a lifejacket and made sure they were both harnessed properly. Half an hour later the sky turned black. Dense sheets of rain poured down and the wind increased, whipping the water into whitecaps. The boat ducked and dipped, heeled and creaked; then, an hour later, the squall passed and the sun came out.

They were under sail all the way to Delos – even when the sea became choppy again later in the evening, as they approached the island. Then they came into the Delos strait, between Rhenea and Delos itself. Here, the waters welcomed them and the island, bathed in moonlight, appeared like a hazy jewel on the silvery sea.

Through it all Damian had remained cool and efficient. Oriel had never been seasick but that afternoon she nearly was – until he provided some tablets that immediately did the trick and she was saved the humiliation of being ill. Strangely enough, at no time had she been afraid. Damian's obvious skill at sailing his boat and his constant reassuring words left her confident that they were never in any real danger.

He had remained as calm and cheerful through the whole day as he had been that morning. When he bade her goodnight, after they were safely moored in the harbour, he did so in an almost impersonal way – although there was never a break in the kind solicitude with which he treated her. It was as if the *Drákon* Damian side of his personality had been cleansed entirely from him, washed away by the salt breeze and the sea spray.

When Oriel awoke the next morning, the sun was already up. It was a hot day and there was no hint of a breeze coming through the open porthole. She showered quickly – she was certain that Damian had been long awake and was keen to show she was a match for him. After putting on a pair of old denim shorts and a peach spaghetti-strap top in thin cotton, she slapped some sunscreen over any bare skin. Armed with a sensible hat and her sunglasses, she hurried up on deck.

Tour boats were just beginning to arrive from neighbouring Mykonos and Damian was nowhere to be seen. Leaning against the mast, Oriel surveyed her surroundings. Stark Delos, crossed by long streaks of golden morning light, stretched before her. The virgin island, the fabled birthplace of Apollo, was suffused with a divine light and she was conscious of a strange lull in the atmosphere, as though the island were under a spell.

She was about to abandon her vantage point when she saw Damian striding towards the boat: an impressive, masculine figure, lean, tall and confident. He looked every inch a part of these surroundings with his thick black curls and strong-boned face. She sighed to herself quietly as he approached.

He waved to her and, moments later, joined her on the boat. '*Kaliméra ómorfi kopéla mou!* Good morning, my beautiful!' He seemed in great form, an easy smile lighting his face. 'Did you sleep well?'

'Yes, wonderfully, thank you.'

'Have you had breakfast?'

'No, not yet.'

'Me neither. I went down to catch the delivery launch that passes by every day from Mykonos. I bought us lobster sandwiches and a bottle of white wine for lunch, and a few salad things for our supper.' Damian tapped the large cool bag he was carrying. 'I'll improvize something for us tonight.'

'That sounds lovely,' Oriel beamed.

His gaze fell on her straw hat and dark glasses. 'I see you're well equipped. Glad you're wearing sensible shoes, we've got plenty of walking today. Let's have some coffee and yoghurt, then we'll be on our way.'

'Are you really planning to carry that bag around with you? It's so hot and it's going to be heavy with those bottles,' Oriel remarked as she watched Damian stow two large bottles of mineral water and a bottle of wine in the cool bag.

Damian chuckled and smiled at her. 'It's not heavy, *agápi mou,* but thank you for your concern. I'm taking everything with us. We could have gone to the air-conditioned restaurant but it will be packed with tourists. They're already arriving, as you can see. No, I figured we would enjoy our lunch more sitting on a slab of ancient marble, surrounded by the gems of history. The *meltémi* isn't blowing today but a gentle breeze will pick up, you'll see.'

'I'd love to have a picnic, it sounds perfect.'

Damian's smile broadened into a grin. 'After lunch we'll make our way to Mount Cynthus. The tourists will have left by then and we'll have the island to ourselves. Sundown is late at this time of year and we'll have plenty of time to visit most of the interesting sites on the island. In the early evening we'll climb up the mount. It's not that high and there's a good path. There's an impressive view of Delos and the surrounding islands from the top.'

'It sounds great. Where will we set down for the night?'

'The best thing is to pitch our tent near the Sacred Port. I might even move the boat there. That way, if you're not comfortable camping under the stars you can always sleep in your cabin. But I'm guessing you'll choose the open air. Sleeping out, with the sky as your ceiling, is one of life's great pleasures, I always think.'

'You're preaching to the converted. I've no problem with camping. A friend of mine has a caravan and we've often taken off during the holidays.'

Though Damian didn't say anything, Oriel felt him stiffen.

'Vicky and I grew up together,' she clarified, suppressing a slight smile. 'She's a botanist and loves being out in the fresh air and nature.'

He visibly relaxed and shot her a dazzling smile. '*Kalós!* I'll make some coffee, then we'll go.'

* * *

Oriel wanted most of all to visit the place that had been the beginning of everything – the Sacred Lake, where Leto had given birth to Apollo – so she and Damian headed towards the north of the island. En route, they walked through the Sacred Way, a wide, paved road lined with marble plinths that had once supported votive statues. There were also the remains of benches, which had been provided for the pilgrims who had travelled the route since ancient times. There was still an annual procession during the religious Delia festival held every year to celebrate the birth of Apollo.

A maze of dry, meandering paths led them across the island. On either side crumbling stone temples, toppled columns and the remains of statues told a story of the once-great sacred island. Damian and Oriel were greeted by something new at every bend. Whether it was a view of the sea or the debris of an ancient dwelling with the most magnificent mosaic floors open to the sky, glittering in the sunlight, the beautiful treasures were endless. The sun burned down on them from the great blue dome of the Apollonian heaven with a dry, brilliant but bearable heat, with the hot Aegean wind wrapping itself about them at every turn.

Sometime in the late morning they paused to have a drink and sat on one of the old walls of a large ruined villa. A pine tree offered much-needed shade and away from it the glare was intense, almost blinding. The air was a dancing, quivering flame, seeming to reflect light off the white marble of the building. In what must have been the main room of the villa, a huge mosaic floor had been laid and even now, two thousand years on, it was still almost complete. Oriel stood up and went over to inspect it more closely. Bright turquoise and black, it depicted a sea with bulbous-eyed fishes. The little coloured tiles made it seem almost as though the creatures were moving sinuously with the current as the hot sun danced and winked on the mosaic.

'Look!' Oriel gave a cry and Damian, who had been packing away their water, came over to join her. 'It's the trident! See?'

In each of the four corners of the great oblong floor was a representation of Poseidon's three-pronged trident, which Oriel had come to know so well over the past few days. There it was – the trader's insignia of Marcus Sestius, with the serpent entwined around the shaft.

'*Né*, that's it,' said Damian, and there was something in the tone of his voice that made Oriel look up to scrutinize him. Behind his dark glasses his face was impossible to read.

'You knew it was here, didn't you?'

'Yes. I contacted François, my friend on the French team here, when I knew we were coming to Delos,' he explained, his mouth trying but failing to suppress a smile. 'He knew of the place and told me about the floor … describing exactly where it was. I thought I'd surprise you.'

Oriel beamed at him, excitement lighting her features. 'So this is where Sestius came after the destruction of his business in the earthquake.'

'Well, he can't have lost everything. This villa is certainly a fine one,' said Damian. 'He must have had money squirrelled away elsewhere. He was a lucky man not to have been cast into a watery grave, along with his argosy.'

Oriel took out her camera and circled around the patterned mosaic floor, taking shots from different angles before coming back to him. 'Perhaps we can meet up with François and swap information about Sestius. It would be useful for our report on the wreck for the Ministry next week.'

Damian nodded. 'We can drop in tomorrow to the team's site office. He did mention we could help out if we wanted, as they're short of people at the moment.'

Oriel smiled. 'Great. Do you know, I can't wait until we dive the wreck and see the statue of Poseidon again,' she said wistfully, putting her camera back in her bag. 'Although it won't carry the same thrill as it did when we first set eyes on it. That giant face shining through the water was incredible.'

Damian shrugged the bag on to his back and grinned. 'Well, you won't have to wait long. We'll dive together with the Ministry inspection team after the weekend. Then we'll both enjoy the looks on their faces when they catch sight of the statue. And don't worry,' he added, 'I won't let anyone from the Ministry take over. The site is yours. There'll be seasoned archaeologists trying to muscle in, but you discovered it and made all the connections, so it's only right you lead the team.'

'Thank you,' Oriel said simply, her green eyes sparkling up at him. The day just couldn't get any better.

They walked on and, apart from the tourists milling around, nothing broke the stillness of the countryside. The landscape was parched, with thistles and barley grass growing thick among the ruins, but for Oriel the shimmering presence of something almost supernatural gave the island a sense of enchantment that was almost palpable. Here, history and myth vibrated as one. She took off her sunglasses, preferring to appreciate the view in its full glory. Damian had been right: the sunlight over Delos had such brightness and penetrating clarity that she now had her answer as to why the ancient Greeks had chosen it as the birthplace of Apollo. What could be more appropriate for the great sun god?

As for Damian himself, he was not only good company but also an excellent guide, pointing out things that Oriel would have missed had she had been on her own, and always animating his information with legends and anecdotes to amuse her. He was very attentive, making sure they stopped to rest every now and again and insisting she drink water regularly so she wouldn't become dehydrated.

It was lunchtime when they arrived at the Sacred Lake. According to legend the sacred swans and geese of Apollo were once kept within its oval expanse, but it was now drained. A lone palm, its magnificent branches swaying in the sea breeze, stood at the centre surrounded by a low stone wall, marking the place where Apollo's mother, Leto, had supposedly laboured for nine days. Oriel could almost imagine the girl clutching the trunk of the tree, bracing her knees against the sweet meadow grass as she gave birth to the sun god.

She looked across to the famous Terrace of the Lions. The five elegant beasts, carved from Naxian marble, stood poised and snarling silently, guarding the sanctuary and looking out to the Sacred Lake. They reminded her of the ones that watched over the temple of Karnak in Egypt. By now, Oriel's eyes had become accustomed to the glare, and the view around her had ceased to be like that of a golden chalice seen through a sheet of gauze or lit by flickering candles. The hordes of tourists had moved off and the place was deserted save for these ancient relics; an absolute peace crept over her while beneath it all, humming in her veins, was the thrill of being alone with Damian.

'It's time we had something to eat, you look as if you need it,' he said, watching Oriel from behind his sunglasses as she took off her straw hat and wiped her brow with the back of her hand. 'I hope I wasn't going too fast for you.'

'I'm fine, just hot.' Oriel smiled and looked around her. 'What a lovely place,' she murmured. 'It's as if the years have rolled back and we were still living in those times.'

'It's even lovelier in the spring when it's a mass of wildflowers with whole sheets of multi-coloured anemones, bluebells and poppies.'

'I've seen photos of Delos with people walking around on marble paving slabs and red, purple and yellow flowers sprouting between the cracks.'

'By this time of year they've mostly gone. The heat kills everything and it's been such a hot May. There's another legend that says that Delos was a nymph who had attracted Zeus's attention. Out of respect for his wife Hera, she became a star and fell to the sea, transforming herself into an island to escape Zeus's favours. To punish her, he made the island barren and parched.'

'Delos might appear to some as a dusty, baked desert, home only to lizards and murmurs of long-gone civilizations but, for me, it's a treasure trove,' Oriel replied. 'A place where ancient memories are distilled … you can even detect their faint smell.'

Damian smiled. 'I knew you'd have a natural affinity for the place, Calypso.'

Oriel sipped from her bottle of water and smiled back. 'You're right, I have.'

They both sat on a rock in the shade of a pine to have their lobster sandwiches and a glass of wine, which was light and refreshing in the midday heat. Huge, vivid-emerald lizards, like mottled mini-dragons, strutted and scuttled about the stones as if they owned them.

'Mind you, there *are* an awful lot of lizards running around,' Oriel remarked, her eyes following them as she bit into her sandwich. 'I wonder why?'

'They're called *stellions* and, according to Ovid, these lizards originate from a boy who derided Ceres and, for this, was turned into a lizard by the goddess.'

Oriel laughed. 'Amazing! Your knowledge of Greek myths really does surpass anyone's I know, even my old lecturers. How do you do it?'

Damian spread his hands in a very Greek gesture and grinned. 'Simple, I grew up with them.'

'Well, now that we're here, will you tell me the rest of the Apollo legend?'

'You really do like stories, don't you?'

'To give the devil his due, you tell them well.'

Damian had taken off his glasses and the ice blue of his shirt reflected in his eyes as he looked at her. He gave a low laugh. 'The devil is always present in your phrases when you're describing me. Is that how you see me, the devil, *koucla mou*?'

Oriel gave an awkward laugh and felt herself go pink. 'The word "devil" in English doesn't have the same inflammatory religious connotations as here. I forget how it sounds in your country. I was actually flattering you with the saying but, if I have offended you, Damian, then I'm sorry.'

His white teeth gleamed in the sunlight as he threw back his head and laughed again. 'Now I've embarrassed you and made you blush. I'm not offended. Let's go back to myths and legends, though. Much safer ground for conversation, eh?'

Oriel looked at him sheepishly and nodded. 'You never told me the last part of Leto's story.'

'Well then, here goes. So, as you know, now Delos had been created as a place of sanctuary for the pregnant Leto. Her confinement lasted nine days and as the time of birth approached, she held on to the trunk of an ancestor of this very palm tree. The *Homeric Hymn to Delian Apollo* mentions that Leto was leaning against Mount Cynthus when she gave birth to the sun god. Other writings claim that two huge waves rose against the island at the moment of his birth.

'Anyhow, in the simpler, first version, many goddesses gathered on the island to help Leto, except for Eileithyia, the goddess of childbirth, whom Hera kept prisoner in a cloud on Mount Olympus, with the help of Iris, the goddess of rainbows. In the end, the goddesses were able to bribe Iris with a gold necklace, persuading her to fetch Eileithyia. They got back just in time to help with Apollo's birth.'

Oriel's eyes turned to Mount Cynthus, imagining the girl crouched in the throes of labour, her celestial midwife ministering to her.

'Don't look at it now. It seems artificial in sunlight but you'll find that in the moonlight it takes on a truly mysterious and romantic aspect. You'll see it tonight. Later, when it's cooler, we'll climb the mount. The view from up there is breathtaking.'

'I'd very much like to go up there but if you've done it before, do you really want to see it again?'

'It's been a few years. I'd like to repeat the experience.'

Oriel couldn't help but wonder with whom Damian had climbed Mount Cynthus. Yolanda, Cassandra, maybe one of his other women? But she knew better than to ask.

A dry wind had started up, whispering among the ruins and shivering the brown grass. The *meltémi* was doing its work, stirring up the sea around the island. Soon the waters would be a churned-up boiled pot of white foam. Oriel's gaze shifted from Mount Cynthus to the fermenting waves, feeling as though her emotions were suffering the same turmoil. An inexplicable sense of unease settled on her like an invisible cloak.

Damian lit a Gitanes and blew out a plume of smoke that curled into the air like a question mark. Oriel gave a nervous start when, a moment later, a cool glass was placed in her hand. She heard Damian murmur: 'You're a million miles away. Anything the matter, *agápi mou*?' The aroma of his cigarette clung in the air along with his question and she could feel him studying her profile.

She turned to face him and her heart missed a beat. It was the first intense look they had exchanged since the night before, when Damian's eyes had been hot with desire. She remembered, too, that his voice had been icy with scorn then soft with determined compassion. It had been easy to hook into his emotions and it brought her closer to him, even when it was frustration she read in his eyes. All day she had missed those eyes, which had been hiding behind their dark shades. Now that he had removed them, the silver pupils were still unfathomable and Oriel felt as if she had lost something precious.

'I was thinking about this lake,' she said, quickly aware of the colour running up to her hairline, betraying the lie. 'It's such a pity that it's been left to dry up.'

'It was drained in 1925 because it was a breeding ground for mosquitos carrying malaria. In winter, after the rain, it takes on another aspect and one can hear the croak of green tree frogs in the ancient cisterns.'

A couple of wasps came hovering around them, attracted by the food. Oriel shrank away from them with a little gasp.

Damian shooed them off her. 'You mustn't be afraid of them, they're part of nature.'

'I've never liked wasps.'

'The interesting thing about the countryside is that there's always something going on in nature. Look at that queen wasp there, busy making paper.'

'Making paper? Where?'

'On that shrivelled-up, diseased olive tree stump right beside you.'

Oriel could see the bright-yellow-ended insect at once.

'If you listen carefully, you'll hear her chipping away and pulping up the fragments of wood. Once she has all she can carry, she'll take it back to her nest to make the first cells of the comb, where she will lay her eggs.'

'Somehow I didn't expect you to know this much about life in the country.'

'I love to watch nature at work, always have done.'

Oriel savoured every moment of the present alone with Damian, spending time in easy conversation until they had finished their sandwiches and the bottle of wine. Once or twice she had been tempted to steer the dialogue towards more intimate subjects but she always refrained from it, fearing to draw a cloud over this beautiful day.

The afternoon went by as if in a dream. The ruins near the lake were beautiful, full of primitive echoes and the amazing phosphorescence of Apollo's light. Oriel found herself walking softly in this enchanted land, as if the ghost city could still feel and hear. She listened to Damian telling her what each edifice would have been – and he spoke so vividly that she could see them in her mind's eye, in all their former splendour: the temples, the stoas, the luxury villas, like the House of Masks and the House of Dolphins. And walking among the ancients would have been Marcus Sestius, the Roman who became more Greek than the Greeks, according to what little they knew of him.

As Damian spoke, Oriel could imagine the rise and fall of the power of these people; the coming of pirates, the devastation as the island was looted and plundered, falling gradually into decay.

'All we have now are these ruined buildings ... and the myths, of course,' she said faintly.

'And the myths have served a purpose through the centuries,' remarked Damian. 'I know, as you've studied them, you'll be perfectly aware that the stories were told to caution the public against immoral behaviour. Incest, adultery, that sort of thing ...' He gave her one of his devilish smiles. 'That is why, *agápi mou*, we are such a moral people today. Believe it or not, the old laws still hold sway over the emotions of the Greek people. The worst aspects of civilization haven't yet ruined our sun-drenched land.'

Oriel gave him a sidelong glance, wondering at her own sense of protective caution. 'So what do you do when all your senses, all your instincts, compel you to do something you know is wrong?'

The breeze ruffled Damian's hair and he lifted his head. Oriel's question seemed to have disturbed the mask he had kept on all day. His eyes suddenly looked dark and turbulent with emotion, his jaw tightened a little and, for a moment, she was almost tempted to forget everything but his obvious need of her. It would be so easy to tumble into his arms, let him make love to her and experience once more the rapturous thrill only his possessing her could bring. But she couldn't let that happen – not now, not after the lecture she had given him the night before on the boat. Where was her dignity, her self-respect?

'Oriel,' he breathed, and his eyes were narrowed and sensual, alert to every nuance of her expression. 'What are you saying?'

Again she was afraid of what might happen, of what she might not be able to control. 'Don't read anything into my words, Damian. I was curious, that's all. A woman's prerogative.'

His features hardened into the neutral countenance he'd worn since their talk and the slight bow of the head he gave her told Oriel that he would continue to respect their pact. As he got to his feet and moved over to hoist the rucksack on to his back, she stayed on the rock for a moment, staring at his lithe body topped by broad shoulders, the muscles flexing under his shirt. That hard, stern back was like a stone wall shutting her out for his own good, she thought with a heavy heart.

They walked silently for a while in the late afternoon and, for Oriel, the day seemed drained of its earlier beauty. She no longer heard the cicadas or saw how passionately blue was the sky or how turquoise the sea, with its white horses racing each other. From time to time she threw Damian a furtive glance only to see a cool and distant profile. An icy reserve had descended upon him as if he didn't want to speak or be spoken to, and she respected his silence. How could she handle him in her present state of nervous tension when she had fared no better the night before?

As they came to the stone-cut staircase that provided access to the summit of Mount Cynthus, Damian stopped. 'I think it's really worth your while to climb to the top. The view will be one you'll always remember. Shall we do it?'

Oriel's first impulse was to say no. He was regarding her, his face grave, waiting for her answer, not elaborating on his last few words. Damian had said the same about the sunset at Santorini and she hadn't been disappointed. This would be another souvenir she would be able to recall when she'd left the island … Greece … Damian.

'I would like that very much, Damian.' She had spoken softly, her face upturned to him, her eyes wanting to read his, but they were once more hidden behind his sunglasses.

They started up the trail. There was so much rubble around it was almost impossible to imagine that it had once been honeycombed with sanctuaries and temples to various gods. Although the ascent was gentle, the grade was difficult because of the gravel that made the going slippery. It wasn't helped by the *meltémi*, which blew relentlessly, assaulting them with violent rushes of howling air that could make them lose their balance at any moment. Oriel stumbled from time to time and, although she tried to ignore it, Damian's protective hand was always within reach if she wanted to steady herself.

Along the way, a path cut through groves of ancient, truncated pillars. They passed a sanctuary of the Egyptian gods, with its façade largely intact, and then, treading on fallen Cyclopean masonry, they came to the Grotto of Heracles, a cave formed by five pairs of enormous stone slabs.

'This place is considered the oldest site on the island,' Damian told Oriel. 'It's probably where the oracles were delivered, although the most important oracle of Apollo, as you know, was the one at Delphi. Archaeologists found fragments of a statue of Heracles in the cave, so they knew it was formed in his honour.'

'It belongs, I suppose, to those Hellenistic times when they were returning to nature and more ancient forms of worship.'

'Exactly. Would you like to go in?'

The entrance faced towards the harbour and a round, white, stone altar stood just outside, embedded in the tufts of dry grass. Oriel peered up at the gigantic stone slabs, fascinated. 'Yes, if you don't mind.'

Inside, the space was darkly ominous, with natural grey granite walls and a great opening in the slabs at the back that let in the sunlight. The stone plinth in the cave was the base for the statue of Heracles, which was now, according to Damian, safely housed in a museum. There were some plants growing at the back of the cave and there the atmosphere was fresher than outside.

Damian and Oriel came out of the cave and, just as they were going to move off to continue their climb, they saw crouching on a step a shrivelled hag – a gaunt, forbidding figure with a hooked nose and parchment-brown skin. Tousled grey hair, like that of a Skye Terrier, hung over her forehead, half concealing a pair of coal-black eyes.

As Damian and Oriel approached she stood up, scrutinizing them, and barred their way with a claw-like hand. She was much taller and stronger-looking than she had first appeared when seated, and it was as if her presence suddenly seemed to take up the whole of the island: the sky, the rock and the surrounding sea.

Damian immediately put a hand into his pocket and drew out a handful of coins. 'Here, take these and get yourself a hot drink and something to eat.'

'Keep your money, silver-eyed son of Aphrodite and Ares. You are generous hearted but Delia does not need your handouts.'

Damian leaned in to Oriel, murmuring in English: 'I've heard of this woman, they call her the Oracle.'

The woman's deep voice echoing in the wind seemed to be coming from the underworld. 'You are well named ... a tamer of men ... but you could just as well have been called Achilles, Heracles, Jason or Perseus for the feats you have faced. And those you will still have to meet. Your journey is long, handsome Odysseus, in your toil for happiness. It might be in reach but treachery, fire and destruction surround you. I can sniff the scent of death in the air, coming from afar. Only your courage and your determination will carry you through the dark times ahead.'

Damian's face was an unreadable mask and Oriel noticed he seemed completely unfazed by the antiquated speech of the old woman, which was as oblique as if she had been the Oracle of Delphi herself. 'And the outcome?' he asked.

'*Tò peprōménon phygeîn adýnaton*, it is impossible to escape from what is destined.' This woman was straight out of a Greek tragedy, like a modern-day priestess of the gods, and Oriel saw in Damian's eyes that he was taking her seriously.

'What is my destiny? Will I know how to deal with these dark times you predict?'

'Man is the measure of all things.'

The shrewd black eyes turned and fastened on Oriel's face, which had grown pale at the Oracle's prediction for Damian. She knew she shouldn't believe a word of such nonsense, nonetheless something about the woman sent an uncomfortable prickle down the back of her neck. 'You have the fair skin and soft hair of those born to luck and love. It's normal that the fair be attracted by the dark and the dark by the fair. But *eínai polloí mia olísthisi metaxý tou kypéllou kai tou cheílous*, there's many a slip between the cup and the lip.'

Oriel felt the powerful energy emanating from the woman overwhelm her. Suddenly she wanted to run away, fearing what this strange creature was going to say. The disquieting prophecies surrounding Damian were unnerving enough, she didn't need any more spine-chilling omens. 'Please, don't go on,' she protested. 'I don't really ...'

But the old woman, Delia, lifted her hand and Oriel felt a strange radiation emit from it on to her face, rendering her mute.

'Your fortune is changing, mermaid of the North Sea. Your Christian name begins with an O, the O of amazement that men utter at your beauty. A beauty that captures their hearts and twists them in knots that can never be undone. And though your beauty can be compared to that of Calypso, the fair nymph of Ogygia, or Selene, goddess of the moon, your fate could be that of the dark and passionate Antigone if the gods are not on your side. They are silent today but remember, it will not always be summer. Gather the harvest while you can.'

Oriel's brows knitted. 'What are you saying?'

'You are looking for water in the sea.'

Having said her piece, the Oracle moved aside to let Damian and Oriel pass. Taking her place on the step again, she once more became the shrivelled-up, gaunt old woman, a faint shadow of what she had metamorphosed into a few moments earlier.

Damian didn't seem rattled by the encounter. He held out his hand to Oriel and this time she took it, too shaken by the uncanny words of Delia to protest about anything. His hand was strong and comforting, his fingers transmitting a natural warmth that spread up her arm. Her heart fluttered treacherously and danger signals rushed through her veins. She knew exactly what her senses were saying. How could she ever resist?

She felt secure with Damian. The Oracle had been right about one thing, for sure: he really was the personification of all those brave gods Delia had named. Oriel remembered the words Yorgos had told her, describing his boss on the first day of her arrival at Helios: *master, tamer and conqueror … he hunts in the moonlight with the wolves, and swims with the sea monsters in the deep and dark waters surrounding the island*. Characteristically dramatic, like many of the islanders' utterances, but somehow it fitted Damian's dominating and charismatic persona.

Still, even though Oriel knew she was protected from the outside world when she was with Damian, how safe was she from the emotions that bubbled between them?

The *meltémi* had quietened down and it was almost sunset. They moved much more quickly now that the wind had subsided and Oriel's holding on to Damian's hand helped their progress too.

'Do you believe in all this mumbo jumbo?' she asked suddenly.

Damian drew a deep breath. 'You need to read between the lines.'

'So what does she mean by all those blood-curdling omens she was dishing out to you?'

'Don't worry about it, *agápi mou*. It's business as usual, I'm used to that sort of ominous prediction. This is Greece,' he said wryly.

Damian might be used to the double-talk of oracles but Oriel was definitely not; Delia's gibberish had filled her with a deep sense of foreboding.

When they reached the top of Mount Cynthus the sun was already low on the horizon, flushing the sea with rosy, pearl hues; the sky was striped with green, pink and smoke-grey. At the summit the plateau was adorned with small, simple stone shrines and dedications to Apollo from modern pilgrims.

'It's unbelievable!' Oriel murmured, catching her breath as she stood in wonder, feasting her eyes on the spectacular view. The sun slipped out of sight and the mellow colours of dusk spread over the island. She turned to look at Damian. He had taken off his dark glasses and was watching her intently. The undeniable love she read in his eyes filled her with such emotion that she moved towards him with an impulse to throw herself into his arms. He did take hold of her but only to push her gently from him, his arms rigid barriers preventing any movement.

'*Oyhee*, no Calypso, not again, not tonight.'

Oriel spoke then, stammering. 'But I am … I mean, we are …'

Damian winced. 'Yes, we've been lovers and I do love you more than life itself. At this moment you're moved by beauty so you are overcome by passionate feelings, that is all. At other times, if I so much as touch your arm to help you over rocky ground, you flinch. Sometimes it's as if you'd rather sit in any chair but the one beside me. Forgive me, but I don't like being made to feel my touch is distasteful to you, even if you happen sometimes to want it.'

Her lips parted in dismay. 'But Damian, I don't … you know …'

'Hush, *agápi mou*, let's remain just companions for a while.' He smiled. 'Come, look at this wonderful view. Enjoy it … there are not many that equal it … at least, that's what I think. Our sunsets

440

are the most beautiful in the world and, if you let me, I will take you to watch all of them.'

Oriel stared at him uncomprehendingly for a few seconds. Her wide green eyes questioned him earnestly. He was telling her he didn't want to take her in his arms, didn't want to make love to her. Somewhere, deep down, she was hurt. Yet what did she expect? She had only herself to blame.

The first blush of a rosy-bronze moon had risen across the water, sky and sea mingling in a universal softness. The evening light was radiating over the islands of the Cyclades, dancing like a chorus around the sacred isle of Delos. Looking down from their promontory, Damian and Oriel could see alternate strips of indigo sea between ridges of land and, in this, the peculiar beauty of the landscape lay.

Damian had moved a little away from her and was now standing, arms crossed, looking out to sea. Oriel felt suddenly abandoned, missing him even though he was still there. But then his voice came softly out of the silence and he began to tell her about Apollo, the god of pure sunlight, patron of music and poetry, who at the age of four took his bow and arrow and went out in search of the snake that had tormented his mother during her pregnancy and, finding Python, killed it.

'Listen carefully,' he whispered without looking at her, 'and you might hear the musicians and pilgrims, their music and paeans echoing among the stone as the great procession moves slowly into the Temple of Apollo. Close your eyes, Oriel, can't you hear the lyre and the chorus?'

And then he began to recite Callimachus's verses in the original ancient language of his ancestors, which she was able to understand:

> *The sacred isle its deep foundations forms*
> *Unshook by winds, uninjured by the deep.*
> *High o'er the waves appears the Cynthian steep;*
> *And from the flood the sea-mew bends his course*
> *O'er cliffs impervious to the swiftest horse*
> *Around the rocks the Icarian surges roar,*
> *Collect new foam, and whiten all the shore*

Beneath the lonely caves, and breezy plain
Where fishers dwelt of old above the main.
No wonder Delos, first in rank, is placed
Amid the sister isles on ocean's breast.

There was silence as Damian's sonorous voice died away. Oriel opened her eyes, feeling that her heart might burst with the wonder of it all. She would always be grateful to him, grateful for the most beautiful memory that nothing could ever erase from her mind. She turned to Damian but for a moment was unable to speak, and then smiled ruefully. 'I could listen to you forever but it frightens me. It's so lovely here now, just listening to the peace.'

'Come, *agápi mou*. It's late and you must be tired. The night is warm so we'll be able to sleep under the stars without a tent. We can bring the boat round to the Sacred Port. You can have a shower, if you fancy, then I'll light us a fire, and I'll dive for our dinner. Later, you can choose if you want to sleep on the boat in a proper bed.'

'No, no,' she said quickly in case Damian decided to leave her alone on the boat. 'I love camping.' Tonight, Oriel wanted to be next to him … She had discovered so much about this man who, only two weeks ago, had been nothing more than a nostalgic memory.

* * *

Later that evening, on the lower slopes of Mount Cynthus next to the shores of the Sacred Harbour, Damian decided that they would use a tent after all. 'You might prefer to have some privacy,' he told her when Oriel lifted enquiring eyebrows.

After they'd retrieved the camping bag from the *Alcyone*, she had watched him work, his movements swift and efficient. His back muscles rippled as he shifted the equipment around, fixing her a bed for the night in case she preferred to sleep in the privacy of the tent. He wouldn't let her help him so, sitting on a slab of marble, she had followed him with her eyes, every nerve inside her quivering.

The tent was pitched next to a clump of sea pines, where the ground was covered in tufty yellowed grass and bushes. Damian gathered some dry twigs and pine cones for kindling and had soon lit a fire. Oriel made them a salad with the tomatoes, cucumbers, peppers, olives and feta that had arrived on the boat from Mykonos that morning while Damian went off to catch a fish for their dinner.

He soon returned with a beautiful gilt-head bream and tended silently to their supper, his profile – the well defined cheekbones, the high-bridged nose and his lean, sharply defined jaw – outlined against the flames. It was the face of a strong and subtle man and, together with the confidence that endowed his every movement, Oriel was unable to take her eyes off him.

There was an unreal quality about the moment – in the brilliant masses of stars showering the navy-blue velvet sky above and the twinkling lights of Mykonos, seen across the calm expanse of water. Everything was still under the majestic calm of this warm May night, with the moon peering through the branches of the pines like an inquisitive golden eye.

'It's almost ready,' Damian called out and his gaze was upon her before she could pretend to be looking elsewhere. Now their supper was cooked, he built up the fire and the smoke rose up in a tangy column, causing the hovering insects and moths to fly off for the moment. She and Damian took their places opposite each other, leaning their backs against the dried-up trunks of a couple of gnarled trees.

Oriel had imagined she would be too strung out to swallow a morsel but, to her surprise, she was enjoying her meal. Damian had opened a bottle of wine that had been chilled in the yacht's fridge all day. 'This fish is delicious,' she murmured between mouthfuls. 'The flesh has absorbed the taste of the smoke and the fragrance of the pine cones.'

'Pure air, good water, sunshine, the beautiful surroundings of nature … these are God's means for a great life.'

Never had Oriel felt so strongly that a love of these islands was in Damian's blood, at the very core of his heart. 'You love the wildness and the mystery of it all, don't you?' she noted.

'I belong here,' he said simply. 'For generations my family has lived here on the islands … I am Greek, and proud to be so. The pulse of the place beats in me.' And Oriel saw in his dark, handsome face that strain of disdainful arrogance inherited from generations of haughty forebears.

It was peaceful by the fire. The flames leapt and danced. Now and then Damian threw on extra kindling or a pine cone, and there would be a sputtering hiss as the fire soared then settled.

Oriel watched the orange glow and the dark figure of the man outlined dimly by the firelight. The wine had loosened her up and the tension that had pulled on her nerves all afternoon – especially after their encounter with the Oracle – had been replaced by a feeling of wellbeing and languor.

'You seem to have done a lot to your island.'

'We say in Greece that a society grows great when old men plant trees they know they will never sit under.'

'Come on, you're not an old man. How old are you, Damian?'

'Age is not counted in years, *agápi mou,* but in the lessons life has taught you.'

His face was in shadow but Oriel didn't need to see it to know that the burden he was carrying in his heart was heavy. She knew all too well the pain that caused the bitterness she had perceived in his voice just now. Life hadn't spared Damian – from an early age, tragedy had followed him like a shadow. And if the witch on Mount Cynthus was to be believed, it seemed that calamity was not about to abandon him any time soon. Although his ill fortune appeared to have strengthened him, Oriel guessed that behind the stoic mask this man was vulnerable. Since their conversation on the boat, he had kept his word, raising a wall between them. Yet she felt that tonight, if she probed just a little, Damian would open up to her.

'Has life taught you so many lessons?' Oriel ventured quietly.

'Let's just say I've had my fair share of knocks.'

'Would you consider it insensitive of me if I asked you about those knocks?'

Damian did not answer immediately. Instead, he lifted a piece of wood and threw it on to the flames with a violence that, to someone who was ignorant of the circumstances surrounding his life, might have seemed unjustified. Oriel waited patiently.

'I was nine when I saw my father shoot my mother and his brother, who was her lover,' he declared bluntly.

'I'm sorry,' she whispered. 'A horrible experience. It must have left its mark.'

'You never forget. But I was the lucky one, I managed to bury it.' Damian sighed heavily. 'Helena was five and she's never walked since. Her mind became unbalanced and when she was younger, my family put her away in an institution in Athens for a while, until I got her out. She needed protecting, not locking up.' He shook his head slowly.

'Pericles, too, didn't escape unscathed. He started to shoot up heroin from the age of fifteen … You probably know the rest, I can't imagine island gossip hasn't filled you in. He was murdered by an unknown hand …' Damian raked frustrated fingers through his hair. 'He wasn't alone …' Again there was a pause, and then: 'He was with my wife … they were lovers.' His voice was barely audible and he ran a hand over his eyes, as though to blot out the gruesome scene.

This terrible truth was indeed no revelation to Oriel. 'Your wife and your brother, that must have hurt,' she said softly.

Damian shrugged, his gaze shifting to the flames. 'Cassandra was like a luscious over-ripened fruit, beautiful on the outside but rotten to the core. It hurt because it was my brother and, in some way, it brought up all the pain of the past. But Cassandra and I never loved each other. Our marriage was largely one of convenience, I suppose, so I wasn't surprised when, after my accident, she rejected me.'

Oriel couldn't imagine how any woman married to this man could possibly reject him – her whole body cried out to be touched and held by Damian. She cleared her throat. 'Mattias told me about your accident and how brave you'd been. Were you not afraid?'

'It wasn't an act of bravery, I think I've never been so afraid in my life. But you see, Mattias and I go a long way back. I couldn't have just left him there and saved myself. It was an instinctive act, I didn't stop to think. How could I have lived with that on my conscience? At the end of the day, saving my friend was more important than the fear I felt. A man has to do what he has to do.'

'I still think it's brave. There must have been warriors among your ancestors.'

'Yes, many men in my family fought for the independence of this country in 1921 and took part in the revolution and various other skirmishes.'

She smiled. 'So it goes without saying that you would turn out to be strong and courageous.'

Damian gave a bitter laugh. 'Not necessarily. From a thorn a rose emerges and from a rose a thorn, we say in Greece.'

'Meaning?'

'Meaning that an honest, respected man's son may turn out to be a criminal and vice versa. I think it was more the knocks I've had in my life that formed my character. In this instance I had no choice but to do what I did. As I've told you, Mattias and I go back a long way. He's always been a loyal friend when others who were supposed to be much closer stabbed me in the back. There was a time when I thought life wasn't worth living, and Mattias was there to give me hope and help me back up the slope ...' Damian's face seemed to darken in the flickering firelight and his phrase remained suspended in the silence of the night.

'There's a chill in the air,' he said, abruptly changing the subject. 'I'll make us some coffee, then I'll move the boat.' Suddenly he seemed tense, with an unusual nervousness. Although it was dark, the moon and the glow of the flames projected enough light for Oriel to see that there was a shift in Damian's mien. He pulled himself up with an effort. His shoulders had slumped a little and his silhouette in the penumbra was almost that of an older man as he went towards the tent to fetch the supplies.

Although he had spoken candidly about the various incidents that had marked him, Oriel had detected only the barest hint of bitterness edging Damian's voice ... until now. She had no doubt that this sudden change in him was prompted by whatever it was that Yolanda had done, and that Mattias had half alluded to. Maybe the hurt of Yolanda's leaving him in pursuit of her career went too deep for him to express. Maybe, too, he didn't want to raise the subject of her because he was still torn ...

Minutes passed and Oriel was just about to go looking for Damian when he reappeared. He was smiling now, and she might have put his sudden tension down to the flickering light and a trick of her imagination had she not been so sensitized to his every changing mood and expression.

'I was looking for the *briki*,' he explained, brandishing the longhandled coffee pot, shaped like an hourglass. 'Will you have

446

Turkish coffee with me, or would you prefer the less-strong instant?'

'I'd love some Turkish coffee, please.'

'How do you like it? *Glikós, métrios* or *sketos*?'

'I'll have it métrios, *medium*, thanks.'

'Purists will tell you that there are thirty-six different degrees of sweetness.'

'I can't see how that can be when Greek coffee cups only hold about two inches of liquid.'

'When we were studying for our finals, my friends and I used to make big mugs of Turkish coffee to keep us awake all night and less sleepy when we got up in the morning.' Damian grinned. 'Those carefree days are some of my best memories.'

Oriel watched him mix the coffee with sugar and water in the *briki*, which he placed on the smouldering ashes. He boiled the brew until it almost foamed out of the pot then poured it in a glass.

'I don't have the right cup for this here, sorry. I have some on the boat but the *kaimak* on your coffee is nice and thick, and the more foam, the better the coffee will taste. Hopefully, it'll still be good.'

Oriel laughed. 'This has been a luxurious dinner, thank you. Much better than anything I've ever experienced camping. I don't think I'd dare to complain.'

Damian now proceeded to make his own cup. 'We've been talking about me all evening. What about you, Calypso?' he asked. A lighter inflection had appeared in his voice.

Oriel shrugged. 'Oh, I've had a very straightforward life, no ups and downs really.'

'You must be missing London, the glitter and the lights. It hasn't been much fun for you on Helios.'

'Oh, I wouldn't say that. You've wined and dined me almost every night.' Her voice was deliberately breezy. 'I love my job, as you know, and I can't say I've been short of excitement these past few days ...'

He grimaced. 'No, you're right, we haven't made it easy for you. I blame myself for that.'

'On the contrary, it makes a change.'

'You seem to have such an adventurous nature, how come

you've been able to keep yourself out of harm's way?'

'I don't go looking for trouble.'

'And trouble has never found you?'

'No.'

'Until I came along, eh?'

'You said it, Damian.' Her smile flickered to him and away, like a moth uncertain of where it should settle.

Damian laughed deep in his throat. His eyes held that diamond brilliance, the irises so enlarged they were like mirrors reflecting the leaping flames – but to Oriel, they were unreadable. 'Are you cold? I can always take you back to the boat if you'd rather sleep there,' he wanted to know.

'I'm fine with camping. I've told you, Vicky and I used to do it regularly.'

He chuckled. 'You might change your mind after this.' But he didn't stay to catch her expression, instead busying himself with building up the fire and putting away their supper things.

What was he implying? Excitement raced through her veins, making her pulses flutter. Surely he wouldn't? For that, Damian would have to break their pact. Either that, or she would have to admit to him that she was falling in love. For that was what was happening to her, Oriel knew that now.

She'd known it all along, even before the night they'd spent in the Room of Secrets, a truth that in her stubbornness she had refused to acknowledge. Certainly Damian was a handsome devil, unpredictable and exciting – but her feelings ran much deeper than infatuation or chemistry. She loved his strength, his bravery, his knowledgeable brain, his integrity; she loved his loyalty and kindness but, most of all, she loved his vulnerability, which he went to such pains to conceal.

Oh God! How blind I've been not to see what he means to me.

The eerie encounter with Delia also filled her mind. What had she meant with her reference to Antigone? Sophocles's play had seen Antigone yield to the fate of the gods, not the laws of man. Although decisive and courageous, she had still come to a tragic end. So what did it mean? It made no sense at all to her. Or was it about Antigone herself? Some scholars believed her name meant 'opposed to motherhood' or 'against men'. But Oriel had no antagonistic ideas towards either. On the contrary, she had always thought she would marry and have children, she just hadn't met the right man … until now.

She was surprised but happy that Damian had opened up to her. Was it their strange surroundings that induced this mood of amity? Despite the flickering flames of the fire, the darkness had masked them from each other and perhaps it was easier to speak honestly that way. Still, he had not spoken about Yolanda and, until he did so, Oriel couldn't completely relax. It was as if her trust in Damian would never be entirely wholehearted until he came clean about his childhood sweetheart, with whom he still seemed to share some sort of bond.

As Oriel watched Damian nurse the campfire – he was so close to her now that she felt the impact of him, the masculine attraction pulling at her like a lasso. She realized that every inch of her body felt alive, her senses acutely aware of him. How she longed to kiss that sculpted mouth, to run her tongue over those sensual lips; she ached to hold him and feel the hard strength of him, taste the satiny skin of his broad shoulders, run her fingers through the mass of his black hair. It was all she could do to restrain herself from reaching out and touching him.

Damian paused in prodding the fire and his eyes ran over her. He made as if to move towards her, then checked himself immediately. There was a tortured silence and where there should have been a reaching out, a clasping of hands, a mingling of bodies, there was inert hollowness, an echoing cavern … and it was all her fault, Oriel thought dismally.

Damian quickly broke the moment, sensing their mutual discomfort, and perhaps misreading her reactions. 'Shall I heat you some hot milk?'

Why did that suggestion bring tears to Oriel's eyes? Maybe it was because if she had only let him into her bed the night before, when he had so thoughtfully brought her milk, she could have snuggled into his arms tonight. Being next to him like this, knowing that he wanted her as much as she did him, and not being able to do anything about it was torture. He had rebuffed her earlier that evening and her pride would not allow her a new attempt.

'Anything the matter, *agápi mou*?'

Oriel shook her head mutely.

Damian didn't push her further. 'I'll make you that nightcap, it'll help you sleep on the hard ground.'

He went into the tent and came back with a small pan and a bottle of milk.

'I'll do that,' Oriel offered, taking them from him. She knelt next to the fire and poured some milk into the pan. 'Would you like one too?'

'I think I need something stronger,' he said in a hoarse voice, 'but wine will have to do for tonight.' After emptying the bottle into his glass he pulled a packet of Gitanes from his shorts' pocket. He lit a cigarette and drew deeply on it.

Although she wasn't looking at him, Oriel could feel that he was watching her, and an unanswered question hovered on her lips. She needed to get to the bottom of it before she could give full rein to her love. She lifted her head. Damian was leaning against the tree, facing her, but his face was in the dark. She took the milk off the fire and poured it slowly into her mug. She hesitated then took a sip of the warm brew as if to give herself courage. 'Damian,' she said suddenly, deciding to take the bull by the horns. 'Last night, and this evening on Mount Cynthus, you said you loved me.'

His voice came low out of the dark. '*Né, agápi mou*, and I will keep repeating it until my last breath.'

'What about Yolanda, your childhood friend?'

Oriel felt him stiffen.

'What about Yolanda?'

'I understand that the time wasn't right when you were young but you're free now, and she's a great diva, loved by the islanders … and it's obvious she's crazy about you.'

Damian stared at the ground for a few moments before looking up again. 'All that is in the past, *agápi mou*. You must believe me,' he said finally, his voice trembling a little.

Though she couldn't see his eyes, Oriel guessed they were filled with pain. She took a long breath. 'She came to see me at the staff house and told me you're still lovers. That even if you stray from time to time, you will always go back to her.'

With a raise of an eyebrow, his mouth curled in a bitter smile. 'Trust is a fragile thing. Once broken, it can never be fixed. Yolanda knows that full well.'

'What do you mean?'

'My love for Yolanda died when she—' Damian broke off abruptly, then whispered hoarsely, 'Why do you want stir up the ashes of the past, Oriel? Isn't it enough that I assure you that I love you … that I will always love you … that I loved you from the first minute I laid eyes on you? But back then when we met it seemed an impossible love, and because I wanted to have children, I married Cassandra. We say in Greece, *Mé kheíron béltiston*, the least bad choice is the best. Apparently I would have done better staying on my own.'

Oriel sat looking into the fire, saying nothing. Damian was hurting, she knew him well enough to tell. She could have gone to him, put her arms around him and told him how much she loved him, but she was tongue-tied, fearing he would mistake her loving impulse for a sign of compassion or even pity.

'Does that satisfy you?'

She nodded silently. Inside, though, she felt the questions still had to be answered: what exactly had Yolanda done? What was the thread that tied the pair? What bond did they share?

* * *

Damian sat above the shore, looking out to sea without seeing it. The night was warm and he'd pulled on his denim shorts but hadn't bothered with his shirt so he could let the faint breeze soothe his skin. His eyes were full of the scene in a recurrent dream that had haunted his nights for a long time but had left him alone these past years … until tonight. A shiver shot through him and he smothered the choking sob rising in his throat.

In his nightmare, a newborn child was lying in a beautiful blue cradle. It was dusk and the room was full of shadows. Through the wide-open window he could hear the faint whisper of the sea that was as smooth as a sheet of silk. There was an eerie calm in the atmosphere; the air was still and not a bird was in the sky.

Suddenly Yolanda was in the room and a line of clouds had ominously appeared on the horizon. She was arguing with him about her career and the baby, and it was as if she had gone raving mad. All at once, like a wild beast, she leapt on the child in the cradle and before Damian could stop her, she had thrown their little boy from the window into the sea. Immediately there was thunder and lightning, but his baby's scream as he flew through the air topped the explosive noise of the storm and, like seashells that retain the sound of the ocean, the cry remained in Damian's ears even after he'd woken up.

Yolanda had placed a knife at the core of their love. Although he had found a way to get along with her, his feelings for her were dead. There was not a day that passed when he didn't think of the child; the ache never left him. Did that tiny beating heart know what was happening to him? Had he felt unloved? Had he suffered any pain? The boy would be almost nine today; what would he be like? Each time Damian came across a child of that age, a knot would form deep in his bowels and the hurt would resurface as acutely as the first day.

And now he felt two arms around him. He looked up into Oriel's beautiful eyes, filled with alarm but still dazed with sleep. She was there; his fair angel, her body sleek, her hair that drove him mad with desire tumbling all about her.

'Damian, what's wrong? Can't you sleep? I heard you shout out.' She dropped suddenly to her knees before him and put her arm around his neck.

But he looked away and gritted his teeth to stop the tightness rising again in his throat, almost suffocating him. Feeling Oriel against him so soft, so sweet and so loving was bringing up emotions that alarmed him. He must control himself.

'Tell me what's wrong, my love,' she whispered.

He looked up, staring at her starkly, searching her features. He was silent for a moment then began to speak. 'Before my twenty-fifth birthday, when I was supposed to take possession of my inheritance, Yolanda became pregnant. I had a big row with my whole family, including my uncle Cyrus. He was my guardian and running Helios at the time. I told them all I would marry Yolanda, whether they liked it or not. There was no choice now anyway. We were quietly engaged so as not to provoke gossip, and Cyrus sent both of us to Athens.

'After a couple of years we planned to return when no one would ask questions but five months later Yolanda received an offer of a recording contract. There was talk of a Hollywood film … it was an opportunity, she said, that would never come again.' His jaw tensed and he turned his gaze to the dark waves hissing at the nearby shoreline.

'I told her she had to turn it down, pleaded with her, if not for the sake of our love, at least for the child. But Yolanda flatly refused to listen to reason. She flew to America to sign the contract behind my back. She found someone to give her an abortion, a backstreet affair. She was already four months pregnant.'

'Oh my love.' Oriel cupped his face with both her hands and looked deeply into his eyes. Her tenderness was too much for Damian and uncontrollable tears ran down his cheeks. 'She killed my child,' he said in a choked voice. 'She killed my baby.'

'Hush, my love … hush. If you want, we'll make plenty of babies. I know it'll not be the same child but it will be a part of you and a part of me, a consecration of our love.'

'What are you saying, Oriel?' He looked at her, unable to tear his eyes away from hers – so liquid, so beautiful, so mesmerizing – and they gazed at each other without speaking for a moment.

'I'm saying I've been a fool and that I do love you. I've loved you from the first moment you appeared to me out of the sea, like one of your Greek gods. Oh, Damian, hold me …'

'*Agápi mou!*' Damian reached for her, drawing her against his naked chest. He felt the thunder in her heart, felt the fullness of her breasts, the torment of her nipples grazing across his flesh under her thin nightdress. He'd been aching to hold her and now she was finally in his arms.

His fingertips ran lightly along Oriel's cheek as if committing her face to memory, much as a blind person does when they seek to know another by touch. It was as though merely seeing her was not enough: he wanted all the knowledge of her that his senses could give him. The very sound of her voice went through him like a strange, thrilling whisper.

He brushed Oriel's lips with his, covered them, engulfed them – softly at first, then demandingly, enjoying the way her mouth opened against his and her fingers splayed against his bare chest. He recognized the flicker of desire in her eyes – the same craving that was running unchecked through his own body – and the ache within him deepened.

'*Sas thélo tóso polý agápi mou*, I want you so much, my darling,' he whispered as his mouth touched the very delicate vein of Oriel's throat, his hands covering her breasts and encircling them, the pad of his thumbs rolling over the taut, tender buds of her nipples beneath the cotton. And then, dipping his head, he pushed the loose neckline to one side and tasted the tip of one with his tongue, cherishing its fullness with fiery, liquid caresses.

'I want you too, my love,' she murmured softly, her fingers digging into his hair.

'Come,' Damian breathed huskily in her ear, sweeping her up into his arms, his mouth moving back to hers as he carried her to his sleeping bag, which he had spread open on the ground earlier, and laid her gently on the soft bedding.

Damian watched as, stretched out before him, Oriel unbuttoned the rest of her flimsy cotton nightdress, through which he could glimpse the curves of her body, and let it fall from her shoulders. Standing straddling her, heart beating, he stared over her slim, shapely, perfect length. The soft glow of the moon reflected on her creamy skin and the firm swell of her breasts as her tender pink nipples ripened beneath his gaze and her stomach fluttered slightly in anticipation. Damian let his eyes slowly drift downwards over its peach-smooth curve to linger over the soft mound of pale curls that crowned her slim thighs.

But Oriel was not lying there inert. As he was lowering himself down, she stopped him, lifting herself up to his crotch with the graceful movements of a sylph, her green eyes intense with desire, fixing him with an unambiguous message that sent a hot stab of heat and hardness within him as he waited, desperate for her touch.

But he could see that she was playing him at his own game, making him wait as she knelt against him. He unzipped his shorts and let them slip to the ground. His mouth went dry. Her lips, teeth and fingers followed the curve of his body, moving sensually over the muscled flesh of his thighs and hips, stroking his groin, telling him how much she loved tasting him.

When Oriel finally cupped him delicately in her palms and began fondling him, Damian let out a gruff gasp as the shattering sensation filled him like lightning. He groaned aloud all the while her hands, her mouth and her tongue played havoc with his nerve ends. The volcano erupted, the world exploded and he cried out her name as he poured into her hands, his body shaking with a fit of convulsions such as he had never before experienced.

CHAPTER 13

Oriel and Damian woke with the dawn and the sky was still all pinks and oranges as they made their way back to the boat. They had slept in each other's arms under the starlit sky after hours of passionate lovemaking that had swept them once more into a mindless world of delirious sensations and ecstatic pleasure until, their sanity lost, they had finally collapsed and fallen asleep, satiated and at peace.

As they went below deck, Damian pulled Oriel against him. 'Let's have a shower together.'

'We'll have that tonight but this morning shouldn't we drop in on the French team? Besides, any more of these frenzied orgasms and I'll be like a zombie all day!' She gave him a kiss on the lips, grabbed a towel and disappeared into the tiny shower cubicle.

Oriel stood motionless for a few seconds, grateful for the hot water, letting it trickle down her face and body. For the first time in her life she felt calm, happy and secure. Oh yes, she loved Damian, and she had no doubt now that he loved her too.

He was what she wanted, she knew that now … from the very beginning, ever since that electrifying moment when he'd audaciously barred her passage on the shore of Aegina. While it had infuriated her, it had also made her want him. His arrogance made him seem all the more virile; his determination and courage showing him to be a born leader of men, with those broad shoulders to carry out his responsibilities. And if from time to time he overstepped the mark, she would make allowances.

The proud blood of generations of Greek rulers ran in his veins, already making him an extraordinary man, but on Helios it seemed to brand him a god among men. Life would be a challenge there, having to cope with Helena, Yolanda and who knew how many other snakes that lurked in the shadows of that beautiful, primitive island, but Oriel didn't care: she'd make a go of it, she had little doubt of that.

Oriel gasped aloud as the shower curtain was suddenly pulled back. She turned to find a naked Damian standing behind her, his silver eyes sparkling with dangerous intent. His dark head came down and he took her mouth with his.

'Don't do this to me,' she whispered between kisses as the deliciously warm water cascaded over them. 'I won't be able to talk coherently to the French team later, let alone work.'

'You don't need to, *agápi mou*. I will work for both of us.'

'Oh no, you won't! I'm not going to be left out.'

Damian chuckled. 'Always the professional, Calypso. François isn't expecting us at any particular time. Look at me, I only have to be near you and my control is shot to pieces,' he said and pointed to the evidence of his words. 'Are you going to be heartless and leave me like this?'

Oriel felt desire flood her and she soon found herself breathless as both Damian's touch and the water started to arouse her to a peak. With brimming hunger, she pulled him against her with a moan. But Damian pushed her back against the wall. Hands on her hips, he lifted her, bringing her against his rigid shaft, urging her to wrap her legs around him. 'Take me inside you,' he said, his mouth on hers, hot, wet and delicious, his tongue licking up the water that trickled down her face and throat. He had awakened in her such a heightened sensitivity that as he kissed her it was as though a fire leapt across her heart.

Oriel put her arms around his neck and squeezed her thighs against his hips, dizzy with the sweet sensation of his burning kisses and of his stiff velvet tip pushing against her, stroking, caressing and sliding relentlessly against where she was already slick with desire. A soft moan escaped her lips as he suddenly thrust, swift and hard, into her, again and again, driving her wild, the speed and movement creating a storm that burst inside her.

Pure primitive pleasure seized Oriel. As before he stripped away all her inhibitions – everything but love. This was no civilized lovemaking, it was a savage act of consummate possession; he was her adored pagan god and she surrendered completely to him. Her fingernails bit into his back as his teeth grazed her satiny shoulders and their bodies locked together, moving as one.

Still clasped to Oriel, Damian barely paused, only enough to carry her to the bed and lie her down. She was still straddling him, her knees grasping his waist, and his movements inside her resumed, becoming stronger and more forceful. Her hands slowly ran over his flat midriff and slid below, between their bodies, to find the smooth pouches hiding in the rough-haired expanse of his crotch. Damian made a deep harsh sound as she stroked them lightly and she felt the clench of his taut muscles under her caress. The more he responded, the more Oriel gave in to her impulses, intensifying her own pleasure.

As the waves of pleasure built up in her, Oriel forced her eyes open to look at Damian. His pupils were dilated, his lips parted in a gasping breath, the taut mask of frenzied desire that had spread over his features making him look even more wildly attractive to her – Damian was hers in those moments, all hers. She could feel his heart beating out of control under her fingers.

When it finally came, her release ripped through her like a tornado. Damian joined her seconds later with a long, thick groan, his breath rasping through his throat, his eyes enormous and glittering, trembling and crying out her name, which had never sounded so beautiful to Oriel's ears. She felt his warmth flood her, making her peak again and again, leaving her shuddering, dazed and shaken. And as she drifted back to earth it was like freefalling through the air. All the need and loneliness of the past few years had exploded now into this moment, like imprisoned birds released into the endless blue sky.

Although they knew they should get up, they lay there for a long while, bodies entwined, the languor too deep, too somnolent for them to raise themselves.

Oriel woke after a short dreamless sleep to see Damian pulling on a T-shirt and shorts. He turned his head, conscious of her stirring, concerned that he had woken her. 'Go back to sleep, *agápi mou*,' he told her tenderly. 'I'm just going to check the engine's in good order for later, no need to get up.'

'Don't worry, I'm awake now,' she said, sliding out of bed, suddenly shy as she became aware of her naked body under Damian's hungry scrutiny. 'You go on up,' she added. 'I'll join you in the cockpit.'

A few minutes later she made her way to where he stood at the wheel. He was bent over the ship's radio, speaking with a quiet urgency, his face pale, jaw set in a grim line. When he had finished speaking, Oriel went to him, concern etched on her face. 'What is it, Damian?'

'That was Stavros. We've had a fire at the factory.'

She looked at him, horrified. 'Oh no! Is anybody hurt?'

'I don't think so. They've put most of it out but there's been a lot of damage. You'd better go and pack your bag. I'll call François, let him know we won't be seeing him. Stavros is flying down in my plane and he'll be here in an hour.'

The Oracle! Oriel thought, but she decided not to say anything. Damian was upset enough without her adding superstition to his troubles. Nonetheless, she couldn't help admitting to herself that it was an uncanny coincidence. 'When did this happen?'

He looked pensive. 'Last night. Stavros was surprised I hadn't heard from Yorgos yet.'

'Don't worry, I'm sure they'll bring the fire under control. What's going to happen to the boat?'

'Stavros will sail it back and I'll fly you home.'

'I'm glad you're not going to be on your own,' she said. 'It must have been a terrible shock for you.'

Damian stroked Oriel's cheek. '*Né ksehro*, you don't realize the difference that makes to me. With you, I can conquer any disaster.'

'Hush, darling. It's probably not as bad as you think. I'll go and get packed.'

* * *

They were back by twelve. The hot noonday sun bearing down on Helios was a blinding glare, and the world shimmered hazily as Damian dropped Oriel off at the staff house in the Jeep. He told her that she might as well spend the morning exploring the island while he went to the factory to take stock of the damage. Handing her a car key, he explained where the Volkswagen cabriolet was parked behind the building. Oriel wanted to accompany him but he gently rejected her offer; he'd be more focused without her there, he added with a smile. He would meet her at six o'clock at the staff house to

459

take her back to Heliades.

When she protested, he insisted that she couldn't continue to live at the staff house and that he would explain the situation to Helena, making sure neither she nor her loyal staff troubled Oriel again. She didn't demur further, realizing that Damian had enough worries without her adding to them.

A few minutes after he left, Oriel had already slung a few things into her canvas bag and left the house. The drive in the open Volkswagen cabriolet was cool and refreshing. She headed for the stretch of coast where Mattias had told her there were some interesting isolated coves where she could swim without being disturbed. Although some were only accessible by boat, she was sure she would find a path down to one of the beaches. She parked the car not far from Manoli's, having decided to explore from there.

It was warm for walking but she had taken a hat with her and was carrying her bikini and *peignoir* in her bag. The journey along the dusty road made her hot and sticky. Still, there was a cooling breeze. After half an hour she came to a bluff that jutted out over a small half moon of pure white sand. On one side Mediterranean pine trees shaded the edge of the beach, where rocks tumbled steeply into the deep blue sea with the great conical mass of Typhoeus behind them. Along the rocky side of the coast, she could see the cavernous dark entrance of a cave, lying just beyond the shoreline.

The view from here was magnificent. Oriel stood a moment on top of the cliff with a new awareness of Damian in her heart as she watched the white sails of outbound yachts in the distance, billowing out before the steady breeze. She had sailed with him across that same stretch of ocean just three days ago, with the wind on their faces, and now she marvelled at how much things had changed in that short space of time.

It had been only an hour since she'd left Damian and already she was missing him as if she had lost a part of herself. She stood a while looking down on the bay, at the changing colours of the water as it reached outwards from the shore. It merged from palest green to turquoise, then to the deep, deep blue beyond the reef, so inviting that she couldn't wait to plunge into the clear, cool water. Surely over there – just beyond the cave – was a track, zigzagging its way through the rocks and vegetation. It looked very steep but it would be worth the effort. Oriel made her way along the bluff until she found the path. She scrambled down it then ran across the sand, stripping down to her bikini on the way and throwing herself into the calm water.

Oriel swam far out into the bay, towards the reef that she could make out in the distance. The water was crystal clear, making it possible for her to see right to the bottom where the reflection of the sun-kissed waves rippled the smooth white sand. Revelling in the warm blue-green water, she paddled leisurely, allowing the gentle swell to caress her cheeks and chin as thoughts about Damian and the hours they had spent together making love washed over her. It was clear out towards the rocks too, a brilliant turquoise blue with a gold dusting of sunlight on the surface. The sea was so placid there was no danger. Oriel reflected contentedly that it was well worth the dusty walk to be allowed to swim in peace. Everything today felt new and sparkling – a wonderful world, just for her – and she swam quite far out, aware of a new vigour in her strokes.

After she had come out of the sea, Oriel sat on an outcrop of rock and dried herself in the sun, shaking her wet hair free. It fell in thick damp strands over her face and she combed her fingers through it with slow, leisurely strokes. Then she paused, suddenly aware that something in the air had changed. It felt heavier now; the breeze had gone and a deadly hush weighed down the atmosphere.

It was then that she realized that the crickets were silent and the birds had stopped singing; a palpable stillness surrounded her as if Nature herself was waiting with bated breath for some tremendous catastrophe. Now, looking out across the sea, not even the shadow of a ship broke the silver sheet of water stretching to the vague horizon's rim. It was time to go back to the car.

Then abruptly the sky grew dark, as though a cloak had enveloped the island. A moment later, a sudden wind tore into the bay, swelling the sea so that strong waves began to hurl themselves at the rocks. Suddenly frightened, Oriel made her way quickly along the small beach, watching the pine trees on the far side shiver and sway under the dark storm clouds. It began to rain, in great heavy drops that hammered their way like bullets strafing the sand. Oriel grabbed her bag and clothes and, bent almost double under the driving rain, she headed quickly for the cave, thankful for any shelter it might offer.

She paused at the entrance and reached into her bag for her *peignoir*. There was no point in putting her clothes back on: they were soaked. She shrugged it on over her bathing costume and looked out at the hell-world that had erupted outside. The storm was turning circles in the bay; the sea that roared and beat itself against the cliffs of Helios was a furious monster and bore no relation to the smiling, placid water she had swum in half an hour ago. She looked at the pines, under which the cool shade had seemed so inviting before. Now the wind and rain were bending their branches in a violent assault, knocking the cones to the ground like a hail of huge stones.

Inside the cave a cool dankness prevailed, its customary dark pierced by the flickering, ghostly light cast by the white sheets of lightning. Oriel stood under the lip of the entrance for a while, looking out through the curtain of rain, gnawing her lip and staring at the pandemonium Nature was creating outside. Although the sounds of the storm filled the air, she turned suddenly and looked upwards. There was a rhythmic beat coming from above her – one that had nothing to do with the rain. It wasn't loud but she could distinguish it clearly above the hissing and wailing of the tempest.

Every muscle in her body stiffened instinctively. For perhaps a couple of seconds it was quiet and she could only make out the sound of the wind howling outside. Then, clear and unmistakable, she could hear steps echoing. There was someone in the cave, maybe more than one person, she thought with a shiver, her imagination working at one hundred miles an hour. Had she stumbled on a smugglers' den?

Her mind flicked to Damian and Mattias's conversation in the taverna the night of the sponge divers' farewell. There had been talk of boats slinking through the water like dark shadows in the night. Pirates, too.

Don't be foolish, she chided herself, but all the while the cave seemed increasingly lonely and sinister in this eerie half light. If only she hadn't parked her car so far away ... but the storm was raging and she knew it would be pure idiocy to venture outside. Maybe she hadn't been alone on the beach before and these sounds came from other beachgoers stranded in the storm like her, who had taken shelter before her. But even as the thought crossed her mind, she knew she had been alone in the bay.

There were more steps now and then a shuffling sound, as though something was being dragged. Then the noise stopped.

It was very quiet – *too* quiet, Oriel felt – with no sound other than that of the blustering tempest and the sigh of a chilling breeze spiralling upwards to the vaulted roof of the cave. Her nerves tensed, waiting for something to happen. Then she remembered something and delved quickly into her bag. The day after Damian had ridden out on horseback to find her in the dark, she had put a torch in among her things. Here it was. She took it out and turned it on, aiming the beam at the back of the cave … Except the cave didn't seem to have a back, it looked as if it went deep into the cliff. She ventured a few metres into the cavern. With every step, the air grew more damp and musty. The floor was no longer rock now, but earth. Oriel could hear the angry scream of wind but it was a little fainter now, howling down the crevices and in through the cracks in the rocky wall, punctuated by loud claps of thunder with barely a break between. The storm must be right overhead.

Suddenly she was aware that the cave had widened out and she could see some steep, narrow steps carved into the rock wall ahead. She hesitated and then, leaving her bag on the ground and plucking up courage, put her foot on the bottom step. Oriel could definitely hear movement above her and, being careful to avoid any noise, moved up stealthily. Before even reaching the top – her eyes just peeping over the edge – she took in just how large the space above her was. The great cavern seemed to be part of a veritable warren, with more than one tunnel leading off it.

Straining her eyes, Oriel saw that great cave was full of cases of bottles set in an orderly array. It was an impressive number, quite a stash. She moved cautiously into the room and went over to one of the cases. She stooped and picked up a bottle, aiming the beam of her torch at its label. Her brow creased in puzzlement: it was *affioramento* olive oil, the Lekkas's best. What was it doing here? Surely Damian wouldn't have stored these bottles in this place – why would he? He had shown her the storage rooms at the factory. On the other hand, maybe they had been brought here after the fire? Still, it was rather a long way from the factory and, as far as she knew, Stavros hadn't made any mention of the fire being bad enough to need to move the stock. The factory had certainly not burned to the ground. In fact, hadn't Damian told her that the only room destroyed was the one where the fire had started: the office where they held the accounts and archives?

Oriel stood still. Now she could definitely hear voices coming from one of the short tunnels leading off the room. She took a breath. If something untoward was going on here she needed to tell Damian about it. There were, she noticed, more steps leading up from the tunnel to a level above – probably another storage room.

Slowly she continued her progress up the stone stairway, taking careful steps and hesitating at the slightest sound. As she stood at the top in the semi-darkness, back against the wall, she caught sight of a movement in the shadows at the far end of the short tunnel. She thought she could make out the shapes of three blurred, bulky figures, and they were talking in muffled tones. Her heart was thumping wildly and as her eyes grew accustomed to the dim light, Oriel recognized a familiar stocky frame.

Yorgos!

She didn't call out, the feeling in the pit of her stomach warning her against doing so. But still, she had seen enough. Damian's estate manager, whom she had distrusted from the start, was definitely up to something. All she could think of now was how to get out of the cave as quickly as possible so that she could warn Damian.

Retreating quickly, Oriel had just started to climb back down the steps when her sandal caught on an uneven edge. She tripped and the torch flew out of her hand, toppling with her down the remainder of the stairs. She found herself sprawling on the floor of the cave below, her hands clutching the dirt. Winded, she lay there a moment, then gingerly pushed herself up to a sitting position: she was shocked but not badly hurt.

Fortunately, the torch hadn't broken. It lay on the ground, casting a faint glimmer on the wall. She picked it up with her right hand and as she did so, she became aware that her other hand, still clutching at the dirt floor, was resting on something hard. It was hurting her palm and she shifted it, wincing a little. She aimed the torch at the offending object – which might have been a stone, she supposed, but didn't feel like one. In the feeble light she saw a large square sapphire earring with diamond surround. She recognized it instantly. The last time she had seen that blue stone it had been dangling from Yolanda's ear on the evening she had visited Oriel at the staff house.

Oriel barely had time for the meaning of her discovery to sink in before she heard the soft echo of footsteps: someone was coming down the stairs. She looked up, the piece of jewellery still in her open hand. She gave a small gasp and swallowed convulsively.

Yorgos was standing on the steps above her.

'What has *Despinis* Anderson been doing in this cave, eh? Curious, eh?' he asked with a smile that didn't quite make it to his lizard-like eyes. 'Have you never heard our Greek proverb? *Min rotate schetika me oti den sas aforá, kai pote den tha echete kaka prágmata sti zoi sas,* if you don't ask about what doesn't concern you, bad things won't happen to you.'

Oriel didn't like the sound of Yorgos's voice. She managed a shaky smile and hastily thrust the earring and the torch into the pocket of her *peignoir,* praying he hadn't seen them. 'I was caught in the storm. Luckily for me there was this cave. I was just exploring it.'

Yorgos's hoarse voice was menacing. 'Exploring the cave, eh? But there isn't anything to see down here, *Despinis.*'

Except for an impressive amount of affioramento olive oil, which I presume you're trafficking, Oriel thought to herself, but refrained from saying. 'No, nothing at all.'

Yorgos's thin, unpleasant face smiled. He took in Oriel's dishevelled state. '*Despinis* fell down the steps, eh? You need to take more care.'

'I didn't go up them,' she retorted rather too quickly. 'I was about to but tripped over the first step. The edge of the stone is broken and it got caught in my shoe.'

'The edge of the stone on the bottom step is not broken,' Yorgos said drily, shining his torch over it. He gave Oriel a hard stare. 'I think that the *Despinis,* if you don't mind my saying, was eavesdropping upstairs. Then, as she was hurrying back down, she stumbled. You just couldn't keep your little nose out of other people's affairs, eh? You're all the same, you women.'

Oriel had never liked Yorgos, finding him ingratiating and sly, but now, standing on the stairs looking down on her, he seemed downright sinister. The bones of his skull made shiny patches on his cheeks where the skin was tightly stretched. It looked like a death's head, she thought, her imagination working overtime – not helped by the eerie torchlight in the cave. But Oriel was more than simply unnerved: she was afraid, really afraid.

Yorgos came down the rest of the steps slowly on noiseless feet. 'You must understand that I can't let you go, not now. Not like I did that snivelling Frenchwoman.'

Oriel's eyes widened. 'Chantal Hervé,' she murmured.

'*Né*, she wasn't worth worrying about.' A vacant smile was fixed to his pockmarked face like a mask. 'It was obvious she'd leave the island and wouldn't talk, mouse that she was, so I didn't need to get my hands dirty.' He cocked his head to one side, his eyes gleaming malevolently. 'But you're different, you have the *Kyrios*'s ear. I knew you were trouble the minute I met you. Typical pig-headed sort of woman, the worst type. At least that other nosy little bitch just needed money to keep her mouth shut.'

Oriel stared at him. Her panicked mind told her to keep him talking to buy herself some more time. 'The Dutch student … so that's why she left. She found out about all this too, didn't she? How you were betraying Damian.'

'Betraying?' Yorgos gave a nasty laugh. 'Ah yes, the great *Drákon* Damian. He always thought he was better than me, always looking down his nose. If Pericles had only lived, I'd have been his right-hand man. Then I'd have got the respect I deserve.' He paused with a self-righteous squaring of the shoulders. 'Look at it this way, I'm just taking what I'm owed.'

Yorgos took a step towards her. Oriel's heart was pounding but she tried not to let her fear show. He stopped in front of her. 'You think you're so intelligent, eh?'

He knelt down and shone the torch in her face for a moment, making her wince and screw up her eyes against the light. 'Not so clever now, are you?' He lowered the beam and looked her in the eye, and Oriel glared back at him. 'It'll be different for you, *Despinis*. I'm afraid it won't be a quick end.'

He made a movement with his hand nervously, the large gold

watch glinting on his wrist in the torchlight. 'I'm a little squeamish about blood, you see, so I can't put you out of your misery with a knife to the throat or anything like that.'

Yorgos watched Oriel as the sickening realization of what he planned to do dawned on her. 'Ah, you see now, don't you? All I need to do is tie you up. And as no one knows where you are, they'll never guess you're down here. Come to think of it, you'll be dying a perfectly normal death of starvation and thirst.'

'It'll be murder. And they'll get you for it, Yorgos,' Oriel said with a cold fury. 'Damian will hunt you down. You'll never get away.'

Yorgos's eyes shifted uneasily. His hands gripping hers were hard, soil-roughened, and he spoke with a kind of nervous intensity. 'It's too late. I can't let you go, you understand. You know too much.' His grasp tightened sharply and Oriel cried out, screaming with all her might.

Her terrified shriek seemed to bring out the sadist in Yorgos and he laughed. 'Stop howling like a hyena,' he ordered and, with one hand in her hair, he jerked Oriel's head back to expose the long, vulnerable column of her throat. The other he placed over her mouth, forcing it open, trying to shove his handkerchief between her teeth. Fuelled by anger, Oriel bit him hard. He smothered an oath and slapped her twice across the face – so hard she thought he'd cracked her jaw. Momentarily stunned, she allowed him to gag her, the kerchief he had removed from around his neck strangling the wild scream she tried to utter.

But Oriel didn't give up. Although trembling violently, she still fought Yorgos, trying to push him away with her hands, but it wasn't long before he caught them in his without any great difficulty – he was so much stronger – and he bound her wrists together tightly with a small coil of thin rope that he took out of his pocket.

'Always useful,' he muttered, as if to himself.

Meanwhile Oriel continued to fight, kicking out with her feet, but he forced her to her knees and tied her ankles together. She knew then she was beaten. Only her eyes continued to snap, burning with a fury denied her limbs. Yorgos, who had been crouching beside her, now stood up and straightened his back, hands on hips. He looked down at her with such malevolence in his black eyes that she shuddered, involuntarily recoiling, her back against the wall. Then he turned and headed in the direction of the cave's entrance.

It was very quiet when he had gone. Where were the other men? Presumably they had left by a different route. Oriel remembered seeing at least two other tunnels upstairs. From what she could see, it was a large operation – a roaring trade, no doubt.

She thought of Yorgos and his equally ambitious sister, who was clearly embroiled in this wholesale theft of what was rightfully Damian's. They were like leeches, she reflected bitterly, sucking on his blood, willing to stop at nothing to shore up their own wealth and position on the island. As for Yorgos, some part of her had always sensed that he envied Damian's power and standing, jealousy eating him up. It had been evident in every sideways glance or insidious comment he made; even his ostentatious watch seemed to broadcast what kind of a man he was.

And now he had left her here to die. A macabre thought struck her: how deeply ironic – here she was, a woman who had forged a career sifting the dirt, hunting for hidden artefacts of long-forgotten people … and soon … she could hardly bear to think of it … soon she would be just one more nameless pile of bones for someone else to discover once all other traces of her story had been blown away by the winds of time.

Stop thinking like that! she rebuked herself. *Use your head, don't give up!*

There was blood trickling from Oriel's mouth where Yorgos had struck her. She swallowed hard, her jaw pounding with rhythmic throbs of pain. She tried to guess what time it must be now: probably four o'clock. Damian would be coming over to the staff house at six. In two hours … surely he would be worried if he didn't find her? But even if he looked for her in all the obvious places, would he think to search this cave?

Then she thought of her car, parked at the top of the cliff. True, it might take him a while to find it, but find it he would. She realized such was her trust in him – in his capabilities, as well as his love for her – that she felt instantly soothed by a warm glow of confidence. Of course he would find her!

In the meantime she decided to do what she could to escape. First, she tried to get rid of the kerchief that was gagging her, but

Yorgos had done a good job of tying it. Her wrists were bound just as strongly, as were her ankles. She shuffled across the earth floor to the stairs, the shape of which she could just make out in the near-darkness, then set about sawing the rope that bound her wrists against the edge of the bottom step. At least Yorgos hadn't tied her hands behind her back; that was something.

After several minutes a few threads had frayed but she hadn't made any great progress. All she had managed to achieve was cramp in her forearms and a nasty friction burn on her wrist. She gave up and sagged against the cold stone wall. She had to admit it now: there was nothing she could do until Damian or someone else came to her rescue. So she waited, her mind a tumult of emotions … Fear for herself, anger at Yorgos and Yolanda, and – the one pure thing that kept her going – love for Damian.

* * *

Damian was first alerted to something being wrong by the un-accountable behaviour of his dogs. He had been sitting on the terrace, going through a pile of paperwork pertaining to the accounts of the olive factory, when both his hounds started to whine and growl. Usually they would sit: Peleus comfortably, with his head on Damian's foot; Heracles more alert – keeping guard at the steps that led from the terrace to the garden. Now they were shifting uneasily: the former cringing against his leg, the latter pacing nervously back and forth across the stone flagstones. At first Damian barely registered the change in his dogs, so absorbed was he in working out what might have caused the factory fire.

It had supposedly stemmed from an electrical fault in one of the offices that stored the accounts; and every last file, he had been told, was now destroyed. Damian fingered the papers thoughtfully. He could have understood it if the fire had originated in the area that housed the machines but this simply didn't make sense. Yorgos seemed to think that this was a disaster waiting to happen because the place had badly needed rewiring but Damian's gut told him that arson was the cause … and he wasn't the only one who thought so.

A week ago, he and Stavros had discussed the comings and goings of a ship that was regularly, it seemed, making its way in and out of one of the more secluded coves on the island. Damian had noticed the phantom shape on the water without its port and starboard lights and, according to Stavros, there had been other reports of the stealthy vessel. Stavros said that he had mentioned the matter to Yorgos, who had promised to take it up with Damian. But the estate manager had mentioned nothing.

Someone was stealing from the island.

Damian had immediately decided to get in touch with an old police contact of his in internal affairs on the mainland. His tiny local *gendarmerie* was insufficient to tackle a smuggling operation of any size and he had a sense that if local islanders were involved, it would be safest to keep any ongoing investigation quiet.

Stavros didn't actually say that he suspected Yorgos of foul play concerning the office fire but, when he had left Damian an hour before, it had been written all over his face. He'd never pretended to get on with Yorgos but he was professional and fair-minded and kept his dislike to himself. As for Damian, he had always relied on his estate manager's efficiency – the man always seemed to run things smoothly – but in all the years he had worked with Yorgos, he had to confess that he had never grown to like him either. The man had a chip on his shoulder, which irritated Damian, but if he got the job done, he reasoned, that was the important thing.

He had employed him, initially, out of loyalty to Pericles. Yorgos had been his brother's friend and sidekick since childhood and that, surely, counted for something. Still, it had to be said, the lad had never been a stabilizing influence – Yorgos had always snickered at Pericles's scrapes and excesses – and in adulthood, Yorgos had become Damian's brother's general fixer. This included, he strongly suspected, procuring drugs. Nonetheless, when Pericles died it had seemed only natural to see Yorgos properly provided for with a job. Residual feelings of fraternal duty made Damian feel – rightly or wrongly – that he had a brotherly debt to pay and through the years he had gone on paying it.

Until now, there had been no sign at all that Yorgos hadn't been entirely trustworthy when it came to the management of Damian's various businesses. But the man led a playboy existence when he wasn't working that, to an extent, could never have been funded by his salary. At first Damian had accepted without question Yorgos's vague allusions to family property and business interests on Corfu, but now he had doubts … serious doubts. He was relieved that he had made a discreet phone call to Stelios at the station. At the time he'd felt guilty even mentioning Yorgos's name as a possible suspect, having no concrete evidence of any wrongdoing. Now he was glad he had.

Damian drummed the table in frustration as he flicked through the papers, his brow furrowed. Inside, he cursed himself for being so naïve. He'd need to question Yorgos properly about the fire, as well as filling in the police fully, because the smuggling and the factory arson could well be connected. He straightened in his chair and stretched, then glanced at his watch: it was only three-thirty – just a few hours to go before he would be with Oriel. He couldn't wait to take her in his arms again. Tonight he would ask her to marry him.

Just as he was imagining what her reaction might be a breeze picked up, so sudden in its strength that it almost snatched the file of papers from Damian's hand. Peleus whined, still hunkered close to his side, and he ruffled his ears distractedly. Would Oriel accept his proposal? Might she feel that it was some kind of moonlight madness?

Deep down, Damian still felt that tiny nagging fear that their happiness was too good to last. He worried that even though she loved him, Oriel would refuse to become his wife because she knew that the day would come – after the first euphoria had passed – when she would resent the restrictive life on the island, the heavy load that Damian carried, which she would have to share. Maybe too – although she claimed not to be superstitious – Oriel might come to fear the tragedies that had beset Damian since childhood would strike at her – at their love and their family – and who could blame her?

Standing at the top of the steps to the garden, flanks quivering, Heracles gave a low rumbling growl. His master raised his head from the uneasy thoughts that had begun to circle his mind and saw dark clouds rolling across the sky, pushed on by an unseen wave, the light fading as if the island was at the centre of an eclipse. Then, as he looked out across the olive trees, their leaves shivering, a gust hit him full in the face. He found it surprisingly warm – it burned the back of his throat and nostrils like a desert wind. Then, as quickly as it had materialized, the cloud broke and the sun shone down again from a blue sky. The wind seemed to pause for a moment – everything hanging motionless, as if suspended – and then it returned with a vengeance. Black clouds shadowed Damian's face, the like of which he had never seen before.

He looked down into the garden. It was usually teeming with all sorts of insects and birds at this hour but now everything was unusually still. Then he heard the first crackles of thunder and the skies opened up, pouring down torrential rain. Damian hurried into the house. His first thought was of Oriel. She had said that she might go for a swim; she hadn't said where … *Damn!* He'd better go and check she was back safely at the staff house.

He called to his dogs, shut them inside the house and ran out to his Jeep, which was standing on the driveway. As he drove along the coast road he never once questioned the sense in his decision to be outside in what was gearing up to be one of the most ferocious storms he'd ever seen. By now the Jeep was being buffeted by enormous gusts of wind as thunder roared over the cliffs like captive lions. Great crashes made the ground under his wheels shake, as if the foundations of heaven were being torn apart, and sheets of lightning struck in constant waves, illuminating the island in whirling flashes. It was afternoon and it might as well have been midnight.

When Damian reached the staff house, Oriel's Volkswagen wasn't there and neither was she, nor any of the men. Warring with his instinct to rush out and search for her, he decided to wait inside, afraid that if he went looking, he would only miss her. Burning with frustration, he stood at the kitchen window looking out at the haze that hung over the sea. The swell had never been so dangerously high. Hopefully, she would have left the beach at the first sign of a storm, in which case she would be there in the next few minutes, surely.

After pacing up and down, he decided to make himself some coffee. As he was pouring the steaming liquid into his cup, his hand shook and a feeling of vertigo seemed to take him over. The movement was slight at first but it quickened, rising in a crescendo of vibrations. His knees almost gave way as he was suddenly propelled against the opposite wall, the ground lurching and bucking underneath his feet. What was happening to his legs? It couldn't be vertigo, the sensation was too intense … He grabbed the window frame and stared out at the trees that were swaying on unsteady trunks, at the rainstorm of rocks and rubble that had come loose from the scarp and were bouncing towards the house. The window was shaking so hard that the glass seemed about to break. He looked up: the ceiling lamp was swinging back and forth.

He had to get out of the house. If this was an earthquake, then it was probably safer to be outside, even taking into account lightning bolts and falling trees. Everything was moving – the floor, the shelves and the china, which was sliding and clattering in the cupboards until the doors finally burst open and it spilled out like a cataract. Plaster fell from the roof, powdering Damian's head, and the heavier furniture next door groaned as it moved across the open space in the hall and living area. The whole house rocked, the wind slamming against it as he staggered to the front door. And then, just as he reached it the quake died away, as stealthily as it had begun.

But he wasn't staying here: he needed to be out there, doing something to help … finding Oriel …

* * *

Oriel had thought things couldn't get worse but she soon realized she was wrong. Suddenly, she felt a violent rumbling and shaking of the ground beneath her. The whole cave pitched back and forth as though on a huge vibrating bed; the very earth was trembling. Next to her, a vast crack split the stairs, then rocks began to tumble down, some small, others enormous. Her wrists were still tied but she needed desperately to get up, determined not to be in the cave if the ceiling fell in.

Then there was a loud crack above her. Looking up, she dimly saw something shift. She screwed up her eyes, trying to pierce the gloom, then realized with a sickening lurch that it must have been the lintel over the doorway at the top of the steps splitting in two because just then the entire structure caved in, collapsing in a shower of stones and earth. Chest heaving with fear, she gave a cry of horror. One escape route gone and the other – the steps back down to the original cave – almost completely blocked by boulders. She could see the dark mass of them covering what had once been a vague source of light.

Then she realized she was slipping; the floor beneath her had tilted violently. She dug her fists into the soil and scrabbled with her bound feet for a toe-hold. But there was none, only crumbling soil that gave no purchase. Then the earth seemed to close overhead, rushing past her and raining down, carrying her with it. In endless moments of nightmare, she was crashing down, helpless, into darkness.

Oriel lay still, only blackness around her. Above the creaking, grinding, rushing sounds of rock and earth, the sound of gasps reverberated in her ears, gasps she soon realized were her own desperate gulps of air. Flat on her face, half buried in choking clouds of dust, she moved her head to one side so that she could take a proper breath but winced as her ribs stabbed at her lungs. She became aware at that moment that her gag must have been torn loose; that was one positive, at least, in the absolute horror of it all. But the thought was quickly obscured by a blind panic that took her up and squeezed the remaining breath from her lungs. She lay still, unable to move, feeling the earth shake around her, her ears filled with the roaring and explosions erupting outside her subterranean prison.

Oh, Damian! Where are you now when I need you?

How long it was before a measure of sanity came back, Oriel couldn't tell. She managed to raise her head finally and lifted her wrists to meet it. Sheer desperation, coupled with a dogged determination, kept her going and she set about gnawing and tearing at the knot that secured her wrists. After an interminably long time, it seemed, she felt it coming loose and finally she was able to pull through one of the ends of rope. Moments later, her arms were free and she wriggled them in an attempt to restore circulation. After that, it wasn't long before she had freed her ankles, too.

The effort of it all made her dizzy and she stopped for a moment, her eyes closed, taking painful, shallow breaths. As she did so, a thought distilled in her fractured mind and ominous waves of warning chased up her spine. Was this an earthquake? Had it cut off all escape routes to the outside world? Or, even worse, had Typhoeus, who had lain dormant for so many years, raised his monstrous head in fury?

When things seemed to have calmed down a little, the dust and debris around her settling, Oriel attempted to move again. She did so carefully, prepared for sudden stabs of pain. There was nothing broken, she realized; her ribs were hopefully just bruised and her lung wasn't punctured, judging by her normal breathing. There was an unpleasant stickiness on one knee as well as grazes on her arms. No doubt sundry bruises would soon make their presence felt but what else mattered, other than that she was now untied and still in one piece … safe. *But was she?*

Gasping and sweating, Oriel staggered to her feet. She groped around her and then remembered that she had hidden her torch inside her *peignoir*. A glimmer of hope lit up in her mind and, trembling, she fumbled in her pocket, her fingers searching for the small object. There it was. She registered briefly that Yolanda's earring had gone before dismissing the thought from her mind. What did it matter anyway? The only important thing now was to get out of there. Anyway, hopefully the torch was still working. She pushed the button. The flicker of light was like sight to a blind man and she moved the tiny beacon in a slow circle.

Oriel noted that the falling earth had formed a soft bed, cushioning her headlong fall from the chamber where the bottles of olive oil were stored. She now found herself in the clammy darkness of a small, rocky, underground cave. How it fitted into the warren of tunnels and chambers that smugglers had no doubt used over the centuries she didn't know, but it seemed to be a narrow fissure in the rock. It was almost impossible to get her bearings but what she did realize was that she had been lucky to avoid a very serious injury. A jagged spur of rock jutted from the wall, not two feet from her right hand. She shuddered, imagining herself skewered on it, forced to die a slow and agonizing death.

By moving only a few short paces it was possible to trail her fingers round the enclosing walls of rock in a circle. She discovered that it was complete but for one narrow gap and, higher still, another, much larger opening. She looked up. There was a ragged shaft of subdued light. No sky was visible and she supposed that ferns and undergrowth would obscure any sunlight. She tried to resist the tremors of panic that assailed her. What use was it if she couldn't climb up to reach the crack? The silence around her was remote and unfriendly and Oriel shivered. This was like the most dreadful nightmare that imagination could devise. Everything was there – the terror, the nameless danger, the throbbing darkness holding her back – so that her crawling steps towards safety seemed to measure out eternity.

How long before Damian found her? And suppose he didn't, suppose he had been hurt by the earthquake? She had no rope, nothing to help her climb up. She was alone … and alone she must try to get out of this place, she told herself, mustering all the courage of which she was capable.

'Don't panic,' she encouraged aloud. 'Think, girl, think!'

Turning on her torch again she surveyed her prison, slowly moving around it, feeling every step carefully before trusting her weight to it. She was standing in what appeared to be a clean split in the rock itself. Whether the fissure led to any other tunnels or caves in the warren she wasn't sure. Underfoot, the uneven surface of the floor sloped steeply downward. Was it even sensible to wander further into what might be a labyrinth deep in the heart of the cliff, the walls of which – unsettled by the earthquake – might cave in at any time? Or should she wait for help? Still, what if nobody came to rescue her? Sweat began trickling between her shoulder blades. What had the Oracle on Delos called her, Antigone? In the Greek tragedy hadn't Antigone been buried alive? No, she couldn't just wait there passively … she *had* to find a way out.

Cautiously, Oriel moved along, feeling her way falteringly down the passage, inch by inch, facing the uninviting gloom as she moved deeper into the tunnel. Weaving her torch slowly to and fro, she fought down the fear that was making her heart thud painfully fast, trying to persuade herself that it was only a matter of time before Damian or someone else rescued her. She had to believe that – she had to believe that he was unhurt and would come for her sooner or later.

Talking aloud to herself in ridiculous muttered phrases of encouragement, Oriel groped round the walls, raising the torch from time to time to see if there were any gaps she could slip through without having to climb too high, praying the battery of her torch wouldn't die on her. As she directed its beam ahead of her, she could see in the wavering light that several other fissures branched off from the main passage, and she knew that each of these must be examined before she dared to go on. The rocky walls gleamed in the torchlight and delicate ferns grew in the crevices. The air seemed to be getting thinner and, though she progressed slowly, Oriel found her breath coming in hard gulps that hurt her chest. Terror and hopelessness made a mockery of any attempt at optimism: she was lost.

Still, she plodded on for what seemed miles, sometimes plunging into invisible puddles of water, at others bumping into sharp spires of rock. Occasionally she found herself descending to depths where she wondered how she was able to breathe at all, the air was so fetid. But she forged on, hoping that up ahead there might be an opening, one that would lead to blessed freedom.

Oriel could only guess at the time but it seemed to her that she had already been hours in the cave. The path had narrowed until it was no more than a ledge running along a wall of crumbling rock. She was hungry, but most of all she was thirsty. Not to mention cold … the icy chillness of the damp penetrated the walls of the cave, which even in summer could never be warm. She cursed the loss of her canvas bag, in which were her clothes and a water bottle. She pulled her *peignoir* more closely round her but she was beginning to shiver now, the cold and the eerie deep silence adding to the growing horror of her predicament. She caught a strange smell in the air – almost like smoke but not quite. Dust? Ashes? She couldn't tell.

Suddenly an object hurtled out of the darkness, uttering a terrifying shriek as it winged past her face. Oriel screamed – a last terror-crazed effort born of sheer desperation that ripped, high-pitched, from inside her. Even after she had vaguely registered it was a bat, she continued to scream until her throat rasped sore but her cries echoed mockingly, bouncing through the caverns and reverberating against high walls and fallen boulders. She had no way of knowing if it was still daylight outside; she was in a void of darkness and time, wherein nothing seemed to matter any more.

Pain assaulted her from every angle. Her head felt as if it had split in two and her knee had swollen to such extent that she had increasing difficulty in moving forward. Weariness hit her, unreasoning panic bringing tears at last. As the strength ebbed from her, Oriel suddenly sank to the ground, uncaring of the cold, uncaring even if bats flapped at her face or rats scuttled over her. She was just too exhausted to continue further and too frightened to even pretend bravery.

What if the earthquake had caused so much damage she had to stay in the cave all night? ... Or even for days? ... She didn't want to think about what that might mean. If she closed her eyes, she could go to sleep and then all the pain would go away.

* * *

As Damian got into the Jeep, the wind almost tore the door from his hand. He sat for a moment in the driver's seat, heart thudding, looking across at Typhoeus. A black cloud sat tight on the volcano's rim but, in the brassy light, the fire-eating dragon looked indifferent.

Fear suddenly overtook him. Oriel ... where was Oriel? What if her car had been swept off the cliff? Or a tree had fallen on it? He must find her.

He took a breath, trying to quieten his panic. Oriel had a sensible head on her shoulders; he had to trust that she would do the safest thing and that she was now out of harm's way. In the meantime he needed to survey the damage left by the quake. Had many of the islanders been injured? They would need to use the church hall as a makeshift clinic if the little island hospital proved inadequate.

Damian started the engine of the Jeep, his thoughts now moving in a calm and logical progression. Pulling out into the road, he was relieved that the rain had stopped and the wind had died down a little, but the sea was still tossing from the storm, waves slamming over the parapet that separated the road from the shore. As he drove along, heading for the town's main square where the hospital and fire station were situated, he took in the extent of the wreckage. He could see that trees had come down here and there; some of the poorer-built cottages had been knocked about and had lost parts of their roofs or walls. There were piles of dust and rubble everywhere; the roads were peppered with broken brick, tiles and glass.

At one point he stopped the Jeep to give a lift to an elderly couple, both dressed in dusty black clothes and standing haplessly at the side of the road. They were silent in the back of his vehicle – whether from trauma or stoicism he couldn't tell – but he was glad of the quiet, knowing that time and a clear head were both precious commodities when it came to disaster management. The tremors had been brief but they had also been strong, and it was obvious there would be much rebuilding to do.

Eventually the old man asked Damian if he could drop the pair of them at his nephew's house in the next hamlet. Having delivered them into their relative's care, Damian had just returned to the Jeep when he looked up at the volcano. His worst fears were confirmed: up through the black cloud and erupting high into the sky above it came a burst of flame, higher than any fountain gush, brighter than any firework. The fire was thrown up from the very heart of the earth, from its sulphuric core, into a sky that had suddenly deepened to an angry red. The flames lit the sea and the shores, and the livid, crimson scene seemed to him like a vision from the Bible: God's judgement on earth by fire. He could hear the mighty roar as Typhoeus shot its blazing infernal torrent a thousand feet into the air, sending down a rain of sizzling stones and burning lava and diffusing its poisonous sulphurous breath over the island.

Panic struck Helios. People and animals were running in all directions, jostling each other in their rush to get to safety. The confusion was indescribable as Damian drove into the town's outskirts, and he made his way carefully now: through rocks and rubble, twisted iron, piles of debris, uprooted trees and shrieking human beings. More than once he had to move to the side of the road to make way for Jeeps and emergency vehicles carrying the injured and infirm.

With only one fire engine and two ambulances available to the tiny island, they would need every available vehicle to help evacuate and rescue any hurt or stranded islanders. Damian had never spared any expense in buying rescue equipment and training the islanders in first aid and rescue procedures – indeed, he had recruited some of the most bright and able-bodied to form what he'd named the Emergency Club of Helios Rescuers. He could see some of them now, issuing instructions, at the wheels of Jeeps, helping the inhabitants of ruined cottages to safety. But even though he had known that one day the volcano might erupt and had done his best to prepare for such an eventuality, now it had actually happened he wondered just how they were going to cope.

As Damian drove on, it was as though this sudden shaft of doubt that had pierced his confidence allowed for an onslaught of horrific thoughts, which hurtled once more through his mind. Where was Oriel? If she had been on the road, he might have seen her, but he hadn't. What if she had crashed her car? Was she injured and lying somewhere on the island, alone and incapacitated? Helios wasn't that big, and he didn't think that she would have ventured too far. He wished he had asked her where exactly she had been preparing to go, but he'd been too preoccupied with the fire.

Damian's heart turned over painfully. Who else might know where she was? Mattias … Yes, probably she had gone to visit Mattias … Oriel was quite close to the fisherman. He would try to ring his friend from the hospital, although he doubted whether many telephone wires were still intact.

Suddenly he saw a Jeep coming in the opposite direction. At the wheel was Stavros, who waved his arm, signalling for Damian to stop. He looked exhausted and grim-faced, his khaki drill shirt and shorts crumpled and stained. He jumped out of the vehicle and ran to Damian even before the latter had time to turn off his engine.

Damian knew immediately that something terrible had occurred; something personal to him, some awful calamity that had perhaps nothing to do with either the earthquake or the volcano's eruption. A cold sweat ran down his back as his thoughts immediately turned to Oriel …

'What's up, Stavros? It's Oriel, isn't it …?'

But Stavros shook his head. '*Ochi, den eínai i Anglída*, no, it's not the English woman, it's *Kyria* Helena, your cousin.'

Damian almost breathed a sigh of relief before his brow furrowed. 'What's wrong?'

'You need to come with me … I'm afraid there's been an accident.'

'What do you mean? Is she all right?'

'I'll turn my Jeep around. Follow me, it's not far.'

'What's happened?'

'She was out with Marika. They were caught in the earthquake. A tree fell … just missed her maid, but Helena … she was trapped under one of its branches. She's conscious but took a nasty blow to the head.'

'*Theé mou*! Oh my God! Has she been taken to hospital?'

'The ambulances were already attending to islanders but a res-

cue team is trying to move the tree off her. She's in bad shape ...
keeps calling for you ... there's no time to waste.'

A doctor, with Marika, was attending to Helena when they
got there: taking her pulse, covering her with a blanket, mopping
the blood that was trickling from her mouth. When the man saw
Damian, he moved out of the way to let him get near his cousin.

'How bad is she?' asked Damian grimly.

'I'm afraid there's not much we can do, I don't think we can
move her.'

Damian swallowed hard, a lump in his throat choking him, and
sank to his knees beside his cousin. He slipped an arm under her
head then, realizing that Helena was attempting to say something,
he drew very close. Her lips were moving and at first he couldn't
make out any words, so quiet was her whisper.

Her hands gripped his arm. 'I must tell you everything,' she
panted, trying to lift her head. 'You need to know the truth. I have
to tell you ...' She stared into his eyes beseechingly.

'Shush, Helena, you mustn't talk ... you need to save your
strength.'

'... about Pericles and Cassandra ...'

'It's over, they're gone. You're not to worry about it ...'

Instead of his words calming Helena, she seemed to become
more agitated, breathing in short rattling gasps. 'The truth ... I must
tell you the truth ...'

'Don't worry yourself, Helena, please.' Damian's voice was
trembling.

'I'm a sinner ... the worst sin ...'

'Shush, keep calm, *agapiméno mou*.'

'I saw them together ... so horrible ... I couldn't stand it, you
see. How could Pericles? ... That harlot ...'

Damian tried to calm his cousin again but to no avail. Her eyes
were wild but her speech was becoming more fluent now, as if she
was engaged in one last desperate rush to the finish.

'The devil possessed me, the devil of jealousy, of hate ... I
promised Beshir ... if he killed them, I'd build him his own little
house. It wasn't his fault ... you see that, don't you? ... I'm the
murderer,' she said, tears streaming down her cheeks. 'Forgive me,
Damian ... The devil, the devil ... forgive me ...' Helena was pre-

vented from saying more by a fit of coughing that racked her slim body. Stunned, Damian drew back as a stream of blood trickled from her mouth, and moved out of the way to let the doctor attend to her.

A sudden rush of tears blinded Damian's eyes; there was an ache all round his heart, a gnawing pain as a sinking feeling came over him. Stavros stood at his side dutifully. Like Damian, he must have heard Helena's confession but tactfully made no sign that he had done so, delicately avoiding his friend's distraught eyes.

Damian then noticed Marika standing at the side of the road. She was wringing her hands, watching her mistress helplessly. He had never liked the dour servant but now his heart went out to her. She had looked after Helena since birth and had very much been a mother to the girl. He went over to her and placed a hand on her shoulder.

'*Aftó eínai to thélima tou Theoú*, it is the will of God,' he whispered. She didn't move or look at him and her black eyes, wet with tears, maintained their steady vigil.

Damian walked back to Stavros and raked a hand through his dishevelled hair. 'How's everyone out there?' he asked quietly. 'I was on my way to the hospital but I can't leave Helena now …'

'There's a lot of damage but it could have been much worse. We don't know how many casualties there are, but the team is in place, they know what to do. They're surprisingly coordinated considering the shock of it all, though the islanders are in a blind panic.'

'Have you managed to get word out to the mainland?' asked Damian.

'Luckily not all the lines are down. Helicopters are on their way, apparently. In the next half hour we'll start getting supplies, tents, food, bottled water … whatever they reckon we'll need.'

'It's a blessing Typhoeus is on the edge of the island. There are few houses to worry about, and most of the lava will be falling into the sea. Anyhow, glad to hear that everything is under control.'

'Yes, thanks to the Emergency Club people like Mattias's son, Elias. He's been invaluable,' added Stavros. 'Mattias too.'

'Ah, you've seen Mattias,' said Damian, an intense urgency in his tone. 'Was Oriel with him?'

'No, I haven't come across her. I was with Elias when all this broke out and we went by their house to grab his uniform. I would have seen Oriel if she'd been there.'

Damian's face creased into a frown of worry. Then, before he could ask anything else, the doctor approached.

'*Kyrios* Lekkas?'

Damian turned quickly to the man. '*Mahleestah?*'

'I'm afraid she's gone.'

The whispered words failed to register for a moment. Then Damian lifted his head and looked into the doctor's eyes. 'You mean …?'

'Massive brain injury … there was nothing I could do. I'm sorry.'

Damian nodded his head sadly. 'I see … I'll have a Jeep take Helena back home to Heliades. Marika can go with her and see to what needs to be done.'

'Yes, of course,' said the doctor courteously, before adding: 'Now, if you don't mind, I'd better get on to the hospital. They'll be needing my help there.'

'Of course you must.'

The man gave a quick bow of his head. 'My condolences in your time of trouble, *Kyrios* Lekkas.'

Damian thanked him then quickly made the necessary arrangements with Marika and the rescue team. Finally, he turned to Stavros. 'We need to find Oriel, my friend. Let's go back to the staff house first. If she's not there, we must send out a search party.'

'It's getting dark, you know. We might have to wait until tomorrow.'

'No, we'll work all night if needs be. We *must* find her.'

Stavros's eyebrows rose but he nodded. 'You're the boss, *Kyrios*.'

Damian and Stavros went back to the staff house to find no one there. After that, they visited the hospital – maybe Oriel was injured and had been taken there. But she wasn't there either. Damian was beginning to panic now.

It was dusk when they finally started their search at the harbour. Dense clouds of smoke made the place too dark to attempt a serious investigation of the area. Damian tried to assess the crumpled cars that were lying in a huge pile of tangled steel, as if flung by a giant's hand. In the obscurity it was difficult to distinguish anything but he was pretty certain Oriel's Volkswagen wasn't among them. Mattias's son, Elias, had joined them by this point and it was he who finally managed to convince Damian that they were better off sparing their efforts for an efficient full-scale search of the area the next morning, as soon as the sun was up. In the meantime he would organize a team of men with dogs, which would make the task easier.

But Damian couldn't rest and did his best to take his mind off Oriel by helping out at the hospital, coordinating the efforts of doctors and rescue workers. The two island churches and one large church hall had already been commandeered, and they were now temporary accommodation with rows of sleeping bags on the floor. Spirits were surprisingly high among the islanders, Damian thought to himself – Blitz spirit, Oriel would doubtless have called it. It felt as if he alone was stretched like a taut string on a violin, so tight it felt like his sanity would snap. He was vibrating with a tension he had never felt before.

At one point in the night he left to join Marika in her solitary vigil over Helena's body. He climbed straight up to Heliades' little church, which stood on a cliff among old olives and umbrella pines. Built in a rectangular shape, in the form of a ship, with a bell tower over the entrance, it looked out over the Mediterranean, which tonight was veiled in a thick ashen haze. Damian walked inside to breathe in an atmosphere tinctured with the scent of burning incense and candles, of musty prayer books, metal polish and flowers; and it comforted him.

Helena's body was lying in state beneath an iconostasis, a wooden wall of elaborate carvings and rare icons painted in gold, brilliant ochre, blues and reds. Next to it she looked pale, drained of all colour, which seemed odd somehow, after a lifetime of passion and frenzied mania. Damian wished it had been possible to at least have flowers to honour her passing but the church seemed to be doing its best to make up for that, and he was grateful for the colourful high-arched windows of stained glass and the bright paintings decorating the walls – a visual encyclopaedia of the orthodox religion. Looking now at the scenes from the final weeks of Jesus's life, he wondered what lessons he could take from the familiar story, but his mind was unable to make sense of anything that night.

Damian walked over to Marika, who was sitting as immobile as a dark-eyed sphinx, weeping soundless tears at the loss of her charge. He spoke a quiet word to her before taking a handful of candles and distributing them among the large candleholders on either side of the altar, before which Helena was laid, and in a sandbox on the floor for the souls of his departed ancestors. Then he straightened and took a step towards his cousin. Seeing her so peaceful made him remember the tender, gentler side of her, which had made increasingly rare appearances as mental derangement had taken over. He wanted to reach out to the spirit of his cousin but found himself unable to focus on anything at all, his grief struggling with his other distractions.

All he could think about – worry about – was Oriel. It was as if his very life depended on finding her safe and well. Damian couldn't bear the thought that she might be lying somewhere injured, cut off from the outside world, buried under the rubble and debris that was strewn over the island. As he sat there beside the waxen-faced body of his cousin, who in life had been animated by strange and psychotic passions but in death looked so fragile and still, all he could think of was Oriel crying out for him, trapped and injured: *Damian, help me!* He could almost hear her terrified voice echoing around the church, haunting him in a waking nightmare. He wanted to run to her but he was thwarted at every turn and that, in itself, felt like the stuff of bad dreams, too.

He couldn't bear the stillness of the chapel any longer. Silently he asked Helena to forgive him for such a short visit then he turned abruptly and strode out of the church.

He drove to Mattias's cottage, deciding to wait with his old friend until first light when he would drive back to Heliades to meet the rescue team. Damian knew he would never be able to sleep and, in any case, he wanted to quiz the fisherman in case there was anything – the slightest clue – he might have as to Oriel's possible whereabouts.

Mattias met him at the door of his cottage and closed it after him quickly so as to avoid letting in any more ash and dust than necessary. 'It comes in through every crack, settling on everything. I keep telling Anna not to worry. If she dusts it off, it'll only be back, so why bother?'

He ushered Damian into the living room, lit by the dim glow of a pair of hurricane lamps. Anna, who was sitting at the table, knitting by the light of one of the lamps, stood up to bid Damian welcome, her round face creased with concern.

'I'm sorry, but I cannot make you coffee, *Kyrios*. We have no electricity, you see,' she explained. 'But let me bring you some water and a piece of honey cake.'

'Please don't trouble yourself on my account,' Damian said. 'A glass of water would be welcome. I don't think I could eat a thing, to be honest.'

Mattias had drawn a couple of chairs up to a small side table, on which stood one of the lamps. On the table were two small painted wooden replicas of the Virgins of Chora. A little earthenware vase of Greek basil had been placed in front of the icons and a candle lit in their honour.

'Ah, our ladies of March and May,' said Damian bitterly as he sat down. 'Where are you now when we need you?'

Damian saw the pity in his old friend's eyes. Mattias knew him well enough to sense immediately the extremes of anxiety he was suffering, so great was his desire to find Oriel.

'The harbour's been the most badly hit, Elias says,' Mattias told him. 'Not surprisingly, the coast took the worst of it.' His expression then became grave as he placed a hand on Damian's shoulder. 'I'm sorry about your cousin, *Kyrios*. Elias told us what happened. God rest her soul.'

Damian gripped Mattias's arm, silently nodding his thanks.

The older man sighed heavily. 'The saints be praised that hardly anyone else was hurt.'

Damian thought of the fishermen's huts on stilts ranged around the harbour. They must have folded in on themselves, toppling like flimsy card houses. 'It does seem miraculous we haven't sustained many casualties, from what we can see,' he agreed.

'Any more news of Oriel?' Mattias asked.

Damian gave a sigh more like a shuddering sob. 'Mattias, I don't know how I can bear this! I will do anything, make a pact with the devil if I have to … I just have to find her. Where the hell could she be?' His slate eyes were like a grey sea dashing against storm-riven rocks. 'Do you know of any beach she might have gone to?

Somewhere she wanted to explore?'

'You need to calm yourself, *Kyrios* Damian,' said Mattias sooth-ingly. 'We'll find her, you'll see. I think she might have been exploring one of the secluded coves I told her about. You know, the ones on the north side of the island. That's where I'd look first in the morning if I were you.'

Anna brought the men water and, after that, the three of them sat quietly, the old couple occasionally offering some new idea or word of comfort. For the most part they prayed silently, their eyes on the icons of the *Maytissa* and the *Martiatissa*, who had rescued the island from pirates but hadn't prevented the great Typhoeus from raising his monstrous head and disgorging a great stream of fire and ash into the sky.

At times Damian felt utterly defeated, his faith struggling, and then his prayers sounded hollow to him. In those moments he ques-tioned if there were a God out there at all. It seemed to him that he and the islanders were nothing more than the tiny inhabitants of an anthill, scurrying about while careless boys poured boiling water on their home.

And why had this happened? he asked himself. Just now, when everything was good for the first time in his adult life. Was it really to be his fate forever, to be struck down each time after he had just picked himself up again? Would the curse never lift? Before Oriel had come into his life again he had felt able to bear anything – shielded by an armour of numbness, not caring. But now he had found someone so precious, the pain of thinking he might lose her was unbearable.

Finally, just before dawn, Damian made his farewells, Mattias and Anna both embracing him warmly with words of encourage-ment, and drove to Heliades. There had been no further eruptions of Typhoeus – and no more quakes or even tremors. He hadn't slept at all and hadn't eaten since lunch the day before; he was vibrating with a nervous energy, desperate for the search to begin.

As agreed, ten men with dogs in three cars arrived at the house at first light, complete with the digging equipment they had used in the rescue operations elsewhere on the island. They were joined by Damian's own hounds, Peleus and Heracles, who paced and sniffed at their master's feet, sensing his agitation. He had found a scarf of

Oriel's and now let the dogs pick up her scent from it before pushing it into his pocket.

Damian was sure that Mattias's hunch was right so they immediately went to the harbour to start from there and work their way north. In the cool light of dawn they revisited the scene of the previous evening and this time they were even more appalled. Everywhere they looked, the devastation was plainly to be seen. Ash and dust covered the landscape like cold, dead snow. Windows were broken, leaf-barren trees felled and cars overturned. A couple of old buildings were nothing more than a tumbled heap of splintered wood, their beams distorted out of all recognition. On the quay and in the streets, bits of bedsteads, broken chairs, wooden babies' cradles ... Every kind of domestic household item was strewn about and there was something about the sight that was infinitely pathetic.

The shore was littered with the wreckage of smashed boats, while others still lay at their moorings, every one of them minus their masts or waterlogged and sinking. Here and there, a yacht lay on the sand, tossed ashore by the raging floodwaters and the huge waves of the storm. The whole shoreline was a tangle of fallen trees and telephone wires, even dead livestock that had yet to be removed. It was a depressing sight.

It was mid-morning when, finally, Damian spotted Oriel's car. He had detached himself from the group and was leading his own investigation with Stavros, out by Manoli's bar. As he came to the place where Oriel had parked her car, he noticed that the road was badly scored, as if something sharp had been dragged across it, and there were a few fragments of glass in the sand. He looked over the precipice, and there was the Volkswagen: it was lying on its bonnet on a bluff, having been blown off the edge of the escarpment. It was halfway down the cliff, upturned and crumpled.

'Over here,' he shouted to Stavros, trying to keep the strong emotion he felt under control. 'Get the others!'

Please God let her be alive, he prayed, and then he was off, his hounds at his heels, clambering along the flank of the cliff, the sharp points of rocks and the thorns of dried-out bushes tearing at him as he went. He had no breath left now for issuing orders but trusted Stavros would organize the team. Damian himself was nothing more than a panting, sweating automaton that could not stop, would *never* stop – his only thought was that of his one goal: to find Oriel.

Once he had established she wasn't in the wrecked car, Damian looked anxiously around him but still there was no sign of her. The ash caught in his throat, choking and bitter. He cupped his hands to his mouth and called out her name twice … three times, but there was no movement or sound anywhere on the clifftop or down the long stretch leading to the beach. The ground sloped downwards steeply on the far side, the rocks piled anyhow, as if from some prehistoric explosion. The trees that had fallen were very old, their roots exposed but still alive. It was a strange scene – the sun, usually brilliant above a turquoise sea, shrouded in a grey haze – like looking through filmy, cinereal-coloured muslin. At any other time he might have enjoyed the strange and savage beauty of the place – even in its devastation – but now he was only conscious of his own dismay.

He and his dogs had now been joined by Stavros and Elias, and together they hurried across the rough patches of brush and thorn, scrambling over boulders and piles of grey scree in their haste to get to the cove. All three men bellowed Oriel's name and listened anxiously, but only the wind answered their harrowed calls.

In the minutes that followed, the frenzy of the early morning gradually ebbed from Damian and he began to be tormented by doubts. There were many moments when despair flooded him and he had to fight to prevent the torrent of tears, which were bottled up inside, from overwhelming him. His stomach was clenched so tightly it was like a boulder in his abdomen. He had quit yelling orders, his mind too occupied with horrific images of Oriel lying at the bottom of a cliff under a thick layer of ash, her limbs broken, eyes waxy and unblinking. Or had her beautiful body tumbled from the cliffs and into the sea, to join the wrecks in the depths of the ocean that she so liked to explore?

Now the other members of the team had joined the three of them and their bloodhounds were moving through the undergrowth with Damian's dogs, zigzagging hither and thither as they picked up first one scent, then another. As soon as they reached the beach, Damian paused for a brief moment to survey the devastation. He remembered it well, the half moon of white sand where he and Yolanda used to play as children, which later became a lovers' trysting place. Now it was covered in a grey film of ash, tumbled driftwood and a mass of seaweed, grey and snakelike as the writhing, grizzled locks of Medusa.

He shuddered. A thought suddenly struck him. *There was a cave, wasn't there? Yes, there it was.* The entrance was covered by rocks and the branches of broken trees. The bloodhounds were making a beeline for it, sniffing and growling before digging frantically among the boulders and earth. Then they stopped and barked.

Damian's heart leapt, suffocating, into his throat. Elias issued an order and the men – their faces blackened, smarting eyes red-rimmed, clothes covered in dust and ash – got to work with spades and shovels, clearing an opening big enough for a man to get through. After speedy deliberation it was decided that Damian, Stavros and Elias with one dog would enter the cave while the remainder of the team stayed outside. Damian insisted that a small group went back for a stretcher and medical supplies so that no time would be lost in waiting for help, should they find an injured Oriel. A surge of fresh hope had risen in him now. The dogs had indicated that she was somewhere in the cave and he wanted to believe that she was hanging on in there, waiting for him, knowing that he would come for her. Oriel was a fighter and if she was there then Damian was certain she wouldn't give up.

Inside there was lonely darkness and the dank smell of rocks and earth kept perpetually damp. Gasping and coughing as their lungs filled with the various fumes that had built up in the cave, the men struggled, scrambling their way through the narrow rocky path of the tunnel with their torches. They called, but still there was no movement, not the slightest sound. Damian's disappointment flooded him like a wave of nausea. *What did you expect?* he asked himself roughly, *Oriel sitting there, enjoying a picnic?* Yet in spite of that empty darkness, he went on, feeling that somewhere in the warren of caves leading deep into the cliffside she might be crying for him.

'Oriel!' The thin thread of Damian's control almost broke and his shout cracked in his throat but he moved on relentlessly with the bloodhound, straining to pierce the gloom ahead. Then he stopped, holding his breath, absolutely still as if a gun were pointed to his head. Had he heard something? But the dog, nose to the ground, dragged frantically on his leash, pulling Damian forward, as if eager to lead him on towards his quarry, beckoning him like some canine will-o'-the-wisp. He quickened his step, Stavros and Elias hurrying to keep up, and together they stumbled down the path that was dropping more steeply at every pace.

'Oriel … Oriel … Oriel …' Damian shouted, his heart thumping so fast he thought he might lose his breath. The echoes chimed and danced back to him, cascading down an unearthly scale. Then he caught sight of another entrance half blocked by rubble.

The dog stopped and barked … Silence … then again small staccato barks, which were met with only more silence.

* * *

She must have slept or lost consciousness for a long time but now Oriel was suddenly brought back to reality by the excruciating pain of sudden cramp in her legs. She straightened them, which only seemed to make the pain worse. She was conscious, too, of the dryness of her mouth, her throat parched as sandpaper. Now she wondered, with the passing curiosity of conscious thought, how long it took to go mad. As she did so, Oriel thought she heard the echoes of a man's voice travelling through the darkness.

She must be dreaming … Like the wings of a captured bird eager to fly, yet hesitant of release, her eyelids fluttered.

Damian? Yes, it *was* Damian, calling out her name! Attempting to scramble to her feet, Oriel began to cry hysterically. 'Damian, Damian, over here,' she sobbed, realizing as she did, that her voice was barely more audible than a whisper.

Please let him hear me. He's got to find me!

'Hold on, *agápi mou*,' she heard him say through the haze in her head. There was a lot of banging and scraping and then, soon enough, Damian's torch was shining on her face. In her semi-consciousness Oriel was aware of powerful arms around her and his voice assuring her that she was all right. She knew then that her sanity was restored and felt the exquisite comfort of his grasp. Her teeth chattered as she was seized by violent fits of shivering and all she could do was lean helplessly against his powerful chest, feeling the safe haven of his encircling arms.

EPILOGUE

Oriel ran a temperature, sometimes delirious, and slept for most of the week that followed. In her dreams, the cave and Yorgos merged together in confusing and sometimes terrifying fragments. Thoughts clamoured for admittance into her mind but she resisted the urge to remember, sensing the experience might be painful. She was aware of Damian giving her medicine, helping her to drink water or silently sitting by her bed every time she opened her eyes and it made her feel secure.

Now and again, when she had seen him at her side, she'd tried to communicate but her heavy lids had always fallen back down and she'd been unable to speak. With his dark head resting against the pale upholstery of the armchair and his eyes closed, his face looked haggard and drained of colour. He was blue-jawed, as if shaving had been a sketchy affair, accomplished swiftly – whether because he begrudged time away from her side or was just too tired to care about the way he looked, she didn't know.

That morning when she opened her eyes, Damian wasn't in the chair where he had sat religiously day and night. Instead, Irini was sitting in his place. And now, for the first time, Oriel made a conscious effort to look around her. This was neither her room at Heliades nor the one at the staff house. The pale jade-green ceiling, the black-and-white mosaic flooring and frescoed walls, and the two tall niches that harboured precious statues of ancient divinities had nothing to do with either dwelling. Where was she?

'*Kaliméra, Despinis,* you look so much better today.'

'*Kaliméra, Irini. Efharisto,* I do feel much better,' Oriel said as she sat up slowly, propping herself against her pillows. 'But where am I?'

'You are in the *Kyrios*'s house on the island of Paxi.'

Oriel knew a moment of panic, which must have shown on her face because Irini immediately tried to reassure her. 'Don't worry,

Heliades is fine. Helios will survive. Typhoeus is asleep again, that's what the islanders are saying.'

'But where is *Kyrios* Lekkas? And why am I here on Paxi?' Oriel asked.

'The *Kyrios* will be back this evening,' the maid replied. '*Oh yiatros eepeh*, the doctor said you needed a change of air. Helios is not a healthy place at the moment, the air is still full of dust and ash.'

Oriel looked at her doubtfully. 'Did the *Kyrios* leave a note for me?'

Irini smiled at her, a mischievous glint in the depths of her dark eyes. 'No, *Despinis*, but before leaving he prepared you this dish which he said to keep in the warming oven until you woke up. You haven't eaten for many days and the *Kyrios* thought that today you would feel much better because your fever broke during the night.' She placed a tray in front of Oriel. 'The *Kyrios* also said that it is a breakfast dish very similar to the one you eat in your country … po … po … por something.'

Oriel laughed, a little reassured. That sounded just like Damian. 'Ah yes, porridge.'

'That's it por*ee*dge! This is a Greek version of your por*ee*dge, called *kykeon*. The *Kyrios* made it himself with semolina and a white cheese that we make on Helios, mixed with eggs and honey.'

'*Efharisto*, Irini, this looks great, and I *am* hungry this morning.'

There were so many questions going round in Oriel's mind. She had a vague recollection of what had happened after Damian had found her and she was aware that disaster had struck the island, but she wanted to know more.

As the maid turned and was preparing to go, Oriel called out to her. 'Irini, has there been much damage on the island? I remember now there's been an earthquake and the volcano erupted, didn't it?'

'*Né.*'

'It seemed so sudden.'

The maid shrugged and made a moue. '*Poios xérei*, who knows? My cousin who lives quite close to Typhoeus says he heard a moaning coming from the depths of the volcano. And he's not the only one. It's the spirits of our ancestors and the souls of those who perished long ago when the volcano destroyed the island. They were trying to warn us, you see.'

Oriel thought of the Oracle's predictions. Maybe, after all, there was something in what most people dismissed as mumbo jumbo.

'It could have been worse,' Irini went on. '*Efharisto ton Theó,* thank you, God. But we've lost two from Heliades. Beshir was found at the bottom of a cliff and …' Irini paused, eyeing Oriel carefully. 'Did the *Kyrios* not tell you?'

'Tell me what?' she asked, apprehensive suddenly.

Irini looked stricken, clearly torn between the desire to tell and concern that her master might be angry if she did. She hesitated then spoke, crossing herself. 'His cousin, *Kyria* Helena, may God rest her soul, died too.'

Oriel's hands flew to her mouth. 'Oh no! How did it happen?'

'She was out with Marika. The earthquake caught them by surprise and while they were trying to get back to Heliades, a tree fell on her. The *Kyrios* was there when she died. In fact, that's where he is now: at his cousin's funeral.'

'Oh no … I must go to him!' Oriel cried, setting aside the breakfast tray, throwing her covers off and attempting to get out of bed. But the room soon shifted in front of her eyes and she fell back against the pillows.

'*Ochi, ochi parakaló,* no, no, please, the *Kyrios* will be very cross with me,' the maid exclaimed. 'You are still very weak. He gave strict instructions that no one should talk to you about the casualties on the island or about anything that happened.' Irini's eyes were wide with alarm.

'But I can't just sit here …'

'*Parakaló,* please be reasonable, *Despinis.* Up until yesterday you were still running a fever. You have eaten nothing for days but some spoonfuls of broth. You will collapse and we'll all be in trouble. The *Kyrios* will be coming back soon and I have already said too much.' Irini smoothed the covers over her and moved the tray back on to her lap. 'Eat your breakfast that the *Kyrios* prepared especially for you.'

Oriel sat back and began to eat her porridge.

Irini smiled. 'That's better.'

'I know you're not meant to unsettle me with talk of the disaster but there is something I want to know: what happened to Yorgos? I didn't see him among the men that rescued me, but maybe I was in too bad a shape to notice all the people around me.'

'*O kakós ánthropos!* The bad man!' Irini exclaimed, shaking her head disapprovingly. 'Crates of olive oil were found by the dogs in one of the caves. Apparently there was oil running down the main tunnel. Yorgos and *Kyria* Yolanda were caught trying to board *Kyria* Yolanda's yacht. He had a suitcase full of dollars. As the saints are my witnesses, he was stealing from the *Kyrios*.'

'How did they know it was him?' asked Oriel.

'I think the police were asked to put a watch on him. Or maybe one of Yorgos's gang gave the game away,' Irini explained. 'Whatever it was, they managed to seize him before he got away in the chaos of the earthquake.'

Oriel shuddered. 'Thank goodness they got him,' she almost whispered.

'Poor *Despinis*! You must have suffered a lot. Though you were delirious and your thoughts were confused, you spoke about what happened to you. The police already suspected Yorgos had a hand in your disappearance. When they caught him at the port, at first he denied it but he admitted it in the end.'

'It was a horrible nightmare. I'm happy he was caught. Was Yolanda aware of her brother's dealings?'

Irini shook her head doubtfully. 'Though I think they suspected her too, the police couldn't charge her because they had no proof.'

Oriel smiled ruefully to herself. She'd had proof for a while – the square sapphire earring with diamond surround – but it had become lost in the rubble and dust where she would leave it to lie, like sleeping dogs.

'After her brother was arrested, Yolanda left the island.' The maid paused and then asked: 'Do you need anything more?'

'No, I'm fine, thank you. I'll get up in a bit and go for a walk outside.'

'The grounds are huge. You won't need to leave the property,' Irini warned. 'If you need me, just ring the bell. It's next to your bed.'

'*Efharisto*, Irini.'

The maid paused at the door and looked back at Oriel with a knowing smile. 'Forgive me if I speak out of turn but the *Kyrios* seems a different man. Despite all that has happened … his many

496

troubles and sleepless nights… his face is serene and his heart is warm. Up until now he may have been luckier than his neighbours, with riches and women at his feet, and I'm sure many envied him, but he still was not happy. We who see him every day know that. Something has changed him … it is you, *Despinis*.'

'It's very sweet of you to say that, Irini.' Oriel looked warmly at the maid, who said no more, and merely nodded with a smile and was gone.

Once Irini had left the room Oriel finished her breakfast quickly – she quite liked this sweeter, smoother Greek version of porridge. She drank two cups of coffee, too. The hot brew revived her somewhat and she was able to climb out of bed. She thought of poor Helena. Although Damian's cousin had tried to harm her, Oriel found that she harboured no ill feelings towards the invalid. How could she when the poor woman had had a miserable life, and an equally miserable death? No one deserved that.

Oriel went on to the veranda outside her bedroom, which looked out on to the bright green turf of the lawn that stretched along the back of the house. She could see fields of scarlet poppies edged with olives, cyclamen growing wild, hills brushed with myrtle and the holly-like ilex to the east. To the west, cypresses speared up blackly out of the silver-green groves and villas were arboured with green pelmets of grape leaves.

Beyond, the turquoise Ionian Sea lay calm as a mirror bordered by sandy beaches; nearer to her, in the grounds of the house, a fountain splashed through its centrepiece of copper turtles. Green ramblers with purple flowers were growing up the sides of the granite terrace walls at the side of the house. The scenery was too stunning for words. What was this paradise Damian had brought her to? She must go down to explore it.

She went to the bathroom and took off her nightdress before stepping into the shower. As memories of her ordeal came flooding back, Oriel scrubbed herself from head to toe, eager to eradicate any residue of the experience, almost as if the hideous smell of the dank cave might still be stuck to her skin. Other memories also crowded her mind: recollections of the day she had arrived, of her first dinners with Damian, of their lovemaking, the Epiklisi festival and the islanders, of Mattias, the wise fisherman. She hoped that he had come to no harm. His son, Elias, she knew, was one of the men who had rescued her with Damian, but then her thoughts turned to Helena, who was now dead … Poor beautiful, crippled Helena.

After she had stepped out of the shower, Oriel studied herself in the mirror. Her hair, newly washed, was soft and shining but her face, innocent of make-up of any kind, looked suddenly pale and oddly naked. When she applied a hint of lipstick and blush it looked hard and too bright so she wiped it off and decided to leave well alone.

She found her clothes, which must have been brought from the staff house, nicely tidied away in the cupboard and drawers. Oriel glanced at her watch, it was only late afternoon – Irini had said that Damian would be back in the evening. She had time to explore the garden.

It was glorious outside. Oriel gazed back at the glistening white façade of the villa, built of Parian marble. It was pure Renaissance in style and yet there was something ancient about the site; perhaps a Greek temple had once looked out across these groves on the one side and the sea on the other. At the back the incline was sharp and a stone balustrade ran along the bluff, protecting the property from the steep two-hundred-metre drop to the bottom of the cliff. Now, as she looked down upon the Ionian Sea in the late afternoon, the waters displayed a different set of colours – stripes of Parisian blue and amethyst – than those she had perceived earlier from her window. In the distance, small boats drifted to and fro on the undulating sea. Oriel felt light-hearted. It was odd how quickly she had recovered her spirits.

She found an old swing hanging from a big plane tree next to the ground-floor terrace. Oriel hadn't been on a swing since she was eight years old and now she sat on the rough wooden seat and kicked off jubilantly. The feeling was marvellous and she closed her eyes and swung higher and higher, thoroughly enjoying the sensation, until the sun started to slip down and Irini called out to her to say that Damian was on his way.

* * *

The night was still and calm and the scents of the island filled the air: the mingled fragrances of earth and trees and salt, iodine and sea. A magical summer's night. The frogs in the creek that ran through the garden at the back of the house were setting up their nightly chorus and a large, hot moon glowed in the dark bowl of the sky overhead, blanching the pale olive grove. With the added sprinkling of iridescent stars, the firmament resembled a sparkling velvet coat. Oriel had always felt that these bright pinpoints seemed to know that the beautiful land they looked over had once been a sacred country, and now they shone with a thousand glistening tears as they looked upon the remains of Greece's past glory.

She walked along the balustrade at the edge of the cliff in a long Grecian dress of thin lilac chiffon that Damian had left for her and Irini had laid out. She didn't feel the slightest chill and her heart was warm, so warm. Now she could hear the boom of the sea clearly. The feeling of height, the great expanse of open water below her, gave Oriel the impression she was up in a balloon.

Damian would soon be there. He'd rung from Helios to say he was on his way in the two-seater plane that had flown them to Santorini. That night seemed such a long time ago. Once she had thought there were too many reasons against her loving Damian, too many differences between them to hold them together … but now she knew that they completed each other. It could never have been different; their love was inevitable from that moment they met on Aegina.

Oriel strolled back to the swing where she had spent such happy moments in the afternoon. Through the trees she could see the lights of the house through the windows. They were like friendly yellow eyes in the blue night.

She was swinging far back into the heart of the branches and was about to plummet forward again when a shadow moved into her line of vision, silhouetted against the night sky. Unable to stop, she swung right up to the figure and let out a little shriek, worried she was going to hit whoever it was, but he stepped deftly aside and she heard a low chuckle: Damian.

Swinging forward again, she dragged her feet on the ground to slow herself and he reached out and caught one of the ropes so that she jerked to a stop. Damian's other hand caught the second rope and Oriel was imprisoned between him and the seat.

'Oh, Damian ...' she whispered.

They stared at each other as though hypnotized. The leaves above them fluttered in a sudden breeze. Damian's face loomed very close to hers and then he dropped his hands from the ropes and folded them tightly around her trembling body. Through the thin chiffon of her corsage she could feel the tight muscles in his arms and, as he drew her closer to him, Damian's warmth seemed to flow into her like a burning tide. She gazed into his eyes, her mouth opening on a gasping sigh of sensuality.

Oriel said his name again in a wild plea of longing. Damian's lips met hers suddenly and passionately. Like the breaking of a dam too long under pressure, the force of his ardour erupted and she was caught, submerged, drowned by waves of delight as they kissed in a frenzy of desire.

When at last they pulled apart, a little breathless, Damian smiled and tucked her hand into his arm. 'Shall we walk? I'm cramped after flying for an hour in that small plane.'

They strolled for a while in silence up a small avenue of plane trees towards the orchard at the side of the house. Oriel noticed a gazebo there, and they made their way to it.

'I'm sorry about Helena ...' she said eventually, once they'd reached the wrought-iron hideaway with its peaked roof and sides smothered in sweet-smelling roses. 'Irini told me about the accident.'

'Hush, my love. Let's not talk of it now ... She's in peace at last, God rest her soul.'

'Are Mattias and Anna all right?'

'He's very glad that I made him move to a well built cottage. So many other fishermen's homes have been destroyed.'

'Were there many casualties?'

Damian turned around a little towards the light of the moon and drew Oriel into his embrace. 'Hardly any, but let's not talk about unpleasant things tonight. Thank God you're safe. I died so many deaths wondering if I would ever see you again. I thought you were lost to me forever.' He took both her hands in his and carried them to his lips. 'Life without you would be a prison of loneliness.'

Damian pulled Oriel towards him, his arms firm and strong around her, communicating his vow to never let her go. His head tilted towards her upturned face and he kissed her with an ever-growing intensity. His fingers weren't content with moving over her dress; they slid underneath it and she caught her breath sharply as she felt the burning touch of his hands against her bare skin, that touch that made every nerve silently quiver, that touch she had missed, which was now putting life back into her body.

His hand floated upwards, one palm brushing against her breast, his fingers curling around its soft curve and nipping at the hard peak clamouring for his attention. A dozen different sensations burst through her, spiralling down to where her need for him was intensifying by the second, and she pressed herself against him to sense that part of him that she yearned to feel within her.

'I know you are shaking inside, *agápi mou*,' he murmured, his voice low and hoarse.

'Yes, yes, Damian,' she breathed against his mouth, his words fuelling her desire to an unbearable ache. 'Touch me, I want to feel you inside me. I've missed you so much.'

'I want you too, *matia mou*,' he replied, as slowly he lifted his head and drew a little away from Oriel, leaving her trembling and somewhat dazed. 'I am not being cruel,' he assured her, placing a peck on her nose. 'Anticipation will only make the reality more enjoyable. Tonight, *móno i agápi mou*, I promise that I'll make it up to you. I'll take you to rapturous places you've never been before. But for now, there is something I would like to share with you.'

Damian took a little box out of his pocket. He opened it and placed the ring it held on to the third finger of Oriel's left hand and, once again lifting her hand to his lips, brushed it with the whisper of a kiss. His eyes as he looked directly into her face were bright though infinitely serious. His voice, too, when he spoke again, was vibrant with sincerity.

'This was the only thing that survived the shipwreck of my Albanian ancestor. It belonged to his mother and he wore it on a string around his neck, a golden ring set with a pearl and a diamond. A lovers' ring that symbolizes the best of all that is between us, the pearl for purity and the diamond for solidity. I love you, Oriel, with all the shocking lust and tenderness I am capable of. Ever since I set eyes on you I wanted you to be my wife, my companion, my mistress, the mother of my children, the one with whom I would grow old.' His gaze devoured her, its ardent fire holding a promise that embraced her now and for all the years to come.

'I love you, too, Damian,' she breathed, her eyes shining with happiness, her voice husky with emotion. 'I will love you until my dying day, and beyond the grave if that is at all possible. I will be your wife, your mistress, the mother of your children and your companion in our winter years.'

Damian hesitated, lifting a finger to trail it gently down her cheek. 'How do you feel about my island … my home? After all that's happened, will you be able to live on Helios?'

Oriel studied his earnest features. Helios … Was there ever a place like it? Beauty and horror, grim tragedy and sheer beauty walked hand in hand there. Helios had frightened her, horrified her, given her ecstatic happiness, intrigued and tortured her, but it had also stolen her heart forever. Vivid, amazing Helios. Terrible Helios … But oh, so dear!

Damian read the answer in her eyes and let out a breath, smiling. 'You know, you're going to be a part of the island's history now,' he said. 'I had a call from the Ministry. They're falling over each other with excitement. They've studied the photos I sent and even before inspecting the site they're almost certain it has to be the lost city of Helice.'

'I can't even begin to take it in somehow,' said Oriel dreamily. 'The city I used to imagine as a child when I lay in bed, unable to sleep … I'd try to picture its temples, its great bells tolling … and I'd think of Poseidon glaring out over the waves, magnificent and glittering in the sunlight.'

'And now it's your home, my love,' he said tenderly. 'So you think you could be happy at Helios and *really* love it, and regard it as your home, not only mine?'

The humility and stark simplicity of his question seemed to tear her heart.

Oriel smiled up at Damian. 'Your island, like the dragon that rules it, has captured my soul, *Kyrios*,' she said simply. 'What more can I say except to go on repeating that I love you, that I am home when you hold me in your arms … home when you kiss me and say I'm yours. Is that a good enough answer for you, *agápi mou*?'

She could see the surge of emotion that had risen in him at

her answer and knew that he was on fire to touch her. 'Yes, quite enough!' He drew her back into his embrace. '*Tóte eíste sto spíti gia pánta*, then you are home forever,' he whispered against her mouth, his hold on her tightening.

The moonlight streamed on to Oriel, standing before him in her lilac chiffon, her hair sweeping her shoulders.

Damian smiled down at her. 'Remember always, *matia mou*,' he said, his tone tender and intimate. 'There's no room for pride in our love. There should be no secrets between us, no quarrels that cannot be bridged. Other people may find causes to quarrel and separate over, but never us. Our love is too big for anything or anyone to part us. You must believe that you are my first and last love. It is a precious thing that holds us together, one we must guard eternally because a one-time love can never be repeated. Come,' he murmured, taking her hand. 'Let's look out to sea, out towards Helios … our home.'

He led her slowly towards the beautiful carved balustrade. Below lay the blanched and moving waters of the Ionian, creaming and foaming on the rocks, with the sand and pebble beaches and the far-off islands all frosted by the moon.

Oriel smiled up at him radiantly. She had come into Damian's kingdom, Helios, and they would be returning there soon – to the living present, the ghosts of an unfortunate, unhappy past and the burning hope of an endless future. They were at the start of their journey, which she knew would last a lifetime. The curtain was coming down on the first act of her Greek drama but her romantic adventure was just beginning.

And Aphrodite wept, finally, for joy.

THE END

AUTHOR NOTE

I chose two real-life sites as inspiration for my underwater archaeology story.

The first is a famous wreck of a Roman galleon, first explored in the early fifties by Jacques Cousteau and his team. It had been discovered by a lobster gatherer near a small island, Le Grand Congloué, situated across the water from Marseilles on the southern French coast. The galleon had been carrying a mixed cargo, including amphorae filled with wine. Cousteau actually tasted the two-thousand-year-old wine, still sealed in one of the earthenware pots his team brought to the surface, although it had long lost its alcohol content. He reportedly declared it to be 'a poor vintage century'.

On the seals of these large amphorae were stamped the owner's trademark – SES – which identified the cargo as having belonged to the Roman shipping magnate Marcus Sestius in the third century BC. Sestius was an intriguing character, who had settled on the Greek island of Delos, where he had built up a sizeable export business. He became almost more Greek than Roman over time, changing his name to its Greek version, Markos Sestios, in 240BC after he had been granted Delian citizenship, which would have been a great honour. A group of ruined Roman villas on the magical island of Delos today includes one, the House of the Trident, with a beautiful mosaic floor on which is depicted a trident, complete with two Ss forming a bracket in the space between the tines. Archaeologists have speculated that this was Marcus Sestius's insignia (because his trademark also included a basic trident shape).

The second piece of history that set my imagination on fire is the sunken seaport of Helike (or Helice). In the seventies, when my story is set, this port was still thought to be located under 10 metres of mud in the Gulf of Corinth. This Greek city was mentioned by Homer when he listed the powerful cities that assembled against Troy. What we didn't get from Homer, however, is where the city lay. We hear of its location from another writer, Pausanias, who describes coming to the river Selinus and 'about 40 stadia from Aegium is a place called Helice near the sea'. It was a very important city, he tells us, and the Ionians had built there 'the most holy temple of Poseidon of Helike'.

We know from Strabo, a Greek geographer writing a half century before the birth of Christ, that Helike was overwhelmed by the waves in the winter of 373BC. Strabo gives an account of Eratosthenes, who was alive a century after Helike's destruction, visiting the scene of the disaster. The boatman who ferried him over the spot told him that in the midst of the drowned ruins could be seen a massive bronze statue of Poseidon, holding aloft a hippocampus, a mythical beast with the head and torso of a horse and the tail of a fish.

The famous diver-explorers Cousteau and Peter Throckmorton each separately tried to locate the lost city but it was only in 2001 that Helike was rediscovered, buried in an ancient lagoon near the village of Rizomylos and not in the Gulf of Corinth after all.

In *Aphrodite's Tears* I've connected the Roman trader Sestius and his wrecked cargo to an island of my invention, Helios. Although Sestius was actually trading a century or so after Helike was submerged, I've rewritten history – as purveyors of fiction are often wont to do! In my story, Sestius's business was destroyed by a massive tidal wave following an earthquake, his ships stranded in the harbour, lost beneath the waves until our hero and heroine make their exciting discovery.

Because there was much seismic activity over the years in the Mediterranean, Helike was by no means the only city to be submerged by a tsunami but it is my favourite. Who can resist the legend of a vast, glittering-bronze statue still waiting to be discovered beneath the waves?

Hannah Fielding
January 2018

A Letter from Hannah

Dear Reader,

Thank you for reading *Aphrodite's Tears*. I hope that Oriel's and Damian's wildly romantic story of rediscovered love and unforgettable passion kept you turning the pages long into the night.

If you did enjoy the story, I'd be eternally grateful if you would write a review. Getting feedback from readers is incredibly rewarding and also helps to persuade others to pick up one of my books for the first time.

For news of my next releases, please come and visit me at my website – www.hannahfielding.net or join me on Facebook or Twitter @fieldinghannah.

Best wishes,
Hannah

Q and A
With Hannah Fielding

A Greek Odyssey

What drew you to Greece as a setting for your new novel?

Greece is very special to me. I grew up in Alexandria, Egypt, at a time when it was a very cosmopolitan place. Many of my parents' friends and my school friends were Greek. As Greece is a Mediterranean country, the sun, sea and warmth appeal greatly. So too, of course, does the mythology.

The ancient Greeks left such a rich inheritance of legends – stories full of wisdom, with a god or goddess for everything from love and war to wine-making. Add to that the many antiquities, each with its own tale to tell, and it's easy to see the fascination for a storyteller such as myself. To this day, the culture and traditions of Greece are rich and diverse, reflecting its location bridging East and West.

What I love most about Greece, though, is that it is such a romantic country. I bought my wedding dress there and my husband and I honeymooned on Rhodes and Santorini, where, like Oriel and Damian, we saw the most spectacular sunsets.

What Greek qualities do you most admire?

Joie de vivre: Nowhere is this more evident than in the traditional dances and songs performed by both men and women. They are filled with such passion and exuberance that it is impossible to watch without yearning to join in.

Hospitality: Whenever I travel to Greece, I am struck by the friendliness of the people. Many a time I have been welcomed warmly to a restaurant, taverna or shop and have ended up chatting for ages with the proprietor and, quite often, his or her family, too.

Sentimentality: Like Damian in *Aphrodite's Tears*, the Greeks are a people who feel deeply and are not afraid to show it – they are wonderfully open, which is something I like very much.

Importance of family: The close-knit family is an important part of Greek culture. As you see in *Aphrodite's Tears*, the Greeks can be fiercely loyal to their family members and feel a strong sense of duty to protect and support them, which I very much respect. I especially like their strong traditions when it comes to marriage (a man still asks a father for his daughter's hand, which I find very romantic).

What aspect of Greek life did you most enjoy exploring in the book?

The mythology springs to mind – because I so enjoyed revisiting all the stories I'd been told as a child – but for this book I also really enjoyed learning about Greek cuisine.

Greek food is the perfect example of the traditional Mediterranean diet. It's based around a variety of colourful and flavoursome foods that are high in nutrients and low in animal fats. Greek cuisine incorporates a host of fresh ingredients, among them garlic, onions, fennel, zucchini, grapes, apples, dates and figs, into a variety of local dishes, some of which can be traced back to ancient times.

The *mezedes* of which Oriel and Damian are very fond, and which appear often in my novel, are appetizers, served before or with the main dishes. They come in individual small plates with various dips such as *tzatziki*. My favourite of them all is *dolmades*, vine leaves stuffed with rice and vegetables, and *spanakopitakia*, small triangular filo pastries filled with spinach and feta. I have learned to make these myself using ingredients from my kitchen garden, and my guests always ask for more.

On Heroes and Heroines

What traits are inherent in your romantic heroes?

After a lifetime of romantic imaginings, I have no absolutely problem dreaming up all my heroes' swoon-worthy qualities. A hero
is handsome, usually with a rugged edge, and he takes care of his
physique, which is strong (deep down, I think all women respond to
strength). He is intelligent, hard-working and tenacious; he is confident and he has a good sense of himself. He is, of course, very
sensual, virile and passionate.

But he is not perfect! How could the heroine, a flawed human as
we all are, have a hope of building a future with a god? A hero may
be arrogant, he may be secretive, he may be tormented. He may,
like Damian in *Aphrodite's Tears*, have a touch of machismo about
him: strong masculine pride and a traditional mindset. Of course,
when taken to the extreme, there can be a downside to this but for
Damian, leader of Helios, it rather comes with the territory.

How important is a career to your heroines?

All of the heroines I write are career women. I believe it's important
for a heroine to be following her own course in life, reliant on her
own talent and hard work, so that while she may fall in love with
a man, she need never be dependent on him. Some traditionalism
may be present in their relationship – for example, I believe the hero
should be a gentleman, opening a door for the heroine or lending her
his jacket on a cool evening – but they are both on an equal footing.

In *Aphrodite's Tears*, Oriel faces a real challenge because, as
an archaeologist in the 1970s, she is a woman in a man's world.
Although she is excellent at her job, Oriel feels she has to prove
herself. Falling in love with her employer complicates matters, of
course, but that doesn't mean she will be anything less than the consummate professional and earn the respect that is rightfully hers.

Packing Up My Suitcase

How important is travel to your writing?

Absolutely essential!

Experiencing a new culture is a common theme in all my novels.
I take a young woman out of the comfortable, safe (and perhaps a

little staid) life she has always known and plunge her into a brand-new culture: one that is colourful, vibrant and appealing but also, by the nature of being foreign, somewhat alien and overwhelming at times. Emotions run high as this new environment challenges the heroine to her very core. Who is she? Where does she belong: in the new world or her former one? Where will she choose to live – in what cultural landscape? Most importantly, what kind of man will she fall for: one from her past or one from this heady new place?

The journey that my heroines take is one with which I identify strongly. I grew up in Egypt and because the government put my family under a sequestration order, we were not able to travel for many years. As a child that didn't concern me too much – Egypt has much to occupy the mind of a little girl with a big imagination. But by the time I was a young woman, with a degree in French literature from the University of Alexandria, I had a deep-seated need to see the world.

In my twenties, I spent several years travelling, predominantly in Europe, and then met my husband at a drinks party in London. Ever since, we have lived something of a cosmopolitan life, moving between different cultures. In the year I wrote *Aphrodite's Tears*, for example, we divided our time between our homes in Ireland, England and France, travelled to Egypt to see family and also went to the Greek islands as part of my research for the novel.

For me, experiencing different cultures and their people is as essential a part of life as reading and writing. As Moroccan traveller Ibn Battuta said: 'Travelling – it leaves you speechless, then turns you into a storyteller.' Travel makes me the writer that I am. That is why all my novels are infused with a passion for experiencing new peoples and places – and also with a love of coming home to wherever it may be that you truly belong.

A Writer's Life

Why do you write in the third person?
I have always written in this style – as the narrator, not speaking as the characters themselves. The third-person narrative is as old as time. Imagine ancestors telling stories at the fireside – fairy tales such as *Cinderella* or *Aladdin* – the storyteller always told the story

in the third person. There is an intrinsic sense of comfort in hearing (or reading) a story in which the narrator is one step removed and not a part of the tale. As a little girl, I lived for story time and for me that meant listening to tales. My governess would challenge me to come up with my own stories, and I did. So my first steps into storytelling were in the third person and as a result, when I write now, it feels right and natural to tell a story this way.

The third-person narrative allows me occasionally to move into the hero's point of view as well. It's important to me that he should have a voice, a perspective on the love story – and it helps the reader to see the heroine from another angle. It also allows me to follow the hero to different locations and focus on his interaction with characters other than the heroine, enabling me to paint the world of my romantic protagonists as vividly as possible for the reader.

From where do you draw inspiration for your characters?

My characters are products of my vivid imagination but they are shaped by an essential – although covert – pursuit: people-watching.

I think all writers are observers of life. Truthfully, few are happier than when ensconced in a café with a favourite drink and a notebook, quietly watching the world around them. There, in a place where people come and go, the writer can find a new voice, type of behaviour, motive or look for a character. They can think up a new plot direction or twist, or perhaps discover a means by which to navigate around or obliterate a stumbling block. Writing is a solitary pursuit but people-watching offers solace as well as inspiration.

The beauty of people-watching is that, over time, you build up a great understanding of human behaviour and you have an ever-growing resource from which to draw as you write. Films, books, plays, photographs and painted portraits are wonderful sources of inspiration but you want the characters in your story to feel real, and to achieve that you need to shape them with first-hand knowledge of real people.

My aim is always to write tangible characters that make the central love story believable; characters who make you feel, as you're reading, that you too could meet a man like Damian and even become mistress of an island like Helios. I think it is that ability to believe in romance that makes reading romance novels such a compelling pleasure – it is not merely an escape but a restoration of hope.

Find out more at www.hannahfielding.net

About the Author

Hannah Fielding is an award-winning romance author, who grew up in Alexandria, Egypt, the granddaughter of Esther Fanous, a revolutionary feminist and writer in Egypt during the early 1900s. After graduating she developed a passion for travel, living in Switzerland, France and England. After marrying her English husband, she settled in Kent and subsequently had little time for writing while bringing up two children, looking after dogs and horses, and running her own business renovating rundown cottages. Hannah now divides her time between her homes in England and the South of France.

She has written five other novels, all featuring exotic locations and vivid descriptions: *Indiscretion, Masquerade* and *Legacy* (the Spanish Andalucían Nights Trilogy); *Burning Embers* (set in Africa); and *The Echoes of Love* (set in Italy). Hannah's books have won many awards, including the Gold Medal for romance at the Independent Publisher Book Awards and the Silver Medal for romance at the Foreword Reviews IndieFab Book Awards (*The Echoes of Love*), and the Gold and Silver Medals for romance at the IBPA Benjamin Franklin Awards (*Indiscretion* and *Masquerade*). *Indiscretion* has also won Best Romance at the USA Best Book Awards.

ALSO BY HANNAH FIELDING

Burning Embers
Hannah's mesmerizing debut novel.

Set in the heart of Africa, *Burning Embers* is a tale of unforgettable passion and fragile love tormented by secrets and betrayal.

On the news of her estranged father's death, beautiful young photographer Coral Sinclair is forced to return to the family plantation in Kenya to claim her inheritance.

But the peace of her homecoming is disrupted when she encounters the mysterious yet fearsomely attractive Rafe de Montfort – owner of the neighbouring plantation and a reputed womanizer, who had an affair with her own stepmother. Despite this, a mystifying attraction ignites between them and shakes Coral to the core as circumstances conspire to bring them together.

It is when Coral delves into Rafe's past and discovers the truth about him that she questions his real motives. Does Rafe really care for her or is he hiding darker intentions? Should she listen to the warnings of those around her or should she trust her own instincts about this man with a secret past?

Paperback ISBN 978-0-9955667-9-8
Ebook ISBN 978-0-9929943-1-0

The Echoes Of Love
Hannah's award-winning novel.

Set in the romantic and mysterious city of Venice and the beautiful landscape of Tuscany, *The Echoes of Love* is a poignant story of lost love and betrayal, unleashed passion and learning to love again, whatever the price.

Venetia Aston-Montague has escaped to Italy's most captivating city to work in her godmother's architecture firm, putting a lost love behind her.

Paolo Barone, a charismatic entrepreneur whose life has been turned upside down by a tragic past, is endeavouring to build a new one for himself.

Venice on a misty carnival night brings these two people together. Love blossoms in the beautiful hills of Tuscany and the wild Sardinian maquis; but before they can envisage a future together, they must not only confront their past but also dark forces in the shadows determined to come between them.

Will love triumph over their overwhelming demons? Or will Paolo's carefully guarded, devastating secret tear them apart forever?

Paperback ISBN 978-0-9926718-1-5
EBook ISBN 978-0-9926718-2-2

Indiscretion

The captivating first novel in the Andalucían Nights Trilogy.

Indiscretion is a story of love and identity, and the clash of ideals in the pursuit of happiness. But can love survive in a world where scandal and danger are never far away?

Spring, 1950. Alexandra de Falla, a half-English, half-Spanish young writer, abandons her privileged but suffocating life in London and travels to Spain to be reunited with her long-estranged family. Instead of providing the sense of belonging she yearns for, the de Fallas are riven by seething emotions and in the grip of the wild customs and traditions of Andalucía, all of which are alien to Alexandra.

Among the strange characters and sultry heat of this country, she meets the man who awakens emotions she hardly knew existed. But their path is strewn with obstacles: dangerous rivals, unpredictable events and inevitable indiscretions.

What does Alexandra's destiny hold for her in this flamboyant land of drama and all-consuming passions, where blood is ritually poured on to the sands of sun-drenched bullfighting arenas, mysterious gypsies are embroiled in magic and revenge, and beautiful dark-eyed dancers hide their secrets behind elegant lacy fans?

Paperback ISBN 978-0-9926718-8-4
Ebook ISBN 978-0-9926718-9-1

Masquerade

The heartstopping second novel in the Andalucían Nights Trilogy.

Masquerade is a story of forbidden love, truth and trust. Are appearances always deceptive?

Summer, 1976. Luz de Rueda returns to her beloved Spain and takes a job as the biographer of a famous artist. On her first day back in Cádiz, she encounters a bewitching, passionate young gypsy, Leandro, who immediately captures her heart, even though relationships with his kind are taboo.

Haunted by this forbidden love, she meets her new employer, the sophisticated Andrés de Calderón. Reserved yet darkly compelling, he is totally different to Leandro – but almost the gypsy's double. Both men stir unfamiliar and exciting feelings in Luz, although mystery and danger surround them in ways she has still to discover.

Luz must decide what she truly desires as glistening Cádiz, with its enigmatic moon and whispering turquoise shores, seeps back into her blood. Why is she so drawn to the wild and magical sea gypsies? What is behind the old fortune-teller's sinister warnings about 'Gemini'? Through this maze of secrets and lies, will Luz finally find her happiness … or her ruin?

Paperback ISBN 978-0-9929943-6-5
EBook ISBN 978-0-9929943-7-2

Legacy
The thrilling conclusion of the Andalucían Nights Trilogy

Legacy is a story of truth, dreams and desire. But in a world of secrets, you need to be careful what you wish for.

Spring, 2010. When Luna Ward, a science journalist from New York, travels halfway across the world to work undercover at an alternative health clinic in Cádiz, her ordered life is thrown into turmoil.

The doctor she is to investigate, the controversial Rodrigo Rueda de Calderón, is not what she expects. With his wild gypsy looks and devilish sense of humour, he is intent upon drawing her to him. But how can she surrender to a passion that threatens all reason – and how can he ever learn to trust her once he discovers her true identity? Then Luna finds that Ruy is carrying a corrosive secret of his own …

Luna's native Spanish blood begins to fire in this land of exotic legends, flamboyant gypsies and seductive flamenco guitars, as dazzling Cádiz weaves its own magic on her heart. Can Luna's and Ruy's love survive their families' legacy of feuding and tragedy, and rise like the phoenix from the ashes of the past?

Paperback ISBN 978-0-9932917-3-9
Ebook ISBN 978-0-9932917-6-0

Made in the USA
Las Vegas, NV
23 March 2022

46194611R00299